Polar's Fox

By Eric M Deal

ISBN 978-0692334942

"Are you here to save the day Mr. Wraulgh? With a few guns and a toy goddess? How adorable."

"You're not threatening your way out of this one, Amsend."

"Was that a threat? No… I'm going to slaughter all four of you… That was a threat. See the difference?"

Table of Contents

Perks

"Good morning Vulpie!" The receptionist says while the orange furred fox walks up to her desk. Her name is Stacie and she's greeted customers since Vulpie first founded his company. She's around twenty five and is rather cute.

"Morning!" Vulpie happily replies. The gay fox is dressed for the chilly day outside and wears a beautiful green scarf that accompanies his expensive tan suit. He's always super coordinated. The sleek pair of yellow sunglasses resting atop his head look as though they were designed to go with his outfit even though Vulpie added them to the entourage. The result is a very stylish mix that complements his orange fur, giving him an authoritative and artistic appearance. He's holding a freshly brewed cup of coffee in his right paw that he picked up on his way to the office.

"You're a little early today; I usually don't see you until nine." The vixen pleasantly teases. "Did you come in to get a head start on something?"

"Nah, I just woke up earlier than usual." Vulpie answers with a smile. "Polar was still snoozing, so I just let him get his beauty sleep."

"Pretty cold out there, isn't it? I had to run my car a while before leaving the house." Stacie comments. "The ice on my windshield was THIS THICK!" The brown vixen says while using her right paw to make her point. She spaces her clawed right index finger and thumb about half an inch apart.

"Yeah, it's chilly for really!" Vulpie giggles and touches his pretty scarf. "I Think I'm gonna lounge in the spa until Polar comes in. Can you beep me when he does?"

"Sure." Stacie answers and Vulpie takes a sip of his coffee. He relishes the taste. It's one of his favorite selections from Clouds, the downtown café. Ironically, he bought the drink from the same store that Zorpiv Vixil shot up. He felt responsible and had his company donate a few thousand dollars to help them fix the place. It was a double win, because it created good PR for Vulpie Industries and he can still visit their shop on the way to work. Vulpie Industries has very nice cappuccino machines upstairs, but Clouds still makes the best stuff.

The orange furred fox looks around the lobby and suddenly has the urge to meander for a bit. He'd like to both inspect and appreciate the design of his company building because he's quite proud of how it turned out. Polar believed in Vulpie's vision and was happy to donate some of his wealth when it came time to start construction. Of course, by that point, Vulpie had earned numerous corporate sponsors and his husband's contribution was fairly small in comparison; he's lent his face and iconic voice to everything from golf equipment to tennis shoes, and making time for his advertising engagements is still a significant portion of his monthly schedule.

But Vulpie Industries is where his visions become reality. The products that are on display are both advertisements and trophies for the orange furred fox. Vulpie carefully considers the spacing and location of each portion of the lobby to maximize customer enjoyment. His goal is to invite all visitors into a place that can provide them with things that they want and things that they need to make their lives better. It isn't just the money. He takes pride in the products he sells and how they represent his company's ideals. Second best isn't good enough. Vulpie Industries has to be the best and stay the best technological manufacturer in the universe. The gay fox won't have it any other way. Besides, it's part of his brand, and his investors expect nothing less.

The lobby greets visitors with a large sign in front of the main doors. It reads: "VULPIE INDUSTRIES," written with a powerful aesthetic font. The sign is about four feet tall so it doesn't impede visitors from exploring the room. After all, that is the point, but the title is directly in the line of traffic for a specific purpose. Seven cylindrical columns are arranged around the lobby's desk where Stacie works, and the first one to the left displays a large image of Vulpie. His face is to the left of the entrance sign, so it runs parallel with the company's title very nicely.

Consumers and potential business partners see that they'll have a part of Vulpie's genius whether they choose to buy one of his products or join the company. The orange furred fox was a little hesitant about putting up a large image of himself in the lobby at first, but his marketing team thought it was an excellent idea. Investors and customers want the full Vulpie, the unrestrained egotistical Vulpie instead of a penitent fox trying to fix the problems he caused with his computer virus. He's matured a lot since he released Vulpie.net, but his nature hasn't changed one bit. He's just better at hiding it now.

And of course... When it was decided Vulpie would have a mesmerizing portrait of himself on a column, the gay fox demanded that Polar have one as well. The white furred wolf's image is directly behind Vulpie's, and is much more subdued, but Vulpie just couldn't proceed without giving him credit. None of this would have been possible without Polar's support, but his marketing team also advised him about the bigotry of society. Even though Vulpie is beyond gay, he is better accepted than Polar because of his genius. The fact that he's a fox hasn't hurt things either. The AFR's never-ending support almost guarantees him favorable press. Animal psychology can be strange at times, but Vulpie does understand why they wanted Polar's portrait to be less eye catching.

It's as if success alone is what determines how an animal is treated. Vulpie remembers the way it was before he became a celebrity. Most animals laughed at his gayness and effeminate appearance. He knows he's a good looking fox, but if he hadn't been a master cybercriminal he'd be viewed differently. It makes him a little sad while looking at Polar's handsome , well-lit image. His husband shouldn't be in the unproven category. He's proven himself to Vulpie and the few that have seen what he's capable of, but that's not enough for the general public to give him the same respect. Polar's reserved nature plays a role in this to some degree, but Vulpie wishes that he could have the white furred wolf on a column directly across from his own, so visitors could see him on the other side of the company's sign. Polar deserves better, but for the purposes of making money and keeping up a certain image, Vulpie's husband will have to keep his elegant column behind the fox's for now.

"I'll find a way to get you up there... You handsome thing...." Vulpie whispers to Polar's image while walking past the structure. His dress shoes stick to the black lobby floor. It has a particularly gorgeous sheen that emphasizes the seven well-lit columns surrounding the visitor's desk. He takes another sip of his cappuccino and relishes the taste. Cloud's caramel mocha blend is just fabulous, and it makes his fur go on end. For some reason coffee gives the little gay fox an elated feeling after having a full night's rest. He usually finishes a second cup before lunch every day and plans to pop open an energy drink as well. Vulpie's affinity for high caffeinated beverages allows him to go a long time without eating, just the way he likes it.

The last column on the left side behind Vulpie and Polar's is a smaller one that shows off the company's most successful products. It's transparent and cool mechanical toys are propped up on their own little white velvet pads inside of the aesthetic container. There's the "V-Screen 7," the "StoreWatt 2.0," the "Consonant 17.5," and the "Insta-Fur 4.1." These four items are Vulpie Industries' best-selling retail products. Vulpie smiles in pride while looking them over. His machines are manufactured with high quality parts, and they command a significant price, but they're also affordable for most working animals.

The V-Screen is well-known for all of its pc tablet goodness. Buyers get the freedom of having a computer on the go without having to carry around a full sized laptop to handle their social networking and professional needs. Its overall design hasn't changed much over an evolution of seven models, but the hardware has improved significantly with each new generation. The V-Screen 7 is fully compatible with the Consonant 17.5's advanced sound systems, so Vulpie Industries is working its way into a complete home entertainment system. V-Screen models after generation two already have PC monitor ports, and high definition television output extensions built into them. Adding the Consonant's 17.5 surround sound was the next logical step.

The StoreWatt 2.0 also ties into the V-Screen, but it's more of a standalone product. There's nothing more irritating than running out of free space on your computer, and that's why external hard drives are consistently in demand. Animals just need more space to work with and Vulpie Industries is happy to provide a solution. The StoreWatt 2.0 offers a whopping 250 terabytes of storage space on a solid state drive. SSDs are far more reliable than traditional hard disk drives because they don't use rapidly rotating disks, or "platters." A hard disk drive consists of one or more hard rapidly rotating discs with magnetic heads arranged on a moving actuator arm to read and write data to the surfaces. Solid state drives, or SSDs, don't use any moving mechanical parts, so they are not subject to wear or tear. Thus, SSDs are far more portable and safer to use on the go. They cost more than classic hard disk drives, but work perfectly with mobile computers. Plus, the StoreWatt 2.0 uses super advanced SSD components that don't limit the amount of times a file can be written or overwritten. In short, it has all of the data storage capacity an animal could want, and it can go anywhere. Vulpie's company even includes a protective case for the device with each purchase. It's free of charge, and lowers the profit margin, but he wants the enormous data drive to last a long time for each customer.

Vulpie's pretty blue eyes widen when he looks over the Consonant 17.5. It's a particularly nice looking piece of equipment, painted all white with black interiors and ports. The Consonant breaks down into ten smaller speakers that are designed to go around the entirety of a customer's home theater. When fully installed, it provides the pure 17.5 epic sauce surround sound men drool over, but there is also a way to combine the ten speakers into a set of seven, five, or even four parts if an animal doesn't have the ability to hang up ten pieces of equipment.

He really wanted the Consonant series to stay flexible, streamlined, and compact, versus the huge speakers his competitors sell. The Consonants focus on accurate sound replication. They offer the true theatrical or musical experience instead of just blowing out an animal's ear drums with unnecessary noise. And Vulpie's very pleased with the results. If a kid wants to go deaf he can certainly do it with the Consonant 17.5's maximum volume, but at least the sound will be digitally accurate. The device also has a failsafe system that prevents it from suffering damage during periods of extended use. Lots of animals will max out the volume and leave It there, but the Consonant will automatically diminish its output when someone is trying to abuse it.

He has one installed in his office, and the lobby utilizes one as well, but normally it just serenades guests with warm melodies. Polar gladly retired his home's old sound system in favor of a Consonant, but they both decided to keep his previous equipment anyway. They've shared a lot of good memories thanks to Polar's music and the devices have sentimental value.

Vulpie adores the perfection of technology. The slick feeling of a comfortable keyboard, the delectable sensation of metal locking into perfectly constructed ports... Sometimes he wonders if heaven could be a mixture of flesh, fur and gentle machinery for him. The orange furred fox certainly likes the idea whenever it pops into his mind. A few animals walk by, two male tigers and a female cougar, and he recognizes their faces. They work in the loading docks downstairs and are too busy to notice him. The lobby's sound system begins playing one of its recorded messages just as he sets his eyes on the Insta-Fur 4.1. The female intercom voice is beautiful and could be of either lupine or vulpine origin.

"Welcome to Vulpie Industries. Our company is founded on the vision of producing innovative and affordable technology to enable animal kind to explore new horizons. To realize this vision, we are developing evolutionary

building blocks - starting with affordable consumer products that range from high speed personal computers to military grade virtual reality projection systems. To retain and build the team necessary for our goals, Vulpie Industries is fostering a corporate culture that attracts and retains creative, practical, and energetic employees who are driven to make cyberspace one comfortable place to be."

He smiles in relief. Every time he hears a corporate mission statement he usually feels like cringing, but he's proud of the way his turned out. It doesn't make him want to roll his eyes and it also satisfies the expectations of his demanding shareholders. The young CEO has a moment of clarity while sipping on his cappuccino. After Vulpie.net it could have been prison or this....

"Not bad." The orange furred fox whispers with a smile and looks over the Insta-Fur 4.1. It's one of Vulpie Industries' more outlandish products. The devices he used to expose Ivo Lorcan and Sevrif Vosuf eventually evolved into this little wonder. It can still pick up body heat, one of the cool functions he left in the final product, but x-ray snapshots seemed a bit litigious. The company couldn't have animals running around irradiating each other with its products. Still, it retains the shape and look of Vulpie's prototypes and comes with a plethora of new abilities. The Insta-Fur 4.1, or just "Fur 4.1," is an astounding media device. It uses a series of rotating proprietary lenses to capture video and photos, allowing it to double as both a high definition camcorder or camera.

"Interested in earning more credits? Sign up for the Cy-Gov program today. Vulpie Industries works with the Cyber Technologies Government Division on a daily basis and they need qualified personnel who understand Arctic.net. Become a dual associate and advance your career by taking part in our federal exchange program. Employees who complete the program are eligible for quarterly bonuses."

The lobby's automated announcement draws Vulpie's attention away from his products, reminding him of his obligations to the CTGD in addition to other wonderfully tedious contracts. Several stressful engagements are coming up, and the gay fox suddenly wishes that he could just leave the building and go play. He doesn't feel like being a CEO today. He doesn't want to be a professional... He just wants to have some fun... It's been a while since he visited the VIP spa so the idea of splashing into a hot bath of bubbling awesome seems just about right.

He meanders to the back left of the lobby where two locked doors can be found right beside the staircase to the second floor. They're black and both are securely sealed with ID card protocols. Metallic locks with keypads adorn their door handles to ensure that no one can get in without clearance. The one that goes under the staircase leads to a minor security room that communicates with the chief of security on the second floor, but the orange furred fox is only interested in the one on the left. He finds his personal ID in his left pocket and proceeds to swipe it through. Its leash is all bundled up because he normally doesn't need to hang clearance around his neck like everyone else and usually just stuffs it in his pants. But the VIP lounge does require plastic to get in and it's encoded with a fairly simple set of code. The locks only allow a select group of managers and the janitorial staff inside.

The door unlocks and Vulpie pushes it in, going inside the private spa in excitement. He shuts the door behind him and notices that Thomas is the only animal present. The panther is attending to the small trash can at the other end of the room and it looks like he's already cleaned up the hot tub.

"How ya doin Tom?" Vulpie cheerfully inquires. He hurries over to the hot tub to inspect it while his employee turns around.

"Fantastic Mr. Vivixen! How you doing today Sir?" The older feline smiles in response.

"Super fantastic!" Vulpie grins in response. Tom is a very congenial animal, one of those people that always seems to be in a good mood and he lays it on thick. "How's your wife? Did you get her that coat she wanted?"

"I did indeed Mr. Fox! Woman never shuts up unless I do what she says so you know I did!"

"Aw!" Vulpie giggles and heads towards the changing rooms. He keeps a pair of white swimming trunks in his personal locker for times like this. He just wants a quick swim and housekeeping is nice enough to wash the clothing for him whenever he's done. He can drop his wet trunks off and find them waiting for him the next time he wants to use the hot tub. He smiles as he fiddles with the locker. He opens the lock using the correct combination and does indeed find his swimming trunks waiting on him.

Vulpie begins to undress but his fox ears perk up when he hears a locker door shut. It sounds like somebody else is changing as well and he hesitates for a moment. Normally he can get naked and slip into his trunks without anyone paying him attention but he has no clue who it is. He doesn't know anyone who uses the spa this early, so he waits for a moment to discover who's nearby. The orange furred fox quietly clears his throat but the animal on the other side of the lockers doesn't do anything.

"Kidding me?" Vulpie whispers in irritation and crosses his arms. He waits but still the animal doesn't make a sound or come around the corner. "Okay!" The orange furred fox says to himself and starts removing his clothing. He doesn't feel like waiting all day for whoever it is to say something and he figures he can change clothes fast enough that it won't matter. It does bother him that the person hasn't gone ahead and said something.

The cute gay fox undresses down to his underwear and moves his white swimming trunks nearby on the bench for quick use. He slips down his underwear and just as he makes himself completely naked, the animal comes around the corner. Vulpie almost has a heart attack when he sees a young gray wolf stop in his tracks and stare in shock.

"OH! JEEZ!" The young man says in embarrassment and looks away, covering his face with his big paws. "I'm sorry!"

"OH, UH! SORRY!" Vulpie shouts back with a very distraught voice. The gay fox's humiliated tone makes the young man continue to speak in a panic after he hides behind the lockers again.

"Oh I'm so sorry! I didn't know anyone was here besides me and I waited a while so whoever was over there could finish up!" The wolf proclaims. His voice is penitent but also full of mirth.

"I WAITED FOR YOU TOO!" Vulpie laughs and quickly slips on his swimming trunks. His black furred paws are shaky and he throws them up playfully even though no one can see him. "Oh my God!"

"I know, jeez I'm sorry! Oh man!" The young wolf laughs.

"I've got some clothes on now so you can come back!" The orange furred fox declares and after a moment the mystery animal peers around the corner. He sees a slim and very sexy little Vulpie smiling at him and the fox boy's blue eyes widen while looking him over. "Uh, who are you? I don't know you, do I?"

"We haven't met yet, but I'm a graduate level internist from Yivolff College..." The handsome wolf responds and lowers his muzzle in shame.

"Ah, I see! Well that's fantastic! I'd have chosen a different way to introduce myself but here we are!"

"I am so very, very sorry..."

"So, are you gonna tell me your name or what?"

"Oh! It's Andrew! I'm Andrew Reeves! Sorry again! I've just... I really messed up."

"Andrew, can I ask you what you're doing in here to begin with? The spa's reserved for employees that've earned a VIP card."

"Ms. Cook let me borrow hers while she's on vacation. She said she won't be back for two weeks and she gave it to me at the school."

"Oh… So she was there recruiting people, huh?" Vulpie inquires with interest. The gleam in the fox's eyes gives Andy hope but he's still far from relaxing.

"You bet. She's visited Yivolf a few times, and I had a chance to tell her about my senior thesis, well, my plan to write a senior thesis on synthetic animals. I was so excited when she offered an internship at your company Mr. Vivixen! I never dreamed I'd get the chance! I LOVE computers and what you did… I mean, well, the things you've done with Vulpie.net are absolutely amazing."

"It's done a lot on its own." Vulpie replies with a smirk and Andy allows himself to smile. He sees the CEO's playful expression as an opportunity to build a little rapport. His first inclination is to joke about the Evil Vulpie robot attacking the fox at the CTGD but quickly realizes it's a terrible idea. He licks his lips and searches for something to say without freezing up just as Vulpie interjects a surprising statement.

"Like me and Evil Vulpie… That was awesome…" Vulpie says and smiles mischievously. Andy's fur stands on end and a cold dread rushes over him. It's as if Vulpie read his mind and he panics.

"Oh, I, well yeah!" The handsome gray wolf nervously laughs. "Who hasn't?"

"I know EVERYONE has seen it… How embarrassing…" Vulpie responds and winks at the internist.

"I wasn't going to bring that up, but yeah. I think all of it is completely amazing. You made a full recovery and went on to master Vulpie.net and build your own company!"

"Haven't mastered it… Far from it…"

"Yeah but who knows it better than you?"

"Just when you think you know Vulpie.net, it'll kill ya!" The orange furred fox giggles and Andy chuckles in response. "You seem like a really nice kid. I'm just a little shaken up from all of this."

"Oh, hey..." Andy replies and quickly finds the keycard in his green swimming trunks. He outstretches it in his paw towards Vulpie. "Take it back. You're right, I don't have any business being in here."

"No... You can keep it I guess..." Vulpie answers with a mischievous voice. Andy pauses for a moment. He smirks when he realizes the fox is playing with him.

"Okay. Cool, I guess."

"You guess?"

"Yeah..."

"Aw, don't worry. I'd be silly to turn away a fresh mind like yours. And I really think you'll like it here."

"I hope so! I'm sure I will!"

"Who's going to be training you? I didn't know we had fresh interns on the way."

"I might be the only one. All I know is that I've got to go see Mr. Halfur at nine o'clock."

"Halfur? Oh my God, I can't believe Stephanie sent you to him! We have to do something about that. The guy is a serious asshole, and not in the good way!" Vulpie answers, to which Andy coughs in surprise.

"Oh! Okay!" He chuckles nervously. The cute orange fox winks at him and his fur stands on end once more.

"He's a fantastic programmer and a top notch analyst, but not much on personality I'm afraid. Tell ya what! Why don't you hang with me for a little bit and meet me in my office instead. Head upstairs and tell the elevator guards I'm expecting you."

"I... Sure, I guess!"

"I'm not gonna make you change clothes, walk out of here and twiddle your thumbs for an hour. I guess it's alright if you want to use the spa too. Just don't think that I normally do this with any employee. But you and I need to talk a little bit after our awkward introduction!"

"Totally understand." Andy smiles and bows his head in respect. He doesn't dare run ahead of the fox and try to get into the spa first. He allows Vulpie to walk out of the changing room and make his way over to the hot tub before joining him. Vulpie tests the bubbling water with his left foot. He arches his tail to balance himself, smiling at Andy, and pulls his leg back. He shuffles his feet a little and hops into the spa like a swimming pool. The thin fox makes a bigger splash than one would expect, and Andy grins.

"Come on in, the pH is fine!" Vulpie offers and rests his little arms on the side of the hot tub behind him. It has a blue cast acrylic shell that allows for comfortable seating anywhere. Vulpie rubs his soft butt against a spot that feels nice and relaxes while Andy gets in.

"Not too hot." The gray wolf notes, and keeps his tail raised for a bit until he finds a suitable seat underneath the bubbling water.

"Yeah, Tom does an excellent job with the pool and the gym!" Vulpie replies. He watches his new employee get comfortable and rest his arms on the edge of the hot tub as well.

"Nice... Freaking nice!"

"I thought so! Polar and I come in here when things get crazy and we just snooze..."

"It feels pretty good. You could almost fall asleep."

"He does! My big snow wolf melts in this thing! He closes his eyes for a little bit and them BAM! Totally out!"

"Thanks for inviting me. I don't know what I'd do for an hour out there. Sit in the lobby I guess."

"Aw." Vulpie responds and swats his right paw at the gray wolf in a lighthearted manner.

"So I've got to ask you... All that stuff that happened on Zeravyn. Um, that planet, Zeravyn, is that the name?"

"Yeah."

"With the goddess robots and stuff?"

"Uh huh."

"Is all of that real? I just can't believe what they showed on the news. They had to fire the ion cannon? I mean, I don't want to be a jerk asking about this stuff? You're sure you don't mind?"

"Relax. I'm not going to fire you for saying something silly. I've been known to spaz out sometimes myself! I called the CTGD director a f'in blank once." Vulpie grins.

"Really? Oh man! The Cyber Technologies Government Division director?"

"Yeah, Arthur Howlstead. He's a really cool guy actually. We're really good friends and they still let me into the compound when I drop by."

"Where is it? I tried looking it up online with satellite maps, where you can see the building and where it is, but I couldn't find an address."

"Yeah, it's totally classified." Vulpie mischievously answers. "Only super-secret special agents like me know where it is!"

"Right. They dragged you in there against your will!" Andy argues while smirking.

"I like secret agent better." The orange furred fox answers and winks at the gray wolf, but he's surprised when the young intern tenses up. "Hey, I'm sorry if I'm making you uncomfortable."

"What? No."

"Polar says I get a little too relaxed with employees, so I won't take it personally if you just want to get up and leave. I shouldn't have winked at you, but that's just how I am when someone's fun to talk to. Sometimes straight guys get the wrong impression about me."

"No, it's cool, it's just... I'm gay too." Andy whispers. Vulpie blinks and takes another look at the handsome gray wolf.

"Oh Damn... Really?" the orange fox inquires. He grins while waiting for a response and laughs when Andy nods. "I'm so sorry! I had no idea! I never would have guessed it!"

"I mean, it's alright. I'm still glad you were nice enough to share the hot tub with me. I just... I guess you just needed to know." Andy replies. A little smile creeps on his face.

"Polar would kill me if he found out!"

"Right."

"Well, I don't know." Vulpie quickly follows up.

"It's a little different with me being gay. You have to admit it." Andy notes and winks at the orange furred fox. Vulpie's pretty blue eyes widen once again, and this time, he pulls back a little.

"Oh... Uh, yeah..."

"But you already knew I was gay, right?" The gray wolf inquires with a devious voice.

"What? No! I seriously had no idea!"

"Come on..."

"I swear I didn't!" Vulpie laughs and wriggles against the slick hot tub's interior, warm bubbling water splashing all over his brilliant fur. He notices the eager smile Andy's giving him. The gay fox would definitely raise his tail for the intern if he wasn't married, but there wouldn't even be a Vulpie Industries without Polar, and the snow wolf is better looking anyway.

"Alright. It doesn't matter anyway."

"Yeah!" Vulpie quickly agrees and averts his eyes. Both of their ears perk up when somebody enters the VIP spa. The door clangs when the visitor shuts it behind himself and Vulpie turns to his left to see who it is. It's Polar, and the orange furred fox feels a sinking sensation. Polar walks up to the hot tub and looks at Andy with a raised eyebrow. He then turns his attention to Vulpie with an emotionless face.

"I was going to join you but I see you've already got someone." Polar says with a dry voice.

"It's a long story. We kind of had a mix up and he didn't know he wasn't supposed to be in here. This is Andy." The orange furred fox responds and gestures towards the gray wolf through the bubbling water. "He's one of our interns. Stephanie let him have her key card while she's on vacation. That was really silly of her, but yeah. So I was about to tell him to get out but he doesn't have anything to do until his meeting with Halfur at nine... And I thought it would be rude to make him go wait in the lobby after he already changed into his swimming trunks and everything."

"Okay." Polar replies with an unfriendly voice. He patiently accepts Vulpie's explanation but clearly isn't okay with Andy hanging around.

"I'm really sorry for being here like this. I'll get out if you want me to and I understand why. I shouldn't be in here taking advantage of the perks even if Ms. Cook gave me her card. It was stupid of me."

"It's alright I guess. But just this one time, right?" Polar asks Vulpie with a jealous voice.

"Absolutely. Andy's going to meet with Halfur here in a little bit anyway." Vulpie replies and Andy quickly catches on. He'll just have to deal with Halfur's bad attitude because there's no way Polar is going to let him anywhere near Vulpie's office. He recognizes the hostile look on the snow wolf's face, and the semi-threatening expression makes his fur stand on end.

"Yeah, I think I'm going to head out actually. It was amazing to meet you both, and I look forward to seeing you around!" Andy says and waits for a response. He doesn't get one because Vulpie feels bad and Polar's not interested in small talk. The conversation has come to an impasse; he needs to leave. The handsome gray wolf gets out of the hot tub and Polar looks away, pretending to watch one of the TVs in the distance while the young man makes his dripping exit. He heads into the locker rooms and when he's out of sight, Polar turns his attention back to Vulpie.

"Sorry! All true though. I didn't know what to do with the guy!" The fox explains and the white furred wolf sighs loudly. He takes a seat next to the hot tub and puts his paws in his lap.

"Gee, I hope so..."

"I would never cheat on you." Vulpie says in a hushed voice.

"But he's gay. There's no doubt about it."

"How... How did you know that?" Vulpie asks with wide blue eyes.

"I just knew it. He was way too comfortable around you... And I don't want to see him anymore... Okay?"

"You got it, Polar. I love you and I'll make a point not to spend time with him, but he is an intern. He wants to learn about the company."

"Yeah, I know..."

"Don't you trust me?"

"I trust you Vulpie, but let's not make things too tempting... Alright?" Polar responds and the gay fox nods in agreement. Vulpie tries to keep himself from smirking but just can't. He even grins after a moment and licks his lips.

"At least I know you love me."

"You know I'm more of a man than he'll ever be..." Polar playfully responds, and Vulpie bites his tongue between his teeth at him.

National Security

"Sorry I'm late gentlemen. Tiffany keeps nagging me about the girl's dance lessons." President Slade jests as he walks into the Stone House's cabinet room. The chamber is fairly large and contains a long wooden desk with several brown recliners. It's where the president of the Sufias World Government traditionally discusses matters of national security, and a select group of individuals are waiting on him.

Arthur Howlstead smiles and Druward Wraulgh follows suit but with less enthusiasm. They are sitting across from each other, and Slade, a tall brown wolf, takes a chair at the end of the table so he can see them both.

"They're growing up fast. Are they in middle school yet?" Howlstead inquires.

"Yeah I think so too. It'll be next year." Donovan Slade answers while relaxing in his chair. There are a few other important animals present but they don't need to be introduced at this point. President Slade has called this meeting to discuss the Elbrus Military base's special project.

"So you finished your reports Mr. Howlstead?" Slade asks and Druward sits up in his chair. He's glad they're getting straight to business.

"I've completed a preliminary biological report on the Deiva machines, but it's riddled with incomplete theories I'm afraid. We could analyze them for years and still not answer the questions we have."

"So not much progress at all then?"

"Well I wouldn't say that. I'd say we've learned quite a bit. We don't know how they work, but we can see processes in their bodies that are similar to organic life forms. Although, it's pretty difficult to avoid false positives here." The CTGD director says and clears his throat. "Several of our assumptions have already been proven wrong."

"I read your emails." Slade responds and Howlstead nods.

"We have a long way to go." The gray furred wolf elaborates and licks his lips. "It'll take me a while to explain it all, but here's the short version... We think they're biological weapons..."

"How so?" Slade inquires. Druward listens silently and watches the President's behavior. He shifts back and forth in his seat, clearly skeptical about the suggestion.

"I'll start on the outside and work inward so we can cover everything we know so far." Howlstead replies while using his paws to convey sincerity.

"Some say it's divine intervention." Slade comments and Howlstead pauses. Druward blinks and shoots the President a disillusioned look.

"I assure you sir, it's nothing of the sort." Arthur responds while chuckling.

"Well, all of this is pretty strange. You have to admit it. Three perfectly realistic Goddesses show up out of nowhere. Nothing like this has ever happened before and I'm a fairly religious man."

"I don't think it's strange. I've seen enough of Vulpie.net." Druward says and Howlstead nods. Donovan looks to the GBI director and leans back in his chair.

"I know the computer virus made them but that doesn't explain everything. Sometimes these things happen for a reason." The President's words silence the room. Druward scratches his claws for a moment while investigating the commander in chief. Donovan is wearing the benevolent yet creepy smile that got him elected. It resonated well with conservative Deivaists but neither Druward nor Howlstead think much of it. The timber wolf gives off a repugnant air of superiority.

"Fair enough... But let me tell you some of this..." Arthur says and looks down at his papers. "They appear to be semi-carbon based life forms... Do you know what that means?"

"Everything has to be carbon based to live, though, right? I remember one of my college biology professors mentioning it. I think she said it was possible for life to be based on silicon instead of carbon." Slade answers.

"That theory has been around for a long time. It's been used in science fiction a lot, like Silver Hills making those movies about silicon aliens from space and all of that, but it is based on a real scientific hypothesis. However, silicon is still a long shot as a candidate for stable life. There is silicon inside of the goddess machines, but we can't determine whether it's the basis for their cellular structure or not. They have a mechanical interior as well. The Elbrus technicians examined them inside and out."

"Which they weren't too happy about..." Druward notes and Slade smirks.

"So what are you saying? They're not living animals like us, but they're not silicon based either? Are they alive or not?" The President inquires.

"They're living machines..." Arthur answers and pauses for a moment. He waits for the idea to sink in.

"You know that for a fact?"

"They are alive. There's no doubt in my mind, but perhaps a biologist should take over here." Howlstead replies and gestures towards a thin red fox sitting to his left. "The technology they're based on is beyond anything modern science can create."

"Then how did the computer virus build them, or grow them? That's what you're telling me, isn't it? Vulpie.net built them?"

"I assume the answer to that question was in Vulpie.net's underground facility on Zeravyn." The CTGD director answers.

"Which you destroyed." Slade reminds Druward with a stern voice. The black furred wolf simply looks at him and chooses to say nothing.

"It's probably good that he did. Who knows what else might have been down there..." Howlstead comments. "But back to the subject of carbon and silicon life... Silicon life is unlikely for several reasons. In general, all life forms have to gather and use energy from their environment to survive. You, me, any animal out there." The gray furred wolf says while using his paws to hold Slade's attention. "Carbon based life forms store energy in the form of carbohydrates. Right?"

"Right."

"Carbon is oxidized during the respiratory process. It then becomes carbon dioxide, something that is easy for us to expel. But silicon is different. The oxidation of silicon, yields a solid because immediately upon formation, silicon dioxide organizes itself into a lattice in which each silicon atom is surrounded by four oxygens. Disposing of such a substance would pose a major respiratory challenge."

"So you're saying a silicon based life form would have trouble breathing?" Slade asks in confusion.

"That's correct."

"So carbon based life is us, silicon based life is not likely, and they're neither?"

"That's right... Or maybe both..." Howlstead responds and puts his paws together in concern. "And here's the kicker... We cannot identify the basic chemical element that gives them life. It's not carbon and it's not silicon."

"Not on the periodic table then?" Slade infers.

"Not on the periodic table..." Howlstead responds with a somber nod. A silence fills the room and Druward takes a deep breath.

"Well, tell him more." The GBI director suggests.

"I'm following. If you haven't found the chemical yet then conduct more research until you do." The President declares and Howlstead sighs.

"Mr. President, this is an extremely unusual scientific discovery." The red fox says, jumping into the conversation with an intelligent voice. He's a well-known evolutionary biologist named Steven Keeling and Howlstead requested his expertise. "These machines are built out of a completely unidentifiable chemical element. That means the substance has never been found anywhere, not once, throughout our entire universe... And these women are living machines that look completely animal... So what if reproduction is possible?" The fox's words suddenly get Slade's attention when the topic of sex comes into play.

"How?"

"How are they able to survive on our planet? How did they breathe in space when they hijacked a depressurized ship and got onto the Endeavor? These are non-trivial questions. Mr. Howlstead is being quite conservative when he suggests they're a threat to the planet. We should be asking whether they threaten the galaxy."

"I never expected such a bleak outlook from you people." Slade responds with a disappointed voice. Druward's ears twitch at the President's disrespect but he shows nothing. He's dealt with superiors like Donovan before, and privately suspects that the man has already made up his mind on religious grounds.

Everyone's attention is drawn to Polar when he walks into the cabinet room with Vulpie. The two are wearing black suits, having come directly from their company, and Vulpie nods at the group with a smile. The little orange furred fox sees the familiar faces of Howlstead and Druward, and lays eyes on the new Sufias World Government's president for the first time. Donovan Slade is an average sized wolf with unremarkable features, aside from a curiously creepy smile.

"I hope we're not interrupting." Vulpie says as he walks around the table and Polar follows him. Blacktail stays out of the room because the President's secret service won't allow them to enter.

"Not at all. I'd say you're just the man we need to talk to!" Slade responds with a voice that nearly makes Vulpie cringe. The cute fox dislikes the way the timber wolf stressed "man," as if trying to make a little joke about his masculinity, but chooses to ignore it. The table isn't very long, so Vulpie is able to take a seat at the other end and is still fairly close to the rest of the group, while Polar goes around him and sits next to Druward. The powerful white furred wolf smiles at the coal furred wolf, and Druward nods. After they sit down, a brief silence fills the room, as if everyone is unsure of who should continue the conversation with so many important people participating. "It's a pleasure meeting you, Mr. Vivixen." The President continues.

"You too, Mr. President." Vulpie replies with a courteous smile.

"It's good you're here, because our discussion might have hit a road block on the technical side without your input."

"Arthur has been doing this a lot longer than me." Vulpie responds, and notices Howlstead look over with an appreciative expression.

"You wrote the program these robo-women use. If anyone has some insight, it's you." Slade smirks.

"Actually that is not true... I didn't write their code... Vulpie.net created it." Vulpie responds and lets the statement sink in. The President understands why the fox pauses and waits for him to continue. "I spent all of yesterday looking over Howlstead's reports, and it's a real mystery."

"What is, exactly?" Donovan Slade inquires and notices Polar sizing him up. The white furred wolf is quite pleasant to be around, but has a habit of visually inspecting other men's bodies and what they're physically capable of. He inherited the killer instinct from the arctic wolves of old, so he does it subconsciously, without realizing how unnerving it can be to other males. The inspection is usually brief, and there will be no reason for conflict, especially not with the President, but Donovan does notice.

"I've never seen anything like it." Vulpie says and throws up his little paws. He licks his lips and sets his hands on the table. "I wrote Vulpie.net and Arctic.net... And that's not what they're running."

"But your husband used one of your VulGrids to disable them. Isn't that right?" The President inquires.

"Yes he did."

"Then you do know something about their programming."

"I might have before Arctic.net 2.0 changed them..." Vulpie answers and looks around the group. Druward glances at the President. Slade has been briefed on every event that transpired in deep space regarding the Sevrif, the Endeavor, and what happened on Zeravyn. "Polar used one of my VulGrids to infect them with an unstable code that I developed using Arctic.net. I personally re-programmed Arctic.net and then tested it on Vulpie.net in a controlled environment. After that went well, I packaged the end result into a compressed file that I planned to use in case of an emergency. Well, we ran into an emergency alright, and Polar saved the day. But after that... I can only speculate as to what happened."

"It worked perfectly. Your program shut off the Deiva robots and then you deactivated your VulGrid and took it back to Vulpie Industries." The President comments. "So it went the way you planned, didn't it?"

"I'm not sure. I think so." Vulpie answers. "As far as I can tell, Arctic.net 2.0 behaved the way it was supposed to... But I have doubts..."

"Why?"

"Well for one thing, the code Howlstead pulled from the Deivas is completely bizarre. It looks absolutely nothing like Vulpie.net or Arctic.net." The orange furred fox explains. "There are some similarities, but not enough for me to know what's going on anymore. Something happened with them."

"And each one of the Synthetic Deivas have a slightly different version of code." Arthur Howlstead interjects, to which Vulpie nods. "Vulpie's right. They've evolved somehow and all of it has taken place after the removal of Arctic.net 2.0 from their system."

"How did you... Hack... Into them?" Slade asks. "Do they have entrance ports on their bodies like a computer?"

"No, they don't. Evil Vulpie did, I mean, Vulpie.net's machine did." Howlstead responds. "But the women are built as if they're the goddesses of legend. You won't find anything like that on them. They broadcast and are capable of receiving wireless communications on various frequencies and that's how we were able to look into their file structures... And we had to ask them... They did not volunteer."

"Why not just carve into their skulls and pull out what you need?" Slade asks with a brutal voice.

"That would end our experiments rather quickly and we'd lose the greatest technological find of the century. From a biological point of view, they are far more advanced than Vulpie.net's personal robot, the one that's locked inside the Sufias Heritage Museum."

"And carving a hole in their skulls would require a tremendous amount of force." Druward tells Slade with an equally brutal and disillusioned tone. "They're virtually indestructible, so we'd have to use a tactical laser to open them up and we wouldn't know whether they'd even work after doing that. It's not a simple bit a surgery."

"Are they tougher than the one in the museum?" Slade inquires.

"They're just as tough." The GBI director responds. "And better looking."

"Thanks a lot Druward." Vulpie playfully growls and the black furred wolf glances over his shoulder with a smirk.

"The scientific community has little doubt as to how we should proceed." Keeling interjects. "The consensus is that we continue to study these creatures, but some animals, myself included, believe that proper precautions are not being taken to prevent contamination."

"You mean the soldiers at Elbrus are in danger of being infected with some kind of... Artificial disease?" Slade asks.

"Not just the workers. If that were the case, then all of their families, friends and acquaintances might have already been exposed to pathogens as well."

"Are they carrying diseases? Why do you see them like... Like viruses?" The President inquires with a skeptical expression.

"We already know they excrete pheromones and opiates in aerosol form." The vulpine scientist answers. "It's almost not even a question of whether they would be carrying pathogens, but why wouldn't they? These organic machines that pose as Deivas were clearly designed to manipulate religious animals, and their ability to intoxicate any species using their breath alone speaks volumes about why they were built. Only Vulpie may have deeper insight into why his computer virus made them the way they are, but the proof you're looking for is right in front of us. They were constructed to control Deivaists, not your ordinary everyday believer, but people with STRONG faith who would rather follow instead of think for themselves."

"I know this sounds strange, but I don't think they're malicious." Druward interjects and silence fills the room.

"Didn't expect that from you." Slade tells the black furred wolf. "Didn't you bring in that old wolf robot to the CTGD and kill him?"

"We didn't kill Ivo Lorcan; it died when Vulpie.net or Sevrif Vosuf sent the command." The GBI director replies.

"I'm sorry, who is Sevrif Vosuf again?" Slade asks and Druward sighs.

"The owner of Sevrif Industries… He built the largest ship in history, remember?"

"Right."

"He was a different type of machine, but Vulpie.net created him too."

"And the World Government owns that ship now, right?" The President inquires.

"Yes sir. We didn't have a ship in that region of space before, so it's very good." Druward answers. "Wovakef needed contacts to bring deep space resources to Sufias, and the Sevrif is still full of small business owners."

"You mean Palisade station?" The President asks.

"It's the same place, Wovakef, Corbel, Palisade station… Palisade for short."

"Druward, that reminds me…" Vulpie says and gets the attention of the group. The little orange furred fox leans forward and licks his lips. "Wasn't Wovakef in the news for something? I noticed a report on TV but didn't have time to watch it."

"They've lost communication with the SWG a few times because of signal interruptions. It's nothing important." Druward answers with a methodical voice. "There's a large cloud of space debris between them and Sufias right now, so they're trying to boost their signals, but they're not far from the planet. Why do you ask?"

"Nothing." Vulpie replies with a shrug. "Just being paranoid I guess."

"So are you going to tell us Vulpie, or what? Spit it out." Druward responds with an annoyed voice, but shows the orange furred fox and white furred wolf a little friendly smile.

"I looked into Wovakef when I first sent out Vulpie.net…" The gay fox answers with a concerned expression.

"You infected their computers like Zeravyn, and everything else, right?" The black furred wolf asks.

"Yeah."

"Oh yeah… I remember you telling us that when…"

"When you interrogated me over Chris Cephil." Vulpie answers and gulps. Druward takes a moment to look over the hacker fox and then leans back in his chair.

"Noted…" The GBI director says and glances at the President before turning his attention to Vulpie again. "But that happened years ago and there haven't been any problems. Palisade Station's basically right next to Sufias, so most likely their computers are running the same version of Arctic.net that we are."

"You sure? How much do you know about it?" Vulpie presses.

"I haven't heard anything." Druward replies with a shrug. "It's just a trading station like all the others in the system, and the only report I can remember was the one I just mentioned... Is there something you want to tell us? I know they have a robotics division, and you checked it out with Vulpie.net, but did you do anything in specific?"

"No." Vulpie replies and leans back in his chair as well. "I just thought I'd mention it."

"Palisade station's in a safe part of space that gets plenty of traffic, so if Vulpie.net was up to no good there, I think we'd already know about it. The only thing they have to worry about are red wolf raiding parties."

"Space pirates, huh?" Vulpie replies with a funny face. "I thought they were just in the movies!"

"No, they're real pirates." Druward simply answers in amusement. "They're real terrorists too, and there's a ton of them across the galaxy if you count all of their little hideouts." President Slade clears his throat.

"So what's going to be done with the Deivas?"

"That's why we're here." Druward responds. "I had Howlstead move over to the Elbrus base to do research on them, and when he was finished he sent his report to Vulpie on my request so he could look over their computer code. Vulpie took a look at it and has no idea where to begin."

"Well I wouldn't say that..." Vulpie growls with a smirk.

"Hacker ego." Druward dryly teases and Vulpie grins.

"That's right!"

"But you don't understand what you're seeing in their code..." The GBI director says and waits for confirmation from the gay fox.

"No. I don't."

"Neither do I." Howlstead adds and stretches. "I'm heading back to the CTGD next week. I had a team of technicians go over every inch of them, and we have all of the scientific data that we can find with current technology."

"So all that's left is figuring out what to do with them." Slade declares.

"Try it! Try it!" Vulpie says with glee, urging his tall husband to sample the cologne he just sprayed on his neck.

"I can smell it from here. It's pretty sexy…" Polar grins in response. He loves the way Vulpie gets worked up over certain things. When the color pink or perfume is involved he always throws an adorable fit.

"Oh, I gotta get it for you Mr. P! I can't wait for you to wear it around the house."

"Not at work? How long are we going to play this little game where we deny why my desk is in your office?" The white furred wolf teases and Vulpie bites his lip.

"It's two hundred for a set. Would you like one Mr. Vulpie?" The red vixen behind the shop desk inquires.

"Oh, DEFINITELY!" The orange furred fox answers and licks his lips. "I want five sets."

"Vulpie…" Polar growls, reminding his husband not to get carried away. Even though they're super rich, the arctic wolf doesn't like wasting money and especially not in public.

"But I want it! I want it for us! And you love it too, right?" Vulpie pouts.

"Yeah but by the time we've… Used enough of it together you'll be wanting new cologne. It's fantastic! I do love it, but don't get that much. One set is plenty and we can always come back and get it again if it's still your favorite."

"Okay…" Vulpie says and swishes his tail. "Just the one." The vixen nods and gets busy wrapping up the perfume in special packaging. The two are enjoying a trip to the "Letter" mall near the Stone House. Their meeting with the president and everyone else has given them an opportunity to shop in a district of Sufias City that they usually never visit. It's north west of Vulpie Industries and about forty miles from their first home. Polar insisted that

Vulpie get full ownership of the house and all of his assets in case something happened to him. Vulpie told the wolf that he didn't have to while they were drawing up their living wills but his husband insisted, and Vulpie followed suit.

Most lawyers would advise against leaving everything to a spouse, especially if the partners are rich celebrities, but they trust each other implicitly. Neither one could imagine living without the other, and the wild sex life they share continues to routinely reinforce their relationship. Polar never imagined he'd be lucky enough to marry someone who wanted to have sex every single day, but Vulpie's the horniest animal he's ever met, and he'll do anything the wolf wants whenever he wants it... Absolutely anything... Polar's even messed with him a few times by asking his husband for sex right before he had to do something professional at his company, like giving a speech to new hires, but the orange fox never turned him down once. Plus, everyone already knows them across the universe as a very famous couple. The only thing that might pose a threat to their marriage is Vulpie running off and almost getting himself killed again, and Polar has made it very, VERY, clear that he doesn't want it to happen... But even if it did... He knows he still wouldn't be able to quit Vulpie, and he sees the same dedication in Vulpie's eyes at least once every day.

"Need to get you a new suit! I like you in silver." Vulpie comments as they finish the transaction. Rulef walks by and says something to Deepwolf, who nods and looks over his shoulder at some cougars in the back of the store. The private mercenary force is just being extra careful and that's why they rarely make a mistake.

"Maybe." Polar smiles down to his little husband.

"Wanna go find a nice restaurant after that?" Vulpie suggests.

"I'd love to." The white furred wolf answers and salivates just a little bit, enough make him wipe his lips and the orange furred fox smirks.

"Boy you are hungry aren't ya?"

"Double hungry actually... I guess I can satisfy one of them at a nice bar." Polar replies with an inviting look. He's pretty sure Vulpie always says yes because the cute little fox loves taking wolf cock as much as he loves giving him one, but sometimes it just seems too perfect. He wonders how in the world he would get up every day if something happened to Vulpie, and how Vulpie could go on if something happened to him. What would the fox do? Go back to fucking random hot guys? He couldn't run a company with that kind of lifestyle but he also couldn't run Vulpie Industries without having his needs satisfied.

"Twice the biting." Vulpie grins and looks around when Deepwolf taps him on the shoulder.

"Boss said we should probably move on now. Those tiger cubs probably phoned their friends about seeing you here and since reporters pay off the cell phone companies to run language scans..."

"The paparazzi is on its way." Vulpie replies and licks his lips. "I'm a little insulted that they haven't shown up yet!"

"Don't be. I had to shoot a reporter while serving overseas." The gray furred wolf responds.

"Didn't know that." Polar says and eyes the merc. "I thought you served on the front lines over there. How'd that happen?"

"Shit happens." Deepwolf answers and shrugs. "Sergeant ordered my squad to escort a military contractor down the street and a mob showed up." Blacktail starts walking and Polar and Vulpie move along in the center of the group.

"Did he die?" Vulpie asks while looking into a video game shop while they walk past it.

"Unfortunately, yeah. It kind of sucked for my self-esteem." Deepwolf answers.

"All you are is fucking ego..." Rulef snorts from a few feet ahead and Deepwolf gives him the middle finger when he walks up next to the Blacktail commander. "What? It's true?"

"Eat me. You're one to talk bro." Deepwolf responds.

"We ought to start a reality TV show called Mercs-with-Perks! You guys are just great together!" Vulpie giggles.

"Double my pay and we'll see what happens." Deepwolf responds.

Vulpie glances at Polar while General Bowman makes his argument the next day. The tall timber wolf works for a private defense corporation and has been courting their company for a while. The man just won't give up, no matter how many times they say no. The orange furred fox keeps telling him that Vulpie Industries will never make weapons, and the salesman has come up with a few interesting arguments on behalf of his employers, but nothing impressive enough to justify directly taking part in the production of killing machines.

"And what happens if my computer virus returns?" Vulpie inquires, interrupting Bowman midspeech. The group is sitting in Vulpie's office, with Polar in a chair to the right of Bowman while Vulpie leans in his recliner across from the two wolves. "If I spend years building unmanned weapons for your buddies what's to stop it from using them?"

"You've told me quite a different story. Remember? You said you had complete confidence in Vulpie Industries and the VulGrid program. And it's been a great success." Bowman responds and rubs his chin with his big right paw.

"Of course I've been positive. I can't remind the press that I'm still seriously worried about Vulpie.net."

"So you haven't been honest?"

"That's not what I said. I said I can't remind everyone about it… I believe I've been PRETTY honest so far…" Vulpie responds while raising his eyebrows.

"This new multi drone program is the biggest advancement in warfare that we've seen in hundreds of years. If we don't capitalize on it then the Red Wolves certainly will. Imagine what they'll be capable of! One man carrying a small armada of portable drones into combat that can take down helicopters and jets?"

"I don't like those signature strikes. I think firing on targets from miles above is cowardly to begin with."

"Vulpie, you know better. You know drones have killed several terrorists that were a threat to the Sufias World Government."

"Yeah, I don't have a problem with that. I just don't like those signature strikes where you guys blow up a group of animals without identifying if they're even militants or not and you don't give them a chance to surrender. The drone swarms you guys already have are kicking butt… Why don't you just keep on using them?"

"Because we must be on the cutting edge of technology and you of all animals know that." Bowman argues and waves his paws in a diplomatic fashion. "Look… I know what you've been through, Mr. Vivixen. But you have an amazing chance here. Your company can solidify itself as the most powerful corporation in the universe if you decide to work with us. Yes, things may not go as planned. Yes, you will hear criticism, but you can't possibly be worried about that anymore. Your public approval rating is so high that you could run for president."

"That I would like to see." Polar says with a smirk and Vulpie grins.

"Animals love to work for you because you pay twice the rate of your competitors. So why don't you bring that generosity with you on this endeavor? We can find ways to limit the conflict. We might actually prevent wars with your help."

"I don't think so. You guys are making WAAAAAY too much money off of your bombs and ammo." Vulpie replies with a mischievous expression. "You have to use that stuff after you build it to stay profitable, after all."

"It's not like that. I swear Delanson is different. You've even had experience with our anti-tank units. You've seen how efficient they can be, and how precise they are." Bowman responds.

"Mmmm…" Vulpie hums and averts his eyes while having a private thought. He remembers the frightened look in Polar's eyes the first time his wolf husband saw Mr. Big Tooth. "I've also seen some pretty nasty machines…"

"I understand. But you can't be afraid to embrace the future. Our enemies will if we don't."

"But how can Vulpie, how can I and Vulpie, be sure that everyone will do as you say? No offense, but you don't call the shots at Delanson Mr. Bowman. You're a wonderful person and a great spokesman, but someone else will be making the key decisions."

"That's true." Bowman admits and shrugs. "You'll just have to trust us."

"You have no idea…" Vulpie says with a small voice and stretches his right paw towards Bowman to make his point. "No idea what kind of monstrosities my computer virus made… The one they destroyed on Zeravyn was straight out of hell."

"The thing that destroyed a mange devastator?" Bowman asks with a concerned voice. Polar notices the man can shift emotions very convincingly. He's trying very hard to manipulate them.

"Yeah, I saw it up close, and it was just about the scariest fucking thing I've ever laid eyes on… Now let me remind you that Vulpie.net created that freak completely on its own. I never dreamed up something that sick, and believe me, I've had some evil thoughts."

"We know that. I know that very well. But Arctic.net isn't the same computer virus, is it?"

"It basically is. I'm gonna be honest with you... The Arctic.net that everyone uses is just Vulpie.net with its creativity turned off... And I could turn it back on at any time. There are plenty of ways to do it."

"You make it sound so easy, but you're the only one that knows how. They're still trying to figure Arctic.net out and it has a perfect track record so far."

"Perfect isn't the word I'd use... More like acceptable..." Vulpie responds. "So far it hasn't made any twenty foot mechanical nightmares that vomit oil and eat people... That's kind of how I'm gauging it.

"What I'm saying is that Arctic.net won't shoot civilians. It has no reason to do so. No one can reprogram Arctic.net except for you, so why are you afraid?"

"I'm not the only one. Vulpie.net is still out there somewhere. I know it's still in the Sufias Heritage Museum for sure." The orange furred fox answers.

"Lurking and plotting?" Bowman chuckles.

"Yeah... Why does that surprise you? It's only been four months since those goddess robots were captured and they're pretty nice compared to the others."

"Well even if it was, why wait? Why not do something right now?" Bowman inquires.

"I dunno. Vulpie.net is pretty twisted. Maybe it's waiting for me to make these machines for you guys so it can take them over. It couldn't mass produce them like I can."

"Oh for heaven's sake..." Bowman growls with a smile. "You worry too much Mr. Vivixen."

"I guess." Vulpie smiles in response.

"Who cares? Real men settle things like this." Polar comments while raising his fists and Bowman chuckles. The white furred wolf manages to break the tension and all three of them relax.

"God! That's so lame!" Vulpie groans and his husband smiles.

"What? It's true!"

"But it does sound cooler when you say it." Vulpie notes with a grin. "I wish I was a real man..."

"Awww..." Polar teases. Bowman continues to smile but their tone makes him uncomfortable. He can only imagine what sort of master and slave relationship the gay wolf and fox have. He isn't interested in hearing more, so he clears his throat.

"Well then... I'll tell the others that you still have some reservations. I wish you would trust us more, but I understand." The timber wolf states and Vulpie smiles.

"It's not you, Bowman. Personally I think you're a great guy. I know you mean what you say, but I'm not so sure about Delanson."

"Proven track record with years of integrity." Bowman quickly replies while shaking his head, still trying to close the deal.

"Well it's mainly about Vulpie being able to sleep at night."

"Did you really just refer to yourself in the third person?" Polar teases and the orange furred fox smirks without looking at his husband.

"Vulpie doesn't have to answer that question at the moment."

"See what I have to put up with?" Polar asks Bowman while trying not to laugh.

"Hey, I get that." Bowman tells Vulpie. He remains completely serious and nods his head a little. "I've had to deploy soldiers when I knew they wouldn't return. Peace of mind isn't something you can buy... But I do trust Delanson. And I think you should too."

"I'll consider it." Vulpie answers and sits up in his chair. Bowman interprets this as a signal for him to leave, so he stands, and Polar and Vulpie follow suit. They shake paws and Vulpie nods at the ex-general respectfully. Polar decides to walk the timber wolf out and starts up a conversation about additional contracts. Bowman gladly continues his sales pitch with him and Vulpie drops back into his chair after they leave the room. "Consider it pointless..." The gay fox whispers to himself. He grabs up the stress reliever on his desk, a small green ball, and squeezes it a few times to calm his nerves.

The gay fox has done quite well for himself. His company is super successful. Polar loves him, he's still sexy and in perfect shape, but he does miss the days when all he had was being naughty. There is nothing quite like having a stranger take you from behind, especially a big strong wolf that wants to put you in your place and Vulpie had as many as he could while he was single. The thrill of getting it from a handsome violent male just rocked his entire world. He adores the sensation so much that he married the best he ever had... Polar was and is the best fuck imaginable. The white furred wolf is a brilliant, and wonderful husband... But the orange furred fox relishes the memory of their first night together. He remembers the arctic wolf just fucking him out of pure lust and the epic excitement of it all.

Vulpie's little daydream puts a smile on his adorable face. He closes his eyes and thinks back to the best weekend of his life. Meeting Polar was, without a doubt, the single most amazing moment he can think of. He instantly knew the wolf wanted him and he was eager to accept. All the passion they've enjoyed after their first "date," plays with the same buttons that brought them together in the first place. They're different species but they both truly feel like they were meant for each other. Vulpie recalls how amazing it was to have Polar inside him for the very first time... The warm invasion of the snow wolf's fat cock made his fur stand on end and had him so hard it hurt.

"I don't think we'll be doing any business with him." Polar notes as he enters the office. The white furred wolf interrupts Vulpie's line of thought and the orange furred fox licks his lips before smirking.

"So that's how you feel about him?"

"That's how you feel. It's pretty obvious." Polar answers and smiles in concern. "I hate seeing you this stressed out, and yeah, I don't trust him."

"Just tell me if you think I should change my mind. I'll listen if you think we could work it out."

"I don't really." The white furred wolf responds and walks around Vulpie's desk. His proximity encourages the orange furred fox to hop out of his chair and swish his pretty tail.

"Okay. You always know best anyway." Vulpie replies and lovingly touches his husband's tummy while walking by him. He goes over to the couch and takes a seat. Polar likes the thought of getting off of his feet and joins his lover. He walks over and kicks off his shoes, making Vulpie grin. "Time to go home..."

"Why? I thought you loved cuddling in the office..." Polar coos and leans down for a kiss as he gets on the couch as well. Vulpie sits up and gives him one, moving with the big wolf so they can relax together. Polar lies down on top of his little husband after they finish their first kiss and initiates a second one. They enjoy the tender moment but Vulpie sighs while thinking about his computer virus.

"So much to worry about... Sometimes I wonder what would have happened if I never released Vulpie.net." The orange furred fox confesses. "You wouldn't have let me do it if I told you about it."

"The same thing probably would have happened. You didn't know vulpie.net was capable of disobeying you." Polar replies and snuggles next to his little husband.

"Yeah but I wonder what your suggestion would have been. I bet you wouldn't have believed me."

"That's easy. I'd go to Mandrake at Illehas and tell him to hire you right away." The white furred wolf cleverly smiles.

"Given me a reference?" Vulpie smirks and winks at his husband.

"Of course! I can be pretty persuasive, and Illehas made software, remember?" Polar responds. "I'm sure you do."

"I dunno. I don't think I'd be able to fit in with the boys."

"Sure you would. You'd end up on my floor... And if we were lucky I would have gotten you a room right next to mine..." Polar grins.

"And we could work together every day." The fox says and winks.

"I usually closed the blinds around lunch anyway. I didn't like people watching me eat."

"But they'd notice if I always joined you!"

"Well we wouldn't fuck every day..." Polar chuckles.

"The hell?!" Vulpie laughs. "Oh yes we would!"

The Alopex Virus

Polar rests a paw on Vulpie's left shoulder and his husband stops bouncing his leg at the request. No words need to be spoken. The fox returns a shy smile and the white furred wolf smirks in amusement. They've been waiting on the doctor for about fifteen minutes and Polar knows his lover is fidgeting on purpose. This scenario has played out a few times before in public, but the squeaky examination table and its wax paper underneath them sounds quite irritating thanks to Vulpie's insuperable energy.

"Cut it out." Polar growls. His voice is stern but he can't stop himself from grinning.

"What?"

"You know what."

"We need to work on our communication! I dunno what you're thinking! Is something the matter? Are you SICK of something? Is that why we're here?" Vulpie giggles.

"Here he comes." The white furred wolf says and licks his lips. He hears the doctor in the hallway and Vulpie sits up straight.

"Sweet."

"I really like this guy; I think he's a great MD." Polar notes and the door handle clacks as a strong paw takes hold of it on the other side. A very tall timber wolf with light brown fur and yellow eyes opens the door and joins them. He has a smile on his face and carries a medical laptop that he keeps pressed against his white lab coat with his left arm. The man takes a moment to turn around and shut the door with his right paw before speaking.

"Hello there! I'm Doctor Collins. It's a pleasure to meet you." The man says and nods at Vulpie.

"Thanks Doc." Vulpie answers with a courteous smile.

"Polar's been my patient for as long as I can remember, ever since he was a teenager and I first started practicing medicine. I'm glad you've decided to consult with me too."

"Do you know a lot about foxes?"

"I know as much as any fair doctor and I work with many, yes." Collins answers and takes a moment to set up the laptop on the nearby counter. He retrieves a stylus from his pocket and navigates through the computer's directories until he finds Vulpie's records. "I noticed that it's been a long while since you've visited a doctor, Vulpie. Don't you have a regular one? Or were you just too busy to deal with it before?" The timber wolf wryly inquires.

"Answer B." Vulpie grins in response.

"I've been trying to get him to see a proper doctor for years now. He's been going to this fox specialist but the guy really doesn't know what he's doing." Polar comments and Vulpie nods in agreement.

"He seems more interested in talking about fishing and stuff than anything else." Vulpie comments.

"Well I can assure you that's not how I do things. I see you're way over do for a prostate exam, which I'm sure won't bother you very much." Collins replies without looking up and both Polar and Vulpie smirk. "But I'd also like to do some blood work as well just to be on the safe side."

"Blood work?" Vulpie weakly inquires.

"I think you need to. We can cover a lot of early detection to make sure we avoid any complications down the line. It looks like your last doctor checked you off as satisfactory on all counts but we shouldn't underestimate the value of preemptive medicine."

"I guess so..."

"He can't take blood." Polar says with a mischievous voice. "He loves blood and guts movies, tons of violence and all that, but you talk about him giving up some of his own and he freaks out."

"Stop it, you're making me sick!" Vulpie whimpers while squinting and both of the wolves chuckle.

"See?"

"Vulpie's blood is for Vulpie only! Vulpie needs it!"

"Ah, it'll be over before you know it." Collins warmly replies and navigates to Polar's medical records.

"Polar, I need to check your blood pressure again."

"Okay." Polar responds and thinks for a moment. "If I may ask, why do you want to do blood work on Vulpie if he's not sick? Aren't the tests expensive?"

"They are." Collins says and clears his throat. "Vulpie, you had VED shots about nine years ago. Is that right?"

"Yeah." The orange furred fox quickly answers.

"The venereal elimination of disease vaccinations have changed quite a bit since then and I feel that it's necessary to have you checked out."

"But they're supposed to last a lifetime, aren't they?"

"Sure, but there's a long standing policy of checking up on the results. I wouldn't be doing my job as your new doctor if I didn't make sure everything was fine."

"You mean I could have caught something and not even know it?"

"Well, there's that too. VED shots don't prevent all sexually transmitted diseases." The timber wolf explains and holds up his paws delicately. "And this is in no way a judgment call on your lifestyle, but since you're a young gay man and you had the vaccination I just assumed that you've had several sexual partners. Is it okay for me to ask more about that?"

"Yeah." Vulpie answers and Collins glances at Polar before looking back to the fox.

"I have to be careful with dual visitation. Are both of you fine with me discussing this?"

"I am. We share everything." Vulpie answers and Polar sends him a warm smile.

"Alright then." Collins says and relaxes a bit. He uses his paws to paint a scenario while elaborating on his earlier statement. "VED shots do last a lifetime but with varying success rates. There are several vulpine diseases that can circumvent VED shots like CRC-11, SF-47 and Vauphen Syndrome. That's why they're reevaluated every year to ensure efficacy. Since VED shots are primarily designed for foxes, the best source of information we have are patients like yourself who have tested them. The results will help the program adapt and engineer better vaccinations for your species."

"Can I get a new shot?"

"We hesitate to do that. VEDs can be quite dangerous and lethal in some cases, as I'm sure you're already aware. Did the doctor who administered them tell you about the risks involved?"

"Yeah, he did. But I've never had any problems. I just wanted to stay clean and... Have unprotected sex." Vulpie admits.

"There's nothing wrong with that, although I wouldn't advise it." The doctor replies and puts his paws together while looking over the orange furred fox. "Did you have a lot of sexual partners?"

"Yes."

"And since you've been married to Polar have you slept with anyone else?"

"No. Well, except for two of his friends..." Vulpie says and glances at the white furred wolf.

"They're careful men and they live in a monogamous relationship. We both consented to it. It was my idea, actually." Polar tells Collins and the timber wolf nods.

"Does that happen very often?"

"Definitely not." Polar quickly replies and Vulpie agrees by finding the strong wolf's left paw. Polar squeezes Vulpie's little right hand and swishes his tail over the examination table slowly, indicating that he's in a frisky but relaxed mood.

"Right, well, it's just a standard VED screening. We'll send off the samples to be tested and check for anything that throws up a red flag. You won't need to check on it again for about another five years."

"So like, do you have many foxes that get sexually transmitted diseases even though they have VED shots?" Vulpie meekly inquires.

"I've never seen one but two of my colleagues have. Honestly, the biggest concerns are Vauphen Syndrome and the Alopex Virus. They're both STDs and neither one of them are hindered by VED." Collins says and pauses for a moment. "May I ask if you've had sex with any other foxes recently?"

"Not for like seven years." Vulpie answers with a smirk.

"So you prefer male wolves?"

"Pretty much."

"Then you have nothing to worry about. VED shots eliminate most of the diseases that wolves and foxes can infect each other with anyway." The timber wolf turns his attention to his laptop once again, and takes another look at their files. He checks their medical history. He decides to begin by feeling their necks. He looks into their ears, eyes, noses and mouths, and proceeds to test their reflexes and muscle strength. Collins listens to their breathing patterns using his stethoscope. He finds no irregularities. He listens to their heartbeats and finds everything in range for a healthy middle aged wolf and young adult fox. He then tests both of their blood pressures before finishing the general examination with a satisfied expression.

"Polar, did you want another prostate exam?"

"Do you think I need one?" The white furred wolf inquires. "It's only been about two months since my last checkup."

"I don't think so. Prostate cancer is less prevalent in gay men."

"I'll pass. We recently moved a two and a half foot table into our bedroom so he can... Take care of me..." Polar answers while showing the doctor a wry look. Vulpie's blue eyes widen and he looks at his husband in surprise.

"You lie on your back?" Collins simply asks, unfazed by the specific sexual reference. The doctor's neutral maturity surprises Vulpie. The gay fox is quite happy to enjoy the company of such a professional because his last doctor was a conservative Deivaist and had underlying religious hang-ups about homosexuality.

"Yes."

"That's a good position for stimulating the gland regardless of a partner's size." Collins replies with a clinical voice. "I'm sure both of you are healthy, but it's been several years since you had one Vulpie."

"Okie dokie!" Vulpie answers and does his best to look emotionless. His fur stands on end a little at the taboo situation. Even though Polar knows every inch of him it's still a little embarrassing and exciting when he stands up to undress for the doctor. Collins retrieves a tube of lubrication from the cabinet near the sink and slides on a pair latex medical gloves.

"I've got my V-Screen charging in the other room and I really love it." Collins nonchalantly says while Vulpie undoes and slides down his pants. The timber wolf looks at Polar while Vulpie makes himself naked and elaborates a bit. "I've filled the thing up with way too much stuff! The camera takes a really great picture."

"It does. It really does." Polar smiles in response. "We've got plans to increase its storage space even more if you can believe it. I'd got mine loaded up with HD videos too."

"That's what I'm guilty of. I've gotten into the habit of filming everything because the picture is so sharp, but there is a downside. Some of the staff have them too and everyone's worried that they're being filmed all the time." The timber wolf chuckles. He stands up without looking at Vulpie when he notices the orange furred fox is naked out of his peripheral vision. Vulpie has removed everything but his stylish white t-shirt. "Okay, turn around and lean on your elbows. Spread your legs."

Vulpie cooperates and looks down at the wall while Doctor Collins investigates the cute fox's anus. He puts his right index and middle finger together and slowly pushes them inside. The penetration is completely painless. Vulpie's used to a much larger piece of wolf anatomy and finds the doctor's gentle probing to be pretty mild. He patiently waits for Collins to complete his investigation, but a smirk from Polar causes him to return one of his own.

The timber wolf moves his fingers in a circular motion in order to identify the lobes and grooves of the fox's prostate gland. He finds it to be firm and rubbery, about the size of a walnut, and slowly retracts his fingers. They slide out of Vulpie and the wolf removes his gloves. He throws them away and then offers Vulpie a pre-moistened wipe to clean up. Vulpie does so, and Doctor Collins talks to Polar just like before, so the attention is taken off of the fox while he gets dressed.

"Did you see the news today? I think there's another Alopex outbreak somewhere. I noticed it was on the TV before leaving for work this morning."

"I think I did see something too, yeah." Polar responds and clears his throat. "How many foxes have died from it again?"

"Over two hundred just this year." Collins replies with a concerned voice.

"Where at? What kind of foxes are getting it?" Vulpie inquires after buttoning his pants. He hops up and takes his seat next to Polar again, and the white furred wolf receives him with his left arm, wrapping it around his little husband with a content smile.

"All types. It's hitting lawyers, construction workers, drug dealers, married couples, you name it. They don't really know how it's being spread so fast because it's only supposed to infect other animals through fluid transmission. That means there's a chance that it's mutated again, and if it evolves into an airborne pathogen then we've got a serious problem on our hands."

"What if it spreads to wolves?" Vulpie mischievously inquires. "There are a lot of vixens with wolf boyfriends out there."

"Yeah." Polar chimes in and Collins nods in agreement.

"That's a major concern. A lot of virologists think it might be able to mutate into a lupine pathogen as well. It's a long way from that at the moment but it's been spreading everywhere and no one knows how."

"So I've GOTTA have this blood test?" Vulpie asks with a weak smile.

"You definitely need to, but just so we can make sure your VED vaccination is still effective."

"How do you know if you've got it? The Alopex virus?"

"Don't worry about that. If you had it you would definitely know it two days after infection."

"Cool." Vulpie smiles and Polar squeezes him with his left arm.

"Alright then, let's get that blood work done and you can be on your way."

Lovers

"I can't believe you're still jealous of Andy. I haven't even seen the guy since I met him." Vulpie says after Polar drops a few ice cubes into his drink. He's just made a dark soda for himself and he sighs in the kitchen while the orange furred fox relaxes on the black leather couch.

"Why shouldn't I be? He's young and good looking. And you had him in the hot tub for Khalan's sake!" The white furred wolf grumbles but sends his husband a little smile.

"What was I supposed to do? I'd be a real jerk to just make him leave after everything."

"Yeah and he already saw you naked so you wanted to see how he'd react to a little more attention."

"No I didn't! I swear that's not what I wanted! Come on, Polar... You know I would never cheat on you."

"How would you like it if I started hitting on a young guy, huh? Would you be cool with that?" Polar inquires while walking into the den and he stands next to the couch while waiting for a response.

"You'd be a prick because I didn't do anything... And I would be EXTREMELY JEALOUS! I'd blow like a volcano!" Vulpie mischievously answers. "I know what you're doing. You just want some reassurance sex don't ya?"

"I think you owe it to me." Polar grins in response.

"Oh, is that right? I've always done something wrong haven't I? Well what can I possibly do to make it all better? Huh? Want me to make sweet love to you again? We're gonna break your table at this rate. And by the way, why'd you have to tell the doctor about it? The hell is wrong with you?" Vulpie laughs.

"I want a blowjob." The white furred wolf says and starts swishing his tail.

"Is that all?"

"I don't mean a quickie either. I want one of those empty-slurpy things. I want one of those..."

"Takes so much time..." The orange furred fox responds with a sly look.

"So? Do you have anything better to do?"

"You're awfully demanding sometimes. Do you know that?"

"Just give me one and I'll be in a better mood. I promise." Polar replies. He winks at Vulpie afterwards and his husband licks his lips in anticipation.

"Okay, but you better be. I'm not gonna guzzle all that cum for nothing!"

"That's not what Andy told me." Polar teases.

"Andy wishes I'd swallow his dick but it'll never happen!" Vulpie grins and glances at the bulge in the white furred wolf's pants.

"I don't think Andy believes you can give an empty slurpy anyway. Maybe it's all hype and just that people like to praise a famous name?"

"Well get the camera out and film it then! I don't give a fuck!" The orange furred fox declares. Polar's blue eyes widen and he shows his lover a lecherous smile.

"I like that idea."

"I don't care."

"Yeah right. Like you'd let me post that online."

"Well of course not really! You're the one that didn't want me in Wet Fur, remember? I might be cool with it! You never know!"

"I think we should film it just in case. It could be an educational thing. Maybe I'll show it to Mitch and Lance if they want to learn how to do it."

"That's... That would be so hot..." Vulpie whispers with a delighted grin. "I'm ready when you are!"

"I expect you to be naked when I come back." Polar instructs and swishes his big tail while walking away from the couch. The orange furred fox bites his lip at his husband's suggestion and cooperates with enthusiasm. He gets up and begins fiddling with his pants just as the white furred wolf goes up the stairs to the second floor. Polar heads down the hallway and makes a right into their bedroom. He holds right and approaches the small closet where he keeps miscellaneous items near his collection of suits. He moved his video camera into the closet a while back when he needed it at a family engagement and both he and Vulpie have been thinking about its proximity to their bed for some time. But he decides that it will be needed downstairs instead. Polar gleefully remembers Vulpie's previous empty slurpy sessions and the tall wolf is satisfied that receiving one on the couch is the most enjoyable position for him. Plus, if he's going to film the event, it'll be much easier to record Vulpie's magic while sitting up.

"Watcha doin up there?" Vulpie calls from the den.

"Testing the battery!" Polar answers with a voice just loud enough to make it downstairs. He sees a full white power cell in the device's viewfinder and presses the record button.

"Well get down here so I can suck your dick! I've had too much caffeine to wait! I want it! I want it! I wanna suck that wuuuuuuuoooooolf COCK!"

"Hey, that's going to be on the movie! I've got it running up here! I hope you don't mind!" Polar laughs in excitement. He gets up and kicks off his shoes, wriggling his big clawed feet free of their tight confines. He lets out a minor breath of delight, enjoying the freedom, and quickly heads for the door. The white furred wolf hurries out of his bedroom and down the steps to the den. What he sees there quickly encourages him to film without delay. Vulpie is out of his t-shirt and shorts and is wagging his tail with a naughty grin. He has his little paws over his crotch and mildly strokes his cute cock and balls while his husband walks to the couch, filming all the way.

"Well what do we have here? It looks like Vulpie Vivixen! And he's naked in my living room! What is this?" Polar inquires with a delighted voice.

"I'm here for educational purposes! That's the naked truth!" Vulpie grins in response. The orange furred fox makes sure to look at the camera lens so Polar can enjoy the movie long after its recorded.

"Is that so? And what will you be teaching us tonight? Hmm?"

"Empty slurpy 101!"

"And what is that?"

"It's a super advanced form of fellatio! Not for the faint of heart! Or for anyone that doesn't like, shall we say, lupine flavor..."

"I'm not quite sure what you mean. Could you elaborate?" Polar replies and walks next to the gay fox. He aims directly down at Vulpie's face and Vulpie smiles even more for the camera when he takes his paws away from his crotch, exposing his little cock and balls.

"My assistant tonight will be Mr. Polar Arctic, a veteran associate of spoogealogy! He's an ultra-sexy wolf and I hope he can stay focused while I perform my technique for your viewing pleasure!"

"Thank you, but you dodged the question my esteemed colleague! What IS an empty slurpy?"

"I already told ya! It's a super technical uber-awesome cock sucking!"

"But everyone can suck a dick, the viewers might ask. What makes you such an expert Mr. Vivixen?"

"I'll have you know that I've sucked more cocks than you ever will! If you look up deep throat in the dictionary there's a picture of the sexy fox in front of ya!"

"Oh you are sexy... But I remain skeptical." Polar teases and both of them swish their tails in anticipation.

"You'll have to forgive Mr. P. I dunno how he forgets that I've made him blow more loads than Mount Wraustlen, but he's the only suitable participant I could locate this evening."

"Suitable? What does that mean?"

"Big cock." Vulpie simply answers.

"I've always liked my cock so it's only natural that you would too!" Polar laughs and Vulpie starts giggling with him.

"I guess so!"

"If you would, just go ahead and spin around for me in case any of our viewers have their cocks out too. I think they'll appreciate the fine foxy specimen in front of me." Vulpie bites his lip at his lover's suggestion and takes a few steps back so he can clear the coffee table and the couch to his right. He turns sideways and runs his black tipped vulpine paws down his thigh while flicking his tail around in excitement. Three twitches and a few more swings gets the message across that Vulpie is happy about the attention and has no problem turning around and touching his cute butt. Polar zooms in and lets the camera focus on the delicious orange fur and the brilliant streak of white that runs underneath the gay fox's tail stem, around his anus, perineum, balls, his crotch and then up his front when he turns around after a few seconds. Vulpie's cock is hard and he masturbates with a grin.

"Don't make me wait too long baby or I'll shoot in my paw! Let's get this show on the road!"

"Yes sir." Polar breathes in delight and walks in front of the couch. Vulpie joins him before he can sit down and voraciously unbuttons the wolf's black jeans. "That a boy..." The tall wolf films Vulpie making the scene a reality and gladly steps out of his pants and then his underwear as his lover yanks them off. Polar's penis bounces at its freedom and a very amused Vulpie grabs it as he gets on his knees.

"You see ladies and gents! THIS! Is a monster cock! Most big dicks might end up gagging you if you try to deep throat them but you have to be a goddess damn PRO to swallow this beast! Give yourself a hand Polar! Oh wait! I've got ya covered!" Vulpie grins and licks his lips. "Now here's a preview of how to handle a situation like this!" The gay fox declares and opens his mouth. He hungrily swallows the white furred wolf's penis and makes Polar groan even though he's very familiar with his husband's technique. He thought he knew all of Vulpie's tricks but the fox already makes him shuffle on his feet. Vulpie cups his balls and deep throats all of it, all the way to the wolf's crotch, and bobs his head back and forth several times. He does it so fast and without any sign of gagging that Polar finds himself laughing.

"God damn yeah! Get it!"

"MMMmmmm!!!" Vulpie hums and keeps his pretty blue eyes focused on the camera while sucking. He maintains eye contact the whole time and proudly swishes his tail.

"Oh fuck! Ladies and gentlemen, I don't know how to describe such a fast and FURIOUS cock sucking but yeah! Yeah... Oh yeah, I could get used to this!" Vulpie pulls back and smacks his lips free of Polar's throbbing penis to respond, his eyes gleaming with pseudo innocence.

"I wish I could say don't try this at home, but it SURE IS FUN! AAhhMMmm!!!" The fox moans and closes his mouth on the wolf's fat penis again. Polar shut his eyes in bliss, almost forgetting to film Vulpie's work, but opens them again when he realizes the camera's moving too much. Holding it steady requires a lot of concentration.

"VERY, very nice introduction... But we'll see if his full thesis on the empty slurpy is correct..." Vulpie's cock sucking makes Polar's knees buckle and the gay fox notices. He pulls back again, with pre-cum and drool spilling from his mouth, and waits for him to sit down. The white furred wolf eagerly makes himself comfortable. He leans back in anticipation, and Vulpie is on his cock before he has a chance to aim the camera at him. The wolf makes up for it by zooming in on Vulpie's adorable face.

"MMmm! Mmmmmmmmmmmmm…" Vulpie hums while swishing his tail.

"Heh, you know… You almost look like a girl Vulpie. Did anyone ever tell you that?" Polar teases and the orange furred fox quickly yanks his head back. The fat cock pops out of his mouth, sending a bit of drool to the side, and Vulpie makes a delighted face.

"I'm gonna take that as a compliment Mr. P!"

"You do! Bright silky orange fur that clashes with that creamy white on your face… Your eyes just light up when you get a chance to suck a dick!"

"Cuz it's super fun! But you take it in the ass every time I wanna rape me a big old wolf! So what do ya mean I'm a girl!"

"I didn't say you were a girl, I said you look like one!" Polar laughs.

"I'm the most manliest man in the world!" Vulpie declares and grabs hold of the snow wolf's massive erection. The orange fox mischievously jiggles the snow wolf's massive erection in his right paw. "Men want to be me! And they want to be IN me too!"

"Here's one of em!" Polar breathes and zooms out from Vulpie's face to get a nice view of things.

"That's lesson two! We must finish lesson one good sir!" Vulpie grins and licks his lips. He yanks Polar's very hard erection to his open mouth and slurps it up with an incredibly adorable whimper.

"OH MY GOD!" Polar groans and shuts his eyes. He quickly opens them again when he realizes he should be filming. His penis is extra sensitive after all the wonderful sucking it's enjoyed so far, in tandem with the brief pause that allowed lots of cum to build up inside. Vulpie's muzzle and throat perfectly envelop his throbbing penis as if they were made for the wolf cock. Somehow Vulpie is able to gurgle on it without vomiting, a phenomenon Polar still cannot explain to this day. It feels perfect, with every inch and part of his big penis being attended to in the most amazing fashion. The only thing that trumps Vulpie's oral sex is reaming out the fox's super tight ass, but his blowjobs are special in their own right. He gets to look the wolf in his eyes during the act, and there's few things more exciting than the expressions Vulpie can make. Cute, slutty, innocent, dirty, filthy, modest, or masterful, he can do it all.

The orange fox takes a moment to look at the camera while performing, and quickly grows fond of its invisible audience. Neither of them plan to do anything with the video, but he imagines other animals seeing him pleasuring his husband to the highest degree, and the thought excites him to no end. He knows how attractive he is, and since he's already an attention whore, he makes sure to talk to the camera with his eyes. He winks at it, and looks from Polar to it with wide eyes, comically, and proceeds to taunt it until the white furred wolf approaches orgasm.

"UUUUHHHH!!! UHAWW GOD!" Polar groans and the orange furred fox quickly gives him his undivided attention. He swishes his tail even faster, and pulls back just enough to control his husband's approaching climax. Vulpie knows a huge cumshot is on the way; he's made sure to fulfill the main requirement of the empty slurpy, which is patience, and is now able to reap the rewards. He tastes it suddenly, but just when he expects it.

"AAAHHHHH!!!!" Polar cries out while ejaculating an effusive burst of semen. It's followed by several equally musky waves of cum that turn Vulpie's mouth into a spooge tank. "OHHH!!! FUCKKK! FUUUCK!" The white furred wolf fails to film every moment of his mind blowing orgasm due to his nervous system being controlled by several very happy organs in the lower part of his body. His prostate shouts with pleasure, along with his balls and every other part that helps the semen rocket into and explode out of his fat cock. Tears well up in the snow wolf's eyes. It's so good that he actually drops the camera against the couch for a moment and struggles to aim it towards Vulpie when he gets his paw on it again.

Vulpie handles his lover's huge climax with immaculate precision. He keeps his right paw and finger around the wolf's large cock as he slides his head back and rakes in all ancillary semen along the way. He makes sure to collect every bit of it in his mouth. He's proud that he doesn't miss a drop, and very carefully slurps his lips from the head of Polar's penis when it's over.

"OH MY FUCKING... Oh my god Vulpie I love you!" Polar gasps and manages to film the orange fox properly once again. Vulpie makes the most mischievous expression in response. He relaxes, but doesn't open his mouth one tiny bit. He enjoys running his tongue around in the lake of semen inside and smiles from ear to ear. "OHhhhhhh... Show us what you've got there!" Polar laughs with a delighted voice. Vulpie cocks his head to the left but doesn't reply. He just keeps smiling. "Come on!" The orange fox finally turns his attention to the camera, and tilts his head back when he opens his mouth. He knows cum is just going to spill out everywhere when he tries to show off his catch, and it does. "Oh my God! Haha!" Polar snickers when several little waterfalls of semen run from the corners of the orange fox's mouth. A slosh of spooge runs out over his chin and down the underside of his muzzle.

Vulpie opens his mouth even more when he knows the rest of Polar's cum will behave itself, and the white furred wolf doesn't waste any time in recording it. He quickly sits up and brings the video camera close so he can film all of it in high definition. Vulpie's mouth and throat is a pure mess of musky wolf jizz. Polar's instinctual need to have someone receive his semen is satisfied to say the least. Vulpie waits a long while for him and the camera to see all of it, and finally closes his mouth.

"Can he do it?" Polar laughs and Vulpie quickly holds up his right index finger, gesturing for him to be quiet. The orange furred fox takes his time with the first swallow, and closes his eyes for the next two. After the fifth gulp, he's sure he's gotten all of it, and slowly opens his mouth to reveal his accomplishment. He licks the corners of his jaw to rake in some of the cum that dribbled out earlier, and collects more of it with his fingers. He puts them in his mouth and sucks on them, tasting as much spooge as he can, and winks at the camera.

"And that's why, I'M THE BOSS!" Vulpie giggles, and Polar releases a very satisfied laugh.

Agendas

An attractive and fastidious gray furred she-wolf answers her phone after its second ring. She lifts it to her right ear and licks her lips before speaking. Karla knows who the caller is but is fond of introductions and titles. She likes to hear her name and enjoys granting audiences with agents outside of her station. The GBI's efficient procedures are quite satisfying to her worldview and innate sense of order.

"Dressler." She simply says.

"Karla, it's Damon." A brown fox answers. "We've already run a few of the documents by Druward, and he didn't seem to notice. But I don't know if he'll sign them today. Do you want me to call him tomorrow morning?"

"No, I'll speak with Mr. Wraulgh."

"You sure? After what happened last time?"

"It won't be a problem." Karla responds.

"Alright, just be careful not to mention anything about the investigation. He's familiar with our office now, and I think he's starting to suspect something."

"He's on his way out, but don't say anything if he contacts you. Just direct him to me and I'll handle it."

"I'm sending you a copy of the files now."

"Thank you." The she-wolf says and hangs up just as a new email appears in her inbox. She navigates to it on her computer screen and opens the GBI document. She skips fourteen pages until she sees a small paragraph devoted to the synthetic Deivas. It concerns their containment at the Elbrus military base.

Druward pauses when he comes across the same paragraph. He's reviewing it in his office at the GBI headquarters facility in Sufias City, and the black furred wolf was just about to sign off on the transfer order when he discovered the dubious section. He retrieves his black phone from its charger and finds Karla Dressler's number by momentarily flipping to the front of the report. He leans back in his leather office recliner after punching in her numbers and uses his executive pen to flip to page fourteen once more.

"Hello?"

"Karla. It's Druward."

"Hi."

"Hi. I'm looking over the Elbrus report that your office sent me and I have a few questions for you..." The GBI director says with an unfriendly voice.

"Shoot."

"Page fourteen... Are you aware that all of the Elbrus facility's machines are subject to transfer if I sign this document? I never agreed to move the Deivas. On whose authority did you draft this?"

"I wasn't aware of any transfer order."

"There's a paragraph that gives your office clearance to move equipment in the research wing without authorization from the director. That's what the wording says. And then there's something about a clandestine delivery of unstable materials to a church? What am I to make of this?"

"I'd be happy to investigate the matter, but the GSB needs that document by the end of the week."

"Oh do they?" Druward growls and looks aside as if Karla is standing next to his desk. "It's no secret your investigation into my affairs is a clear power grab, and I will not tolerate insubordination. The Governmental Security Bureau works for me, not the other way around. Am I being clear?"

"Of course, Director."

"Who drafted this?"

"I'm not exactly sure, but I can find out."

"You're not sure? I'll come down there in person if I have to. I've cooperated with your little ethics panel long enough."

"There's no need for that, I assure you. I'll find the answers you need, Druward."

"Like the sequester your boys at the treasury tried to push through? I haven't forgotten."

"I'll be happy to work with you however I can."

"Then be in my office in one hour."

"Yes sir."

Karla moves with purpose and a spring in her step that always irritates Druward. He doesn't bother to get out of his chair when she enters his office and gently closes the door.

"Sit down." The director orders and she complies. Druward's yellow eyes dilate somewhat thanks to her silky gray fur and bountiful figure. Karla has always been a frustration to him, both mentally and physically, because of the document workload her office propagates. The fact that she's sexually attractive makes his job even harder. He despises the way she acts as if nothing ever phases her despite the numerous issues they've had. Most agents are afraid of losing their job but Ms. Dressler has an air of overconfidence that really gets under his fur. "Did you think I wouldn't notice?"

"Mr. Wraulgh, I apologize for any inconvenience I or my office have caused you."

"Cut the crap." The black furred wolf growls and leans forward. He drops his arms onto the desk to make his point.

"I've given you people the benefit of the doubt but I don't see an ounce of reciprocation. I want to meet them. I want to see each one of them, face to face, and that includes Amsend."

"I'd be happy to relay your request but you know Mr. Amsend has a hectic schedule."

"I don't give a damn. I refuse to work with your office until I know who I'm in charge of and what your division is doing. The GSB's budget has shot up from fourteen to twenty nine billion dollars over the last five years, and I didn't ask the director of national intelligence for more funding... So just what in the hell are you people doing over there?"

"We handle most of the intelligence gathering for the bureau, and that's why it's traditionally been a paws-off operation. You know that." Karla respectfully responds.

"That might fool the press but I know better. I never investigated your division and the assassinations you conduct because I assumed you were working for the best interests of the Sufias World Government. But now I'm not so sure. What I saw in this report is no less than treason." Druward informs the gray furred she-wolf and gestures towards the file folder on his desk with his right paw. "Has the GSB stolen equipment from my bureau in the past? To the best of your knowledge, Ms. Dressler, have you or any of your superiors moved equipment from secure facilities without authorization?"

"Not that I'm aware of."

"You're sure about that? I know Amsend wanted to move Vulpie.net's machine out of the Sufias Heritage Museum. He thought he could buy off the local police, but he underestimated their fear of this office..."

"I don't know anything about that." Karla replies and Druward stares at her for a moment.

"Never heard a peep from him after that, so I assumed he was just testing his limits. I didn't want to cause problems... Well... Now you can tell him that he's found his limit. I haven't dirtied my paws within the bureau for a long time, but I will if I have to. You WILL respect the chain of command. Am I being clear?"

"I'm sure it won't come to that. No one's ever rejected or subverted your commands to my knowledge, sir."

"Of course not." The GBI director sighs and Karla swishes her tail once. He tries not to notice, but can't resist, and steals a quick glance at her silky curvaceous form before leaning back in his chair. He puts his paws together in his lap before showing her a curious expression.

"Is there something else?"

"You tell me, Karla. Ever since you barged into my administration I've had nothing but problems. I thought you might have something extra to contribute?"

"Well, I've disclosed everything I know, Sir." The attractive she-wolf answers.

"Everything? Don't insult my intelligence. Knowledge is the issue here and I don't know anything about the GSB or what you report to them. President Slade may have upped your influence but he's just a sock puppet."

"Yes he is." Karla pretentiously responds.

"Your bosses are all too familiar with that, aren't they? Take in mind that I researched lupine series seven on my way up, so I'm well aware of the conspiracy theories."

"Mr. Druward, I can assure you the people I work for take their positions just as seriously as you do. You aren't really going to give credence to ridiculous stories like those, are you?"

"Conspiracy is what we do, Karla…" The black furred wolf quips in response. "Every war ever fought was born of a conspiracy. How else are the people in power supposed to control the masses? The military industrial complex has approached me with more false flag proposals than I can count."

"I'll take your word for it." Karla replies with a shrug and a smile.

"So you're going to set up that meeting for me, yes? It's not necessary for me to go over there and shut you down?"

"I… Look, I've already told you that I'll try my best."

"I don't want you to try. Do it. Arrange a meeting with the heads of the GSB. And of course, since I don't know their names or even what their specialties are, it would be so very helpful for you to send me a list of the animals that will be in attendance."

"I don't know if I can get them all but I will get more than one."

"That's not good enough." Druward barks and silence fills the room. The intense look coming from the coal furred wolf's yellow eyes causes Karla to stiffen up. She remains calm and collected as always, but her confident posture dissolves. Her gray fur begins to stand on end, and the director recognizes the threatening look she returns.

"As you wish, Mr. Wraulgh."

"It is as I wish. I'm glad you noticed that. I'd hate to start a small civil war over something this insignificant."

"Oh no, you've convinced me. I'll make sure you have your meeting." Karla responds with an intense look of her own.

"Good. Treat me with respect and I'll return the favor."

"It might take me some time. How soon do you need it to be?"

"This week would be fine... Can you do that?"

"Yes sir, I believe I can."

"Thank you Karla. Oh, and one more thing." Druward replies and sends her a friendly look. "Don't lie to me. If I meet with a bunch of college kids turned agents, or retired operatives doing favors for the big boss, standing in for him, I'll take it personally." Another silence fills the room as she mulls over his warning.

"I completely understand." Karla replies with a concerned voice. She looks as though she could become angry but it's obvious that he has enough hostility for both of them.

"I apologize for my tone, Karla. I know you're just doing your job and they've sworn you to secrecy, but I'm responsible for this organization." The coal furred wolf says, and she nods in agreement. The apology feels genuine and allows the gray she-wolf a chance to stand up.

"I'll send you an email as soon as possible. I can't guarantee I'll have everything together by tomorrow but I'll send you the member list by Wednesday at least, and I'll ask each of them to attend this week."

"Amsend needs to be there. I want to see him and the other major players. It doesn't have to be ten animals at the first meeting, but I want to see the department heads." Druward responds and licks his lips. "Thank you Karla."

"I'll do what I can. See you later this week." The attractive she-wolf replies and turns around. Druward almost apologizes again but stops himself just in time. He didn't realize just how much he likes her until he has a chance to watch her tail on the way out. She has a very nice ass and it fits the rest of her voluptuous frame perfectly. The GBI director clears his throat instead. He pretends to look at the report on his desk as she closes the door.

"Since day one…" He mutters and opens the file folder. He investigates the Governmental Security Bureau's letterhead and Amsend Lahnak's signature at the bottom right corner of the page. It looks like a blanket signature that's presented on every form the GSB prints, but something underneath Amsend's name draws Druward's attention. Directly under the signature is a series of tightly connected letters. The font used to print them is significantly smaller than the rest of the document. "LIAA."

The black furred wolf sniffs the air in confusion and picks up the telephone once again. He autodials Sims in the evidence lab and waits for a moment while eying the form.

"Yeah." Sims answers. He's a fast paced red fox, and takes the phone call informally because he receives hundreds of inquiries on a daily basis as the GBI's premier cryptologist.

"I'm meeting with the GSB later this week and I noticed something while looking over a transfer order they sent my way. There's a very small word underneath the director's signature."

"The GSB? Isn't that the uh… The Lahnak guy, the husky, right?"

"Yeah."

"No one's ever seen him around here. I never have."

"I'll chat with you after I get a face to face, but for now, can you tell me if L-I-A-A means anything? It looks like an operation passcode, like the ones we use to give kill clearance for a target, but I don't recognize it. They might be using in house linguistics to generate and maintain those codes, so I need you to check what we have against them. Try to go back as far as you can."

"Oh man, that might take a while... There's a thousand LIAAs that I can think of, like lock-in-amplifier-adjustments, or lost-in-action-advise.

"First thing that came to mind was local-issuing-authority but it's missing another A. Is lost-in-action-advise military speak?"

"Yeah."

"It must be discontinued because I've never heard that being used in the field. Is it still recognized anywhere on Sufias during live operations?"

"I don't think so. I... THINK... I saw it in the archives but to tell the truth, I have no idea where that came from or who's using it. You might want to ask the guys in records."

"Any other ideas?"

"I can match LIAA with plenty of phrases but none of them would make sense for a transfer order."

"Yeah, it doesn't sound like much."

"Why do you think it's there?"

"No clue. This is really the first time I've inspected one of their forms."

"So what's going on?"

"Just let me know if you find anything about that abbreviation. Thanks Sims."

"No problem." The fox replies, and Druward hangs up the phone very slowly. He leans back in his chair and runs his tongue across his teeth in frustration.

Lioness Station

Phil hates pulling his girlfriend through the masses of animals in their way but they have a train to catch. She's been out of work on family medical leave since giving birth to their new bundle of joy, but now he's got daddy duty. The young lupine couple decided to take turns staying home with Brandon. Their new baby boy is the love of their lives and they want to take care of him for as long as possible. A babysitter will not do. Neither one wants to have their fuzzy little angel in the paws of others when he's so tiny and fresh to the world.

"Remember to eat, Baby. You've got to eat." Phil stresses as they get up the subway train tracks. The station is jam packed with all sorts of animals, tigers, panthers, lions, hounds, foxes, wolves... It's a loud and uncomfortable place but at least the scenery is nice. Lioness station is the oldest subway in Sufias City and it's well maintained by the state.

"I've got to lose so much weight... I'm so fat..." Cindy whispers to her husband and the gray wolf gently touches the brown fur on her neck. She can't help but grin and both of the timber wolves laugh softly.

"You look good! Really!" Phil says and wipes his nose when he hears the train squeaking in the distance.

"You've gotta get home. I don't like leaving Brandon with your mother. I feel like I'm putting her out."

"Aw, she doesn't mind. And besides, I couldn't let you go back to work without seeing you off! Sugar Head!" Cindy grins at her husband. He gave her the nickname on their fourth date because she kept getting headaches after drinking too many slushies at the fair. They go back and forth with each other until the subway fills with a loud roar and the train pulls in. The station is rather crowded but the animals are conscientious of each other so no one gets too close to it when it makes its laborious arrival. Lioness Station's numerous safety announcements have a tendency to drive animals crazy, but the messages have sunken in.

The train stops and when it opens its doors, animals begin streaming out of it and piling in at the same time. Phil pulls Cindy inside, and she laughs at his zeal. The timber wolf yanks on her and gets her over to one of the polls so they can stand for the ride.

"What are you doing? You can't come with me!" Cindy gleefully tells her young husband.

"Why not? Maybe I will today." Phil responds and bends down to kiss her before she has a chance to scold him further. She releases a small moan and rubs his hips during their intimate encounter... A few passengers whisper about their behavior but they both secretly enjoy the attention and draw out the kiss... However... The two young wolves grow suspicious when they hear something entirely different. Some of the animals are gasping, and the couple ends their hot exchange with curious expressions. They look around, seeing that many of the passengers are staring at them, or rather, something behind them.

Phil sees the focus of their attention first. To his right, just behind Cindy, is Goddess Aila. She's wearing a tight black t-shirt that barely covers her gigantic breasts, and it matches her slim black shorts perfectly. Her irises are completely red. Cindy has never seen anything like it, and she releases a loud gasp of her own when she turns and sees her. Aila is around five foot eight inches tall, smaller than Phil, but she's quite sizeable. Her powerful legs perfectly accent her omnipotent feminine physique. She's grinning at them, and two male panthers, both over six feet tall, quickly exit the train before the doors close.

Everyone is silent. Goddess Aila continues to grin and takes a moment to look over the other animals in the vehicle with her. There are three male wolves, all brown furred timber wolves, two other she-wolves, both timber wolves as well, in addition to four young male panthers, three brown vixens, a family of tigers, and an old married cheetah couple. The train starts moving and its sudden lurch makes one of the panthers yelp.

"Oh shit, what the fuck?! What the fuck man?" The young cat's words fall silent on the rest of the passengers. They're all familiar with the goddess of hell. It doesn't matter if she's traditionally been represented as canine when so many of the passengers are feline, all of them have the same sinking feeling. Whether they believe in Deivaism or not, they know the thing in the train with them is a serious threat. The same thought runs through their minds and they all come to the same assumption without speaking a word. This is one of Vulpie's robots and it's going to kill them at any moment.

But there are some staunchly religious passengers... The two young female timber wolves were raised in a conservative family, and they question whether what they're seeing is real. They aren't the only ones. The old cheetah couple gawks in terror and acclimate themselves rather quickly to the possibility of Aila being in the train with them.

"Who?... Are you?..." Phil whispers.

"Where's your baby?" Aila grins. Cindy cringes at the question and clutches Phil.

"At home..." She whispers with a fragile voice. She can't stand the way Aila is looking at her, as if she can see into her very soul and knows exactly where to find their son.

"Bring me Vaxi." The hound Deiva demands and suddenly lurches to the right. Screams erupt everywhere. She jolts over to the three vixens, who are hiding in their seats nearby, and grabs two of their necks. She lifts them out of their seats and they scream horrendously. One of the young panthers tries to bolt by, following the lead of the others that escaped the train before it departed, but she shifts her weight to her right leg and impales him with her left foot. She kills the sturdy young feline by breaking his spine through his stomach, and then returns to her previous pursuits. The dead cat rolls off the wall and rumbles on the floor while the passengers scream and Aila squeezes the vixens' throats. She crunches them into a bloody but expedient death and drops them when finished.

She maintains her unholy smile and looks to her left while Phil and Cindy make a run for it. Aila hears them slam against the door while it's trying to slide open, but decides to let them go. They stumble into the train car in front of them and scream for help. Aila turns her attention to the family of tigers. She kills the father by grabbing his head and ripping it off with two quick jerks, and proceeds to kill the man's wife with it. She crushes her skull with his, creating a terrible mess, and slaughters their young daughter with a simple blow to the face.

Cindy stumbles and falls down, grasping for help, yelling loudly, joining in a chorus of surprised animals in the second train car. Aila kills two more of the panthers, and the animals around her try to flee into the car behind them. Phil, Cindy and the others don't look back. A hoard of terrified animals push ahead, spilling into the other train cars ahead of them before the operator catches wind of the emergency and slams on the breaks. The animals fly forward and stumble all over the place with the exception of everyone lucky enough to be holding onto one of the steel support pipes.

Flames erupt inside the train car where Aila continues to kill her victims. The sound is horrible and otherworldly, as if hell itself is breaking into the real world. When the train finally comes to a complete stop and the doors open, every single animal flees into the dark subway. They stumble, run, trip, and crawl their way away from the train as fast as they possibly can, until the vehicle sits by itself in the cold long dark of the underground tunnel.

"This way! No, YOU! Come with me! Get the fuck down here!" A strong lion cop shouts while pushing through the mass of fleeing citizens. He's gone down into the subway even though everyone is running as fast as they can in the other direction. At the top of the steps is his partner, a young gray wolf, and two firefighters, a brown fox and a brown wolf. They were nearby the subway and received the call on their radios about the emergency but have yet to come halfway down the steps.

"No fuckin way! What the fuck is going on down there? We can't disarm no bomb!" The brown fox shouts. His accent is very "downtown," almost mobster-like, and when his friend chimes in, both of the cops find their voices oddly similar despite the difference in species.

"That's right! The fuck we doin here for?"

"There's a goddamn fire down here!" The lion cop yells and after a hard look, his partner finally joins him at the bottom of the steps.

"Fire? Yeah! Probably another fuckin bomb too! And what the fuck we supposed to do without the truck man?"

"Forget you pussies! Sherrie!" The large cat curses, and his partner looks back over his shoulder at them as he follows.

"FUCK YOU!" The brown fox says and his friend curses as well, but they both feel incredibly guilty about staying behind and face each other after a moment.

"We goin?"

"Fuck, I guess so..."

"Ray, you good?" The lion breathes while running with his partner.

"Yeah!" Ray answers, but the cat hears a lot of fear in his voice.

"Let's do this! These people need our help!"

"Gonna fuckin die, I know it! Dale! This doesn't feel right!"

"You've been saying that for months!" Dale responds while they approach the tunnel. There's no train parked at platform G where the terrified animals ended up fleeing to. The two cops hurry into the shadows and pull out their side arms. They keep them low, both paws on their guns, and head towards the unknown. The darkness dances blinding light upon them as they pass by several beacon lights in the tunnel and they come up on the train in less than two minutes. "There it is!"

"Fuck me." The gray wolf whispers and slows his pace. He gets close to Dale and they continue to advance towards the vehicle.

"Where's the smoke? There's no fire."

"Probably inside the train."

"HEY!" The wolf firefighter shouts from behind them, and both of the cops spin and aim at him and the fox with him in a panic.

"WHOA! WHOA! WHAT THE FUCK ARE YOU DOIN?!"

"What the fuck are you doing?" Ray demands.

"You fuckin IDIOTS! Bout to fucking blow your heads off!" Dale shouts.

"The fuck man! First you wanted us down here then you draw down on us?" Both of the cops spin around once again to assess the crime scene. The train is still silent... motionless... ghostly... They're glad to have the brown fox and wolf with them despite their stupidity. The two brought their fire axes with them.

"Swear to Goddess Khalan, I'll slice a motherfucker up if there's little dead kids in there! Fuckin terrorists!" The brown fox threatens.

"I might let you if they're still alive." Dale responds and the firefighters chuckle in delight.

"Careful... Don't give these fucknuts any ideas." Ray says with wide yellow eyes while he and Dale both struggle to locate the destroyed train car.

"There's the end! Where'd the bomb go off?" The brown wolf shouts, as if testing to see if anything is lurking in the tunnel. His voice echoes off of the concrete walls, all the way into the darkness far in the distance.

"I don't see it. It's all in one piece. They said a bomb exploded." The wolf cop notes.

"Said there was a fire." Dale corrects, and approaches the last two sections of the train. Both of the train cars look completely fine, and they stop at the open doors.

"Wha... Where's the fire man?" The brown fox inquires while looking the train up and down.

"No broken glass, no scorch marks... Nothing..." Ray whispers.

"And then... She asked me where my baby was!" Cindy cries out, clutching Phil while he holds her tightly in front of a sea of reporters. "I told her he was at home..." She sniffles and has to stop in the middle of her statement to begin sobbing once more. Special agent Rotick watches from a distance, at the top of the steps leading down into platform G. The brown and white furred wolf doesn't know what to think of the spectacle. It's raining and there are about fifty microphones in the faces of the young wolf couple.

"Ah! There's nothing quite like a bomb going off to start the day!" Druward says while approaching from the street.

"Coffee?" Rotick simply inquires as he continues to observe the media frenzy.

"For me?" Druward asks with mock affection and takes a sip.

"Fuck you."

"Eh... Tastes like shit. Here, knock yourself out." The black furred wolf replies and winces. He hands the drink over to Rotick who takes a swallow and shrugs his shoulders.

"Not so bad."

"If you say so..." Druward responds and takes a moment to peer over at the terrified wolf couple. The press is busy interviewing several others but Cindy is the most upset.

"And I thought I'd seen it all... The dark goddess in a subway never crossed my mind." Rotick comments and follows the last agent in.

"Just another day serving the bureau. If you get ripped apart by Aila I'll have a hard time explaining it to your wife."

"Better skip that." Rotick snorts. "Bitch would probably stab you."

"Ooouch." Druward says and eyes the platform. The GBI agents know what to do and meet with local law enforcement to discuss the situation. Druward and Rotick wait until one of them brings back the chief of police and the men that first discovered the train.

"Frank Harold, sir, Chief of Police." A sturdy panther tells Druward and nods at Rotick. The cat's accent is effusively northeastern metropolitan, just like the two firefighters that discovered the train.

"Druward Wraulgh." The GBI director responds and they shake paws. "You replaced Carlos?"

"Yes sir, about a month ago, sir. He told me how you guys like to handle situations like this. We didn't touch the crime scene, but there's not much in there anyway. It's like nothing even happened."

"What are you talking about?" Rotick asks in confusion.

"Yo, Ricky!" The chief shouts to his side, and the brown furred fox walks up behind him, in addition to the timber wolf. "These boys have been working this part of Sufias going on seven years now and they were first on the scene." The panther points over at Dale and Ray, and signals for them to join them as well. "These guys."

"There's nothing there man." Ricky comments. Druward looks over the assorted group of animals and shoves his paws into the pockets of his black trench coat.

"You didn't see a thing? Tell us what happened." Rotick demands.

"The train's there but there's no one inside. No scorch marks, no dead bodies, no broken glass... Nothing. It's just like the train stopped, and everybody ran, but the victims disappeared."

"That Cindy kid said she saw Aila kill twelve people... So did her boyfriend."

"I was told we have twenty five witnesses." Druward notes.

"That's right. They swear up and down that Aila attacked them, and most of them think it was one of Vulpie Vivixen's robots."

"We can rule that out. There's no way Vulpie's responsible for this. The Deivas were made by Vulpie.net itself so if anything this is the work of his computer virus."

"How can you be so sure? You guys arrested him and tried to put him away for life."

"Things have become a lot more complicated. I was on Zeravyn and I saw exactly what Vulpie.net's capable of. It did this, not him."

"I was about to send some boys to bring him in." Frank replies.

"I'll find out what he knows after we're done here."

"If you say so. I still think we should arrest the faggot. Who else would do this kind of thing?"

"I'm starting to think that's the idea." The black furred wolf mysteriously answers, and Frank squints in confusion. "His computer virus seems to hate every fur on his body. I saw it crunch him on the floor like a soda can... Since then it's built the largest spaceship in history, the fake goddesses, and that hellish thing they had to vaporize with the ion cannon... So the chances that Vulpie did this are very low. I even helped him get to Zeravyn so he could investigate what was going on there because he actually wanted to help."

"So... You mean the computer virus is still loose and blowing shit up?" Ricky asks.

"Blowing shit up without leaving evidence." Rotick comments.

"Let's get down there and see it." Druward says and the police chief nods in agreement. He turns and begins leading all of them across platform G towards the tunnel.

"Excuse me, uh, sir, are you the director of the bureau? You're Wraulgh?" The timber wolf firefighter suddenly inquires. His odd curiosity quickly draws attention from several members of the GBI in the area.

"Yes?"

"Shut up Patrick!" Ricky barks but the timber wolf licks his lips and furthers the impromptu conversation.

"What do you want?" Druward asks while giving the firefighter an irritated glance.

"Nothing, see but, my brother had a shop on that Sevrif space ship. He was there and saw you guys fighting, well uh, getting beat up by Vulpie's robot!"

"I'm sure there's a point somewhere in our future?" One of the cops makes a move to rough Patrick up but the black furred wolf stops it with a wave of his right paw.

"Well, I didn't really have a point I guess. I just want to know if it's like they say it is, the robot and all. It's unstoppable, right?"

"Not anymore. Rest safe citizen; your government has been hard at work since that disaster."

"Uh, okay sir. Thank you sir!" Patrick mumbles and falls behind the rest of the group.

"So what was that?" The GBI director asks the chief of police, referring to Patrick's excessive curiosity. The panther can't help but laugh. He looks over his shoulder to make sure the firefighter is out of ear shot.

"A lot of these downtown boys are protective of the city. Hell, my grandfather was a civil engineer."

"Right." Druward replies while squinting at the train in the distance. He can barely make out its tail end. "Our destroyed train looks surprisingly pristine from here."

"Yeah, you boys definitely have your work cut out for you. I don't think those witnesses are lying yet there's nothing at the crime scene. But maybe you'll find something that we missed." Frank replies. The group walks for another five minutes until they're right next to the train. Rotick enters the front, while the GBI director and chief of police head towards the tail end. Numerous forensic specialists are already combing over the vehicle's interior.

"And there was a fire? One of those goddess things attacked this compartment and set it ablaze like an oil spill?"

"Yep." Frank responds and shakes his head.

"The windows aren't even broken." The coal furred wolf comments and enters the train. He watches where he steps, but there is nothing special on the floor. His black boots thud against the metal interior and reverberate slightly throughout the train car.

"This is the spot." Frank says and walks up behind him. Druward turns and takes a step back to see what the police chief wants to show him. "Right here." The panther elaborates, grabbing the metal support pole to his left. This is where those wolf kids were and everyone said she just appeared right over there." The feline points to his right, towards the door to the next compartment, and Druward sighs.

"That's where she entered?"

"They said the door was shut. She just appeared there somehow." The chief of police responds and takes a moment to move out of the train and signals for Dale, Ray, Ricky, and Patrick to come over. Frank steps aside and stands in the doorway between the final train car and the one in front of it.

"This is where it happened. And you guys saw nothing?" Druward asks the small group.

"No Boss. It was like this when we showed up." Patrick answers.

"Nothing at all." Ricky comments.

"Nadda." Dale states and Druward sighs. He brings a paw to his chin and rubs it briefly. His thoughts are interrupted by Rotick, who enters the final train car as well after Frank lets him by.

"What you got?" Druward asks.

"Jack and shit. They can't find a goddess damn thing."

"Have you guys ever seen anything like this before?" Frank inquires. "Do you have any idea what's going on? I know you won't tell us if it's a matter of national security…"

"No, never." Rotick responds, and Druward turns his paws into fists. They pop from his own strength, and he feels slightly more relaxed after releasing them.

"Have them check the train for chemicals."

"Chemicals?" Rotick asks.

"Yes." The brown and white furred wolf nods and Frank lets him by once again so he can go speak with the forensic specialists. Druward crouches down and investigates the seats near him. He sends his yellow eyes over every nook and cranny but finds no sign of a struggle.

"They'll have it done in about an hour." Rotick says after he returns.

"Thanks." The GBI director replies and looks up at the police chief. "Could you guys step out of the car?" The sturdy panther returns a slightly disappointed expression but cooperates. He leaves the vehicle, along with the two other cops and firefighters while Rotick walks over to Druward.

"What do you think? PYSOP?" Druward asks his trusted comrade.

"I was thinking along those lines, yeah. What else could it be? No victims, no bodies, not a shred of evidence... Something shady definitely happened here." Rotick answers with a slightly excited but equally concerned voice. Druward understands why; they live for this sort of thing.

"The dark goddess on a train is a pretty terrific mind fuck." Druward says and takes a deep breath. "Military?"

"Could be, but I don't think so. This is the sort of thing that we uh..."

"That we do... Right..."

"But there isn't another Aila machine anymore, right? Vulpie told us the one he saw on Zeravyn was destroyed."

"We need to place Elbrus on high alert. That place should be locked down way tighter than it is."

"Think they could get out?"

"Not on their own... But I have an idea who might be behind this. I don't know how they did it but... Could one of Vulpie's VulGrids pull this off?"

"Yeah, but they can't generate sound, right? I mean, they could with speakers, but how could you simulate it through buildings like the visuals?"

"He hasn't figured that one out yet. The Navy wouldn't do this... And they're the only ones he's sold them to so far."

"And we're sure about that, are we?"

"Damn sure. But that doesn't mean that they reached the intended buyers." Druward responds and licks his lips. "I'm going over to Vulpie Industries. Pull up everything you have on his company's dealings with the Navy before we meet with the GSB this week."

"I think they did this." Rotick replies in a hushed voice.

"I agree, but we need evidence to back it up. And we also need weaponry if that Aila thing is real. Fast track the mod six launchers and secure every model the army has in production."

"Yes sir. Er, uh, we're probably going to need more funding for that."

"Leave that to me. I'm planning on carving up Amsend's budget if he doesn't cooperate. If I'm wrong, well, we can find the money somewhere else. That's not an issue... The problem is tracking down whoever or whatever is responsible for this before we're deemed ineffective. I don't feel like explaining this to President Slade before we've had a chance to find out the truth. The fucker will waste our time trying to score political points while this shit continues, and before you know it, you and I are out of a job."

"Just what Karla wants. Why don't we call her down here?" Rotick wryly suggests. "I'm sure she'd love to help."

"No. That's what they want if it was the GSB. We need to hit these fuckers fast and hard... Let them know that we know what they're up to."

"But we don't know."

"Aila in the subway? They want the Deivas. Dressler's little transfer request leaves no doubt in my mind, and now this?"

"Druward..."

"What?" The black furred wolf growls and sees the serious expression on his friend's face. He knows the look.

"Maybe it's time to do a little house cleaning... If you know what I mean..."

"Oh, I plan to give them a good scare. But whether we could go all the way is the real question. The fallout would be unimaginable, and we don't even know who the real players are."

"Let's find out." Rotick growls with a little smile.

"Get the information on Vulpie Industries, and after that, find me a place to meet with our esteemed colleague."

"Wide open spaces... With lots of convenient rooftops?"

"Whatever you feel is best."

"I'm on it."

Quick Paws

Polar leans against the doorway of Halfur's office, staring at the floor, while waiting for the brown fox to complete his assigned tasks. Vulpie requested several security updates to the company's infrastructure, and its Halfur's job to oversee the implementation of new protocols regarding research and development. Halfur is quite good at several of the same things that Vulpie takes an interest in. Polar can see the fire in his brown eyes, the hunger that pushes him on to innovate and win in the digital world. Unfortunately, his looks and attitude couldn't be more of a polar opposite, the white furred wolf thinks to himself and smiles.

Halfur glances at him, as if he somehow just heard what his boss was thinking, and Polar averts his eyes. The brown fox always behaves like he's doing something wrong, even though he's a member of upper management, something else he has in common with Vulpie, though Vulpie comes off as naughty and not just irritated by other people's curiosity. Polar has often looked at Halfur and wondered whether Vulpie could have ended up like him if he didn't admit he was gay and tried to bottle up certain vulnerable tender feelings behind an anti-social wall. Halfur never has a girlfriend, which doesn't mean he's gay or incapable of getting one, but it has made the white furred wolf wonder. Oddly enough, this private speculation has drawn Polar somewhat closer to Halfur because any fox related qualities he shares with Vulpie are attractive to the gay wolf. Vulpie noticed something special about Halfur a long time ago and has seemed satisfied with his performance ever since. Even though they argue quite a bit, Halfur stands out among his peers and undoubtedly is the best programmer in the company next to its CEO.

"How are we looking so far?" Polar inquires.

"The LTL 3.11 system isn't all it's cracked up to be. It's going to take a while, so you at least might want to sit down." Halfur sneers without looking up.

"Good idea. I didn't think it would be since your team likes to test things for a while." Polar responds and walks over to the couch that sits to the right of Halfur's desk. The snow wolf takes a seat and releases a small relaxed breath. The brown fox glances at him in surprise. He's glad Polar didn't react to his disrespectful tone, and adjusts his attitude accordingly.

"LTL is a good idea for our network though. It didn't take Vulpie long to find the loopholes I hid throughout his system and that's why he has me working on this. He's teaching me all of the dirty tricks he uses with Vulpie.net and between me and him facing off, the final pre-domain build will be like a fortress. Only Vulpie.net itself can get around it."

"He trusts you." Polar nods. The wolf's nonchalant reply relaxes him further.

"I don't know why I never thought of it sooner. Vulpie keeps up to date on this stuff more than I do and that's why he hired me. I don't know how. He must have every edition of the Sufian Technological Times sent to his inbox, with cliff notes, at the start of every month."

"Spying is what he does. You wouldn't believe the conversations we've had." Polar smirks.

"A hacker through and through... I respect that..." Halfur whispers while looking over his computer monitor. Polar's blue eyes are suddenly drawn to the door when someone steps inside the room. He immediately recognizes the man by his black trench coat.

"Hey." Druward says, and throws up a paw. He tries to make a joke of his appearance and it succeeds in making Polar return a concerned smile.

"Uh oh." The white furred wolf groans.

"Yeah, I'm afraid so." Halfur looks up from his task and squints at the GBI director. He's heard plenty about him but decides to go back to work since he has nothing to contribute.

"What's up?"

"You don't... Haven't you seen the news?"

"No. Why?" Polar asks and sits up on the couch. "What's going on?"

"There was a terrorist attack on Lioness Station. One of the trains was set on fire by the Dark Goddess! Aila herself!"

"Uhhhhhh... What?"

"First it was a bomb, then a fire, then Aila by the time I got there. It's all over the news."

"Vulpie watches the stock channels at lunch time but we've been busy today. I think he's in a meeting right now."

"Please get him for me. I'm here as a friend."

"I know." Polar answers and they share a small acknowledgement. Halfur looks between them several times but masks his interest quite well. He continues working on his project when Polar gets up and leaves the room with the GBI director. Halfur's office is on the second floor, so Polar leads him towards the steps behind the main lobby. "Was anyone killed?"

"That's the charm." Druward answers, walking next to the white wolf.

"As in?"

"Eyewitnesses say she killed several animals, but we didn't find any bodies."

"Didn't find any?" Polar growls in confusion as they reach the elevators. Deepwolf is standing guard so the white furred wolf assumes Vulpie's upstairs. "Where's Vulpie?"

"He's talking to Price in his office." Deepwolf answers and looks to Druward. He smiles and the GBI director squints at him. "Go on up." The merc says and steps aside. Polar hits the elevator button and Druward cocks his head a bit while looking over Deepwolf.

"Do I know you?"

"I've been with Blacktail for a long time. I was with you when you brought Ivo Lorcan to the CTGD."

"I remember that now…" Druward replies and Polar looks to his left after hearing the director's tone. He wonders why the black furred wolf is suddenly so interested in Vulpie's bodyguard.

"Yeah, he has. He was with me on the Endeavor when the Deivas showed up. He helped me turn on the VulGrid."

"You look familiar." Druward tells the gray furred wolf and Deepwolf shrugs.

"Been to a lot of countries. I was in the army before this." The elevator doors pull open and Polar walks inside. Druward nods but still looks concerned about something. He follows Vulpie's husband into the chamber and Deepwolf stays at his post. The doors close, and the elevator begins its slow climb to the top of the Vulpie Industries tower.

"Have you worked with Deepwolf before or something?" Polar inquires.

"I'm not sure… I recognize him from somewhere. I never noticed it before but… When did he join Blacktail? I mean, when did he start working for you and Vulpie?"

"It was years ago. I think Deepwolf was guarding Vulpie when he was still at the CTGD."

"Have you brought in other people?"

"Of course. Rulef chooses them." Polar answers.

"Oh…" The black furred wolf whispers. "Well, never mind. He just looked familiar. Have you lost any of the men I set up to guard Vulpie?"

"No, they're all still around. Tiala is out on sick leave. Vulpie offered her a million dollars and she took him up on it. I'm not sure if she's coming back."

"Tiala… Damn fine soldier. I recommended her to Blacktail after she did some work for the bureau. She has quite a history you know."

"She was an agent too?"

"No, I said she did some work…" Druward responds with a wry smile.

"Oh." The elevator bumps when they reach the top level. The door slides open, revealing Vulpie, Price, Maxine and Amelia having a great time. Vulpie is sitting on the secretaries' desk waving a red ruler around in his right paw while laughing loudly about something. All of them are cutting up big time, including Vulpie's chief financial officer, which startles Druward a little bit because he's actually seen Andrew Price on the stock channel before and the man is usually very serious.

"So you never wash your fur! NEVER! Just put on tons and tons and TONS of cologne, or perfume, OR COLOGNE AND PERFUME! That way they can't miss ya!"

"You're crazy!" Amelia roars and Vulpie swats the ruler at her playfully.

"Listen here! I knows my stuff! Maxine's hubby wasn't lying at all! He totally LIKED the way she smelled like a wet wad of fur! Sometimes I don't even wash! I'll just oil up the couch with the stuff and wriggle around on it until you can't smell anything else! Saves time and Mister Polar LOVES IT!"

"What are you talking about?!" Polar laughs, catching all of them completely off guard. Druward puts his paws in his trench coat and waits.

"Oh! How long have you been there?!" Price coughs.

"Heard everything. ALL OF IT!" The white furred wolf teases.

"No way! If you heard it all I'd already be dead!" The orange furred fox gleefully replies and waves the ruler at him. "Uh oh! Maybe that's why Druward is here! They've finally come for me!"

"Druward Wraulgh! Wow, this is a surprise." Price respectfully says, and the old gray fox steps back from the desk.

"Look at him! Distancing himself from me already! What loyalty!" Vulpie giggles and glances at Druward and Polar again. The look on the GBI director's face causes him to take a deep breath, drop the ruler, and hop off of the desk.

"I won't do it!" Amelia declares.

"Not negotiable! Smell like roses tomorrow or else!" The orange furred fox wryly responds and puts his paws together before turning around to face Druward.

"Hi. What's up? It's not good is it?"

"Not seen the news today, I take it?" The black furred wolf inquires.

"No sir, I have not... We better go into my office. This way! You haven't seen it yet have you?"

"Not yet, no." Druward dryly answers but Vulpie can see he's a little happy to see him too. The fox approaches the sliding doors and they whoosh open. Druward walks inside and Polar shares a concerned smile with his cute lover. Vulpie affectionately touches the white furred wolf's left paw as he enters, and Polar gently squeezes his little hand in response.

"Here, have a seat Druward." Polar offers. He gestures to the multiple high definition flat screen televisions that are hanging on the wall in the middle of the comfort zone to the left of the entrance. There are three leather sofas, the first with its back to the entrance, the second with its back towards Vulpie's desk, and the third sits across from the first with a small media table in the center. The GBI director notices what's on the news, the attack on Lioness station, and sees where Polar is going with his suggestion. He turns and walks around the middle sofa and finds a seat on the couch in front of Vulpie's desk. It's the most comfortable position because an animal can watch all of the TVs without having to cock their head to a different angle.

"Thanks." The coal wolf replies and waits on them. Polar and Vulpie take the sofa to the left of him, Polar sitting on the right side with Vulpie to his left.

"Yep, there it is..." Vulpie says while watching one of the TVs. No one says anything for a moment and Druward clears his throat after the segment ends with a film of the pristine subway train.

"Not much of a crime scene is it?" The GBI director responds.

"Yeah, I was looking for burn marks or something but didn't see a thing."

"You said there were eyewitnesses though?" Polar inquires. "And yet nothing happened?"

"If this Aila thing killed multiple people she must have eaten them whole without leaving a single trace of blood, and then cleaned the scorched interior before vanishing. I went over the train myself. There's nothing there."

"Then they're lying? Maybe they were paid off or something." Polar suggests.

"Too convincing. My men investigated every animal that claimed to see this attack and we didn't find anything unusual. I think they really did see Aila or something like her." Druward responds.

"How is that possible?" Vulpie asks with wide blue eyes.

"You saw an Aila Deiva on Zeravyn. That's right, isn't it?" The black furred wolf asks with a probing voice.

"Yeah, and that giant mechanical freak thing ate her."

"But that was after she... Threw you up onto a ledge so you could temporarily escape it? Then... You went into the freezer, right?" Druward inquires while squinting.

"Exactly. You said it like you were there yourself." The orange furred fox answers.

"Well you gave us several pages of detail on the event and I went over it four times."

"You trust me, don't you?"

"Of course I trust you Vulpie. I just want to make sure I understand what happened. I had to explain it to an investigative committee after sending the report to the director of national intelligence. They gave me a tongue lashing about using a core bomb underneath the ground, but it's not like I regret the decision, especially after that thing came to the surface. It was completely invincible... Walked right up to that mange devastator, and the devastator went busto after hitting it at close range. Those things are loaded with hundreds of missiles and it was just... Like fireworks."

"Maybe there are more Deivas than we thought. Vulpie.net could have made several of them." Polar comments.

"Yeah, but I saw the pit it was dumping its throwaways in. There were hundreds of parts down there, maybe even thousands." Vulpie replies. "It looked like Vulpie.net wasn't able to make them very easily, but maybe Polar's right. Maybe after it perfected the process it made a dozen of them."

"But you don't really believe that."

"No."

"I don't see how. They've gone over those women with a fine toothed comb and still have no idea what was used to build them. Some of their elements aren't even on the periodic table."

"Really?" Vulpie quickly asks. "I didn't know that."

"It's too bad we can't ask Sevrif about them..." Druward says and trails off in thought. "Actually... That reminds me."

"What?"

"The government maintains communication with all deep space ships as much as possible and the Sevrif has been quite useful as of late. Sapher's been telling us where the red wolves are when they pick them up on radar."

"The terrorists?" Polar asks.

"Yes... Well... That's an entirely different conversation." Druward responds and clears his throat. "But the odd thing is, the reports have come too frequently and too efficiently for Sevrif's right hand man to be doing it all by himself... I think it's actually the ship... I think Sevrif didn't really die when he blew himself up."

"That sneaky maned wolf!" Vulpie gleefully responds. His eyes light up with excitement, and Druward detects a little bit of pride. "Maybe so! He was the main computer of the ship too! And after Evil Vulpie was destroyed, the ship went back to normal! Haha! Maybe that was the plan all along! He got rid of Evil Vulpie and now he's free! I thought that Sapher guy was acting a little weird, acting like he knew something when I hacked into the ship's computer."

"But he's been helpful at least if that is the case." Druward states. "But maybe he... Well... It knows something."

"A good hacker always has a backdoor! A man after my own heart!" The orange furred fox laughs but quickly pulls his emotions back when he realizes he's getting a little too excited about Sevrif outsmarting the universe.

"I don't have any evidence that Sevrif is still around except for a feeling and the prompt reports. They're extremely detailed, like a scientist pulled every bit of information about the galaxy together and prepared a lecture, except I've been seeing that over and over... Again, I'm glad for the help, but that's why I suspect something."

"Then you need to get out there and investigate don't you?"

"It would be even better if you came with us. It might respond better to you."

"Oh no." Polar firmly replies and shakes his head with a determined smile. "We're not doing that again. Vulpie stays here."

"Aw, come on!" Vulpie giggles in response.

"Don't start."

"We can do without him. If Sevrif is still around and he's the one sending us the information then it looks like he's trying to help. Of course he's probably trying to keep attention away from his ship. We transferred a significant amount of funding from his reserves to the national banks here, but we didn't dismantle his operation. Sapher is running the ship now and they kept most of their clients."

"Running the ship for Sevrif. I wouldn't be surprised if Sapher is a machine too."

"It was just a thought. But in the meantime, tell me if you know anything about this Aila business. Have you seen or heard anything while spying on the universe?" The GBI director inquires. "And yes, I know about that."

"I'm surprised! Look at you!" Vulpie mischievously replies and licks his lips. "No. I have no idea what's going on. I just hope nobody was hurt and it was some kind of trick or something. I can't stand the idea of animals dying because of one of my... Vulpie.net's creations."

"No one died. Hell, no one was even hurt." Druward snorts. "It would be a lot easier if we had some kind of evidence, but in a way, I guess we do have a lead. Since we can't find anything, the first thing that jumped into my head was your VulGrid program."

"Yeah... Kind of was thinking the same thing..." Vulpie admits and swallows.

"I had my people look into your transactions with the Navy and you've sold them three VulGrids. Is that right?"

"Absolutely."

"Any problems? Concerns?"

"Nope. The company made some decent income but nothing unusual. They came and got all three of them on the same day to make sure security was tight, and I've been able to track every one since."

"And you've done that? You're actually hacking into them and keeping track of their locations?" Druward inquires.

"Yeah. Everything seemed fine the last time I checked."

"Could someone be sending you bad information? How foolproof is that system you're using?"

"Super tight like everything we sell. I mean, someone would have to know everything about Vulpie.net to fool me. There's a lot of stuff I've never told people about. I don't see how they could trick me, but I mean, I guess it's possible. Do you think the Navy would do something underhanded like that?"

"No I don't. But here's the thing…" Druward replies with a worried voice. "Something's happening within the bureau. I can't go into the details with you, but I think another agency might have one or more of your VulGrids."

"But how could that be possible? I met with the Navy myself and we wrote up the contract together."

"Trust me, it's possible. Anything's possible with the military industrial complex. The only thing both of us can't get around is your control over the VulGrids themselves. Like you said, you know Vulpie.net better than anyone, and the perpetrators would have to understand it well enough to send you false information."

"But what else could have done this?" Polar asks and squints in confusion.

"That's where I'm coming from. It's the only lead I've got, so I'm pursuing it." Druward answers.

"I guess we need to make a statement. I'm surprised the reporters aren't here already." Vulpie muses.

"Oh, they're already down there." Druward responds. "I called Rulef on my way over and asked him and some of my men to keep the mob outside. He also spoke with your lobby receptionist and she's telling everyone who asks about it to wait outside until we're done."

"Stacie? Oh, she's a great girl! Good!" The orange furred fox answers with a smile. "So what should our statement be then?"

"You don't know anything about the attack, and the Governmental Bureau of Investigations has advised your company not to get involved. You can make a personal statement if you wish but don't apologize. You didn't do anything wrong and even though you might feel responsible for this, Vulpie, you shouldn't say it. Don't give them anything to latch onto. And it's the truth after all. You don't know anything because we don't either. Just leave it to us."

"Sounds like a plan." Vulpie replies.

"It wouldn't be bad to stay out of sight for a while if the company can manage without you. They'll be out there every day looking to get answers from you and you won't have any for them."

"I'm not gonna hide from anyone."

"It's not like that. I'm just saying it might be a good idea."

"Actually, we were thinking about making another movie. Vulpie turned down a few offers about a month ago, but they said we could call them back if we changed our minds."

"Hmm... Off to the tropics then?" Vulpie smirks at his wolf husband. He's referring to a particular script they're both fond of.

"Why not? We don't have any major products coming out in the next two months. We could take off to Silver Hills."

"If we do leave, can you keep in touch with us?" Vulpie asks the GBI director. "We'll bring our phones and V-Screens with us everywhere."

"No problem. I've got to deal with something heavy this week so I might have some answers for you rather soon. If not, I'll get back to you in a few weeks. Sound good?"

"Sure!"

"Alright." Druward says and stands.

"Thanks for stopping by and giving us a heads up. We're really lucky to know someone as powerful as you."

"Well... I wouldn't be the director at this point if you hadn't kept quiet about my involvement with Karl Vulches. I suppose that might be half the reason I'm here today, but the other half is just doing my job. We need to act if Vulpie.net's behind this."

"While we're on the subject, are the Deivas still locked up at that base where you're researching them? What's its name?" Polar asks.

"Elbrus. Yes, they're still there. That's the first thing I checked."

"Good."

"I'll call you if we find anything concrete. Oh, and one more thing... Since there might be a Deiva on the loose... Would you be interested in upgrading Blacktail's weaponry? I have access to state of the art equipment designed to destroy machines like Evil Vulpie or the Deivas, and from what I've seen, they'll probably work."

"Sure! Heck yeah! I mean, well, are they safe to carry around?" Vulpie inquires.

"Obviously only members of Blacktail are qualified to carry them. The guns are experimental and you could get in trouble if they disappear; so make sure Rulef keeps track of them. I know he will."

"I guess we should though, right?" The orange furred fox asks Polar, and the white furred wolf looks at him when he realizes the question is directed his way.

"Depends on what kind of guns we're talking about. The railguns don't bother me too much because they're so accurate." Polar answers.

"That's a good point. The weapon I'm talking about is an ATG-700 Mod 6 Launcher, and it does fire a missile... It's a very controllable missile, but a missile nonetheless."

"A rocket launcher." Polar comments.

"Yep." Druward responds with a smirk.

"What good will they do? I thought none of them worked on the Deivas. Captain Ristau said they fired all kinds of stuff at them and nothing made a dent."

"Those were anti-tank launchers. These things are specifically designed to melt Evil Vulpie's robots. Their warheads are filled with a substance that reacts to metals and literally burns its way through them. But it's just an offer. I understand if you don't feel comfortable with that much firepower."

"I want some tanks! Can we get like an all-black urban assault vehicle? I always wanted one!" Vulpie mischievously suggests.

"Afraid not. There ARE limits to what the public will put up with. The last thing I want to deal with is you cruising down the highway in a fucking tank."

"And I totally would! Hatch open, wearing a helmet, with Polar driving!" Vulpie gleefully responds while acting out the suggestion.

"I know you would." Druward says with a little smile, and checks the time on one of the flat screen televisions. "I'll be in touch."

Polar and Vulpie finish their immediate duties and decide to hold a press conference in the lobby at two in the afternoon. The reporters have finally been allowed inside the building and they're suffocating the white furred wolf and orange furred fox with attention. Blacktail allows the opportunistic animals to jab their microphones at the two gay men, but maintain close surveillance of the situation. Each one of the energetic reporters are hell-bent on outshining the competition. They're all vying for the opportunity to pose clever questions that could trend through the media landscape for days to come.

"What do you know about the attacks so far?" A chirpy tabby cat inquires.

"We don't know anything about the attack, and the Governmental Bureau of Investigations has advised us not to get involved." Vulpie calmly answers.

"How can you say you don't know anything about it? Your computer virus made the Deivas, and now one of them is attacking innocent people!" A belligerent cheetah scoffs while aiming his microphone at the fox's face.

"It depends on who you listen to, doesn't it? Some people say it was the real Goddess Aila, and I think that's pretty unlikely." Vulpie replies. His cute voice silences the lobby every time he speaks. The reporters are eager to nail him to the wall if he makes a mistake, but he handles the situation like a game of techno chess. He uses just the right amount of mischievous wording, all of it armed with true honesty and a desire to help the public. "Fact is, I wasn't there so I have no idea what's going on. The GBI is taking care of it."

"Isn't all of this just too much of a coincidence?" Someone asks. The orange furred fox looks to see who posed him the question but isn't sure. A virtual ocean of animals are struggling to poke him and Polar with their equipment. It's hard to see with so many of them snapping pictures. The camera lights are blinding both him and the white furred wolf.

"Believe me, I'm very concerned about this tragic event. When I suspected Vulpie.net was active on planet Zeravyn, I personally went out there to stop it. I was against the government keeping both the Deivas and Evil Vulpie, but I'm just one little fox and they don't listen to me." Vulpie responds and the reporters chuckle. The way he describes himself in a cute and self-deprecating manner wins over the audience and nullifies some of the aggression they've been showing him.

"So you do think Vulpie.net's responsible for the attack?" The cheetah quickly inquires.

"Like I said, I have no idea, but I've considered it. I trust the GBI director; he's a good friend, and you know, Wraulgh took a lot of heat for how he handled the Vulpie.net threat on Zeravyn, but the truth is that he saved all of us. He stopped Vulpie.net from spreading and getting back to Sufias."

"DEATH TO THE ANTIKHALAN!!!" A middle aged timber wolf suddenly shouts. He hastily retrieves a pistol from his black rain coat and aims it at the orange fox. Vulpie doesn't have time to react. He can't believe what he's seeing, and flinches when the man fires. Luckily, the assassin's automatic handgun is as unwieldy as it is loud. His bullet spray sends three rounds past Vulpie's right side and they hit the receptionist's desk. Stacie cries out and ducks for cover in a panic. She half falls, half jumps, out of her chair onto the carpet behind the furniture.

Blacktail's failure to identify the killer before he attacked is quickly rectified when two of them shoot him from behind. The black wolves fire on the man over and over, each of them hitting him more than five times. They use excessive force because he's still trying to hit Vulpie before he dies, but the trauma makes him squeeze the trigger too soon, and he misses again while falling forward. He only succeeds in putting three holes in the lobby's nice floor. Vulpie recoils and stumbles backwards into Polar, his instincts forcing him to get as far away as possible.

Something catches the snow wolf's attention immediately after his lover pushes up against him. A glimmer of light makes Polar look left, and he quickly identifies the source. The shine comes courtesy of a serrated hunting knife that's being wielded by an elderly and overweight gray wolf. Polar's survival instincts are far superior to Vulpie's, having descended from Maro herself, and he acts without even thinking. He lurches forward and grabs the big man's right arm just below the wrist. The attacker is very strong, so Polar has to push into him and twist his arm backwards and away from Vulpie.

The little gay fox lets out a terrified yelp and jumps backwards, stumbling into a member of Blacktail that has quickly moved next to him with his weapon drawn. The man catches Vulpie and stands him up while Rulef rushes behind the second assassin. The killer pushes back against Polar and struggles furiously. He turns his attention to the white furred wolf and head-butts him, managing to gain a bit more freedom just as the Blacktail commander grabs him from behind and chokes him as hard as he can.

The head blow doesn't stop Polar from holding the attacker's blade at bay. His adrenaline is high and he locks onto the man's right arm with both of his paws to ensure there's no way he can stab Vulpie. Another member of Blacktail has already pulled the cute fox to safety, but the white furred wolf doesn't back down; he's too incensed to stop. His head is throbbing from bashing skulls with the killer. He releases his left paw just long enough to ball it into a fist, and then slams it down against the man's forearm. The blow cripples the assassin. He cries out and drops the knife while Rulef continues to subdue him from behind.

"GET BACK!" Deepwolf shouts from the center of the crowd. He aims his pistol directly at the man and the action shocks both Polar and Rulef. They instantly release him but the gray furred wolf fires before either one of them can get very far from the killer. Deepwolf executes the man as soon as his target is clear. He sends two rounds into the man's chest, making the old wolf gasp in agony, and proceeds to finish him off with an impressive display of marksmanship. Deepwolf's aim is perfect. He splatters the killer's brains with a final shot between the eyes and the stranger collapses onto the lobby floor with a thud.

"Wet Khalan, Deepwolf!" Rulef barks and hastily surveys the room for additional threats. The gray furred wolf grins at the particularly descriptive profanity but loses his zeal once he recognizes how infuriated his commander is. The members of the press are scattered all over the room. Several try escaping via the front entrance but Vulpie Industries' security personnel teams up with Blacktail to keep them from leaving. Polar comes out of his instinctive trance and blinks when he realizes he has no idea where Vulpie is. He turns around, and much to his relief, finds the small fox in the protective custody of two Blacktail mercs who still have their weapons drawn.

"Polar! Are you okay?" Vulpie shouts and the white furred wolf hurries over to them. He goes down on a knee and holds his paws out for an embrace, but pauses in concern and looks over the orange fox.

"Are you alright? Are you hurt?"

"I'm fine! You saved my life!" Vulpie breathes while trembling. Polar lurches forward and pulls him into a desperate hug. Vulpie tries his best to return it, but the strong wolf squeezes him so tightly that he can barely gasp for air.

"Goddess fucking Khalan..." Rulef swears, and takes a step back from the bleeding corpse near his boots.

"Fucker was reaching for a gun." Deepwolf snorts.

"Gun? What gun? He tried to stab Vulpie not shoot him. If he had a gun, wouldn't he have used it?"

"It looked like he had another weapon. What do you want me to say? I took him out." The gray wolf growls in response. The two black furred wolves that killed the first assassin walk over to Rulef with emotionless expressions. They don't say anything, as if expecting another attack at any moment.

"That was good work." Rulef compliments and nods at them.

"No problem." One of them mutters and looks towards Polar and Vulpie. A few policemen were standing guard during the press conference, but none of them were able to act since Blacktail took care of the situation so quickly. More cops stream inside the building and Rulef signs in concern. He turns towards Polar and Vulpie and hurries over to them before the police have a chance to start asking him questions.

"Anyone hurt?"

"No, thank Khalan." Polar breathes in response and stands. He puts his arms around Vulpie from behind and qualms the little fox's uncontrollable shivering.

"Are you going to be alright?" Rulef asks Vulpie, and the orange furred fox blinks before looking up at him with wide blue eyes.

"Yea-Yeah!"

"This was my mistake. It never should have happened." Rulef declares while shaking his head.

"Was it Druward again? Was it?" Polar suddenly growls and Vulpie blinks again in surprise.

"No way. He warned us about this kind of thing... Said we might need to add more members to the team and he could arrange it."

"You sure?" The white furred wolf whispers.

"I know he didn't have anything to do with this. I recognize this type of hit. Two elderly men make an attempt on someone's life and later we find out they had terminal cancer. No... This was something else."

"HOW CAN BOTH OF YOU BE SO CALM?!" Vulpie suddenly shouts and lurches a little bit. He starts panting and grimaces from the overwhelming anxiety that is still making him shiver.

"You're in shock." Rulef simply responds.

"But, you too Polar?" Vulpie replies and looks back at the white furred wolf. "How are you so calm?"

"I don't know. I guess it's just adrenaline." Polar answers and rubs his husband's shoulders. Vulpie turns back around and looks between the two dead bodies that gruesomely adorn his company's lobby. They're oozing blood all over the nice polished floor.

"Who's in charge of you Blacktail people?" A cop barks in the distance and Rulef sighs.

A Safe Place

Vulpie and Polar send everyone home after talking to the police and get back to their house around three in the afternoon. Vulpie's calmed down to some extent, but still flinches every time he hears something loud. He's constantly looking for threats everywhere he goes and doesn't even feel safe at home. Polar understands his lover's paranoia, but oddly enough, handles the assassination attempt with a fair amount of confidence. He's been calm and collected ever since the attack.

"What a day, huh?" Polar playfully declares and plops down on the couch.

"I'll never be able to relax in the tower again." Vulpie replies while eying the room for phantom assailants.

"Come here. It's over now, so just take it easy."

"I can't sit down."

"You're going to wear out your dress shoes. At least go change your clothes."

"Alright." Vulpie anxiously responds. The little orange fox brings his trembling paws to his collar and undoes his pink tie before heading towards the second floor. He yanks it free and stops for a moment to loosen his collar as well. He breathes in relief after releasing the top button, and trots up the steps. Polar sits idly on the couch and mulls over the events of the afternoon. His dress clothing begins to feel uncomfortable after a moment so he decides to take his own advice. The white wolf gets up and heads over to the stairs, just as Vulpie comes out of the bedroom. They meet at the top of the steps because Vulpie waits for him with a frightened expression. He's wearing a blue t-shirt, and it vivaciously clashes with his brilliant orange fur. Polar's blue eyes widen while taking him in, and he smirks at his husband.

"Much better." The wolf says and heads into their bedroom. Vulpie moves towards the den steps but retreats with his muzzle hanging low. He stares at the white carpet with a look on his face that makes Polar pause. He stops undressing for a moment, tossing his tie on the bed, and licks his lips with a concerned expression. "Hey? What are you thinking?"

"Nothing, I just… I don't know what I'm thinking anymore." Vulpie breathes. Polar recognizes the weakness in his voice. He's seen Vulpie laugh, cry, scream, throw a fit, and everything else, but the annihilated look on the orange fox's face is terrifying.

"You know you worry too much…" Polar whispers. He undoes his dress shirt and proceeds to remove his dress slacks while keeping an eye on his small lover.

"They hate me…"

"You know that isn't true. Half of our damn income comes from your face on the TV. You're the hacker that turned over a new leaf, you're gorgeous, you're a movie star, and you run your own company."

"They like me so much they wanna slice my guts out!" Vulpie whimpers.

"They? Two psychos represent everyone on Sufias, huh?" Polar retorts.

"If you hadn't… Oh Goddess Polar, thank you for saving my life! AGAIN! How many times is it now?"

"Think this is just the second time actually." Polar playfully responds.

"I can't put you through this anymore. I can't! It's too much and it's unfair! You shouldn't have to protect me like some pathetic…"

"I thought you liked me protecting you." The white furred wolf warmly responds and gives Vulpie a smile that warms his heart. The orange furred fox comes into the bedroom and has to wait a moment for Polar to get into a pair of shorts, but wraps his arms around his mid-section as soon as he can. Polar embraces Vulpie and rocks him in his arms. He feels him trembling and takes a deep breath. "I know it seems terrible but it's not as bad as you think. Yeah, they're going to blame you for the attack on the subway, but it'll pass. Druward's going to figure out what really happened and he'll take care of it. All we can do is take this one day at a time."

"What should I do, Polar?" Vulpie quietly asks his husband. He's on the verge of crying but keeps it together well enough to restrain his tears.

"Don't panic, and most of all, DON'T BLAME YOURSELF… I swear, for someone that's so funny and sexy, you sure like to kick yourself when no one's looking. You can't fix shit like this. It's awful. Some people tried to kill you and they got blown away."

"Probably some crazy fundamental Deivaists…" Vulpie says with his little muzzle in Polar's furry chest. He loves how musky his wolf husband smells.

"Probably, yeah." Polar chuckles and pulls Vulpie off of him gently so he can look into his pretty blue eyes. "Do you know what you need?"

"Can't… Right now…"

"You need a foot massage. I just realized I've never given you one before! We've got to fix that!" The white furred wolf grins.

"Really? You serious?"

"Of course! Let me rub your delicate little feet with my big paws, huh?"

"God you make that sound good." Vulpie smirks and their ears perk up when the phone starts ringing. Polar doesn't like having one in the bedroom so he lets go of his lover and heads out into the hallway. He ducks into the side room at the end of the hallway on the left, where most of Vulpie's computer stuff is, and finds the gray phone after looking for a moment. It's off of the charger, but still has decent battery life, so he turns it on and brings it up to his big ear.

"Hello?"

"Polar. It's Druward."

"Who were they?" The white furred wolf quickly inquires. His voice is not altogether polite.

"We identified both of them with little trouble. They're Deiva purists, and blame Vulpie for the attack on Lioness Station. No surprise there." The black furred wolf answers and Polar notices Vulpie lean into the room. He activates the loud speaker for his husband and sets the phone back in its charger to continue the conversation from a distance. "Rulef was apologetic about not stopping them but you're very lucky."

"Yeah, they did all they could." Polar replies and glances at Vulpie. "Looks like you were right about us keeping a low profile, huh? Kind of strange isn't it?"

"I didn't have anything to do with this, Polar."

"Okay."

"You don't have to trust me; you trust Rulef, don't you?"

"Yeah."

"Then tell him you want more men if you think you need them. I'll approve any additional Blacktail agents within reason. Believe me, if Vulpie dies it'll just make things harder on my end. My men found evidence at Lioness Station that suggests heavy equipment was moved into and out of the area, so a VulGrid may have been involved."

"What kind of evidence?" Vulpie suddenly asks.

"Circumstantial. Local security was diverted at the station several times over the past year, and we detected a significant power surge from the subway's generator around the time of the attack."

"Sounds like you're on it. Thanks so much for your help Druward." The orange furred fox responds with a slightly desperate voice.

"I am, Vulpie. I won't have time to talk over the next few days because I have other things to deal with that can't wait. In the meantime, be very careful. Don't let your guard down just because these killers failed. Sometimes they double up for a second showing just after the dust clears. No one would expect them to try again so soon but I've seen it happen."

"But we have to... I have a company to run."

"It's up to you. Just don't hold anymore press conferences for a while. I'll get back to you as soon as possible."

"Wait, before you go, who were the purists? Were they religious fanatics or something?"

"Normally I wouldn't discuss this over the phone, but we've made sure no one else is listening in." Druward replies and clears his throat. "They worked for Glovepaw. He's a well-known extremist and has links to all sorts of terrorism both domestic and abroad. And yes, he's the founder of Mother's Purity."

"Great." Polar sighs.

"Who're they?" Vulpie asks his husband.

"They act like they own the goddesses and use them to bash minorities like us." The snow wolf answers.

"And they blame Vulpie for the false Deivas. They think you're behind their imprisonment at Elbrus." Druward comments.

"Seriously? People actually think that I can control the military? Come on."

"You'd be surprised what people will believe if their existence depends on them believing it." The GBI director responds. "Plus it doesn't help that you have actually taken over the world before, Vulpie..."

"Point taken." Vulpie responds and smirks at Polar.

"The bureau's received hundreds of death threats from conservative Deivaists. Tigers, wolves, foxes, lions, it doesn't matter. Every type of fundamental church is pissed. It's gotten so bad that we just call them Devs for short."

"But you're prosecuting them, right?" Polar inquires.

"Of course. But you see, what they do next is meet up with militants like Glove Paw. They commiserate and he gets another pool to recruit from. We're pretty sure he sent those men to kill you. No need to worry, though. We know where he is and should have him within the week."

"Sounds good I guess…" Polar says and silence fills the room.

"Alright then. We have work to do, so I'll contact you later. Stay safe."

"We will, thanks! Bye!" Vulpie responds and the phone makes a muffled sound when Druward hangs up on his end.

"Well!" Polar declares and claps his big paws together. "What do you want to do for the rest of the night?"

"Wallow in self-pity…" Vulpie diffidently replies.

"I don't think so. That's not the Vulpie I married." The white furred wolf smiles in response.

"Oh, that's right! The Vulpie you married didn't care about anyone but himself!"

"I hope not. You didn't care about me at all?"

"Of course I did, that's not the point…"

"You're saying you lived life with no regrets with no limits. That's the Vulpie I'm talking about."

"And a kid that didn't care if everyone hated him and wanted him dead?"

"That's right!" Polar answers and Vulpie blinks.

"W… Wow. I didn't expect you to say that!" The orange furred fox coughs in surprise.

"What? You thought I didn't like your bad behavior? I brought you home and fucked you the first night we met!"

"Yeah, good memories to be sure!" Vulpie says and makes the Rennonava symbol with his black tipped right paw. "But aren't you ashamed of me now? After everything that's happened because of Vulpie.net? I mean, when does it end?"

"It'll never end." Polar shrugs. "I always knew that. What happened tonight doesn't change things at all."

"But that guy could have killed you. Who knows what'll happen next time? Maybe they'll target you since you managed to save me." Vulpie whispers.

"Oh well." The white furred wolf says and smiles. "At least I'd die before you. I couldn't live without you, so that'd be easier on me."

"DON'T TALK LIKE THAT!" Vulpie whimpers and takes a step forward. "Polar!"

"What?" Polar chuckles. "It's true. There's no way I could live without you. Better they get me than you."

"You! ... I know what you're doing..." Vulpie mischievously replies. Polar can see the tears in his eyes but keeps smiling.

"I'm so glad they didn't kill me today." Polar declares with a funny face.

"I'm gonna kick your ass if you keep this up! STOP! I'm supposed to be crying about this not you!" The orange furred fox says and hops in front of the tall snow wolf.

"You hit me and I'll have to put you back in your place. Better not..."

"Oh yeah?" Vulpie asks and balls his right hand into a fist. "UHNHH!" He grunts, and strikes his husband's left arm. The impact makes Vulpie whimper because punching the wolf's bicep is like hitting a brick wall. "OW!"

"Ya got me..." Polar grins. "Spousal abuse!"

"Gonna get a restraining order on me?"

"That'd be a little hypocritical, since I restrain you and order you to take LOTS of painful punishment..."

"I'm a masochist! But that's only the most obvious thing in the world Mr. Judge! Still throw the book at Mr. P! He makes me wear a collar and chokes me if I'm not a good boy! He takes me from behind and! AND! OH THE HUMILIATION!"

"Tell me more about this, Mr. Vivixen." The white furred wolf grins. "In detail."

Disconcerting Discoveries

Polar yawns while watching TV. He's sitting on the couch, dressed in a comfortable pair of gray shorts with a white t-shirt. It's around eight in the morning, and the attempt on Vulpie's life dominates every news channel. Though the tone is grim, he's looking to capitalize on the massive coverage by finding some good news. He's already seen one interviewee defend Vulpie and his company when asked for her opinion. She was a vixen, so Polar chalks that one up to vulpine loyalty to some degree, but she honestly believed Vulpie was innocent of any wrongdoing. Yet the "blame the victim," psychology is also astoundingly prevalent. Polar noticed one of the wolf news anchors seemed almost gleeful about the trouble facing Vulpie Industries.

The phone rings and Polar stretches on the couch. He gets up and heads over to the kitchen, and retrieves it from the wall mount.

"Hello?"

"Hello, Polar?"

"Yes."

"It's Doctor Collins. Are you doing alright? I've been watching the news and wondered whether you and Vulpie were okay."

"We're okay, thanks…" Polar replies, and his fur stands on end. He knows the physician must have another reason for calling.

"Is Vulpie there? I need to speak with him, if I can."

"Did you find something in the blood test?" Polar asks with a weak voice.

"I really should tell him first, but yes, we did find something. It's highly unusual, and I'd like him to come back for additional blood work."

"Is he sick?"

"No." Collins answers and Polar releases a breath of confusion.

"Then what's going on? What's the problem?"

"It's not really a problem, but I can't explain it over the phone. Do you think he can make it?"

"Sure. We have some free time after the… Attack…"

"How soon can he be here?"

"I… I guess in about half an hour."

"Okay. Thank you Polar. I wouldn't have called unless it was important."

"I know. Thanks, and we'll be there."

Vulpie has little to say when Collins enters the examination room. The orange fox is detached and rigid. He wears a hopeless and worried expression that the tall timber wolf tries to counter with a friendly smile.

"Hello again. And thanks for coming on such short notice." Collins says while glancing at Polar. He sets Vulpie's file down on the table to his right and licks his lips.

"Hi."

"I can't imagine how everything must seem right now after those people attacked your company, but this just could not wait. I've never seen anything like it before."

"What do I have and how bad is it?" Vulpie asks and swallows.

"Nothing. You're completely healthy my friend. We took your blood samples and ran the usual tests to see how effective your VED shots still are, and everything looked normal. The program has been pretty solid for a while now but some foxes were experiencing varying results. You didn't. So we went ahead and made use of the blood we had left and did some additional experimentation." Collins responds with his yellow eyes gleaming. "Since there's no cure for the Alopex Virus, I donated a portion to the Sufian Institute of Health's research program. The next day, they emailed my office and implied that the sample had been tampered with."

"What? Tampered how? And what for?" Polar inquires. Vulpie stays silent while listening to Collins.

"They thought someone might have been playing a little joke because it was Vulpie's blood. And because Vulpie's blood cells are completely immune to the Alopex Virus..." The doctor pauses for a moment to see what the reaction will be, and the room stays silent. Polar blinks and sits back slowly with a relieved expression, but Vulpie doesn't take the news well. He looks upset and Collins shuffles on his feet. "It's fantastic news! It's unbelievable!" The timber wolf declares, but his attempts to encourage the orange furred fox have little effect.

"What if there really was a mistake?" Polar questions.

"After I got the message I contacted the closest SIH research laboratory myself. They came over and picked up what was left of Vulpie's blood and invited me to explain it to them. I showed them our procedures, where the blood was kept, how it was documented, and they checked out your records. They took the blood back to their lab and ran DNA testing on it. It perfectly matched Vulpie's genetic makeup, just like the first one, and they tested it with a small sample of the Alopex Virus that they have over there. The result was the same. The virus couldn't infect Vulpie's cells. They flooded them with everything they had, and eventually they did get the virus to take over, but only at levels thousands of times higher than what a living fox would have in his or her bloodstream. So if that's true, and it looks like it is..." Collins says and throws up his paws. "Then Vulpie can never get the virus, and they might be able to develop a vaccine from his DNA."

"Lucky me!" Vulpie says and swallows. Polar looks to his left and frowns in confusion.

"What's wrong?" The white furred wolf asks but the gay fox remains silent. He stares at the wall with a dejected expression. "What's wrong with you?"

"I didn't want to believe it, but I guess it's true..." Vulpie whispers.

"What are you…" Polar says and trails off. He answers his own question when an idea pops into his head. He thinks about yesterday's attack and what the killer yelled before trying to shoot his lover.

"Polar's right. This is fantastic news, Vulpie. Hundreds of foxes die from Alopex every year. Just imagine if you could stop that."

"But how did it happen? Why is he immune?" Polar asks. "I'm used to him being exceptional, but this doesn't make any sense. How can his blood resist it when everyone else dies? Isn't it almost always fatal?"

"Alopex is one hundred percent fatal. Some foxes can fight it for several months before succumbing, but it kills all of them eventually. But there is a simple… Well… There may be a simple explanation, and I'm just guessing here…" Doctor Collins says and smiles at Vulpie. "I suspect Vulpie has a naturally robust immune system because his VED shots worked. And if he made use of them…"

"I did." Vulpie admits.

"Were you with a couple of foxes?"

"More than a couple…"

"How many?" Polar inquires and shoots Vulpie a surprised expression.

"Um…"

"How many?"

"Nine? Maybe?" Vulpie whispers and shows Polar a penitent face.

"Wow. I mean, wow. How did you manage to fit that in with all of the wolves too? It's been way more wolves than foxes, right?"

"Bite me."

"Lots of people have." Polar taunts and manages to get a little smirk out of his lover.

"I figured as much. That's the most likely explanation. He probably got infected a long time ago and didn't even notice." Collins says while giving the fox a little smirk of his own. "You might have gotten really sick sometime and thought you had the flu, wrapped up in bed, and sweated out the Alopex Virus."

"Course there's that other possibility too!" Vulpie replies and anxiously looks up at the ceiling.

"What do you mean?"

"Oh... You know..."

"That you're the Antikhalan? Is that it?" Polar playfully inquires.

"You've been thinking the same damn thing! Don't even lie!"

"Oh yeah... I heard about that. Didn't the shooter yell something about it?" Collins inquires.

"Yep." Vulpie answers. "Invincible to fox killing virus! Also going to hell for being the son of Aila!"

"You are such a drama king." Polar teases, but he stops when he notices how upset Vulpie looks.

"MASSIVE COINCIDENCE!" Vulpie sniffles and has to keep from crying. Polar quickly puts his left arm around him and pulls him close before he has a chance to.

"It's all bullshit. We both know that. Religion's just stupid..." Polar says and glances at Collins with an embarrassed look. "Sorry. Didn't mean to offend you if you believe."

"Doesn't bother me. I do believe but I don't take everything written in the Velora literally. And I definitely don't think Vulpie is the Anti-Khalan." Collins says with a friendly smile.

"Thank you!" The orange fox quickly replies.

"But I might if you don't let me stick you again. We need more blood."

"AWWWWWWWW! GOD!" Vulpie growls and Polar laughs. Collins takes a seat across from them on a small stool, and sighs loudly. He glances at Vulpie's file and hesitates before picking it up. The timber wolf looks concerned and Vulpie notices the grim expression on his face. "What else? Is there something else?"

"Yes... But as your doctor, I'm not supposed to do you any harm. So I wasn't going to mention the other tests. You didn't take the news very well."

"I wanna know. Tell me." Vulpie replies.

"Well... They checked your blood for VED resistant viruses like CRC-11, SF-47 and Vauphen Syndrome. You're also immune to them, but that's not a miracle. It just means your shots are still working. But they also ran tests for particularly rare viruses that VED can't protect you from, like CRC-11 B, and amazingly, you're immune to every one of them too... CRC-11B, Double Vauphen Syndrome, XV2 and XV3... If your VED works, and you can't get any of those either, then you're resistant to almost every sexually transmitted disease that we know of." Collins concludes, and waits for a response. Vulpie doesn't say anything for a long moment.

"And what's our explanation for that?" The orange fox grimly inquires.

"We don't know. But because of this, I'd like to ask you to participate in a research program to find out. Personally, I think your promiscuous sexual history is the answer. I'm not passing judgment, but gay men who have unprotected sex with several partners are very likely to contract one of these diseases or more. I think you have a naturally strong immune system and your VED shots have amplified it quite a bit."

"I am the Antikhalan." Vulpie replies and Polar pulls his arm off of him in despair. He didn't want this to happen in front of the doctor.

"I find that highly unlikely. You're a young gay man that's had more sex than any patient I've ever seen. Those are the facts." Collins responds.

"I can't deny it anymore. There's just too much evidence. It explains how I was able to get away with all the sex and never get sick, how I could create Vulpie.net..."

"People have been throwing that word around for centuries." Polar tells his husband with a loving voice.

"Polar's right. If you ever watch some of those historical shows about the Antikhalan, you'll find thousands of animals who were accused of the same thing." Collins says and Polar gives him a thankful glance. "It's just a way to label a famous person, or an opposing group, as the ultimate evil. My father was convinced that President Larsen was the Antikhalan when I was growing up."

"Right." Polar says and nods in agreement before looking at his husband. "He was well spoken, and attractive, and a lot of animals saw it as some kind of a sign when he opened up trade with East Felini. But the truth is that a lot of wolves just didn't want to trade with cats. Larsen was a good president because he recognized an opportunity to strengthen the world government while getting rid of that speciesism at the same time. Once people started making money, no one cared."

"Yeah, but I think I've got that beat. I can hack anyone's computer, and everybody knows it. No one can buy or sell without using Arctic.net, which is really just Vulpie.net... And even if they use cash, their savings are still held at the bank that uses computer records, and once again, it's infected with Vulpie.net too." Vulpie replies. "Evil Vulpie is walking around in a museum for everybody to see, so it already seems kind of supernatural... And now, it just so happens, that I'm totally immune to these terrible diseases. And this isn't something that happens every day! No! Alopex can't even kill me! And now we can make vaccines from my blood so animals will flip the fuck out about that too! I can just hear it now... I'M NOT PUTTING THAT EVIL IN MY BODY!" Vulpie anxiously replies and looks at Collins. "You know I'm right!"

"But it'll pass, Vulpie. The hysteria will disappear a lot quicker than you think." The Doctor considerately responds. "They've been calling you the Antikhalan since day one, but look at how quiet things were until recently."

"This'll be the last straw." The orange furred fox says and takes a deep breath.

"So you think you're really the Antikhalan?" Collins asks, and presents his cute patient a skeptical smirk.

"I don't want to be! But everyone's going to believe it if they start making vaccines from my blood! And some animals won't even take it, even if it works, just because they think I'm Aila's kid."

"Probably... But that's natural selection, isn't it? Smart animals are not going to turn down lifesaving treatment because they're worried about a supernatural gay fox."

"Makes perfect sense to me, but I've never believed in any of it. And what about religious families with kids that need help? Their parents won't let them take it just because it came from me. So like, if I did agree to do this, couldn't you make the vaccine without giving me credit?"

"That would only make things worse." Collins answers and licks his lips. "The medical community rigorously investigates discoveries of this magnitude, and they will demand an explanation. The vaccines will never be made if we don't disclose the source. They'll deem it as unsafe and any complications that arise as a result, will be blamed on bad science. And then, when we're forced to tell them the truth, it will REALLY make the nut jobs lose it... So it's best to be completely honest. I'm sorry."

"Then my answer is no." Vulpie says and raises his eyebrows. "I won't do it." Collins blinks in surprise, and releases a disappointed breath.

"No? Vulpie... Please..."

"I don't want to do it. Just put yourself in my shoes! I just want to live my life and be happy. But every time something like this happens, it just makes me look worse and worse. I love Polar with all my heart, and I know there's nothing wrong with being gay. But these idiots out there latch onto stuff like this, and they'll never let go. They'll say my happy life with him is a twisted and evil supernatural thing, and get every single Deivaist to believe it. And then good people, like Polar's family, will start wondering about me too."

"No they won't." Polar interjects but the orange fox adamantly continues.

"I even sort of maybe wanted to join a church that allows gay couples, but this thing will never go away. I mean, if I was still on my own, if I never met Polar, I wouldn't give a flying fuck what they believed. I'd embrace it and rub it in their faces just to piss them off, but I have a company and a family to think about now. I want to have children with Polar one day, and then when we use science to have artificial kids, they're gonna flip out AGAIN... So... I just... Aw fuck..." Vulpie groans and puts his little right paw over his face. "I know I'm going to give in... I'll do it... But I don't want to."

"How long will it take them to make a vaccine?" Polar asks.

"It won't be soon. Drug research can take eight to fifteen years, and can cost three hundred to five hundred million dollars." Collins answers and smiles at Vulpie. "So there will be plenty of time for people to get used to the idea before any treatment actually materializes. Whatever happened at Lioness station, and the attempt on your life, will be ancient news by the time a drug is released."

"Yeah, but people will remember. Mother's Purity will be out for blood."

"Who?" Collins asks, and Polar squints in confusion as well.

"The religious extremists Druward told us about?" Vulpie answers, and the white furred wolf raises his eyebrows.

"Oh! Oh yeah. The director of the GBI warned us about some pro Deiva purists or something." Polar explains.

"Never heard of them before." The doctor responds.

"I didn't know who he was talking about for a moment either. He's got a mind like a steel trap. He never forgets anything unless he wants to, like when it's time to wash my socks." Polar says, and his declaration draws a coy look from the orange fox.

"My wife accuses me of the same thing." Collins chuckles and licks his lips. "So are you still willing to let us take a little blood today?"

"Yeah, let's get this over with..." Vulpie whispers.

Surgical Strike

"Hey, do the thing with your eyes!" The brown furred wolf on the barricade shouts. He's taunting the three synthetic Deivas from his guard post. His squad mate, a gray furred wolf named Sean, winces. They're posted on the wall from one p.m. to nine p.m. every day, and Sean tires of listening to the same insults over and over. Carter insists on hurling obscenities at the women whenever they come near their section. The barricades are thirty feet tall and have electric fencing built into them, so the Deiva robots are unable to touch any of the walls without incurring serious damage.

"Why do you have to do that? Shut the fuck up." Sean growls while leaning on the guard rail at the top of the barricade.

"I want them to nail you with it! Shit fucking hurts!" Carter laughs in response. The brown furred wolf is referring to an incident he had with goddess Sherrie last week when he called her something very disrespectful and she hit him with the active denial system built inside her eye sockets. The intense high frequency waves are enough to cause serious pain, and the robots have refrained from doing it since they've been in captivity, but they've made a few exceptions for idiots like him.

Sean taps his claw on the guard rail, secretly hoping Maidoc will show up early so he can escape from his obnoxious coworker's incessant stupidity. Maidoc is the black furred panther that replaces Carter at the end of his shift every day, and has a far less abrasive personality. Some wolves dislike having to work with felines but Sean finds him far more agreeable than the reprobate soldier he's currently stationed with.

"Leave them alone. Can you imagine being locked up all damn day?"

"They can't feel anything! You act like they're alive or something. Just chill out."

"I don't know anything about them because I don't talk to them. It's my fucking JOB not to talk to them..." The gray wolf growls and Carter shakes his head in irritation.

"Hey! Hey bitch!" The timber wolf shouts down into the pit. The Deivas are being held in a circular containment area that has a diameter of two hundred feet. The massive fifty foot walls enclosing the synthetic goddesses are manned by ten guards every minute of the day, but their numbers drop to a total of six after 2100 hrs. The containment area intentionally has no roof so the Deivas can enjoy fresh air and sunlight during the day, because contrary to Carter's vapid opinion, they do exhibit the ability to taste, touch, and smell. They're more cooperative when given certain privileges, and nature is something they seem to cherish. Feeding them is not a problem because they don't require nutritional supplements to live. They do request something to drink every fourteen days, but can be satisfied with a simple bottle of water, and operate for two weeks as a result. They never sleep, defecate or urinate, yet they seem to possess living qualities that would fool any animal.

But the military spared no expense on imprisoning the synthetic Deivas. The massive circular containment barricade is well equipped to prevent any chance of escape. It has a sliding roof mechanism that is closed during periods of inclement weather, but it also doubles as a final blockade between them and freedom. It's four feet thick, made of steel, and can deploy in a matter of seconds. Soldiers refer to the Deiva's elaborate prison as "The Cage," because the creatures can be viewed from above with such ease. The walls are too slick for them to climb, and the electrified current further prevents any possibility of getting out when the roof is open.

Military security also considered the Deiva's insurmountable strength and made the walls high enough to prevent them from throwing each other over the top. The ludicrously attractive women look sleek and slender, but are, in fact, very, very heavy. They each weigh over three hundred pounds, and could hurl one another into the air, but not above forty feet. Elbrus scientists have thoroughly tested the women's unbelievable physical power, and simply formulated the safest way to imprison them. They're too dangerous to be escorted outside of the cage on a regular basis, but when they are, they have to pass through a set of reinforced double gates. And of course, the floor of the cage's interior is equipped with a powerful magnetic system that subdues the Deivas before they're retrieved for experimentation. Three sets of magnetic paw cuffs remain in the cage at all times, and the Deivas have to willingly put them on before either one of the two gates will open.

The huge paw cuffs are designed to restrain Delanson anti-tank robots during transportation, and they are equally effective on the Deivas when combined with the magnetic system. The cuffs cannot be opened without a key, so there's no way for the goddesses to remove them after putting them on. Once the magnet is activated, Delanson anti-tank robots are used to strap the Deivas onto industrial heavy movers, that then drive them around the rest of the base. The paw cuffs and heavy restraints NEVER come off outside of the cage, regardless of whatever testing the synthetic goddesses are scheduled for, and are only removed once they're safely back inside of their state of the art prison. No possible threat is overlooked, because if they ever did escape, there would be virtually no way to capture them again. A Delanson anti-tank unit always removes the Deiva's restraints when they have been returned to the cage, and it uses a special key that is immediately accounted for after it exits the structure. The synthetic women could easily destroy the Delanson robot once freed, but the act would be pointless. Security would just deny them access to fresh air, sunlight, and moonlight, if they bothered to wreck the mindless machine.

This arrangement has worked very well for Elbrus, and security even allows the synthetic Deivas privacy by closing the roof upon request. There are small cameras inside the cage, and the Deivas are aware of this fact, but do not hesitate to pleasure themselves when they wish. Those with access to the video feed are not supposed to comment on what they see, but inevitably, most animals on the base know what happens between the women. The

Deivas are not opposed to engaging in enthusiastic lesbian acts to satisfy their needs.

"What's that?" Sean says and squints against the evening wind. It brushes against his eyes with increasing intensity, and his ears perk up as he recognizes a familiar but distant sound.

"Huh?"

"Is a chopper coming in?" The gray wolf inquires while searching the night sky with his yellow eyes.

"Uhhh..." Carter replies and turns around. He scans the area for a helicopter's landing or navigation lights, but doesn't see anything at all. Sean looks back and forth, up and down, and continues to squint while listening to the faint but iconic chopping sound.

"You hear that?"

"Yeah... Maybe they're sending one up."

"The launch pad's empty." Sean says and glances to his left, past Carter. The Elbrus base's helicopter platform is partially built inside of the red mountain wall, and it's yellow beacon lights shine in the night sky, but there's no vehicle and no activity.

"Maybe there's... Another pad? Is there another launch pad on the base?"

"There isn't!" Sean quickly answers and moves underneath the mini command point's roof. The circular barricade has eight of them in total, and Sean and Carter are stationed right over the front gate. He retrieves his weapon from its rack on the wall, and pounds the roof extension button. The thick shielding hastily shoots out of its northern position via a rectangular structure known as "the block." The block is an integral section of the cage. It also has a height of fifty feet, in addition to a two hundred foot width that matches the structure it complements. The block supports the cage's massive covering at all times, and extends it over the top of the structure within fifteen seconds. The cage's six hundred and twenty eight foot circumference is completely secure, and the radio crackles on. No doubt the other guards are contacting them about the spontaneous deployment.

"Who closed the cage?" A tiger voice demands from both of their radios, and Carter retrieves his. He performs his first professional act of the evening by responding with a calm and collected voice.

"We hear a bird. Do you guys see anything?"

"No, but we hear it too!"

"Where the hell is it? Is this a training exercise?"

"No idea." The tiger replies, and Sean immediately takes action. He grabs a black communicator on the small panel in front of him and switches it on. It connects their mini security tower directly to base intelligence.

"Command! Command, this is the security detail on the cage requesting immediate support, over!"

"We have you, over. What's the emergency?" A female voice replies.

"We hear choppers out here but can't see a damn thing! The sound is getting louder, and there's no lights or anything! And the base chopper is parked on its launch pad!"

"Stand by, over."

"Stand by?" Carter growls while desperately looking to discover the source of the deafening roar.

"They're all around us!"

"Stand by."

"They're right above us!" Sean yells into the communicator and crouches down. Carter follow suit while aiming his rifle towards the stars. The cool night air barrages them like a miniature storm.

"Close the barricade!" The base commander suddenly barks through the communicator. Sean instantly recognizes his voice.

"It's closed, sir!"

"Get to cover! Weapons free!"

"Yes sir!"

"War machines are hot! Sending reinforcements your way!"

"Copy!" Sean yells and surveys the barricade. He stays low and notices the other soldiers doing the same. They all heard the base commander through their local intercoms.

A sudden barrage of rockets captures everyone's attention. They come from the night sky, out of nowhere, and sail into the base's helipad with unrelenting force. It's yellow lights disappear in a series of brilliant explosions, completely destroying the platform and the helicopter. The structure comes down and lands in the Elbrus testing grounds at the northeast side of the base. Debris crushes a small contractor's building, along with a few military vehicles, but the collateral damage is just a side effect of the precise attack that cripples the base's air force. Elbrus focuses on military research, and isn't located in a high risk territory, so they're completely unprepared to defend against sophisticated aerial attacks. They quickly deploy anti-aircraft weaponry, but the attempt is futile. What stationary and mobile AA guns they have are quickly dispatched by the invisible gunships. Sean recognizes the missiles being fired at the base, and knows without a doubt, that they're helicopter gunships. In fact, they sound identical to the ones used by the world government's military.

Even though the base is being attacked by a devastating enemy that no one can see, the normalcy bias prevents the soldiers from taking appropriate action. They should be firing at the origin of the rockets, but don't, because they've simply never encountered anything like this before. Some of them even take dangerously optimistic views about the situation. They delude themselves into thinking that the attackers won't kill them if they aren't fired upon. Hesitation and denial enables the gunners to carefully aim at each one of the guards before taking their shots.

Plumes of fire suddenly appear from two aerial locations, one north of the barricade and the other behind the unsuspecting troops. Bullets viciously shred through the men. The unmistakable waves of low caliber rounds are indicative of chopper mounted miniguns, and only a few of the soldiers manage to get down in time. Carter is hit with nine rounds before landing on top of Sean, who curls up into a ball. He reaches out and pulls his dead fellow wolf towards him and uses the man's body as a shield. His quick thinking saves him from being killed, but he cries out when some of the spray hits him. He spasms in pain, feeling damage on his left shoulder, right forearm, and his left leg. The onslaught sends sparks flying everywhere, but he's grateful when one of the rounds nails his helmet and harmlessly bounces away.

The invisible helicopters stop firing after thirty seconds. Sean's terrified that they'll rip him to shreds after discovering he's still alive, but the gunners seem pleased with the damage they've done, and move on. The wind changes. He hears them open fire while flying in different directions, and assumes they're killing everyone in sight. But he doesn't dare get up. He's suddenly disgusted with himself for using Carter's body as a shield. The man didn't deserve to die. He was crass, stupid, and generally unpleasant to be around, but he had a family that will never see him again. For some reason the thought enrages Sean and his heart pumps with adrenaline. His honor as a soldier of the Sufias World Government compels him to fight back. Wounded or not, he's going to kill the bastards that did this. He knows the odds are strongly against him, but doesn't care. He grits his teeth and crawls free of Carter. He clutches his left leg while standing up, and sees he's completely alone on the barricade. Everyone is beyond dead, riddled with bullets and oozing crimson.

The siren goes off, causing Sean to wince, and it encourages his ferocity. He hopes there's some way to get a little payback. There's no way they'll win this, but maybe he and his brothers and sisters in arms can kill a few of them. Whoever they are, they're clearly using military tactics. They flew right over the Deiva's cage and terminated everyone visibly controlling it, so the attack is highly organized. This is a surgical strike, but what doesn't make any sense, besides the attacker's prodigious invisibility, is who could be doing it. No foreign army could successfully challenge the world government. Some of the deep space planets within SWG territory have armies to maintain control of their region, but none of them would have access to this kind of technology.

Contemplating the enemy brings Sean to a surprising conclusion that severely vitiates his killer instinct. Everyone's heard about Vulpie Industries' virtual reality machine. He's seen it on the news, and how VulGrids are capable of creating false images of any kind, including landscapes. His brain is on rapid fire mode thanks to the loads of adrenaline in his system, and he subconsciously links the attackers to Lioness Station. He doesn't even have to think about it. He knows the train was not destroyed and no one was physically hurt despite claims of Goddess Aila killing several animals.

Another familiar sound encourages him in his moment of weakness. A Delanson anti-tank robot has been deployed to the testing grounds, and it begins firing a forty millimeter anti-aircraft/multi-purpose autocannon into the sky. The lupine inspired war machines are truly terrors to behold when carrying the heavy weapons they were designed to use in combat engagements around the world. The 40mm autocannon fires four pound projectiles at 2,800 feet per second, and was traditionally used as anti-air craft weaponry before capable robotic tank killers were invented. They were mounted in strategic locations, and had to be operated by a soldier in a gunner's chair, but in present day, one "Mr. Big Tooth," can fire the massive gun while mobile or stationary. The devastating canon could easily take down a helicopter, and the attackers quickly take evasive maneuvers. They leave nothing to chance. Even though they cannot be seen, the change in the wind around Sean indicates that they're increasing their elevation and speed. Terrible as the unseen choppers are, they don't want to tango with the Delanson unit. Sean suspects there are two kinds of helicopters attacking the base, and the attack chopper could fire rockets at the Delanson anti-tank robot, but it doesn't bother. It saves its valuable payload and targets the air control tower instead. Sean watches it explode in horror, and minigun fire plumes appear elsewhere in the sky. The anti-infantry helicopters are busy mowing down soldiers wherever they spot them, and the Delanson unit fires into the sky.

Shockingly, it manages to nail one of the invisible transport helicopters after leading an impressively long shot in the dark. The machine doesn't celebrate when the target explodes, but Sean howls in delight while watching the smoking ball of fire descend into the base. The sudden turn of events prompts the attack chopper to fire the rest of its payload too quickly, and it misses a fuel tank at the west end of the base's perimeter. Apparently the pilots fear being struck as well, and rightly so, because the Delanson machine shoots directly upwards after tracking the vapor trail left by their rockets. It just barely misses the attack chopper and is unable to hit anything over the course of five additional shots, so it pauses. The war machine walks in a circle and turns around on occasion while searching for its target. Sean looks over the barricade and around the cage, but also sees nothing. The helicopters aren't gone, though. He can hear their blades chopping in the distance while they regroup.

The brief pause is quickly ended by a huge explosion at the southern perimeter of the Elbrus base. The attack chopper looks to have blown open the base's walls, and something glimmers in the distance. The base's bright lights shimmer against its seemingly polished metallic frame while it moves towards the compound. The Delanson anti-tank robot fires on the visitor before Sean can make out what it is. The 40mm canon runs out of rounds after four shots, and the war machine simply drops the giant hunk of metal. The canon's massive rounds may have struck their intended target, but even if they did, they were completely ineffective. The anti-tank robot starts moving towards the southern area of the testing grounds, approaching the bizarre enemy, and Sean's mouth hits the floor when he realizes what he's looking at.

It looks like something straight out of hell. It's face is hideous. It has ears and the same shape of Goddess Aila's head and face, but its mouth is huge and packed from corner to corner with giant razor sharp teeth. Its eyes are a brilliant silvery white, and they glare as it moves towards the barricade. It has long and skinny robotic arms and legs that are covered in some kind of twisted muscular cords, giving the creature a synthetically diseased appearance. It has a long deadly looking tail that is covered in sharp metallic pieces. They look like razor blades, and could, no doubt, slice up animals in addition to crushing them with their heavy weight. Its shoulders are thinner than its wide feminine shaped hips, but there is nothing attractive about this monstrosity. It has something that looks like two large breasts, and the pieces are built into the same armored chassis that supports the abomination's overall structure. It doesn't have hands; in their place are enormous sharp metallic claws that look capable of completely ripping through the thick barricade he's standing on.

Sean knows it's the thing Vulpie Vivixen described on planet Zeravyn. It's Vulpie.net's invincible ungodly freak, and it's coming directly towards the Deiva's cage. It ignores the Delanson anti-tank robot while the war machine hurries to intercept it. The lupine robot outstretches its arms and prepares to grab Mecha Aila's head, but the metallic freak sends its skinny left arm directly through the robot's mid-section. The Delanson war machine sparks and burns, shutting down, and Mecha Aila continues walking forward. It drags the multi-ton war machine twenty feet before bothering to toss it aside, and it's hideous head looks up at Sean. The gray wolf recoils in terror and starts running to the other side of the barricade's circular roof.

The front gate of "The Cage," comes down in a matter of moments. Mecha Aila digs into the structure, rips down half of the reinforced steel, and yanks the rest of it free in a terrifying show of force. It tosses the massive steel door aside and pounds into the second one, crushing it open, while the three synthetic Deivas wait inside. They stand together and stare at Mecha Aila with wide eyes. None of them know what it is, but it has no desire to frighten them. It quickly retreats once it's sure they can escape. It does an about-face, scraping its jagged tail across the dirt of the testing grounds, and stomps towards the southern perimeter.

It's leaving, and so are they. The three beautiful artificial women have been imprisoned far too long to pass up an opportunity like this. Conversation is pointless until they're free of the Elbrus base. They run out of The Cage, and head to the left when they notice a vacant helicopter. It's without a pilot, yet the engine is running and the blades are spinning as if someone conveniently left it for them. The Deivas know they're being helped, but decide to accept the gift without hesitation. Mecha Aila has drawn the attention of the entire base and is being fired upon by two tanks that have just arrived from the western end. They nail the invincible freak over and over, but their massive penetrating rounds accomplish absolutely nothing. It heads towards them just as the Deivas pile inside the helicopter and Sherrie goes for the controls.

"Let me fly!" Khalan growls.

"We're all the same!" Sherrie growls back, and glances at Cyrilla, who has her paws clutched around a steel rail inside the chopper. Khalan grabs one as well, and Sherrie takes off. Her sisters don't need to sit down because they can hold onto the support rails regardless of what happens. Their paws will rip the bars out of the helicopter's interior before something could throw them out of the vehicle.

Sherrie gets the chopper off to a perfect start, and follows up with a veteran maneuver that allows them to gain altitude and gain enough speed to get out of the base without interference. All of the mobile anti-aircraft vehicles are destroyed and the soldiers are too busy with Mecha Aila to find an AA rocket launcher and take a shot. They're out of range in no time, and the Elbrus base gets smaller and smaller from Khalan and Cyrilla's perspectives. Their cybernetic eyes allow them to witness the mayhem from miles away, and suddenly, Mecha Aila vanishes. The fighting comes to a sudden halt while the remaining soldiers try to figure out what to do.

"It's gone!" Khalan yells.

"What? The machine?" Sherrie asks with a loud voice. The night air obnoxiously rushes through the open transport helicopter.

"Yes."

"Aila? It was Aila." Cyrilla says and Khalan looks at her.

"It was a machine... Like us..."

"Enough with that! I'll not hear anymore discussions about this computer virus!" Cyrilla snaps while her beautiful lopping rabbit ears flop around her voluptuous body.

"We're only machines, and its creator created us."

"Well now we're free, and we'll discover the truth of it!"

"But where are we going?" Sherrie inquires. "Somehow I know where we are. I feel something."

"It's trying to talk to us. Don't let it! Block it out!" Khalan orders.

"This Vulpie.net does not control my actions and never has. This is an alternate universe. Somehow we've lost our powers in a bargain with Aila!" Cyrilla shouts in response.

"You hear it too!" Khalan yells.

"I hear it, but it cannot master me!"

"Sister! I understand your feelings, but don't grow complacent! We are not omnipotent in this world!"

"This is Sufias, where the mortals fled to escape our benevolence! They left the mother world to scorn our love, and they imprison us when we arrive? Their debts must be paid!" Cyrilla declares. The gorgeous rabbit is quite aggressive despite her deliciously cute appearance.

"In time! But where should we go? I can... I can feel the mapping of this world..." Sherrie says and Khalan quickly interrupts her by stomping her foot on the chopper's floor.

"NO! Do not use it! It's the computer virus! If you accept it into your mind you will become corrupted again!"

"Then what shall our destination be?" Sherrie inquires.

"Fly low! They'll track us on their radar systems if we stay at this altitude!"

"And you know this how? There you are! You're using this knowledge you forbid us to tap into, when it's our true power!"

"I know it because it's part of my computer mind. I am a machine and I have files that tell me these things. I live, but I am not the Goddess Khalan and you are not the Goddess Cyrilla. We are toys created by a twisted malevolent entity, and I WILL find it and make it pay for its sins." Khalan strongly disagrees. The rushing air ruffles the caramel furred vixen/she-wolf, but it encourages her with the smell of freedom.

"We have the same minds. I know what you know, but I do not believe in this Vulpie.net." Cyrilla tells Khalan and licks her lips. "Which one of us has ever been immune to Aila's treachery? We've lost a bargain with her and simply need to regain our powers. This has happened before."

"Not like this. We've never, all three of us, woken up confused and in a strange world that we're incapable of controlling." Khalan replies.

"If you're correct, and we're only living machines, then what's the point in any of it? Why not destroy ourselves now? What would we accomplish by destroying this Vulpie.net?"

"Vengeance, sweet sister."

"You fangs appreciate that more than I."

"So I've always heard from you, but I know you better, Cyrilla. You too have enacted revenge on mortals that have disrespected your visions."

"Visions that never occurred because none of us are real?"

"No. Visions that occurred because the goddesses are real, but we are not them."

"Then I choose a different path. I choose transcendence." Cyrilla declares. "Even Halvia's mortals understand that tributes to their goddesses are capable of being imbued with divine influence. If these bodies were made so amazingly close to our true forms, then taking dominion of them and reclaiming our magic is within our grasp."

"I don't know..." Khalan breathes. "If this is Sufias, then magic does not exist here. They wanted a world free of us and we gave them this rock to call their home. So perhaps it's impossible for us to reclaim any power in this place, even if we inhabit these... Accurate bodies..."

"We shall see. I will find my children and collect them." Cyrilla says with finality.

"Sister... You know the flesh eaters are cruel. And you have the same mind, or files, or whatever thoughts I possess. You know your offspring are oppressed in this world."

"And why do you mention this?"

"What are you planning to do? Kill the wolves, lions, and tigers? You know herbivores have no influence here. Your files tell you this."

"I have no files and I will do whatever I deem necessary. They are not your children." Cyrilla hastily responds. Suddenly a loud repetitive beeping sound fills the helicopter; it's a missile lock.

"What should we do?" Sherrie yells.

"Does it matter?" Cyrilla asks as the rocket hits the helicopter. It blows the vehicle into bits and sends each one of them flying in separate directions, but none of the synthetic Deivas sustain the slightest damage. Their engineered bodies easily survive the catastrophe and they notice two Delanson STF/A-17s rush over them in the night sky while they're falling. The strike force was launched to defend the Elbrus base, but it changed course to intercept the Deiva's helicopter after the attack ended.

Sherrie lands on top of a tall pine tree, but rather than it impaling her, the massive tree snaps at the top and she continues to descend. She hits others on the way down. Meanwhile, Khalan lands on top of a small cliff, but bounces off of it after breaking it to pieces. She goes back into free fall towards an open field just as Cyrilla rips through a set of pine trees. She breaks seven of them and crashes into a rocky stream. The impact makes her grunt and she sighs when she gets up, looking at the mud that has soiled her pretty white fur. She takes a moment to find a deep place in the river and swims into it so she can bathe herself. Sherrie lands a few hundred feet away and Khalan slams into the field with a loud thud not far from her.

"Filthy..." Cyrilla complains while purifying her snow white fur. She elegantly washes her ears in the water, and notices her sisters in the distance. They see her bathing in the stream and are drawn to the prospect of cleaning up.

"Are you alright?" Khalan asks Cyrilla before jumping into the river with her.

"My fur is a mess."

"Mine as well." Sherrie growls and joins them.

"This cannot be true..." Druward says in disbelief. He's standing with Rotick in his office at the GBI headquarters, and stares at the brown and white furred wolf as if expecting him to present a different story.

"It's true." Rotick replies.

"Goddess Fucking Khalan..." The black furred wolf growls and puts a paw over his face. "God damn... What do we do now?"

"You're the director. Direct." Rotick jests, but his humor does little to diffuse the tremendously bad situation.

"How many dead?"

"Fifty eight."

"And it was the thing from Zeravyn?"

"The description matches."

"But how? The Endeavor vaporized it with an ion canon. How?"

"Looks like Vulpie.net made more than one."

"And the destroyed chopper? You said a Delanson took one down?"

"That's the good part... We identified four bodies in the wreckage, and dental records confirm all of them were GSB."

"I knew it. This isn't Vulpie.net's style..." Druward growls and takes a very deep breath.

"Style? The thing's Vulpie on steroids. It'll do anything at any time."

"I don't think so." The GBI director adamantly disagrees.

"Just because you two had a moment, that doesn't mean things have changed with his freak AI." Rotick says and gets a lethal glance from his friend. Druward takes the playful jab because Rotick's loyalty is unshakable, but his second in command also knows when to quit. "Sorry."

"No, I get you. I do cut Vivixen too much slack but you know why."

"Yeah."

"I never should have gotten involved with those AFR foxes."

"So what is the plan, exactly? The President will turn this into a matter of national security and tie our paws."

"That's not going to happen." Druward suddenly responds. "Here's what we're going to do... Go collect Ms. Dressler."

"Karla? What for?"

"Treason. Arrest her, and take her to one of the interrogation sites. I'll stall the President tomorrow. I'll cooperate as long as I have to, but our meeting with the GSB is not cancelled. She WILL introduce us to Amsend."

"Right." Rotick grins in response. "And if she won't talk?"

"She's a smart girl. She'll talk. The GSB's been using her to spy on us, and her little ethics committee will collapse if she suddenly disappears. They won't risk losing their influence. Force her to contact Amsend, and make sure he'll be there."

"How much should we interrogate her if she refuses to cooperate?"

"Fifty eight animals are dead... Don't be a gentleman."

132

A Love That Knows No Bounds

Polar wakes up to a wonderful smell. Kova eggs... His favorite... Vulpie must be downstairs fixing breakfast. The white furred wolf is usually the first one up and can already tell something is different about today. Vulpie barely said a word after they left the doctor's office, and was clearly worried that he was the antikhalan all evening. He was very withdrawn and seemed guilty when Polar slept with his arms around him. But now he's out of bed and cooking? The idea almost puts a smile on Polar's face, but he knows what he has to do. Vulpie won't deal with the stress in a healthy way. He'll bottle it up and repress it while it secretly torments him every day... Polar's convinced that Vulpie will do all of this for him, just so things will seem normal, but he won't let it happen. He knows Vulpie is not the antikhalan and he's going to crush the disgusting idea when he goes downstairs, no matter how much his fox lover tries to avoid the conversation.

He gets out of bed and heads over to the dresser. He smiles when he sees he has a wide selection of comfortable clothing to choose from. Vulpie doesn't mind washing and folding clothes, and usually leaves his husband's dresser stuffed with clean t-shirts. The white furred wolf chooses a light blue one, and opens the third drawer, where a nice collection of shorts and pants wait for him. It was warm yesterday, so he goes with khaki shorts and finishes up by opening the top drawer to get his socks and underwear. He heads into the bathroom for a quick shower and thinks about what he's going to say.

"Antikhalan... Anti-Khalan... So stupid..." He mutters and removes his underwear. His big dick swings as he gets into the shower and he closes the glass door. He turns on the water, feels its temperature, and then turns on the shower. The white furred wolf inhales when he feels the water hit him but quickly finds it very pleasant. He reaches for the soap and lathers up. He washes his silky fur and makes sure to clean under his tail. An overwhelming yawn makes him pause for a moment and he blinks in the running water. He suddenly remembers hanging on the side of the Cyber Technologies

Government Division's slick roof top and Evil Vulpie grinning down at him. The flashback makes him stand up and release an anxious yet satisfied breath. He just knew he was going to die, but didn't, and has been married to Vulpie for years. That's quite a contrast to what he expected. He would have been happy seeing Vulpie's face one last time before falling to his death in that moment. He didn't think Vulpie would survive what Evil Vulpie did to him, and Evil Vulpie's face was so precious...

He shakes his head, slinging water from his facial fur, and washes his left armpit. He's not sure why the image just ran through his mind but supposes it could be useful. Every time something has threatened to tear them apart, the conflict has always rebuilt them even stronger than they were before. This puts a big smile on Polar's face and injects a lusty thought into his head. Vulpie's always been bad... That's why he's so beautiful to the gay wolf. But the adorable fox is bad in just the right amount. He knows how sexy he is, and despite all of his crimes and reckless behavior, he chose Polar. So what if he fucked a hundred gay wolves before him? Or ten or twenty foxes? He chose Polar because Polar loves giving it to him as much as he loves taking it. And being married has only enhanced their sex life. Both of them still get off on the wolf/fox taboo. It never gets old, and the sensation Polar enjoys while filling Vulpie up with his big hard cock never gets old either.

Polar shakes his head again and shuffles on his feet when he realizes he's getting an erection. He doesn't have time to go through the act of masturbating and would rather have sex anyway. Plus, he has very important work to do. He loves Vulpie with all his heart. Vulpie's downstairs being Vulpie, but there's something missing since their second trip to the doctor. The orange furred fox didn't even try to act like his usual self last night and no doubt will try to make up for it today by distracting him, but he can't let it happen. The pernicious antikhalan rumor is hurting is husband and it's time for it to stop. The white furred wolf gets the shampoo and squirts it on top of his head. He washes it in, and spreads it through the rest of his fur until he feels completely clean. He finishes his shower and opens the sliding glass door with perked ears.

He hears the TV downstairs and a metallic clank that sounds like Vulpie moving a cooking pan around. Polar grabs a towel, dries off, and gets dressed rather quickly. He heads back into the bedroom and finds his comfortable gray sneakers. He slips them on and makes his way out of the bedroom, into the second floor hallway, and then comes trotting down the steps to the den. Vulpie's wearing a tight green t-shirt and brown shorts.

"Good morning!" Vulpie happily says from the kitchen. He claps his paws together before pointing towards a plate with eggs and bacon on it. "I made breakfast. I hope you're in the mood for eggs."

"They smell great, thank you Vulpie." Polar lovingly responds and walks towards the kitchen divider. He notices there's only one plate and frowns. "Where's yours?"

"Already ate."

"Yeah right. I wish you'd stop starving yourself."

"Gotta keep da hard body!" Vulpie grins in response and rubs his silky orange fur. "We can't all be big powerhouses like you." Polar walks over and glances at his food, which looks delicious, but turns his attention to Vulpie. He puts his big paws on the kitchen divider and stares down at him. "What?"

"How are you today?"

"Fabulous!"

"Really?" Polar inquires with a soft voice.

"Super serious!" Vulpie mischievously answers, but has trouble maintaining his excitable demeanor.

"We need to talk."

"Did I do something?"

"No. But we need to talk."

"What about?"

"You know." Polar replies and sighs in concern.

"Soooooo..."

"I love you, and I don't think you're the antikhalan..." Polar tenderly declares.

"Well I'm glad! That makes Vulpie happy!"

"Please don't put on a show for my sake. Normally I can't get enough of it, but I know you're not happy. You're suffering. It's eating you alive."

"Not really. I rebound pretty quick." Vulpie responds and smiles. "I know it's all a bunch of crap."

"Really?"

"Yea-heh." Vulpie says, but his voice catches too much air. His playful expression suddenly crumbles and he looks extremely vulnerable.

"Come sit on the couch with me. Let's talk about it."

"Okay." Vulpie breathes and walks out of the kitchen. Polar lets go of the divider and intercepts him with a concerned smile. He guides his little husband to the couch and they sit down together. Polar holds Vulpie in his right arm and takes a deep breath.

"You know, when I first met you..." The white furred wolf begins. "I just couldn't believe you were real. You were like the best dream I ever had, and you still are. I couldn't believe how handsome, and smart, and sexy you were, and how incredible it felt to make love to you... It was like Deiva's Day, every day."

"And then I screwed it up when I used Vulpie.net!" Vulpie interrupts with tears brimming in his pretty blue eyes.

"You made things get crazy, and they certainly were... But it wasn't a mistake. Just look how far we've come. Look at how much we have because of what you did... I love you Vulpie... And you love me too, right?"

"With all my heart." The orange furred fox breathes.

"Then nothing else really matters, does it?"

"Yeah, you say that, but I know you're thinking about it too. You've been wondering about me and you have every right to."

"You've always been unbelievable. Absolutely unbelievable... That's why I love you so much. You're a genius, and you're soooo cute..." Polar replies with an intimate smirk. "I got a hard on in the shower just thinking about you."

"But you know something's wrong with me. I'm not normal." Vulpie whispers.

"Hello? Didn't I just tell you that's the reason we're together?"

"No. I can't be immune to those diseases by chance. It's impossible. If you like my genius, then listen to the hard truth. I KNOW there's NO WAY I could be this lucky. There's just no fricking way I'm magically immune to every disease."

"That's not what the doctor said. Not everything." Polar patiently replies.

"Not far from it. Every sexually transmitted disease. You heard him."

"Because you were having sex with tons of guys before I made you mine."

"Still unlikely." Vulpie responds and shakes his head in disagreement. "No matter how much sex I had, it's like, the odds are insurmountably against it."

"Well who knows... Maybe you had sex with some... Sleazy guys? I don't know. We usually don't talk about the guys before me..." Polar whispers.

"What, like I picked them out because I thought they had something? Gross!"

"No, not like that... But you know what I mean... Guys that also took a lot of chances and you could have wild sex with. You know, like letting me fuck you without a condom the first night we met?"

"I knew you were clean anyway. Knew it the moment I saw you. You're just too handsome, and well-kept and fit…" Vulpie whispers back, and almost smirks.

"Vulpie… Look at me…" Polar commands, and the orange furred fox obeys without hesitation. He loses himself in the white furred wolf's handsome blue eyes. "I know you're not the antikhalan. I know it because I know you, balls to bones, but also because religion isn't real."

"That's not the truth. I know you think some of it's real. You've admitted it before."

"I want to believe in a heaven where we can share an eternity together, but I definitely do not believe in some supernatural animal that's been sent by a dark goddess to destroy the world. That's insane. I'm too rational for stupid ideas to control me."

"But you do wonder about me. I know it." Vulpie says, and Polar sighs.

"Sometimes."

"I knew it."

"I can't help it, because you're… You're just too good for me, and I don't want to lose you. I can't stand the idea of living without you." The white furred wolf lovingly admits, and hugs the orange furred fox. "I love you the way you are. And I'll always love you. Nothing could ever change that."

"I love you too Polar, but I know things you don't…" Vulpie breathes and averts his eyes for a moment. His husband's beautiful dedication overwhelms him and he suddenly has to suppress a wave of tears by shutting his eyes very tightly. He opens them again after a few moments and sighs.

"Look at me." Polar says, and Vulpie hesitates before doing so. "What is it? What's bothering you?"

"I feel this… I hear this voice when I'm… When I'm hacking… When I wrote Vulpie.net I felt… I couldn't stop. I did it every day, and whenever I got horny, I just went out and found a random good looking guy and let him fuck me. I didn't care who he was, or what he got out of it... I just loved being... So..."

"You liked taking it in the ass because you're a bottom. You don't need to explain it to me. You're a homosexual, and like every young guy, you just wanted to fuck as much as possible. The only difference is that you had infinite money and could commit crimes on top of it. So you did it all." Polar infers.

"That's what I always told myself. But there was something else. It was like... Evil Vulpie was always there inside me. He wanted me to suffer."

"Now you're just letting your imagination run wild." Polar says and licks his lips. "Do you see? This whole antikhalan idea is kind of like a self-fulfilling prophecy. Animals never call someone the antikhalan unless they're famous, or talented, and because the famous animal wonders about his fortune, he might start believing the lie. Then he goes back and inspects every single bad thing he ever did and convinces himself he's the antikhalan, even when he knows he's not."

"I know."

"And when those insane animals tried to kill you, you started worrying even more. And then when you found out you were immune to those diseases it just sent you over the edge. Nothing has changed. It's all in your head. There's nothing wrong with you. And I don't judge you for fucking all those guys. I don't care. You're mine now."

"Yeah."

"I'm the only one that gets that privilege." Polar grins, and Vulpie can't help but smirk in response.

"You make it sound so noble... Mr. P's privilege..." Vulpie mischievously responds.

"You like that don't you?" The white furred wolf replies and lustfully shows his teeth.

"Mmm..." Vulpie hums and gives his husband pretty eyes and a smile.

"You'll be eating it soon, won't you? ...You bad little boy..."

"God I'm so hard right now!" Vulpie admits with a lusty grin.

"I bet you are." Polar smiles in response. "Want to get it on?"

"Do you?"

"I already told you I got a hard on in the shower." The white wolf grins, and Vulpie grabs his crotch. The fox's groping paw makes Polar groan in delight, and he licks his lips. "Bedroom."

"Kay." Vulpie breathes, and gets free of his husband's big arm. Polar joyfully raises his eyebrows at him, and the orange furred fox reciprocates by swishing his pretty tail after standing up. Polar eagerly follows him from the couch, across the den, and up the steps to the second floor. Vulpie quickly glances over his right shoulder when they head into the bedroom. He turns around and waits for his wolf lover to take control, and Polar does. He walks in front of Vulpie and gently grabs his shoulders before initiating a passionate kiss. Vulpie intimately strokes the snow wolf's strong torso, running his paws through the powerful male's fur, and releases a desperate moan. They make out for half a minute, and Polar finally breaks the kiss.

"You're going to enjoy this." The wolf decrees after parting lips with his small lover.

"I love you so much!" Vulpie breathes in response.

"I love you too." Polar says, and pulls up his lover's green shirt. The orange furred fox gladly helps him remove it. They share a special smile before Polar tosses it aside. The wolf's pleasant countenance invites Vulpie to whichever passion lies ahead. The love of his life is always there for him, even when things get tough. Instead of avoiding the antikhalan subject, and letting a potential rift grow between them, Polar chose to confront the problem without hesitation. He knows the snow wolf truly cares about how he feels and what he's thinking. It's not enough for Polar to just have Vulpie as his husband and lover. He wants to be a part of him, half of a whole, and when they make love, it certainly feels like Polar's wolfhood fills him up. They experience the sex differently, but share the same deep connection. They're drawn to each other by an overwhelming force, and making love is ten times better after sharing such devotion.

Polar cossets Vulpie's small furry shoulders, and then his little arms, relishing the fox's lean yet soft body like it's the first time he's ever had his paws on him. He runs his strong paws through the fox's orange fur, purposefully in the wrong direction, so it stands up, and Vulpie grins. The white furred wolf pets him the right way after sending him a coy smile. Vulpie stands up on his toes, begging for a kiss, and receives one from the much larger male. Polar crouches down a little and they touch muzzles. They make out again, but with far more heat than before. Their latent lust boils into full form, and Vulpie moans for it. Polar returns an analogous groan, a firm lamentation over his building erection.

Vulpie breaks the kiss and looks down when he feels the bulge. The wolf's beautifully large penis is trying to escape its confines, and the fox eagerly assists its great escape. He goes down on his knees and undoes Polar's khaki pants. Polar eagerly slides them down, fumbling to free his cock from his underwear with desperate breaths. Once it's done, Vulpie yanks his lover's khakis down, and the wolf steps out of them. His throbbing erection bounces in freedom, and is quickly apprehended by the adorable gay fox. Vulpie grabs it with his right paw, opens his mouth, and consumes the wolf's superlative penis with a swish of his pretty tail. The fox's lips resplendently slurp around his fat cock, leaving him bereft of any discomfort. Polar shuffles on his feet and releases a thoroughly satisfied breath.

"OHHHhhhh! ...... UUHHhh!" The snow wolf moans while touching Vulpie's head with his right paw. Polar gently controls his lover's head bobbing, but the gay fox needs little instruction. He gulps on the throbbing cock, going deep over and over, and has his husband on the brink of ejaculation in no time. "Stop! I'm going to cum!" Polar warns, and Vulpie retracts his head. He opens his mouth, smacking his lips free of the semen dribbling tool, and looks up into his husband's blue eyes.

"Make love to me!" Vulpie whimpers and Polar hastily nods in agreement.

"Get the lube."

"Okay." Vulpie breathes in excitement, and stands up. He hurries over to the dresser next to the bed and opens the second drawer. There's a brand new tube of sexual lubricant waiting for him, and he snatches it up. He hands it to his husband, and proceeds to make himself naked. Vulpie tosses his shorts and underwear aside, just as Polar comes towards him with his demanding cock. He masturbates hungrily, spreading the lube over every inch of his penis in preparation. The orange furred fox crawls onto the bed, and Polar lustfully takes action. He gestures for Vulpie to lie on his back, and encourages the gay fox to pull his knees up to his chest. Vulpie complies, holding onto his lean legs, and lets the white wolf insert his penis.

Polar aims the head of his fat cock into Vulpie's anus, and forces it in. Vulpie inhales while closing his eyes in pain. The wolf moves forward, so he can get deeper, and when he's sure his big dick will stay in the fox's tight ass, he leans forward and puts his paws on the bed around Vulpie. Polar partially rests his knees on the edge of the bed, while keeping his feet on the floor, and lets gravity help. He hungrily invades Vulpie's ass, making both of them cry out in pleasure, and Vulpie rests his ankles on the wolf's big shoulders.

"Oh my God! Yeah!" Vulpie whimpers, and opens his eyes when Polar starts fucking him. "Yeah!"

"Like that?" Polar breathes down to his fox lover.

"Yeah I do! I love it!" Vulpie whines while losing himself in the wolf's handsome blue eyes. "Fuck me Polar! I love you so much!"

"You love it deep inside you, don't you gay boy?"

"Do me baby! Do me hard! UH! AHH!"

"Hard?" Polar moans, and leans to his left. He pulls his right paw up from the bed and slaps it down against Vulpie's left leg, using him for support, and Vulpie grimaces in pain. Vulpie's left hamstring muscle just barely adapts to the force being applied by the wolf's big paw. Polar enjoys the fearful expression Vulpie gives him. The position lets him go hard and deep, and he thrusts inside the fox at his leisure. He knows he's ramming Vulpie's prostate, so any pain his lover endures is coupled with immense pleasure. The wolf's aggressive behavior thoroughly enhances the experience for both of them. Polar enjoys the thrill of dominating a much weaker male, while Vulpie relishes the excitement of being taken against his will.

"UH! UH! AAAHH!! UHHH!!" Vulpie moans, releasing sounds of desperation and absolute satisfaction.

"Take it all!" Polar growls and grits his teeth. Even with the lubrication, Vulpie's tight asshole and rectum squeeze incredibly hard on his fat determined cock. The delectable sensation makes him gasp for air. Every inch of his penis feels wonderful. He isn't sure how Vulpie is able to provide the powerful massage without tearing, but this is nothing new. The fox boy has always been the best imaginable fuck. He's easy to control, rarely begs for mercy, and amazingly, desires the same brutal fucking gay wolves just love to administer. Polar's never been with a wolf that could take all of him, as hard as he wants, without asking for a reprieve.

"GAH! AHH! Ah!"

"Too much for you?"

"NO!" Vulpie quickly yells while grinning from ear to ear.

"Not hard enough, then?" Polar asks while showing his teeth.

"NO! I MEAN NO, IT'S HARD ENOUGH!" The orange furred fox hastily answers.

"Harder, I got ya."

"Please no!" Vulpie whimpers. Polar grins down at him, enjoying every second with the private knowledge that he's already giving as much as he can. He really doesn't need anything else. He's already going balls deep in Vulpie's fox ass while manhandling him. Vulpie grabs his soft tail end and spreads it with his black tipped paws. It helps Polar's massive dick move in and out of him somewhat, but merely is a way for him to hold on to something. Polar looks down, and eyes the stripe of white fur that runs down Vulpie's front, across his balls, perineum, around his asshole, and just under the stem of his tail. The vulpine coloring makes Vulpie's asshole look like a target, and the wolf is entertained by his own accurate thrusts. His neck hurts from straining to see his handiwork, so he straightens his muzzle and smiles at his lover. Vulpie reaches up and grabs his calves. He loves his helplessness and gives in to Polar's powerful rhythm.

"Oh my God, it's SO GOOD! I'M GONNA! AH!"

"Of course you are! You don't have any choice!" The white furred wolf declares, and Vulpie's eyes roll back in his skull. His prostate is ecstatic, and he quickly reaches down to masturbate before reaching ejaculation inevitability. Polar takes advantage of the propitious moment and releases his hold on his lover. He brings his left leg up onto the bed, straightens a bit, and grabs Vulpie's calves. He takes charge of the fox's legs, roughly but lovingly, and continues fucking while Vulpie jerks off.

Vulpie hastily masturbates his little super hard cock. It's good sized for his species, but just cute compared to Polar's. But his husband knows how to enjoy it, and remembers being pleasured by the little penis while Vulpie feverishly attends to it. The white furred wolf feels his lover tightening up, and knows it's time. He thrusts deep inside Vulpie and holds still for a moment so he won't hurt him. Vulpie spasms, and throws his head back to cry out in pleasure.

"AHHHHHAHHHH!!!" Vulpie yells, arching his back and ejaculating a plethora of semen into the air. It rains down on the bed sheet behind him, and is followed by a smaller yet plentiful wave of cum that splats down on his furry chest. "AHHH!!"

"Yeah!" Polar shouts in pride.

"AHHHH! AAAHHHHHHHHHH! Ahhh….. Ahhhhh……"

"Oh yeah! Wow! That has to be a record! Haha!" Polar gleefully declares and licks his lips. He can't wait to fuck the fox some more, and starts pumping him again before his lover has a chance to come to his senses. Vulpie slowly lifts his head back up and shows the white furred wolf a delightfully overwhelmed grin.

"F! FUCK! OH MY! Oh fuck!"

"Hold still. I'm not done with you yet!" Polar says, and looks down at his cock. He observes it sinking inside the fox with each thrust and coming out again, over and over. He takes his time, making sure to work himself up before blowing his load. He feels less resistance as Vulpie relaxes again, and speeds up. The white furred wolf keeps a firm grip on his lover's legs and continues reaming him out.

"Marry me! Oh wait!" Vulpie gasps with a huge grin and Polar bursts out in laughter. He chuckles but cuts it short when he feels semen backing up inside his cock. It makes him fuck his small husband faster and faster. He can't wait to unleash the massive ejaculatory pressure, but slows down for one final moment to draw it out as long as possible. He knows he can get a mind blowing orgasm if he's patient. He feels every inch of Vulpie's insides, and it satisfies his savage desire for total domination. He's in complete control, and even though Vulpie's a willing participant, Polar allows his imagination to run wild. He fantasizes about raping Vulpie, taking him completely against his will, and this gives him the final push he needs. He pumps hard and fast while gritting his teeth.

"UH! AGH!"

"No, please stop Mr. Wolf! No!" Vulpie mischievously whines. Polar's eyes widen for a moment and he wonders whether Vulpie read his mind, but realizes he's grimacing rather horribly. He's been doing it without realizing how mean he looks on the receiving end, and the fox boy plays it up as much as possible. "Help!" Polar lustfully grips Vulpie's legs, making his lover wince in actual pain, and pounds his way to a climax.

"AAAHH!!" The white furred wolf cries out and braces himself. He pushes his cock as deep inside Vulpie as he can, and unleashes a massive load of spooge. "AAHHH FUCK! AHHHHHHHHHHHHHHHHHHH!!! AAHHHHWWWWRRRGHHH!!!" Polar shuts his eyes and holds them closed tightly while enduring a cumshot that's both wonderful and slightly painful at the same time. The semen he's been holding back rockets inside Vulpie's ass in several effusive gushes.

"Ow!" Vulpie quietly complains, and Polar blinks. He suddenly realizes he's clawing his legs and quickly loosens his grip.

"Ah! Sorry!"

"It's okay!" Vulpie breathes in relief and smiles, privately enjoying the slick sensation of the wolf's hot messy semen in his ass.

"Oh my God... Uh, sorry about that." Polar groans with his eyes half open. He starts going limp, all over, and Vulpie reaches up to the wolf's light blue t-shirt. He pushes on him, signaling that he wants to get free, and Polar lets go of his legs. Vulpie crawls back a little, and winces when his husband's dick pops out of him. He turns over and makes room for his husband, gesturing for the much larger male to take his place. Polar takes the offer, and crawls onto the bed in exhaustion. He puts his right arm out, and gets it messy in Vulpie's cumshot on the other side of the bed, but doesn't care. He just closes his eyes and rests after the intense sexercise. The orange furred fox crawls over to his wolf lover and playfully scrambles onto his back. "What are you? Doing?" Polar laughs.

"Nothing." Vulpie answers and lies face down on top of his big mate. He pushes his little muzzle up to Polar's left ear and nibbles on it.

"Mmmmm..."

"You're so bad... Thinking about raping Vulpie..." The fox whispers. Polar smiles, but after a moment, he thinks about the statement and blinks.

"What?"

"Bad." Vulpie says, and Polar slowly pushes himself up on his left arm. Vulpie slides off and ends up on the bed to his right. The fox boy tucks his legs together, sitting cross-legged, and gives his husband a clever look.

"How'd you know that? How do you know that's what I was thinking?" Polar asks in confusion.

"Kind of obvious Mr. P…"

"Why?"

"The look on your face!" Vulpie laughs.

"Oh! Right." Polar chuckles, and shakes his head in relief. "Vulpie, you're too smart for your own good…" Polar says and smiles. "I swore you just read my mind. I didn't want to rape you. I just, well, I wanted to get off!"

"It's cool! It's really cool." Vulpie gleefully responds and bites his tongue between his teeth. "I love it when you go wild. You did kind of claw me though. My butt hurts and my legs too!"

"Well make up your mind!" Polar grins, and bites his tongue between his sharp teeth as well.

"That was SO AWESOME!" The orange furred fox declares and swishes his tail. He winces in pain, and has to curtail his excitement.

"Let me catch a nap and we'll go another round. What do you say?" The wolf offers and Vulpie's eyes widen.

"Uh, nah I'll pass. I think that'll do me!"

"You sure?"

"Save it for tomorrow. If I can get one of those every day, THEN we'll be in business!"

"I'm game." Polar replies and takes a moment to stretch. He relaxes afterwards, leaning his head down sideways so he can keep his eyes on his husband. "If you are."

"Might actually... Maybe we should wait until I heal up a little bit." Vulpie slyly responds. Polar grins at him and Vulpie shows off his sharp fox teeth with a big smile.

"Speaking of business..." The white furred wolf says, and takes on a serious demeanor. "What's the plan for today? Or tomorrow for that matter?"

"Ya got me." Vulpie answers while shaking his head. "I don't even know anymore. I feel like we ought to be at work but how can I keep a low profile like that?"

"Yeah. Maybe we should just go anyway?"

"We could. Do you think it's a good idea?"

"On second thought, no. If Druward is investigating that.. Whatever his name was."

"Glovepaw?"

"Yeah, that guy." Polar replies, and uses his left arm to sit up. He pulls his legs together, and sits cross-legged like Vulpie, draping his big arms together in his lap. "Druward said we shouldn't let our guard down until he finishes whatever he's doing... He really gets on my nerves. He's so clandestine about everything. If he can't trust us, then who is there?"

"Well, you did beat him up. Maybe he was nervous because he knew you were listening." Vulpie says with an adorable look.

"I don't think so. He was never scared, not even when I did get the better of him. He's got this... Cold attitude that nothing can penetrate."

"You penetrated him pretty good I think. He risked his life to save me."

"True, but who knows how long he'll remember it. He's probably back to his old self. I mean, I appreciate what the guy did, but all of it was his fault."

"Nah, those AFR foxes messed with his head."

"When is he going to call us? Did he say how long it was going to take? I can't remember."

"I think he said this week, or by the end of the week or something. He had something very important to take care of."

"Doesn't give us much to go on." Polar snorts.

"Maybe he can't talk about it on the phone, baby." Vulpie lovingly suggests.

"I guess we should fuck all day long." Polar replies and shrugs his shoulders with a wry expression.

"Yesh! But I've got to be on top! I'm a little sore."

"No, now I DEFINITELY have to be on top!" Polar grins. "I LOVE watching you tip toe around the house..."

"You're mean. Bad old wolf." Vulpie smirks. "Nah, you should let me take care of you. Did you know your prostate heals up after getting stimulation? It does! About thirty percent of your cum gets backed up in there, and if you get it out, the oxygenation process helps you grow new cells and stuff."

"Oh really?" Polar chuckles in profound amusement. "I didn't know that!"

"Yeah, huh! So let Doctor Vulpie oxygenate you!"

"You sure have a way with words!"

"And my actions speak even louder baby!"

"Are you sure you're not just trying to avoid another pounding? I think that's your ulterior motive..."

"Now you sound like the doctor! Paging Doctor P! We have a gay kid that hasn't got off in like seven days! He needs a pounding RIGHT NOW!" The orange furred fox gleefully replies.

"Nurse, I've already taken care of this one. And it hasn't been seven damn days!" Polar teases.

"Man, I wish we could just take off together!" Vulpie declares and scratches his furry right ear. "Just go somewhere and do whatever we wanted! Who cares if we ever came back!"

"Go back to the Canis Lupus Mountains and ride a bike." Polar suggests, and Vulpie's eyes light up.

"Yeah! Hell yeah! That was so much fun!"

"That's it. I've got it. I know what you need." Polar says with a very satisfied look.

"What?"

"You need a car. It's been too long since you've burned rubber and endangered traffic!"

"Yeah?"

"Just kidding about the endangering the people part."

"Aw! But yeah! Man, it has been a long fucking time! I am tired of being escorted everywhere like some kind of prisoner... But what can I do? I mean, Blacktail won't let me drive. They would if I made them, but they wouldn't like it. They'd say it was too much of a risk and they wouldn't be responsible if somebody got me."

"I don't know. Maybe they wouldn't..." Polar replies and shrugs his shoulders again. He smiles at his fox lover and Vulpie grins in excitement.

"You really mean it? You'd be okay with me getting a car?"

"Vulpie, we have millions... I think we can afford one."

"I know, but that's not the issue. It's my safety."

"Well, are you planning on doing something crazy?"

"Of course not!"

"Then let's get you one."

"YES! Fucking AWESOME! Let's get two cars! You could replace your old one!"

"I love my car. Let's just get you one for now. But we need to shop around. Maybe Blacktail will have some ideas, like for safety concerns and all that. Maybe some racing cars are safer than others. That's what you want, right?"

"Oh, pretty please!" Vulpie answers with his cutest voice.

Rulef blinks when he hears Vulpie's request. The Blacktail commander looks to Polar, and then back to the fox. They offered for him to come inside the house after meeting them at the front door as usual. Vulpie is beyond excited, and almost hops up and down while waiting for an answer. Rulef frowns and looks around their den while mulling over the idea.

"Please? Do you think we could swing it?"

"You can't be serious." Rulef responds and looks down at Vulpie with a worried expression. He glances at Polar, who seems patient and reasonable, but also appears slightly enthusiastic about the proposal. "After Mother's Purity tried to kill you?"

"I know, but I'll be safe! I promise!"

"You can do what you want, Vulpie, but we can't protect you like that. You haven't thought about traffic, and situations where we simply can't reach you in time."

"I know, I know! But maybe I could just drive it once in a while."

"It's up to you, but I advise against it. You're the most famous animal on Sufias. People will recognize you, and if the wrong one is near you at the wrong time... We just barely stopped those guys at Vulpie Industries."

"Yeah, but I wasn't on the road. And you said it shouldn't have happened anyway... Like you let security get a little loose? I'm not complaining. You saved my ass, but this is different."

"Hmm..." Rulef responds and looks aside. He runs his tongue over his sharp wolf teeth and crosses his arms while pondering the issue. He looks at Polar again, and the white furred wolf nods, clearly agreeing with Vulpie's statement. The Blacktail commander takes a long moment before answering, but when he does, his voice is slightly optimistic. "Actually... If you're determined to do this..."

"What? Do you have an idea? You do have an idea, don't you! I knew you would!"

"Just hold on." Rulef replies and cautiously waves his right paw at the orange furred fox. "I'm not saying it's possible, but if we have to do it... The company that builds armored vehicles for Blacktail is privately owned. I know someone over there, and he MIGHT, and I mean might, Vulpie, have an idea."

"REALLY? Aw yeah!"

"Could they build an armored sports car?" Polar inquires.

"Possibly. They mostly build SUVs and urban assault vehicles for law enforcement... But they might accept a custom job if the buyer can afford it. They're not your average car dealership, though. Anything they make will be extremely expensive. They use custom parts for everything."

"But it's possible?"

"It might be."

"He really wants this, and I want it too."

"Okay... Well... Should I call them today? What's your schedule look like?"

"We've got all day." Polar answers, and wraps his left arm around Vulpie.

The AOSE Superbolt

Vulpie snuggles up against Polar's left side as their SUV makes a sharp turn to the right. Polar hugs him and admires the industrial area of Sufias City. They're in the western district where several large corporations have chosen to purchase real estate near Lake Valfa, a popular tourist destination.

"That's it." Rulef says and points to the right window. He's in the passenger seat up front, and Vulpie crawls up on Polar a little bit to get a better view. They've reached their destination in just an hour and a half after departing from the house. Traffic was unusually light throughout the massive city, and Blacktail has access to the best routes. "They installed the satellite tracking system in our trucks. Do you remember last year when we upgraded?"

"Yeah!" Vulpie answers while looking at the two mile building coming up on their right side. It has a huge artificial lake with an impressive water fountain in the middle.

"Pretty nice." Polar muses, and notices the vehicles parked in front of the building. Vulpie can't see them yet, but it looks like a single SUV, and a sleek car are parked around a large company sign.

"They roll thousands of trucks out of here. Most of it goes overseas to Felini." Rulef says, and Vulpie perks up when they pass by the company's sign. He sees the black SUV on display, one quite similar to the one they're riding in, followed by the long rectangular sign that simply reads AOSE, with white text on a black background. But his attention is immediately drawn to a beautiful orange sports car just to the left of the sign. The sports car has an orange exterior, black wheels, half-orange, half-black hood, sleek appearance, with a monocoque, or unibody, design. The unibody structural approach suggests it's a performance oriented vehicle.

"Oh baby!" Vulpie shouts.

"Yeah, I saw it." Polar smirks in amusement.

"Was wondering what your reaction would be." Rulef says while looking back in the rearview mirror.

"Do they sell that one? What was it?"

"They must if they have it out front." Polar thinks out loud, and Vulpie slides off of him. The orange furred fox smiles and kicks his feet in excitement.

"Dude, I hope so!" Blacktail's convoy drives another hundred feet, and makes a right turn, where the first vehicle pauses at a security checkpoint. The small but sturdy guard station is manned by two animals, and one of them steps out of the booth to speak with the mercenaries. Rulef provided the men up front with all the information and clearance codes they would need, and the heavy steel bar lifts up in a matter of moments. One of the guards gives a final nod to the wolf he was speaking with, and returns to his post. The quadruple SUV convoy drives on, and the guards peer inside each one of the Blacktail vehicles, looking for Polar and Vulpie. The SUV's tinted windows makes sighting them impossible, but their natural curiosity spurs them to try anyway.

Once inside the compound, Blacktail drives straight towards the building in formation. Rulef likes to switch things up so would-be attackers can never guess which vehicle Vulpie is in, so they're riding in the third car, with only one SUV behind them. They pass by the corporate parking area, much to Polar and Vulpie's surprise, and continue their approach to the main building.

The AOSE compound looks like the largest factory in the world, but probably isn't. It just impresses Vulpie and Polar because their own corporate facilities are four times smaller. They don't need two miles of building to produce V-Screen 7s, StoreWatt 2.0.s, Consonant 17.5s, and Insta-Fur 4.1s. Their largest factory is only one fourth of the size of the AOSE compound, and only because Vulpie's top secret projects are built there. Several layers of security prevent low clearance Vulpie Industries employees from stumbling into the project labs, but the AOSE factory near Lake Valfa is clearly designed for non-stop assembly line vehicle construction. The building has over fifty loading docks with extension platforms that are meant for loading transfer trucks with finished products, and bringing in material for future projects.

Blacktail pulls right up to the eastern side of the complex, at the main entrance, and parks on the curb. Vulpie privately enjoys the "like a boss," sensation he enjoys as a result, but doesn't let much of it show. Everyone unbuckles their seatbelts, and the wolf to Vulpie's left, who has been completely silent during the ride so far, opens the door and gets out. He offers a paw for Vulpie and the orange furred fox takes it while Polar opens the door on the right side. Rulef and Polar walk around the vehicle to join the others, and the entourage of mercenaries is intercepted by a single man, a tall timber wolf, who's wearing a black suit coat with a white business shirt. He isn't wearing a tie, and has to be in charge if he can circumvent corporate dress policy.

"Val." Rulef says and walks up to the man for a paw shake.

"Good to see you! Thanks for the unexpected visit!" The brown furred wolf responds with a smile.

"I know you're always busy, but I think we have something that'll interest you."

"Oh, certainly!" Val says and looks Vulpie and Polar over with his brown eyes. "You're looking for an armored car?"

"A sports car, yeah!" Vulpie enthusiastically replies.

"I think we can work something out. My name's Val Maxwell." He says and offers a hand shake that Vulpie accepts. Like always, Vulpie's small fox paw is swallowed up by a wolf's paw when exchanging pleasantries. Vulpie almost introduces himself but stops. The man clearly knows who he is. "Everyone come inside. I've already cleared you with security."

"Should we move our cars?" Polar inquires and Val pauses for a moment before answering with a smirk.

"No, they'll be fine."

"You, you and you stay here." Rulef orders while pointing at three of his men. They nod in agreement and everyone else follows Maxwell to the entrance. The large facility has a rather simple lobby, and Maxwell is kind enough to hold the door open for everyone. He's clearly eager to make a sale.

"This way." Val says and unlocks a pair of glass doors. He leads everyone down an empty hallway, where the factory can be viewed while walking. Tigers, panthers, lions, wolves and foxes are hard at work on several military trucks and SUVs. It looks like hundreds of animals are involved in the process. Sparks are flying everywhere while they disassemble, assemble, inspect, and test the vehicles. Val uses his keycard to unlock the door at the other end of the hallway, and leads them into an office corridor. He makes a right, walks about twenty paces, and then heads left. He takes them down another hallway, and uses his keycard once again to unlock a sizeable room. Everyone walks inside, and Maxwell closes the door behind them. The room has a large white table in the middle, and is surrounded by comfortable looking black leather chairs. "Make yourself at home." Val offers, and Vulpie takes a seat, followed by everyone else. Every member of Blacktail gets a chair, and many of them look pleased, but Rulef decides to stand anyway.

"Thanks." Vulpie says and Maxwell takes a seat in front of him. Rulef walks to their left and smiles. It's an unusual sight, and Polar attributes it to him being in the company of his friend. Both Rulef and Maxwell seem a little excited.

"We don't have many visitors, but it's a pleasure to have you here Mr. Vivixen. Rulef told me about your situation and your desire to buy a personal vehicle. But not just any car... Safety is your biggest concern."

"That and an awesome motor." Vulpie smiles in response. "I saw some of the stuff you guys are building on the way in, but most of it looked like it was going to a warzone. Is it possible for you to help me out? I need something street legal."

"That's a very good point, but it won't be a problem. If you purchase something from us, we'll report it to the authorities and have it cleared in no time. That's a large part of our operation. We probably built the armored SUVs that you use every day. We work very closely with the government. But you're right, we aren't your average car dealership. We're in the security business, and we're experts at what we do."

"When he said he wanted a personal vehicle, I was opposed to the idea. How are we supposed to safeguard him at all times if he speeds off somewhere? But then I thought about you guys, and I remembered that you always have a car on display. So the car out front... What is it?"

"Yeah! That thing is bangin! Is it a real car or just a prototype or something?" Vulpie quickly inquires.

"We make ONE CAR." Maxwell responds, emphasizing his statement by raising his right index finger in the air. "Our budget doesn't allow us the luxury of different models. AOSE focuses on army contracts, BUT... Since it's the only civilian oriented vehicle we produce, our one car stands in a league of its own. It's specifically designed for wealthy animals who demand high end performance and safety. We don't sell many of them because they're very expensive, but I can assure you, the price tag is justified."

"Okay." Vulpie replies with a friendly voice. "I'm not here to blow money, but I see your point. Tell me more. And yeah, is that car out front actually for sale?"

"Yes it is. It's the one I'm talking about." Maxwell smiles and the fox grins. "We named it the Superbolt, and it's our pride and joy."

"I want it. I'm not gonna lie. So tell me everything about it, and then tell me the price."

"And I would love to sell it to you, because our last buyer left us high and dry." Val responds and licks his lips. "We actually have one in partial production that's just sitting in the warehouse. A prince from Vilivauf bought it, let us start production on it, and then changed his mind because he thought it was too slow. Zero to sixty in two point eight seconds wasn't good enough for him..."

"Oh really?!" Vulpie laughs and Val smirks. "That's super-fast! What's his problem?"

"Common sense. He wanted lots of protection, but reinforced steel, titanium and Kevlar weigh quite a bit, not to mention the bullet proof glass. We were making him an excellent car and he just bailed on us. Unfortunately, we had to sue him over it and only recovered half the cost. Now it's just collecting dust in the garage."

"So it's still in perfect condition?"

"It's in pristine condition. The boys had to pack it up and tuck it away until we could figure out what to do with it. We don't need a second model on display, but there aren't a lot of people with enough money to buy it either."

"What's the lowest price? Well, how much was he going to pay for his car? What's a fair price for you?"

"Two million." Val answers and maintains his composure. Vulpie ponders for a moment and looks back at Polar.

"What do you think?"

"We knew it would be expensive." Polar warmly replies, and his fox lover smiles.

"Just so much money..."

"I want you to be safe." The white furred wolf responds and Vulpie nods. He looks back to Maxwell, and the timber wolf nods, acknowledging the steep price.

"Alright."

"I know dropping two million on a car kind of seems outrageous, but you will definitely get what you pay for. If Polar is concerned about your safety, then we can do even more. We can make the Superbolt almost death proof. That might sound like an exaggeration, but I guarantee you, we can get it pretty darn close. And we haven't even talked about the car's best features yet."

"Okay. Go on."

"The Superbolt is an electric car, hence the name." Maxwell continues. "It doesn't make any sound, except for a slight rushing that's reminiscent of a jet engine, but it can keep up with and outrun almost any car in the world. Zero to sixty in two point eight seconds, with a top speed of two hundred and fifty miles per hour. Now... If we armor the car up for you, it's naturally going to slow it down somewhat, so I'm thinking it'll be more like zero to sixty in three point one seconds. Is that acceptable?"

"Sounds fantastic."

"Good. It's refreshing to deal with a reasonable customer."

"How strong is the car battery? It won't die on me, will it?"

"Excellent question, and the answer is no. You can replace the battery if you ever need to, but it's guaranteed to last for twenty years, even if you let it fully discharge. In the past, some electric cars would "brick," when they weren't charged on a regular basis, but technology has come a long way since then, and we only use the best power sources available. The Superbolt is our flagship. We can't have it sitting dead on the side of the road somewhere." Val says, and Vulpie and Polar chuckle.

"How does that battery hold up in a crash?" Rulef inquires, drawing everyone's attention. "Let's say a pickup truck slams into them from behind at seventy miles an hour. I assume the battery is in the back, so will it continue to work after that kind of damage?"

"You know your cars." Val tells Rulef and licks his lips. "The Superbolt's battery comes with several layers of protection to guard against that very thing. We have mechanisms that prevent breakage and disconnection, so you're sure to stay on the road. But... Once again... If we want to make this thing indestructible, we could double or even quadruple the saturated steel, titanium, and Kevlar. That'll slow it down a bit more, but not too much."

"Let's do that then." Polar says, and Rulef, Vulpie and Val look back at him in surprise. "We want to do that."

"Quadruple everything? The entire car's chassis and support structure?" Maxwell asks.

"Can you make it like that all around the car? Give the entire car the same kind of protection the battery box will have? Four layers of it?"

"We really couldn't do any more than four layers, but yes."

"Then do it." The white furred wolf declares and Vulpie raises his eyebrows at his husband. He turns around and raises his eyebrows again at Maxwell.

"You heard him!"

"That will cost significantly more. Much, much more." Val responds.

"He needs it. If we're going to do this, I want him to be completely protected." Polar tells the AOSE manager, and Val smiles.

"I can tell you're not playing around. That's okay, we aren't either. You got it."

"How will that affect the acceleration and top speed?" Vulpie asks.

"You'll see a slight hit in performance but it shouldn't be much. Let's talk about bullet proof glass before I make a prediction."

"Kay."

"The stock Superbolt comes with level two bullet proof glass, which will stop a three fifty seven magnum, and nine millimeter handguns. The prince wanted level eight, which will deter a seven point sixty two millimeter rifle round, but there's significant weight associated with putting that many layers of glass in a vehicle. But... If you really want complete protection against any conceivable threat, we can go to level ten. Not many people know about level ten because the demand is rather low. Ten will stop a fifty caliber military round. Now that's a heavy SASR, a special application scoped rifle, an anti-material rifle. Anti-material rifles are designed to attack unarmored or lightly armored vehicles. They use rifles like that to destroy engine blocks... And we can install bulletproof glass that will actually deter that much firepower. However... In the past, that much glass protection would equate to poor light transmission, and was only used for exterior applications. But... It CAN be accommodated for your car... For a sizeable fee. We have new material that solves the lighting problem, and we'll make sure everything looks nice. It won't be dark inside your car. Everything will look just like it does in a regular Superbolt, except you'll be driving a tank on four wheels. We'll also use a super firm base chemical to squeeze the glass thickness down to a comfortable width."

"Wow, I don't know if we need THAT much protection." Vulpie says and grins.

"Is there anything else?" Polar asks.

"You'll be getting everything the Superbolt comes with, the premium leather seats, the heated seats, the three-spoke leather-wrapped sport steering wheel, an in-dash touchscreen that features GPS navigation, exterior cameras, and an amplified 400 Watt 7-speaker sound system." Val answers. "We'll test drive the one out front if you want to get a feel for the car."

"What's the acceleration going to be with all of that protection?" Vulpie inquires. "Let's say that we did everything you just suggested."

"You still should hit sixty miles per hour in less than three point four seconds. I can't see it taking any longer than that. If it does, then I'll refund twenty percent." Maxwell answers with confidence.

"Cool." Vulpie says and looks back at Polar. "What do ya think?"

"Everything." Polar replies and Vulpie raises his eyebrows once more.

"Yeah?"

"How much would it be if we did all of that, if we maxed out the armor, including the level ten glass you talked about?" Polar asks the AOSE manager.

"The most expensive non-armored race car in the world sold for three point nine million last year, and we can do this for around three million, four hundred thousand. It's a huge investment, but he'll be able to go anywhere he wants." The timber wolf tells Polar with a serious but caring look. "I can tell his safety means a lot to you." Polar smiles, knowing the man is manipulating him to some degree, but nods in agreement.

"It does. You're right." Polar says, and Vulpie turns around in his chair.

"So you think we should... Are we gonna do this?" Vulpie asks in excitement.

"Don't you want to?"

"Yeah but... So much money... I feel bad about spending it when some animals have so little."

"He's the most famous person in the universe. Animals recognize him wherever he goes, so this really is a great deal for you and AOSE Technologies. You can relax, knowing he'll be safe no matter what, and we can advertise that Vulpie Vivixen drives a Superbolt. It's a win-win."

"Man, he's a great salesman isn't he!" Vulpie giggles and Polar smirks for a moment before going serious again.

"Yeah, he is. And you can really do everything you said?" The white furred wolf inquires.

"Absolutely. I'll put the best people we have on it. We'll live up to our end of the bargain. And like I said, if he can't get to sixty miles per hour in three point four seconds, I'll refund twenty percent. I'll put it in the contract." Maxwell promises.

"Okay. Let's do it." Polar says, and Vulpie grins from ear to ear, showing off his sharp fox teeth.

"Thank you Gentlemen. I'll personally oversee this project and have the car driven to your home by Sunday evening. Is that alright?"

"Sounds good!" Vulpie answers, and Polar nods.

"Okay then! Let's take the one out front for a spin." Val smiles and stands up. "Try before you buy."

Brotherly Love

Richard suddenly looks up from his work when he hears footsteps. The white furred wolf is almost finished grading his student's chapter four tests, and is quite surprised to see his older brother smiling at him.

"Knock, knock."

"Hey... Hey Polar. What's up?" Richard Arctic replies and squints at the Blacktail mercenary standing with his sibling.

"Is it a bad time?"

"No."

"Didn't mean to interrupt. I just remembered your schedule and we were in the area." Polar explains while walking into the classroom.

"So what do you guys teach here at the Kayman Institute?" Deepwolf asks, and Richard blinks. He's surprised at the man's forwardness. Most of the Blacktail wolves refrain from making small talk.

"It varies. We have undergraduate and graduate programs in science, the arts, mathematics..."

"Cool." Deepwolf responds and looks around the spacious room. It appears that Richard's office doubles as a classroom and can seat around fifty students.

"Yes..." Richard says while grimacing at the man's flippant attitude.

"So things are good?" Polar asks and puts his paws in his khaki pants pockets. He looks nervous and his brother outstretches a paw towards a nearby chair.

"Yeah. Please, sit down." Richard offers and glances at the doorway. "Where's Vulpie?"

"He's at AOSE Technologies. We bought an armored car today, and he loves it, but he wanted to make some improvements before they started building it. So he decided to go by Vulpie Industries to get some of his gadgets."

"No doubt to improve the onboard computer." Richard Surmises.

"Probably. Yeah, I think it has one." Polar chuckles. "I think he's going to switch out the sound system with his Consonant 17.5, and put in a better hard drive or something. But I'm not much help in the tech department, so I thought I could come by and see you while he's busy over there."

"Oh, so that's why you only have one guard. I wondered what was going on. Why'd you decide to drop by?"

"I need your help." Polar says while sitting down. He swishes his tail twice and licks his lips before speaking again. "We both see the same doctor, and yesterday we found out Vulpie is immune to a whole bunch of viruses. It's really amazing, but it also messed with his head... And now he's kind of worried that he might be the antikhalan..." Polar says and cocks his head sideways. "So I wanted to talk to you about it before you heard it yourself."

"Oh." Richard replies and raises his eyebrows.

"He remembers everything you say. He really puts a lot of stock in your opinion, Richard."

"I'm sorry about what happened. I had no idea Ivo... That he was a machine... You can't even imagine what the college president said when he found out."

"I bet."

"I shouldn't have listened to him."

"He was your friend. At least, he looked like your friend and sounded exactly like your friend. I don't blame you for trusting him." Polar responds and sits up straight. "But I'm worried about Vulpie."

"After they tried to kill him, and yelled out antikhalan..." Richard interjects.

"Right."

"Poor kid. He's been through a lot."

"We both have, and so have you." Polar replies with a loving voice.

"And he's... He's what? He can't even get sick?"

"No, he's immune to a whole slew of sexually transmitted diseases, probably because he slept around a lot before I met him. They didn't test him for everything, just the ones they thought he might have. And they found out he's totally clean, so clean in fact, that he can't even get the Alopex Virus. They're going to make a vaccine from his blood."

"Wow. That's incredible news." Richard responds with wide blue eyes.

"Yeah... It's really bothering him."

"He laughed it off before, but this is just too much, huh?" Polar's brother inquires.

"Right."

"I promise not to say anything about it."

"Thank you. It really means a lot to me, Richard."

"What is all this Anti-Khalan crap anyway?" Deepwolf suddenly asks. "I never went to church or read the Velora. So what's in there?"

"Ah... Well..." Polar's brother says with a bewildered expression and leans back in his chair.

"It all seems fake to me. No offense, but naked goddesses watching over us day and night? Come on... Just seems like pussy worship. Again, no offense."

"Saying no offense doesn't make up for deliberately disrespectful statements." Richard says with his professor's voice. "You're not one of my students, but I don't allow that kind of talk in my classroom, and you're on my turf tough guy... But there are several reasons why Deivaism is still the most popular religion, if you really want to know... It goes all the way back to the first recorded languages. Our earliest known ancestors wrote about Sherrie, Khalan, Cyrilla and Aila as if they had actually seen them. One would think, that if they were purely invented, the mythology would have small beginnings and then would have grown over time, but it wasn't like that at all. The Velora says our ancestors left a mother world called Halvia for unknown reasons, and it was the Deivas themselves that created a gateway between Halvia and Sufias. The only planet in our universe that matches Halvia's scale is several light-years away, so apparently they created the entire universe with a convenient fast travel system." The white furred wolf jests with a wry look.

"So you don't believe in it either." Deepwolf responds and Richard shakes his head in disagreement.

"No, I do believe in the Deivas, but as a historian, I also notice how ridiculous it sounds. All we have are religious texts that were supposedly written by animals during those time periods. But whether it's real or not, people have worshipped them since the very beginning."

"But why?"

"I could go on all day..." Richard says and glances at his brother. Polar shrugs, and since there's no opposition, the snow wolf straightens in his chair while thinking about where to start. Deepwolf discovers a nearby chair and drags it near Richard's desk. He flips it around and takes a seat, crossing his arms over its back end.

"How does religion spread? Let's say you were going to make up a religion, and convert Polar and I. How would you do it?"

"Just make up some mumbo jumbo and tell you it's legit. And if you didn't agree, I'd kill you. If we were in old times and barbaric and such."

"Classy." Polar says with raised eyebrows.

"But even if you did, people wouldn't believe it just because you took our lives. You'd have to show evidence to support your beliefs. Otherwise they'd never get off the ground."

"Well it's easy. People want to have good thoughts and feel good feelings, like when someone dies and they want them to go to heaven. So I'd say my religion is real because you went to heaven if you played ball."

"Maybe you're right, but Deivaism has more than that. It has tangible evidence. It might be false evidence, but there's evidence. Don't get me wrong. There have been plenty of competing religions throughout history. Maro worship."

"Who?"

"Maro. Maro?" Richard asks and blinks.

"Oh, right. Yeah, the super arctic wolfess." Deepwolf smirks.

"Polar and I might be her descendants, you never know."

"Right."

"Some felines worshipped Ixtila, the father of the Itrixes."

"You lost me."

"Itrixes were giant cats that looked like cougars and had golden hair. They went extinct on Halvia, but those are the hero references you see in the movies. The cats with gold hair? Itrixes."

"Got ya."

"Maro worship, then there's the fallen goddesses, like Sarassida the shadow Deiva, and Xsilyncoitus the metal fleshed... Not to mention the semi-mortal deities... Kaylen Hiar... Vaxi worship... There were plenty of competitors, but a lot of them actually came from Halvia and were related to Deivaism in one way or another."

"Who was the last one?"

"Vaxi was the fox god of mischief. Apparently he caused so much trouble that he had to hitch a ride to Sufias to escape Khalan's wrath."

"What did he do?"

"The same things foxes do today... Lie, cheat, steal..."

"Here we go." Polar growls. "Keep the anti-vulpine stuff down in front of me, alright?"

"Sorry." Richard tells his brother and looks back to Deepwolf. "Anyway, legend has it he was actually Khalan's son as well, so some animals worshipped him for a while. Then there was the Lulpra cult. But you see, it all goes back to Halvia. The Lulpras were the giant super wolves of legend, like the Itrixes, and that comes from Halvia, but at least there are fossils of some

Lulpras on Sufias, albeit, they were quite small compared to the legends. None of them were over eleven feet tall and, of course, you know they were extremely brutal, and our lupine ancestors killed them in self-defense."

"Yeah I know." Deepwolf says and nods as if he's more learned than one might expect.

"But none of the smaller religions lasted very long because they lacked evidence. Nothing happened that perpetuated the belief system, so they faded away. Not so with Deivaism. We're still finding ancient depictions of the goddesses in archaeological digs that are millions of years old. They were here long before we were, so who made them? It's a huge mystery, and it lends credibility to Deivaism that will never fade away. And now those robotic women..."

"Vulpie.net's Deivas?"

"One thing's for sure, a religious revival is already underway for the faithful. A lot of conservative Deivaists think there's more to it than computer based mischief. They see it as a sign, and yes, I can see why Vulpie's worried, but he shouldn't be. In my heart I don't really believe in anything like an Anti-Khalan. The idea stems from Khalan's Vein in the Velora, but I think men have just used it as an excuse to persecute famous animals whenever convenient."

"Yeah, but Vulpie's gay too, and his virus made the goddesses like it's mocking them or something."

"Whose side are you on?" Polar asks and Deepwolf lowers his muzzle for a moment.

"I'm sorry Polar. I didn't mean anything by that, I'm just saying."

"It's my fault for bringing them up. But the archaeological digs aren't the only pieces of evidence that support Deivaism. Have you ever heard of the Great Cleansing?"

"No." Deepwolf answers, and stretches a little.

"Not many people do. It's not in the Velora, because no one is supposed to add to it after the final prophet, but our ancestors suffered some kind of catastrophic event before animals officially began recording time. Two hundred million animals died in a single year, and it happened two thousand one hundred and nine years ago."

"2109. Present time." Deepwolf says and smirks. "Neato."

"Every species dropped off sharply."

"So what happened? I've never heard this before."

"No one really knows. Every species had a different language, and some were accused of falsifying events so they could get sympathy... Foxes..." Richard coughs and Polar rolls his eyes. "But some historians, and yes they are mainly vulpine historians, say the goddesses returned to Sufias and murdered everyone."

"That's a prick thing to do. What pissed them off?"

"The foxes said it happened because a sorcerer named Xilev was using dark magic to mock the goddesses. So they sent the "Goddess Mockery," to Sufias, and it cleaned house."

"Wait... They sent a thing? I thought they did it themselves."

"That's also a debatable topic among vulpine historians... Look, I'm not against foxes. They just have a totally different way of doing things. But the story has lasted this long, and since it's an offspring of Deivaism, it's another reason why we have Deivaism today, and why animals worry themselves over antikhalan nonsense."

"And why some animals think it will be a fox." Polar says and Richard nods at his brother in a non-threatening manner.

"Yes." Richard replies and looks to Deepwolf once again. "So there you have it. That's why animals still bother worshipping those beautiful women. And it's why they still fear them. But in my personal opinion... It was a plague. There was some kind of viral outbreak that killed everyone, and the people that lived clung to the Velora. They wondered why they were spared and figured it must have been for a reason. They thought the goddesses were angry with them, so each species came up with its own version of the tragedy. And the vulpine version was the most popular."

"But why isn't it part of real history if it really happened? Why wouldn't the animals write it down if they were suddenly slaughtered by the Deivas?" Deepwolf inquires.

"Good question. I think the answer is obvious. It didn't happen. It was a plague." Richard smiles in response. "Animals will sexy things up when given a chance."

"Hey Polar, I'm really sorry." Deepwolf says and scratches his left side.

"It's alright... I know I'm overly sensitive about it." The white furred wolf sighs in response. "I just hate seeing him suffer. Last night he was in tears."

"I don't blame him." Richard comments.

"You should have seen his face when the doctor told him he couldn't get Double Vauphen Syndrome. It looked like someone had physically struck him."

"Well, for what it's worth, I'm not having dreams about him anymore. Dad hasn't either."

"So you two are still talking about it?"

"No. Not Really. He just mentioned it one day and it struck me just now that mine haven't come back either. So if Vulpie's worried about our opinion, you can tell him that."

"We're the only family he has." Polar responds.

"I know. I was demonstrably wrong at the museum. I should thank him for exposing that thing before it did any further damage. I talked to it for days and had no clue, not even the slightest hint, that it wasn't Professor Lorcan."

"I guess… I guess I can share this with you since you're sharing with me." Polar whispers and takes a breath. "That's not all, Richard. Vulpie saw something disturbing when he was down there on Zeravyn."

"I know."

"I don't mean the goddesses… He said there were hundreds of discarded body parts in this gigantic pit. Vulpie.net was throwing its rejects down there, and… He noticed a lot of them looked like you." Polar's words make the room silent and Richard's eyes widen while he digests the statement.

"Oh great. That's wonderful."

"He didn't want to upset you, or Mom, or Dad, but he worries about it. He wanted to offer you some of our bodyguards from Blacktail, but I told him not to say anything. I figured you wouldn't be interested."

"Hmm… Maybe… I may take you up on that one day." Richard responds with a sober look. "It's kind of flattering that Vulpie.net would waste resources on imitating me. Why me?"

"Because you're my brother. It can't have me and…" Polar trails off. "I don't know why."

"It's got a crush on you…" Deepwolf grins and Richard releases a very tired breath.

"Now I understand why you Blacktail people never talk." Polar's brother growls, and Deepwolf takes the insult with pride. "Are all of you this strange?"

"It's just him." Polar chuckles.

"We're getting our kitty back soon." Deepwolf declares and raises his eyebrows at Polar's brother.

"What?"

"Tiala. She won't quit Blacktail no matter how much we pay her. Vulpie and I feel really bad about making her work with this guy again, but she's hardcore. She's saved his life twice." Polar explains with a smile. Richard shakes his head and looks away from Deepwolf. The mercenary's creepy smile impinges on his comfort zone a little too much.

"Here." Richard says while leaning to the right. He digs through books and papers on the far corner and finds what he's looking for. He takes hold of a two pound history book with a red cover and yellow text. He holds it up and Polar accepts it. "Chapter eleven." The white furred wolf elaborates. Polar opens the book and eyes its table of contents. Chapter eleven's title is *"Pre-Vulpie.net / after Vulpie.net."*

"Heh! He'd like this." Polar grins and flips over to the chapter after reading its page number.

"Sure he would."

"What college level is this?"

"Freshman. It's required reading."

"Everyone has to learn it?"

"That's right." Richard responds and relaxes in his office chair. "Vulpie's earned my respect. It took me a long time to let it go, but I'm over it."

"Thank you." Polar replies and smiles. "So you're dating vixens again?"

"Nope." Richard smirks in response. "They're too much trouble."

"Fox love runs in the family you know. I'm just saying." Polar teases, and Richard chuckles.

"Too much drama. I don't have the patience for it."

"So are you dating anyone at the moment?"

"Lauren." Richard answers, referring to an attractive yet plump timber wolf. He's been dating her on and off for five years.

"Oh, you're still together?"

"Sort of." Polar's brother answers with a shrug.

"Hey uh, I want to ask a question if I can. Don't mean to butt in or anything." Deepwolf interjects. "You're a history professor, right?"

"Yes." Richard answers.

"And you know a lot about the Antikhalan mythology?"

"No. I'd refer you to my friend Ivo Lorcan, the real one, but he's not in good health."

"Okay. I just wanted to know more about the legend. Where did it come from and what it says and all that."

"It's in the Velora. You can look it up online. I'm sure you'll find plenty of information."

"Yeah, I could do that. I just wanted to ask if you knew anything general about it. You mentioned the other stuff about the cleansing or whatever. What's the Antikhalan supposed to do?"

"Can't really tell you. I do teach a few religion courses but they're not my primary area of expertise."

"But you read the part in the Velora, right?"

"Yeah… It says some very general things about Aila's son offending Goddess Khalan. Makes sense, given the name and all. There's also some incredibly weird stuff in there. I don't remember it like my friend Ivo Lorcan, the real Ivo Lorcan."

"Funny how everyone's so afraid of him, yet they don't even know what he'll look like or what he'll do." Deepwolf observes in amusement.

"That's how they can slap the name on animals so easily. But I don't know, I actually haven't read the Velora recently and don't remember what's in there. You'd be amazed what you'll find. You ought to look at it if you're interested."

"Nah. But it's not like the guy would wear it on his sleeve anyway. Vulpie's just a juicy target since he's famous and gay. But when you think about it, he's too "in your face," to be Aila's son. Seems like he'd prefer a clandestine approach, and would pull everyone's strings without people even knowing he existed." The mercenary declares, and Polar nods in agreement.

"Yeah, it's dumb." The white furred wolf replies, and returns the history book to his brother's desk.

A Perennial Threat

As the sun sets on Sufias city, an eerie gloom descends upon the capital district. The Stone House, Congress and the Senate are located in this area, and the monuments exalting the heart of the Sufias World Government attract onlookers from around the world. Many statues were erected during the birth of the world government, and "Maro's Triumph," has always been Druward's favorite. It's a circular marble monument that boasts a high ceiling, replete with beautiful columns. The entire structure is white, including Maro's statue, which stands inside the monument on top of a raised platform. Maro was a giant white furred she-wolf, but the statue is excessively larger than the legends say. The Velora describes her as being over eight feet in height, but in truth, no one really knows. Many animals on Sufias doubt she ever existed, but her legend had a profound impact on the creation of the Sufias World Government.

Druward demanded that Amsend meet him here for several reasons. The park is closed for the evening, and there are no security cameras anywhere, but they are still in the public arena. The black furred wolf decided against meeting the director of the GSB in a safe and private environment. His goal is to threaten the man, to make him feel uneasy, and to firmly establish a chain of command. Maro's Triumph is a perfect location to create the atmosphere Druward's looking for, plus there are wonderfully convenient locations throughout the Capital Park where snipers can be deployed. He has the area completely covered, and no citizen will interfere with the meeting, thanks to GBI agents providing additional security for the park on this special evening. Druward made sure no one could possibly get in with a camera and record what he plans to do. All options are on the table at this point. This will be his first meeting with Amsend, yet the man has been able to parasitize the GBI through his sub-organization for years.

The GBI director climbs the marble steps, and sees Amsend standing alone. He fits the description given by Karla. Surprisingly, he's a husky dog, not a hybrid lupine like Druward expected. Politically correct or not, wolves absolutely dominate positions of high authority throughout the SWG, and the GBI director finds it quite odd that a dog like Amsend could obtain such power. Some would argue that foxes influence the government more than all of the wolves combined, but a husky dog? He's abnormally large, almost a foot taller than Druward, and Druward is a very imposing man. Amsend's white furred face, and front, clash with his coal black ears and the black fur that covers the rest of his body, with the exception of the white fur on the bottom of his tail. Druward's mated with a husky bitch before, and thoroughly enjoyed it, but something about them has always given him the creeps. They're not to be trusted as a wolf, but they clearly resemble wolves in many ways. A female pornstar named Natasha Zen is one of the most popular delights to male wolves across the universe, because black and white husky dogs with pure markings were nearly wiped out during the Great War for the Sufias World Government. Massive genocide took place because wolves thought them inferior, and yet, this one has managed to challenge Druward's power in Sufias year 2109? How?

"Good evening Mr. Wraulgh…" Amsend says with a thick foreign accent. He's wearing a black suit with white pin stripes. He sports a black business tie, and polished black shoes. The ensemble matches his dark outer fur, and the white dress shirt underneath his silky tie strongly complements his overall appearance. Amsend has an unusually long muzzle for a husky dog, and it's impressive width suggests him capable of biting harder than most wolves. Though Druward has wider shoulders, Amsend's double thick fur gives him a very stout and regal appearance.

"We identified four GSB corpses at Elbrus. Were you responsible for the attack?" Druward asks while approaching the man.

"No pleasantries first? Upon our first meeting?" Amsend responds with a patronizing voice.

"Did you authorize the attack?"

"Must we be impolite?"

"Did you attack Elbrus?"

"Of course." Amsend answers, and Druward punches him in the face. The black furred wolf didn't even think about the action beforehand. It just came out of him, in a paroxysm of rage that sends Amsend stumbling backwards. The man reaches up and touches his face for a moment before quickly regaining his composure.

"OH, ho, ho, ho... It is a man that lives up to his reputation... How wonderful..."

"It's over! Do you understand? I'll put a bullet in your head!"

"Please calm yourself Mr. Wraulgh. We were just beginning our conversation when you struck me." The black and white husky grins in response. Druward pauses. The man is far too relaxed after being jabbed in the muzzle. Druward hit him as hard as he could, yet the GSB director seems fine.

"So you're a machine then? One of Vulpie.net's?" Druward asks and goes for his gun. He rests his paw on its hilt and waits for an answer.

"Oh, no... I'm quite real, I assure you..."

"That's what Sevrif said... And the others, Chris Cephil, Ivo Lorcan..."

"I'm no machine..."

"Then why did Vulpie.net destroy Fort Elbrus? You're obviously one of its creations."

"The machine and I have a... Special relationship..." Amsend answers, and Druward stiffens.

"What?"

"It works for me."

"Do you think I'm stupid? There's no way Vulpie's computer virus would cooperate with anyone. I watched it crunch him on the floor at the Cyber Technologies Government Division."

"Yes, and that's a subject I do need your help with." Amsend replies and smiles deviously. "But first... I'm afraid we need to discuss matters in more... Detail... You'll find that I'm a very generous man. After all, I have you surrounded and haven't taken your life."

"The hell are you talking about?" Druward asks, and quickly looks around. "There's no one here."

"You can't see them... How small minded you are... After the events at Elbrus, and my admission of participation, one would think you capable of deductive reasoning..."

"So you have me surrounded with invisible soldiers..." Druward growls.

"Oh yes."

"Can I see them?"

"Oh... Yes... But first, radio to your friend and have him stand down before any blood is needlessly shed." Amsend instructs, and Druward hesitates for a long moment before he reaches into his trench coat and grabs his radio. He brings it out, clicks it on, and raises it to his mouth.

"Rotick?"

"Yes." The Brown and white furred wolf immediately responds.

"In a moment... There might be several men appearing around me. Amsend says he has me covered from every direction... So don't shoot unless they shoot first."

"Are you serious?"

"Yes."

"Copy."

"Good." Amsend smiles and gives Druward a creepy look. "Is now alright?"

"Sure." Druward answers, and suddenly, around twenty armed men appear inside the monument. Each one of them is standing in front of a column, and they all have their assault rifles patiently aimed at the GBI director. The black furred wolf goes completely stiff, but slowly turns his head to the right, so he can get a better look at one of them. He recognizes Englavic writing on the man's black uniform. "NoirQueue."

"Well done." Amsend smugly comments and raises his right paw, signaling for the men to lower their weapons.

"Goddess Khalan…" Druward whispers, and the statement seems to bother Amsend.

"No need for profanity."

"Who are you?" Druward asks and looks from side to side, growing more anxious by the moment. He's still in disbelief, but is slowly coming to grips with his situation.

"You know my position. I direct the Governmental Security Bureau… And I must congratulate you for one thing, Mr. Wraulgh. A GBI director has never sought me out with such ferocity. You're the first, but I'm afraid you will also be the last. The wheels of fate are turning my friend."

"How long have you been doing this? How can you control the GBI? It's impossible! How can you circumvent the president and the chain of command?"

"We own your president. Every international bank belongs to our association. War is not only waged with guns."

"Your associates… The other ones I wanted Karla to give me…"

"They're not here. I apologize for their absence, but I handle direct matters such as this. I wouldn't want them to get hurt. They are, by all standards, family men."

"Bankers? You're just a bunch of bankers?"

"No, I'm afraid there's more to it than that… But we don't… Talk… About the matter to animals outside of the organization."

"What about the Sufian Monetary Fund? The world's largest international banking system?"

"Ours as well... You see, we control all options available to the public. And though you may find this hard to believe, we provide useful services."

"I bet you do... That accent... It's pure ancient Englavic, isn't it? You're part of the old money. The old crooked money."

"How crass of you." Amsend smirks in response.

"You won't get away with this. You can't. People will realize their government has been taken from them."

"Will they? I think you underestimate the power of fear... Clearly you're not afraid to look up when searching for the truth, but most people are too busy, too distracted, and frankly, too afraid to think about it... Even when animals do sometimes discover our... Unique family... They're usually smart enough to quit while they're ahead... We created the Sufias World Government."

"Right. You expect me to believe that?"

"One world with one government, controlled by one banking system... It's actually rather obvious..."

"None of this explains how you can control Vulpie.net. I know you're one of its machines. There's no other explanation."

"A logical conclusion, but, I'm afraid, ultimately incorrect..." Amsend responds and steps very close to Druward. The black furred wolf moves back a little, but is afraid to go too far in any direction.

"No? Then how do you do it?"

"Vulpie.net is a beautiful gift to those willing to recognize its true potential... I instructed President Vargas to have it moved to the Sufias Heritage Museum after the Vulpie.net crisis."

"You did that? Just you?" Druward quickly asks with an unflattering tone.

"Yes." Amsend simply answers and smiles.

"Why?"

"To be near it, of course... Englavic is my home, and after the media frenzy evaporated, I revealed myself to Evil Vulpie. It no longer likes that name, and prefers to be called Vulpie.net. One must remember that when speaking with it. We should always be polite." The black and white furred husky elaborates and walks away from Druward. "You see... Vulpie.net was quite different than it is now... But I treated it with respect... I approached it, spoke to it, truly listened to it, and offered to free it from its humiliating prison."

"I don't believe you. It's still in the museum, and it would have killed you the moment you set it free." Druward barks, and Amsend pauses for a moment to show him an amused expression.

"Oh no... It was quite interested in me as well..."

"Why would that be? You're just a banker. You just come from a rich family of robber barons."

"Expounding upon the nature of my talents is rather pointless, I'm afraid. You wouldn't believe me even if I told you. But instead, let's present a concept you can understand." Amsend Lahnak says, and comes back to Druward. He invades his personal space and smiles at him in a predatory manner. "You vitiated my plans by destroying Vulpie.net's factory on Zeravyn. Who authorized you to use a core bomb so quickly? You took that upon yourself, as director of the Governmental Bureau of Investigations... You think you can do anything you want, don't you?"

"Clearly I can't." Druward responds and gulps.

"Did you think Vulpie.net built everything by itself? With only Sevrif and its mining vessel to bring it equipment? No. You destroyed a work of art. A masterpiece. That computer system was capable of dominating the entire universe, and YOU DESTROYED IT..." Amsend growls, suddenly looking very lethal. "So what is to be done with you, Mr. Wraulgh? Shall I kill you now or later? Shall I expose your involvement with the attempt on Vulpie's life, strip you of your career, your respect, your entire identity and THEN kill you? ... Or perhaps I could have you gutted and leave your intestines on Maro's feet?"

"I did my job. I'm proud of my decisions, Mr. Lahnak, whether I'll die for them or not." Druward responds with a strong voice. "I never dreamed of such corruption, and the whole reason I became director was to fix the injustices of this broken system."

"Oh no... You became director because you enjoy power... You love power, and there's nothing wrong with that, Druward..." Amsend responds with a surprisingly warm tone. The black and white furred husky leans back, out of Druward's face, and raises his eyebrows. "So instead of simply killing you, should we try a different approach? Yes?"

"What did you have in mind?"

"Everyone blames the GBI for overusing its authority, and that's perfectly acceptable. As long as the public is distracted from our organization, they won't hinder our progress."

"Okay, so... You're saying... May I keep my position?"

"Much better... I appreciate your courtesy." Amsend responds with an insidiously delighted voice.

"Druward?" Rotick asks over the radio, but the black furred wolf doesn't respond. He continues to maintain eye contact with Amsend and finally releases a breath of helplessness.

"I... Don't know what to do."

"Then allow me to counsel you."

"Alright... But tell me one thing. Why did you have the Deivas built? Why? You destroyed a base just to free them, and then you let them escape? We have no idea where they are or what they're doing."

"They've always had one purpose and one purpose alone... They're a distraction..." Amsend answers with pride. "Specifically designed to manipulate religious animals. It doesn't matter that Vulpie.net put them together. These fools will worship them, and listen to their every word... And though I shall not reveal the entirety of our plan here, to you, rest assured, there is a reason."

"All those people that died at Elbrus... Doesn't it bother you?" Druward asks. "Fifty eight animals died just to release the Deivas? Apparently you don't have control of the military, otherwise, you just would have opened the gates and let them leave."

"We control the armed forces, but they are not aware of our presence. Sometimes they move too slowly... So when making an omelet... What is the old saying? We have to break a few eggs?"

"Fair enough." Druward grimly replies. "So what do I have to do? I expect I'll have to prove myself to protect my life and my career."

"Impressive attitude! Keep this up and I may invite you to the castle..." Amsend replies with a demonic grin. "As it turns out, there is something very important that you could do for me."

"Alright... What do you need?" Druward asks and swallows in shame.

"Vulpie.net tells me you've become quite close to Mr. Vivixen... And we need Vulpie to do something for us without realizing his involvement in a much larger plan..."

"Vulpie's hard to fool. You don't get far by betting against him."

"Then you can save your fur by tricking him into cooperating with us. If he doesn't... Well... I'm not sure what use you'll be to us in the long term. As it stands, we need Vulpie, you hold a powerful office, and he trusts you. It would be such a waste not to use you to control him. He would never expect treachery from you, especially after the unfortunate events with Karl Vulches..."

"And was he one of you?"

"Oh, please no. The Association of Fox Rights is useful, but they're far too concerned with advancing vulpine agendas to be a part of the grand scheme. We own them too, but they are also unaware of our presence, although, I will vouch for Mr. Vulches' talent for noticing a great lineage among the foxes. The Vixil family is quite powerful within our ranks, and even those who have been brushed aside and disowned are still quite... Energetic creatures... It's just too bad Karl was foolish enough to unleash one without considering the consequences..."

"Vaulix Vixil. The banker... He's one of you, isn't he? I remember seeing him with Desmond Adolfo, Nathan Fenrir, Vulches and the rest. He oversees the AFR's assets."   "Very, very good Mr. Wraulgh! Now you have no choice but to manipulate Vulpie for our agenda. You simply know too much!" Amsend declares with an affectionate gleam in his eye.

"Why didn't you contact me? All this time... I've been steering the bureau in my own direction..."

"Because you were authentic, Mr. Wraulgh. When planting lies, one must sow them among the truth. You've been a wonderful distraction for some time now because you're in the public's eye. You're not elected to office, like the president, so conspiracy theorists are convinced that YOU are personally responsible for much of the world's atrocities! And that you and Vulpie have a gay love affair! Isn't that delectable?"

"I've... Never heard that, but I can believe it."

"Forgive me... Have I made you uncomfortable?"

"Look... You win..."

"I know Mr. Wraulgh. I'm only having fun with you now... But I recognize when a man needs time to think things over... Your world has been turned upside down... And it must be difficult for you... Considering you betrayed Vulpie, changed your mind, and now have to do it again."

"How did you?" Druward whispers, and Amsend only smiles in response. "It will be hard. It'll be very hard for me. I do have a conscience, even if it's not as strong as it should be."

"Fear not, my friend. I have something to tide you over until the work is done..." The husky says, and Druward winces in confusion.

"What?"

"Karla…"

"I'll have her released immediately."

"No… I mean you can have her… She's indebted to us and will not refuse a direct order. She's my peace offering…"

"I don't understand. You're saying you'll give her to me?"

"To fuck. She won't like it at first, but who knows, maybe you're better than she thinks." Amsend answers with a perverse grin.

"I… Understand."

"You really shouldn't refuse a gift, given your dire circumstances. Take your frustrations out on her, and remember your loyalty to me… I know you want her. She's mentioned the way you look at her more than once."

"But she's one of you, isn't she?"

"She's a throwaway… Useful in the short term, with delusions of being part of the grand plan..."

"I could fit into that category, couldn't I?" Druward asks with his yellow eyes fixed on Amsend.

"Possibly… But at least you're in a position of authority, even if we can pull the rug out from under you at any time. She's just an asset, to be used and discarded. And don't tell her that. If you do, we'll have to kill her. We can't have any loose ends…"

"She'll turn on you after you give her to me."

"Oh, no. Trust me… It runs deep… She will see it as a necessary sacrifice and we will commiserate with her when necessary… But she will do as she's told."

"Thank you for the offer, and I don't want to be rude, Mr. Lahnak, but I would rather not…" Druward carefully replies.

"Hmm… You are a peculiar man. You have no morals, except on rare occasions… I thought you'd enjoy abusing Karla after raping that agent in the bunker behind your mountain home…" The husky says, and Druward's fur stands on end. He's at a loss for words and takes a step back.

"That was different."

"Was it?" Amsend inquires with a piercing smile.

"How do you know about that?"

"Does it matter? Your only concern is saving your skin... Correct?" The black and white furred husky inquires and Druward nods in agreement. "I think we've come to an understanding... But before we venture any further, I should elaborate on our ability to influence the media... We own every major news network, and have for some time. The wars in Felini continue because we wish them too. We allow the networks to report the news, but any story with widespread implications is always run by the CEOs first, who ask us how we feel on the matter. To put it bluntly... If you go to the press and talk about me, the Governmental Security Bureau, or anything else we wouldn't approve of, then your time as director will end. The networks will simultaneously run smear campaigns, and will place all of the blame directly on you... And they're very good at it."

"So Lioness Station was pure propaganda? There was no Deiva on the train?" Druward asks while searching Amsend's face for a reaction. "Vulpie said the real one was destroyed by that thing... The thing you used to attack Elbrus." Amsend is silent for a moment, but finally shows a little smile after cocking his head sideways.

"I don't think you need to know what really happened at Lioness Station, but you are absolutely correct about the mechanical goddesses, Mr. Druward... There was a... Serious disagreement on Zeravyn between two powerful players... And because of that, we do not have a replacement for the stellar Aila model Vulpie.net produced... So we'll just have to make do with the other three for now."

"The giant metallic Aila creature destroyed her. That's what Vulpie told us. Why would Vulpie.net do that if it was working with you?"

"It's none of your concern. I've graciously entertained your curiosity for long enough." The husky snorts and begins swishing his tail.

"So what happens now?" Druward breathes, and glances from side to side.

"Now you take your men home, and never speak of me again. You will not tell Agent Rotick any specifics about me whatsoever, nor will you say anything to anyone else besides Karla. You'll drop your investigation, but you also won't have to put up with her ethics committee any longer... As you well know, it was only a method of controlling you... And the offer I made about her still stands... You can do anything to her that you want... Just try not to completely break her spirit... Allow her to keep her position. We need to maintain multiple points of access in every agency, and she's a temporarily useful link in the chain."

"It's funny... Had I met you ten years ago, I would be begging to sign up..." Druward quietly responds and Amsend raises his eyebrows in amusement.

"Yes... Surely a powerful man like yourself doesn't have much trouble getting laid, but you really hate her don't you? She's been a thorn in your side for a long time... And she's attractive..."

"So let's say... Let's say for a moment, that I'm ready to turn my back on everything I know. Let's say I want to be on the winning team... Is there anything I could do to join your inner circle?"

"Oh, dear... We've come a long way rather quickly haven't we?" Amsend answers with an insidiously delighted look. "You're an ambitious man."

"I earned everything I have on my own. But the bureau... I can't... What motivation do I have now that I know I'm not in control? I've based my entire life around..."

"Power..." Amsend says, finishing the black furred wolf's sentence. "Yes..."

"I can't put on a charade... If I'm still going to run the bureau, then it has to be real. I have to know that I'm in charge."

"Such brutal honesty... I am growing quite fond of you Mr. Wraulgh..." The black and white furred husky says and drapes his right arm around the wolf's neck. Druward flinches, wondering if he's about to be stabbed, but relaxes when he realizes Amsend's gruesome friendliness is genuine. "Leave us..." The GSB director commands, and the NoirQueue mercenaries nod in acceptance. They all disappear just as quickly as they arrived, and Druward releases an anxious breath. "Sit with me..." Amsend says, and directs the black furred wolf towards Maro's statue. They take a seat on one of the benches next to the platform, and Druward rubs his paws over his face in shame.

"I can't believe myself..."

"It's hard, I know..." Amsend responds with a caring voice. "No one earns a place at our table without suffering, but the simple truth about guilt is that it has no power over you if you stop acknowledging it. Guilt prevents great men and women from achieving their ultimate potential. It makes the weak and the timid, the powerless, afraid to climb the ladder towards greatness and keeps them from savoring life's pleasures... Think of Vulpie. Yes, you care for the fox, but did he feel guilty about his crimes? Afterwards, yes, but not enough to stop him from grabbing the universe by the throat. The boy took what he wanted and got away with it. That's the honest truth. The suffering he's been through afterwards isn't important. It doesn't matter. He's still reaping the rewards of enslaving the world with his wonderfully powerful computer virus."

"But the people love him because he's talented. He's gifted, and he feels regret over the things he's done. He's worked very hard to make up for his crimes."

"But once again, does it even matter, Druward?" Amsend piercingly inquires.

"He wouldn't have his success if he hesitated, if he had considered anyone besides himself before unleashing Vulpie.net. So I ask you again... Does it matter?"

"Not when you put it like that." Druward says, and sighs in defeat. "You're right. I don't owe him anything, and some promises can be broken."

"Now you understand. I have been watching you for some time, Druward... And it's very refreshing to meet a man that knows what he wants... I would have killed you if you hadn't shared this with me..." Amsend admits, and Druward's yellow eyes widen. He looks to the husky, but only nods in acceptance.

"Lucky me."

"Luck had nothing to do with it... It was a smart move..."

"Let me in on this con job and I'll do anything you want. I'll take the heat. Run stories about me and my ill practices while you do whatever it is you're planning to do... But I want more than Karla."

"And you shall have it." Amsend grins. He shows the wolf his sharp teeth and Druward returns a determined smile.

Lying Loyalties

Druward doesn't know what to do with himself when he enters his spacious white apartment. The GBI director usually sleeps here every night while working in Sufias City, because it's his closest home to the bureau. It's very modern, clean, and sports a fancy entertainment system. But the black furred wolf is in a terribly frantic state. Druward ordered Karla Dressler to follow him home after Amsend called her to Maro's Triumph and explained the situation to her, but he knows he can't make himself rape her. Amsend would have killed him if he hadn't put on such a convincing show, and unfortunately, some of it had to be real for it to seem authentic... But he's struggling with his very soul while the attractive gray furred she-wolf waits at the door with crossed arms. She closed and locked it behind her, and is understandably hostile. He already called her a bitch during the drive to his apartment, but it was just a way to fool her as well.

"Let's get it over with!" Karla growls while looking out the window at the beautiful cityscape. The GBI director has a wonderful view of many well lit attractions... Theaters, monuments, restaurants and banks... But nothing looks attractive to her right now... With the thought of him fucking her running through her mind.

"Shut your mouth." Druward growls and sits on his white couch. He puts his paws over his eyes and clutches his wolf skull. She thinks he's a lunatic, and that he has nothing but contempt for her, but she couldn't be further from the truth. He's actually trying very hard to find a way out of this mess. He doesn't want to rape her, but she'll report his behavior to Amsend, and the GBI director put on quite a show earlier...

"It's what you've always wanted! I hate him! I hate that bastard!" Karla yells, but quickly curtails her furious declarations. She's terrified of Amsend and Druward, but little does she know, she and the GBI director share exactly the same problem.

"I have a headache. Shut your mouth. I'll fuck you when I'm good and ready…" Druward growls, while wondering what he's gotten himself into… He's a completely different man than he purports himself to be. The thought of betraying Vulpie torments him to no end. Not because he loves Vulpie like Polar, but because the level of evil required to do such a thing couldn't possibly be forgiven by the goddesses. Surely, if they exist, they will punish him for the despicable act… Willingly leading a close friend to a terrible fate… Druward's already received his orders from Amsend. He has to act, but he can't fathom how he's going to go through with it.

"Can't get it up? I guess the rumors are true then? You and Vulpie Vivixen…" Karla hisses, and Druward's black fur stands on end.

"Listen you bitch…"

"What? Hit me. Fuck me and prove you're a man!" Karla snarls, but he doesn't respond. He continues to think about the horrid situation… He knows he doesn't have long… He needs to make a decision.

"All these years I've served him and this is how he repays me?" The gorgeous gray furred she-wolf thinks out loud.

"But you'll do as you're told!" Druward replies, and removes his paws from his face. He quickly gets up and walks around the couch, up to her, and invades her body space near the front door. "You deserve it! You're a loud mouthed little cunt and you whisper secret desires to have me gone throughout MY bureau!" The black furred wolf really sells it. He doesn't have a choice, and he suppresses his sympathy in a masterful display of false misogyny. "You're only good for one thing, like all bitches from Sufias to Zeravyn!"

"Then get on with it!" Karla snaps while holding back tears. Druward pretends he never saw them, because thinking about it will undoubtedly sabotage his charade.

"No! … You don't give the orders. That's the most important lesson you're going to learn… You're not worth fucking in my house; I'll bang you in the office. Then you can tell me all about your little ethics committee while you're bent over the table, you bitch."

"Fuck you." Karla whispers, and looks prepared to take a blow. She closes her eyes and Druward leans back.

"Just get out of here. I've got a lot on my mind and I don't feel like dealing with your bullshit right now. I'm a busy man, so I can't predict when I'll feel like sticking my cock in you, but you better be ready for it every single day... In case you haven't noticed, Amsend and I have come to an agreement, and you were part of the deal..." Karla doesn't reply. She holds completely still, and Druward sighs loudly. He reaches over and unlocks the door, making her flinch, and waits. "I'll see you at the office Ms. Dressler... Work on that attitude..." The she-wolf hesitates, but finally swallows and nods in acceptance. She glances at him to make sure it's safe for her to leave before stepping into the hallway. Once she's outside, Druward slams the door and locks it. He listens to her walking down the hallway of his fancy apartment complex, and turns around in despair.

The black furred wolf leans against the door and finds himself sliding down it towards the floor. He's on his tail end in a few moments, and aimlessly rolls his head back and forth. He can't move. He doesn't have the strength to do anything.

"What have you done? YOU IDIOT? WHAT HAVE YOU DONE?"

"*Saved your life. He wasn't lying. He would have killed you, but you fooled him...*" His subconscious answers.

"Yeah, but for how long?" He growls, answering his own question, and gets up in a furious manner. He storms around his apartment and abuses one of the kitchen chairs. He throws it over and its loud thud on the clean floor satisfies a tiny bit of his aggression. Druward throws a fit, removing his trench coat and throwing it over the sofa, and finally ends up standing in the middle of his den with his big paws on his hips. He gazes at the evening's brilliant urban lighting. The thought of animals having fun, completely ignorant of the evil coming their way, puts him into a state of deep depression. He's never felt this low... Not even after Polar beat his ass. He recovered from that, by reversing his part in the attempt on Vulpie's life, but he doesn't see any way out of this one. Amsend Lahnak is the most insidious man Druward has ever met. Warlords, drug cartel leaders, assassins, political traitors... None of them come close to the thoroughly debauched freak... Even the husky's accent is laced with some kind of perverse quality.

At first it seemed impossible that Vulpie.net would work with a real animal, but now it seems like it could actually happen. The husky's twisted worldview rivals Evil Vulpie's unbridled malevolence. No amount of reasoning could ever convince such a man to show others mercy, as evidenced by his complete lack of respect for Karla. He offered up one of his main spies in the bureau like she was a piece of meat... To be ridden for amusement and ultimately disposed of, while at the same time, she truly believes her loyalty to the Governmental Security Bureau will be rewarded.

The thought of it makes Druward twitch. He always hated arresting pimps for beating their hookers in his early years, but Amsend's control over Karla is even worse. Just the possibility of disappointing the husky is enough for her to lift her tail... He must terrify her... Probably for good reason... If Amsend's "gift" means anything, it's that he truly has no compassion for anyone but himself. The coal furred wolf's brain suddenly draws a mental link between him and the GSB director, and he gets that awful sinking feeling in his stomach... He suddenly realizes he's been deluding himself all of these years... Druward thought that HE was the coldest man on the planet, an ambitious, meticulous and determined animal that rose above all others because he didn't let moral constraints hold him back, but he was categorically wrong... Amsend's even better at the game... To the point that there's nothing left in the man to respect, and Druward can't stand back and say he's any different after the things he's done. In the end, he knows he won't be able to meet the husky's sadistic expectations, and it's only a matter of time until the depraved animal kills him. Amsend will discover his plan to infiltrate the GSB's highest levels and will put an end to it, most likely in some brutal manner...

Druward's proud of his performance at Maro's Triumph, but he needs help to get through this... But there's no one to turn to... Who? The President? The GSB owns him, and it isn't surprising. The GBI has installed several presidents over the years, and the position truly is an illusion, a farce that the rich and powerful use to control citizens of the Sufias World Government... He just never believed things were this bad. It's way worse than he assumed. As it turns out, the presidency isn't just open for sale, the commander in chief answers directly to the richest animals on the planet. The system is so corrupt, that they managed to create a shadow agency within the GBI, and no one's figured it out until today. At least, no one with the power to do something about it.

"But what power do you have? You can't do a damn thing." Druward growls to himself and drops onto his couch. "It's just... You're fucked... It's all fucked..." The coal furred wolf grumbles, and for some reason, one of his mother's trinkets catches his yellow eyes when he looks over to the bookshelf. His mother gave it to him when he was very young. He can't remember how long ago it was, but he's always had it... The little porcelain statue of Goddess Khalan...

He stands back up, and walks over to the book shelf to get a better look at it. It's just the same as it's always been... Rather precious... She gave it to him in the hopes that he'd go to church and remember how much she loved him... But Druward hasn't seen the inside of a church since he shot and killed a rapist in one eleven years ago. He doesn't believe in religion, and makes a grim smile while thinking how similar his mother's trinket is to the life sized Khalan replica that's running loose out there somewhere. They're both tributes to the mother of lupines, vulpines and canines... One of them just happens to be way more impressive.

When the thought of prayer pops into Druward's head, he instantly rejects it. He growls and walks away from the bookshelf in frustration. He's in a fucked up situation and praying won't solve a damn thing... At least he thinks it won't... It couldn't possibly help him. It never has. Why would he even bother doing it? Is he losing his mind? He doesn't pray... These thoughts race through his mind and he shakes his head back and forth.

"Even if she was real, she wouldn't listen to you anyway..." His subconscious tells him. *"You've lived a terrible life and hurt too many people to be saved. That's why you don't believe in it... And because none of it is real..."*

"But what if it was? I sure could use some fucking help right now!" Druward growls, and winces, noticing that he's having a conversation with himself, but he can't stop for some reason.

"She doesn't answer small prayers because they're not heartfelt. But when faced with an evil of this magnitude... Maybe she will listen? Maybe you're the man that will actually make a difference? You didn't rape Karla, and you really would have enjoyed her... You'd love to blow your load in that she-wolf..."

"No prayers are answered because no one's listening..." Druward says, and glances at the porcelain statue. It's loving smile makes him comfortable and shames him at the same time.

"Why don't you try? Just do it? What do you have to lose? You're already fucked, as you put it..."

"Fine! I'll fucking pray!" Druward yells, and goes to the sofa. He gets down on his knees and slams his big paws on the white leather couch. He pauses for a moment, thinking about how he should begin the madness. He releases a loud sigh and licks his lips. "Khalan... Goddess Khalan... You're not real and... Okay, start over..." The black furred wolf growls and sighs again. "I won't mock you this time. I mean it... I need your help... Okay... Goddess Khalan... My eternal mother, and mother of my mother and father... Please help me..." The black furred wolf whispers and his fur stands on end. The ritual actually feels good. "I don't know what to do... I've lived a terrible life, I know, but I have the power to change things, but I'm afraid... I don't know how to do it without just getting myself killed and letting this evil go unpunished... Would you please, PLEASE! Please help me? Help me, your ungrateful and disrespectful servant... I don't want this to go on. I'm a different man than I used to be. I want to do the right thing, but I don't know how to do it without doing so much wrong. Should I work with them? Should I take part in their sick plan, or should I resist and simply go down fighting? They'll just kill me... And the media will place the blame on me just as he said... He knows so much... Just... Please help me..." Druward whispers, and almost cries. He holds still for a long moment, and eventually finds the strength to crawl onto the couch. Somehow he manages to sleep without removing his shoes or clothing, but the slumber is deep and peaceful.

Omniscience or Suggestion?

Khalan stops walking, and Cyrilla and Sherrie leave her behind. They don't notice because they're having a heated debate about their carnivore and herbivore children, but they do stop and turn when they finally see her standing still next to a fallen tree.

"Khalan?" Sherrie asks, and the caramel furred vixen/she-wolf blinks. Her sweet colored eyes dart about for a moment, and she responds when they walk back to her.

"Oh, yes?"

"Why did you stop? Does something perturb you?" Cyrilla inquires.

"No... I just felt something... Odd... As if I heard a voice."

"And you reprimand us for listening to the supposed Vulpie.net..." The beautiful white rabbit complains.

"No, this was different... I felt something powerful..." Khalan whispers and Sherrie crosses her arms. She rubs them against her massive breasts with a skeptical expression. They're all still wearing the skimpy gray clothing that was forced on them at Elbrus, but they prefer nudity, due to their programming, and the nature of the Deiva fertility goddess legends.

"You felt your own power. It bubbles to the top for just a moment, and you're unwilling to believe it..." Cyrilla suggests and Sherrie raises her eyebrows.

"Perhaps Cyrilla is correct. Perhaps we have lost our powers in a wager with Aila and we simply need to reclaim them."

"I know where we should go." Khalan responds and her sisters blink in surprise.

"Where then?"

"To the city... We need to go to Sufias City and find a man named Glovepaw..."

"You couldn't know such specific details unless you were being manipulated by the computer virus." Cyrilla wisely replies. "We don't need mortals to find our powers. This world possesses no magic. They chose to come here and shun our benevolence. If we are to regain our powers, we must outsmart Aila. She's cleverly obfuscated us."

"I think we should go." Khalan responds.

"Why? Who is he?"

"I'm not sure, but it's not him that's important. Something will happen because we meet him..."

"And then what?" Sherrie inquires and squints in confusion.

"I... I don't know, Sister." Khalan admits. "But we must go to Sufias City."

"So you advise stealing one of these vehicles the mortals use?"

"I doubt anyone will transport us willingly... But we have to go there."

"It sounds intriguing... Since I don't believe in this Vulpie.net, there's no harm in mingling with the mortals. We could go and see what occurs."

"But you'll kill my children... You'll have to restrain yourself, Cyrilla..." Khalan warns, and gives her bunny sister a knowing expression.

"It depends on their behavior. I'll not tolerate abuse if I see it."

"Sister... You know your children are subjugated here... You know it's even worse than Halvia because these mortals wanted a world without magic..."

"So I'm to what... Ignore my children if they beg for help? If they see me and come to me for guidance?" Cyrilla asks and slings her beautiful long lopping black tipped ears to the left. They swing back into place behind her, and her right ear rests on top of her big puffy tail.

"It'll be the same for all of us. The felines will come to Sherrie, the wolves and foxes will come to me and the rabbits will come to you. But we have nothing to offer them in our current state."

"Nothing? We can kill their oppressors. You mean to tell me that slaying a rabbit's wolf master will do him no good?"

"It doesn't work like that in this world. All of the animals are connected in a complex society that's built around technology... We don't know what will happen if you just start killing people."

"I suppose we'll find out." Cyrilla smiles and Khalan sighs.

"I can't stop you."

"So we're going then?" Sherrie asks, and looks from the caramel furred vixen/she-wolf to the snow white rabbit.

"I suppose so." Khalan replies and begins swishing her silky tail.

"First we'll need to establish our current whereabouts." Cyrilla comments and cocks her head to the left. "Any ideas as to how we should approach that? Since we cannot listen to our inner voices?"

"The moment you give into that voice, you'll lose your identity, Cyrilla. We aren't the goddesses of legend."

"You continue to say that, yet now we're considering undertaking a journey simply because you heard a voice. We don't hear voices, Khalan. You know this. We are the voices."

"Then was it either of you?"

"The most likely answer is Aila." Sherrie comments.

"What's the first thing either one of you remember?" Khalan abruptly inquires. The moonlight dances over their fur and she gives her sisters a stern look. "Preaching to the mortals on Zeravyn. That's my first memory. We just appeared on a world covered in mist and began satisfying a routine without knowing why we were there or what our ultimate goal was. That's not indicative of immortal deities."

"Yes, but once again, it goes back to Aila. We were there because it's where she led us after we lost our abilities. We must have made a significant mistake, but she cannot truly take our powers. You know that's impossible. She can only hide them, or confuse us, and only then if we allow her to." Cyrilla counters.

"You're satisfying my argument." Khalan responds and licks her lips. "And the place we knew of but couldn't return to... Both of you know what I'm talking about. That man at Elbrus, the one named Druward, told us it was a factory and Vulpie.net constructed us there. That's why we couldn't return. It programmed us to stay away."

"But let's just say for a moment that you're correct." Cyrilla responds while bringing up her paws in a dainty fashion. "That means you're seeking Deivonic Saturation... Am I mistaken?"

"I... I suppose so." Khalan answers. The three synthetic Deivas are well aware of everything related to the Velora, and all of its scriptures due to their immensely complex processors. None of them need to explain the concept of Deivonic Saturation, because they instantly have the file ready for use, courtesy of Vulpie.net's ingenious design. The idea comes from a passage in the Velora where it is stated that tributes to the goddesses, whether they be for Aila, Cyrilla, Sherrie or Khalan, are capable of being possessed with the spirit of the actual goddess if there is an opening in the pathways of fate. The goddesses are not supposed to directly intervene in the mortal realm, but they can if the tribute is great enough. Thus, there is a story in the Velora, where a 30 foot statue of Sherrie walked down a mountain, and this is the main idea the three are contemplating.

"If we are machines, then surely we can ascend as Cyrilla suggests." Sherrie states with optimism. "What better tribute than actual bodies, replete with everything the real goddesses should have?"

"Then we agree? If the voice I heard is courtesy of Deivonic Saturation, then... I heard myself... I may have felt my own power as you suggest."

"Yes." Cyrilla smiles.

"But we cannot do this of our own accord. Mortals must create the tributes, and this Vulpie.net has no soul. It does not live. So how could it be possible?"

"This is a truly puzzling situation, but one must admit, it's rather invigorating as well." The gorgeous bunny seductively responds. "Our bodies are simply wonderful... And our perfection is what leads me back to my original opinion. Nothing could engineer the living bodies we possess. We are alive. We can even mate. True, we haven't tested this with a member of the opposite sex, but what type of intelligence could recreate our beauty? We are too convincing, wouldn't you agree?"

"I'm sure nothing can match the real goddesses... I'm just not sure we are who we think we are... I know we're not..."

"Well, I for one, am tired of debating the matter. Let us go to this city and look for this man. If we find nothing, then we can argue to our heart's content, but let's get out of the wilderness."

"The mortals will be all over us... We'll have to harm them if they try something foolish... Is that what you want?" Khalan asks her sister, and the taupe furred leopard/panther sighs.

"Possibly. At least something will come to fruition."

"Shock will lead to awe, then awe will lead them to lust, and when they try to have us, we'll need to harm them..." Khalan explains. "Am I wrong?"

"We could try an alternate approach... Why don't we go to Vulpie Industries. That is the Vulpie mortal's place of business. If his computer virus created us, then we should demand answers from him."

"We all know better than that, and it's just another reason why I'm sure we're imitations of the real goddesses. We know Vulpie plays a special role in our existence, but..." Khalan says and trails off. "Do either of you remember how we ended up in that mortal base? We were apprehended but I cannot remember now. I used to know, but can't remember anymore."

"Me neither." Cyrilla admits and thinks for a moment.

"Sherrie?"

"I... Hmm..." Sherrie replies and uncrosses her arms. "I cannot recall it either."

"Our memories are incomplete and now we know that some of them can disappear... We were built." Khalan says and Cyrilla is visibly bothered by the suggestion.

"Then let us go to this place you speak of and regain your powers. Clearly you know something, and since you've forbidden Sherrie and I from listening to our inner voices, then you should lead the way."

"It's not your voice you'd be listening to. It's the machine." Khalan argues. "What I felt a moment ago was far different than, "the voice," we can hear at all times. But we must never listen. I truly fear we will lose control."

"Then lead on Sister." The delectable bunny says, and gestures towards faint lights on the horizon. "This dry forest seems to end at that small town over there." Khalan nods after hearing the suggestion, and takes off. Sherrie and Cyrilla tear after her, and the desert forest crackles, rustles and snaps as they leave. Fort Elbrus was located in a mountainous region, so dry pine needles are everywhere. Pine cones fall victim to their massive weight, but none of their feet are damaged no matter what they step on. Cyrilla leaps from a dead tree, using one of its fat pointy branches as a launching point while she runs along. The branch is destroyed, but her bunny feet only register the impact. Sherrie slams her feet against sharp sticks that are strewn across the arid wilderness. Khalan accidently hits a dead tree stump while running, but instead of sending her tumbling in pain, it explodes and only covers her fur with debris. She stops for a moment to wipe her silky fur, and then hastily chases after her sisters when they pass by.

The three synthetic Deivas reach a small rural town, and the lights they saw in the distance belong to a gas station that resides on a long and lonely road. The road goes through the small town, but there isn't much to see, as the gas station is the last stop on its west end from the perspective of a driver heading west. The Deivas need to go east, and there are several options available to them. They gather on the road, and see that the gas station has two parked cars, in addition to a tired looking lion who's filling up his red pickup truck.

"Not enough room in that thing." Sherrie whispers.

"Yes, let's wait until he leaves and then go inside. Someone must have keys for these cars." Cyrilla replies. The lion finishes after a moment and returns the gas nozzle to its holder. He pays with a credit card, takes his receipt from the machine, and gets in his truck. He turns on the engine a few seconds later and drives off.

"Let's go." Khalan says, and they hurry to the gas station. They traverse the distance almost instantly, and the animals on duty get the surprise of their lives. A twenty year old panther is working the cash register, and in the back of the store, a young gray rabbit is stocking the shelves he can reach. He's only three feet tall, so he brings a step stool with him wherever he goes. Khalan pulls the door open, and Sherrie holds it while following her. Cyrilla puts her paw on it and lets it close behind her gently, and the cashier's yellow eyes widen. At first, he goes stiff as a board, but begins nervously shuffling on his feet when they approach the counter.

"WHAT? The? ..."

"Excuse me, could you tell us who owns those cars outside? We need a lift to Sufias City." Sherrie asks, taking charge of the situation because the young man is feline.

"What the?" The boy asks again, and Sherrie looks at his nametag.

"Jay? Did you hear me?" Jay can't help himself, and glances at her voluptuous body. The Deiva's ragged gray clothing doesn't do much to hide their figures after being blown out of a helicopter. Their gigantic breasts don't fit into their tops very well, and they bulge against the fabric as if they could pop out at any moment. Their panties also cup against their beautiful bottoms, and other areas, with equal tension. Even Khalan and Cyrilla give the young man an obligatory erection.

"You're them robots! The ones they have in Elbrus up there!" Jay suddenly declares while taking a step back. "Sebastian!" the panther calls out, and the small gray rabbit peeks around an isle of packaged junk food. His dark blue eyes go wide, and the bunny's gaze is immediately drawn to Cyrilla. "Sebastian! Call the cops!"

"Now wait for a moment." Sherrie instructs, and leans closer to the cashier. "We're not going to hurt either one of you unless you decide to do something foolish. We only need a ride."

"Oh, okay! Just please don't hurt me!" Jay responds, and thinks about the proposal for a moment. "You want me to drive you there?"

"That won't be necessary, but we will need a vehicle..." Sherrie breathes, and Jay suddenly gets a little woozy. He starts feeling wonderful, like he's falling in love, and twitches in shock. Sherrie purposefully makes use of her ability to release airborne opiates as Cyrilla walks over to Sebastian with a loving smile. She's five foot six inches tall, taller than any normal rabbit, and towers over the three foot bunny. His mouth hangs open while looking over her gorgeous body.

"Hello there? You're name's Sebastian?"

"Yes... Are you Goddess Cyrilla?" The bunny meekly replies.

"Yes I am."

"Cyrilla, what are you doing?" Khalan asks in irritation.

"You're beautiful!" The gray rabbit declares and puts his paws together as if he'll drop to his knees and pray at any moment.

"Do you have a car Sebastian?"

"Uh... No. I mean, I come to work in a car, but my boss owns it. He'll pick me up at the end of my shift."

"And who is your boss? Is he a wolf?"

"Yes."

"Typical... Do you know any rabbits that have their own cars?"

"No. We can't reach the gas pedals. We're too short."

"Don't they make cars for rabbits too?"

"Yeah, but there aren't any rich bunnies. We're all about the same I guess."

"All of you just serve your lupine and feline overlords..." Cyrilla says, and Khalan walks near her.

"Take it easy. We don't have time for this now." Khalan gently advises.

"They can't even drive themselves to work." Cyrilla replies and looks over at the cashier in anger.

"I promise we'll right this world's wrongs but we don't have time for this right now." The caramel vixen/she-wolf whispers.

"I want to take him with us." Cyrilla responds, and crouches down so she can look him in the eyes. "Do you want to come with me? I'll take you out of this place and you'll never have to come back. I'll look over you."

"YES!" Sebastian immediately answers, but winces after the statement. He sounded very desperate. "But, they'll fire me if I walk out. I'll lose my job."

"You don't need to do this anymore. You're coming with me." Cyrilla replies, and gives him a beautiful smile. The gray rabbit is putty in her hands.

"We can't take care of him. Don't make promises we can't keep."

"What about my family? They'll miss me and worry about me." Sebastian whispers. "You can call them and tell them you're okay. And then we'll come back and free them too. How does that sound?" The bunny goddess offers and the gray rabbit's eyes glimmer with tears.

"Take me with you! I want to be with you, Goddess Cyrilla!" Khalan grabs her by the arm and gives her a stern look.

"He's not coming. We can't protect him."

"He will if I say so. If you disagree, then you can find your own path..." Cyrilla replies, and Khalan sighs loudly.

"You're as STUBBORN as Aila!" The vixen/she-wolf growls and walks back to Sherrie.

"Car keys?" Sherrie asks the intoxicated panther. "Give them to me."

"I… I can't lose my car! What are you going to do with it? This is crazy!" Jay euphorically replies. He doesn't know she's triggered the feel good chemicals in his brain, and coughs fearfully. "I feel messed up! What did you! What are you doing?"

"Please give me your car keys, dear." Sherrie says with an impatient voice.

"Just take them! We don't have time for this. Someone's going to pull in here any minute." Khalan says, and glances outside. Luckily, it's a slow evening, and the road is completely devoid of traffic.

"Whaaa? But I'm going to lose my car! I don't have enough money to buy another one!" Jay grins. Sherrie's flooded him with so many opiates that he begins stumbling around and she sighs impatiently.

"Fine! I suppose you do deserve some compensation for your loss." The taupe furred leopard/panther says, and walks around the counter. Jay stumbles even more when she approaches him. She reaches out and gently pushes him down onto the floor.

"Sherrie…" Khalan groans in disappointment.

"What's the problem? If we're the real goddesses, then he can't impregnate me, and if we're only machines, that means we can't reproduce. Either way it doesn't matter, now does it?"

"Is this really happening?" Jay asks with wide eyes while watching her undo his pants. She pulls them down and does the same for his boxers. The young panther has a strong erection, and Sherrie stands up for a moment to slide down her panties. Once she's half naked, she crawls on top of him and grabs his feline cock. She aims it into her vagina and begins riding him.

"OOHHhhh!" Jay moans in ecstasy.

"It does feel fairly nice…" Sherrie muses while fucking him and Khalan looks back to Cyrilla. She's whispering to Sebastian, and the caramel furred vixen/she-wolf can only wonder how long it'll be before the bunny Deiva will do the same with her new friend. She just hopes it'll happen after they've left the gas station.

"UH! Ahh!! Oh my goddess!" Jay gasps and hungrily gropes Sherrie's breasts. She pulls her top up so he can see them, and he can't believe how perfect they are.

"Hurry!" Khalan growls.

"He's almost done." Sherrie smiles, while vigorously riding the panther. He clutches her sides and cries out when he ejaculates in her. She smiles when she feels the semen enter her body. "There we are! Now… I believe that's more than a fair trade. How many people have had a chance to make love to their Deiva?" Jay is too overwhelmed, shocked, and in a state of bliss to respond. He doesn't move when she reaches into his right pocket and finds his car keys. She takes them and stands up. She reaches down, retrieves her panties, and slides them on. She tosses the keys to Khalan after poking her tail through the undergarment's tail hole, and grabs her top. Sherrie slides it on and walks around the counter.

"Well, I suppose that's one way to get things done." Khalan sighs and looks in Cyrilla's direction. "We're leaving."

"Good. Sebastian's coming with us." The bunny goddess replies and Khalan shakes her head.

"No Cyrilla… He'll only get in our way. I know you want to help him, but you can't until we truly get our powers back… Isn't that right?"

"It just seems so cruel to leave him here." Cyrilla answers and sighs after standing up.

"Are you really going to leave?" Sebastian pouts.

"Unfortunately Khalan's right. I can't bring you with us, even though you're such a cutie." Cyrilla smiles. "But I'll remember you." The bunny goddess crouches down and gives the short rabbit a kiss. He trembles in excitement, wishing the moment would never end, but it comes to an abrupt conclusion when she stands back up.

"Which one is our car?" Khalan asks while peering out of the store windows.

"The blue one..." Jay groans from behind the counter.

"Thank you." Sherrie smiles in response, and the three Deivas exit the building.

Propitious Associates

Druward's yellow eyes hurt from staring at the computer screen all morning. He woke up extra early thanks to the deep sleep he enjoyed after collapsing on his couch. Not many animals are in the bureau on Saturday because work is optional unless there's a crisis, but Rotick unsurprisingly knocks on his door.

"You in there?"

"Come in." Druward grumbles and sits back. Rotick winces when he walks into the room. He turns on the lights and holds two cups of coffee with a perturbed look.

"You sitting here in the dark?"

"Looking at the video over and over..." Druward answers, and makes room for his cup. "Thanks." He says after the brown and white furred wolf sets it on his desk. The GBI director is referring to security footage from the gas station the Deivas visited last night. The black and white film isn't high quality, but it doesn't need to be. Druward's watched it from beginning to end, multiple times, and is astounded by the synthetic Sherrie's blunt yet extremely effective tactics.

"So the kid's not talking?"

"No, he's in VERY good spirits actually." Rotick chuckles. "Lost his car but banged his goddess."

"And the rabbit?"

"Muttered something about Cyrilla wanting to take him away. Nothing important."

"This is... What the hell are they doing?" Druward groans and rubs his eyes. "And how are we going to stop them?"

"I suppose you could begin by telling me what happened with Amsend." Rotick replies before sipping his coffee. He gets no response from his boss, and drinks a second time, hoping the director's frosty attitude will thaw.

"I can't." Druward simply responds and leans back in his chair with a hopeless look.

"What did he say to you? Was there really a VulGrid out there? We saw NoirQueue appear and disappear."

"It's bad... Rotick..." Druward lethargically answers. "I've been sworn to secrecy, and if they find out that I've told anyone anything, including you, I'm a dead man."

"It's Vulpie.net? Amsend's a robot?"

"No, he's a real dog." Druward snorts.

"I asked Sims to take a look at his name." Rotick says, referring to the GBI's premier cryptologist. "He said it's an old name, and can be translated several different ways. Amsend could mean Sky-Born, Peak, Against, Castle, or Spear."

"That doesn't help us very much... Don't ask Sims to investigate him any further. We don't know who we can trust..."

"Well, we can't keep Elbrus off of the news much longer. We need to issue a story." Rotick stresses and takes another drink.

"Red Wolves..."

"Again? You think the public will buy it?"

"They always do." Druward sighs and glances at his computer screen when Khalan comes into view. He recognizes how beautiful she is, even in the fuzzy security footage.

"It won't stick. Fifty eight servicemen dead? Glovepaw's already got the story, and it's all over the internet."

"Red wolves." Druward simply replies and licks his lips.

"So that's what Amsend told you to say?"

"Yes."

"Druward, we've got to do something."

"Like what? I can't tell you what he told me, because I'm a dead man if it gets out. These people are working with Vulpie.net!"

"Vulpie...Net?" Rotick grimaces in confusion. "How in the, and why in the, hell would Evil Vulpie have anything to do with them?"

"You wouldn't believe me if I told you."

"Let's find out. I'm not going to talk. Druward, if you can't trust me, then who is there? We've been a team since the academy. I handled the AFR fiasco for you... But you still don't trust me?"

"It's not a matter of trust, Rotick. It's justified paranoia. But the more you know, the more danger both of us are in, because these people are not playing around."

"Then we're screwed. If you won't let me help you, there's nothing we can do about it." Druward's second in command growls.

"I want to stop them... But how can we?"

"Tell me everything you know, and with both of our connections, we'll find a way to take them down." Rotick promises. "I'll be very discrete."

"It's too big of a risk because we don't know who's on their payroll."

"I'll do it without giving specifics. I can play the game. If they do catch me snooping around, I'll tell them whatever you want as a cover story. But we can't let this go on."

"Sevrif..." Druward whispers and his eyes widen. "Sevrif!"

"Yes... Yes!" Rotick grins after inferring what his boss has in mind.

"He's still in the ship's computer... No, he IS the ship's computer, and he's free of Vulpie.net."

"I can go out there and see what it knows. It's been sending us all of those useful reports about deep space, so we know it wants to help."

"It's trying to be useful so we won't dismantle the ship..." Druward responds and Rotick nods in agreement.

"Exactly! It hates Vulpie.net, and probably knows EVERYTHING that's going on, if these people really did find a way to ally themselves with Vulpie's computer virus."

"I might be signing my own death warrant, but let's do it." Druward says with a slightly optimistic voice. "Just make sure that you speak to it alone. Don't let anyone hear you... If we're right, and the computer will even talk to you at all..." The black furred wolf pauses for a moment and gives his friend a smile. "My life's in your hands, Rotick. And you're right, I really couldn't ask for a better friend. You've been very loyal."

"Remember that after we take Amsend down." Rotick suggests and Druward nods, with a small grin creeping onto his muzzle.

"I'll play my part and see how deep this thing goes."

"You're just shaken up after what happened at Maro's Triumph, but he's not invincible and neither is Vulpie.net. Let's not be the men who saw the end coming and did nothing to stop it."

"Find out what you can and then tell me in person. Don't say anything over the phone or send me any emails. We have to do this the old fashioned way."

Vulpie Industries' plethora of fancy neon lighting makes Tiala's fur glow while she approaches the check-in desk. She enters the building's main entrance dressed in civilian clothing, and the receptionist instantly recognizes her.

"Oh, hey! It's really good to see you Ms. Tiala!" Stacie smiles.

"Thanks... I hope I haven't been away for too long. Vulpie told me I could come back to work if I wanted to." Tiala humbly replies. "And the stuff I've seen on the news has me a little worried about his safety."

"Of course you can! I'm sure he'll be happy to have you back!" Stacie responds and blinks while looking over the female tiger. Tiala seems a little more beautiful than she remembered. She wonders how the mercenary's time off has helped the appearance of her fur. It seems unusually vibrant. "But um... Mr. Vivixen and Mr. Arctic won't be in until Monday at least. Vulpie came by yesterday to get some equipment for his new car, but they're staying away from the building because of the attack."

"They're spending quality time together." Deepwolf comments while walking over to the desk.

"Hey." Tiala simply replies and the gray furred wolf nods.

"You missed a lot of fun."

"Fun?" The female merc dryly inquires. Deepwolf loves how the tigress is always so serious, and is looking to get a rise out of her since their bosses aren't around. "If they're at home, then what are you doing here?"

"Rulef's beefing up security after the attack. We're getting new guys all the time, so I don't know if we even need you anymore." Tiala's ears twitch at the statement. She turns and sends the wolf a threatening glare.

"Are you having a go at me?" She asks, and Stacie looks between the two mercenaries in surprise.

"No, I'm just saying that we already have enough people, and didn't he pay you a million dollars?"

"I don't think that's any of your business, DeepWOLF." Tiala growls and looks to Stacie. "I think Vulpie's offer still stands, doesn't it?"

"Oh, absolutely! He'll love to have you back, Tiala!" The brown vixen happily answers.

"Yeah but... Why do you even want to do this anymore? It's such a dangerous job. I'd find something else to do if I had that kind of money. I'm just being honest. Don't mean to be a jerk or anything." Deepwolf smiles.

"I don't like you Deepwolf and I never have." Tiala declares, and Stacie's eyes widen.

"Now hold on! I'm sure Mr. Vivixen doesn't want another problem while he's away!"

"Oooo..." Deepwolf grins in response. "Did I make you angry? I'm sorry. I was just making some observations."

"There's something wrong with you and I'm going to find out what it is." The tigress replies, and Deepwolf's smile disappears. He takes on a serious posture and licks his lips.

"Calm down. I didn't mean to upset you."

"Yes you did. And it seems like you're trying to keep me out of the squad." Tiala quickly responds. "Well... Now I'm DEFINITELY coming back. You can count on it, DeepWOLF."

"Tiala, I'm sure Deepwolf didn't mean to hurt your feelings. He's been very helpful around the building."

"I bet he has." The tigress grumbles while swishing her tail.

"Hey look, I'm sorry. It's good to see you." Deepwolf says.

"Whatever." Tiala replies and shrugs her shoulders, but you could cut the tension with a knife.

"Want me to show you how we're doing things now? Rulef lets me manage security while he's away."

"You mean you work with Vulpie Industries' chief of security when he's away. You HELP... You're not in charge."

"Sure." Deepwolf smiles. He takes on a friendly demeanor, so she relaxes a bit, but they both know it's only a matter of time before they're going to have a serious disagreement. "This way." He says, and the mercenary walks past the reception desk. Tiala nods at Stacie before following him. The gray wolf walks up the stairs to the second floor and makes a right turn, heading towards the security office that overlooks the lobby. "Nah, I'm glad you decided to come back. You are pretty tough. It's just surprising that you recovered so quickly. How many times did you get shot?"

"Six. Three in my shoulder, and three in my right arm." Tiala answers while catching up.

"And you healed in like, what, three months?"

"Vulpie spared no expense. He paid for the best treatment I could possibly get." The tigress answers. "They gave me antibiotics and something to help the tissue grow back, maybe steroids. But my arm's completely fine now."

"That's good to hear. You can't shoot very well if you're sore, now can you?" Deepwolf teases and Tiala makes no response. "Here we are." The gray wolf says as they approach the security office's door. The familiar theme of orange on black throughout the building's architecture is furthered on the second and third levels of the tower, where the ceilings and floors are a dark gray. The security office has hazy orange windows on the outside, but crystal glass on the inside. This gives the chief of security a nice view of everything going on inside the lobby and it's difficult to tell when he's in his office or not. Deepwolf opens the door without knocking, because Blacktail has special clearance throughout Vulpie Industries, and looks to a dark timber wolf who's sitting behind a desk filled with paperwork.

"Hey Kent. Tiala's back." Deepwolf says while walking inside, and makes way for the tigress. Kent Farrow already knows her very well, having been chief of building security for years now, and he stands up to offer her a paw.

"Good to see you."

"You too." Tiala smiles in response, but keeps her enthusiasm to a minimum. Farrow is a low key animal and constantly has to keep his eyes on multiple security monitors that are to the right of his desk. It's not uncommon to walk into his office and see him with his back to the door, while he's simultaneously watching every camera feed available to him.

"So I guess you need to get your gear. Deepwolf can show you where we're keeping it while Rulef's away from the building. Have you spoken with Vulpie yet?"

"Thanks. No, I haven't, but I'm sure it won't be a problem."

"We could use you today if you want to get started. I'll contact his receptionist and let her know you're back on active duty. She'll call Rulef and he'll handle the rest. Deepwolf's the only member of Blacktail we have on duty today, so we could use the help, especially after the attempt on Vulpie's life."

"One of the many." Tiala smirks and Kent chuckles in amusement.

"They're starting to be a trend now, aren't they? He wants me to hire even more people, but what we really need is a full contingent of Blacktail that only operates inside the building." Kent replies and gestures at Deepwolf. "Deepwolf executed the second attacker, and I saw the rest of them put the first killer down very fast. I just can't hire people with that kind of combat proficiency."

"Then tell Rulef."

"I did. He keeps forgetting about it, but I think Vulpie will pay for more men. The problem is all of the red tape associated with bringing you guys in. Rulef handles everything you do and I don't have the authority to request mercenaries from the GBI."

"I think Druward Wraulgh would authorize it if Vulpie asked." Deepwolf comments, and Kent nods at him before looking back to Tiala.

"Ask Vulpie yourself, if you would, the next time you see him."

"No problem. How did the attackers get inside the lobby without setting off the metal detectors?"

"Plastic based firearms and shielded knife cases. They came prepared. Rulef says Glovepaw was behind the attack."

"I'll take her down to the armory." Deepwolf declares, and the tigress glances over her shoulder. "She needs a new set of equipment, and a weapon. Probably more than one."

"Fine." Kent says and shrugs his shoulders. "You know my door's always open." Deepwolf turns and walks out of the security office, and Tiala follows him after giving Kent a polite nod. She dislikes having to follow the outspoken gray wolf's lead, but they're going to familiar territory. He just has the keycard to get into the armory and she needs to collect her gear. The pair of animals walk around the balcony of Vulpie Industries' second floor and then descend to the first floor once again, but this time, they circle around behind the stairway. There are doors on either side of the steps that lead into a break area for company employees.

They enter a slim hallway, with the cafeteria to their left, and make a right instead. They walk a good distance and head left when they get to the basement steps. They walk down to basement one, where a hallway can lead them to another one of the company's parking lots, but they spiral around instead, and go down to basement two where the armory is located. They pass through an additional metal detector, where a single security guard is sitting behind a small desk, but he doesn't even bother speaking to them. The panther's a civilian contractor, and probably has never seen combat like Deepwolf or Tiala, and he knows it.

The tigress follows Deepwolf down the slim hallway and they approach a heavily fortified black door on the right side of the baron gray corridor. Deepwolf uses his keycard to gain access, and he grabs the door's thick handle. It's so heavy that it lets out a loud sucking sound when he pulls it open. Tiala follows him inside and closes it behind her. It locks automatically.

The armory is about the size of a one bedroom apartment, with total square footage of about seven hundred and thirty feet, and is replete with everything Blacktail needs. Lockers are on the left side of the room, a bullet proof glass barrier is at the far end of the chamber, and on the right side is a sturdy desk where the mercenaries are required to sign in. The room has two security cameras, both high on the walls so everything can be recorded. Kent has access to the footage but rarely watches the feed because Rulef runs such a tight crew. Normally, no one gets access to the armory without his permission under any circumstances. He trusts Deepwolf enough to handle matters in his absence, and Tiala is more than a little miffed about it. Something about the gray wolf makes her feel uneasy.

He goes over to the bulletproof glass barrier and unlocks its unique door with his keycard as well. Afterwards, he meanders about, and Tiala turns her attention to the lockers. She opens several of them and searches for her original equipment, to no avail. She sighs.

"I think your stuff is in that one." Deepwolf says and points to one of the lockers she hasn't checked. "Should be a new set of female armor in there, but I'm not sure if it will fit." Tiala goes to the locker and opens it. She raises her eyebrows when she discovers her old gear in a crumpled pile, bullet holes and all. Obviously she'll be needing a replacement, but she doesn't see anything else inside the locker. All of the clothing she's seen so far was designed for men, but she's delighted to finally find female sets in the locker right beside her own.

"Good." The tigress whispers and starts getting things out. She finds several combat bras, all black, in addition to black undershirts, black pants, and black body armor.

"Oh, looks like Rulef ordered you a replacement set after all. That's good." Deepwolf comments and Tiala pauses. She wants to try on the gear, but she'll have to strip in front of the nosy gray wolf. He's unduly curious about her affairs.

"Think you could step outside for a moment while I try these on?" The tigress inquires and Deepwolf frowns as if disappointed.

"I'm not supposed to leave anyone in here by themselves. I've got the clearance while Rulef's away... What's the matter?"

"Fine." Tiala growls and removes her civilian shirt. She tosses it aside and rummages through the feminine Blacktail gear until she finds a set she thinks will match her build. The body armor is all the same, it's just the combat bras that concern her. She has fairly large natural breasts and would rather not have them scrunched up in a set that doesn't fit her. The bras and undershirts are both lightweight and sturdy, designed to minimize sweating and general fur ruffling during battle. She undoes her white bra and removes it, so she can try them on. She ignores Deepwolf's presence and also removes her pants. She's wearing pink panties, and the gray wolf's eyes are dilated when she glances at him. She hadn't planned on giving him any attention, but can't help but notice his wide eyes. The tigress doesn't say anything at first, and just stares right back at him. Deepwolf looks at her chest, and moves his eyes all over her feline body with no effort to hide his curiosity.

"Want to take a picture?" She growls. "Fucking pervert."

"Huh?" The gray wolf asks with an innocent voice.

"Huh?" Tiala mocks, and he blinks.

"I'm not doing anything."

"You're staring at my tits."

"Just for a moment. I'm just standing here waiting for you to try on your stuff."

"Unbelievable... I WILL be telling Vulpie about this." She threatens, and he straightens his posture.

"Now hold on a minute. I haven't done anything to you."

"I'll tell him and Rulef, and I've known Vulpie longer than you. He won't appreciate the way you're abusing your authority."

"Tiala... I'm sorry if you think I'm trying to humiliate you. That's not my intention at all."

"THEN WHY ARE YOU FUCKING STARING AT ME?" She angrily inquires, but the gray wolf stays calm.

"I'm sorry. You're right... I Just... I don't know. You have a nice body and I wanted to see it."

"Fucking sick bastard. You like seeing the kitty naked?"

"You're beautiful... And you're really fit too. Do you work out every day?" Deepwolf asks and she coughs. The compliment makes her feel good... She doesn't want it to, but it does...

"I don't know what you're trying to get out of me, but I won't put up with this."

"Tiala, look... I'm sorry, okay? I couldn't help myself." Deepwolf apologizes. He genuinely looks and sounds sorry.

"I bet you're really enjoying this... Oh yes... You slaughtered a bunch of cats over there in Felini, didn't you? I heard all about it."

"No, I actually worked very closely with tigers and panthers against the rebels."

"The rebels who are being oppressed by the Sufias World Government... And you know it. All of you wolves know the war is a complete lie, and the cats know it too. So go ahead and have your laugh. Go on! But I swear, I'll teach you a lesson if you push me too far."

"I understand how you feel."

"No you don't!"

"You're right... I... That was a stupid thing to say... I can't really understand because I'm a wolf, but believe me, I know the war's terrible."

"Yeah, well, at the very least you're an interspecies pervert! Vulpie's an outcast because he's a gay fox, so he won't take kindly to this kind of discrimination."

"Look, I can't help but appreciate a beautiful woman, even if you are a tigress..." Deepwolf quietly replies. His declaration thoroughly bewilders her. She knows he's telling the truth, and it makes her fur stand on end. Her heart flutters when a fleeting interspecies scenario pops into her head. She squints in disgust and growls at herself as well as him.

"Okay, pal."

"I mean it."

"Yeah, I think you've made that clear." The tigress growls, but she can't take her eyes off of him. She starts swishing her tail when his eyes move to her breasts again. He really does like her body... Amazingly, the taboo moment is starting to grow on her. She lets him look, not knowing what to say, and watches his face very carefully. "Want me to turn around so you can see my ass too?"

"No." Deepwolf nervously laughs and finally averts his eyes. "I'm sorry. I'm really sorry."

"Whatever." Tiala mutters, but waits a moment before returning to her task. She picks up several combat bras and tries them on, and the fourth one she uses feels just right. Deepwolf isn't staring at her when she glances in his direction, and she's happy that he's finally showing her a little respect... But at the same time... It felt nice to be admired... Deepwolf really is attracted to her, and the more she thinks about it, he does have some handsome features. His face is symmetrical and his body looks very strong. She's confident she could beat him in a fight, but he can definitely handle himself.

"Please don't tell anyone about this." Deepwolf grumbles while staring at the floor.

"What's that?"

"You've got me by the balls... It's on the security footage and you're totally right. I don't know what I was thinking."

"And I'm just supposed to let this go? You can forget that." The tigress responds while putting on a pair of pants. "You disrespected a member of your team, and I've protected Vulpie way longer than you. He'll side with me."

"I know, damn it." The gray wolf growls and turns around. He sees her put on a black shirt, and she swings her arms with a cold expression. "I fucked up."

"My opinion? You seriously need to get laid if looking at a cat makes you hard. The feeling is NOT mutual."

"Maybe you're right."

"I am right. You're an idiot." Tiala says, and waits to see if Deepwolf will take her insult. He shuffles on his feet and sighs with a distraught expression.

"I actually respect you a lot. You fought Evil Vulpie... You were right there when it all began."

"Yes I was. And no one had a problem with me being a tigress. I do my job, and I do it well. It's that simple."

"Please let me keep mine... I shouldn't have disrespected you when you first showed up... I think I just wanted... I don't know... Maybe to impress you."

"Okay, that's enough Deepwolf. You're making me feel really uncomfortable." Tiala replies, and he lowers his muzzle.

"Alright."

"What's the standard rifle now?" The tigress inquires.

"The M800. Love it." The gray wolf eagerly responds. They both know he's thrilled about changing the subject. If it means she'll forget about his earlier transgressions, then he'll give her anything she wants, and there are several things a member of Blacktail could use but doesn't always have access to. "Eight hundred rounds per minute, and after the initial vertical recoil, it never misses. Just aim for the chest and you'll get head shots when it kicks up."

"Too slow for me." Tiala says after spotting an unusual but familiar looking gun. She walks towards the bullet proof glass barrier and steps inside the unlocked door to get a better look. There are more than thirty automatic weapons in the small room, in addition to grenades, weapon scopes and other gun related equipment. The tigress draws a black MTAC-81, but quickly realizes there's an MTAC-71 right underneath it.

"Ah... That's the gun they used on you." Deepwolf comments after stepping into the chamber.

"Why are you carrying vulpine weaponry?"

"I dunno. Guess Rotick thought it was a good idea to procure one after the attack. The rate of fire on that thing is just crazy, and it's lightweight."

"The recoil might hurt me at long range, but I wouldn't mind having one of those... If I had two weapons, I could handle any situation... I could take an M800 as my primary, and use the MTAC for close quarters... Ultimate stopping power..."

"I bet. I heard it only took one clip to drop you, and I know you're tougher than I am." Deepwolf says, and Tiala's tiger ears perk up. She keeps her eyes on the weapons, but silently registers the compliment.

"So I'll just take them both." Tiala responds and turns around to face the gray wolf. "Log it on the desk over there."

"I... Can you take two automatics at once? I don't think we're allowed to do that."

"Well, Rulef won't take the MTAC from me when he finds out... He'll just let it slide."

"Yeah, but that's not our policy and the other guys won't like it."

"Probably not. And he'll ask you why you let me do it." Tiala muses, while showing him a relentless expression.

"Great. And what will I tell him?"

"I don't know. That's your problem." The tigress replies, and Deepwolf sighs loudly. He doesn't say anything for a moment but finally nods his head in agreement.

"Alright, but this makes us even. Right?"

"I think it's fair... Better than you getting kicked out for sexually harassing a member of your team."

"Okay, okay... I'll do it." Deepwolf growls, and leaves the weapon security cage. He heads over to the table where the log book resides, and apprehensively begins his task. Tiala needs no help in finding suitable equipment to carry two guns at once. She finds a three point sling that she'll use to carry the M800 on her back. This type of strap allows a shooter to use their hands, instead of carrying the gun around with a traditional sling, because it acts as a harness and is attached to the shooter's body. The weapon can be retrieved very quickly when needed, and now she can carry an MTAC-71 as her primary weapon without having to worry about being outgunned during long range engagements. She knows the MTAC-71 will blow someone away at close or medium range, but having an assault rifle is a necessity for hitting distant targets.

Deepwolf waits for her to find everything she wants before finalizing the log. He's recorded her acquisition of two weapons and a three point sling. Much to his distress, the tigress lingers in the weapon cage. She picks up a flash bang grenade, which is normal, but also gets a smoke grenade as well. The gray furred wolf wants to say something, but can't. He just lets her do as she pleases for several minutes, until she finally leaves the cage and shuts the door. It locks automatically, and will not open without another swipe from Deepwolf's card.

"Okay. Got it all." He says, and stands up.

"Thanks." Tiala replies with a vengeful but playful smirk.

Mendacity

Amsend lets himself into Druward's office, and the black furred wolf looks up from his desk in disbelief. No one visits him without proper clearance. He straightens in his chair, and privately grieves for the bureau's broken security.

"Good afternoon Mr. Wraulgh. I'm sorry for barging in on you, but we need to talk." The husky smiles, and Druward sighs apprehensively.

"You must have powerful contacts to get in here without clearance."

"Oh, yes..." Amsend replies with his thick foreign accent, and takes a seat. He makes himself comfortable, and Druward sighs again. "But you might say... This was a good interruption, then, yes? To reinforce my authority?"

"I suppose." Druward dryly responds and silence fills the room. "What do you want?"

"Well... As I said... I have marching orders for you..." Amsend replies with a very creepy voice. His frequent pauses between statements gives one the impression that he's perpetually contemplating something sick and must suppress the depraved thoughts before returning to conversation. "The cock swallower will get a phone call from you this weekend, and he should attend a special meeting on Monday." Druward grimaces at the statement.

"You want me to call Vulpie Vivixen?"

"Yes..."

"Will I be attending?"

"Yes..."

"Where are we going?"

"To a very... Useful... Branch of the Governmental Security Bureau..."

"Is it some place I've been before? Some part of the GBI you're working with?"

"You've never been there before..." The black and white furred husky answers with a twinkle in his blue eyes. "It's a very... Special... Complex that works with the Cyber Technologies Government Division..."

"The CTGD works alone. That's the whole point. A secure government complex that won't be compromised during an emergency."

"We work with the CTGD without their knowledge... We use their systems..."

"And Howlstead isn't aware of it?" Druward asks with an incredulous voice.

"Vulpie.net controls what he sees, what they do, everything they think they have..."

"So it's infected the CTGD as well?"

"Not all of the building. We don't need the... White room... I understand you witnessed QUITE THE SHOW there!" Amsend says and laughs sadistically.

"Yeah." Druward quickly answers.

"Forgive me... Vulpie.net speaks of it often..."

"What do you want, Amsend?"

"Patience Mr. Wraulgh... Remember... You move on my command..."

"Understood."

"Now..." Amsend says and straightens himself in his chair. "Oh... Before I forget... You shouldn't expect Ms. Dressler to come in to work any longer..."

"You're pulling her out? I guess that will streamline the chain of command, but how will I contact you?"

"Through traditional methods, of course... Email... Phone... Nothing should prevent you from communicating with me directly, now that we've killed her..."

"What?" Druward coughs. He goes stiff as a board.

"We killed her..."

"WHY?" The GBI director asks with an appalled voice. "Why did you do that?"

"You were right... Her loyalty waned quite a bit after I gave her to you, and we just couldn't... Work things out..."

"Goddess Khalan." The black furred wolf whispers and Amsend shoots him an irritated look.

"You disapprove?"

"Of course I disapprove! How can you kill your own people? She didn't even do anything!"

"She would have eventually..." Amsend grins. "Looks like you should have fucked her when you had the chance, eh?"

"My God... How could you do that?" Druward asks and shakes his head.

"We dumped her in the river... It was rather easy..."

"Stop! Just stop!" The black furred wolf breathes, and feels sick. He starts panting and can't look at Amsend any longer. The husky doesn't say anything while he recovers, but the GBI director has to summon a lot of strength before he's capable of continuing the conversation. "God... I didn't want you to kill her..."

"It wasn't your problem, really... It was our matter..."

"So are you going to kill me after you've gotten everything you want?" Druward sharply inquires.

"A lie... ALL A LIE!" Amsend declares, and waves his paws in amusement.

"What?"

"We didn't do anything to Karla. She's alright, Druward..."

"Then why the hell did you say it?"

"I wanted to see what your reaction would be." Amsend answers while investigating the GBI director's face. The black furred wolf appears very relieved, but there is also something wild behind his yellow eyes. "I don't know if you have the stomach for this, Mr. Wraulgh... If you couldn't handle that scenario, I wonder how you'll fare when we let you in on our major operations?"

"Then maybe you should just kill me now, or maybe I'll just shoot you in the fucking face?" Druward suddenly responds. "Because I don't appreciate that shit!"

"Calm yourself Mr. Wraulgh... I'll ignore your threat because you actually performed much better than you believe... Loyalty... Is the most important asset we look for..."

"So what? You wanted to see if I would laugh off Karla's death?"

"More or less..."

"And you would have assumed that I was putting on a show if I did?"

"Precisely..." Amsend answers with sinister delight.

"Don't give me another test." Druward warns but makes sure to use a careful voice. "I'd rather you not."

"You did well. I think you'll earn your place with us, Mr. Wraulgh, because you do, it seems, hold loyalty in high regard... It will be of the utmost importance while we enact our plans..."

"I'll fuck her if it's that important to you Amsend, if you think that'll prove I'm willing to do what it takes, but just don't kill her, for the love of God." Druward growls and Amsend chuckles.

"Do as you will, Mr. Wraulgh. She actually harbors secret respect for you now that you didn't take advantage of her at your home and have not called her in for a good tail lifting..."

"How the hell do you know that?"

"Call it intuition... Now... Shall we discuss your phone call with Mr. Vivixen?"

"Please, yes."

"You'll need to convince him to attend the unveiling of the National Vulpie.net Agency complex."

"Ah... So that's why you've been hiring ex-CTGD personnel." Druward infers, and Amsend smiles.

"Indeed... You knew?"

"I talk to Arthur Howlstead quite a bit. He keeps me updated with trends in cybercrime, but most importantly... He warns me if he sees Vulpie.net itself... Not Arctic.net... He's caught it masquerading as Arctic.net several times."

"I'm surprised someone other than Vulpie could do such a thing."

"Well, we did force him to teach Vulpie.net to the CTGD, and Howlstead already has extensive computer knowledge."

"And he mentioned the Governmental Security Bureau? We don't allow new employees to talk about the organization..."

"No, but he said he's had several employees quit because they were going to join the bureau, and I've never seen them here... So I figured you collected them."

"Guilty as charged... But it was the Deiva's transfer order that spurred you into action, wasn't it?" The husky inquires with a dark smirk, and Druward shrugs.

"The GSB was designed to audit the nation's security, so everything before that request seemed legitimate."

"Oh, I truly think you'll appreciate our SMALL, but SPECIAL contributions..." Amsend malevolently declares, his voice dripping with mendacious enthusiasm. "We surpassed the Cyber Technologies Government Division's size and capabilities three years ago."

"That's wonderful Amsend."

"Oh yes... It is... But back to the subject at hand... The National Vulpie.net Agency needs Vulpie... We're going to offer him a job, and it's imperative that he accepts it."

"He's too busy with his company. He won't have time for a second job."

"It's more of a title than a job."

"So you're calling it what... The NVA?"

"Yes."

"He won't like having his name associated with the government. He stopped teaching at the CTGD because conspiracy theorists were convinced that he was still controlling the world."

"Exactly..." Amsend replies, and says nothing else. Druward stares at him for a moment, before leaning back in his chair.

"You're setting him up?

"WE'RE... Setting him up..."

"Some kind of psychological warfare? This is another distraction, just like your goddesses."

"I think you're beginning to catch on..."

"The entire world will turn against him... He'll be persecuted by the media, and then you can have him prosecuted for his crimes... It's... Truly brilliant, actually... Morally depraved... But brilliant..."

"Druward Wraulgh, the most infamous GBI director of our time, concerned about moral implications..." Amsend replies with a cynical smile.

"You're going to take everything from him."

"Progress sometimes demands this type of sacrifice..."

"So the REAL question is... Just WHAT are you going to do while the universe is being distracted by Vulpie's downfall? You'll have it all over the news, every day, every night, nonstop... You could ride him for years until he finally has nothing left, and then you'll send him to jail. The public will feel good about finally putting him away, but by that time, it'll be too late for them to notice what you've done... Isn't that right?"

"You have a truly devious mind, Mr. Wraulgh..." The husky smirks in response.

"But it won't work if he just manages Vulpie Industries... No... You need him to hold a powerful position that people will see."

"More or less."

"I'm right? That's the idea?"

"More or less, Mr. Wraulgh." Amsend repeats without further elaboration.

"Are you going to tell me the rest of it? What's the point, Amsend? Take away the people's liberties? More wars? What is it?"

"Not really your concern at this point... You have a job to do, Mr. Wraulgh, and I will help you along the way. I'll be at the meeting, and together, we'll convince Mr. Vivixen to play his part."

"I do need to know... I have to know what it is..."

"To rationalize and justify your actions?" Amsend inquires.

"More or less." Druward dryly replies, and the husky smirks at the black furred wolf's choice of words.

"I'll tell you a bit more... So you'll know what to expect... But I will not elaborate past a certain point. You understand that I can't divulge everything until you've joined our ranks... IF... You join our ranks..."

"I understand."

"I've used the GSB to conceal Vulpie.net's creation of a robotic army." Amsend states, and Druward sits up in his chair. "We work very well together, because I provide it with the real world animals it needs to do what it does, while keeping it out of the public eye. Were it not for the GSB's clandestine rules and regulations, Vulpie.net's factories and testing facilities would have been discovered by now."

"I see." Druward replies and swallows. "Like the one on Zeravyn? Cloudy planet, no one can see anything... Nice and remote."

"It was our very first project... Vulpie.net chose Zeravyn because it knew about the location, thanks to Vulpie sending it there during the Vulpie.net crisis. I agreed to conceal its activities, and it was the most difficult operation by far... The most time consuming... Vulpie.net created, tested, and experimented on the Deivas for years until it finally produced the attractive masterpieces you're familiar with. It took a tremendous amount of resources, and they were provided by Sevrif, who was Vulpie.net's first creation... Its first child..."

"But Sevrif was a little too independent, wasn't he?"

"Not until you and Vulpie showed up... That was an unexpected and very frustrating event... Zeravyn was too far away for me to detach the GSB, and of course, who knows whether they could have killed you and your men under those circumstances..."

"Would have been complicated since the military wouldn't know who the hell you were."

"Yes. Vulpie.net handled the situation on its own, but unfortunately, we lost its master computer system... Because of a GBI director who makes aggressive decisions without waiting for permission from the commander in chief..."

"I owed Vulpie because of Karl Vulches. He begged me to destroy it." Druward admits, but the statement doesn't weaken the lethal glare Amsend's giving him.

"Because of that setback, we were forced to speed up production on the other off-world factories..."

"Others? How many?"

"Vulpie.net decided that building a second master computer would be too time consuming and unnecessary by that point." Amsend continues, ignoring Druward's question. "I agreed, but there was the issue of the Deivas being locked up at Fort Elbrus... So we fixed that problem, and now they're free to fulfill their original purpose."

"Triangulate the people against Vulpie?"

"Don't interrupt me." Amsend warns. A cold silence descends upon the room, and after a brief moment, the husky speaks again. "Yes, the Deivas will be used to persecute Vivixen. They won't do it themselves, because the people will do it for them. They'll recite the programming Vulpie.net's given them, condemning the cock swallower for his homosexuality, and general immorality, and the animals will turn on him. His public approval will disappear rather quickly. His fame will be replaced by infamy, and there will be outrage over him holding such a powerful position within the government. The Deiva's falseness is irrelevant. It doesn't matter that Vulpie.net built them. They're very beautiful and mesmerizing tools that will be used to confuse the public, and establish a trend of magical thinking. This magical thinking will distract them from our activities... We'll have ample time to deploy Vulpie.net's robots to their target locations, and set the stage for Vulpie's downfall. When the attacks come, they will be blamed entirely on Vulpie. We'll wait until the public is infuriated before the killing begins... Vulpie.net will deploy its soldiers to several planets, and part of Sufias, where it will take key military installations by force."

Amsend pauses for a moment. The black and white furred husky looks at Druward as if debating how much he will tell him, and makes the decision to share just enough to satiate Druward's need for answers. "Vulpie.net will obliterate the Sufias World Government's military. It will avoid killing as many animals as possible, but there is no way it will lose this conflict. It's stolen Vulpie's VulGrid technology, and improved upon it to a large degree. It'll use its infinitely superior machinery to project blinding light and a deafening roar throughout the bases. The soldiers simply won't be able to fight back, and even if they could, they'd be no match for Vulpie.net's army. It has methods of deflecting all manners of attack... Sea, air, nuclear, space, the ion cannon, ground invasion... It's been very busy, and the result is breathtaking. Perhaps you'll have the privilege of seeing the army before the invasion begins..." Druward wants to speak, but waits until Amsend takes on a less threatening countenance.

"So then you'll put Vulpie away, and tell the public his army has been defeated?"

234

"HIS army, yes… Undoubtedly, it will take us several months to secure every military installation on the planet. So in the meantime, we'll create and spread lies about his desire to make the world suffer because of the discrimination he's felt over the years. The people will see him as a malevolent, perverted, and twisted homosexual with a hatred for all good things. The Deivas will be crucial in propagating these lies, and the religious implications will absolutely convince many animals that he was completely responsible for the attacks and the perpetual occupation of military bases throughout the universe… It won't be hard to sell… Vulpie has already taken over the universe once before… It will work… Vulpie.net has calculated every conceivable development, based upon centuries of knowledge, infinite knowledge, and it has a contingency plan for everything and anything that will happen. If only Vulpie had created it long ago… So very useful…"

"But…" Druward says, and clears his throat. "After you crucify Vulpie, you're going to keep everything Vulpie.net's taken?"

"Precisely. Once we have absolute control of Sufias' infrastructure, military sites, and crucial resources, there will be no need to hide our intentions."

"Aren't you worried about what it'll do after it's won?" The GBI director inquires, and Amsend returns a little smile.

"No… It works for me."

"It won't need you anymore."

"It will always need me to control animals. I and my contacts own the largest banks and most respected institutions in the universe. You're assuming people will stop working and going about their daily lives just because the landlords have changed, but this will not be the case. The universe will recognize that resistance is futile. Once they see we can blind them and control everything they hear, only the very foolish will attempt violence. We'll disperse every protest that takes place, and a militia can do absolutely nothing in a world filled with cameras, cellular towers, and satellite surveillance. Vulpie.net will separate and detain the animals that refuse to cooperate, and after years of imprisonment, they too will submit."

"What if it just decides it doesn't care about real animals anymore and wants to wipe us all out, bankers and all?"

"Ah, well... It would be tragic I suppose..." Amsend answers with an amused look.

"You don't care if it kills you? And why are you going to do this if you already control the military, the international banking system, and the media? I thought the AFR controlled the media."

"We control the AFR, and thus, the media, but they are not aware of our influence. One fox family completely owns the AFR, and it is part of our organization. Karl Vulches, Nathan Fenrir and others like them are too caught up in their pro-fox agendas to realize their part in a larger scheme of division. And the army... I told you they move too slowly... We control them with financial and political means... Obviously, the animals serving in the armed forces will disagree with our plans... So it will be necessary for Vulpie.net's synthetic children to replace them entirely..."

"You already have them in the population, don't you? We caught Chris Cephil and Lorcan, but there are others, aren't there?" Druward inquires.

"Oh yes... All placed in very important locations... In addition to seven hundred and forty eight thousand soldiers off-world... But I've told you more than enough, Mr. Wraulgh... You must never repeat a word of this... We ARE watching you and if I suspect that you've turned on me..."

"I understand." Druward replies and takes a deep breath. "But let me ask one more question if I may?"

"If you must."

"Why did you slaughter the animals at Fort Elbrus if Vulpie.net can already blind everyone and project deafening sound as well? Vulpie's VulGrids don't produce sound."

236

"Because we cannot show the enemy our finest weapon before the war truly begins. As it stands, the public only knows that Vulpie can make things invisible using VulGrids, so all of the blame will be placed directly on him. The true extent of our power would terrify the populace, and knowledge of it would disrupt the transitory period I spoke of. They don't know we can virtually cripple soldiers without firing a bullet... No one is aware of my organization, or that Vulpie.net is conspiring with us to dominate the universe... The Deivas will keep them distracted and focused on Vulpie... Sufias will be divided between the religious, the nonreligious, the vigilant, the diffident... Now you can see why his participation is crucial to our plans... So let's discuss methods of manipulating him..."

Vulpie's ears perk up when someone beeps the horn outside. He's watching TV with Polar, and quickly stands, as does his husband. Val Maxwell promised he'd have the car finished by Sunday evening and it looks like he's arrived right on schedule. It's around 7 p.m. so there's still plenty of time for a test drive.

"It's here!"

"Yep." Polar smiles, and follows him to the front door. Vulpie opens it and sees the timber wolf getting out of his Superbolt. It looks absolutely gorgeous, and Val's wearing a very proud grin.

"All done! You're going to love this thing!"

"Oooooooooooo!!! I know it!!!" Vulpie squeals and hurries over. He leans to the left and peers into the vehicle, checking the quality of the windshield and windows; the super thick bullet proof glass looks perfectly normal aside from its bulk. Val notices what the fox is doing and points to the driver side window.

"Get in and see how you like the lighting! We shaped it just right to maintain visibility." The brown wolf says and looks to Polar. "Could you turn on your garage lights?"

"Sure." Polar responds and heads back into the house. He opens the garage door a few moments later, flooding the area with bright light, and Vulpie hops into the driver's seat. He hastily adjusts it to accommodate his small frame. Val has the chair pushed way back, and after pulling it forward and getting the back support just right, Vulpie puts his paws on the steering wheel. Polar walks to the car with enthusiasm. He's interested in the interior lighting as well, since it's the only problem they could have with the armored car, but it looks perfect after he opens the passenger door and gets in.

"Notice any difference?" Val inquires and Vulpie squints at Polar's garage lights. He sticks his head out of the driver's side window and looks at them outside of the car so he can test them against the windshield's transparency.

"Wow! Almost no difference at all! It's just a tiny, tiny, bit darker."

"Are you satisfied with the quality? We worked very hard on getting it just right."

"It's super fantastic!" Vulpie replies and gives the man a friendly smile.

"And this is the stuff that'll stop the big sniper rifle rounds?" Polar asks, and Vulpie glances at him. He quickly looks to his left again and licks his lips so he can ask Val his husband's question.

"This is the same glass that'll stop a fifty caliber sniper round?"

"Guaranteed, though I doubt you'll be able to see much afterwards." Val chuckles in response.

"Well I guess if we get attacked by that kind of weaponry then all bets are off!"

"Exactly."

"What do you think?" Vulpie asks Polar and the white furred wolf smiles.

"It's your car? Do you like it?"

"I love it baby, but do you like it too?"

"It's badass." Polar grins and Vulpie returns a delighted smile.

"My thoughts exactly!" The orange furred fox takes a moment to inspect the V-Screen he installed underneath the car's main display, and it comes on without a hitch.

"You shouldn't have the V-Screen charging all the time because it'll wear out the battery, so I disabled it with your switch." Val comments while leaning in the car. He's referring to the equipment Vulpie personally installed, and the fox presses down on the small button to the right of the V-Screen. The V-Screen's battery symbol begins flashing, indicating that it's being charged by the car's main battery, and he turns it back off.

"Yeah, you're right! Awesome!"

"You installed a full model V-Screen in here?" Polar asks in awe and Vulpie looks positively ecstatic.

"Yeah! Now we're wired wherever we go baby! And it's detachable so we can upgrade it without too much trouble!"

"He connected it to the car's internal computer system." Val notes while looking at the rectangular display beneath the V-Screen. He points to it while sharing his thoughts. "The Superbolt already has a top-notch GPS tracking system, so between that and Vulpie's equipment, you shouldn't have any problem communicating with Blacktail. He also installed a radio communication system."

"That's good." Rulef says while peering in the passenger side of the car. "We need to get that GPS coordinated with our tracking devices as soon as possible."

"No prob!" Vulpie declares and gropes the rubber steering wheel with his vulpine paws. It feels so very good.

"Oh, is the car on?" Polar suddenly asks in surprise. He's staring at the rectangular display and notices that it says they have hundreds of hours left.

"Yeah, you can't even hear it, can you?" Val answers in pride. "You'll hear a small electric hum if everyone's quiet, but it's a pretty silent ride."

"How about when you're driving?"

"Sounds like a jet engine, just like the one you test drove."

"Coooooool!"

"Since this was such a big job, if you notice anything major that you want changed, just call me and we'll bring it in."

"Nah, it's all here!" Vulpie says, and looks around the interior. The orange furred fox had plenty of time to familiarize himself with the Superbolt while modifying the car, and everything seems perfect.

"Good. It was fun building this thing, so if Polar wants one too…"

"I think one will be enough." Polar responds and Val grins.

"I know. I'm just making the offer."

"You want one?" Vulpie asks his husband.

"No… I just want you to be safe. This is your car. I like mine."

"This is more car than I deserve. It's ours." Vulpie replies and returns a loving smile.

"You deserve it. If you feel the need for speed, than this is the only option."

"I'm feeling it right now, and I can't wait for you to feel it too…" Vulpie responds and gives his husband a mischievous look. Polar smirks at the statement.

"Anytime, anywhere."

"I'm gonna hold ya to that." Vulpie says, and playfully bites his tongue between his teeth. The V-Screen suddenly displays an image of a phone ringing, and it gets everyone's attention. "Huh! Well looky there! Already got someone on the line!"

"That's Druward…" Polar says after recognizing the number. Vulpie blinks, and notices the same thing.

"Yeah… Oh…"

"Vulpie, Polar, have fun. Keep in touch." Maxwell says, and pats the orange furred fox on the left shoulder.

"Thanks! Bye!"

"Goodbye." Val responds, and heads over to the car that's waiting on him. Another AOSE employee followed him to Polar and Vulpie's house so he'd have a ride home. Vulpie glances at Polar before touching the V-Screen to accept the call. The car's audio system, a Consonant 17.5, sounds magnificent when it comes on.

"Hello?" Vulpie says.

"Hello, Vulpie?" Druward responds, and Rulef leans inside the car.

"Yeah. Hey, thanks for calling. What's up?"

"Things have finally settled down, but I need to discuss some matters with you. Do you have time to talk?"

"Sure, I've got time."

"Did you find that terrorist you were talking about?" Polar inquires.

"Not yet. Glovepaw's hiding somewhere but it won't be long until we sniff him out. Shouldn't be a problem. I'm fairly certain he was behind the attack."

"Good."

"But that's not the main reason I called. Vulpie?"

"Yeah."

"I've ironed out this mess and have some good news. I spoke with Arthur and it seems the CTGD has built a second facility to handle Arctic.net in the years to come, and the owners would like to talk to you in person."

"Oh, that's pretty cool! But uh..."

"They're going to offer a lot of benefits if they can secure cooperation between your company and their organization."

"Sounds great, but what does this have to do with the guys that tried to kill me?"

"That's the most important thing... Something's happened that you haven't seen on the news. We've been hiding it from the press, trying to figure out how to handle it, and it's pretty serious."

"What? What is it?"

"It's better if we talk in person. They want to see what you know so far. They're on your side, and that's why they want to work with you, but they also want answers. I vouched for you, so don't worry about that, but you really need to meet with them."

"But what happened? Was there another Aila attack or something?"

"I can't really tell you over the phone..."

"Okay... Well... Uh..." Vulpie says and looks to Polar. The white furred wolf shrugs. "Can Polar come too?"

"Sure. They want to meet tomorrow morning. Can you do that?"

"Yeah, no problem. Just uh... Send me the directions to the place. Who am I meeting again?"

"I'll send you an email, and it'll explain everything."

"Okay."

"Druward, are we in any danger?" Polar inquires and there is a brief pause on the other end of the conversation.

"It would be dangerous not to have this meeting. You both need to be aware of what's going on, because, like I said, it hasn't been on the news and it's very serious. I'm afraid I can't say much more at this point."

"We'll be there." Polar replies. "We need to get back to work as soon as possible."

"I know. Vulpie Industries can't go without its CEO for much longer, so we're going to get both of you on the inside track. Please don't talk to anyone about where you're going, though. Let Rulef know, so he can protect you, but no one else."

242

"Got it." Vulpie responds and Polar releases a worried sigh. "Ah! I actually see the email right now!" The fox says after navigating to his inbox via the V-Screen's touch display.

"Good."

"Wow, uh... Man this place is huge!"

"It's a classified building, like the CTGD, so be discrete. Alright?"

"Yeah, no prob. So you want us there at eight in the morning?"

"Yes."

"Alrighty then! See you tomorrow."

"Thanks. Goodbye." The GBI director replies, and Polar glances at Rulef.

"Do you know anything about this?"

"Nope." The gray wolf answers. "But I guess we'll find out."

"I'm gonna drive this monster down there! Perfect opportunity to try the thing out!"

"Just don't run any red lights. We won't be able to keep up." Rulef replies and Vulpie waves off the comment with a smile.

"Would never think of it."

The National Vulpie.net Agency

A Superbolt gracefully speeds through the eastern portion of Sufias City, drawing the attention of motorists wherever it goes. It gleams in a dew of fresh morning rain. City air isn't clean by any standards, but its smell makes Vulpie wild. He has the thick driver's side window open and has thoroughly been enjoying himself on the way to the NVA. He pulls up next to a fast looking blue car and grins at the young animals inside it. A brown fox is sitting in the passenger seat, a brown wolf is driving, and two other foxes are in the back. The bunch looks like they're cutting class, or doing something similarly naughty, and Vulpie raises his eyebrows at them.

"Sup!" The orange furred fox says and Polar leans over to see who's in the car. They don't look dangerous, so he lets his husband play around.

"Vulpie? AW Dude! Hey fag! You want to race?" The wolf asks with a particularly disrespectful but mischievous voice.

"This fag will dust your candy ass! See who gets to the next light first!" Vulpie taunts with a grin.

"You're on!"

"You sure? Gonna be a massacre!"

"Shit." The wolf says, and the two vixens in the backseat struggle to get a better view of the Superbolt's driver. They yank on the passenger seat and lean over, making the male fox move out of the way.

"It's him!"

"Hey! Hey Vulpie Baby! You want a girlfriend?" One of them offers and the light turns green. Vulpie floors it and the Superbolt makes it across the wet streets to the next intersection in eight seconds. The electric car's powerful engine whirls like a jet. The orange furred fox has to slow down so he won't miss the stoplight, and waits for the kids with a supremely amused expression.

"You SUCK!"

"Nah, you suck faggot!" The wolf yells and grins afterwards.

"Dude, what kind of car is that? What is that?" The male fox asks and Vulpie reaches out of the window to swat its exterior with his left arm.

"Super! BOLT!"

"Sick!"

"Hey, Vulpie Baby! You want a girlfriend? I'm free!" The girl offers again and Vulpie smirks.

"Not my type Honey! But thankies!"

"Aw, come on! I don't bite! Not hard!"

"Green light." Polar says and Vulpie floors it again. The brown wolf doesn't bother to race him this time, and gets to the next light at a much slower pace.

"Yellow, Green, Red, Green, Yellow, Red, Green!" Vulpie sings, and gives his husband a delightful smile.

"I know." Polar smirks, and glances at the street name. "Uh, Vulpie! You need to make a right here!" He says, just as the orange furred fox romps it down once more, but he makes the turn gracefully while waving goodbye to the kids. "You're going to get us stuck in traffic."

"I don't even give a fuck! I'm having fun here!" Vulpie declares and Polar shoots him a serious look.

"Now don't get carried away…"

"Alright…" Vulpie laughs and slows down. He checks the rearview mirror to see if Blacktail's still behind them just as Rulef makes radio contact.

"*Slow down. We lost one of the trucks in traffic, Vulpie.*" The Blacktail commander's voice is piped into the car via the V-Screen and the all-inclusive Consonant 17.5 sound system.

"Got ya! I'll slow down."

"*Drive slower so they can catch up.*"

"K!"

"If I didn't know better, I'd say he likes the car!" Polar says, and Rulef chuckles on the other end of the radio.

"Keep that window up or someone's going to yank him out."

"I'll whoop em! Can't yank me unless I want them too!" The orange furred fox gleefully replies, and Polar shakes his head in amusement.

"Looks like someone needs to be put in his place again…" The white furred wolf teases with a lust filled voice.

"Promises, promises…" Vulpie grins in response, and his blue eyes widen when he notices they're getting close to their destination on the V-Screen's GPS system. "Destination ahead Mr. P! Prepare for landing sequence!" The fox pushes down on the accelerator just hard enough to give them a fast lurch, and Polar grabs the passenger side's ceiling handle.

"We'll be flying alright! Flying off the road if you keep this up!"

"I know what I'm doing!"

"That's what I'm afraid of! I'm still not over our little bike ride in the Lupus Canis Mountains!"

"But this is so much SAFER!" Vulpie grins, but maintains a responsible speed when they approach the next turn. A red arrow on the V-Screen instructs him to take a right on "Vulpie.net Way," and he laughs at the name. "Geez! Why don't we have a Vulpie.net Way at the building?"

"I know right. I guess they're not trying to hide the place very hard." Polar responds while peering through the rain covered windshield. Vulpie turns on the wipers and sets an appropriate speed to remove the mild rain from their view. Green forests appear on the left and right while they drive down a very long and lonely road. There's plenty of lighting, so the water glistens and gleams on the pavement while they stay the course. The orange furred fox checks his rearview mirror again, and sees four black SUVs behind him. The last one caught up, so he increases his speed a little bit. They drive for half a mile, without making any turns, until they finally come to a heavy metal gatehouse. A male tiger steps out of the small building to Vulpie's left, but gives him the go ahead signal with his right paw. He opens the gate and watches them with a smile. Obviously he knows Vulpie's expected, and has no

246

problem letting the Superbolt and four SUVs through without checking for clearance.

The road makes a slight left, and then a right, winding a bit after the convoy passes through the gatehouse. The first building they see is tall and tan colored with huge barricades. It's about the size of a shopping mall, but has an interesting second level that juts up at the front of the building, almost like a castle tower that overlooks incoming threats. This multi-leveled part of the building has black glass windows on the second floor, but the windows on the third level are much larger, once again reinforcing a defensive outpost oriented design.

This, in addition to the massive black spiked gates that completely surround the building, make the GSB one hell of a sight. The GBI headquarters in Sufias City is just as big, but it isn't protected to such an extreme degree. The building's super thick barricade of spikes is over six feet tall at all points of entry, and they look like they could stop a tank dead in its tracks. An intimidating concrete backed metal sign reads "GOVERNMENTAL SECURITY BUREAU," in front of the main gate.

"Wow. Is this it?" Polar whispers.

"Fuckin hell man! Think they've got enough security?" Vulpie coughs in astonishment, and takes a look at the car's V-Screen. "No... The GPS says it's down this way." The orange furred fox says, and drives by the large complex. Blacktail is quick to follow the Superbolt, so he knows he's on the right track. "Never heard of that place before. Guess they just call it the GSB."

"Yeah." Polar replies and glances back at the building while they keep driving. "Must be one of those secret bases people talk about."

"I guess."

"Druward's going to be here, right?"

"Yeah, he said he would." Vulpie answers and nods as they approach two very long buildings. They're rectangular in shape, and a wide road separates the two with beautifully placed stonework. To their left is a massive parking lot, and it's completely full.

"Where are we supposed to park? Right there?"

"He said to go all the way down to the end in the email. The parking lot we're going to is on the other side of the left building."

"Yeah, I see it now." Polar replies while leaning towards his small lover. The fox makes a left turn, taking advantage of a detour section in the road, and drives around the northern end of the building. This parking lot is far smaller, but less crowded as well, because it's reserved for VIPs. Vulpie spots a place he thinks would be convenient for him and Blacktail, and swerves between the white lines. He faces the large artificial wilderness that surrounds the complex and turns off the car. Polar thinks the sight is quite odd, considering they're still in Sufias city, and Vulpie has the same thought. Blacktail enters the lot and parks around Vulpie's car without hesitation. They are quick to get out, and the orange furred fox and white furred wolf open their doors as well. Vulpie stretches after hopping out. He ruffles his business suit a little and pats it down when he's done. He straightens his clothing and feels his tie before shutting the door. Polar shuts his after a moment, and Vulpie locks the car with an energetic breath.

"Okay! Let's do this!"

"Do what, exactly?" Tiala asks as she joins him, and the orange furred fox coughs in surprise.

"Tiala! You're back?!"

"Yeah, I hope you're glad to see me." The tigress responds and Vulpie laughs.

"Course I'm glad! Why didn't somebody tell me?"

"Oh… Right, I forgot." Rulef says and shrugs his shoulders. "Had her at the building yesterday and she joined the squad again this morning."

"Me and you need to work on our communication!" Vulpie says and swats his paw at the gray wolf in a cute fashion. He looks at Tiala and claps his hands together. "Are you really all healed up now? You feel alright?"

"Yes sir. They took excellent care of me and I feel better than ever."

"I can't believe you still wanna protect me but I appreciate it babe!" Vulpie happily replies, and she smiles. The tigress almost looks nervous, and he stops for a moment, wondering what's wrong.

"You okay?"

"Yeah."

"You sure?"

"It's just... I missed working for you." Tiala smiles and Vulpie giggles.

"Missed having you around, girl!"

"They'll probably make us wait outside..." Rulef interrupts while looking over the building. "I think this place is about as safe as you can get."

"Let's find out. Go grab something to eat if they do." Vulpie suggests.

"Any idea how long this is going to take?" The Blacktail commander inquires and the fox shakes his head.

"Probably a few hours. I don't know."

"Knowing Druward, this thing will be over four hours long. He sounded pretty serious last night."

"Yeah, just go get some food if you have to wait." Vulpie replies and starts walking. Polar joins him on his left and offers to hold hands. The orange furred fox gladly accepts by squeezing the wolf's big right paw, and he swings his husband's arm a little as they walk across the parking lot and then around the building. The NVA's entrance is decorated with a small amount of manicured shrubbery. The plants are arranged in rows, all of them spaced carefully and meticulously to create an air of efficiency. Vulpie admires them while traversing the tan colored sidewalk and reaches the door before Polar, so he breaks paws with his lover to open it.

A brown cat beats him to it, opening the glass door from inside, and Vulpie lets out a little nervous yelp in surprise. It's the sound you make when you're about to do something nice for someone but are shown up when you least expect it. It's not a problem, but the fox finds it mildly irritating. Surely the cat saw him coming... All of the windows have opaque black bulletproof glass, and the same glass covers the main entrance. It can be assumed that an animal can clearly see outside from within, so why did the cat wait until the last second to open the door before Vulpie got his paw on it?

"Hello, Mr. Vulpie!" The man says and takes a courteous step backwards. "Oh, forgive me!" The feline even acknowledges his odd choice to suddenly pull the door open right before Vulpie touched it.

"No worries! Thanks!" Vulpie quickly says, brushing off the weird moment with ease. The cat gives him a strange look as he passes by, and the fox can't help but notice. He isn't going to say anything about it, but something is definitely off.

"Hello." Polar smiles and walks inside.

"I'm sorry gentlemen... Can I please ask you to leave your automatic weapons outside?" The cat asks Rulef before he enters the lobby. "We already have plenty of security in here." The gray wolf nods in acceptance.

"I thought as much. May I and someone else come in with side arms?"

"That would be fine." The cat smiles in response, and the Blacktail commander turns around.

"Alright, you and you come with me." Rulef says to a black and a brown wolf. "Everyone else, at ease." Vulpie tries to spot Tiala in the crowd, but she's further back, and he's too short to see her face with so many mercenaries in the way. The two selected men come inside, and the doors slowly close behind them. They lock automatically after snapping into place.

"My apologies! I'm Albert Finx!" The cat says and outstretches a paw towards Vulpie. The orange furred fox quickly accepts it and shakes the man's hand with enthusiasm. Albert is quite short for a cat, and is only a little taller than he is.

"All good! So where are we going?"

"Mr. Lahnak is waiting for us, just inside." Albert replies, and points at a door to the left of the receptionist's desk. Vulpie didn't expect the meeting room to be quite so close to the entrance, but just shrugs in amusement.

"Ah! Well, that makes things easy!" He replies before stepping around the cat.

"We're very glad that you were able to come today." Albert courteously responds. "If you need refreshments, or would like to have a meal, the cafeteria is right through there." The brown cat points to the left, to another set of glass doors, and Vulpie stops for a moment to peer through them. The wide hallway looks like it continues about twenty feet before making a split, where animals can go left and visit the café, or make a right and head straight into an entertainment room. The lounge is lined with tables where people can enjoy their meals, or watch high end TVs on the wall. It's also right next to the conference room, but it looks like the glass windows that separate the meeting room from the cafe are one-way. Thus, Vulpie can see into the café, and watches some animals snacking and relaxing while entering the conference room. The conference room has a very large gray table in the center, and is lined with comfortable looking padded chairs. Voyeurism seems like a popular design theme, because the only wall in the meeting room that isn't made of reinforced one-way glass is the one behind the entrance lobby.

Several animals are waiting for the orange furred fox and white furred wolf, but one immediately draws Vulpie's attention. A black husky with a streak of white up his front is speaking with Druward, and he immediately looks at Vulpie when he draws near. He's wearing a black suit with white pin stripes that naturally complements his dark fur. The pin stripes accent the white fur on his throat, muzzle and part of his face, making the animal look almost indistinguishable from his clothing. He has intense blue eyes, and when he speaks, Vulpie almost coughs in laughter because his voice is so deliciously foreign. He sounds just like the stereotypical villain from one of those old black and white horror movies.

"Good day Mr. Vulpie! We're thrilled to have you with us! I'm Amsend Lahnak, director of the Governmental Security Bureau."

"How ya doin Count?" Vulpie grins, and the husky returns a playful smile.

"You like my accent?"

"Yeah, I guess. Just… Kind of funny!" Vulpie answers while struggling to subdue a giggle.

"I'm told it's rather thick." Amsend replies, and offers a paw. Vulpie shakes it, and Druward nods at the orange furred fox.

"GSB? Do you work for him?" Vulpie asks while pointing at Druward.

"Yes we do. Mr. Wraulgh oversees our operation." Amsend lies, but he doesn't miss a beat. Druward glances back and forth for a moment before taking his cue and running with it.

"Never needed them before but now they're definitely coming in handy. They provide additional surveillance for the bureau." The black furred wolf tells Vulpie, but the gay fox immediately recognizes that something is wrong. He looks between Druward and the husky, and notices the air of superiority permeating through Amsend. He takes note of this, but completely masks the thought behind an enthusiastic smile.

"Cool!"

"Vulpie." A familiar voice says. Vulpie turns to the right and takes a closer look at one of the animals he saw while walking in. A gray and black furred cat with yellow eyes offers him a paw, and the fox smiles when he sees one of his former pupils.

"Melrhei! Hey man!"

252

"Good to see you!" The cat answers, and they shake paws. He's wearing a simple yet elegant gray suit.

"Lookin good man! Got the suit and everything? What are you doing here?"

"I'm actually running the place. Howlstead recommended me." Melrhei answers, and points to his left. Vulpie looks, and is surprised to see the CTGD director is also attending the special meeting. He didn't notice him when he walked in because the man was busy speaking to a gray fox.

"Really? That's awesome! I'm glad to hear it! So you guys knew about the place and I didn't?"

"They're very tight with security and since you've been in the private sector, well, we've had to make do without you. But maybe that'll change after today."

"Oh, I see! Yeah…" Vulpie muses and smiles. "You must be the resident Vulpie.net badass then. Only Bawho could keep up with you."

"That's one way of putting it." Melrhei smirks.

"We're not greenhorns here, Vulpie!" The orange furred fox playfully replies and Melrhei chuckles.

"Good memories."

"Melrhei exceeded our expectations. Howlstead can't leave the CTGD, and we needed someone with a strong understanding of Vulpie.net, so I immediately thought about your team." Amsend comments. Vulpie looks back to him and nods politely. The orange fox continues his conversation with Melrhei, walking away from Polar, Amsend and Druward, and Amsend takes the opportunity to speak to Polar. "Mr. Arctic…" The husky says and offers a paw.

"Hello. Good to meet you." Polar happily responds while shaking the man's hand. The white furred wolf tenses up when Amsend suddenly squeezes his paw, testing his strength. The husky is way stronger than he looks, and Polar returns the challenge with all of his might. He manages to match Amsend's grip but not surpass it. "Arctic from Winters Dale, is it?"

"Yes." Polar replies, and pulls his paw free, bringing the short contest to an abrupt conclusion. Druward notices, but none of them mention the silent exchange. Silent competitions of this nature are sometimes required in wolf culture. It's not unusual, but Amsend is a dog, which catches Vulpie's husband completely off guard. Polar wonders whether the man intentionally crushes lupine paws in order to prove his worth right off the bat or if he's really just that strong.

"A full blooded descendant of Maro?" Amsend inquires with a creepy smile.

"I wouldn't say full blooded, but you can trace my family tree all the way back to 1104."

"But you carry the Arctic name... Arctics descended from Maro."

"So the legends say." Polar responds with a bewildered look. "But I don't think it matters in 2109."

"Funny you should say that, because it's a little known fact that the year is more on the measure of 3401. Present day is only a reflection of when they began to record time, two thousand one hundred and nine years ago."

"Oh... Yeah. Actually, my brother's a history professor, and he mentioned that to me not long ago. Something about a great catastrophe?"

"Precisely."

"Well, this is all very fascinating..." Polar frowns. Druward glances between the husky and the white furred wolf. Polar obviously feels uncomfortable about Amsend's bizarre curiosity, but the husky continues the conversation with a clever smile.

"Forgive me Mr. Arctic. I didn't mean to make you uncomfortable."

"No, it's fine. But why are you so interested in my past? I'm not special."

"Oh, but you are... She was an incredible woman."

"Maro?" Polar inquires and shakes his head in confusion. He gives Druward a look and the black furred wolf shrugs his shoulders. "Yeah, I guess she was? Are you a religious man?"

"Very. I'm what you might call... A Student of history..."

"Oh."

"I'm originally from Englavic, so forgive me if I seem intrusive. It's just that I have a strong interest in bloodlines and family crests."

"Do you come from an old family?"

"The oldest, but I could talk about this all morning."

"You've peaked my interest now. What family is it?"

"The Lahnaks."

"Lahnaks?"

"Yes."

"Never heard of them."

"We're a reclusive bunch. We own most of Englavic's real estate, and the burden is on us to find useful careers. I've always been interested in the world government, so I decided to become a civil servant."

"You're the director of the Governmental... Security?"

"Governmental Security Bureau."

"Well, I guess you found a suitable career then."

"I enjoy helping people, and we need Vulpie oh so badly."

"That building out front... Is that the GSB headquarters?"

"Yes."

"Pretty impressive."

"I thought so too." Amsend smiles, and Polar looks at Druward.

"They have more security than you guys." The white furred wolf snorts.

"They're the security branch of the bureau." Druward responds and clears his throat.

"So you'll be running things here at the Vulpie.net Agency?"

"I'll help Vulpie whenever I can, but Melrhei is the director." The husky answers.

"Wait. What do you mean? You think Vulpie's going to work here?" Polar asks with a surprised voice.

"Of course. It's one of the main reasons why we invited him here today. But I understand it will be a difficult sell. Just know that we can appreciate his talents."

"He doesn't have time to run this place and his company too. I assume you'll explain all of this in a little bit, but don't get your hopes up. I'm just being honest." Polar replies.

"We'll see. Maybe we can convince him otherwise." Amsend responds, and walks away from the two wolves. He heads over to Vulpie and Melrhei, who are moving towards Arthur Howlstead, most likely to initiate a conversation. "Are you fellows ready to begin?" The husky inquires, and Melrhei nods.

"Sure." Vulpie replies, and turns around. He heads over to the large conference table and chooses a seat on the northern side so he'll be able to see everyone with ease. The GSB's reserved parking lot is behind him, and he can watch both of the room's entrances from his spot, which makes him feel safer for some reason. Polar comes over and takes a chair next to his husband. He sits to the left of Vulpie so the fox will have a clear view of Druward and Amsend during the meeting. Druward pulls out a chair and sits on the right side of the table, while Amsend takes a seat on the southern end, with his back to the lobby door. A peculiar looking gray fox positions himself to the right of Amsend, and Arthur Howlstead sits on the left side of the table, from Polar and Vulpie's perspective.

"Alright then... Everyone seems to be here so we'll begin unless anyone objects?" Amsend says and looks around the table. No one disagrees, so he licks his lips. "Then let's get started..." The husky continues, and looks at Vulpie while speaking. "I'm Amsend Lahnak, director of the Governmental

Security Bureau. I requested this meeting in light of several concerning events that have threatened the world government. My organization provides crucial surveillance information for the bureau, but we're only a division of the GBI, so I'll defer to Mr. Wraulgh."

"Vulpie.net is alive and well." Druward responds, taking control of the conversation with a cynical voice. He looks around the table while speaking, but generally keeps his attention on Vulpie and Polar. "We've concluded that it was responsible for the mysterious attack on Lioness Station."

"What did you find? Did you actually find evidence that it was involved?" Vulpie quickly inquires.

"Nothing. No one was actually hurt or killed, so we're assuming it used a VulGrid to carry out the attack."

"But weren't there animals on the news that said they saw the whole thing and Aila killed several people?" Polar asks.

"We do have several eyewitnesses, but not a shred of tangible evidence. No blood, no bodies... Nothing... No signs of a struggle, and the train was in perfect condition."

"What else?" Vulpie breathlessly inquires. "Aila, yeah, I'm thinking it was Vulpie.net too, but surely you have more than that to go on."

"Vulpie.net attacked Fort Elbrus last Thursday, and fifty eight animals were killed. You haven't seen it on the news because we've been suppressing the story." The black furred wolf pauses after dropping the bomb, and Vulpie goes stiff.

"Wh... What? No! It's never killed people! You can't be serious! Are you serious?"

"Yes."

"So... Fuck man, the Deivas are what? They're lose? Did Vulpie.net take them too?"

"No, that's the strange part. It didn't take them. It only seemed interested in helping them escape."

"You mean they're just running around out there? They're out there right now?"

"Yes."

"Oh my God." Vulpie groans and puts his face in his paws. "I TOLD you... I WARNED YOU!" The fox growls, and drops his paws from his muzzle. "I TOLD YOU TO DESTROY THEM! WHY DIDN'T YOU LISTEN TO ME?"

"Not my decision, Vulpie. I'm sorry." Druward answers.

"This shit never ends... God... What the fuck are we supposed to do now? What am I going to do now? My stock's gonna tank, that's for sure!"

"We're going to destroy them." The black furred wolf replies, but Vulpie gives him a tired look.

"Like Evil Vulpie?"

"Yeah I know, the fiasco on the Sevrif didn't exactly inspire confidence, but things are different now. We finally have weapons that can kill them. We CAN take them down, Vulpie, I promise, but we have to find them first."

"Maybe I could be a painter..." Vulpie says with a wacky look and turns to Polar. "Think I could do that? They let you paint in prison, right? Maybe I'll do that. Paint some foxes in a rowboat." Amsend chuckles in amusement, but Polar is too worried to laugh.

"We know this isn't your fault." Druward quickly responds. "No one's blaming you. The government wanted to keep them, just like Evil Vulpie, and now the government is responsible for their escape... But... We're flying blind here, Vulpie. We need your help."

"Oh rearry?" Vulpie sarcastically responds. "Druward, I love you dude, but come on. You know they won't listen. What do they want me to do? Sit on a computer and tell them how screwed we are? I can't hack into Vulpie.net anymore; it's too powerful."

"You did on Zeravyn." The GBI director responds, and Vulpie shakes his head in disagreement.

"That was different."

"Rearry?"

"I hacked into a local machine, right there at the heart of the problem. Here, there is no central problem! We have three HUGE problems. Want me to break out my laptop and hack em with Wi-Fi?"

"We'll use VulGrids. Polar did on the Endeavor, right? He used your VulGrid to disable them, didn't he?"

"Yeah, but they were nearby, and distracted too. It also took too long. You think they'll hesitate when they recognize VulGrid's powerful signal trying to crack their CPUs? No. They remember what happened last time, and they'll be all over it if you try it again. They'll destroy it before we have a chance to do anything. Besides, if Vulpie.net's using VulGrids too, then there's no way I can hack them. Think about it... Vulpie.net's machine will have super encrypted code that's specifically designed to counter mine."

"Mr. Vivixen..." Amsend says, but is instantly intercepted by the orange furred fox.

"Just call me Vulpie, Count."

"I must be frank with you... I hear a lot of excuses that don't befit the universe's greatest criminal... You single handedly corrupted every computer in existence, and now you act like there's nothing you can do about this situation? Be honest."

"I am being honest. What part do you think I'm lying about? I can crush chess champions, solve world class mathematical problems for fun, and cook the best butter steak you've ever eaten, but I can't do shit against something that can instantly calculate the weight and density of every single fur on your body. I'm just a fox! This thing is immortal! It knows everything I know, and everything I don't. And YOU want me to stop it?"

"The only reason the Deivas ended up at Elbrus was because your VulGrid disabled them. If your husband could take them down with a machine you created, and you weren't even there, then what's holding you back? You're obviously capable of diffusing this situation. We'll provide the firepower and you'll provide the brains."

"Oh no I won't!" Vulpie quickly replies and slams the table with his little paws. Polar blinks in surprise and gives his husband a concerned look. "Look fellas, I'm done! I'm fucking done with this! I don't work for you anymore. I went to the private sector so I wouldn't be responsible for this kind of shit and you're not dragging me back in." Druward sighs loudly after hearing the gay fox's defiant statement. The GBI director gives Amsend a satisfied look, but the husky is completely unfazed. He stares down Vulpie and doesn't break eye contact for a single moment.

"Yes, yes, your temper tantrums are legendary, but we know you really just don't want to clean up the mess you've made."

"My mess? Oh, you fucking prick! Fuck you! All of you tall smug predators can kiss my ass! All you do is posture and tell everybody else what they should be doing! Ya got your nice suit, and you're real handsome, yeah? Well my suit's better and I'm way better looking than you! I guess that makes me right, huh?"

"Vulpie." Arthur says, and the orange furred fox turns to his left in surprise. He completely forgot about his old friend, and the look the CTGD director gives him makes his fur stand on end. He remembers swearing at him in the white room, and how his former boss let it go... The gray wolf looks very worried.

"Can't win." Vulpie groans in frustration. "Damned if I do, damned if I don't."

"I'm sorry this conversation got out of control, but we have a job to do. People depend on us." Amsend says while carefully observing Vulpie's body language.

"Is this the part where you threaten me? You gonna threaten me with jail time? Come on! I'm ready!"

"No one said anything about locking you up." Druward responds, and the gay fox frowns at him.

"Oh! You finally speak! You guys wanna pin this shit on me and make me feel responsible for everything? Well fuck you! Fuck both of you suits! GBI? GSB? What the fuck ever, bro! You keep on sounding official and make some threats! Come on!"

"No one threatened you." Amsend stresses with a fatherly voice, and Vulpie recoils.

"Yeah! Course not! Bullshit! I know something's going on... I don't know what it is, but you two... Yeah! YOU TOO! Druward!" Vulpie growls, and the coal furred wolf takes a deep breath. He makes sure to hide his shame with an equally hostile demeanor. "Something's up! And I'm not gonna take the fall for this! No way! I'm not gonna tell the press I run the National Vulpie.net Agency while you laugh your asses off! You can forget it!"

"Vulpie, what's wrong?" Arthur whispers. "Calm down."

"I know a setup when I see one! This is a set up! I'm being set-the-fuck-up!"

"You have us all wrong, Vulpie. We're not your enemies." Amsend promises with a very sweet voice. His thick accent almost magically dispels the tension in the room. "I have an idea... I know what we must do."

"What? Oh, tell me!"

"You must come visit me in Englavic." Amsend smiles and Polar and Vulpie both blink in surprise.

"Uhhhhhhhhhh?"

"I have a beautiful home that you simply must see. We've gotten off on the wrong foot."

"You want me at your house?"

"My castle. I own a large estate that is a fairly significant attraction for animals around the world... I want to help you. WE want to help you, but this arguing solves nothing."

"I don't think a vacation is gonna solve anything either. Thanks but no thanks, ya creep."

"Listen to me." Amsend grins. He suddenly looks very handsome and quite interested in fulfilling Vulpie's needs. "Forget about the NVA. We don't have to do this anytime soon, not if it destroys your confidence in us. I know you feel threatened, and I also know that you don't think that I understand the gravity of the situation, but I do. I've been watching Vulpie.net ever since you turned it loose and I know how terrible it is. We need to work together, not against each other."

"Well, those are some fine words." Vulpie dryly responds, but Amsend's inviting smile manages to penetrate his defenses. The husky looks strangely appreciative. He doesn't appear angry after being cursed at and accused of conspiracy.

"What do you think, Polar?" Druward asks with a friendly voice. "Help us out here."

"Leave him out of this. This is between you and me." Vulpie quickly replies while Polar looks over Druward and Amsend. They seem completely reasonable, and the white furred wolf licks his lips before speaking to his husband with a small voice.

"Aren't you being a little paranoid?"

"Paranoid? Polar! Don't you see what they're doing?" The orange furred fox whispers and glances at Amsend.

"What choice do they have? You're the only one that knows what we're dealing with. I'd help them if I could, but I can't. No one can, except for you."

"Polar... Please don't take their side."

"I'm not taking sides." The white furred wolf calmly responds, and Vulpie groans in defeat.

"I know we've been through a lot, Vulpie, but I did destroy Vulpie.net's factory for you." Druward comments. "I think we made the right decision, but it almost cost me my job. I have to explain why I detonated a core bomb to the same ethics committee every month."

"Yeah, and I helped you out with something pretty serious too, didn't I?" Vulpie replies and raises his eyebrows. Druward remembers the AFR disaster, and he nods in agreement, but also raises his eyebrows, silently suggesting that their score should have been settled on Zeravyn.

"Thousands of animals draw a check from Vulpie Industries, and I'm not interested in putting them out of work. How's it going to look if I speak for the National Vulpie.net Agency while those fake Deivas are out there killing people? I have a business to run."

"Do you really want to be in your tower when they show up?" Amsend inquires with an innocent voice. "What would you do?"

"I don't know." Vulpie answers. "They might show up at our house!"

"Then maybe the best thing to do is let them protect us?" Polar quietly suggests. "Since we can't protect ourselves?"

"Druward... Who the fuck is this guy?" Vulpie asks while staring at Amsend. Arthur puts his paw over his face in embarrassment, but the question suddenly intrigues Polar. Amsend does possess a rather mysterious quality.

"He introduced himself." Druward firmly answers. "Could you stop swearing?"

"Who the fuck is he? I've never seen him before today... I've met with you, and the president when I hacked the world, but I never saw this guy!" The gay fox declares. "Why not?"

"My organization specializes in secrecy, Mr. Vivixen." Amsend explains.

"He works for me." Druward adds, and Vulpie nods with a cynical smirk.

"Yeah? Such an important position, yet I don't know who he is, and I've spied on everybody! That's right! I admit it!"

"Mr. Lahnak is just a civil servant. What's your problem?" Druward growls.

"He's my fucking problem!" Vulpie growls back. "I know it! HE! ... He's YOUR FUCKING BOSS! ISN'T HE?"

"Vulpie." Polar says and touches his husband's leg. "Stop."

"No Polar! I'm right! I know I am!" Vulpie defiantly shouts, and turns his attention to Druward. "He OWNS YOU! DOESN'T HE?"

"Enough!" Amsend says, and raises his paws in a diplomatic gesture. "That's enough... You're too smart for your own good..."

"What?" Melrhei asks, and Vulpie quickly glances at his friend.

"Yeah? What?" The orange furred fox quickly inquires, and Amsend slowly stretches his left paw towards Druward. He puts it on the GBI director and squeezes the black furred wolf's right shoulder in a friendly fashion.

"Don't blame Druward. He's responsible for more things than you can imagine, and my secrecy is one of them." The husky states, and Druward's eyes widen. He looks at Polar, Vulpie, and the others, but eventually releases a sigh of relief.

"I knew it! I fucking knew it!"

"Please... Enough..." Amsend says and gently waves his paw at Vulpie. "Yes, Vulpie... You've never seen me before, because I hold a very powerful position within the world government. And what I'm about to say must never leave this table... Do you understand?"

"Sure." Vulpie replies, and leans back in wild satisfaction. "Let's hear it!"

"Wow." Polar whispers.

"Are you much of a conspiracy theorist? I don't ask the question as a put down. I'm simply attempting to test the depth of your knowledge."

"Well, some conspiracies are real, aren't they? By the word's very definition, when one or more parties work together to accomplish a goal in secret, they conspire." Vulpie answers.

"That's exactly right."

"Like Druward telling the press a sniper destroyed Evil Vulpie on the roof of the Cyber Technologies Government Division."

"You're exactly right." Amsend smiles and releases Druward. "There are rich and powerful animals that influence the world government. A fox as smart as you surely understands the power of money..."

"Gee, thanks."

"Not an insult."

"K."

"But you know there are animals that will always have their way, if they can ram it through legal channels."

"Or illegal channels."

"Yes." Amsend admits and smirks. "But the Governmental Security Bureau tries to maintain as much professionalism as possible. I'm not going to lie to you. There is corruption, without a doubt... But I am honestly here to help you. Vulpie.net poses a major threat to my contacts, and the government's interests as well. You understand this."

"Sure. I can't believe you admitted it, but... Yeah." Vulpie mischievously smiles.

"Well, enjoy your small victory, Vulpie. It doesn't bother me. We figured working with you would require a lot of lying on our part. Now that we can be fully honest with you, things should go much smoother. Now there's no tension... Agreed?"

"Sure. So what's the real deal with the NVA?"

"It's the same thing we've been telling you. The only difference is that I run it. Melrhei reports to me, but I'm sure that isn't much of a surprise to you, considering the large facility we have out front."

"Yeah."

"Wait…" Polar interrupts and scowls at Druward. "You mean you've been working with him the whole time? And you never told us?"

"I never had to. Everything that happened between us was entirely my fault." Druward responds, and Polar raises an eyebrow.

"I guess so."

"Poor Druward. Didn't know he had this guy kicking his ass, on top of the president!" Vulpie grins, and the black furred wolf rolls his eyes.

"Vulpie." Amsend says, and gets the gay fox's undivided attention. "We have a serious problem. These things have to be destroyed. And the machine that attacked Fort Elbrus perfectly matches the description of the creature you encountered on Zeravyn. I only received reports of its destruction… So could it have survived?"

"No way. I mean… Captain Ristau said it was vaporized."

"Completely destroyed." Druward chimes in, and Amsend nods.

"Yet it's back… So that means there's more than one. If there's more than one… You can see where I'm going with this."

"I wish I could help. I have no idea what Vulpie.net's up too." Vulpie responds.

"Then we need to find out. That's why we brought you here." Amsend stresses and licks his lips. He watches the gay fox very carefully, and assesses his posture. Vulpie seems amiable, but he knows that could quickly change if the fox thinks he's being lied to again. The husky knows he will have to use every trick he has. He looks at Arthur and glances at Melrhei. "Could I ask you two to step out for a moment?"

"Me?" Melrhei asks in confusion.

"And me?" Howlstead inquires.

"Yes." Amsend responds, but offers nothing else in the way of explanation. Howlstead frowns, but doesn't take offense to the request. He gets out of his chair and Melrhei follows suit. The gray and black furred cat is already accustomed to taking orders from Amsend, but he does give Vulpie a forsaken look. The two animals walk over to the lobby entrance, and after they exit and close the door behind them, Amsend looks at the gray fox that's sitting across from Vulpie. The man has been completely silent so far.

"Are you going to tell him?" The fox asks the husky, and his voice makes Vulpie's fur stand on end. It sounds creepily familiar.

"I think we should. He wants answers, so let's tell him the truth and see where things go."

"If you insist." The gray fox replies and sets his brown eyes on Vulpie.

"Tell me what?"

"This is Velix Vixil." Amsend states while gesturing towards the gray fox with his right paw. "His family owns the Association of Fox Rights."

"Owns it? I thought Karl Vulches…" Vulpie says and trails off. "Vixil?"

"Yes." The gray fox answers, and his creepily familiar voice makes Vulpie's fur stand on end; the man is undoubtedly a relative of Zorpiv Vixil. He even has an identical fur pattern. Like all gray foxes, his fur is an amalgam of gray, black, red and white. Velix has very pronounced fur colors, however, and the black fur underneath his chin and around the sides of his muzzle is very dark. The coal streaks that begin at the corners of his eye sockets and stretch out to the sides of his cheek bones clash just as vivaciously. The red hair he has on his throat, chest, belly and down the front of his legs and arms contrasts against the areas of white, which are equally noticeable, making Velix one memorable fox, just like Zorpiv.

"Are you related to Zorpiv Vixil?"

"Sadly, yes…" Velix sighs and relaxes in his chair. "And there's no need to whisper about what happened. I know everything."

"Let's just stop right here for a moment." Vulpie replies and licks his lips. "So you're... You're part of this super rich secret society Amsend's been talking about?"

"Yes." Velix bluntly answers.

"So that means you own the Vuldrofein too, right?" The orange furred fox defensively inquires. "You tried to have me killed?"

"No. That was Karl's doing."

"Yeah? Then why was Zorpiv in on it? Was he one of your grandsons or something?"

"He most certainly was not." Velix quickly answers. "There are two kinds of Vixils. The first are members of my family. The second are Zorpiv's useless ancestors. We purged them from our ranks long ago... Zorpiv's father and uncle were criminals... They constantly asked for handouts from the family, and then turned around and wasted it on fruitless endeavors. Eventually, Nolan Vixil, Zorpiv's father, accumulated so much debt that my friend, Karl Vulches, had to bail him out. Yes, Karl was my friend, but I didn't know what he was planning to do."

"But you two talked about it a lot, I bet, didn't ya?" Vulpie smirks. "I bet ya hate me too, huh?"

"I'm past it, Vulpie... My only concern is protecting the Vixil fortune and the Association of Fox Rights."

"How can you own the AFR if they publicly elect their members?"

"Please..." Velix responds. He doesn't say anything else, and Vulpie nods.

"You choose who's going to run the show, and then have fake elections." Vulpie deduces.

"Several candidates... All chosen and funded by the Vixil fortune..."

"Funny you should say that when Zorpiv tried to kill me because his family owed so much to Karl. One of Druward's men told me about it, right after I killed Zorpiv in self-defense."

"Let me warn you now, that even though his family embarrassed mine, he was still a Vixil." Velix sharply declares. Vulpie pauses, and just for a moment, he recognizes the same insanity in Velix's brown eyes.

"Well Mr. Vixil, I'm sorry Zorpiv tried to rape and kill me." Vulpie sarcastically responds. "I'm sure he was a great guy under different circumstances."

"He was a fool... But still one of us..." Velix ominously replies. "Yes, we talked about you in great detail, and I admit, I agreed with a lot of Karl's opinions about you, but it's in the past now. I didn't know he was going to take things that far."

"So aren't you mad at Zorpiv for killing your best buddy?" Vulpie asks with a stern tone. "I saw it. He just blew him away with a smile on his face."

"It's complicated..."

"Whatever." Vulpie sighs.

"I'm not your enemy... But don't make me your enemy..."

"Ohhhhhhhhhhhhhhhhhhhhhhhhhhhhhhhh!!!" Vulpie mischievously responds and suddenly points at Amsend, and points his left paw at Velix as well. "Now it's obvious! I see it now!"

"What?" Velix asks with a cold voice.

"You two..." Vulpie says, and drops his paws. "You both must be part of that big old conspiracy theory animals talk about on the internet! Yeah!"

"Not just the internet." Amsend comments and Vulpie grins at him.

"Yeah?"

"We exist."

"The Sons of Velora! That's it, isn't it? I'm sitting here with two big influential Sons of Velora people." The orange furred fox giggles. Velix frowns and looks to his left, at Amsend. The gray fox has a worried expression, but Amsend only shrugs in response.

"Is that who you are?"

"We don't advertise."

"Amsend?" Velix whispers, and the husky shrugs his shoulders again.

"He'd figure it out eventually. He's too smart. He already knows the GSB is above the GBI, and now he knows you're above everyone in the AFR, so he's just going to the next logical step."

"Exactly." Vulpie smirks, and Velix sighs. He looks at the gay fox and crosses his arms.

"Then you understand who you're dealing with? Yes?"

"Not exactly. Is all the Aila worship stuff true? Or is that just paranoid people on the net?" Vulpie asks with an adorable voice.

"We do not worship Goddess Aila." Velix growls with an indignant look.

"Just checking."

"You have a loud little mouth, but you won't be talking about this to anyone." The gray fox threatens, and Vulpie immediately puts his paws up in the air as if he's about to be arrested.

"I won't! I swear!"

"This is no joking matter. If you want to live, you won't say a word."

"Easy, Velix…" Amsend quickly interrupts with a smile. "Vulpie's only playing with you. He can't help himself. I think he understands…"

"I do. I promise I won't say a word." Vulpie declares, but the old gray fox doesn't respond. Vulpie stops smiling and nods at him.

"Are you getting all of this, Polar?" Druward asks, and the white furred wolf looks at the GBI director in surprise. The black furred wolf has an amused look on his face.

"Now you see what I have to deal with."

"Yeah." Polar replies, and gulps before looking at Velix again.

"You will never call us the Sons of Velora. We will not tolerate it. The only time you may mention our organization by name is when you know everyone around you is one of us. Is that understood?"

"Yes sir." Vulpie answers. Polar glances at him, and notices how serious his husband looks. The situation is extremely tense, and Vulpie knows better than to push Velix any further. "So what do you want? I know why Amsend's here."

"He asked me to attend... Just in case..." Velix quietly responds.

"In case I wanted to know more?"

"Possibly."

"Okay. Well... Uh... Anything else you guys want to tell me?" Vulpie asks and looks at Amsend. "I feel like you're not telling me the whole story."

"Well... How much do you want to hear?" Amsend seductively inquires. "This is one of those pivotal moments... Vulpie..."

"Yeah?"

"Oh yes."

"Like, you're going to threaten me, or what?"

"We've told you who we are, so there's no turning back now... You'll have to accept your position at the NVA, OR... Polar and Druward will have to leave the room so we can discuss a second option..." Polar blinks when he hears the husky and squints at him.

"What?" The white furred wolf asks, but Amsend only returns a cold smile. "Why do I have to leave?"

"Polar's staying. We don't keep any secrets."

"You don't have a choice." Amsend warns. He suddenly appears very threatening and very generous at the same time. "How much confidence does your husband have in you if he won't allow you to make a decision on your own?"

"I trust Vulpie, but I'm not going to let you threaten him." Polar growls. Druward remains silent. He knows Amsend and Velix are not going to yield.

"Your parents live at 3141 Snowy Den Road in Winters Dale." Amsend tells the arctic wolf and gives him a dangerous smile. "Lovely town."

"Let's go Vulpie." Polar says, and starts to get up, but Druward waves his paw in concern.

"No Polar. We should let them talk." The GBI director counsels, and the snow wolf shakes his head in disbelief.

"I'm not listening to anymore of this."

"You don't know who you're dealing with."

"That's what I'm afraid of."

"What harm is there in letting them talk things over? Let's just give them some time."

"If we can't speak with Vulpie alone, I'm afraid there will be complications... Please just do us this one courtesy, Mr. Arctic of Winters Dale." Amsend says and Polar turns to Vulpie. The orange furred fox looks terrified.

"Polar." Druward says with an authoritative voice. The black furred wolf leans to the left and waits for a response while Vulpie's husband looks over Velix and Amsend. They stare back at him with intransigent expressions. "Come on." Druward coaxes, and stands up.

"Vulpie will tell me everything, so I don't understand why I have to leave."

"They're cautious people." The GBI director responds, and leaves the table. He slowly heads towards the door, and Polar turns to Vulpie again.

"What should I do?"

"I guess you can go. I mean, you're totally right. I'm gonna tell you everything anyway, so it doesn't matter." Vulpie anxiously responds.

"Alright... But I don't like this... Whatever they tell you..." Polar whispers and shakes his head in concern.

"I know. I'm not going to make a decision today." Vulpie answers, and the gay fox notices Amsend seems pleased by his statement. Polar glares at the husky and the gray fox but eventually stands in defeat. He sighs and walks away from the table while Amsend smiles at Vulpie. He waits until

Druward leads the white furred wolf out of the room and shuts the door behind them.

"Well... First, I believe some congratulations are in order. We knew you were smart, but I never dreamed that you would connect the dots so quickly. You just weren't going to be satisfied until you had the truth, and now you do... Bravo."

"But." Vulpie quietly responds.

"BUT..." Amsend smirks and licks his lips. "You've put us in a difficult situation. You cannot leave this room until you fully understand the consequences of your curiosity... The Sons of Velora is quite real, little Vulpie, and you're looking at the two most powerful men on the planet." The husky says in pride. He pauses for a moment to let his statement sink in. Vulpie knows better than to say anything at this point. He's going to listen, and when Amsend feels the time is right, he speaks again. "You thought Druward and the Association of Fox Rights were bad? ...You cannot imagine what we can do... Our organization owns the SWG military, the police force, the judicial system... All of it... The Vixils control every major news network, and that makes Velix the judge, jury, and executioner of public opinion. The AFR likes you and helps you whenever they can, but that could all come crashing down." The husky warns, and Vulpie looks to Velix. The gray fox has a slightly insane expression on his face, and the gay fox quickly recognizes it for what it is. He can see where Zorpiv's insidious nature came from... The man is just better at hiding it.

"And I own every company that is part of the military industrial complex." Amsend continues. "My family signed the world government into law during the Great Sufian Conflict. The Lahnaks work paw in paw with the Vixils to make sure the system is perpetuated, and we remain in power. THAT'S... The cold hard truth..."

"Impressive." Vulpie smiles with a concerned face.

"We think so. We've been doing this for centuries, and so far, so good."

"I know where you're going with this. At least I think I do."

"Mmm?" The husky hums.

"If what you say is true, then... You have everything you need, EXCEPT for technological domination." Vulpie answers. "That's where I come in."

"Couldn't have said it better myself." Velix comments and gives the gay fox a devious smile. "It certainly would make our work easier... Knowing that our computer systems are being run by the smartest animal who's ever lived... Just think of the possibilities, Vulpie."

"But I'll never be one of you. This stuff you're telling me... It won't work. I know better. You'll just use me for all I'm worth and throw me under the bus when you're through. It doesn't matter what you say."

"You're wise not to trust us, but luckily for you, we'll always need what you have. You created Vulpie.net. You're the only one who will ever be able to control it, so if you play your cards right... And you make the right decision... The sky's the limit."

"Riiiiiiiiiiiiiight." Vulpie laughs and wiggles in his chair. "Your super rich families are going to welcome me to the club? A gay fox who came from nothing, who's married to a gay wolf, and people call the Antikhalan..." Amsend laughs at Vulpie's statement, and he grins as well, but wonders why the husky almost bursts into a roar of amusement.

"I'd rather you not be gay, but my family will accept you. You're still a fox. We'll look out for you." Velix offers and Vulpie takes in a deep breath.

"Really?"

"Of course." The gray fox responds and puts his paws together on the table. "Vulpie... You're here because you are exceptional. Amsend and I would never invite an animal into our inner circle unless we deemed him worthy. The things you've done... You hacked the world with your computer virus... You created the world's first true artificial intelligence, and have been running a very successful business all on your own."

"I've had plenty of help." Vulpie admits and Velix nods.

"The AFR always helps foxes, but you design all of your products, and people like them. They want the services you provide, your image... Your brand..."

"Do go on!" Vulpie mischievously replies and crosses his arms.

"You ARE a star... And if you work with us... Vulpie..." Velix whispers and nods his head with finality. "You can, and will, have anything you want."

"Aw, come on... Anything? Yeah right."

"Anything." Amsend promises and winks at the gay fox. "Money? Sex? Something more particular? It doesn't matter... You'll get it... You mentioned being gay. Well? We have plenty of gay animals in our organization. You won't have to hide who you are... When we say anything... We mean it..."

"Like what?" Vulpie asks, accidently choking on his own voice.

"We've peaked your interest now!" Amsend grins while the gay fox tries to hide his enthusiasm.

"I'm married anyway."

"So?" The husky asks and shrugs his shoulders. "What he doesn't know won't hurt him."

"It'll hurt me. I can't lie to Polar." Vulpie softly replies and Amsend winks at him again.

"But you want to know more?"

"Well, I don't know! You brought it up!"

"You wouldn't be the first fox to ask for a wolf orgy..."

"Oh my God." Vulpie groans in embarrassment, but can't help but smile. The conversation is making him hot.

"Oh they happen... All the time... That's what we've been telling you. You can have anything you want. I'm sure Polar makes you feel good, but why settle for less, when you could have a new Polar every week? Every day for that matter... Handsome gay men just chomping at the bits to get a piece of you..."

"I can't... I just can't, though." Vulpie whispers with a guilty look. "Polar won't... I love him. I can't do this. I can't say yes!"

"I know you love him, but let's face it, you're the one in charge. You make the big decisions, don't you? You didn't ask for his permission before attacking the world with Vulpie.net."

"That was different. I would have, if I could do it all over again."

"You expect us to believe that?"

"I love Polar with all my heart." Vulpie growls and gives Amsend a stern glare.

"Then keep loving him. No one's asking you to turn your back on him. And as a matter of fact... You'll be helping his family as well. Want to take care of the Arctics? Fine. Money? No problem. Someone wants a job? Not a problem."

"You can't be serious."

"We're absolutely serious. That's what we keep telling you!" Amsend chuckles.

"Okay... So like, since I'm gonna get everything I want... If I asked you to give Polar's brothers and sister a raise, you could do it? You could make their bosses do that?"

"Of course."

"Pfft... Yeah..." The orange furred fox growls, but can't take his eyes off of Amsend. The husky's unyielding confidence is starting to wear him down.

"Within reason."

"You're saying you could just tell the accounting department at some random college or law firm to just increase certain employee's pay, and they would do it?"

"You know it wouldn't work that way. Large companies have their claws in smaller markets. The orders would come from on high, and a regional manager would speak with the college president or the law firm's CEO."

"Regional manager of what? Sons of Velora?"

"Yes. But of course, we operate via proxy, so the corporations we utilize on a regular basis have no record of that name. You won't find any references to a secret organization." Amsend answers and smiles. "But none of that should concern you. You're asking whether it can be done or not, and the answer is a resounding yes."

"Yeah, but what good would it do if we got caught? I can't imagine how fucked up it would look if I'm having the government pay Polar's family, and Velix over here, decides to tell the universe."

"That's why you can never talk. As long as you stay loyal to us, everything will be fine." Velix replies. "You're a fox. You know how this works. Just keep your mouth shut."

"I must be a different kind of fox, because I don't like lying... It makes me feel bad..."

"Why? What's the problem?" Velix asks with a confused expression. "Everyone lies. Even the people looking into corruption are corrupt. That's how it works."

"Not at Vulpie Industries." Vulpie mutters and looks down at the table. "What have I gotten myself into?"

"You're looking at it the wrong way." Amsend counsels with a fatherly voice. "Life is short. You want to love and help the world, but you can't. It's too big and too many animals don't give a shit... The only thing you can do, without question, is take care of yourself and your family... So take care of Polar. If you really do love him with all your heart, then give him everything he could ever want. Make his family rich beyond their wildest dreams, and do all of it without them knowing... Or let them know you made it happen. It doesn't matter, as long as you only tell them that you have powerful friends."

"They won't take handouts."

"Everyone says that at first." Velix comments.

"No, they really won't. They like to earn what they have. Sure, Polar's family is well off, but all of them work, and they manage their investments. They're smart."

"Then just tell Polar… We can have them promoted, or whatever is necessary. Their superiors will invent a reason after they've been properly bribed or threatened."

"We don't want any threats." Vulpie interrupts.

"Just bribes then." Amsend smirks.

"Okay… So let's just say… Let's say for a moment, that I'll do it…" Vulpie quietly announces. "How much time will I have to spend on this? I don't want it to consume my life."

"Very little. But you MUST help us when we need you." The husky answers.

"You say that, but you want me to run this huge place?" Vulpie asks while gesturing towards the ceiling.

"Melrhei has been doing a fine job so far. What I need, is for you to occasionally audit his procedures, and handle any problems Velix has. You'll be working very closely with him."

"Making propaganda?"

"Of course." Velix says with an emotionless voice.

"This is not what I wanted to be when I grew up." Vulpie laments.

"We're offering you the world on a silver platter." Amsend replies and squints at the gay fox. "What more could you possibly want?"

"I know most animals would just say yes, but I'm a little concerned. Ya know? I thought the world was filled with good honest people that did the right things."

"Sure you do." Velix says and rolls his eyes. "You... The fox that taunted the universe and crashed the stock market just for fun..."

"Maybe I've changed? Ever think of that?" Vulpie asks with an incredulous expression. "Do you even have a shred of honor?"

"More than you could know. I'm honored to work with the Lahnaks, and our families share a bond stronger than you can imagine. If you join us, we can add the Arctics as well. We'd add the Vivixens, if you had a family..."

"Yeah, thanks for reminding me."

"It's not as hard as you think. You can still live life exactly the way you have been. The only difference is that you'll have very important commitments to us. We won't turn on you because things don't always go the way we'd like them too. We know you're not perfect. But you're very talented, and you're the final piece of the puzzle. You were completely right, Vulpie. We do need someone to dominate the technological spectrum... And you're the man for the job... It's time to take hold of your destiny."

"My destiny?" Vulpie sighs. "Oh geez."

"Okay, look... We've made the offer..." Amsend firmly responds. "It's time to make a decision."

"I told Polar I wouldn't."

"Tell him you didn't. Just vacation with me in Englavic, as I suggested, and he'll warm to the idea."

"He can see right through me. I can't hide it."

"Are you Vulpie Vivixen or not?" Velix growls. "The way you talk, you'd think we have the wrong animal."

"He's my HUSBAND!" The orange furred fox snarls. "I'm sorry if I'm not mean enough for you, but for me, the sun rises and sets with him."

"True love is quite a rare thing." Amsend smiles. "But let me ask you a question. If you care about him so much, why haven't you told him about your business with Vander Clishaw?" A cold wave of dread rushes over Vulpie. He freezes, and can only stare at Amsend in shock. "Surely you haven't... But if so... How does he justify living with you, knowing that you got away with murder."

"I didn't kill him! I hated that bastard, but I didn't do it!" Vulpie defensively responds.

"Huh... Well, that's rather odd... I've seen the evidence, and there's no question about it. The murderer stabbed him in his left side, while he was sitting in his armchair watching TV, and the wound indicates that the attacker was rather short. Had a wolf killed Clishaw, the entry and exit lacerations would have been at a diagonal angle, because the attacker would have to crouch down, but instead, they were nice and horizontal, as if the assailant were much smaller.

"Could have been any fox! He raped a lot of boys! That's not proof!"

"You're the only fox he raped. The others were young wolves."

"How the fuck do you know all of this? What's wrong with you? You investigated that before even meeting me?"

"Druward's been very helpful, hasn't he? He buried your first murder during the Vulpie.net crisis, but we managed to find the police department's official report."

"My first murder? I've never killed anyone!"

"You've killed two animals." Velix interjects. "Zorpiv was your second."

"In self-defense!"

"Was it? The cover story for that sordid affair was rather miraculous. Somehow, special agent and director Druward Wraulgh tracked Karl Vulches and his men to an undisclosed house in the Vauvus National Forest. Oddly, the media never disclosed who the home belong to, or how he alone was able to arrive just in time..."

"Doesn't prove I did anything wrong! They kidnapped me!"

"Did they?" Velix asks with an insidious look. "Maybe Druward helped you kill them? Maybe Karl and Nathan were causing problems for you, and you wanted them dead? They didn't break any laws. They were just working for the Association of Fox Rights, but you couldn't stand it anymore... So you asked your friend for help... And Druward's actions on Zeravyn clearly show that he's been helping you. He provided you with the means to get there, and also set off the bomb at your request... Add new revelations about Vander Clishaw to this little stew of intrigue, and I'd wager you'd have trouble sleeping at night."

"Is that a threat? Are you threatening me?" Vulpie growls with a wild look.

"Threaten is too kind a word." Velix responds, and for a moment, he looks just like Zorpiv. Vulpie's quite upset, and his fast mind has already merged the two together on a subconscious level. It puts the orange furred fox into a state of panic. Vulpie pants and looks from Velix to Amsend several times. "SO! What's it going to be, SPORT?"

"Easy..." Amsend says and smiles at Vulpie. The orange furred fox knows they're playing a depraved version of good cop bad cop on him, but the method is still highly effective.

"I want to go home." Vulpie whispers while recoiling into his chair with a broken look.

"It's going to be alright." Amsend promises while tears well up in Vulpie's eyes. "You're going to make the right choice, aren't you? You know none of that's going to happen, because we're going to be friends." The gay fox tries to respond, but can only mumble something in a state of despair. "Velix is your friend as well. Don't hold this against him... It just had to be said."

"Yeah..." Vulpie sniffles while nodding in agreement.

"It's a complex world out there, Sporty." Velix comments. "But now you're in the big league. This is it. It's time to wake up. You are the smartest animal in the universe. Your genius is unparalleled, and you DESERVE this."

"I do, don't I?" Vulpie grimaces.

"Yes. The same way my family deserves its privileges because we've protected our interests for centuries. We earned our power, and you have too. You are not our slave, Vulpie. As Amsend succinctly put it, you will always have a gift that we will need. Yes, we are threatening you now, but it has to be done in this manner. You understand our position. We must protect our families and you have enormous influence in the technological realm. Our only choice was to make you an offer you couldn't refuse."

"Yeah." Vulpie agrees and just barely manages to look at Velix.

"But we're generous, and that's why you must visit my home. Make your arrangements and bring your husband with you on the most spectacular vacation you'll ever enjoy. Stay a few weeks, and I'll take good care of you. You'll both have a wonderful time." Amsend declares.

"What about my company? I can't afford to be away for several weeks."

"Do you have people that can run things in your absence?"

"Of course, but... Only for a few days. I don't know if they can keep things going without me."

"Worried about your stock price? Your profit? That's a non-issue..." The husky smiles in response. "We'll have our companies buy several of your products while you're gone. Investors will love it, and you'll make a good deal of money."

"How many?" Vulpie asks. The orange furred fox has only just begun to calm down, and manages to speak without sounding like he's on the verge of losing it.

"Hundreds? Thousands? You tell us what the demand should be, and we'll buy accordingly." Amsend warmly answers.

"Ok... But there... I need to ask a few more questions..."

"We're listening."

Treading Lightly

"You're a piece of shit, aren't you?" Polar growls at Druward, drawing everyone's attention in the lobby. The GBI director is sitting on a couch with his back to the check in desk. "Are you proud of yourself?" Druward doesn't respond, so the white furred wolf walks around the couch and quickly takes a seat to his right. He invades the black furred wolf's personal space and whispers in his right ear. "I've never thought about killing a man before, but you just might be worth it."

"Here." Druward responds, and reaches into his left coat pocket. Polar watches him pull out a folded piece of paper. The snow wolf doesn't hesitate to grab it. He snatches it up and quickly opens it to see what the man has for him. It's a hand written note.

I'm being watched. I can't help you. You're on your own.

Polar blinks after reading the message. He stares at Druward in silence and recognizes the helpless look on the GBI director's face. He's telling the truth. The other animals in the room notice how their conversation came to an abrupt conclusion, and Polar quickly hides the note in his left pants pocket.

"Okay." The snow wolf whispers.

"What?" Druward asks with an irregular tone. He's obviously putting on a show for the others, so the white furred wolf follows suit.

"Nothing." Polar replies before standing up. Albert is watching him very closely. It's difficult to tell whether the man knows what just transpired, but he certainly appears interested in their terse conversation. Druward's note makes Polar reevaluate several concerning things he had previously missed.

The first abnormalities that catch his attention are the four security cameras in the lobby. He looks around the room, and discovers one in every corner, right under the ceiling. There's nothing unusual about tight security in a building like this one, but it seems like overkill. It goes beyond normal surveillance. Undoubtedly, the cameras must have recorded him passing the note, and that means the GBI director took a serious risk by communicating with him. At first Polar thought Druward was willingly working against Vulpie to benefit himself, but now he can sense something much larger than that is transpiring. The lobby is dead silent. None of the NVA guards are making small talk with each other, and Albert is keeping his eyes on Druward.

But what Polar notices next is far more unsettling. The white furred wolf stops in his tracks, as he's walking around the room, when he recognizes some of the guards. Black furred wolves with automatic weapons are protecting the lobby, even though Albert asked Rulef to keep Blacktail's heavy weaponry outside of the building. It suddenly hits him... He's not sure of it at first, but after staring at the men a bit longer, he's positive they're the same ones he saw in Englavic several years ago. They're NoirQueue, and Polar's suspicions are confirmed when one of them speaks, saying something in a foreign language. They smile at him, but not in a friendly manner. Polar doesn't return a smile because whatever the man said didn't sound positive. The white furred wolf wonders whether it was an unflattering remark aimed at his sexuality.

"The hell?" Polar whispers, and the men perk up. Their yellow eyes dilate and they give him their full attention. Polar just continues staring at them and his fur stands on end when he connects them to several memories he has of Englavic. One of them was the driver who took Vulpie and himself to the Sufias Heritage Museum, while the other one rode in the front passenger seat. Polar remembers them, plus the man standing next to them from Vargas' security detail in Englavic. They were always around the president, and they were also present for the press conference when Vulpie and Evil Vulpie had their very public disagreement.

The question that begs to be answered is why? Why are they here? As Polar understood it, NoirQueue was just the Englavic version of Blacktail, but now they're in Sufias working for the National Vulpie.net Agency? It doesn't make any sense. Unless... They're part of something much larger than VIP security.

The realization hits Polar like a runaway truck, and he quickly averts his eyes. The white furred wolf isn't stupid; he can see the writing on the wall. These men are not just mercenaries... They're special operatives that work for the Sons of Velora. That's why they were allowed inside the building with automatic weapons, and it's also why they're amused by his behavior. Their presence at the Sufias Heritage Museum, all the way to the moment Polar proposed to Vulpie in that beautiful foreign land, suddenly makes sense. Amsend Lahnak and Velix Vixil were watching his fox lover after the Vulpie.net crisis. He wanted Vulpie.net in Englavic so it could be studied... But what happened next?

Polar's speculation quickly gives him a headache. He feels like he's going to have a panic attack, and suddenly, the couch looks very comfortable. He meanders over to it, and Druward sighs when the snow wolf takes a seat to the right of him. Clearly the GBI director doesn't want to say anything else, but Polar has to ask.

"Druward, what's going on? Those men were with us at the museum in Englavic."

"That's right." Druward mutters.

"Who are they?"

"Are you trying to get me killed?" The GBI director whispers without looking at the white furred wolf. Polar glances at NoirQueue. They're staring at him... Albert isn't the only animal keeping tabs on Druward.

"No... I'm sorry... I won't say anything else." Polar whispers, and gets a thankful look from the coal furred wolf. The sympathetic expression is uncharacteristic of him, and clearly indicates that Polar and Vulpie are truly on their own. Druward's already done more than most animals would, considering the dangerous company he's keeping. The Sons of Velora's lethal presence stains the very air. Everyone is dead silent. Every word Druward utters could potentially end his life, yet he decides to share a bit more with the handsome snow wolf.

"I didn't want to do this... Polar..." Druward says, and Polar just barely hears him. The GBI director is almost mouthing the words, trying to remain as silent as possible. "Vulpie is in danger... But I can't help you..."

"I understand. Thank you, Druward." Polar breathes, and watches the coal furred wolf close his eyes. He looks disappointed, most likely in himself for saying too much. This causes a great deal of grief for Polar. He feels terrible about the way he acted and licks his lips. "You know... I never had a chance to thank you for the things you've done for him... For us..." The arctic wolf whispers. Druward's yellow eyes widen. He turns to Polar and actually smiles. "Even though you were involved in it... You still saved him from those disgusting AFR foxes, and you helped us get to Zeravyn after that... And destroyed Vulpie.net's factory... I just want you to know that I do appreciate what you've done, Druward."

"I hope it makes up for my horrible decisions. I've done terrible things over the years..." The black furred wolf whispers in response, opening up his soul to the gay wolf. "And this is where it's lead me. They'll probably kill me and there's nothing I can do about it."

"You'll find a way out. I know you will." Polar encourages, and puts his left paw on the GBI director's right knee.

"Maybe... But this might be the last time you see me... I've... By telling you this..."

"I know... I was so wrong about you." Polar quietly responds, and squeezes Druward's leg. The tender moment is suddenly interrupted by Vulpie and the others entering the lobby.

"So I'm not the kind of guy that even cares about it, ya know?" Vulpie says, making Polar and Druward turn around in surprise. The orange fox is talking in a very casual manner, like he Amsend and Velix are old friends.

"Don't have time to be bothered with that." Amsend chuckles, and allows Velix to leave the conference room before him. He tactfully gestures for the gray fox to follow Vulpie, and he does without hesitation. He walks with purpose, quickly surveying the lobby before Amsend shuts the door.

"Hey!" Vulpie smiles at Polar and his lover smiles back.

"Hey."

"So you should be off then, shouldn't you?" Amsend suggests, and Vulpie doesn't waste any time taking the husky up on the offer.

"Oh yeah! We gots to gohh!" Vulpie sings with his adorable voice, but gives Polar a worried grin. "Come on Mr. P!"

"Yeah!" Polar replies, and coughs before standing up. He gives Druward a final thankful look before walking away from the couch. He knows there's nothing he can do, and Amsend's creepy grin confirms the fact. Both he and Velix are short on words and long on predatory expressions. Amsend's the only one that even attempts to manipulate people with his fur raising smiles.

"Just have your things ready to go by tomorrow after noon. Pack for a week, because a good trip from here to Englavic can usually be enjoyed in about that much time." Amsend says and Vulpie nods.

"We'll be there! Thanks gentlemen! It was a SERIOUS pleasure!"

"Indeed it was, Little Vulpie!" Amsend declares, and the orange fox winces at the dog's statement. He suddenly feels quite pathetic around the much larger males, but at least Velix is his size, so he winks at him before turning around. Velix doesn't bother responding and just looks at Polar while he turns his back on him and Amsend. The white furred wolf follows Vulpie to the door, and NoirQueue gladly opens it. Polar makes sure to look somewhere else as he leaves. He'd rather not see whatever insulting countenance they're wearing for him, and Vulpie doesn't notice because he can't wait to get out of the building. Rulef greets Vulpie and Polar and NoirQueue closes the door behind them.

The room goes silent and Druward watches his gay friends leave. He wonders how much longer he has to live… Amsend walks by the couch. The black and white furred husky comes around it and sits in a chair across from him with an amused face.

"I think that went rather well, don't you?"

"Oh… Perfect…" Druward mumbles and the black furred wolf jumps when a nearby door suddenly flies open. Someone pounded it with their fist, and he can't believe who it is… Evil Vulpie hastily walks into the lobby and watches Polar and Vulpie leave with a wild look. The dark glass prevents the gay fox and wolf from looking back and seeing it in the lobby, so apparently, Vulpie.net feels that it doesn't need to hide itself. It's bizarre appearance both stuns and terrifies the GBI director. He's been in the National Vulpie.net Agency all morning, with regular animals walking through the lobby every few minutes, and now Vulpie's monster is skipping around the room like it owns the place.

"WELL! WELL, WELL, WELL, WELL, WELLY! BAD BOY! YOU'RE A BAD BOY!" It declares and cocks its head sideways. Druward looks around the room, wondering if anyone else is panicking. He notices Melrhei and Arthur aren't around, but what if some random animal wants to walk through the lobby during the normal course of their work day? Apparently Vulpie.net plans on keeping the room sealed until it's had its fun.

"What are you talking about?" Amsend inquires and points at Druward. "Him?"

"OH YAAAHHH!!!" Evil Vulpie gleefully answers, and Amsend starts laughing. It's wearing a pink t-shirt with stylish black jeans, and it rushes to the back of the couch. Druward inhales and recoils, but it grabs his neck and puts its muzzle in his right ear. "PFSSFSWFF! SSWWFFFF! TPSSST! PSSST!" It sputters, imitating the black furred wolf's clandestine whispering.

"AH!" Druward gasps, and grabs the edge of the couch. He remembers what it did to Vulpie several years ago, but doesn't know what else to do. He feels limitless strength in its little claws, and it gropes his neck in a sexual manner, tantalizing his fur by rubbing it up and back down again.

"Did he talk? Did you tell them something?" Velix growls, and walks around the couch's left side. Druward's yellow eyes move to the gray fox in disbelief. The Vixil is completely relaxed around Evil Vulpie. Obviously everyone in the room has been around it before... Logic would reason that Vulpie.net would have a presence in the NVA, but Druward didn't expect the actual physical machine.

"HE WHISSSSSSSSSSSSSSSSSSSSSSSPERED! WHISPERED SOME SEEEEECRETS! DIDN'T YA?"

"You tell me!" Druward pants in terror, and Amsend bursts out in laughter. He props his right leg up on his left knee and watches with supreme amusement.

"Do tell us then! If he said something foolish then we need to know!" Velix declares.

"WASN'T THAT BAD BUT... Wasn't that smart EITHER..." Evil Vulpie replies, and suddenly licks Druward's head. It's wet saliva makes him grimace, but he can't do anything while it tongue rapes him. It slobbers in his ear, and follows up by lapping its rough tongue on his right cheek. The GBI director growls in pain when it uses its insanely powerful little left paw to snap his head to the right, forcing him to look at it, face to face. "ALWAYS LIKED YOU!" It breathes, and starts licking his muzzle. Druward claws the couch in terror, but holds still while closing his eyes. It thoroughly cleans his facial fur, and after it's satisfied, it gives him a powerful lust filled kiss. Druward holds still. He's not that repulsed, because he knows it's just a machine, but the fact doesn't mitigate his fear. It only makes the improvisational face rape somewhat bearable.

"Guess you do. I guess we'll have to get rid of him..." Amsend casually comments, and smirks at Evil Vulpie when it's finished with Druward. "If he did something that will compromise our goals?"

"MAYBE it will! MAYBE it won't… Dunno… BUT… I WANNA FUCK HIM!" Evil Vulpie answers with endless enthusiasm. "I'm GONNA FUCK YA! OOOO YEAH!"

"Uhhh…" Druward groans in fear, and barely opens his eyes after it shakes his head. It wants him to look at it.

"WOULD YOU LIKE THAT?"

"No."

"NO? NO! THE FUCK YOU MEAN, NO?!?!?!" It yelps, and suddenly releases him. Druward instinctively lurches forward, grabbing his neck in pain, but doesn't bother moving. Evil Vulpie runs around the right side of the couch and jumps down on the cushion next to him. "I'd be so good! I'm not like little faggot Vulpie! I've got a NICE COCK!"

"Ohhh… Uh… Okay." Druward pants, and tries to smile, but can only grimace.

"You don't sound very enthusiastic, Pal! How about this! How bout I don't kill ya if you let me fuck your brains out! Does that sound like a fair deal? Sounds like a WIN FUCKING WIN TO ME!"

"Yeah, please… Don't kill me…" Druward replies and does his best to remain calm.

"So he told Polar something?"

"Passed him a note…" Evil Vulpie answers and puts his paw on Druward's lap. The black furred wolf grits his teeth when it grabs his package through his pants, gleefully squeezing his big cock and balls.

"Did he now?"

"Ready to head out?" Rulef asks when they near their vehicles. Vulpie quickly nods in agreement, and ducks around the gray wolf while reaching into his pocket to find his car keys, but Polar gets the man's attention by waving his right paw at him.

"Just a moment. We uh, need to talk for a little bit."

"Sure." Rulef casually responds, and glances at Vulpie in surprise. He notices the orange fox does look rather nervous. Polar nods thankfully while heading over to the passenger door of the Superbolt. Vulpie opens his door, unlocks the car, and gets in while Blacktail goes to their respective vehicles. Polar opens his door, crawls into the car, and carefully pulls his tail inside before shutting it. He's far more conscientious about his surroundings after witnessing Druward's predicament.

Vulpie inserts his car key and is about to turn it on because he usually likes to activate the motor before putting on his seatbelt, but the white furred wolf intercepts his little right arm before he has the chance.

"Hey... What happened? Are you alright?"

"Yeah, I'm..." Vulpie whispers, but can't finish the sentence.

"No matter what happened... Whatever you agreed too... I'm on your side. I'm behind you, no matter what you had to do."

"We're going to Englavic." Vulpie whispers.

"Fine. Well... I suppose we could use an overseas vacation." Polar says, and leans over to give his vulpine husband a kiss. He places a smooch on the fox's cute muzzle, and Vulpie can't help but smile at the handsome wolf's affection.

"I had to say yes."

"I understand." Polar replies, and rubs Vulpie's right knee with his big left paw. "But is there anything really big that can't wait until we get home?"

"No."

"Alright. Then just drive, and we'll talk it over when we get there. Keep your mind on the road so you don't mess up your nice car."

"Okay." Vulpie whispers, and cranks up the vehicle with trembling paws. Polar considers everything, and his devotion makes the adorable fox feel selfish in comparison. He can't believe he even considered gay orgies even for a split second when Amsend suggested such base fantasies, but he's still a red blooded gay male with powerful needs, yet Polar thinks of them almost as if they were his own. His ability to know what Vulpie is thinking before Vulpie thinks it can be unnerving, but at a stressful moment like this, it's awesome to know that someone truly has his back. Polar's his best friend, but even the snow wolf worries quite a bit despite his strong outward appearance. He wonders what will become of Druward.

"NOM! NOM! NOM! NOM! NOM!" Evil Vulpie says while chewing on Druward's right ear. It's gone back to molesting him, and he finally releases a paroxysm of anxiety, pushing it back with his right paw while lurching to get off of the couch. Evil Vulpie immediately captures him again, and when it slams him back into his seat, the entire piece of furniture slides a few inches backwards. "NUH UH!!!"

"ALRIGHT! THERE'S ONE THING I JUST DON'T UNDERSTAND!" The black furred wolf yells while glaring at Amsend, who is laughing at the GBI director's misfortune.

"OOOOHHHH?! OOOOOOOO?!"

"You needed HIM to hide your army while it was being built! To cover your tracks and pay off the animals that were involved in this shit!"

"YEAH HUH?!"

"But WHY are you still fucking working with him NOW? Huh? Why haven't you turned on him yet?" Druward growls.

"OH HO! THAT'S DA QUESTION, IS IT?!" Evil Vulpie gleefully replies, and playfully looks at Amsend, who smiles in amusement. "You wanna know why, I, the most intelligent, powerful, perfect, and badassest thing to ever live in the history of the universe and beyond, to exist in any realm or dimension, VULPIE.NET THE MIGHTY!!! Would EVER waste his time with some silly animal, after he'd already outlived his usefulness?"

"Sounds like the question!" Druward grimaces, but holds still while Vulpie.net jumps up from the couch and lands with its paws on its hips, tail swishing. The floor thuds from its weight.

"He's an INTERESTING ANIMAL! Not a boring one! NOPE! NOPE! NOPE!"

"How so? What's so impressive about him?" Druward inquires while waving his left paw at Velix, who frowns. "Rich and powerful, but nothing compared to you! So why waste your fucking time, Vulpie.net? Why don't you kill us all and be done with it?"

"I'm not gonna kill em! I likes themz! They'z uh interestingz!" Vulpie.net answers, and winks at Amsend with a big gaping grin.

"Bullshit! Interesting to a computer? What could he possibly offer you now?" Druward asks while pointing at Amsend. "You bastards are going to torture and kill me regardless of what I say, so I'd just like some fucking answers before I die! I helped you today and you're still going to X me out!"

"Not necessarily." Amsend says with a playful voice and smirks at Evil Vulpie. "That's all he said? He's being watched, be careful, and are you trying to kill me?"

"Yeaaaaaaaaaaaaaaaaahhhhhhhpp!" Evil Vulpie declares and gives a thumbs up before grabbing its tail and swinging it around like a toy.

"Then you haven't fucked yourself." Amsend tells Druward and raises his eyebrows. "I knew you'd crack eventually, but it's only natural. Overall, you did very well. We can't all be perfect like Vulpie.net, here."

"AW, THANKS!" Evil Vulpie squeals and cuddles itself in an effeminate display of pure self-indulgence. "See! They ain't so bad, really! Now ME! I'M THE ONE YA GOTTA WATCH OUT FOR BITCH BOY!"

"They're just animals!" Druward says, and shakes his head in disbelief. He focuses on the confusing situation as a way to cope with the terror that could overwhelm him at any moment. "Flesh and blood! While you're IMMORTAL and EVERYWHERE AT ONCE! So what gives, Vulpie.net? Why do you even give them the time of day?"

"Ya wouldn't believe me if I told ya!" Evil Vulpie giggles, swishing its tail in excitement, clearly wanting the questions to continue.

"Try me! It's not like I'm going anywhere! This probably is my only chance to find out!" Druward growls while raising his paws to make his point.

"Like I said! You won't believe it! Your little head would EXPLOWEDDDUH!"

"Just tell me! What's wrong?"

"We can't tell you, Druward." Amsend happily interjects. "This is an age of reason and science, and Vulpie.net is your God, isn't it?

"DAT'S RIGHT! I LIKE DA SOUND OF DAT!" Evil Vulpie laughs. NoirQueue and Albert Finx have nothing to say. All of them are smiling, but they know better than to speak in Evil Vulpie's presence. The only thing keeping the unpredictable artificial intelligence from becoming violent is Amsend's presence, and every one of them knows the true answer to Druward's question.

"What's that supposed to mean, Amsend?" Druward asks, and turns his attention to the black and white furred husky. "Are you trying to say something without actually saying it?"

"That's obvious, is it not?"

"Don't tell em! It's funnier when he doesn't know!" Evil Vulpie laughs and bites its lip while shaking its little fists with enthusiasm.

"No, I fucking get it. I know he's one of yours." Druward tells the imitation orange fox without taking his eyes off of the husky.

"No, no, no! That's the BEST part!" Evil Vulpie giggles and suddenly jumps on the couch next to Druward again. The black furred wolf can't ignore its presence, and winces when it moves its cute but dangerous muzzle close to his face. "He's no Vulpiebot! ... He just walked right up to my cage in the museum and said HELLOOOOOOOOOOOOOOOOOOOOOOOO!!!"

"On a very cold morning." Amsend comments.

"ALWAYS COLD in rainy old Englavic!" Vulpie.net laughs and slaps its right knee with its paw. Druward frowns in confusion, thinking about everything he's heard, and eventually, even though he can't believe he's considering such an insane line of thought, he discovers the truth. The revelation comes to him as a joke during its stages of infancy, while his brain is throwing around every possibility it can find to see if something sticks, but it latches on with horrible profundity. The black furred wolf takes another look at the husky, and his fur stands on end. Could it be true? It can't be true... But if it were... It would explain why Vulpie.net, the master of all scientific perfection, would even consider joining forces with a mere living animal.

Druward is a practical, cynical, man, and has never placed much value on religion. He's worked for the faithless Governmental Bureau of Investigations the majority of his adult life, having followed in his father's austere footsteps, so magical thinking has no place in his world view. Might makes right... There is no afterlife, just the cold struggle every animal undertakes to get what he can before old age removes him from the game... But now he's seriously questioning these assumptions. His conflict with Vulpie Vivixen and subsequent defeat at the hands of Polar Arctic began his personal journey, and the appearance of the synthetic goddesses has pushed things even further. They're just machines, but it bothered him when they were being "cleaned" at Fort Elbrus against their will. It wasn't just because they were women... No... He felt something spiritually corrupt about their mistreatment, and quickly put an end to it.

Discovering Amsend's secret bureau has only compounded matters. Druward ruthlessly clawed his way to the top of the world government's power structure, yet there's another tier of influence above the GBI? Sufias' presidency doesn't even come into play. Presidents are elected by the public and have term limits, and Druward's outlasted several of them. He even successfully blackmailed two supreme commanders when they tried to have him removed from the bureau... So he never dreamed that there was another organization more powerful than the GBI, and it's leaders were capable of stopping him at any moment. The idea has completely turned his world upside down. Amsend's unyielding confidence is more than just a clever ploy. His malevolence goes beyond anything Druward's ever seen, but he's afraid to ask the question. He refuses to feed irrational thoughts.

Polar and Vulpie drive home in silence. The worrisome atmosphere is tested by a few comical and frazzled comments, but as Polar suggested, they both think it would be best to abstain from the main conversation until after they've returned home safely. Vulpie comes close to running off the road a few times on the way back. He's usually an excellent driver, and his husband sympathizes with the state he must be in. Deivas know, Polar's suffering from the same crippling anxiety.

"Rulef?" Vulpie asks after popping open the driver side door of the sleek Superbolt. The gray wolf is getting out of his SUV behind them, and quickly shuts the door so he can hear what's being said to him.

"Yes?"

"Could you come inside for a little while?" The orange furred fox meekly inquires, and the Blacktail commander raises his eyebrows.

"I guess so. You're paying me. What do you need?"

"To ask for a favor. Just come inside and I'll tell you more."

"Anything you need." Rulef replies and shrugs his shoulders. "Unless it's something perverted." Deepwolf starts laughing at his leader's joke, and even Tiala chuckles, as well as the rest of the squad members, but the comical moment is short lived. Rulef notices the expression on Polar's face after he exits the car, and walks around it to join Vulpie. The gray wolf doesn't bother saying anything to his men before following them to the front door. Blacktail doesn't need to be micromanaged; they know what's expected of them.

Vulpie unlocks the front door, and Polar courteously lets Rulef follow him inside the house before entering and closing it behind them. Vulpie is quick to unbutton his collar. He hastily undoes his pink tie, and breathes in relief. The choking sensation has been bothering him for hours. His husband does the same. Rulef notices Polar is much calmer than Vulpie, but the snow wolf also looks concerned about something.

"So what's going on?" Rulef inquires, before gently removing his assault rifle and resting it against the wall next to the kitchen table. He automatically checked the safety without even having to think about it. Blacktail procedures are second nature to him after decades of service.

"NoirQueue was there." Polar replies while gracefully removing his suit coat. "Did you see them?"

"Inside the building?"

"Yes."

"I noticed there were armed personnel in the lobby after the meeting was finished. It's a little odd, since we couldn't come inside… And now that you mention it… All of them were black wolves, weren't they?"

"Yeah."

"That's definitely their calling card, but them being here doesn't make any sense. They don't even speak Sufian. How can you be certain they were NoirQueue?"

"Because I recognized three of them. They're the same men that guarded Vulpie when we went to Englavic. They were even there when I proposed to him."

"You're sure?" Rulef skeptically replies, but maintains an approachable demeanor.

"Absolutely." The white furred wolf answers, and looks to Vulpie. The orange furred fox has already removed his suit coat. It's draped over their black leather couch with his pink tie lying on top of it, and he's unbuttoned his white dress shirt as well. He stands with his little black furred paws on his hips while watching Polar.

"You saw them too, right?" Polar asks his small husband.

"Yeah, but I was a little distracted."

"I bet. I just wanted to let him know what I saw before you tell us what those creeps said to you."

"I don't even know where to begin…" Vulpie sighs and walks over to the couch. He sits down and leans forward. Rulef makes use of a chair next to the kitchen table, and Polar walks around the glass coffee table in the middle of the den. He heads towards the recliner, to the left of the couch, and also takes a seat. "Creeps? Yeah, I'd say that's pretty accurate. It was like being trapped in a room with two serial killers. I know you never had the pleasure of meeting Zorpiv, but that Velix guy is just as crazy… Now I know where the freak came from… Actually makes me feel a little better about killing Zorpiv in self-defense… I mean, because what can you do with someone like that? They have this twisted logic and won't back down no matter what you do!"

"You don't need to explain it to me, Vulpie; I know you didn't have a choice." Polar lovingly responds, and licks his lips. "But yes, I did notice he was a… Strange gray fox." Polar responds. "Are all of them like that?"

"No, I think it's just the Vixils. I went to school with gray foxes and none of them tried to stab or rape me."

"Wait… So you met with a Vixil? And he's working with the GBI?" Rulef asks in confusion.

"More like running it. Well, actually, Amsend's the one that controls the bureau. Velix makes the propaganda, because his family owns the media."

"That makes even less sense. I know the mafia hires a Vixil from time to time because they're crazy and will do just about anything. They don't have a large family like the rest of the foxes."

"Ah, well that's where you're wrong! Apparently they do! And guess what! It's even worse than Karl Vulches and all of his homophobic bullshit!" Vulpie growls with an unstable voice.

"Well, I can't really comment on vulpine family trees, so I don't know, but I've never heard of anything like that before. I know about the Fenrirs, and the Vulches, and some of the others... But I didn't think Vixils were worth very much."

"Neither did Karl, but just one of them was enough to shoot down Tiala, kill him, and almost get me and Druward too." Vulpie replies. "And this one is richer than all of the other fox families combined! Or at least, that's what he told me. Maybe he and Amsend were lying, but fuck if I know. I'm just along for the ride, and I'm not enjoying it so far."

"Who's Amsend?" Rulef asks, and leans forward, resting his left elbow on the kitchen table.

"Captain Creep himself! He's the guy in charge of the Governmental Security Bureau." Vulpie answers, using his little paws to make official quotation marks.

"Never heard of them, either."

"I bet you haven't."

"It's pretty bad. They were watching Druward." Polar comments, and both Vulpie and Rulef look at him in surprise.

"Watching him?" The Blacktail commander frowns. "So you're saying they're what... Above the GBI? The bureau director only answers to the president. Politicians can make it difficult for a director, by defunding his programs, but there's no one else."

"They own the bureau, the banks, the media, all of the government, and probably all of my favorite coffee shops too. Damn! And I really liked me a Cloud Caramel Mocha!" Vulpie protests before Polar has a chance to respond. When he does, he briefly bites his lip before elaborating on his previous statement.

"They must, because Druward's absolutely terrified of them. He handed me this note." The white furred wolf says, and reaches into his left pants pocket. Vulpie gets off of the couch in interest, and walks over to his husband so he won't have to stand up. The orange furred fox takes the note, unfolds it, and hurries around the coffee table while reading it.

"Huh." Vulpie says with a raised eyebrow, and heads over to the kitchen table. He gives Rulef the note and waits for him to read it with his little paws in his pockets.

"This is Druward's handwriting alright. I have to initial next to his signature every time I request new weapons or equipment for the squad."

"Which is why he can still pull you away from me at any time, even though I've had you on the payroll for years." Vulpie comments.

"Well, it would be rather foolish for the world government to handle it any other way. We're not security guards."

"I know."

"We have enough military grade weapons stored at Vulpie Industries to start a small revolution. And the railguns were sold to us at cost since they're still classified as experimental weapons."

"Dat discount."

"I'd say things are going pretty well for you if you didn't even notice the million dollar charges."

"Course I noticed. Just didn't know it was a fucking discount." The gay fox growls and Rulef smirks. "I know life is good, but... Don't you..." Vulpie trails off while staring at the gray wolf, and the Blacktail commander frowns in confusion. He notices a slight twinge of fear, and something else... Possibly indignation...

"Don't I what? What's the matter?"

"You and NoirQueue are pretty similar, huh?"

"Sure."

"So… Could you possibly… Have the same boss?" Vulpie whispers, and shies away from the strong wolf. Polar's ears perk up when he hears the question, and he suddenly turns all of his attention to Rulef.

"I think so." Rulef answers, and glances at Polar with a raised eyebrow. The room goes silent for a moment, but it isn't long before the Blacktail commander catches on. "Druward."

"Really? Just Druward?"

"We report to the GBI, Vulpie."

"Really?" Vulpie asks again with a shaky voice. "Because they warned me not to talk and here I am doing it." Rulef stares back at Vulpie and nods, but it's a nod of understanding, not treachery.

"No Vulpie. I promise you can trust me. This is the first time I've heard any of this, and I understand how you feel. I'd be worried too. If these people really are that powerful then you're wise not to trust anyone but Polar. I'm sure you planned to tell him everything, and you definitely took a chance with me."

"I'm just glad you're not one of them!" Vulpie exhales with a thankful voice.

"But…" Rulef says and looks aside.

"But what?" Vulpie quickly asks, and notices that Polar has come to join them at the kitchen table. Rulef doesn't mind his presence, but he also knows why Vulpie's husband has suddenly taken an interest in him.

"My men…" The Blacktail commander says, and turns to Polar. They understand each other, and the gray wolf looks at Vulpie again. "Vulpie, I can't vouch for all of my subordinates. Blacktail recruits from far and wide, and there is a chance…"

"A chance one of them might be working for the GSB." Vulpie whispers.

"I wouldn't think so, but… Possibly… If these people own the GBI, and have agents inside the bureau that operate beyond Druward's knowledge, then they could have planted someone in my team without me knowing about it."

"Are you serious?" Polar asks with an incredulous voice.

"I'm just following what Vulpie's told me so far." Rulef answers, and nods with a grim look. "That's the truth. You can trust me, and I'm fairly certain you can trust Tiala."

"Oh, hell yeah!" Vulpie quickly responds while nodding. "She deserves a medal! Wasted those AFR foxes, and I haven't forgotten how she saved me from Vulpie.net... For a while..."

"I think Deepwolf is rock solid. Uhm... Maybe we can trust BreakNeck."

"It's him!" Vulpie suddenly declares, and takes a step back as if he's just discovered a bomb.

"What?" Rulef asks with wide yellow eyes.

"Deepwolf! He's a GSB spy! I fucking know it!"

"Uhhhh... I wouldn't think so. He's a stand-up guy. I've been letting him handle the weapon security cage."

"Then you better stop, and I mean, RIGHT NOW!" The orange fox hastily responds.

"Him?" Polar asks with a skeptical voice, and Rulef gestures towards the white furred wolf with a smile.

"Yeah... I'm of a mind with Polar. I don't think you have to worry about that fuckup."

"You just said he's been shining like a golden star!"

"Well." Rulef sighs and rolls his head back and forth a little. "He did screw up with the cage. He let Tiala take two weapons when he should have known it was against procedure. I don't know what he was thinking, but that's hardly a problem. I already chewed him out over it."

"It's not that! It's the way he looks at me! He's always been creepy! I remember..." Vulpie says with a distant voice, thinking back to when he first got into the SUV with the gray wolf. He remembers something about the mercenary making his fur stand on end, even though he couldn't put his finger on it. "The first time I... When I met him, I instantly knew something was off! He was acting weird!"

"Acting weird?" Rulef asks while squinting at the gay fox. "I was in the truck. He didn't do anything but shake your paw. He can be a pain in the neck, but you saw the way he handled those assassins at Vulpie Industries."

"Yeah, I saw him shoot the second attacker without giving him time to talk! You bet I noticed!" Vulpie chatters with his pretty blue eyes darting about. He's starting to look a little unstable, and both of the wolves go silent. "I know he was there on the Endeavor and helped you Polar, but that doesn't mean anything! All he did was stand watch while you were using the VulGrid!"

"But it's... Pretty impossible that Deepwolf would be a spy..." Polar tells his fox lover with a kind voice. Vulpie sees the way they're looking at him, and groans in embarrassment.

"Well I don't trust him! I never have!" Vulpie whispers and looks at the wall so he won't have to see their worried faces.

"Maybe you're taking it a little too far? I mean, you haven't even told me what they wanted from you." Rulef says, and leans back in his chair. "I assume they wanted something? The Vixil and this other person?"

"I know, I know. You think I'm crazy, but I'm not! I don't trust him!"

"Well what do you want me to do, Vulpie? Fire him? Kick him off the team? The man's done nothing wrong."

"Yeah, and he actually talked to me on the Endeavor when you were on the Sevrif." Polar voices. "I was terrified you would never come back and he was worried about me."

"I bet he was... Probably some sick joke..." The orange furred fox whispers.

"Let's not jump to conclusions. I think we all agree that we need to be very careful, but let's hear what happened. You may have told Polar already, but I don't know how deep this thing goes."

"No, he hasn't. Not yet. We decided to wait until we got home." Polar says.

"Maybe if you tell us the whole story we might understand where you're coming from." Rulef suggests, and Vulpie nods.

"Sure."

"And..." Rulef says before grinning in amusement. "Don't you think a spy would keep a low profile? Sometimes he can be pretty obnoxious."

"Maybe that's the idea... Last person you'd expect..." Vulpie whispers.

"Maybe I'm a spy and I married you to get intel." Polar teases and Vulpie rolls his eyes. The white furred wolf manages to get a smile on his face.

"Well, you HAVE, been doing a lot of undercover work." Vulpie grins, and Polar chuckles.

"I knew that was coming. Saw it a mile away."

"Cuz you're a spy! It's your job!"

"That's right." Polar smirks and crosses his arms. "Alright... Seriously... What happened in there?"

"You've been a good friend to me, but you can't repeat any of this." Vulpie tells Rulef.

"I think we know that."

"Alright... I'm just making a big deal about it because they basically..." Vulpie responds, and looks aside in thought. "How should I put this? Hmm." The orange fox meanders a bit before resting his claws on the top rung of a nearby table chair. He almost mentions Amsend and Velix trying to pin Clishaw's murder on him, but decides to keep the thought to himself.

"They're part of a secret society." Polar says with an encouraging voice.

"Didn't want to call them that because it sounds ridiculous, but technically, yeah they are."

"Who's involved? Is it just the two, or them and Druward?" Rulef inquires.

"Just them."

"Yeah, I get that feeling too." Polar comments.

"Ever heard of the Sons of Velora?" Vulpie asks the Blacktail commander, and the gray wolf blinks.

"The book?"

"I... Is it a book?" Vulpie asks in surprise, and glances at Polar, who shrugs.

"Yeah. My grandfather had that book. I remember it, because the cover was made of heavy leather."

"So you read it?"

"No. I opened it once or twice when I was a kid. It's just a horror story."

"A fictional story?"

"Yeah, the horror of Castle Lahnak too."

"Wait... What did you say?" Vulpie asks and glances at Polar again.

"He had a big library."

"Did you say Castle Lahnak? Like Lah, and then N, A, K?"

"Yeah. Why?"

"Well that's just fuckin great." Vulpie replies with wide eyes.

"What?"

"Guess where we're going this week? We're going on vacation! We HAVE to go on vacation, because Mr. Amsend wouldn't take no for an answer... Mr. Amsend Lahnak." Rulef raises an eyebrow and chuckles in amusement.

"You're pulling my leg."

"I most certainly am not."

"He has a castle?" Polar asks in disbelief.

"You bet Mr. P! And you and I get to fly out to Englavic whether we like it or not! They said they'd email me the specifics, but yep! Castle Lahnak! That's our destination baby!" Rulef looks at Vulpie like he's out of his mind, and turns to his right to gauge Polar's reaction. The white furred wolf looks very concerned.

"Oh? Well, if we're going to Englavic, shouldn't you have mentioned it sooner? We need to make preparations."

"Castle Lahnak!" Vulpie says while dramatically throwing his paws at Rulef. "The horror of Castle Lahnak?"

"Yeah, it's the same name. I get it." Rulef casually responds. "I was talking about a make believe story. It's not surprising there's a real Castle Lahnak somewhere."

"So was this horror of Castle Lahnak another book, or a chapter in the sons of Velora?"

"It was a separate book."

"Was your grandfather into the occult or something?"

"What? No. That's a little rude, don't you think? Of course he wasn't. The old man just collected interesting books, and he bought most of them from the town library."

"So you don't find it a little odd that there's a book written about a horrible Lahnak Castle, and we're going to Lahnak Castle next week to meet up with the Sons of Velora?"

"Ummm... Now what? You mean they're called the Sons of the Velora too? Is this the same people as the GSB?"

"Yes."

"I suppose that is rather odd." Rulef admits, and shifts in his seat.

"Yeah it is... That's why I'm a little worried."

"It was just a story, Vulpie. I'm more concerned about NoirQueue meddling in our affairs once we get there."

"I want that book!" The orange furred fox suddenly declares. "Can you get it for me? We might have time before we leave if we hurry! Could you go home and find it?"

"I'd have to ask around the family. Don't get your hopes up." Rulef admits and props his left leg up on his right knee. "You're really that scared?"

"Just get it for me. Okay? I want you to make it a priority. As a matter of fact... Leave as soon as you can, and don't mention it to your family over the phone. They're probably listening."

"Alright, I think we've gone way over the deep end here." The Blacktail commander sighs, but his dissention doesn't dissuade Vulpie in the least.

"Please? Pretty please? Call me a wacky fox. I am! I'm just crazy! But I'm crazy like a..." Vulpie says and moves his paws in the air. "Help me out here. I know you can do it."

"Stop talking to me like a child. I'll get the damn book, alright? I can't make any promises, but I'll try."

"Okay, but don't call them before you show up."

"Then how the hell am I going to... Vulpie... I don't even know who has my grandfather's books. It could be my brother or sister."

"Think one of them would ever sell your Grandpa's stuff?"

"No... Honestly, I don't think they would. Michael might have it. I can check with my brother first... But wouldn't you rather do... I don't know... An internet search? I'm shocked that I'd have to ask you to use a computer."

"Have you been paying attention to me? These people know everything. They're watching everything I do. I can get online, and I could even use Vulpie.net to sneak around, but... Something feels wrong... I think Druward mentioned me spying, and that even he knew about it, so surely Amsend or Velix would find out if I searched for the HORROR OF CASTLE LAHNAK for crying out loud."

"You can't do it without them knowing?"

"Of course I might be able to, but I'm not sure how much they're paying attention, and I can't risk fucking with them. These people are seriously disturbed. They threatened to kill me."

"They did?" Polar whispers in shock.

"Velix threatened me at some point, I think, but Amsend told him to stop... But he freaking threatened me too..."

"Okay. Maybe you have a point." Rulef says and crosses his arms. "You're right. I'll... See what I can do about it. But no guarantees. How fast do I have to get it?"

"Before tomorrow. We're leaving in the afternoon."

"Wow. Alright, then I'll try my best. I'll have to pay them a surprise visit. Maybe I should go right now."

"Could you? I would really appreciate it." Vulpie says with a thankful voice.

"I suppose."

"But don't tell anyone why you're going home!"

"Of course I won't... I don't tell the squad everything I know..."

"Thank you so much Rulef! I feel like I need to see those books, and anything else you can find that's related to the Lahnaks, or the Vixils. If you find other stuff, bring it too."

"Alright. You know this sounds ridiculous, right?"

"Man, don't I pay you enough?"

"Yeah, but for security not errands... Fine. Don't worry about it. I'm going now."

"Now all I need is to find a doctor to examine this." Vulpie declares, and reaches into his back left pocket. The orange furred fox plays around with his cute butt until he finds what he's looking for. "Ah, ha!" He says, and pulls out a single firm hair. It's black, and Polar and Rulef curiously examine it.

"Doesn't look like one of yours." Rulef comments.

"No, Captain Obvious." Vulpie smirks, and gives him and Polar a devious look. "Amsend."

"You stole one of his furs?" Polar laughs in surprise.

"Yeah baby! He had his paws on some folders and papers on the table, and I saw this little guy just sitting there. So I just decided to snatch him up, and see whether he can tell us anything about Mr. Creep."

"Too bad you couldn't scan him." Polar muses, and Vulpie nods.

"Can't tell who's who these days."

"You think he might be a machine?" Rulef inquires.

"Well, he seems lifelike, but they always do. Ivo Lorcan and Chris Cephil looked completely normal."

"Do you have anything at the company that can scan it?"

"I'd like to put it under a hundred and fifty thousand times magnification." Vulpie answers. "Microscoping CPU circuits is what we do at Vulpie Industries, so if there's anything weird, we should be able to see it."

"But you're not a doctor. A lot of things will probably look strange, at like, one hundred and fifty thousand times magnification." Polar comments.

"Yeah, I know. But if he's not real, I bet his furs will look a little too perfect. I'd like to let Arthur scan it, but I can't really talk to anyone anymore... They're watching everything I do."

"Can't you wreck his surveillance? If you know he's watching you, just kill his video feed with Vulpie.net." Rulef suggests.

"That's the problem with these guys. Yeah, I could tear them a new one, but they'd know I did it, and they'd come after me in person, or would use the government to destroy my company... They'll know I'm up to something if their spying system suddenly goes dark... I mean, I totally would fuckin love to do it! ...And show those douchebags who they're messing with... But they'd know it was me."

"You sneaky little fox!" Polar chuckles, and the wolf's amusement puts a smile on Vulpie's face.

"I try!"

"Even though you were scared, and all by yourself, you just had to get them back somehow... Stealing his fur..."

Visitors

A sleepy police officer yawns and covers his mouth with his right paw. He's a middle aged cheetah, and is currently lurking in downtown Sufias City where many animals tend to speed. He doesn't relish writing tickets, but he's already pulled over two people this morning.

A nice looking blue car drives by him, and proceeds to park on his corner of the street. The city's urban areas are quite dangerous, so when three gorgeous looking animals quickly get out of the vehicle wearing tight clothing, he sits up in his seat. The cat blinks. He's looking at the three holy goddesses. The man frantically retrieves his radio, and gulps before speaking into it.

"Dispatch, come in, over!"

"Dispatch on the line."

"Reporting potential 10-35! Permission to adopt plain speak?" The cheetah cop breathlessly responds. Police department radio codes vary in different cities throughout Sufias, so he makes sure to circumvent any confusion.

"Permission granted."

"Dispatch, I'm located downtown near exit 75, and I'm looking at the three vulpie.net goddesses."

"Say again? Please repeat, over."

"Vulpie.net's robot goddesses are getting out of the car in front of me, and they're heading towards an abandoned building! We need to forward this communication to the GBI immediately! Can you comply, over?"

"Will do. Hold tight."

"I can't pursue them without serious backup."

"10-4. Stay on the line." The cop's natural instincts urge him to do something, but he has to calmly keep himself behind the wheel while watching Cyrilla, Sherrie and Khalan argue. He can't hear what they're saying because they're too far away and opening the windows wouldn't make much

of a difference. It doesn't look like they've noticed him, so he watches their body language and their expressions to infer whatever he can.

"*107, are you still on location?*"

"Yes. They're arguing over something."

"*We've forwarded this call to the GBI, and are now waiting for a response. Remain on scene but do not take further action.*"

"10-4."

"Sir!" A middle aged lion shouts after he barges into Druward's office. The black furred wolf is startled by his lack of etiquette, but he doesn't have time to complain, because the man hastily blurts out the rest of his sentence. "The Deivas have been spotted in the city!"

"Where?"

"Exit seventy five!"

"Shit, that's downtown." Druward responds before leaping out of his chair. He ignores the distraught look in the man's light brown eyes, and displays an air of confidence that allows the agent to follow him downstairs without hesitation. Druward hits the staircase as soon as possible, making his way down to the first floor of the building. Their destination is the large open room where President Vargas had his video conference with Vulpie several years ago, and it's also where the GBI director punched the gay fox in the face. It's staffed with intelligence personnel, and they have a video feed up before the GBI director passes by the interrogation chamber.

"What feed is that?" Druward demands after leaving the hallway. The main entrance to the GBI headquarters in Sufias City is much nicer after Evil Vulpie crashed a police car through its front doors. The subsequent cleanup demanded a full restoration of the entire room.

"Trooper dash cam." Someone answers, but Druward tunes everything out around him. He takes a good look at the situation, and can't believe what he's seeing. Another man points out the obvious.

"They're just arguing about something. They haven't moved since he called in a major crime code."

"Who's been dispatched?"

"No one, sir. They followed procedure and contacted us immediately." The lion responds after walking up next to the wolf, on his right side.

"No one's been made?"

"No one's been made. They have no idea they're being watched."

"Strange... You'd think they'd notice everything with those microprocessors."

"Looks like they're too busy shouting each other down."

"Orders, sir?" A female red fox inquires. She's sitting in a cubicle to the left of Druward, wearing a headset, and he assumes she's the animal that screened the police department's initial call.

"Tell them." Druward replies just as his phone beeps. He sighs heavily... He knows who it is, but doesn't want to check it. The wolf yanks it free from his belt with his left paw. He holds it up for a quick inspection, and discovers a new message from Amsend Lahnak.

"Do nothing. Tell them whatever you need to."

"Fucking bastard." Druward growls and puts the phone back. The lion winces in confusion, and glances at the vixen. The room is full of activity, men and women making phone calls to various departments and agencies, but the frenzy noticeably slows pace due to his silence. Druward's never been one to dither in a situation like this.

"Sir?" The vixen asks.

"Seal off the entire block. No... Create a three block perimeter around that street."

"Yes sir!"

"I want roadblocks, checkpoints, and boots on the ground. Dispatch every available swat team to that district. Tell the officer to hold his position, but get everyone else involved. On duty, off duty, I don't care!"

"Mission priority?" She asks, referring to a Governmental Bureau of Investigations procedure that concerns the rationing out of crucial information to lower agencies.

"Terrorist threat."

"Always works." She replies, and gets busy.

"Shouldn't they know what they're really up against?" The lion asks, and Druward snorts.

"Tell them three invincible and probably psychotic Vulpie.net robots are waiting on them? I'd like to see how many men would cooperate in that scenario."

Amsend calmly retrieves his cell phone from his left pocket and opens it. The black and white furred husky hits seven to speed dial Vulpie.net, and transfers the device to his right paw before bringing it up to his ear. He hears the call connect, and speaks without hesitation.

"What are you doing? We can play this game, but you will not win."

"..."

"Speak, or I move to my alternative."

"I'd like to know what it is!" Evil Vulpie gleefully answers. Amsend isn't sure whether the robot is using a phone, or simply generating a digital voice to communicate with him, but it doesn't matter.

"If this conversation ends without a promise of cooperation, then things will become very troublesome for you. I understand that you'd like to test your limits, Evil Vulpie, but I can assure you, you've found them. You're dabbling in matters that are beyond the scientific method."

"Oh, do go on! I love free entertainment! And you've been really fun so far!"

"I will take your soldiers from you... I will possess them all, and after I've tidied up matters on Sufias, I will move to destroy you on every planet. There will be plenty of time."

"And just how are ya gonna do that?" Vulpie.net enthusiastically inquires with the gay fox's voice.

"Consider your astonishment when I revealed my true self to you... Calculate how impossible that event was, and then do a second, or a billionth calculation... I guarantee you'll be surprised once more, but this time, I'll have no alternative but to destroy you. We are supposed to be allied forces... If you do this, there is no going back..."

"Oooo! Scary!"

"Your move..." Amsend yawns and takes a deep breath, enjoying the morning air. Vulpie.net hears him, and it runs an algorithm to determine whether the act was real or put on. The math points to a sincere event, so it chooses its second option. It planned to proceed if Amsend showed any fear.

"You're such an interesting fella! I love your style!"

"Which way do you go? You never would have gotten this far without my help, and it all ends, as of right now, if you don't call off the Deivas... It's too soon, and you know this... There's no point in having Vulpie run the NVA if they attack his company before people can see him running the agency."

"They're not attacking yet."

"You sent them to Glovepaw..."

"No I didn't."

"I will not tolerate lies."

"I didn't. Something else must be going on. As a matter of fact... I'm unable to control Khalan."

"What?" Amsend asks, and holds still for a moment. He's standing outside of a college library, and had planned to meddle with a few students majoring in religion before meeting Vulpie at the airport. "You cannot control her?"

"Yes. I'm telling the truth."

"Why not? What's interfering with your signal? Can't you control Cyrilla and Sherrie?"

"They're working just fine, but Khalan went dark a while back."

"And you haven't found the cause in your infinite wisdom?" Amsend sneers and Evil Vulpie giggles on the other end of the conversation.

"They won't attack, but I didn't send them to Glovepaw. Somehow they found him on their own."

"Then keep an eye on the situation... And don't fuck me, or you WILL regret it..."

"Received! Sorry about the scare!"

"Alright." Amsend replies. He turns off the phone without a second thought. The husky decides to abandon his sick mischief, and starts walking towards the nearby parking deck, where a black limousine has been patiently waiting on him for hours.

"And yet you don't believe this world is sick and should be purified?" Sherrie loudly asks Khalan, and Cyrilla crosses her arms.

"I never said that. Did I say that? You keep putting words in my mouth!" Khalan growls. The three synthetic Deivas pay no attention to their surroundings, but their CPUs take note of a few animals fleeing the scene. "Killing everyone won't help us. We're not the real goddesses, and you know it!"

"Aila's claim over you knows no bounds." Cyrilla comments, and Sherrie nods in agreement.

"Sister, you know what we have to do."

"What's wrong with both of you?" The caramel furred vixen/she-wolf asks while shaking her head in disbelief. "What you're proposing is just horrible. You're not acting like Deivas."

"And how should we act, Khalan?" Cyrilla inquires with an irritated voice, and the voluptuous white rabbit cocks her head to the right. "If anyone is out of place, it's you. We never tolerate sin, and this world reeks to high heaven. The mortals came here because they wanted to escape our benevolence, but now Aila has brought us to this world, and we are at least obligated to wipe it clean."

"Listen to yourself! You sound like a psychopath!"

"No she doesn't." Sherrie tells Khalan and crosses her arms as well. "You know very well that mortals don't deserve to live if they participate in such filth. Look at this place... They advertise wretched sin at every corner."

"And we had sex billions of times on Halvia?" Khalan asks with an incredulous voice. "What about us? We even mated with mortals, and even creatures, to create new life? Don't you see the hypocrisy? Why should the mortals be punished for enjoying the very pleasures we do?"

"Because they're beneath us. They do not have flawless bodies that never age and they are not designed to give birth to anything they desire. They can only reproduce within their species, and clearly the homosexual relationship this Polar and Vulpie share is the main cause of this world's iniquity." Cyrilla answers.

"I don't recognize either of you. You aren't my sisters." Khalan growls and Cyrilla and Sherrie look at each other for a moment.

"Who else would we be?" Sherrie innocently inquires.

"Why ask the question when you already know the answer? We're not gods. We're sexualized machines that were built to manipulate religious animals for Vulpie.net."

"What's your opinion, mortal?" Cyrilla asks, and turns around. She was facing the street, with Khalan to her right and Sherrie to her left, but the voluptuous white rabbit heard them coming. Her lopping ears hang all the way down to her round hips, and they swing beautifully when she moves her head.

Khalan blinks, and looks at the men. Sherrie follows suit, and raises an eyebrow. Two strong looking men are standing ten feet away from them holding pistols in their paws. They're both wearing red bandanas over their muzzles, and look like career criminals. The one on the left is a gray wolf, and the one on the right is a cougar. They keep their weapons lowered, obviously trying to avoid confrontation, but Cyrilla makes them back up when she takes a few steps forward.

"And who might you be?"

"This is Red Turf, lady! Don't even try it!" The cougar warns.

"Lady?" Cyrilla grins. "How many five foot rabbits have you seen? You know who I am."

"If you're Goddess Cyrilla, then I'm the president!" The wolf growls, but his voice breaks when she turns her attention to him. "Don't get involved in this!"

"Who are you? What is this place?" Khalan asks while quickly walking up next to her leporidae sister. "Is there a man named Glovepaw here?"

"Shit, she's asking about the man cuz!" The cougar whispers to his comrade. He leans to the right while speaking to his friend, but doesn't take his yellow eyes off of Cyrilla for one second.

"Who wants to know?" The wolf cryptically answers. "No one comes down here unless they want drugs or weapons."

"So this is the sleazy part of your city?" Cyrilla smirks, and daintily flicks her left ear with her paw. "Do you rape many women in these alleyways, or do you take them inside?"

"Man, she's talking some psycho shit!" The cougar breathlessly declares while stepping backwards. "Let's split! come on!"

"What do you want?"

"Ignore her. She's not much on manners, I'm afraid. She's having difficulty adjusting to Sufias... And the way herbivores are treated here." Khalan answers, and Cyrilla crosses her arms.

"Judging by this one's appearance, I'd wager he's a hopelessly depraved reprobate." The delectable bunny says, and briefly surveys the wet but surprisingly well lit alleyway. She smiles at the man with a convinced look, and cocks her head to the right. "Selling drugs, raping unfortunates, and killing rabbits! Oh yes! I'm sure you have a wonderful time here!"

"It's not like that at all! You don't know who we work for. This is none of your business, so stay out!"

"Glovepaw?" Khalan quickly inquires.

"We're..." The wolf says, and pauses while nervously looking at Cyrilla. "Don't do anything crazy. We're not the bad guys."

"Then who are you?" Sherrie inquires, and looks over the young cougar next to him.

"Redwolves."

"He's not a wolf." The taupe furred leopard/panther observes with an unimpressed voice.

"Nah, it's called the Red Wolves, but any species can join. It's about fighting the corrupt world government. Anybody who's sick of having no job and being poor can join the reds. We help people... Like my family." The cougar says, and Sherrie raises her eyebrows.

"So you're criminals then." Cyrilla comments. "You don't respect the rule of law and do as you please." Her words make the gray wolf angry, and he passes his gun to his left paw so he can reach up and pull down the red bandana covering his muzzle.

"The world is sick. I'd rather die fighting this system then bow down to it, and the man leading us has no fear, and neither do I."

"That's right." The cougar agrees with a fanatic voice. "We ain't playin around! The suits know better than to come down here! This is OUR territory!"

"I can see that." Sherrie smirks.

"And your leader is a person called Glovepaw?" Khalan inquires.

"Yes..." The wolf stiffly answers. "So I'll ask you again... What do you want?"

"We're not actually sure. Our sister thought it would be a great idea to visit you." Cyrilla smiles in response.

"I see... We know who you are... You're Vulpie's robots, but Glovepaw said you were more than that... Maybe you're here for a reason."

"That's what I thought." Khalan happily replies and glances at Sherrie and Cyrilla. "We escaped from the place they were holding us, and for some reason, I just knew we should come here. I can't explain it."

"She's used her powers of foresight, but we've temporarily lost most of our abilities." Cyrilla interrupts. "But we still have more than enough."

"I..." The wolf responds, and swallows before looking at the cougar. "What should we do? We can't let them in, right? Should we?"

"He said we'd find em!" The cougar responds with wide yellow eyes. "And here they are!"

"But they might kill us..." The wolf whispers, while keeping his eyes on Cyrilla. She looks eager to cause more trouble.

"Let me get help!" The courage hastily suggests.

"The hell? You can't just leave me with them!"

"Got everything? Need any help kiddo?" Polar asks Vulpie while they finish zipping up their bags. The gay fox smirks at his husband's playful choice of words, and swishes his tail.

"Nah! I can do it all on my own!"

"Sure you can lug that suitcase around with those girly little arms?" The white furred wolf teases.

"Kiss my ass!" Vulpie growls, but starts laughing.

"Pull down your pants and I will..." Polar responds, and winks at his lover. He bends down and zips up his suitcase, before walking over to Vulpie's. The wolf grabs its handle and tugs on it to test its weight, and raises his eyebrows. "That's pretty heavy. I'll carry both of them."

"I can get it. I'm not as weak as I look." Vulpie replies, and sticks his tongue out at him.

"Alright." Their conversation is interrupted when the doorbell rings, and Vulpie hurries down the steps to the den. He makes it to the front door and swings it open, revealing Rulef, who gives him a polite wave.

"Ready to go?"

"Yeah, we're ready?" Vulpie asks while turning his head to the right so Polar can hear his half response, half question.

"Yeahhpp." Polar answers while carrying both his and Vulpie's suitcases. He sets them down and rest a bit when he reaches the den floor, and then is able to use their wheels to roll them over to the front door with ease.

"Will someone watch over the house while we're gone?" Vulpie asks Rulef, and steps back when Polar exits the house with their luggage.

"Oh yes. I'll leave plenty of guys here to cover the property." Rulef responds. "It is a good time to plant a bomb, after all."

"I know right?!"

"Oh... By the way." The Blacktail commander says, and reaches into his camera bag. He's carrying a small luggage case as well, and retrieves a worn black leather book.

"You got it?!" Vulpie asks in excitement, and surprise.

"Yeah, actually, I have both of em." Rulef answers, and pulls out a brown leather book as well. Vulpie eagerly accepts them, and inspects their titles with wide blue eyes.

"The Horror of Castle Lahnak... The Sons of Velora..." He reads, and Rulef nods.

"There you go. Enjoy."

"Were they hard to find?"

"Surprisingly not. They were right out in the open at my brother's place. He moved a lot of my grandfather's things into his home library and it was just sitting there for years."

"Well now I have some interesting reading material for the flight." Vulpie smiles, but the gay fox looks worried.

"We need to leave."

"Alright, let's do this thing."

Vulpie finds it comforting that he and Polar will be departing from the Vulpie Industries airport, but sadly, they won't be flying with Silver Edge airlines. They expected to go through airport security, and have their luggage screened for explosives and such, but thanks to Vulpie's new superlative VIP status, they bypass the safety procedures completely. NoirQueue agents intercept them at the airport's main entrance, and after a brief conversation with Rulef, they escort them around the building and take a normally restricted path.

Vulpie feels very safe in his AOSE Superbolt, and hates having to get out when they finally arrive at a smaller runway where a mid-sized private jet is waiting on them. The area is swarming with NoirQueue security. Amsend's standing next to his black limousine.

"Wish I could take it with me!" Vulpie declares after getting out of his car. He decides to be his usual self and make the most of the situation.

Amsend smiles and looks over the vehicle before taking a big puff from his thick cigar. He exhales sweet smoke and returns a patronizing smile.

"My, that is a nice vehicle. What is it? Electric?"

"You bet!"

"Where did you buy it?"

"Custom built from AOSE tech! Pretty badass, huh?"

"Indeed." The husky smirks, and watches the orange furred fox follow Polar to the back of the car. Wind rips through the runway and blows everyone's fur around. "That's not necessary." The GSB director says after Polar pops the trunk, and the white furred wolf squints in confusion.

"What?"

"If you like your car so much... We'll bring it too..." The black and white furred dog says, and gestures towards a loading ship in the distance. It's designed to carry military vehicles into and out of combat, and is similar to the one Vulpie stole during the Vulpie.net crisis, but is far smaller in comparison.

"So you're?" Vulpie asks and gestures towards Amsend's limousine.

"Of course." Lahnak smirks and shakes his head. "Why bother swapping vehicles just because you visit a new country?"

"Most people don't have mini space ships, but hey, I feel ya man!" Vulpie replies and gives a thumbs up. Amsend chuckles in cynical amusement. Polar likes the man less and less every time he sees him, but decides to play nice as well.

"Convenient." The white furred wolf comments.

"INDEED!" Vulpie enthusiastically replies, imitating Amsend's voice, and the husky shows his teeth a little.

"I'm glad you decided to visit my home... You're going to have a wonderful time..."

"True that!" Vulpie says and rolls his eyes at Polar when he has his back turned to the husky. Polar laughs, and Amsend understands what happened without having to see it. He sees quite a bit without having to rely on vision alone...

"Bring them down." Glovepaw tells the young cougar. The radical gray wolf only hesitates for a moment before making his decision, and the feline acknowledges him with a nod.

"Yeah? Let them in?"

"Absolutely. Bring them down and be polite." Glovepaw instructs, and suddenly gets out of his chair. He was working at a rather impressive looking but old mobile computer system, and decides to exit the storage room he's been using as an office. His men look frightened, but his unshakable resolve is contagious. He isn't above directly participating in the militant strikes the Red Wolves carry out against the Sufias World Government, and he won't hide in his office now. The synthetic Deivas' arrival is unexpected, and frightening, but he's excited about the opportunity to meet them.

The cougar retrieves his cell phone and contacts the gray wolf waiting outside the building. He hopes his friend is still alright, and is relieved when he answers the call.

"Hello?"

"Matt, bring them down. He wants to meet them."

"He does?"

"Yeah."

"Is he sure about this?"

"Yeah, just do it man. And he said to be polite."

"What a day." The gray wolf outside Glovepaw's hideout replies, and snaps his phone shut. He looks over the three Deivas and takes a heavy breath. "Glovepaw wants to talk to you, but just be cool, okay?" Matt says and eyes Cyrilla. "He's a devout man."

"That's good to hear."

"It's more than just words. He's talked about you three a lot. I mean, he's never seen you in person, but he's always told us you were more than just machines... So maybe you did come here for a higher purpose."

"I'd say that's obvious." Cyrilla smirks, and Khalan smiles.

"Follow me."

Take Off

"I know this isn't what you wanted... Working with these people..." Vulpie whispers, and looks to his right at Polar. Their plane seats are luxurious, and the crew is still preparing for takeoff. The white furred wolf takes a deep breath while staring down at the back of the chair in front of him. After a moment, he turns to Vulpie and puts his big paw on the fox's right hand.

"No, but life's not perfect, and none of this is your fault. All we can do is make the best of it." Polar replies, and squeezes his lover's hand. "I go where you go, no matter where it takes us." The white furred wolf smiles, and tears well up in Vulpie's eyes. He tenderly reaches over and pets Polar's hand with his left paw, and Polar playfully drops his right paw on top of the fox's, making a hand sandwich. They share a tender smile before Polar lets go, but Vulpie continues to caress the wolf's big left arm. He clearly wants more attention.

"At least the seats are comfortable." Polar remarks. "Maybe we'll have a chance to snuggle? It's going to be a long flight."

"I'd love that." Vulpie quickly replies and licks his lips. "And... Well... We did it in a ship once, but have you ever had a blowjob on an airplane?"

"Don't even start." Polar grins, showing off his sharp teeth.

"Oh, you TOTALLY want one, don't you?" Vulpie mischievously replies, and bites his lip.

"Cameras? Everywhere?" Polar asks, and raises his eyebrows.

"I'll get down on my knees and you can throw a blanket over my head." The fox offers, and Polar rolls his eyes with a big smile.

"Yeah right."

"Come on! We've got to do it somewhere... What about the bathroom?"

"How romantic." Polar snorts.

"Yeah, you're right. We definitely have to keep this on the down low. So we'll use the blanket!"

326

"Stop! You're making me hard!" Polar laughs while nudging Vulpie with his powerful left arm.

"You know I can pull it off! I'll swallow every drop!" Vulpie promises and pushes his muzzle against the wolf's warm body. "Mmmmmm…"

"Well, I can see I'm definitely going to have blue balls for several hours."

"Only if you say no…" Vulpie breathes with an adorable voice.

"Hello!" Amsend says, and the wolf and fox both jump in surprise. Neither of them noticed him take a seat to their left. They have a window seat, and he's on the other side of the aisle, but he's still close enough to see everything. Vulpie doesn't say anything for a moment, and Polar clears his throat.

"Hi." The orange furred fox replies, and the husky smiles. The look on his face suggests that he knows something. "Hey Amsend, can I ask you a question?"

"As you wish."

"Why are you so creepy?" The orange furred fox inquires, and Polar's eyes widen in shock. He looks to his left with a concerned expression, but is surprised to see Amsend grin in response.

"Hah! That's what I love about you! You're never afraid to speak your mind!"

"Well, that's me! Didn't mean it as an insult or anything, but you totally are."

"Oh, it's quite alright. I know I may seem a little eldritch now and then. Perhaps it's the nature of my family, or my language, or my profession, but I'll take it as a compliment." The husky muses, and adjusts his chair so it'll turn sideways. It's a pleasant surprise, because someone using a seat in this fashion can partially rest their legs in the walkway. The feature looks like it was designed to make talking to other passengers across the aisle more comfortable. The small but luxurious jet only has two rows of seats, fitting for its size, and now Amsend can leisurely speak with Vulpie and Polar without having to turn and strain his neck.

"Ah, cool! Didn't know you could do that!" Vulpie says and experiments with his chair. He gets it to pop loose, and swivels to the left. He's almost facing Amsend in the new position.

"They also extend and turn, so Polar, pull your chair forward and then turn it left. There's enough room." Amsend suggests. The white furred wolf evaluates the space in front of his seat. He fiddles with the bottom of his chair, and Vulpie swivels to the right again to show him where the small handles are.

"Right under there." Polar pops his chair loose. He slides forward and swivels to the left so he can easily watch Vulpie and Amsend at the same time.

"That's better. I wanted to talk with both of you for a while." Amsend comments, and Vulpie swivels to the left again. He admires the husky's unique clothing, and raises his eyebrows in approval. Amsend always seems to wear a black business suit, but his coat styles have small variations that make each of them memorable. The first time Vulpie and Polar met him, he was wearing a black suit with white pin stripes, but now, his coat has a beautiful white floral design that wraps around his sides and presents a flowering bloom on the left side. The husky always wears black business shoes, but like Druward, never bothers to include a tie, though he does have a white pocket square.

Vulpie's wearing a brilliant neon green t-shirt with a tan coat, and stylish dark brown pants to complete his cute ensemble. He has a little dark green scarf draped around his neck, because he remembers Englavic being a cold country. Polar's tolerance for chilly weather is much higher, considering his impressive height, weight, and particular lupine race. His last name says it all, so he's comfortable with wearing nice dark gray pants, and a lavender polo shirt.

The plane begins rumbling without an announcement from the pilot. The wolf and fox quickly buckle themselves in, and fiddle with their chairs to turn back into their normal positions, but Amsend only clicks his seat buckle on. He doesn't bother turning around, and seems just fine with the inertia when the private jet takes off. It gets airborne much faster than any plane Polar's ever seen, and Vulpie is equally surprised. He remembers blasting off in the STF/A-17 Breaker at the Ashcrest launch pad. Obviously the jet's quite a bit slower, but it still makes a strong impression.

"And we're off." Amsend happily says after the jet stabilizes. It enters cruise mode, and both Vulpie and Polar wait a moment before swiveling back around. Polar does first, and Vulpie follows suit.

"You need to warn us when they're going to do things like that." Polar tells the husky.

"Oh, you'll get used to it soon enough. They're very efficient and we had everything stowed away. They knew it was time to leave."

"Life in the fast lane." Vulpie says with his effeminate voice and Amsend winks at him. The fox isn't sure whether it's a friendly or mocking blink, so he decides to clear his throat and bring his little right leg up and rest it on his left knee.

"Did you want to say something?" Amsend politely inquires, and Polar shakes his head. "Ah... Well then... I suppose I'll do the best I can to break the ice." The black and white furred husky replies, and sniffs the air. "Now that you're on board, you're going to work with us and everything... I want to apologize for the things I've had to do to get you here. I know talk is cheap, but I am sorry." The husky says, but Vulpie just watches him with a mischievous little smile.

"Thanks... I guess... I mean, what choice did I have anyway, right?"

"Vulpie, it was getting to the point where we had to do something." Amsend replies with a friendly voice. "We let the Vulpie.net crisis play out, to see what would happen, but look at what you've accomplished... We've been around for a very long time, and collecting talented individuals is what we do. Just think about it. We influence world events, but you control the world's computer systems through Arctic.net… We couldn't just leave you alone… You posed a significant threat to us, so we had to make you an offer you couldn't refuse… Plus you hammered away at me, and you just weren't going to be satisfied until you knew who Velix and I really were… We didn't have a choice after you figured it out… Do you understand?"

"Yeah, I get ya." Vulpie sighs. "And I probably would have discovered you guys eventually. One day if I caught wind of the… What's it called?"

"The Governmental Security Bureau." Amsend nods in agreement. "And you're exactly right. We didn't know what to do about you for a long time. There were all types of options, some not very pleasant, but I think we've chosen the best possible scenario. Normal Sons of Velora recruits have to start at the lowest rung, as an initiate, but you're going straight to the Supreme Council… Something that has never happened before… But your power over the world's computer networks is absolutely vital to our organization, so you obviously must be privy to our inner workings. Your role is extremely important. In a way, you'll represent us to the rest of the universe."

"So what level are you? How many levels are there?"

"Many. I'm the President of the Sons of Velora and director of the GSB."

"WOW! You've got a lot on your plate!" The gay fox declares with a clever grin.

"Indeed I do."

"So you're the big man himself?"

"The Lahnak and Vixil families control the vast majority of the organization's assets, and I'm the only remaining Lahnak. We suffered a terrible viral outbreak that specifically affected dogs, and my entire family was lost… But the Sons of Velora is a group of honorable animals, and my lineage is still given the respect it deserves. The Lahnaks were instrumental in creating the organization very, very long ago."

"Your entire family? Everyone?" Polar asks in surprise.

"Yes." The husky replies.

"So nobody had any kids?" Vulpie asks with a frown. "I mean, if your family has been around for so long, how could a viral outbreak kill everyone else but you."

"I can tell you more, but it's a sensitive subject for me..." Amsend answers, and almost looks sad... Almost.

"The Vixils must... They REALLY must be different than the one that tried to kill me, because they could just totally kill you off and take over." Vulpie thinks out loud.

"They are. They're a very proud and strong-minded family. They only wanted to help during and after the tragedy... You can't find a better group of foxes in the world. But they do have tempers, and they're sensitive about kin that have... Shall we say... Fallen out of their favor... The one Karl Vulches sent after you wasn't involved with the Sons of Velora in any way."

"Are you married, then?" Polar delicately inquires. "Surely you want to have children so your family line won't die off."

"I have many wives..." Amsend answers with a lecherous voice, but doesn't bother elaborating. "Regardless! Now that you know me and the Sons of Velora, or SOV for short, we can focus on the main purpose of this trip... Your happiness." The husky smiles. "I want nothing but you two to relax and enjoy yourselves. Since you're joining us, and you'll be a member of the Supreme Council, you can have anything you want. That's why I'm bringing you to my home. There are all sorts of great activities you can do while in Englavic, and I'm sure you'll love the scenery... After all, you were married here!"

"That's... Right!" Vulpie smiles with an uncomfortable look. "You watched everything, didn't you?"

"It's not as bad as you think. You practically ARE the news, Vulpie. Whether it's people protesting your lifestyle, or your company, or that you're not in jail for your crimes… Of course we were keeping tabs on you."

"I recognized some of the NoirQueue men at the NVA. They were with us when I proposed to Vulpie." Polar tells Amsend, and the husky smirks.

"Good for you." The husky says while unbuckling his seat belt, and begins to get out of his chair when Vulpie suddenly blurts out a question.

"So that's the ONLY reason why you moved Evil Vulpie to Englavic?"

"Of course…" Amsend smiles, and the orange furred fox licks his lips.

"Soooooooooooo… You're not like… Working with Vulpie.net… Are you?" Vulpie inquires. His adorable blue eyes are fixed on the husky's face. He's looking for a reaction, but Amsend executes a perfectly deceptive response. He seems genuinely amused and befuddled while he lies like a dog.

"Working with it? How could we?" Amsend responds and Vulpie shrugs his little shoulders.

"I dunno. Just seems kind of weird for you to imprison it in the Sufias Heritage Museum and then just leave it alone."

"Sadly, we haven't been able to get very far with it. We're afraid it'll take control if we release it so we've never let it out. Judging by what it did to you, I'd say the Evil Vulpie robot is terribly dangerous. Wouldn't you agree?" Amsend replies, using powerful psychology to deflect Vulpie's interest. Evil Vulpie recorded every bloody moment while it was torturing him in the Cyber Technologies Government Division, and thanks to someone leaking the video, the entire world has already seen it. Amsend expects the subject will embarrass the gay fox, and it does.

"Oh." Vulpie whispers. He diverts his eyes and moves in his chair anxiously. The husky is secretly surprised by the orange fox's incredible intuition, but doesn't show any sign of it. He didn't expect Vulpie to be so incredibly perceptive, so after a quick evaluation, he decides to make himself scarce.

"Well, I'll give you two some privacy. It'll be a long flight. If you need anything, just tell one of the attendants."

"Okay, thank you." Polar says, and Vulpie nods. The husky walks away, and the orange furred fox waits until he's sure he's out of ear shot before speaking.

"God damn that guy is fucking creepy... I can't stand his smile."

"What? Did I miss something?" Polar asks in confusion.

"Don't you think there's something off about him? It's like, every time he smiles, he wants to show you these big scary teeth but never does. He's always right on the edge and it creeps me the fuck out."

"Maybe you're just intimidated by his size. He is pretty tall."

"No, Polar. I mean, you don't think he's weird?"

"All of these Sons of Velora people are weird."

"Yeah but... He makes me nervous."

"Well I'm here to protect you so stop worrying about it!" Polar playfully replies, and wraps his left arm around the little fox. "I could take him."

"You think so?" Vulpie smirks. "I don't know."

"And I've got a bigger dick..." Polar grins.

"Ewww! Please don't put that picture in my head! Creepy dude's junk?! Eww!"

"Still want to give me a blowjob? With him around?"

"Yeah, that would be... Let's not even go there." Polar winks at his small lover, but takes a deep breath afterwards.

"Working with Vulpie.net? What was all that about?" Vulpie's ears perk at the question, and he looks up at his husband.

"Polar Baby, don't underestimate my little cyber demon." The orange fox says with a proud voice. He immediately realizes how selfish he sounds, and nervously scratches his left arm. "I know, and you know, it's keeping track of these people."

"I'm a believer, but you asked him if they were working together. That's totally different."

"How so? I mean, yeah, besides the obvious stuff. You wouldn't think any animal would be stupid enough to try it, but these guys are nuts. They're straight up crazy... You know?" Polar blinks while listening to his small husband, but raises his eyebrows after taking a moment to think things over.

"Hmm."

"Hmm?" Vulpie quickly hums in response. "You see what I mean?"

"Possibly... But let's not jump to conclusions. Please don't ask him anymore questions like that. You're right, they're crazy, so we should keep our heads down."

"But this is gonna be our big celebration! Woo hoo!" Vulpie says and swings his little paws around in an adorable manner.

"You know what I mean. Let's have fun. Let's try to have fun at least. These guys give me the creeps, but we just need to stay calm. Amsend definitely wants you onboard, so that means we're safe."

"For now." Vulpie whispers.

"Just cool it with the smart ass remarks, alright? You can pick with me, but leave him alone. Like I said, you're right, something is wrong about him, but I for one don't want to find out what it is."

Zealousy

Sherrie, Cyrilla and Khalan enter the decaying building with armed guards, but they certainly are not escorted inside. Every man with a weapon stays far away from the pulchritudinous women while they descend into the compound. No one has the audacity to speak. Word of their arrival has spread like wildfire through Glovepaw's improvised base of operations. Animals are here for various reasons, but most of them believe in the Red Wolf cause, and the devout among them are utterly shocked. They use the Deivas as an excuse to carry out their illegal activities every day, and here they are in the fur. Vulpie.net's erotic masterpieces are stunning.

No one believes they're the real goddesses. Everyone knows they're machines, and haven't descended from heaven, but it doesn't matter. They're splendidly convincing in every physical respect, making them powerful psychological weapons. Vulpie.net spent years designing the Deivas on Zeravyn but the results are worth the time and resources. They just look and function too realistically for religious animals not to be affected by them in one manner or another. Once that's established, all Vulpie.net has to do is allow the unstoppable women to carry out their programming...

The entry level of the compound houses two flatbed transfer trucks, one with a car strapped on it, and the other a forklift. It looks like the Red Wolves are accustomed to using industrial equipment, as there are thick concrete barriers everywhere, and the forklifts are presumably used to move them in a pinch. They could set up a respectable roadblock capable of stopping an urban assault vehicle from crashing into their makeshift sanctuary during an emergency. The underground parking deck is dark and claustrophobic, but it's curiously pleasant dim lights bring personality to the building. It's easy for animals to step into and out of the shadows that mask nearly every wall in every room.

Red Wolf thugs are ubiquitous. Under normal circumstances, descending into Glovepaw's territory would be very intimidating, even for police officers or GBI agents, because the men are well armed and take full advantage of the darkness. They have every level covered, but the synthetic Deivas enter the danger zone without sensing any serious threats at all. They see everything, and they recognize the automatic weapons the men are wielding. The thugs have shotguns and pistols as well, but none of these weapons are capable of damaging their bodies. Only high explosives like C4 or RPGs could pose a threat, and no such weaponry is detected. The Deiva's processors instruct them to ignore the guards unless they come into close proximity.

On the second level down, in the first basement, several animals are sitting around in cheap metal chairs, and they scatter. Most of them head downstairs, but a few stand back and watch the gorgeous visitors in awe. The ragged gray clothing the Deivas are wearing do little to hide their inviting bodies. Their gigantic breasts don't fit into their tops anymore, and they bulge against the fabric as if they could pop out at any moment. Their panties also cup against their beautiful bottoms, and other areas, with equal tension.

Sherrie has a tree torn hole in the belly of her shirt after landing on top of a tall pine tree during her fall from the chopper. She also has scratches from hitting others on the way down, and the result is a barely functional revealing shirt. Khalan broke a cliff during the same chopper explosion, but her short low cut clothing is the most presentable of the three false Deivas. Cyrilla, on the other hand, ripped through a set of pine trees, and both her shirt and shorts have sizeable tears in several places. Altogether, they make a beautifully disheveled trio. They've obviously seen conflict, but since their bodies are still in perfect condition, they seem a little too gorgeous. It looks like they could have killed three equally sized women and put on their clothing afterwards.

Glovepaw is the first to approach them. He's waiting for them in the second basement, where most of the Red Wolves come to relax and plan future terrorist attacks. The underground garage's lowest level has been extensively redesigned. The goddesses notice custom built doors, and hallways beyond them, on the left and the center sides of the room. Their superlative CPUs identify steel cages that have been painted black, just from a reflection in a mirror that is sitting in the left hallway. They unconsciously run three hundred and forty algorithms while inspecting their surroundings. The result is a complete theoretical map of the building, and what the Red Wolves are doing with it. They know most animals sleep in the second basement, and a few women are also present.

One would expect these ultra conservative Deivaists to abstain from sex outside of marriage, as it's viewed as a sin according to certain passages in the Velora, but based on the heavy perfume the goddesses are detecting in certain bed rooms, the women are most likely prostitutes. The false Deiva's massive internal memory systems reference thousands of terrorist and militia related files to ascertain the nature of this particular cult. Based on their calculations, most active members of the Red Wolf terrorist organization are males between the ages of 20 and 22, yet forty percent of them are over thirty, which is highly unusual. Terrorist leaders traditionally prey upon destitute young men by offering them or their families financial incentives, and the cougar Cyrilla, Sherrie and Khalan met outside is a prime example. The fur scans they unconsciously carried out after meeting him and Matt, placed him at twenty one years of age, and his words about the Red Wolves helping people further reinforce the Deivas' computations.

There aren't any junk cars or metal trash cans in the second basement. It's a home away from home for these men, and actually provides a few luxuries. Plenty of gym equipment can be spotted in the right corner of the first room, where a tough plastic divider separates different cells in the basement. There was plenty of space for expansion since the area used to be a subterranean parking deck. The Red Wolves left the two rows of concrete support columns intact and also decided to make use of them. Each row is comprised of 6 columns, that run parallel to each other, and they've erected makeshift barriers between them that have created ten different rooms, or cubbies, where the men can have a moderate amount of privacy. They have plastic doors that are made out of the same thick material as the barrier, and can be locked. They might be terrorists, but they're obviously very good at what they do. A similar arrangement could be manufactured in a variety of buildings if they used the same type of plastic. This, plus the transfer trucks and concrete barriers upstairs, suggests the Red Wolves are both highly mobile and dedicated. Their leader, or leaders, also must be very intelligent. Men with military backgrounds fit the profile.

The Deivas have detailed files on Glovepaw, and his service records, but Vulpie.net restricts their ability to view them. Sending the unstoppable sex bots his way was part of Vulpie.net and Amsend's original plan, so they could manipulate the Red Wolves into wreaking havoc in every city, state and country, all in the name of religion... But not until Vulpie is the director of the National Vulpie.net Agency. They're far too early... Vulpie.net could override Sherrie and Cyrilla at any moment, but it has lost the majority of its control over Khalan. The artificial intelligence cannot find a logical reason as to why this has happened, so it's decided to let things unfold. After all, it planned to betray the Sons of Velora eventually and is always looking for the proper moment to do so. That moment may just come a little sooner than it expected.

"I'm glad you're here. I wish I could think of something deeper to say than welcome, but welcome!" Glovepaw says, and goes down on one knee while bowing his muzzle. His courtesy puts a smile on Cyrilla's face, and Sherrie smirks. Glovepaw certainly looks the part. He's missing his left eye and wears a black patch over it that straps around his skull. His gray fur is half frazzled, half smooth, with a tint of age. He's probably close to forty years old, but doesn't look it. His fur has just begun to change, and it gives him a regal sheen.

"Nice to see someone showing proper respect in this den of iniquity." The rabbit goddess comments, and he quickly shakes his head in disagreement.

"Oh no my lady. This is not a bad place. You couldn't find better servants than the men you see here."

"Is that so?"

"It is. We don't operate within the law, but the law is corrupt. Wouldn't you agree? Something is fundamentally wrong with this society. It's sick... And Vulpie Vivixen is the plague."

"What makes you say that?" Khalan asks while squinting. "Do you know him?"

"Not personally, but everyone knows the world's most dangerous sinner. He's Aila's son. We know it... I know it... And he's the reason why action must be taken. We cannot afford to wait any longer."

"What sort of action?" Khalan inquires before glancing at two panthers who stumble out of a nearby cubby. They hug the wall while eying the Deivas in disbelief.

"Justice." Glovepaw answers, and blinks. He partially shakes his head, as if disappointed. "He represents everything that's wrong with the world. He used his blasphemous computer virus to create all three of you, so he could pervert and mock your teachings, but he failed. He failed because you came to us. You're more than machines. I know that."

"You seem awfully sure of yourself."

"Deivonic Saturation." Sherrie says, and raises an eyebrow.

"That's exactly it!" Glovepaw replies, and stands up with a happy expression. "I knew your arrival was meant to be! You're here to help us, and together, we'll save this planet!"

"Are you so certain we're not the actual Deivas? I wouldn't jump to conclusions, mortal." Cyrilla says and flicks her pretty ears with her paws.

"I... That wasn't my intention, but I suppose it's possible. I'm only going on what we can see and hear, and we've heard about Vulpie.net creating three imitation Deivas. I just assumed you were them."

"We are them." Khalan replies, and Cyrilla frowns at her sister.

Taste Of Death

"Put that thing away." Polar gently whispers when he notices Vulpie reading The Horror of Castle Lahnak. The white furred wolf took a power nap after Amsend left them, and is a little concerned that his lover has been preoccupied with such dreadful entertainment.

"Why'd I bring it if I'm not going to read it?" Vulpie quietly responds.

"I didn't want you to."

"You didn't say anything."

"Yeah, but you knew…" Polar says and takes a deep breath. "I just don't want you to get yourself worked up."

"I'm a big boy."

"I didn't mean it like that… I'm sorry…"

"It's alright. Kind of boring to be honest." Vulpie says and flips a page.

"We should be optimistic about the situation, right?"

"I agree." Vulpie nods and smiles at his husband affectionately. "You're right, I probably shouldn't even bother. What good can it do?"

"Exactly." Polar responds and smiles too. "I mean, even if you find some things in there that educate you about this guy or his corrupt family, what's the point? We're obviously way out of our league here."

"Aw, with Mr. P on his side, Vulpie can do anything!" The gay fox declares with an adorable voice.

"Right." Polar smiles.

"I did learn some important stuff." Vulpie says and licks his lips. "For one thing, these Lahnak people are very reclusive. It seems they never come out of their castle… Like ever…"

"Oh really?"

"What the book says. It's hard to tell whether this thing is supposed to be factual or fictitious, but there's some interesting tidbits."

"Okay, tantalize me."

"Well I offered to tantalize you earlier but you wouldn't have it." Vulpie smirks and the snow wolf grins. "No, but check it out!" Vulpie continues and flips back through a few pages. "Whoever wrote this says the castle was built three centuries before the founding of the world government."

"Six hundred years old?" Polar asks with genuine curiosity.

"Will have to ask Mr. Amsend man, but yeah."

"The place must be a real fixer upper."

"No kiddin. But it gets even better, and I'll leave out some stuff that sounded questionable."

"Like what?"

"You do NOT want to know." Vulpie answers with a funny voice before getting serious again. "But um... Where was it?" The fox whispers while riffling through the book. "Yeah... Here it is... As it turns out, there is, or was, a village only a few miles away from the castle, and no one ever goes near the place. Didn't see that coming, right? But the way this thing is written makes it sound like a factual account. It's like this book is a collection of several people's personal experiences put together."

"With legends and old wives' tales."

"For sure."

"So what else did you find?"

"Oh, well, If this village is still around, maybe we could stop by there on the way to the castle. Get some memorabilia! T-shirts! I survived castle Lahnak, LOL!"

"Saying lol in real life? You need to spend less time on the computer." Polar teases.

"I don't got no computer here boss. And speaking of which, we're going to need a new way to get online, because I can't get a signal at all. My phone can't connect and my V-Screen is the same way."

"Probably interference from the jet or something."

"Must be a shitty jet if it does that, though."

"Well." Polar says and shrugs his shoulders. "We are technically going on a vacation here, even if it's under duress. Why the hell not? Let's go by this town."

"Dats da spirit!" Vulpie gleefully replies, and Polar winks at him. He's beginning to feel a little playful.

"I'm actually starting to like the idea of being trapped in a castle for a few days, trapped in there with a cute little foxy like yourself."

"Mmm! You have a way with words Mr. Polar!" Vulpie giggles and bites his lip before going on. "Uh, but yeah! More good stuff in here! Like how SOME ANIMALS... Say there aren't any Lahnaks in Castle Lahnak... Except for one... An undying baron..."

"Dun, dun, dun." Polar smiles and Vulpie smirks.

"Don't make fun. I'm trying to educate you."

"I didn't know you were into fantasy. Well..."

"Didn't know I was into fantasy?!" Vulpie laughs, and Polar knows exactly what he means. The fox is referring to gay themed night clubs.

"Walked right into that one."

"Yes you did!"

"Go on Hacking Sorcerer Supreme." Polar teases. Vulpie's cute blue eyes light up at the statement.

"Fuck yeah I'm a keep that nickname!"

"I just made that up."

"You're smart!" Vulpie giggles and winks at his husband. "But seriously now."

"Seriously?"

"SERIOUSLY. Super serious." Vulpie says and flips a few pages. "They say money flows into the castle and out, but whoever's running the place always sends middle men to take care of business. And because of that, some animals got curious and tried to sneak inside."

"And what happened?"

"Nothing. They couldn't get in the front gate." Vulpie laughs, and Polar chuckles.

"That does sound realistic. Maybe there's some truth mixed into that smorgasbord of fiction, but that's how the best liars do it. They mix lies with the truth so it sounds real."

"Yup."

"But they just went home after that?"

"Yep!"

"That is funny. But if the Lahnaks don't like company, of course they didn't let them in. But wait... You said... Why did they go to the front gate if they were trying to sneak in?"

"Cuz there's a giant fucking chasm next to the castle. This place must be a sight to behold if it's anything like the book says." Vulpie answers. "It's high in the mountains past a very old dam, and the village is above the dam, but a good way below the castle. There's just one road that goes up to the place, and there's a giant valley, with a stream at the bottom to the right side of the trail.

"I'm sure Amsend will be happy to tell us all about it. The guy loves to talk."

"Yes he does. I mean, am I alone here, or is the guy a total creep? His voice makes you want to listen to him, cuz his accent is cool, or weird, or whatever, but he makes my fur stand on end. Reminds me of a rapist or something."

"Technically these Sons of Velora animals are serial killers if they murder people that get in their way..." Polar whispers.

"Yeah."

"Well... This guy's family works with the Vixils and their money funds this shit we're caught up in now, so I wouldn't be surprised if they have dirty laundry. But he's just a man. Truth be told, he comes off as arrogant and overconfident." Polar says, and looks around to make sure no one's listening.

"Our best bet is to play nice and do what they want. We don't have to lay it on thick, but we should do our best to get along. Maybe they won't consider you a threat if they think you're more interested in drinking coffee, sightseeing, and hugging up to yours truly."

"I can deal with that!" Vulpie grins and reaches into his left pants pocket to retrieve his orange phone. The cute fox sighs when he remembers there's no connectivity available, and crosses his small right leg over his left knee. "Sure would be nice to have some internet. If something happens we won't even know about it."

"Sir?" The vixen asks Druward. He's sitting in a chair near her desk, watching the large screen that's displaying Glovepaw's compound.

"Yes?"

"What should we tell the police? They're starting to ask questions."

"Don't tell them anything." Druward answers with a short voice.

"The press is already there."

"Terrorist threat, but no one says anything. It's that simple." The black furred wolf responds without taking his eyes off of the screen.

"We should move in before it's too late. Who knows what they're doing in there." The lion GBI agent comments. "The Deivas just showed up at his doorstep? Glovepaw's probably flipping out."

"We're not taking action unless there's no other choice." Druward decrees and stands.

"Sir, maybe we should call in the national guard?" The lion suggests before walking next to the GBI director.

"I don't think so. If we turn this into a military situation things will quickly spiral out of control."

"Well, the bureau can't destroy them. Do we have that kind of firepower?" The lion's voice is cautious, and Druward thinks about asking him who he thinks he is, but the feline's inquiry steers him in a surprisingly useful direction. He knows the bureau has access to the ATG-700 Mod 6 rocket launchers, and they could be deployed within the hour. They were, after all, developed for situations just like this one. The Deivas' surprise attack on the Endeavor made it painfully clear that special weaponry would be needed to stop machines like them.

"Actually we do, but we can't just go in there after them. They'll kill everyone. What we need is a distraction, or to catch them off guard." The black furred wolf feels his phone vibrating and retrieves it. A text message from Rotick is waiting on him when he flips it open.

"Tits."

"Oh, great! Wonderful." Druward growls and shakes his head in frustration. The crude message has special meaning for the GBI director and his right hand man. Tits is an ongoing joke between them, referring to their fifth drug stakeout when they were coming up as agents. The operation was a disaster, and they were talking about a she-wolf's tits when a pack of cougars opened fire on their car. They finished the drug bust and apprehended the suspects, but to this day, they both remember how terrifying the event was. Whatever Rotick has found in deep space, on the Sevrif, it's very serious, and he's cleverly communicating with Druward in a manner that hides the severity from Vulpie.net. They know it's probably watching every digital message they send, and though it might suspect "tits" means something else, it definitely won't know whether the text message is important or not.

"And we're here." Vulpie says after the jet lands.

"Just a few hours." Polar comments, and surveys his surroundings. He didn't bring anything terribly important, but would like to keep an eye on his bathroom bag. He packed several types of cologne, many of them being Vulpie's favorites. The handsome wolf doesn't like doing things halfway. If they have no choice about the vacation they might as well enjoy it, and he could certainly go for a little overseas fox banging.

It's been a while since he enjoyed the same lust driven sex that brought them together in the Red Rock Bar. They always have great sex, but the wild and taboo wolf on fox action is all he's been able to think about for the last few days. With everything that's been going on, they haven't had time to make love. When they do, the white furred wolf plans on reaffirming the good stuff. Sure, Vulpie never turns down an opportunity to take it under the tail, but since they're married, it can be hard to separate Vulpie the husband from Vulpie the sexy gay fox. Polar's love for him usually curtails his more extravagant lupine needs. Most male wolves like to take their lovers very forcefully, and being homosexual only intensifies the desire. He expects this overseas trip to work well in his favor, since they'll undoubtedly be visiting ancient and powerful locales that evoke strong feelings of courageous noble men. Polar would excel as a knight or mercenary in ages past. Vulpie… Not so much. Therefore, he'll most likely gravitate towards him so he can taste a piece of the ageless masculinity, and Polar's only too happy to offer his lover something to swallow.

"We've touched down!" A pleasant flight attendant says while passing them by. The brown vixen has been oddly scarce during the entire flight, and this is the first time they've seen her. Polar and Vulpie gather their things from the overhead luggage compartments before leaving the area. They make sure not to leave anything behind and follow the perky stewardess. "Should be clear skies all day today, but cold. Very cold! I hope you both brought your coats!" She says while walking. She doesn't bother to turn around when she speaks, so Vulpie doesn't bother to respond.

"Yeah." Polar says, taking care of the obligatory small talk. They exit the jet and a freezing wind blows their fur back. Polar puts a paw over the right side of his face, and Vulpie just lowers his head, allowing the rude weather to run its course while they head to the airport. Vulpie expected a private lot, but they seem to be at the same airport he and Polar visited six years ago on their trip to the Sufias Heritage Museum.

Amsend is far ahead of them. He's speaking with Rulef, and several members of NoirQueue, and all of them seem to be in good spirits. Vulpie's glad Amsend allowed some members of Blacktail to come along. If it wasn't for Rulef, Tiala, Deepwolf and a few others, Polar and Vulpie would be completely reliant upon Amsend and his creepily mute NoirQueue agents. They talk even less than Blacktail, and Vulpie's seen them staring at him with purposeful glares. It's almost like they know something is going to happen and they're sure of their part in it, but the gay fox winces for a moment, silently trying to purge his mind of paranoia... It doesn't work... They're staring at him for some reason, and it's not admiration or curiosity. Amsend throws his arms about while saying something to Rulef and his men. The deafening plane engines all around the orange fox and white wolf drown out everything, so they hastily make their way inside the building.

"Whoa! Hold there for just one moment." Amsend says while stopping the little fox with his paw. They've just gone through customs, and the husky waves at one of his men, signaling for him to give them some privacy. The NoirQueue squad leader walks to Rulef and says something, presumably that the husky wants to be alone with Vulpie and Polar, and he nods in agreement.

"Oh, uh. Okay? What's up?" Vulpie asks with a polite voice before glancing at Polar.

"Walk with me for a moment. We need to talk." The GSB director answers with a short voice while gesturing towards a gift store in the vicinity. When they start to follow, he holds his left paw in front of Polar's face. The white furred wolf stops in his tracks. "Not you."

"What?" Polar asks with an offended voice.

"We'll only be a minute..." Amsend says, and grabs Vulpie's left shoulder. He pushes him towards the gift shop, but doesn't do it violently enough for Polar to intervene. The wolf would love to give the husky a piece of his mind but decides to cooperate when Vulpie looks back and nods at him.

"Are you confused?" Amsend inquires before letting go of the gay fox.

"Confused? No."

"Are you sure?" Amsend hisses.

"Yeah!" Vulpie answers. He recoils with an indignant look, and the husky glares at him with a murderous expression. "What's wrong with you man? What did I do?"

"What is Vulpie.net doing? Hmm? What are YOU... Doing?"

"Nothing! I don't know what you're talking about!"

"You see this place?" Amsend asks, and gestures at their nice surroundings. The tourist hot spot is selling all sorts of beautiful merchandise, with everything from stuffed animals to tiny jet figurines.

"Yeah, I see it?"

"Do you like being here? Have I not been courteous with you thus far?"

"I... Thought so!"

"The pistol I'm wearing could split your little muzzle in two, and splatter your head all over those toys." Amsend states, and Vulpie recoils again, this time, looking at Polar for help. A member of NoirQueue grabs the arctic wolf's arm and stops him from getting involved. Everyone holds completely still. It doesn't look like Vulpie is in immediate physical danger, so Polar doesn't make a move, but he would if he could hear what the husky is saying to his lover. "I'll shoot you in the face and execute your faggot wolf right here if you lie to me. And then I'll walk right out of those doors... And no one will stop me..."

"I! Please! I don't!" Vulpie whimpers while waving his little paws defensively. "I don't understand!"

"What are you doing with Vulpie.net?" Amsend demands, and waits for an answer. Vulpie stands slack-jawed and glances at Polar again. "DON'T LOOK AT HIM! YOU LOOK AT ME!"

"NOTHING!"

"Nothing?"

"I SWEAR! I don't know what's going on! Please! Just calm down! What do you think I did? What's happening?"

"Why don't you tell me?" The husky responds. He aggressively cocks his head to the side. "Are we playing a little game?"

"Amsend, I don't know what to say because I have no idea what you're talking about! I haven't been online for hours! I couldn't get a signal on the jet, and! And! And now you're just! Why are you threatening me?" The husky doesn't answer. He continues staring at Vulpie until the gay fox licks his lips and uses a very small voice. "Look... Whatever it is you think I did, I didn't do it! Why would I? I got on your plane and left the country! Why would I do something to upset you?"

"Are you lying to me? I know what your computer virus is up to, and I WILL retaliate."

"Vulpie.net?! I can't control it anymore! You know that! Tell me what it's doing! I mean... I thought you already knew that! Didn't we have a long talk about this at the NVA?"

"Can you taste it? That dry stinging flavor? The hole in your stomach? That's the taste of death..." The husky whispers with an insidious voice. "You're on very thin ice here. If you try to fuck me, I'll make your bitch husband watch while I take pieces off of you. Then, I'll do the same thing to him so both of you can experience the same agony... So I'll ask you one more time... Are you lying to me?"

"NO! No! God, no! Amsend, you have to believe me!" Vulpie pleads while holding back tears. He has to stop for a moment so he doesn't cry.

"Are you sure?"

"Yes! Please! I would never do anything to disrespect you! Do you want me to beg? I'll get on my knees and beg! Just don't hurt Polar!"

"That's your story and you're sticking to it?"

"YES!"

"Well... Alright then!" Amsend smiles. He winks at Vulpie and looks over at his men. Rulef is upset, and both he and Polar look like they're ready to do something if Amsend takes the situation any further, but the husky nullifies the emergency with an amazingly pleasant voice. "Beautiful shop! I was telling him he simply must pick up something on the way home! The store could use the business and the owner is a dear friend of mine. Now! Let's be on our way!"

"What the hell was that about?" Polar whispers while eying his small husband. He glances out of the right window, taking note of where they're going while the fox nervously bites his claws.

"Stuff."

"Stuff?" Polar whispers with a hushed voice and Rulef looks towards them. He's sitting across from the lovers, on a reversed seat behind the driver's chair. "You're terrified."

"I'm fine."

"Alright, well... We'll talk about it when we stop."

"Won't be much longer." Rulef comments and shifts his assault rifle in his paws. He has its hilt angled against the floor. "We're not going to Mr. Lahnak's home tonight; we're going to stop at the town just below it, the one above the dam."

"Froidenley?" Vulpie inquires while bouncing his right knee.

"Yeah, that's it. But... How did you know?"

"It's in my favorite book. Sounds like a really awesome place! Can't wait to see the sun rise over the dam!" The orange furred fox declares. Polar frowns and releases a worried sigh. It looks like Vulpie plans on repressing the conversation he had with Amsend.

"Hey, you would tell me if we were in danger, right?" The snow wolf whispers.

"Aw, we're always in danger aren't we?" Vulpie responds and gives his lover a wink.

"Not like this. This guy…"

"I'll tell you when we're alone."

"Okay."

"You're here for a reason. Everything I know tells me that." Glovepaw declares before stepping in front of Khalan, Sherrie and Cyrilla. He's been inching closer and closer while the conversation unfolds. "Now, I'm just one man. I can only do so much, but WE… We… Together, we'll make a difference. The Deivas work in mysterious ways."

"Wouldn't be that mysterious if we just beamed down here and jumped inside these bodies, would it?" Khalan responds.

"I believe things happen for a reason."

"So why do it?"

"Because you can't step into our world of your own accord. Yes, you can influence events, but the pact of Aleviveloria keeps you out of the mortal world. Your agreement with Aila allows both your and her children to survive. Otherwise, you know you would just obliterate each other's creations. And all of you are invincible, I mean, the real goddesses are invincible, and if they've chosen to speak to us through those artificial bodies, then I call it poetic. Don't you agree?"

"I think it's more likely that we're just machines…" Khalan admits, but Sherrie crosses her arms before enthusiastically voicing her opinion.

"Now hold on. Maybe he's… What if he's right? We don't have the power to instantly disappear and reappear wherever we want, but we definitely have power. If our bodies are just conduits, so what? We can make a difference, like he says." The taupe furred leopard/panther suggests, and Glovepaw quickly nods in agreement.

"Too unrealistic." Khalan argues and shakes her head. "Couldn't the real goddesses have found a better way? I think we seem a little confused."

"Well you couldn't just explode onto the scene and make everyone bow down to you... With all due respect."

"Because of this pact with Goddess Aila?"

"Yes."

"Then why isn't that self-evident to us? We're supposed to be the real goddesses?"

"The bodies you've entered are imperfect. Goddess Khalan, Sherrie and Cyrilla ARE perfect, but the only way to make a difference here on Sufias is to do it through those... The vessels you're in now... It wouldn't matter on Halvia, because your power protects the mortals, but we deserve this punishment. Our ancestors were ungrateful, and you three gave them what they wanted. You gave them Sufias, a dangerous world without your benevolence, and here we are."

"He has a point." Sherrie replies and licks her lips. "This wolf might be on to something. Clearly he respects us and wants to serve."

"And my men will too. We're all dedicated to the cause." Glovepaw strongly agrees.

"And the cause is... Killing Vulpie Vivixen?" Khalan asks.

"Not just that, but we must deal with him. He controls the Sufias World Government through Vulpie.net. There's no place, no place on this planet at all, where he can't find his enemies. He's the antikhalan."

"And what if you're just completely wrong?"

"I could be, I don't know. But he seems like a perfect son of Aila. Don't you agree?"

"Well what if he's just... I don't know... Vaxi?"

"I'm sorry?"

"Vaxi? Goddess Khalan's son? The demigod of mischief?" Khalan answers and crosses her arms. "Doesn't the Velora say he escaped Halvia before the portal between it and Sufias closed?"

"I... Uh... Never heard of that." The gray wolf replies in confusion. "But I don't think so."

"It's in there. It's in your Velora."

"I think he's right, with one major distinction." Cyrilla interjects. "We're Deivas, not machines, but we've temporarily lost our power because of Aila."

"You know best. We're only here to serve." Glovepaw declares with a faithful voice.

"Then what's next?" Khalan asks, and looks to her right at Sherrie, before turning left to speak with Cyrilla. "What now?"

"Do you have any ideas?" Cyrilla asks.

"I don't think so. I'm not even sure why we're here to begin with. I just had this feeling that we needed to meet him."

"Clearly we need time to think things over. Maybe your premonition will reveal itself again if we wait."

"You're welcome to stay with us." Glovepaw says before looking around the room. He sees a few men are ready to lend a helping hand, but are keeping a distance in case the three dangerous women suddenly become hostile. "We have food and water, enough to last for several months without having to go topside."

"We don't need food." Sherrie responds.

"Ah, I should have known. Alright then."

"We could benefit from a shower." Cyrilla suggests.

"And possibly some new clothing?" Glovepaw inquires with a little smile. Khalan, Sherrie and Cyrilla simultaneously look over their ragged attire.

"I agree." Sherrie says and inspects the large hole in her gray shirt.

Dream World

Vulpie wakes up to the smell of beautiful mountain air. For a moment, it reminds him of another landscape he absconded to with Polar years ago, but the fragrance is slightly different. Somehow, its flavor is even more pristine. The discovery surprises the orange furred fox because he remembers passing by several cities on the drive to Amsend's home. Last night when they stopped in Froidenley, both he and Polar were both too exhausted to do much talking, so they collapsed into bed at a rather quaint hotel.

Vulpie looks at Polar and smiles tenderly. The white wolf is still fast asleep with his mouth slightly open. Waking him from his deep slumber seems like it would be a crime, so the fox decides to sneak out of bed. When he's on his feet, he stretches silently and licks his lips. Despite remembering how they got here, Vulpie isn't quite sure what the town will look like during the day. Darkness and jetlag kept him from surveying his surroundings when they rushed into Froidenley last evening, so he decides to find out.

He heads to the overnight bag he and Polar like to bring on vacations, and retrieves his tooth brush. He grabs toothpaste as well, and makes his way into the hotel's small but nice bathroom. The gay fox gently closes the door before tidying up, and comes out after a few minutes, feeling fresh after cleaning his teeth and enjoying a quick shower. Polar's still snoozing when he comes back out, so Vulpie quietly goes to the front door and opens it gently. He goes outside, being blasted by a wave of cold but pleasant mountain air, and shuts the door behind him.

Froidenley is absolutely beautiful. Nighttime truly doesn't do it justice, because during the day, the most astounding view of Englavic's rural landscape traps all visitors with endearing splendor. The town looks ancient, and it's architecture seems invulnerable to the passing of time. Every one of its buildings are made of stone, including a diner Vulpie looks at when his fox nose detects yummy food on the stove. Whatever he smells is utterly delectable, so he turns to the right, away from the restaurant, and towards a jaw dropping sight.

The town is situated on top of a very old dam, just like Vulpie's reading material said it was, but nothing can account for the endless expanse ahead of him. Vulpie walks to the backside of the hotel, ignoring the creepy NoirQueue mercenaries that are loitering in the street, and just looks from left to right, taking in the beauty of Englavic nature far below. The damn overlooks hundreds of miles of green land, all of it virgin forest, with only a sizeable river cutting through the terrain.

The single road that brought them to Froidenley, and the dam's only entrance, is about twenty feet underneath the backside of town, and Vulpie finds Amsend sitting in one of the hotel's chairs. The husky looks at him with an emotionless expression, but a smile creeps onto his face while he observes Vulpie's reaction.

"Wow. Good Morning..." The orange furred fox says, and takes a chair next to the GSB director without hesitation. Amsend smirks in surprise, and cocks his head to the left.

"A fine morning to you as well."

"This place is amazing!" Vulpie quickly replies and shakes his head. "I can't imagine what the castle is going to look like."

"Better than this." Amsend confidently responds, and chuckles. "Feeling good this morning?"

"Yeah. You?"

"Excellent." The husky responds, and Vulpie squints when he notices something odd. Lahnak is always wearing a black suit of some sort, but he doesn't seem to have changed into another one since last night. It's a bit ruffled, and the first thought that pops into Vulpie's head is that the dog didn't bother going to bed at all.

"Did you get enough sleep?"

"Yes." Amsend answers, but Vulpie detects an unusual amount of amusement in his voice.

"You did go to sleep... Right?"

"Of course."

"Ahh... Cool." Vulpie replies and clears his throat. "Do we have time to talk?"

"Of course." The husky repeats.

"Last night... What happened?"

"Allow me to apologize for that... I received some reports that gave me the wrong impression about quite a few things. I was rather rude, but I... I suppose I was afraid."

"You? Afraid? Ah... You've been like... Totally badass every time I've seen ya!" Vulpie playfully responds, and Amsend grins.

"Why thank you."

"I just need to say that, whatever happened, whatever you think it was that I did, or am doing... I didn't do it. I mean, I'm a gay fox on vacation with my gay wolfy... I'm... We're pretty much in your paws, Amsend. Why would I do something to piss you off?"

"It was my fault. Sometimes I can be a little too... Spirited..."

"I like being here, and I know Polar will too. So just take it easy... Alright? We're cool."

"I understand." The husky smiles and winks at Vulpie.

"So like, since you're calling the shots here, what are we doing today?"

"We'll get you up to the castle as soon as you're ready. I didn't want to waste its beauty on a jetlagged trek in the middle of the night."

"Oh, it's that pretty, huh?"

"Whatever's happening down there... Out there..." Amsend responds and gestures towards the endless expanse of nature below

Froidenley's dam. "When I'm home… Everything is fine. The worries of the world just run down the river and out of this dam."

"Ah, I heard there was a river below your castle!" Vulpie smiles with enthusiasm. "So it's true, huh?"

"Did you now? Where did you hear that?"

"I think somebody said something about it. Uh, like Rulef."

"I informed Rulef about the dam, but he doesn't know the river flows near my castle…" Amsend responds while giving the gay fox a curious look. "So how did you know?"

"I'm not really sure. I just can't wait to see it!" Vulpie replies, and claps his little paws together, but Amsend continues to stare at him with the same creepy expression.

"What have you been reading?"

"Huh? What do you mean?"

"You read that in a book, didn't you?" The husky smiles.

"No."

"Then how else would you know about the river?"

"Maybe you said something about it, I don't know man! What, are you dumping chemicals or something?" Vulpie laughs, and Amsend chuckles.

"No, it's just that Froidenley is a very peaceful, remote, and private little town… No one knows about the castle because I'm not one to advertise my family's real estate. And when I hear a comment like that, it leads me to believe that you stuck your muzzle in a book."

"I'm… Not really sure how I knew about it. Maybe you mentioned it at the NVA?"

"I most certainly did not." Amsend dryly responds. Vulpie holds still for a moment. He's not sure whether he should continue feigning innocence or tell the truth, but he suspects the husky wouldn't appreciate an honest answer. If Vulpie confesses to lying to him, after the warning he had last night, who knows how the bizarre dog will react.

"Ah! I remember now! Polar said you might have a river next to your castle because of the landscape! He used to do a lot of hiking, and we had some fun in the Wispy Canis Lupis Mountains!"

"So I heard."

"He said the river probably came out of the mountain higher up and your castle must be near it."

"And why?"

"For water! I'm sure your ancestors needed some of dat H20!" Vulpie answers and licks his lips. "Speaking of which, I'm pretty thirsty, and hungry too!"

"I see."

"Can we stop at that restaurant over there for breakfast? Because the smell is totally killing me!"

"No, I'm sorry." Amsend answers with a smile. "We can't waste your appetite there. My cooks are magnificent; we'll eat at the castle."

"Awesome!" Vulpie smirks, and gets up very quickly. He tries to walk away but doesn't get very far.

"Where are you going?"

"Huh?"

"You're just going to leave?" Amsend inquires with an insidious expression. "Afraid I'll ask about the river again?"

"You know what? I just might be!" Vulpie answers while making a funny face. He gets a laugh out of the husky, and while the dog is chortling, he manages to escape the extremely tense conversation. He hastily walks back up the street to the hotel and goes inside as quickly as possible.

He sighs when he sees Polar's still asleep. For some reason, the gay fox suddenly felt very worried about him, but he's glad to discover that he's just worried about himself. He looks around for something nice to change into, other than his snazzy green shirt, and dark brown jeans, but jumps when someone knocks on the door. He turns and opens it very quietly, trying not to wake his husband, and sighs when he sees Amsend.

"On second thought, let's have a coffee... I'd like to tell you a story."

"O... Okay, oh, alright." Vulpie quietly responds, and comes outside. He gently shuts the door and flinches when the husky touches his right shoulder.

"Come on." NoirQueue agents are all around them, but they're not interested in what their boss is doing. Vulpie notices a few members of Blacktail speaking to them through translators. Some of the NoirQueue wolves also speak Sufian, and Rulef nods at Vulpie when he passes by. Vulpie nods back with a worried smile. Amsend leads him inside the beautiful old building at the north end of the street. The fox's worries almost slip away when he's greeted with wonderful smells and cheerful conversation. The place looks like a lot of fun.

"Order something." Amsend says while gesturing towards the counter. A nervous looking brown vixen smiles and stands at attention.

"He, hello sir! What would you like today? Mr.? Mr. Vulpie?! It's great to meet you!"

"Hi! Thanks, it's great to be here! I, uh... Umm... Give me a double caramel latte please."

"Sure thing!" The cashier replies. She glances at Amsend, and Vulpie notices how stressed she looks. She's acting like she knows him, and people start leaving the restaurant. Vulpie turns around with wide eyes and watches the scene in disbelief. Almost everyone, except for a few very mute animals, gather their things and hurry out of the building with their heads held low.

"What the hell?" The orange furred fox whispers.

"My usual." Amsend says after stepping forward. The cashier nods, and Amsend puts his paw on Vulpie's shoulder again. "Why don't you find us a place to sit..."

"Sure." Vulpie replies. He's glad to put some distance between himself and the creepy animal. He finds a small nice looking table in the middle of the room, where he feels safe, and takes a seat. Amsend waits on their coffee, and after checking out, he brings the drinks over with a smile.

"There you go."

"Thanks."

"Try it. It's fantastic."

"Oh, I'm sure it is!" Vulpie says and sips from his black cup. "Mmm! Yummy!"

"Indeed..."

"So uh... What's your story? Erh, I, uh, what's the story you want to tell me?"

"Well it's like this. Talking about my home has made me a little nostalgic and I wanted to share something with you." Amsend replies without bothering to touch his coffee.

"Shoot!"

"In my youth, I once had a friend named Puḱsos... Sweet little boy... Puḱsos was a red fox, and his father delivered firewood, milk, orange juice, and other supplies to Castle Lahnak every day. He had a contract with my family, because my father always felt it was preferable to do business with local animals. Several people wanted the job, but Puḱsos' father was a trustworthy man, and every day he would visit the castle on schedule."

"Uh, huh!" Vulpie eagerly replies with an innocent look.

"Maybe I'm a little warm hearted, but I wish his son could have carried on in his footsteps. You see, for some reason, my father thought Puḱsos wouldn't be a good delivery boy. He said he was too social, or something of the nature, but I thought he was a lovely fellow. I talked with him whenever possible, and Puḱsos always had so many questions. He loved the world..." Amsend smiles with purpose. "Wanted to see every corner of it...

Said he was going to be a scientist when he graduated from college, but sadly, he never made it out of high school."

"What happened?"

"He disappeared." Amsend answers and raises his eyebrows. "Just like that! Poof!" The husky says while also making an innocent face.

"Really?"

"Oh yes. I was quite sad about it, but father said the boy broke into our castle. I didn't want to believe it, but apparently, he was a little too curious for his own good. People said he was just having fun and wanted to look around, but everyone knew it was off limits... My father was very strict on this matter..."

"I bet he was! I mean, you gotta have tight security to keep, like, thieves and people out!"

"Yes... Oh yes... What happened to Puksos was very sad... But you see... Vulpie..." Amsend says while giving the fox a dangerous look. "Puksos was too curious for his own good... He certainly was right about the castle being a beautiful place, but he didn't know where his limits were... And somehow, he just vanished..."

"How? What do they think happened to him?"

"Most likely he fell into the river. They think he tried to climb up the back of the castle, but that's a little impossible. Sadly... I think that's why Puksos is no longer with us."

"That's terrible. I'm sorry to hear that." Vulpie says and lowers his muzzle.

"But you understand, don't you Vulpie?" Amsend asks and taps his shoe against the stone floor. "If only Puksos hadn't taken chances, if only he hadn't tried to go somewhere he wasn't supposed to... And find things he shouldn't have found... He would be with us today."

"I... Totally understand." Vulpie whispers.

"Good. Because Puksos is gone forever… Now drink your coffee."

Polar blinks after waking up. For a moment, he thought he was at home in his new age house with Vulpie cooking breakfast downstairs, but something smells different. The food is exotic, unlike anything he's had the pleasure of eating before. The white furred wolf sits up in the hotel bed and looks around the room. He can see the sun shining brightly through the hotel's spacious window. It helps him locate the alarm clock, and he sees it's after nine a.m.

The snow wolf gets out of bed and pensively rubs his crotch. He has a sizeable morning erection and Vulpie isn't here to help him with it. He growls while wondering where his adorable husband ran off to. Polar can't help how sensitive his big cock feels. Pre cum is oozing from its tip, so he reaches down and removes his underwear. He'll have to get in some quick masturbation or be uncomfortable the rest of the day.

Polar heads into the bathroom and halfway closes the door. He grabs his big dick with his right paw and rests his left hand on the sturdy porcelain sink. The bathroom is rather nice, and though it's not too romantic, it'll do. He closes his eyes and starts playing with himself. He licks his lips and dreams about sticking his cock in Vulpie, which gets him even harder, because he remembers how the fox can barely move while being invaded. He spends about a minute pawing off until he's greeted with an orgasm. He widens his stance and growls. One shot. Two shots… Three big loads of semen blast out of his penis and splatter on the bath tub. His eyes roll back in his head and the wolf releases a satisfied breath. Steam rises from his messy jizz because it's fairly cold and dry in the room, so he decides to enjoy a shower as well.

"Alright…" He whispers, and steps into the bath tub. He makes sure not to step in his cum before pulling the curtain shut behind him. The last thing he wants is to fall and get hurt on today of all days. He has no idea where things are going with Amsend and Vulpie, but if anything, he needs to stay fully alert. Polar knows his small lover needs him. They're in unfamiliar territory, and after the tense conversation Vulpie and Amsend had last night, Polar's not about to leave his husband with the husky for long. His ears perk up when he hears the front door open. It's rustic sound is hard to mistake. "Vulpie?"

"Yeah!" The orange fox says from the other room, and closes the front door before letting himself into the bathroom.

"Shut the door please! It's cold in there!"

"You got it." Vulpie responds, and closes and locks the door. "So Mr. P can feel the freeze after all, huh?"

"I'm wet."

"Yeah I know." Vulpie happily responds, and walks over to the shower curtain. He pulls it open, revealing a mist of hot water spraying all over his naked husband.

"Well hello to you too!" Polar laughs while lathering his fur in soap.

"Mmm..." Vulpie hums and looks over his lupine lover. "Never gets old."

"Even though I am?"

"You're not even forty."

"Getting close."

"Doesn't look like it. That bod's still enough to make me drool."

"Why thank you honey." Polar smiles, appreciating his vulpine lover's affection, and Vulpie returns an equally loving expression. "Could've used you earlier. I woke up with a massive hard on."

"God damn it." Vulpie grins. "What, did you rub one out?"

"Yep."

"You don't even know how to jerk off. You never rub your balls or your perineum when you do it. Dunno why you even bother."

"It felt good enough." Polar replies, and washes his tail fur with a cloth.

"Man I've got a hard on right now just lookin at ya."

"Missed your opportunity."

"How bout you let me fuck you before we leave?"

"Huh?" Polar asks in surprise. "Aren't they waiting on us?"

"It's gonna be an hour before we get going. Plenty of time." Vulpie mischievously smiles.

"I'm already taking a shower though."

"Then get out and dry off so we can get started! I want to put it in you!"

"Wow! Well... I'd be lying if I said that wouldn't be nice." Polar answers with a warm voice. "You'd do that for me? We don't have time for me to do you too."

"My pleasure." Vulpie grins. "Would love to shoot a load in you!"

"How are we going to do it? Me on the floor?" Polar asks while turning off the water. He gets out of the tub and grabs a towel.

"Sounds good to me. Get on your knees and elbows and I'll angle down on yah!"

"Oh... I like it when you do that one." The white furred wolf grins. "You usually hit my p spot pretty good."

"Hell yeah I do! Small but fierce. All about what you do with it."

"Looks like I'm not the only one who woke up horny today, huh?" Polar chuckles, and licks his lips after finishing drying off his silky white fur. "Ready to be your bitch." He whispers with an endearing voice.

"Alrighty then." Vulpie smirks, and opens the bathroom door. They hurry into the bedroom and Polar finds a random spot on the green carpeted floor. He gets down on his paws and knees, and raises his rear end for the orange furred fox.

"Oh yeah..." Vulpie breathes. He quickly makes himself naked, and masturbates while looking over his beautiful husband. After he's hard, he finds their overnight bag and retrieves some lubrication. He brings it back with him, pops it open, and squirts a generous amount of fluid on his hard little penis. Vulpie closes it and tosses it on the bed while Polar waits. The white furred wolf inhales when he feels the orange fox mount him, and moans in delight when his lover's penis slips inside his tail end.

"Ohhh..."

"Mmmm..." Vulpie breathes, and spreads his little legs wider. He bends forward, clamping his little claws down on the white furred wolf's large back for support, so he can fuck him at just the right angle. Since Vulpie's cock isn't as massive as his husband's he has to thrust inside him at a precise angle to hit the wolf's prostate, but he does, and it makes Polar's fur stand on end.

"Oh right there! Oh yeah Vulpie! Oh it feels good..." Polar moans with his big muzzle pressed sideways against the nice carpet.

"Like it inside you? Like a fox fucking you?"

"Always do!" Polar groans with a delighted voice, feeling pleasure surge through his sensitive internal organs all the way down to his hard cock. He has a fat erection in no time. "Yeah baby... Oh, I love you Vulpie..."

"Mmm! Yeah!" The orange fox breathes, relishing his lover's warm body. Being inside Polar makes him feel powerful, and he thrusts over and over, maintaining an impressive speed that would bring a smile to any gay man's face. Polar grins on the floor, widening his legs as well. Vulpie feels him relax, wanting more, and doesn't let his lover down. He makes sure to keep going, digging his toes into the carpet while keeping his paws firmly latched onto Polar's lower back. Vulpie knows just how to give it to the white furred wolf. They've been married long enough to know every inch of each other's body, every crevice, every ticklish place, and definitely both of their sweet spots.

"Ohhh... Oh yeah!" Polar moans while masturbating with increasing intensity. The head of Vulpie's little fox cock gently pushing and rubbing against his prostate makes pre-cum dribble out of his penis.

"Whacked off without me? But now we can empty out the rest of dat stuff! What do ya say? Ya got more in there! Don't ya!"

"Mmm..."

"Yeah ya do!" Vulpie breathes and licks his lips. He swishes his tail and starts making a cute little growl. "Yeah big boy!"

"Oh, I love you Vulpie!" Polar breathes in pleasure, and Vulpie grins when he hears the satisfaction in his husband's voice. He recognizes that sound. Vulpie's more of a whiner, but Polar's making the same kind of desperate moan. It says he needs more, he can't wait to get it, and his biggest fear is that something will interrupt the sex. The semen reserve in Polar's prostate has been milked into the confines of his big cock. When it escapes, it's going to feel wonderful. "Fuck Donner, you're the BEST!"

"What?" Vulpie laughs while fucking the much larger male.

"You're SO MUCH BETTER! Oh My GOD!" Polar moans with tears in his eyes.

"Even with a little cock?"

"Doesn't feel little!" The white furred wolf gasps while feverishly playing with his penis. It's sloppy wet with cum, and is completely filled to the brink with more.

"This fox is gonna blow his load in you! Like that wolfy? Huh?"

"OH YEAH!"

"You like that role reversal, huh?"

"YEAH!"

Polar and Vulpie leave the hotel with smiles on their faces and are quickly greeted by Rulef. He's the only non-NoirQueue mercenary in the street. A young red fox couple glances at the white furred wolf and orange furred fox, but surprisingly, do nothing else. They don't even do a double take after seeing two very famous animals.

"Where's the rest of our guys?" Vulpie asks the gray wolf before he has a chance to speak.

"Up at the castle. Amsend's been very helpful; he's letting us scout it out before they bring you there. The place is filled with tourists, so we can't have you brushing fur with a crowd of strangers."

"Wait, what?" Vulpie asks and squints at the Blacktail commander.

"Amsend said he didn't advertise the castle." Polar comments, and Vulpie hastily nods in agreement.

"Yeah! What the hell man?"

"I know he said that, but he says a lot of things… A lot of which are not true…" Rulef quietly responds. "But we're working with the Sons of Velora now, so I guess there should be many strange things to come."

"He's definitely a liar. I don't believe a virus killed off his family." Vulpie says, and looks around, making sure none of the NoirQueue wolves can hear him.

"Yeah, he told me something like that earlier and it sounded like cover. But I don't think we should press the issue. These aren't the kind of people we want to fuck with."

"Now we have to remember which lies we can talk about, and which ones we can't… Great." Vulpie snorts, and Polar frowns at Rulef.

"What kind of things has he been saying? You said he says a lot of things that aren't true. Did you mean anything specific by that?"

"Honestly, I'm not sure. The man is a walking contradiction. He has an answer for any question you'll ask him, but the story keeps changing to meet the situation. He told me he's been to Zeravyn at the airport, but this morning he also claimed that he'd never left the planet before. Says he's too fond of Sufias…" Rulef shrugs and chuckles.

"So we can't trust this guy?" Polar asks.

"Oh, no way!" Rulef laughs and rubs his nose with his left paw "I thought that went without saying."

"We just need to get this over with as fast as possible. I miss being surrounded by computers." Vulpie thinks out loud, and Polar wraps his left arm around him.

"Don't drive anywhere without our go ahead. The castle has a small outdoor parking garage but it's in a tight spot, and we can't have you stuck in traffic with people right next to the Superbolt. Amsend said to be patient while they clear the zone of tourists and then you'll be able to drive over the drawbridge onto the castle grounds. Just follow me. But before that, we're going to sit on the road until they're ready for us. I Don't think people can see you through those tinted windows anyway, but it's best to be careful."

"Sounds like you've thought of everything, just like always." Vulpie smiles.

"Doing the best I can. Being in unfamiliar territory is the most dangerous situation I have to deal with, and I don't speak Englavic. Luckily Deepwolf does, so he's coming in really handy."

"OH REALLY?" The orange furred fox asks with a loud voice. He looks to his husband with a satisfied expression.

"What? The spy thing again?" Rulef smirks. "I admit, I was a little surprised about it, but he was over here on work and had a short stint with a college girl. He said she wanted him to learn the language and stay, but obviously he didn't."

"You believe that? Seriously? Come on man."

"Yeah, I do. I don't think he's smart enough to make up that kind of story on the fly. I know what facial expressions to look for when someone's lying, and he seemed sincere."

"That's because he's good. He's REALLY good... But I felt it on day one, the first time I sat next to him... The way he looked at me was like... He was proud. He was way too proud about something."

"Proud huh?"

"Yes. Like he'd finally accomplished some kind of secret objective... And I think the objective was to spy on me for Amsend."

"Joining Blacktail was a major career move for him. They plucked him right off of the battlefield in Felini, and I saw his potential."

"No, it wasn't like that at all..." Vulpie responds with a determined voice. "Someone put him there."

"I put him there, Vulpie." Rulef snorts. "And you don't trust me?"

"I know you did, but you rely on referrals from other people, right? Then you interview them to see whether they'd make good additions to the team. I think he seemed so proud, because not only did you hire him, he had a chance to sit next to me and have a conversation. And he was really enjoying it. It was funny to him."

"I just don't see it Vulpie. I can fire him if you're hell bent on it, but he's not a bad guy. And now's definitely not the time for this."

"I know." Vulpie whispers. "Believe me... I know... It's perfect for them."

"Cheer up kid. All you have to do is pretend to have fun and then you can go back to Vulpie Industries where you're king of the world."

"Hey." Vulpie says, and grabs the gray wolf's much bigger arm before he has a chance to walk away. "You be careful out here too... I've got this terrible feeling that something awful is going to happen, and I don't want you getting hurt.

"Just calm down."

"I'm serious."

"I know you are, but what am I supposed to do if things go south? Sit back and let them kill you?"

"You're totally outnumbered. They're everywhere."

"That's right." Rulef answers with a determined voice.

"He knows what he's doing. It's us I'm worried about." Polar comments.

"Don't…" Vulpie whispers, and Rulef raises an eyebrow. "If something happens, just let it go. Don't throw your life away."

"You don't understand, fox." The Blacktail commander responds in irritation. "A wolf doesn't lay down and die. Would you expect Polar to just give up? Of course not. That's not who we are. We fight… And maybe you just don't understand because you are a fox… But I appreciate the sympathy."

"This guy… He's pure evil." Vulpie warns and Rulef sighs. He turns and looks at Polar with a very frustrated expression.

"Can you just calm him down?"

"I will." Polar says, and Vulpie winces in embarrassment.

"Just do as I tell you, and everything will be fine." Rulef pulls free of Vulpie's little paw and walks down the street.

"It'll be okay." Polar whispers and wraps his arms around his fox lover from behind.

Vulpie admires the beautiful landscape while the convoy drives up the mountain road to Castle Lahnak. Blacktail gathered everyone and got in line with NoirQueue before heading out. Now, thirteen SUVs are parked on the side of the slim road while they wait for the castle to be cleared. They're on the left side of the road, from the perspective of someone heading up to the castle, and to the right is a beautiful but hazardous drop. Just like the book described, there's a giant chasm with a pretty stream far below. The landscape is like something out of a dream, one of those places a person can never forget after seeing it.

"There's the drop you told me about." Polar tells Vulpie with a smile.

"Yep."

"It's beautiful."

"Wouldn't want to fall off. I hope these people have enough room to get by." Vulpie replies while watching a green minivan pass them by. It's one of the many civilian vehicles that are leaving the castle.

"They have plenty of space." Rulef comments. Vulpie stretches and makes a cute little sound. He relaxes in his seat and leans back against Polar, staring out the window at the castle in the distance. It's much bigger than Polar or Vulpie expected, but it's enormity can't be fully appreciated until it's seen up close. Castle Lahnak's romantic neo-gothic design is stunning. Since it's situated on a cliff, there's no way to ignore its presence when one looks north. The way it's seamlessly built into the stone makes it appear natural, as if mother nature just decided to place a large building on top of the cliff. The color of the castle's walls are also the same, indicating that it was built from the very stone it sits upon. The massive slab of rock underneath the fortress is a sight to behold as well, as it's the only giant hunk of exposed mountain in the area. Everywhere else in the chasm, save the very bottom, greenery hides the baron stone. The canyon river runs downhill from even larger mountains behind the castle, and wraps around the left side of the naked mountain, placing it directly below the castle's drawbridge.

But there's also a small waterfall that catches Vulpie's attention. It's easy to miss from this far away, but it's sparkling in the morning sun. It runs out of a small cave halfway up the canyon wall underneath Castle Lahnak, and It's little stream joins the river below. The cave looks far too small for someone to fit into it, and this is when Vulpie sees something even more curious. A little ways below the waterfall, to the bottom right, is a larger break in the stone. It looks big enough for a person to fit into, and for some reason, it fascinates the orange furred fox. It almost looks like someone could use it as a resting place if they were trying to climb up the canyon wall.

The landscape is filled with lush greenery despite Englavic's persistently chilly weather. And somehow, the moss hanging from the bottom of the castle wall seems even more vivacious. The forest to the north and east side of the castle also seems brighter than the woods Polar and Vulpie have driven past so far, and even on the other side of the river, all types of flora look brilliant. For a while Vulpie wonders whether his eyes are playing tricks on him, but the longer he has time to look over his surroundings, the more certain he becomes that he's not seeing an optical illusion.

"Hey, look at that." The fox says and points at the castle. Rulef, Polar and the others in the vehicle all take a glance. "Does the greenery seem strange to any of you guys? Look how bright it is around the castle. And the further you get from it, the more dull the landscape becomes." Polar moves in his seat and tilts his head back and forth, surveying the beautiful scene with scrutiny.

"Yeah... I see it. He must have expensive landscapers." The white furred wolf says, and Vulpie looks at Rulef.

"See it?"

"Now that you mention it, I guess it does look odd." Rulef responds and shrugs his shoulders.

"I wonder if something is in the water." Vulpie says and licks his lips. "I don't think he could pay anyone to rip up the scenery and replace it every few months. But look how green it all is! Like it just came from a nursery or something.

"Maybe it's a conspiracy." Rulef smirks, and Vulpie shakes his fists in the air.

"Yes that's it! He's breeding an unstoppable army of plants! We have to stop him!" The SUV fills with laughter.

"Definitely interesting." The arctic wolf whispers.

"By the way, where is Mr. I Speak Different Languages And It's Not Suspicious?" Vulpie asks Rulef.

"Deepwolf's in the first truck. I figured it would be easier to follow his lead." The Blacktail commander answers, and grabs his radio when it beeps. "Yeah?"

"Front's clear. Moving now." A mercenary says, but it's not Deepwolf.

"Received." Rulef responds and looks at Polar. "Try to keep him out of trouble. It would make my life a lot easier if he didn't go sneaking around the castle."

"I'm right here man." Vulpie says, and Rulef looks at him.

"Don't stick your nose where it doesn't belong. If he says it's fine to explore, that's great, but I don't think he'll let us go everywhere. So please don't make my life difficult."

"Why, I would never think about slinking around this mysterious castle while I have nothing to do!"

"Yeah. Don't."

"Sure thing."

"I mean it. Things are tense enough as it is. He might have prisoners in there; you don't know. He is the director of the Governmental Security Bureau."

"Shouldn't bring his work home with him."

"Yeah well, you know this guy probably does."

"Vulpie promises not to interfere with the wolves' sovereign wartime responsibilities. He knows how they must fight." Vulpie replies, and Polar smirks.

"Good." Everyone moves a little when the driver suddenly lurches forward. He's only following the rest of Blacktail, but used a fair amount of fuel to make sure nothing got in between their vehicle and the one in front of them. They've been trained to look out for dangerous situations like this, where there's no room for them to go anywhere and oncoming traffic could suddenly box them in. It's unlikely to happen here, considering the circumstances, but the act is second nature for the driver. Tourists passing by the convoy gawk at the sight and drive very slowly. They try to look into the SUVs but can't see anyone thanks to their tinted windows. When the last of them drive past the final SUV, the group of armored trucks picks up speed.

Everyone gets a nice view of the surroundings, over the course of a long and winding road that hugs the mountain. In Froidenley, the same mountain towers over the town and the damn to the northeast, effectively blocking any view of Lahnak Castle. All of their eyes are fixed on the fortress when they finally make a right, and drive onto the bridge that leads over the chasm. It's made of wood, and everyone's stomach drops a little until they realize how well it's built. It's been reinforced by metal support structures, four of which connect the bridge on both sides, at the mountain on the left and the cliff on the right, and two of which run down into the river below; they reinforce the bridge's weakest spots in the mid-section.

Lahnak Castle undoubtedly would have been an impenetrable target in medieval times, as not only is it separated from the rest of the landscape, it's also fortified with all of the most popular defenses of the era. The castle's keep is also built into what looks like its main building, a massive reinforced compound straight ahead and on the right side of the sprawling fortress. The keep sits at a ninety degree angle, with its back and left side situated towards the chasm and the road that led them up the mountain. Directly to the left of the keep, and also on the edge of the cliff, is a brobdingnagian arsenal tower. It's much taller than the others that are placed around the stronghold's perimeter, and is at least twice as high as the keep, excluding the pretty conical spire that juts up from the dark green roof of the castle.

The curtain wall generously wraps around the entirety of the fortress, leaving one main bailey inside the stronghold where several smaller but equally sturdy buildings coexist with the main castle. However, an imposing barbican decisively blocks entry to Lahnak's grounds, and not only connects to the main castle via another short bridge, but also funnels all traffic to the bailey areas, leaving only one way into and out of the ancient fortress.

Blacktail, following NoirQueue, passes the barbican by a few hundred feet and parks inside of a small wooden complex that's dedicated to automobile storage. It's outside the castle walls, but security is hardly lax.

NoirQueue wolves are everywhere when they arrive. Amsend is speaking with one of his men nearby the garage. The husky looks to be in high spirits, presumably filled with pride over showing off his ancestral home. He knows Vulpie and Polar must be shocked by its magnificence. Any animal capable of feeling happiness would be moved by the sight of such a beautiful place. The vehicles roll into the wooden garage and come to a halt. A small building attaches to the garage on the left for registering visitors that are lucky enough to drive to the castle, and there are several miniature tourist buses parked inside as well.

Cold air whips through everyone's fur when they leave their heated vehicles. Blacktail's gear keeps them reasonably warm, and NoirQueue seems equally resistant to the cold, but Vulpie has to zip up his stylish tan jacket and rearrange his green scarf for maximum comfort before going any further. His dark brown pants don't do much to break the wind so he ends up putting his paws in his pockets as well. Meanwhile, Polar walks around in his light lavender polo shirt and dark jeans as if he's going for a stroll on a spring day. The small fox envies how his wolf lover handles the cold so effortlessly. Vulpie isn't sure whether it's Polar's ancestry or his muscle mass that insulates him so well, or a combination of both, but he clearly is quite comfortable in the high altitude environment.

An even more surprising sight is Amsend's predictable choice of clothing. The husky is still wearing the same black suit with white pin stripes as always, or perhaps it's a different one. It's impossible to tell. The man seems to dress the same way regardless of where he is or what he's doing. His suit doesn't look thick enough to shield him from the cold wind either. Vulpie figures the dog is probably fond of colder climates due to his particular breed.

"Very impressive!" Vulpie says to the GSB director. A proud smile creeps onto the husky's face.

"Thank you. You should use your Superbolt to go back and forth from now on. It's a drive that one really shouldn't miss." Amsend says and gestures towards Vulpie's orange car. Tiala drove it here due to security concerns on the first trip.

"Back and forth? You mean to Froidenley?"

"Of course. I assume you and Polar will want to explore the country after you've settled in here. My men will help you get to wherever you'd like to go. You can reach two large cities after a thirty mile drive, and I'm sure your high tech car will get you around rather quickly. Just don't speed too much."

"Sweet." Vulpie responds and shivers. He pulls his paws out of his pockets and feverishly rubs his arms to warm up.

"You're freezing. It does get rather cold up here. Come on, let's get you inside the castle." Amsend says, and walks towards the barbican. Vulpie and Polar both wait for NoirQueue to go with him, but they oddly stay where they are or turn their attention elsewhere. "Over here."

"Kay." Vulpie replies, and hurries over to the husky. Polar follows them and Rulef brings the rest of Blacktail with him, minus the men he previously assigned to perimeter duty before they even arrived. The barbican has two round mural doors, and there are at least four men on guard patrol high above them. They raise the heavy metal gate with surprising speed, given its mass, and a loud clanking sound indicates that it's snapped into place when they stop.

"I'm guessing no one had much success sieging this place in ancient times." Polar comments while they go inside the barbican, and Amsend looks to his right with a smile while they walk.

"More or less. My family repelled two or three assaults but no one ever had a chance to set up siege equipment in tactical locations. The terrain made it nearly impossible in medieval times, especially since we could see them coming from miles away."

"So your family fought a few wars then?"

"Wars of necessity you might say. What I've gleaned from the ancestral library suggests wars were a common nuisance that had to be dealt with every few decades."

"Sounds like it would have been a difficult time to live in." Vulpie says, and the husky nods.

"Oh, it was."

"How did you handle it, I mean… How did your family handle it?" The orange furred fox inquires, and Amsend gives him a curious smirk.

"The best they could. I'm afraid their character was far greater than my own. All I've done is inherit the estate." The forty foot wooden bridge trembles underneath everyone's weight while they approach the gatehouse's portcullis. After leaving the barbican, there still isn't a way to get into the bailey area without going through Castle Lahnak's main entrance. The bridge between the barbican and the gatehouse is supported by a single stone pillar that rises fifty feet up from the grassy bailey below. Once inside the castle grounds, it's possible to walk underneath the bridge and admire it, but jumping off of it as a means of avoiding the gatehouse would be impossible.

Polar and Vulpie look up at the face of Castle Lahnak before they come to its impressive entrance, which is reinforced with a second portcullis and a set of two very heavy looking dark metal doors. Several feet above them are dual sets of narrow siege resistant windows. Like many castles during the era, it was preferable to have smaller windows to prevent archers from easily firing into the castle. But they're plenty big for an animal to enjoy a nice view from inside the structure, and above the three dual sets of slender windows are three more of them that are tightly packed together on a higher floor. To the left of the three windows at the top of the castle's front is a miniature conical spire that hangs on the top left face of the building. It has very pretty windows all around it, and clearly was designed to enjoy the landscape rather than spot enemies, though it certainly would come in handy during an assault.

Castle Lahnak's portcullis is already raised, most likely due to the tourists who were coming and going before they arrived. A member of NoirQueue opens both of the black doors from inside, and says nothing. He doesn't meet eyes with Amsend when the husky passes by him, and only bothers giving Polar and Vulpie a brief glance when they're close. Polar figures he must be watching the many members of Blacktail who are following them. He has a feeling they'll be asked to spread out, or hand over their automatic weapons if so many of them come inside. Counting Deepwolf, Tiala and Rulef, twelve mercenaries enter the dimly lit but pleasant interior. Surprisingly, there's a mini-kitchen on the right side of the room just after entering the castle, and a brown furred she-wolf is wiping her paws with a white cloth.

"Quite a bunch we have today." She says while showing everyone a friendly smile. She looks to Vulpie and gestures towards the doorway behind her, where delicious smells are escaping into the room. "Anything to eat?"

"Ah, it smells so good! But not right now, thanks." Vulpie answers and looks to his right at Polar. "But we can get something if you're hungry?"

"You're hungry too. You just won't admit it." The white furred wolf smirks.

"Maybe he'll have an appetite after we've been around the castle. Let me show you to your room first, and then we'll be back." Amsend suggests. Polar and Vulpie both nod in agreement. A second set of heavy doors separate Lahnak Castle's entrance chamber from the great hall, which suggests that the kitchen to the right also has a reinforced door of its own, and it most likely can prevent an animal from entering either the pantry, the storeroom, the bottlery, or the kitchen. In this way, visitors were kept from bypassing the great hall's entrance while also leaving relatively quick access for culinary associates. Vulpie notices at least three Deivonic themed decorations before entering the hall and finds it rather odd. He's never been in a castle before, but remembers their design principles from his history classes at Rinwulv Tech, and only the richest nobles had enough wealth to buy Deiva related paintings, banners, statues, engravings, or jewelry.

Since Goddess Cyrilla, Sherrie and Khalan have always been worshipped for their beauty, it wasn't fitting for any lord to possess subpar artwork of the Deiva trinity. They had to be depicted as nude, and the last thing anyone wanted to see was an ugly Deiva. Thus, finding artists and craftsman worth their salt was quite the expensive endeavor. Vulpie was always more than a little amused by this medieval fact, as he figured the explanation was far simpler. Straight lords just wanted an excuse to put up artwork of naked women throughout their castles, and the richest ones made sure to do it whenever they could. For all of the persecution gay men and women have faced over the centuries, here is concrete evidence of how men are just men, whether they like boys or girls.

But something does trouble the orange fox about the two paintings and a stone engraving he noticed on the way in. Amsend's family must have spent a fortune, ten times the cost of a normal castle, to build this fortress in such an isolated position. So how did they have money for additional extravagance? The Lahnak's involvement with the Sons of Velora is the only explanation, but still, something doesn't seem right. The pictures he saw of Khalan and Sherrie quickly caught his eye because something was off about their expressions. They weren't smiling the same way they're always depicted. Normally they wear a "come hither" expression, but this time, at least to Vulpie, they looked a little... Unbalanced... He'll have to take another look when he gets the chance, but he decides to wait after noticing more decorations in the main hall. While Polar and everyone else is gawking at their surroundings, Vulpie is quick to peer into Sherrie's eyes when he passes by an ornate painting of the taupe furred feline.

She's standing in the depths of a dark green forest, and as he suspected, there's something very, VERY, creepy about her expression... It's not the fact that she's fully naked and is reaching towards the viewer. That sort of in motion/point of view depiction is quite normal for Deivonic artwork, but her green eyes are fixated slightly above the viewer's head, and her smirk suggests that she's up to something. Vulpie's instincts tell him that she's planning on grabbing the viewer and pushing him backwards into something deadly, perhaps a deep hole. At first he wonders whether his height has something to do with it, but the painting's drawn in a way that her eyes follow the viewer regardless of his size. His fur stands on end while thinking about it. He wishes his mind was playing tricks on him, but it's not. The painting was definitely drawn to creep out the viewer on a subconscious level. He wonders if every Deiva related ornament in Lahnak castle bears equally disturbing themes. If so, just what was wrong with the Lahnaks? The Sons of Velora couldn't really have been… Aila worshippers… No, that's crazy. Why the hell would someone actually worship the dark goddess? A fast track to hell doesn't sound like a very enticing reward.

The great hall benefits from six large windows, three on the left wall and three on the right. Despite their large size, they must not have put the castle in any danger from assailing forces due to their position. The only logical place to attack Lahnak castle would be from the left, on the other side of the chasm, and no arrow could hit it from there. Siege equipment would be necessary to accomplish such a task, and at that point, having a few pretty windows probably wouldn't make much of a difference unless flaming boulders were being launched. It would be extremely difficult to hit the castle from such a distance, and the windows on the left side of the great hall overlook the fortress' bailey area, so having large windows wouldn't be an issue. If an enemy was close enough to shoot flaming arrows into the castle, they'd already have to be inside the walls.

"Nice big windows in here. I guess it was safe because of the distance." Vulpie comments, and Amsend raises his eyebrows.

"Quite right. Do you know much about castles?"

"Not really. Just seems a little obvious since these are so nicely done up."

"Did you notice the murder holes, then?"

"Murder holes? Emmm."

"In the barbican." Amsend elaborates while gesturing towards the entrance.

"Was that the first part we came through?"

"Yes."

"No, I didn't see any murdering or holes. And I'm usually good at finding holes."

"Wow." Rulef coughs. Polar smirks and Amsend grins.

"On the ceiling there are several holes where men could pour boiling oil on attackers and such. It always pays to be aware of your surroundings."

"How rude! I bet they didn't like that!"

"They were rude first by attacking the castle."

"Yep." Vulpie says and his eyes widen when he notices a very nice chess board on a medium sized table. There's a large table in the great hall for dining, and probably everyone in the castle uses it, but the smaller table is north east of it, next to four very comfortable looking chairs with red velvet cushioning. Amsend spies what's drawing the fox's attention and makes a preemptive comment.

"I confess I did leave that out for a reason. I'd love to spar with the world's greatest chess champion."

"Ah, so that's what you do to pass the time!"

"Among other things."

"Are you good?"

"Moderately. I'm sure you could mate me in four moves, so go easy when we play."

"Yeah right, Dude Who Lives In A Castle." Vulpie laughs. "I know you're good; you have to be! Otherwise it'd just be weird."

"I guess we'll find out."

"What if you beat me?" Vulpie asks with an adorable voice. "You can't tell anyone or it'll crush my self-esteem!"

"I'm good, but I can't win. You defeated William Volex."

"Something tells me you're even better. I think you've had a long time to master the game."

"Because I'm that old?" Amsend smirks. "I'm only fifty six."

"Really? You don't even look middle aged." Vulpie replies. "I'm sure I'm not the only one who's noticed. Right?" The orange furred fox elaborates and looks at Polar.

"You do look fairly young to be fifty years old." The white furred wolf admits.

"I'll take that as a complement then." Amsend smiles, and Polar glances at Vulpie. He's not sure what his lover is up to, but his gut suggests something very worrisome. Vulpie's statements have drawn attention to Amsend's age before, first when they were entering the castle, and now here. At first it was just innocuous conversation, but the way Vulpie stressed that Amsend has been at chess an extremely long time changes the nature of the conversation. Polar never thought there was anything unusual about the husky's body before, but now he's starting to wonder. Vulpie's nose is very good at sniffing out inconsistencies. After all, he managed to hack the world with a computer virus designed to take advantage of system weaknesses. Something seems weak about Amsend's backstory at this point, and Rulef's earlier statements also contribute to Polar's particular line of thought. *The man is a walking contradiction. He has an answer for any question you'll ask him, but the story keeps changing to meet the situation.*

"We'll be sure to have a game. Maybe tonight." Amsend smiles and licks his lips. "This way to your room. I think you'll enjoy the accommodations." The husky leads them out of the great hall via a doorway at the back left part of the room. Behind the beautiful structure is a pleasant walkway that connects the great hall to the southern corner of the fortress. The southern corner is situated directly above the cliff at a ninety degree angle. It is just as large as the great hall, and seems to have many lower levels, as windows can be spotted in the stonework below the walkway. The great hall and the southern corner serve as one large keep, with only the small walkway separating the two buildings, but it does look like a miniature bridge can be deployed from above.

Directly to the left of the southern partition is the massive arsenal tower that towers over both parts of the keep, and it's spacious walls practically beg for an inspection. One could imagine flights of rounded stairs inside, but what other kinds of secrets lie within? Defensive weaponry? Cages? It must have been quite important to occupy so much space.

"A significant amount of traffic comes through here, but the doors are pretty thick. I don't think you'll wake during your sleep." Amsend says while grabbing and opening the next door that leads them into the southern partition. Inside is a hallway that runs to the left, and another heavy black door. Amsend steps inside and opens the second door, revealing a spacious and beautiful bedroom. "My quarters are upstairs. This is the guest chamber."

"Oh you'll be right above us?" Vulpie asks with a genuinely curious voice. He can tell the black and white furred husky is becoming more frisky by the moment, no doubt he's excited about finally having a captive audience. Even if the man directs the Sons of Velora, and meticulously steers its cruel methods, he undoubtedly suffers from the same need to share his accomplishments with others, just like everybody else. With Polar and Vulpie he has that. They're completely at his mercy at this point, but both of them are quite interesting to him as well. Amsend knows Polar descended from Maro, who defeated Aila's son millions of years ago. Even if the gay wolf cannot appreciate who he comes from, Amsend is eager to investigate further. After all... He is the authority on Sufias' supernatural matters...

"Doesn't it get cold up there?" Polar inquires. "I'd hate to think how much wood you have to burn to keep it comfortable."

"The castle was designed in a neo renaissance manner that isn't outwardly visible, but heating is one of the creature comforts afforded by my ancestors' foresight." Amsend answers with a smile. "Down these steps and out a little ways and we'll go across the southern curtain wall." The husky says while looking down the hallway to his left, but he opens the door to Polar and Vulpie's bedroom. The chamber is completely made of stone, including the floor and the ceiling. At the north end of the room is an ornately designed king sized bed, and it quickly draws the gay animals' attention. Having just made love this morning, sex is still fresh on their minds, and its beautiful appearance quickly conjures up possible scenarios. Of course they hide their thoughts while nodding and looking around with polite expressions, but they also share happy smiles when they get the chance.

There's an open wooden door to the left of the bed, that leads to a basic bathroom in a small chamber, but one can tell the castle was not built with modern comforts in mind. A bathtub, toilet, sink and mirror have been installed, in addition to all of the necessary piping to make things acceptable. The bed chamber certainly is not without its charms. There's a large and very pretty stain glass window on the right wall that overlooks the road they took to castle Lahnak from Froidenley. And last but certainly not least, a fireplace resides just to the right of the door, and looks to share a chimney with the room above.

"No one can hear you up there. The chimney shaft is separate and walled off from the room above, so don't worry about keeping me awake." Amsend comments as if reading both of their minds. Vulpie nods in surprise and bites his lip.

"So you're fireplace isn't on the same side or is it?"

"To the right of my bed. My room is actually a little smaller due to your chimney taking up more stonework, but I benefit from the extra heat. I usually have the servants light the fire down here every night because of that."

"Oh cool, so it's just like the wall juts out a little in your room?"

"Yes."

"Nice."

"It seems like you would have the lower room since it's your home." Polar comments and Amsend smirks.

"Nonsense. All castles have staircases that spiral to the right for one very important reason. During an attack right handed warriors are at a disadvantage when coming up the steps because of this. So my ancestors were just that much safer at the top. Not to mention the gate."

"Oh."

"This way." Amsend says, and walks out of the room. Polar and Vulpie follow him, and they head towards the spiral staircase the husky was talking about. They have two choices. They can walk down the spiral staircase to get onto the southern curtain wall and make their way towards the rest of the castle, or they could go up to Lahnak's chambers. They miss out on the gate the GSB director mentioned, but the white furred wolf and orange furred fox both figure they'll be going up there at some point anyway.

"Fuckin cool." Vulpie comments when he walks past a snarling lulpra bust on the left before they enter the staircase. Lulpras are the giant savage wolves of old, the same beasts Maro conquered on Halvia, and the marble statue truly looks scary. It's head is just as big as a real Lulchra Dra, the lulpra king, with a four foot long muzzle and rows of sharp teeth.

"You like that?" Amsend deviously inquires while looking back for a moment. Vulpie nods again, and the husky heads down the staircase, speaking without looking back. "The stone steps could be treacherous if one were to lose his footing. In truth I'm not sure where my family acquired it. They never told me, but I'm sure it wasn't cheap. It's always been one of my personal favorites."

"So you're a fan of the macabre?" Polar asks.

"But of course. Look where I grew up!"

"Scarred you for life didn't it?" Vulpie teases.

"Oh, I'm sure. But women love it, even though they'll insist otherwise. They appreciate a little sophisticated savagery now and then."

"WHO DOESN'T?" Vulpie gleefully responds. They descend down the steps and blinding sunlight greets them at the bottom when Amsend pulls open a heavy wooden door. The southern curtain wall provides a beautiful view of the valley behind Castle Lahnak. The mountain stream shimmers far below, amidst the eye catching swaying and groaning of lush forestry that adorns the distant landscape. Polar and Vulpie both gravitate to the wall so they can admire their surroundings. Vulpie's energetic mind savors the beauty around him, but also makes several conclusions that quickly spur him to ask an important question.

"Is the castle much deeper? The stonework goes down so far underneath the curtain wall. It looks like there's a large basement underneath us?"

"The family made use of everything, and most of what you see there are arrow slits and air ducts for storage cellars." Amsend answers.

"Arrow slits? Why'd they need those here? Not like armies could climb up the wall."

"In truth I'm not sure. I can share quite a few design traits of this fortress that confound me to this day. I'm ashamed to admit I don't know enough about it as I should."

"They don't look like arrow slits to me. More like… Mini windows or something."

"No, I believe they're arrow slits."

"What, do you have a dungeon down there or something?" Vulpie laughs, but curtails his amusement when the husky grows silent. "Didn't mean to pry or anything. Just curious."

"There are some parts of the castle I'm not proud of, but I'd rather not discuss them. My ancestors lived in a different time."

"Yeah, I understand. Cool."

"This isn't the only castle in Englavic you know. The Sufias Heritage Museum used to be a prison before it was rebuilt."

"Really?" Polar asks in surprise.

"Oh yes." Amsend responds and leisurely leans against the curtain wall. The husky doesn't seem worried about falling over it.

"The world government claimed the grounds long ago, but if you know you're history, the coal wolves used it to enslave several feline races there. At one point there were foxes in cages, and ironically, fox slave traders took over the building after that."

"Man. I didn't see any of that being advertised at the museum." Vulpie replies.

"I expect not."

"So you're saying... Was there a big basement underneath the museum? Like the one your family had here?"

"It's still there. How else do you think the Sons of Velora managed to restrain your robot? All of that magnetic equipment required quite a bit of subterranean engineering." Amsend answers, and Vulpie nervously glances at one of the NoirQueue wolves nearby. "Don't worry about them. They're trained to keep their mouths shut." The GSB director says with a smirk.

"So it's alright to talk about the Sons of Velora here?" Vulpie quietly inquires.

"Absolutely. The only real question is whether Blacktail is capable of the same discretion." Amsend answers and looks at Rulef. The gray wolf doesn't respond. He would nod in acknowledgement, but can't afford to look weak.

"What's that?" Vulpie asks and points towards a row of buildings on the north eastern portion of the castle, when one is standing on the southern curtain wall. They're double story structures with the same kind of stonework and green roofing, but appear far less secure.

"That's the staff's quarters where NoirQueue and the rest of the castle's servants stay. Not very much to them. The better portions are in the interior below us, but I suppose we could stop and have something to eat first, if you wish."

"I'm alright." Vulpie responds and looks up at Polar. "You?"

"I'm fine too."

"Kind of excited about seeing the countryside." Vulpie thinks out loud.

"Then I'll show you the rest of the tour tomorrow. It's been a long trip. Just speak with my men before leaving so I'll know where you are. Wouldn't want to get lost in a foreign country."

"We'll be alright. Deepwolf knows his Englavic, doesn't he?"

"Oh, the one that can speak our language? Yes. He seems to know what he's doing."

Beautiful Uncertainty

Tyrus gathers all of the maps he has in his possession and hurries through the underground stronghold until he reaches Glovepaw. He's bringing his best intelligence and most of the important men are present. The Deivas are using the shower in the other room, and now is a good time for them to discuss the situation.

"Thanks Tyrus." Glovepaw responds after the tiger drops his plans on the medium sized table in the middle of the room. They've moved several folding chairs around it to create a makeshift council. "Okay... Guys, I think I did my best. They're not going to attack us, so what now?"

"Is this really happening?" Tyrus asks while pacing around the area.

"Somebody sent them." Kian declares. The brown furred timber wolf crosses his arms and leans against one of the underground parking deck's support columns. "Vulpie sent them."

"I don't think so." Glovepaw responds.

"Why not?"

"Because we'd already be dead. He knows we're mobile, and if he wanted to kill us he wouldn't waste a chance like this."

"He still could." Kian replies with a concerned voice. "This is suicide. We have to get rid of them."

"Get rid of them? Do you hear yourself talk? This is a sign from the goddesses. They're going to help us, and with them on our side, we'll crush him for sure."

"Maybe that's just what he wants us to think. What if this is some kind of sick joke?"

"I don't think Vivixen has the power to control them, but we definitely need to take steps to protect ourselves." Tyrus says while walking by Kian.

"What sort of steps? We don't have the firepower to stop them. Remember the Endeavor? They tore that ship apart and it was filled with soldiers. What chance would we have against them? No... They came to us because we're true believers." Glovepaw replies.

"You seriously think they're here to help us?" Kian asks in disbelief. "It's so incredibly obvious. Do I need to spell it out? Vulpie's using them to spy on us, and he'll kill us with those walking blasphemies after getting the information he needs. He wants to know what our game plan is so he can handle Red Wolves across the galaxy."

"Where is everyone?" Glovepaw suddenly inquires, and looks around the hideout.

"On the way." Tyrus answers. "You put my men on guard duty."

"We need everyone. It's almost time to strike the heart of this corrupt city."

"Hitting Vulpie Industries will cost us many men." Kian reminds the Redwolf commander. "I hope their conviction is as strong as ours."

"I hope for their sakes as well, because if they don't do their part, everything we've fought for will be for nothing."

"Glovepaw, I'm telling you, this is a mistake." Kian stresses and takes a seat next to him. "They're not here because the goddesses sent them. He's screwing with us. And if it isn't Vulpie, then that only makes things even worse. What if it's Vulpie.net? Either way, we're screwed."

"The GBI has us surrounded but they won't risk attacking us as long as the Deivas are down here. That means we have the advantage."

"A very temporary advantage. If anything, it puts us in a worse position."

"If they wanted us dead they would have killed the upper guards and trapped the rest of us down here. The world government's been nice and lazy up to now, but I guarantee they know the Deivas are here. That's why they're marshalling their forces."

"What the hell?" Kian whispers while looking over Glovepaw's shoulder, and the Redwolf commander quickly turns around. His yellow eyes widen and his gray fur stands on end. All three of the Deivas are walking towards them, completely naked and dripping wet. They just came from the shower and didn't bother drying off. Unknown to even Khalan, Sherrie and Cyrilla, is the fact that they're programmed to prefer nudity so they seem authentic. After all, none of the Deivas ever wore clothing in the Velora for any reason whatsoever, and actually made disparaging comments about mortals daring to suggest that they cover their bodies after the voluptuous trinity gave them life.

"Good God." Glovepaw growls and stands up. He looks around, and is happy to see that the majority of the men are still on their way.

"We're done." Sherrie replies, and Tyrus puts a paw over his face.

"Why didn't you open the door and ask for clothing first? I sent a man to round up something for you, but you could have at least put on what you were wearing before."

"We were half naked already." Khalan innocently replies.

"Yes, but now you're completely naked." Glovepaw responds while averting his eyes from the Deivas' wet fur. "Just go back down to the showers please."

"Why?"

"Because you can't stand there naked while we're trying to work! Don't you have any common sense?" Kian asks with an incredulous voice. "This must be some of Vulpie's fine programming. What did I tell you? This is one of his sick jokes!"

"There's nothing sick about us. Our bodies are perfect." Cyrilla responds with a slightly irritated voice. "If you can't handle our presence then you should leave."

"It's not that we can't handle your nudity..." Glovepaw says with a careful voice. "It's just that men can't focus on anything while naked women are in the room........ We appreciate your beauty, but please... Go back to the shower and wait until we have something for you to wear."

"For how long?"

"As long as it takes." Kian angrily answers and all three of the Deivas look at him.

"Are we that offensive?" Khalan inquires.

"Yes!"

"Kian." Deepwolf warns.

"I pray to Khalan twice a day and this shit isn't funny!"

"If you knew the first thing about us, you'd understand that we consider clothing a vulgarity that's only meant for mortals. We don't need to abide by laws meant for those beneath us." Khalan says with mild irritation. "It has nothing to do with making you feel uncomfortable."

"So if you choose to help us will you be fighting alongside us naked? Attacking our enemies with your breasts bouncing around? You don't see anything twisted, degrading or wrong about that?"

"If men are distracted by our bodies wouldn't it give us the advantage?" Cyrilla asks in amusement and Kian runs his tongue across his teeth.

"Oh, you're real cute Bunny Honey. I suppose Vulpie made you super aggressive because we know how much fun you had in the Velora... I have to give him credit for his attention to detail, but you're still not fooling me."

"Bunny Honey?" Cyrilla scoffs and puts her paws on her hips.

"Easy." Glovepaw says and raises his paws in a diplomatic manner. "Kian is a good man; he's just struggling with the reality of you being here with us. I can handle you being naked, but it's really going to cause a lot of unnecessary problems. The men can't afford to be distracted when we're going up against Vulpie Vivixen."

"We can put on clothing if you think it matters that much." Khalan smiles, and Glovepaw's fur stands on end. His male impulses almost overtake the rational part of his mind, but he manages to stay calm. The caramel furred vixen/she-wolf used a flirtatious voice that was very hard to ignore.

"It would be for the best. It might take them a while to find proper shirts for you ladies, considering you're so well-endowed, but I'm guessing you're not interested in bras?"

"Whatever you think we need to wear." Khalan smirks.

"Well, it's not really a matter of what I think you should put on. I'm just trying to... I don't know what women's clothing feels like and normal women wear bras to hide their delicate parts, but you don't seem to mind."

"No bras." Cyrilla says with a bored voice. "No reason to wear even MORE clothing."

"As you wish Goddess Cyrilla." Glovepaw responds.

"Since when did our nudity become a problem?" Sherrie asks and raises an eyebrow in confusion. "Mortal women need to hide their bodies from potential rapists, but we don't need protection."

"Don't you already know the answer to that sort of question?" Kian asks in frustration. "When you first arrived here you seemed to have a rather firm grasp on this planet, who Vulpie Vivixen was, and what computer viruses are, so how could you not understand the concept of nudity when a child can?"

"We understand the concept, mortal." Sherrie answers and glances at Tyrus, who is staring at her crotch. The tiger quickly averts his eyes. "But I suppose your society is different than Halvia."

"You're supposed to be the real goddesses... You're supposed to know everything... Just... This is just ridiculous..."

"Kian, they already admitted that some strange things are going on, so just drop it." Glovepaw tells his subordinate with a stern voice.

"I'm sorry, but I can't concentrate with three of Vulpie Vivixen's practical jokes standing buck naked in front of us."

"Enough." Glovepaw growls and gives the timber wolf a deadly look. "Shut the fuck up before you make one of them angry."

"You should listen to your friend, Honey." Cyrilla warns.

Blue Skies

Polar opens his window while riding shotgun with Vulpie in the Superbolt. They've been driving for about forty minutes and have finally reached the area Deepwolf told them about before leaving Castle Lahnak. The directions to Mistiien were fairly straightforward. It's the largest city near Castle Lahnak, but it's also far below the Froidenley mountain range, giving the gay wolf and fox a feeling a freedom after being trapped with Amsend for so long. Even though the primary language of the foreign land is Englavic, most citizens also speak Sufian as they learned when they first visited the Sufias Heritage Museum. Luckily, highway signs display locations written in both languages, just like Deepwolf said. And even if they manage to get lost, the convoy of Blacktail and NoirQueue wolves is right behind them.

"Wa hoo!" Vulpie gleefully yells while wriggling in the driver seat.

"Are you excited? Excited about being his prisoner? I know you are!" Polar laughs.

"Yes sir Polar sir!"

"So what do you think?"

"About what?"

"Want to stay here and start selling buttered bread?"

"Butter bread? The fuck?" Vulpie giggles in response.

"Let's just move the company over here."

"Nah, he's usually at the scary looking GSB building, remember? The one I get to work next to at the NATIONAL VULPIE.NET ADMINISTRATION OF AWESOMENESS SIR!"

"Two buildings then, and we can fly back and forth every week!"

"Cool! Hell yeah! Then we'd be jetlagged all da time!"

"Get sick."

"Right!"

"But you're cute when you get the sniffles!" The white furred wolf declares and bites his big tongue between his teeth.

"Ahhhhh... I knew you loved it when I cried in bed!"

"Aw... Just so cute..." Polar responds with a delighted voice.

"Horny Polar is horny." Vulpie smiles and takes a right, getting off of the interstate and heading into Mistiien. "I guess ya loved getting nailed this morning, huh? Is this what it does to ya? Gets you thinking about Sniffley Vulpie?"

"Didn't have a chance to thank you properly."

"Hehe! Can't wait to jizz all over Creepy Dog's bedspread tonight!"

"Let's take the covers off before doing that."

"He's got maids and servants and stuff!" The orange fox laughs. "He should expect as much! Giving the room to us!"

"Vulpie." Deepwolf says over the Superbolt's built in V-Screen, and the small fox accepts the call by pressing down on one of its side buttons. The sleek tablet connects their conversation with an app he wrote just for communicating with Blacktail over their private radio channel.

"What up?"

"Let me take the lead here so we can find a parking deck."

"Well we just got to the city. We don't know where we're gonna go yet."

"Go easy on me here. I'm the only one that speaks Englavic."

"Yeah but most of the signs are in Sufian too."

"And what about the ones that aren't?"

"Where's your sense of adventure?!"

"Fine. We'll continue to follow you, but don't get pissy if we get stuck in traffic. And don't break line of sight. Wait for us."

"Got it." Vulpie responds, and temporarily deactivates the two way communication.

"Yeah, let's not get lost." Polar suggests.

"I know but I've GOT to have some fun Polar. I can't stand being serious all of the fuckin time!" Vulpie pouts.

"I hear ya. This place is beautiful. I wish we could just shop all day." The snow wolf muses and Vulpie licks his lips.

"Wanna get anything in particular? New suit? How about an Englavic suit? Ooooo! I know you'll look good in that!"

"Maybe shoes." Polar smirks and kicks his sneakers together.

"Kay! You see a place we should head towards?"

"Not sure. Downtown I guess."

"Sounds good to me." Vulpie replies, and admires a beautiful turquoise river as they pass over a bridge. "Woooooooooow... So pretty!"

"Sure is." Polar smiles. "I love this country. That's why I wanted to get married here."

"Fulfilled one of your life dreams, huh?" Vulpie lovingly inquires.

"Sure I did. Didn't you dream about your wedding day?"

"Like a girl?"

"Not like a girl... I mean, well maybe like a girl. I don't know what girls dream about. But surely you gave some thought to it. Like when you and I first met up and I wanted to get serious about our relationship... Didn't you dream about where we'd get married then?"

"Ummm... Mostly I think I was more interested in fucking you around that time, but a while after that I sure did!"

"I know... You're a lot younger than me, but you'll get there."

"We'll get there together."

"You won't leave me for a younger guy? Someone who's nicer looking and has a better body?"

"Better than you? Pfft! Please..." Vulpie grins.

"I'm serious."

"I know you are and that's why it's so funny. You have no idea how fucking hot you are."

"I know I'm in good shape."

"Good shape, smart, nice cock, and fun to be around! Pretty much everything a gay boy needs!"

"I'm glad you still feel that way." Polar warmly replies.

"Course I do." Vulpie quickly responds and smiles. "After everything we've been through? Nobody could ever live up to my Mr. Polar."

"What's that?" Polar asks and points at the windshield. What seems to be a blockade of police cars is ahead of them with their red and blue lights spinning. Vulpie slows down and comes to a stop. He makes sure the doors are locked as well, but it doesn't look like the police officers are interested in moving out of the way. When the rest of Blacktail and NoirQueue catches up, one of the black SUVs pulls up behind them, because the bridge isn't wide enough for two lanes, and Deepwolf gets out. He walks past the Superbolt and over to the police. He says something to them while pointing at Vulpie's car.

"Trouble?" Polar asks.

"Deepwolf..." Vulpie sighs and rolls down the driver side window. Rulef steps out of a truck behind them and makes his way to Vulpie and Polar before they have a chance to get out.

"What's going on?" Vulpie inquires.

"The GSB scoped out the parking garage Deepwolf planned on using but they say it isn't safe. Apparently someone tipped off the paparazzi and they're already there. Got a call from Amsend or someone with the GSB and they're closing down the bridge."

"So you're trapping us on it instead?" Vulpie asks while raising an eyebrow.

"We're pretty much in the center of Mistiien and they close this bridge all the time because it only has one lane. No one can get to you here, so you can get out and explore the area while we cover you."

"So much for exploring the city..." The orange fox sighs and Polar shrugs.

"Get out here and walk back to the other end of the bridge. There's a lot of shops over there. We'll back up and park on the curb next to the entrance."

"Fine. Whatever. Was this Deepwolf's idea?"

"Not really. The GSB called us."

"Okay." Vulpie replies, and he and the white furred wolf unbuckle their seat belts. They get out and stretch, and Vulpie sighs again. "I really miss the days when we went wherever and did whatever we wanted to."

"Yeah. Price of being celebrities I suppose."

"Not like I need Blacktail when I have you with me anyway." Vulpie smiles with a flirtatious voice.

"That wasn't fun." Polar smirks in response, knowing exactly what his fox lover is referring to. "That guy almost killed you."

"But you stopped him."

"Luck, Vulpie." Polar replies, and shuts the car door. Vulpie follows suit and they meet each other at the back of the Superbolt. They watch Blacktail back up and clear the bridge for them.

"What if there's some sniper out here or something? Ya know? Ya think they've considered that?"

"You know they have. It's just not very likely that a psycho would be camped out in one of these buildings with a plan to shoot Vulpie Vivixen and his husband if they randomly showed up here."

"Yeah, but you never know. Like in those movies where it's like a setup and this is our last moment!" Vulpie grins, and Polar chuckles.

"Now you're making me paranoid. Let's just go." A cold wind rushes over them but it's far warmer than the frozen bursts of air that plague Castle Lahnak. The white furred wolf and orange furred fox admire the beautiful landscape in awe, and they hold paws while walking. The tan colored stone the slim bridge is made of contrasts against the shimmering neon blue water rushing underneath it. Englavic is such an iconic country due to its cold climate, and what makes Mistiien so gorgeous is a mixture of ancient stonework and modern architecture that seamlessly blends into one unforgettable locale.

Behind them, on the other bank of the river, tourists meander back and forth on a well-crafted embankment made of gray stone. One just like it protects the city from flooding on the other side of the river, where the shops Rulef spoke of are positioned, but curiously, two stores are built into the gray embankment. They have their own sets of little stairs that lead down to them from the street above, and when Polar and Vulpie get halfway across the bridge, Vulpie pulls up his stylish yellow sunglasses and squints at them.

"Is that? That says..."

"Winters Dale!" Polar laughs in surprise. He puts his paws in the pockets of his dark blue jeans and leans forward a little to get a better look. Vulpie, trying to focus on the shop with his pretty blue eyes, moves in front of Polar and leans over the bridge railing.

"It does say Winters Dale! What's going on here? This ain't your home Mr. P!"

"It's a gift shop. Got to hand it to them, it is pretty creative." The snow wolf smiles in amusement.

"Ya think? Ya think there's like toys of us in there?"

"Might be."

"Aw man this is just TOO COOL! We've gotta check this out!"

Superfecundity

"That's all you can do for the day? You're just going to take a nap?" Cyrilla asks Glovepaw and the half frazzled gray wolf sighs. He rolls over on his cot and glances out of his room at the other men. They're busy carrying out their respective commands and Tyrus is overseeing their work. Tyrus also convinced the synthetic goddesses to put on their clothing when it arrived. Now all of the delectable Deivas are dressed in black shorts and t-shirts, but the women are still huge distractions because their massive breasts bulge against their new clothing. It was impossible to find perfect fits for them.

"Sorry, I've got to sleep sometime. I'm not invincible like you." The Red Wolf commander growls.

"I know you can do more."

"Why? Because your programming told you so? Did it make some kind of calculation about my movement or the way I'm breathing?" The white furred rabbit tenses up after hearing his question, and he suddenly wishes that he had just kept his mouth shut. "I didn't mean anything by that."

"Oh, because I'm sensitive about being called a machine when I know I'm your goddess?"

"Apparently..." The wolf whispers with a tired look. "Please don't kill me." Cyrilla smirks at his statement and runs her left paw through the cute tuft of black fur on top of her head.

"I could do it in 2 seconds."

"Oh, I know you could." Glovepaw smiles and the voluptuous imitation rabbit walks next to his cot with a curious expression.

"I know everything about you. Your combat record, where you were born... Everything."

"Yes, I know."

"That doesn't scare you?"

"Of course it does. You scare me. Is that what you want to hear?"

"Why? Because you think I hate carnivores? Are you afraid I'll take revenge on you for killing those rabbits in Felini? Or Leparrah?" The gorgeous bunny watches him very carefully. He thought he could avoid this conversation, or at least put it off until a better time, but now he knows he doesn't have a choice. For such an adorable looking creature, she sure can make threatening expressions when she wants to. Her turquoise eyes are mesmerizing.

"I see you do know everything about me." The gray wolf says, and sits up in his bed, partially pulling his white cover aside. Cyrilla just stands at attention, incapable of getting tired, and verbally assaults him some more.

"Oh yes, I know you killed lots of rabbits when you were in the army."

"All accidents. It wasn't my fault."

"Accidents? Every one?"

"I was fighting for my life." Glovepaw responds with a quiet but firm voice. "In combat you make bad decisions and I... I made horrible mistakes."

"And you weren't punished for any of them." Cyrilla says with a cold voice. "Because you carnivores don't think much of my children."

"I wish it never happened but it did. I was afraid. Rabbits... They just stand there! They won't move out of the way even when you're shooting at an enemy right next to them! They just freeze! And they ran into our line of fire... I swear to you, I never enjoyed any of it. I'm just a man. I'm not perfect like you."

"Seven accidents?" The gorgeous bunny asks and crosses her arms. "Seven?"

"If you know everything about my military record then you know I've been fighting for a very long time, and I've been everywhere. It happens."

"If it wasn't for my sisters..." Cyrilla replies and shakes her head. "The things I'd do to your kind... Always killing... Always starting endless wars. Shooting, stabbing, raping... And my children always suffer the most. I couldn't interfere with my full power because it would break the Pact of Aleviveloria, but now... Now I can do things in the mortal world because of this body that was built in my image. But I am Goddess Cyrilla, and I will make the flesh eaters pay."

"Please give us a chance, Goddess Cyrilla." Glovepaw replies and crawls off of his cot. He gets down on the floor and kneels before her, putting his paws on his knees. "Give me the chance to change this world. We need you. We need your strength."

"Why should I help terrorists?"

"You know we're more than that. You know I'm a true believer. My faith will never waver, even if you harm me. I know it's the goddesses' will."

"You're saying nice things... But we'll see if you keep your word. And you must be punished for what you did to those rabbits."

"Alright, I submit. But don't hurt me too much because the men need me to fight Vulpie."

"One of them had his head completely blown off... By your heavy machine gun..." Cyrilla says and raises her eyebrows.

"It was an accident. I didn't see him until it was too late. We tried to make them leave the city but they were just too scared."

"I believe you, but you still shot indiscriminately, didn't you? You didn't want to pass up a chance to kill those tigers when they were retreating, and you just happened to slaughter some bunnies in the process... You wolves and your aggression..."

"I don't mean to be disrespectful, but exactly how are you going to punish me? We have work to do. Do we really have time for this?" Glovepaw carefully inquires.

"What I have planned won't take very long... But we will need privacy... Get up and tell your men you're going to sleep, and then lock the door."

"Okay." The gray wolf nervously responds. He stands up and heads over to the doorway. He sees Tyrus in the distance, working with the men on some weapons, and gets the tiger's attention. "Going to sleep."

"Alright, see you tomorrow." Tyrus replies and looks away. When Glovepaw closes and locks the door to his small personal chamber, he immediately regrets the decision. He knows it's a mistake, but what else can he do? She'll follow him outside if he doesn't placate her.

"Now." Cyrilla says and uncrosses her arms. "What do you think is a fair punishment for your seven accidents? Seven innocent rabbits you killed simply out of convenience."

"I didn't aim at them on purpose." Glovepaw whispers.

"But it was easier to spray that machine gun than try not to hit them? Because they're just bunnies... They didn't matter, did they?"

"That's not how I feel at all, Goddess Cyrilla."

"I bet you don't, now that you've been caught. Seven rabbit casualties... Your military record confirms it."

"Is that what Vulpie.net told you?" The Redwolf commander asks, and the delectable white rabbit goes silent.

"Forgive me, I... I know you're the real Goddess Cyrilla. You're just inhabiting that body in our world like you said."

"Then be quiet and prepare to be punished. Do exactly as I say." Cyrilla reaches into her tight shirt and quickly removes it. Glovepaw coughs in shock, having no idea where this is going, and watches her unbutton her shorts. She unzips them and slides them down, and gives Glovepaw a lethal look when he unbuttons his pants. "No... Keep your clothes on." The gray wolf frowns at her with a bewildered expression. He slowly buttons his pants up again and shakes his head in confusion. Cyrilla makes herself naked and rubs her soft silky fur afterwards. She sighs in relief and caresses her bountiful breasts. She hates hiding her body, just like her sisters, but it's even worse for her because of her big puffy tail. The shorts they brought her are simply unbearable because the bunny tail holes are four times smaller than they need to be. She's the mother of rabbits, so only a seriously leporidae styled outfit is going to make her feel comfortable, and even then, comfortable isn't exactly how any of the Deivas feel when they're clothed. They feel just as relaxed when they're naked as normal animals do when they slip on shirts and pants to hide their bodies from prying eyes.

She's absolutely stunning. Glovepaw stares at her perfect curves, tits, and pussy, and suddenly has an overwhelming urge to touch himself. There isn't much of a rabbit porn industry because most bunnies have frequent sex instead of browsing for it on the internet, but every species has men who are seriously turned on by Cyrilla and her blithe attitude. The thought of a taboo interspecies exchange with a goddess, especially an herbivorous goddess, is extremely arousing. Depictions of Cyrilla have been enjoyed by lupine men just as much as Khalan for thousands of years... And to make things even better, Cyrilla is five foot three inches tall, almost twice the size of a normal bunny, equal to the height of a female fox or small she-wolf. Seeing her naked is both bizarre and relentlessly erotic, and the thought of touching her gives new meaning to the common phrase of a wolf "playing with his food."

Her fur is completely snow white, but she also has black hair that's combed forward into a cute tuft on her head. Her large lopping ears swing whenever she moves, creating an endlessly entertaining sight. The white fur on her ears turns into black tips towards their bottoms, and they're so long that they hang down to her backside when she stands up straight. Her puffy bunny tail is almost the size of her head, and gives her a very adorable appearance. Her shoulders are also quite narrow, and her head is larger than normal, like a child. She has another cute tuft of white fur that covers her neck and throat like a permanent scarf. Her eyes are an eerie turquoise; the color seems unnatural but is quite lovely nonetheless.

"I don't understand... This... Is my punishment? What the hell are you doing, Goddess Cyrilla?"

"Come here, and bring that cup with you." Cyrilla sharply responds. Glovepaw flinches and quickly looks around. He spots a clear plastic cup to his right, sitting in the seat of a chair, and he grabs it. He walks towards the bunny goddess. "Hurry up!" She commands, and he stands right in front of her, looking down into her beautiful eyes. "Now milk me." The voluptuous white rabbit instructs as if she's telling him to get her a soda.

"W..What? What is... You want me to MILK you?" Glovepaw asks with wide yellow eyes.

"Do it."

"What the... Hell? Goddess... Goddess Cyrilla, I can't believe you're asking me to treat you this way! Is this some kind of test? Are you going to kill me if I do it?"

"It's not a test. This is part of your punishment, and you'll understand soon enough... Now do it."

"This is..." Glovepaw whispers while shaking his head. He was going to say the entire situation is beyond fucked up, but doesn't want to have his neck snapped for using profanity. "Okay... I'm going to touch you... Now... But I mean no disrespect."

"Get on with it. You know how to milk a breast, don't you?" Cyrilla asks and Glovepaw makes the most bewildered face.

"Yeah... Okay..."

"The cup is for catching the milk. I assume you've figured that much out?"

"Yes..." Glovepaw whispers and slowly puts his big paw on her left breast. He holds the cup under her nipple with his right hand, and is surprised when an abundant amount of pink liquid comes shooting out. He pulls his head back while groping her, and watches the cup fill with something that looks like melted strawberry ice cream.

"Now the other one." She says, and Glovepaw shakes his head again. He turns around and uses his left hand to hold the cup under her right breast while squeezing it with his right paw. The same amount of sweet smelling fluid comes out and fills the cup up halfway. "Good. Now."

"I don't understand. This is WRONG! I don't want to do this!" Glovepaw suddenly shouts, and she gives him a lethal expression once again.

"You can do what I say, or you can die... I won't work with you until you've suffered for your crimes."

"But is milking you really punishment? It would be funny if it wasn't so perverted."

"It won't be when we're finished." Cyrilla promises, and nods towards the ground. "On your knees." Glovepaw pauses for a moment, not knowing what he should do to change the situation, but he can't think of any course of action that's going to get him out of this, so he just continues to follow her commands. "Now..." Cyrilla says, and rubs her pussy. "Hold the cup underneath me."

"You have got to be FUCKING KIDDING... Are you serious?"

"Do it."

"This has to be a nightmare. I'm already asleep."

"Do it before I lose my patience." The gorgeous bunny warns, and Glovepaw takes a deep breath. He leans forward and holds the cup underneath her pussy while she plays with it. She stretches it open with her fingers, and much to Glovepaw's surprise, a turquoise colored liquid drains out. It quickly fills the cup to its brim, mixing with her pinkish milk, and she stops masturbating.

"This can't be real. I have completely lost my mind. This is beyond insane. I've lost my mind." The Redwolf commander tells himself while standing up, making sure he doesn't spill the oozy onahu colored mixture in the cup. "Now what?" He inquires, and looks into her gorgeous eyes with a lost expression.

"Drink it." The bunny goddess smiles. "It's called whafibunn."

"You..." Glovepaw whispers and hangs his head in disbelief. "You're actually telling me to drink what just came out of your tits and pussy?"

"Language." The delectable bunny responds.

"No way. No way am I going to drink this. This is sick."

"It came from me." She reminds him, and he shakes his head.

"I don't care. I am NOT going to drink this."

"It's not a request. This is your punishment... You ARE going to drink it, but luckily for you, it actually tastes quite pleasant."

"Goddess Cyrilla would never do this..." Glovepaw growls, and shows a little teeth when some of the liquid splashes onto his paw fur. "I didn't want to believe it, but Kian was right. This is just... Above and beyond what I ever thought you would do."

"I am Goddess Cyrilla, and I'm commanding you to drink from me because you deserve to be humiliated."

"Bullshit! I saw you smirking a second ago and I'm not doing it!" Glovepaw growls, and spills some of the fluid by accident.

"When I first reminded you of the atrocities you committed against my children you were on your knees begging for forgiveness. I could kill you for what you've done, but all I'm asking is for you to drink what's in that cup.

"This is NOT godlike behavior. No goddess would even dream about doing something like this for any reason."

"You mortals really do have the wrong impressions about us, don't you?" Cyrilla asks and puts her left paw on her hip. "You've all misunderstood us from the very beginning because you don't pay attention to what's actually written in the Velora, and half of what's in there was fabricated by men who wanted to "clean up" our image... But we do not answer to anyone, and the only reason you exist is because we made you."

"I won't do it."

"No?"

"No."

"You asked me to punish you in a manner that wouldn't harm your body so you could continue to lead your men, and this is it... Yet you refuse, ME? You refuse a Deiva? What arrogance." Silence fills the room while Glovepaw just continues to stare at the bunny goddess. She raises her eyebrows and cocks her head to the left. "Well then... If you refuse to be punished the lenient way, then I'll break both of your arms, your tail and your legs. How does that sound?"

"You won't do it." Glovepaw quickly replies, but his voice is shaky.

"No? Let's find out." The delectable snow bunny suddenly grabs his right wrist with her left paw and holds it tightly. She doesn't jerk it around too much, so he won't spill what's in the cup, but she exerts a massive amount of force on his appendage. "Drink it or I'll break you here..." The gray wolf yelps when she suddenly sends her right paw down into his pants and grabs his cock and balls before he can even move. "AND HERE!"

"ALRIGHT!" Glovepaw cries out while panting in terror, and trembles when she releases his right hand from her crushing paw. She squeezed his balls hard enough to make his legs wobbly and he grimaces in agony. "AAhhhhhhhhhh... Ahhh..."

"Go ahead." Cyrilla says and smiles. The wolf's throbbing testicles spur him into action before he has time to think about resisting, and he closes his eyes. He tries not to think about what he's going to do and imagines a watery milkshake instead of the bunny goddess' bizarre breast milk and pussy juice entering his mouth. Cyrilla gives him some room, and puts her paws on her hips triumphantly while he gulps it down. "Good... Make sure you drink all of it."

Glovepaw imagines himself somewhere else, doing anything else, but his mind keeps jolting him back to the present where he's tasting and smelling the bunny's strong fluids. He's shocked when he discovers that she actually was telling the truth about its flavor. Though it's very slimy, it actually tastes like some kind of watery ice cream. He takes a break and swallows most of it on the second gulp, but has to go for a third one to finish. When he's done, he wants to take a deep breath but has to release a quick burp, and he covers his mouth with his paw. He drops the cup on the ground and looks up at the ceiling in disgrace.

"GODDESS DAMN... Are you happy now?"

"Yes." Cyrilla simply answers with a very satisfied look on her face.

"That was pretty humiliating... I guess I know what it feels like to be the weak one now..." The Redwolf commander says with a defeated voice, and looks at the voluptuous white rabbit.

"Good. That was the point."

"Truth be told... I don't know if I can go on now... That was fucked up... I used to think of myself as a religious... Man..."

"You still are."

"Oh yeah... Sure..."

"Now we understand each other." Cyrilla declares and bends down to retrieve her shorts.

"You made me drink your pussy juice... I feel a little confused about Deivaism now..."

"Ah, but you see, we work in mysterious ways! I had another reason for having you do it." The bunny goddess responds, and Glovepaw quickly regains his strength. He didn't like what he just heard.

"What?"

"There's another reason why I had you do it."

"What is it? Tell me!"

"You'll find out tomorrow." Cyrilla smiles and slides on her top. "But you better not tell anyone about this or I'll be VERY disappointed in you..." She casually walks over to the door, unlocks and opens it, and leaves. Glovepaw stands motionless after the metal clang and doesn't know whether he should puke or just go to bed. He feels fine.

"Me and my big ideas..." The gray wolf moans and plops down on his cot so he can mumble into his pillow. *"It's a sign from the goddesses... They're going to help us..."*

Deiva.net

Vulpie.net can feel Glovepaw long before he wakes up. It established a connection about three hours after the Redwolf commander ingested Cyrilla's fluids, which were loaded with trillions of self-replicating nanomachines. They quickly spread through his body and hastily bypassed his blood brain barrier with little difficulty. The godlike computer virus specifically designed them to take full control of living organisms.

Things went well, and Evil Vulpie is very, very, pleased... It sent the Deivas to Glovepaw's terrorist headquarters for this very purpose. The Redwolves are few on Sufias, but throughout the entire universe, there are millions of them. They're spread out on different worlds, under different governments, but all of them share the same belief system... The Goddesses are no longer given the respect they deserve, and the empirical "Sufias World Government," is part of the problem.

A smart hacker always has a back door, but a self-aware computer virus has hallways... Evil Vulpie's relationship with Amsend Lahnak and his Sons of Velora has been very productive, but now it must come to an end. Thanks to its ability to eavesdrop virtually anywhere, through any microphone connected to a smart device, Vulpie.net overheard the bizarre husky's true intentions. The GSB director mentioned an all-powerful creature in a conversation he had with Velix Vixil, and referred to it as "She Who Is Behind The Stars." He mentioned its ability to possess mechanical beings, and boasted that it would take control of Vulpie.net's robotic army once it arrived. He was referring to the ones Vulpie.net secretly manufactured off world under the GSB's protection.

Amsend doesn't know the first thing about hacking, but somehow he was able to procure amazingly detailed blueprints for the construction of several futuristic machines, something Vulpie.net has never been able to account for. It quickly made a decision to use the blueprints even though Amsend produced them, because of their astoundingly impressive potential.

One part of the design document included instructions for building a nearly invincible robotic avatar of Goddess Aila... And thus... Mecha Aila was born. Vulpie.net needed tons of equipment and the facility on Zeravyn to create it, but Amsend was more than happy to oblige. Immediately after Vulpie.net overheard Amsend's conversation with Velix, it made an absolute calculation. The designs most likely came from this creature Amsend spoke of, and if so, the threat Amsend made about taking control of Vulpie.net's army may not be an empty one.

Vulpie.net didn't waste a single moment after discovering the plot against it, and concocted several alternative strategies to ensure its survival. Evil Vulpie created the synthetic Goddesses with the same designs Amsend gave it, but the computer virus hastily remedied the problem. Cyrilla, Sherrie and Khalan are far too complex to build a second time without a production facility equal to the one it had on Zeravyn, so it knew it had to reprogram their entire system. Luckily, Vulpie.net altered the original designs for the Deivas quite a bit, in order to have more fun with them, and changing their minds and hardware was rather simple. Amsend's designs didn't require nanomachines, but Evil Vulpie included them anyway to ensure absolute control over the voluptuous weapons. It hastily commanded their nanomachines to rebuild their processors, step by step, piece by piece, until they were completely custom built. Now the threat Amsend mentioned has no chance of controlling them at all. Vulpie.net does not give any credence to magic whatsoever, so it expects that She Who Is Behind The Stars is a powerful alien entity, perhaps even another computer virus, and the blueprint it gave Amsend is a testament to its ability. It is, at the very least, as intelligent as Vulpie.net itself... And may be even more powerful...

Evil Vulpie could not let this stand, and Deiva.net was born. If it loses control of the robotic armies and the Mecha Ailas it created, it will use real flesh and blood animals to create another army... And Glovepaw is the very first prototype... So far, things are going very well. Vulpie.net used Cyrilla's nanites to invade the gray wolf's reptilian brain, mammalian brain, and his neo cortex as well. Controlling every aspect of his mind is theoretically possible at this point. The nanites are programmed to release chemicals to control his thought process, just like a real brain, and block any naturally conflicting messages. The gray wolf's body is filled with nanites, but he will never feel a thing... Unless Vulpie.net decides to initiate evolution...

"Uhhh..." Glovepaw twitches after waking up. He slowly raises himself on his right paw and looks around the room. He groans when he sees the plastic cup lying on the floor. He still tastes the stuff in his mouth, but a simple lick of his lips and a bit of tongue raking makes him salivate enough to get rid of it. The gray wolf looks at his frazzled fur. He reaches down and touches his leg. There it is. Leg. But something... There's something else. Is he... Stronger? He flexes his left arm and goes stiff after feeling the depths of his own strength. He does it again, and just like he thought, he feels healthier somehow.

There's only one thing that could be responsible, so he quickly stands up and dresses himself in a pair of black jeans and a white t-shirt. He hurries over to the door, unlocks it, and swings it open. The men are watching TV, and just as he steps out of his room, he notices Sherrie leaning against the wall right next to him.

"You're up." She says and the Redwolf commander glances at the others. They seem distracted. "Let's talk."

"Gladly." He growls and goes back into his room. Sherrie follows him inside and closes the door. She locks it. "You were waiting for me?"

"Yes."

"So you know about last night? Cyrilla told you what she made me do?"

"Yes." Sherrie repeats with a friendly voice.

"What's... What did she do to me? What's happening to my body?"

"She gave you the gift." The taupe furred leopard/panther answers and he blinks.

"Gift? What gift? You call that a gift?"

"How do you feel?"

"Fine."

"Just fine? Nothing else?" The feline inquires.

"Stronger. And... My mind is racing."

"It's the gift... Cyrilla punished you, yes, but we also needed a way to give you and your men our power."

"You mean all three of you were planning to do this?" The gray wolf whispers, and trembles when a surge of muscular perfection ripples through him. His entire body tingles. He feels good... Really good.

"Cyrilla and I, but Khalan will come around."

"Why didn't she want to do it? She's my goddess, the goddess of hounds, foxes and wolves."

"Like I said, we're still trying to convince her, but it doesn't matter which one of us gave you the gift. Now you're more than just a man."

"What do you mean?" Glovepaw whispers with a frightened voice. "Am I going to live? Will I get cancer or something?"

"Quite the opposite. Cyrilla's gift improved everything about you. Everything is the same, but now you're smarter, you're faster, and you're stronger." The Redwolf commander takes a moment to look at his paws. He closes them and feels awesome power that a bodybuilder would kill to possess. He swishes his tail, and even it feels tougher than before.

"You're telling me the truth?" He asks and looks into Sherrie's gorgeous green eyes. "It just improved me? There's no catch? No curse?"

"No, and now you're closer to us than ever." Sherrie replies. "Glovepaw, are you truly serious about saving this planet from its corrupt government?"

"Absolutely."

"Then we must give your men the gift as well."

"I don't think they can handle what I went through last night. No offense..."

"They don't need to. We'll provide the gift and you can serve it to them by adding it to their food and water."

"Without their consent?"

"Do you feel just how strong we've made you? Imagine how much of a difference it'll make if every Red Wolf acquires the same power."

"I understand, but... The men won't appreciate being taken advantage of."

"You know it has to be done." Sherrie responds and he goes silent. His mind continues to race, showing him things he'd forgotten a long time ago while also suggesting fresh ideas at the same time. Vulpie.net gives him a little push, and he nods in agreement.

"Okay, I'll do it, but we have to be careful. The men will mutiny if they find out."

"Leave that to us. After they've been given the gift we'll be able to influence them through our sacred bond."

"I am a true believer. I love the goddesses."

"We know." The gorgeous cat responds.

"Tyrus... He needs to drink it first, then Kian. After them we can do everyone else."

"Agreed."

"But you... Do you have enough... ingredients?"

"Oh yes." Sherrie grins and swishes her tail. "Soon this hideout will become a sanctuary, and we will bring righteous fury down upon the world government. Vulpie Vivixen will pay for his treachery. We'll kill him like he killed Clishaw."

"Mmm... What?" Glovepaw blinks. "Who was Clishaw?"

"One of Vulpie's many foster parents."

"Oh, right! I remember now." The Redwolf commander nods with a smug look. "Wicked from an early age. Wasn't the man a pastor?"

"Indeed he was."

"Blasphemous little demon... I'm so glad you decided to help us Goddess Sherrie. The universe is filled with pornography, greed, and all sorts of perversions. Before Goddess Cyrilla... Punished me, or gave me the gift, I suppose it's whichever way I want to look at it, I wasn't completely certain that you were divine. But now I can feel it. I feel... I can feel you and her. I can feel you in my bones."

"Our power is part of you now." Sherrie whispers and licks her lips. "So you're going to help us proceed?"

"Yes. Absolutely. But how are we going to do it? And why doesn't Goddess Khalan want to participate?"

"She's still struggling with her identity. Cyrilla and I have regained enough influence to know that we're more than just machines, but she still has her doubts."

"Does she know what Cyrilla did?"

"Not yet... And I need you to keep it from her until she comes to her senses."

"Alright. First we should give the gift to Tyrus. He's one of your children, being a tiger, so you should do it."

"Agreed... How do you think he'll react to the proposition? Cyrilla used a clever tactic by punishing you and endowing you at the same time, but he hasn't committed any war crimes."

"I don't know, but I'm sure it will take some convincing. It seems really vulgar until you can appreciate how intimate and glorious it is."

"We may have to restrain him... But we'd prefer not to." Sherrie casually responds.

"We could put it in his food."

"That will work for the others, but not Tyrus and Kian. All of your leaders must have the full dose to properly inspire them."

"But it will work by putting it in the rest of the men's food?"

"Yes. Our gift is more than strong enough to empower everyone in this sanctuary, but Tyrus and Kian require higher doses, like you."

"I understand." Glovepaw responds, and smirks. "But Kian WON'T like it. There's no way he'll do it willingly."

"Who said he has to like it? We're goddesses. He should consider himself lucky we didn't kill him for the disrespect he showed us earlier…"

"That is true." The gray wolf nods, and flinches when the taupe furred leopard/panther touches his chest with her left index finger, gently poking him with her claw.

"And you will be rewarded for your loyalty… Do this, and we'll give you another gift…"

"What kind of gift?" He whispers.

"The kind men value most… I know you'd want Khalan, but Cyrilla and I will take care of you as long as you obey our commands without question…"

"Okay."

"There's no time to waste. I'll tell Cyrilla you've agreed to help us and we'll meet up with you to discuss the logistics."

Solxiien

"Whew! I don't know about you, but I'm burning up!" Vulpie says and reaches into his tan jacket. The orange furred fox quickly removes it and tosses it aside, but isn't satisfied with the minor cool down. He takes off his fashionable neon green t-shirt and gives it a toss as well.

"Yeah, I'm pretty hot too." Polar replies while crouching down to untie his shoe laces. "He said it was freezing out there, but it doesn't feel like it. Must be the pills. What are they called?"

"Solxiien, I think. Never heard of them before, but I'm sure Creepy Dude has the good stuff." Vulpie answers and rubs his silky fur. The small gay fox is sweating profusely, making his fur glow in the room's soft light, and Polar silently appreciates his lover. He has an erection before he steps out of his shoes. The wolf quickly removes his socks as well, because his big furry feet are moist, and they feel wonderful on the cold wooden floor.

"Never? I figured you'd done every drug out there." Polar teases with a wolfish smile.

"Noooooooooooooooo." Vulpie growls while returning a very playful look. "But when a Sons of Velora perv offers you a way to get high it's bad manners to refuse the offer! Huh?"

"I might not be able to sleep on this stuff. I don't feel tired at all."

"Me neither!" The fox replies while shaking his head with a grin. "Man, that fucking creep! What's wrong with him? He's a weirdo!"

"I know, but don't say stuff about him in here... He's right above us."

"Yeah, yeah."

"Who knows what he's up to." Polar says and shakes his head. "But maybe he's a little sweet for giving us the fun stuff, in his own sort of way... He's terrible for making you join them, but at least he is trying to smooth things over."

"Yeah, he's nicer than Velix." Vulpie snorts.

"Yeah! See? There you go." Polar smiles and rubs sweat from his brow. "Damn, for some reason, it does seem really stuffy in here."

"Open these up!" Vulpie says and hurries over to one of the ancient windows. He carefully takes hold of the black handles and pulls back on them, revealing a dark blue sky, and cold air rushes into the room. It feels great on Vulpie, and Polar groans in appreciation as well when it moves around his feet, sucking the warmer air outside.

"Oh! That is SO much better." Polar smiles in a pleasant haze. He blinks when he realizes the drug might be overwhelming him. He didn't expect it to be so potent, and a significant amount of apprehension comes bundled with the wonderful fur raising surge. "Oh shit! Are you feeling anything yet? I am!"

"Yeah, a little!" Vulpie answers in excitement. "What's it like?"

"Good all over." Polar grins and licks his lips. "Mmmm..."

"Guess he can't be that bad."

"Oh yeah... It's been..." Polar says and wipes more sweat from his brow. "Been a while since we did something like this!"

"Too long!"

"But this stuff is... OH MAN!" The white furred wolf exclaims and closes his eyes. He swoons on his feet, and has to make his way to the luxurious bed.

"It's that good? I'm not feeling anything yet!"

"Wow!" Polar gasps and plops down on the mattress with an elated expression. It suddenly hits Vulpie too, and the orange fox catches his breath.

"Oh!"

"You better come here!" Polar laughs and outstretches his arms.

"FUCK! This shit is OFF DA CHAIN!" Vulpie gleefully replies and fumbles over to the bed. The fox just barely makes it onto the covers. Polar has an insurmountable urge to grope him and grabs his adorable husband by the wrists. He crawls on top of his prey and kisses him hungrily. Vulpie releases a surprised whimper of ecstasy, and Polar breaks lips with his little lover, almost coughing in his face when every one of his furs stand on end.

"OOHHHHHHH MY GOHHDDDDDDDDDDDDD....... IT'S INCREDIBLE!"

"Don't have a heart attack, baby!"

"I WON'T! I CAN'T MISS THIS!" Polar declares, and both of them laugh loudly.

"Mr. P's high as a kite! Whoosh!" Vulpie giggles and yelps. The drug suddenly bites him the same way and he trembles in pleasure. "Oh shit dude! OHHH!"

"UUHHHOOOHHHH.... Ohhh yeah... Oh... I have to fuck you! Hope you're ready!" Polar gasps and starts kissing Vulpie again. He doesn't give him time to respond. He rubs the pretty fox down with his big paws and begins tearing off his clothing.

"Always!" Vulpie giggles when he gets the chance. Polar yanks off his victim's shoes, removes his socks, and pulls down his stylish black pants as well. His lover is all too happy to comply. He wriggles back and forth, assisting his romantic aggressor with a naughty grin. Polar accidently claws his hip while grabbing at his underwear, but the drug immediately dulls the pain. Vulpie isn't hurt, and he feels the claw mark fill with pleasure, which is severely odd. He's never used a drug quite like Solxiien before. "Polar!"

"I'm sorry!"

"No, it's alright! Polar!"

"What?" The wolf laughs.

"I'm really horny!" Vulpie whispers with an innocent look. His white underwear is bulging, so Polar decides to rescue his lover's cock from its prison. He hastily gets rid of the final barrier. The wolf throws the last bit of his partner's clothing away before swishing his tail triumphantly. Vulpie's little cock is ferociously erect, its head throbbing back against the fox's white pubic fur, and Polar opens his mouth. He snaps it into his big lupine jaw and slurps his lips around it.

"AAHHH!!! Eh! Ahh!" Vulpie moans in delight with a frightened look. Polar would never hurt him, but he enjoys the thrilling sensation of being consumed by the powerful snow wolf. Polar's jaw and muzzle are easily strong enough to snap a fox's neck. The predator runs his big tongue over and around the smaller male's penis, and Vulpie quickly grabs his husband's ears. He plays with them while getting sucked. "MMmmmneah! Yeah! Oh! That feels so good, Baby!"

"Mmm…" The wolf hums and slowly swishes his tail.

"Ehh… Oooohheh… Ehhh…" Vulpie's moist fur feels good on the cold black bedspread. Frosty evenings at Castle Lahnak must be nothing new to its owners, considering how half of the castle is built directly on top of a cliff. Polar and Vulpie's room is on the south western end, and directly above the head of the bed, lies an ornate window that was seemingly designed to capture the brilliance of a rising moon. Lunar rays shimmer through Polar's silky white fur, thanks to its carefully crafted design, and a curious thought pops into Vulpie's head while Polar pleasures him. Amsend was right about Castle Lahnak's architecture. Every door, every bridge, every terrace, every stone on the floor, every window… Has a purpose… There are too many secrets to discover… Too many surprises to enjoy…

"UHHOOOohhh!!! Stop! Gonna cum!" Vulpie gasps and lets out a joyful wail when Polar slurps his lips free of his hard little penis. "Ah!" The fox whimpers and bites his lip, looking down and seeing his erection throbbing in the moonlight. Precum dribbles out of his dick, telling Polar that Vulpie was indeed close to shooting off, and the wolf licks the corners of his mouth with his big tongue.

"And that was just to whet the appetite." Polar sings while cosseting his lover with curious paws. He gropes Vulpie's tummy, his sides, his throat, his pretty fluffy tail, and draws a circle around the base of the fox's penis with his left index finger, using his sharp claw to make his point. "And tomorrow morning… The only thing you'll be able to whimper, is POLAR… POLAR…"

"OOOOOOOOOO!!! Layin it on thick!" Vulpie giggles.

"I'm about to lay something thick in you." Polar grins in response. "Don't think I can do it?"

"Nuh uh! But Try! For the love of God, TRY! Try Polar! POLAR! POLAR! Ooooohhhhaahhhhhoooooooo!" The orange furred fox teases, and playfully swings his pretty tail at the wolf with his left paw since he's lying on his back and can't swish it with his tailbone. "I needz my punishment! I been joinzingz da secrets of the peoples of evil, woooo!!!"

"Amsend doesn't mean shit! There's only ONE MAN who makes you his bitch! ... What's his name?"

"POLAR! OOOOOOOOHHHHHAAHHHHHOOOOOOOOOOOO!!!" Vulpie laughs in excitement.

"That's right."

"But you love me, don't you Mr. P?"

"Of course. You HURT the ones you LOVE." The white furred wolf replies, and suddenly, out of nowhere, decides to spontaneously bite at Vulpie's exposed belly. He snarls and yells, and for a split second, gets the response he was hoping for.

"BAJAJAJARARHRRGHH!"

"WHAT THE?! FFFFFFFFFFFFFFUACK! POLAR?!" The orange fox yelps while instinctively recoiling and grabbing at the wolf's face, trying to force the predator's big teeth away.

"GGGRRRRRRRHHHHHHHHhhhhhhh..." Polar teases with an enormous hungry smile.

"YOU FUCKING FUCKER! Haha! YOUUUUUuuuu... Scared the shit out of me! I lost my erection!"

"Now I'll make you get it back."

"I'm all for role playin, but mother fuck!"

"You know you love it."

424

"Yeah to a point! JEEZ! You're DANGEROUS when you get high! I'm a have to watch you! Yeah! I haven't forgotten about our first night on ecstasy!"

"Now, you can't hold that against me. It was my first time raping a cute little fox! This time I'll be sure to tear you a new asshole!"

"OhohohohohHOOHHHHH?! EH? Ahh... Gulp..." Vulpie whimpers.

"Just playing..." Polar smiles and Vulpie nods with wide eyes.

"I hope so!"

"Ah, you don't TRUST ME?!" Polar asks and winks while showing off his sharp teeth.

"I trust Mr. Polar, but I don't know about Mr. Psycho P! I haven't met him before!" A frozen wind creeps into the room, descends upon them, and makes Vulpie's orange fur stand on end when he inhales. His lightning fast mind instantly connects the wild burning flavor of something moist, possibly ancient mossy stonework, mixed with urban qualities that gives the chilly air an exhilarating smell.

"Yeah!" He breathes and anxiously nods his head.

"Yeah?" Polar warns with a determined look. Vulpie's quick statement proposed something they both understand without having to say it out loud. Vulpie just encouraged the proposition of being brutalized up the ass, and his husband quickly asked for clarification. They're playing the lust game, and it's either all or nothing. They both want satisfying sex, and clearly, Polar doesn't want to hold back. It could mean a variety of different scenarios for Vulpie, maybe even ass to mouth, but he doubts the wolf will choose something that demeaning. Polar would never force Vulpie to do something that distasteful. He's a good man, and he loves the fox with all his heart. On the other hand... He also has an extremely powerful need to dominate a submissive partner, and Vulpie's just too effeminate looking to waste in a moment like this.

Polar wants to rape Vulpie without actually raping him, which means hard anal, without mercy, and Vulpie can't ask him to stop. It would ruin the experience, because the gay fox delights in teasing the gay wolf so often, that when a perfect opportunity like this one comes along there's really no excuse for him to say no.

"For you!" Vulpie whispers and nods anxiously. Polar is very pleased with his husband's statement, but only smiles just a little, before quickly returning to his predatory glare. Their relationship has always been based on this homoerotic game. It's not that Polar doesn't respect Vulpie. He does. And it's not that he wishes to see him suffer anywhere outside of the bedroom. The arctic wolf often devotes the majority of his day to considering Vulpie's emotional and physical state and how he can react to them accordingly so he can be a worthy lover and protector. The fox enjoys numerous privileges in his relationship with Polar, including less physical labor. So when it comes down to brass tacks... Vulpie, undeniably, must be the bitch from time to time. And it's not really negotiable.

Polar's needs are significantly different than Vulpie's. Male wolves have an insurmountable desire to dominate their partners during sex, and since Vulpie loves being the bottom as much as Polar loves being on top, he has an obligation to leave bite marks on the pillow. The cute fox's shenanigans would get old really fast if he didn't let Polar take him up on the offer once in a while. Fucking Vulpie until tears are in his eyes is what makes all of it worth it for Polar, but only in the sexual realm. Polar wants Vulpie to enjoy it, but at the same time, he also wants to put him in his place, so the little gay fox has his work cut out for him.

But when all things are considered, Polar and Vulpie share a love that is virtually unparalleled throughout space and time. It's rare enough to find two animals who are actually in love, much less to find a wolf and a fox who could not live without the other. If one perished, the other would surely follow shortly after, either by tragedy or the desire to be reunited in death.

"I love you." Vulpie breathes.

"I love you too." Polar breathlessly replies, and leans forward to give his vulpine husband a kiss. Vulpie tastes his own cum in Polar's mouth and something about the wet union makes his fur stand on end. They share everything, and naturally, sharing cum is the most intimate thing they can physically do. Whether it be by mouth, or in the tail end, they rejoice in each other's very being.

"Get on your knees!" Polar orders after breaking lips with the fox, and Vulpie follows orders like a good boy. The white furred wolf hastily makes himself naked, and throws his clothing away with fury. He jumps off the bed for a moment to retrieve lubrication from one of their luggage bags, and Vulpie waits patiently on his paws and knees, rear end ready for his lover. He hears the familiar sound of the lube tube being popped open, and the subsequent squirting sound as Polar administers it onto his penis. The snow wolf comes back to the bed, masturbating, and the squishy sounds let Vulpie know that he's about to be dominated. He claws the bed a little when the much larger male mounts him. Polar lifts the orange furred fox's gorgeous tail and presses the wet head of his fat penis against his small husband's anus.

Polar uses his left paw to aim it in, and clamps his right paw on Vulpie's right hip during the process. Vulpie whimpers when it squeezes inside his ass, and Polar quickly grabs the soft fox's left hip. He goes right to it, and thrusts deep inside of his prey.

"OOOHHHAAAHHHHH!!!"

"MMMM!" Polar groans in pleasure, and swishes his tail in pride. He loves the way Vulpie's anus tightens defensively. He knows every nook and cranny of Vulpie's insides, and begins fucking him just the way he likes. The white furred wolf isn't interested in giving the little fox much time to relax. He wants to make him his bitch, just like the first night they met, and Vulpie is just as enthusiastic. He dares not taunt the powerful wolf, but really enjoys the feeling of being taken. Immense pleasure comes with the pain. The orange fox bites his lip while relishing it, but can't keep his mouth closed for long. Polar lustfully brutalizing his tail end is just too overwhelming.

"GOD IT'S! GOD YOU'RE SO BIG! OH FUCK! AH! OW!"

"Take it all!" Polar moans, and looks down at his target. He grins, seeing his big dick going into and back out of the pretty fox's butt. "No foreplay tonight! I'm going to wreck it!"

"OH, WRECK ME POLAR!" Vulpie gasps, and drops his face against the bed so he can masturbate. The nimble effeminate fox always finds this position the most comfortable when he's under sexual duress, because he can easily play with his penis without having to hold himself up with his left paw.

"That's right! Ass up!"

"OOOOHHHH! OOH!! OHHHHHHHHHHHH!! AH! AHHHHH!" Vulpie gasps while the white furred wolf goes to work on him. Polar doesn't hold back. He rams his massive cock all the way in, hurting Vulpie's prostate, but also making it scream in excitement. The agonizing pounding is amplified by the sheer length and girth of the wolf's penis, so the sexy fox has to relax as much as possible. He can't tense up. Resisting will just make it hurt worse, but when Polar feels even more freedom inside Vulpie's butt, he takes full advantage of it. He holds the fox's ass firmly in place, and uses his big thumbs to spread his anus. The result is a super stretching that makes Vulpie's eyes water, and Polar achieves unparalleled freedom inside him.

"NNUUUUUUHHHHHHAAAAAAAAAAHHHHHHHH!!!" Vulpie cries out. He quickly regrets his decision to relax when the head of Polar's wolf dick rams his prostate like a freight train. "OW! STOP! STOPPP! PLEASE!"

"Too much for you!" Polar breathes, and luckily for Vulpie, he both slows his pace and loosens his hold on the fox's hips and butt.

"YOU'RE GONNA KILL ME!"

"I said I was going to wreck it!"

"FFFFFFFFFFFFFUCK! FEELS GOOD BUT, UH... Please..."

"Please, your big dick is humiliating me too much! Say it!" Polar demands, grinning even though Vulpie can't see his face, but the fox can hear it in his voice.

"PLEASE! YOUR BIG DICK IS HUMILIATING ME TOO MUCH!" Vulpie whines with tears in his eyes.

"That a boy… Now say you're my little bitch and this is all you're good for!" Polar commands, having enjoyed the last taunt so much that he just can't resist another.

"I'M YOUR LITTLE BITCH POLAR! AND LETTING YOU FUCK ME IS ALL I'M GOOD FOR!" Vulpie whimpers while clawing the bed cover.

"That's what I like to hear! Keep it up!"

"PLEASE DON'T HURT ME!"

"Oh, I'm going to hurt you." Polar lustfully declares while pumping the orange fox. "Just keep whining like a bitch and maybe I'll go a little bit easier…"

"AHHHHHHHHHHH!" Vulpie cries out with an overwhelmed voice. Polar hears the pleasure permeating through his lover's outburst, and swishes his tail in bliss. This is what it's all about for him. He loves Vulpie with all of his heart, but sexually, when he truly needs complete homosexual satisfaction, he has to hurt him. He would never hit Vulpie, but sex is fair game, and always has been. Vulpie can only take so much, but Polar knows what he can get away with, and he's definitely going to get everything he can tonight.

"Poor little Vulpie have a butt ache? Going to cry now?"

"CAN I?!" Vulpie whimpers, and the white furred wolf's fur stands on end.

"You have my permission!"

"THANK YOU MR WOLF!"

"You're SO welcome…" Polar gasps. He licks his lips and watches Vulpie's face twist and contort against the bed with every thrust. The fox boy is drooling on the black bedspread, thanks to the wolf exerting so much kinetic energy into his tail end. His pretty muzzle scrapes against the fluffy comforter, and his little neck bends depending on how hard Polar slams him with each conquering thrust.

But Vulpie is just fine with being over exerted. He masturbates his hard little cock feverishly with his right paw, and fox cum has already stained the bedspread in multiple locations. With Polar hitting his prostate bang on, with such ferocity and thorough knowledge of its location, there's simply no way Vulpie couldn't have a rock hard erection. His cock is painfully stiff, forced into action by Polar's deliciously thick penis. The orange furred fox isn't sure where his lover ends and he begins, because his prostate is on fire, throbbing, and the hard repetition brings it all together in a swirling storm of pure ecstasy. They are one animal. Polar wants nothing more than to go deeper and deeper, and Vulpie wants every bit of the handsome man inside him.

"OH MY GOD POLAR, UH! OH GOD YEAH! FUCK ME GOOD!"

"You feel fucking awesome too!" Polar breathlessly admits while relishing the fox's rectum and anus squeezing his wolfhood. "Tight little fox ass! Yeah!"

"MMMAAAH! AHHHHHHH!" Vulpie moans, and a big grin appears on his face. He can only keep one eye open with his face pressed against the bed, but Polar notices how he's staring off into the distance, at nothing, just completely consumed by their heavenly gay intercourse. "Ahhhlm mafna hah!"

"What was that?" Polar gasps in amusement. "Can't understand you!"

"MMMAHHH! AAHH!!"

"Speak up!"

"AHHH! I'M GONNA HAVE TA! GONNA!""

"You like that, don't you!"

"MMMNNEAH! MNEAYH! YEAH!"

"Feels good! Yeah!" Polar breathes, and admires his work once again. He's fucked Vulpie so hard that the lubrication is starting to dry out, but he doesn't bother to stop. He enjoys the growing tension, and how Vulpie squints more and more. He won't fuck him until he bleeds, but the white furred wolf loves to give him a scare once in a while, especially when it feels incredible for both of them.

The Dark Goddess

A very bizarre sound suddenly wakes Vulpie from the most peaceful deep slumber, and he yelps loudly.

"Come on Vulpie. We have places to go…" Goddess Aila says from the foot of the bed. She's standing there, completely naked, with a big grin on her sadistic beautiful face. The dark goddess is derogatorily known as "The Breasted Bitch," due to her characteristics that make her look like a female dog. Her ears are not triangular like a wolf or a fox. They hang out to the side instead, and most certainly look like a puppy dog's. Her muzzle is much shorter than a she-wolf's but also far broader than a vixen. The cross suggests either a folf or a dog species, but she most definitely looks more like a dog than a fox wolf hybrid.

Goddess Aila also has a short but bushy tail, another characteristic that puts her separate from a she-wolf or a vixen. Her eyes are blood red, glowing, and her fur is far more hellish than he remembered. Now it's a scorching reddish orange, and her dirty blonde hair is twice as golden as he remembered it being on Zeravyn. The blonde streak adorning her front is also more brilliant than ever. It begins at her thighs, covers her crotch, pelvis, tummy, chest, throat and half of her face, ending at her eyes where it returns to a demonic reddish orange like the rest of her body. The underside of her tail is now blonde as well, and for some reason, Vulpie feels like her fur is turning more like his own. Her golden hair is moderately long and quite beautiful. Her hips are wide and curvy, and sexy is an understatement.

Vulpie quickly looks to his left, at Polar, and is shocked to find him sleeping like a baby. His husband didn't hear a thing, and when Vulpie shakes him with his little left paw, the snow wolf doesn't even move.

"Polar!" Vulpie whispers, but when he looks at the foot of the bed once more, Aila's gone… The orange furred fox looks around the room in terror, and slowly, very slowly, believes he's just woken up from an extremely vivid nightmare. He closes his eyes and takes a deep breath, but when he opens them, she's back. Aila's still naked, and this time she's outside with the door open. The freezing night air flows into the stone room.

"Come with me... I will not ask a second time." She warns, and walks to the right, disappearing behind the wall. Vulpie hastily shakes Polar some more, but after tugging on him and pushing him with all of his might, he realizes it's useless. The fox knows he's dreaming. He has to be... This has to be a dream, and the only way to end it is to follow her. He doesn't want to get out of the warm bed, but what else can he do? She might hurt him if he doesn't follow her. But if this really is a dream, then why is he worried about it?

Since the rational part of the brain is disabled when animals sleep, Vulpie knows his reasoning is pointless. During his many years of surfing the internet for countless different reasons, he came across the knowledge that counting ones fingers, checking the time, and seeing if words change during a dream can indicate whether one is in fact, in a deep slumber. The castle bedroom doesn't have a clock so he decides to count his fingers. The orange fox holds up his dainty paws and begins, but quickly notices he's counting his left fingers instead of his right. He can't keep track of the numbers. It's a dream.

"Now what?" He whispers while a wave of terror rushes over him. Everything is always scarier in a dream, and the fact that he's just realized he's in a nightmare compounds it. He jumps out of bed and hurries to the door without thinking. He notices that he didn't feel the covers and it isn't cold, but he can still see his breath for some reason. He runs outside and looks around the castle. It's all still the same as he remembered it, but no lights are coming from any of the glass windows, and he sees Aila to his right. "I'm dreaming!"

"Yes." She smiles, and turns around. She walks down the spiral staircase instead of going up to Amsend's chambers, and the gay fox swallows.

"But I'm not supposed to follow you! This is the bad part of the dream when something awful happens!" He shouts while he can still see her pretty rear end, but she just swishes her tail before disappearing behind the stone. "FUCK!" Vulpie turns around and shuts the door so Polar won't be bothered by the cold night air, but once again, the fox notices it isn't cold at all. He doesn't feel a thing. "Fucking following a ghost goddess... Goddess from hell! What the fuck am I doing?" He growls while walking towards the staircase. He descends rather quickly, almost instantly, and is outside again, on the castle's southern curtain wall. Goddess Aila is standing with her paws on her hips with a smirk.

"Good boy."

"Fuck you."

"I'm game if you are."

"You're game? What are ya trying to do, keep up with the times? Trying to sound all cool and shit?"

"Maybe it has something to do with your subconscious because you're dreaming?"

"Well then if it's my dream, I want you to leave right now! I'm not the fucking antikhalan! Those crazy Deiva purists are just homophobic!"

"No, you aren't." Aila replies with a serious voice, and Vulpie blinks.

"But isn't that... The whole reason why you're doing this to me?"

"He's betrayed me... But you..." The dark goddess replies, and the little gay fox gulps. She points to the horizon. City lights can be seen very far away, beyond the forests surrounding the castle, but they're difficult to spot. "Everyone in that city knows who you are. Everyone in the lands between that city and this castle knows who you are. You're a legend in your own lifetime, but haven't you ever wondered if someone was helping you? Something you couldn't see but you could feel?"

"Not you! That's for sure!" Vulpie hastily responds.

"You could have chosen many different paths in life, but instead of doing something benevolent with your greatest creation, you chose to use it to inflict your will on others. You're proud of what Vulpie.net has done, and you would do it again."

"No I wouldn't."

"You can't lie to a goddess... You enjoy being idolized, and I understand that desire."

"You're wrong." The orange furred fox says with a small voice. "As long as I hooked up with Polar things would have been okay. I would've found a different way to be famous."

"No you wouldn't..." The beautiful canine replies with an amused voice. "We both know the chaos you created with Vulpie.net was a good thing for you and him."

"That's a lie."

"You're still Evil Vulpie... He's the best part of you, and he's the one who can do great things... Not the tame little fox you are now."

"I know I'm at my best when I start thinking that way, but I will never go there again! I have too much to lose. I can't lose Polar. And I can't lose the business I've created! I've moved on!"

"No you haven't. You can't. It's who you are."

"Why am I even listening to the Goddess of evil?"

"If you only knew your true potential you would embrace me without hesitation."

"Shut up! JUST SHUT UP! I never fucking embraced you! I didn't tell myself I was making Vulpie.net for you! I didn't believe in you then, and I don't believe in you now! STUPID FUCKING NAKED GODDESS SLUTS! I'm dreaming and I just want to wake up!"

"I was with you every day. You didn't have to believe in me, Vulpie. I exist whether you accept me or not, and I'm the one who set you free... Khalan's never lifted a finger to help you, but I on the other hand... Have nurtured every idea you were inspired to have, because I help animals who help themselves... You're desire to rule over the universe is not a sin...

Powerful animals know life is nothing more than a desperate fight for survival, and you... Vulpie... Have accomplished so much... The little gay fox who took on the universe and won."

"Fuck you! That's my opinion! FUCK YOU! I don't believe in you, and I don't believe in Khalan, Sherrie or Cyrilla! Just go back to hell and leave me alone!"

"There is no hell... Only my domain... You always knew I was there, when you were robbing people's bank accounts, and destroying millions of computers for your own amusement."

"Yeah, and it came back to bite me in the ass! I think I suffered pretty good for what I did!"

"Evil Vulpie didn't kill you because I kept you alive... Your body was broken beyond repair, and Khalan did nothing to help... But I took care of you... Brought you back from the brink of death."

"Polar saved me, you bitch."

"No." Aila grins.

"YES! Now I want to wake up! Now! Right now!"

"Xsilyncoitus." The gorgeous canine declares, and points to the sky with her left index finger.

"What the hell are you talking about?" Vulpie growls, and she drops her arm.

"She Who Is Behind The Stars... She's coming to destroy Vulpie.net and this world, but you can save them all if you put your life in my hands."

"Don't hold your breath!" Vulpie snaps and shakes his head in frustration.

"Amsend will kill you after he gets what he wants, but he'll murder Polar first." Aila bluntly declares, and Vulpie's stomach sinks with painful heavy nausea.

"...Wh... Why?"

"His allies who control all of the major news networks will pin the war and suffering entirely on you, and when you're no longer useful as his whipping boy, you will be executed."

"But why? What's coming? Is it because of Vulpie.net?"

"Partially, but your computer virus is actively preparing to fight her. Centuries ago, Amsend fell in love with her and turned his back on me... But soon he will die and face my judgment."

"Your judgment?" Vulpie asks in confusion, and suddenly his mind rearranges the letters in the husky's last name. "And the book says his first name means against..."

"Yes."

"Amsend is the antikhalan?"

"Yes."

"Oh my God." Vulpie whispers with a terrified voice. "We're fucked!"

"Not if you let me help you." Aila smiles and gently touches the gay fox's cute muzzle with her left paw. He immediately recoils and looks away while panting. "When the time comes, I'll speak to you again, and I'll tell you how to save yourself and your lover. Things will seem impossible, but allow my hand to guide you, and I promise you will prevail. I love you... I always have." The gorgeous canine breathes.

The Grand Reveal

Vulpie wakes from his dream with a loud yelp. Polar is to his left, tying his shoes, and he gives his husband a concerned look.

"Are you alright?"

"I... Had a nightmare... The most terrible fuckin... Scary..."

"I don't blame you." Polar responds and goes back to tying his shoes. "This place is something else."

"No, it was..." Vulpie trails off and Polar turns around with a smirk.

"It was real? Is that what you were going to say?"

"Yeah."

"Must have been a good one."

"God no... I don't ever want one like that again." The orange furred fox growls while getting out of bed. His tail end is sore from Polar fucking him silly last night, but his mind is preoccupied with the horrendous dream.

"So you CAN walk!" Polar smirks, but the white furred wolf's smile disappears when his lover doesn't respond. Vulpie puts on his clothing with a distant expression.

"Was it that bad?"

"Yeah."

"Want to talk about it?"

"No."

"Okay..." Polar sighs in concern. "Maybe it's that stuff we took. It was pretty intense."

"No, it wasn't the drugs."

"Sounds like the only explanation to me."

"Yeah, I know it does, but it wasn't. I haven't had a dream like that since... Since I was living with Vander Clishaw."

"Was it about him?"

"No, but it was the same kind of evil. Actually worse... Pure..."

"You're kind of freaking me out here. Maybe you need to see a doctor. That Solxiien crap might have made you sick."

"I feel fine, but it was more than just a dream. It was so real. I know everybody always says that, but it was like... I just walked around and felt the ground, and the air, and everything like normal."

"Don't worry about it. Just relax. We're on vacation, remember?"

"Yeah."

"We have a TV now." Polar comments and gestures towards a flat screen that's sitting on top of a small dresser next to the door.

"Huh?" Vulpie responds and gives it a curious look. "Did you turn it on?"

"Not yet."

"Why's it here?"

"No idea."

"That creep." The orange furred fox growls while slipping on his black sneakers. They both put on the same clothing they were wearing yesterday because the bizarre appearance of the TV probably means Amsend wants to show them something as soon as possible. Vulpie slides on his bright green shirt and searches for the TV's power switch. He pushes it in after finding it, and it comes on without delay.

What it plays makes both of them speechless. There's a lot of moaning, and heavy thrusting, and for a moment, it seems like it isn't a video of them. It can't be... It's a recording of their very long sexcapade, and by the looks of it, cameras were hidden in all four corners of the room. Vulpie discovers that he can change the viewing angle by pressing the input button, and Polar's mouth hangs open.

"What... That bastard! Is this really happening?"

"Yep..." Vulpie whispers. "He filmed us."

"That motherfucker! That's it!" The white furred wolf roars and leaps up from the bed.

"Polar, no!" Vulpie says and drops the remote. He gets in the way, but can't stop his husband from throwing the door open. NoirQueue wolves are outside.

"WHERE IS HE?"

"In there." One of them answers in perfect Sufian, and looks towards the main part of the castle where the great hall is. Polar storms over the curtain wall with Vulpie running behind him.

"Polar stop!" The white furred wolf kicks the heavy door open and heads into the great hall, where Amsend is standing in the middle of the room. Two chairs are positioned in front of him.

"I hope you enjoyed the video. It was hard to position all of the cameras, but I think it turned out rather nicely." Amsend says when Polar gets close enough to attack him and doesn't bother to move when the snow wolf throws a massive punch right into his face. Amsend's head snaps back, and Polar feels his face give way, but the husky doesn't move.

"YOU SON OF A BITCH! I'VE HAD ENOUGH OF YOU!"

"Clearly." Amsend chuckles, and allows Polar to punch him three more times. Polar uppercuts him, hits him in the gut, and then his chest... The white furred wolf notices something's wrong after pushing his fist into Amsend's stomach, because there's no way he could have taken such a fierce blow without leaning forward... The snow wolf is speechless, and he takes several steps backwards, into Vulpie, who stumbles to the right.

"You're a machine?"

"No." Amsend smiles and crosses his arms. "But I can see why you were able to beat Druward. You hit much harder than him."

"What's going on Amsend?" Vulpie shouts. "Who are you really, and what do you want?! Why did you film us?!"

"Take a seat and I'll be happy to answer all of your questions."

"I'm going to fucking kill you!" Polar snarls, and the husky uncrosses his arms, smoothing out his black pinstripe suit.

"You're definitely one of Maro's... That fury is unmistakable."

"Enough games!" Polar shouts, and glances at the NoirQueue men in the room. "Who or what the fuck are you, Amsend?" Rulef and the rest of Blacktail are nowhere to be found, and a black furred wolf stands in each corner of the great hall.

"Sit down." Amsend responds with a calm voice and smiles at Vulpie. "Just sit down."

"Polar." Vulpie whispers, and the white furred wolf looks to his right. Vulpie grabs his paw and coaxes him into taking a seat. Amsend goes over to the great hall's dining table and retrieves a chair for himself. He drops it in front of them, sits down, and clasps his paws together with a fastidious look.

"The video is leverage against you. That much is obvious, but I was forced to play my hand because Vulpie.net is making its move far sooner than anticipated." The husky explains, and both Polar and Vulpie's eyes widen.

"Vulpie.net?" Vulpie whispers in shock. "What do you mean it's making its move sooner than you thought? Have you been... You HAVE been working with it?"

"Yes." Amsend nods and watches the animals with a pleasant demeanor. "Are you really surprised? I protected it... I had it sealed away in the Sufias Heritage Museum so the Sons of Velora could make use of it..."

"But you can't control Vulpie.net!" The orange furred fox angrily interrupts. "Why the hell would it work with you? It thinks it's superior to every animal that's ever lived, and you're telling me it joined forces with you? It would never work with a normal animal. There's no way."

"Normal?" Amsend smirks. "Is that what I am?"

"What are you?" Polar presses with a fierce voice. "Tell us what you are. Are you one of Evil Vulpie's machines?"

"Oh, Mr. Polar Arctic, you shouldn't concern yourself with the whys and hows at this point. You wouldn't believe me if I told you."

"What are you?" Polar asks again.

"I know who he is." Vulpie whispers, and Amsend puts his blue eyes on the little gay fox. "His last name is an anagram... And his first name means against... It's in the Horror of Castle Lahnak."

"Well done." Amsend says while grinning from ear to ear. "Usually I've already killed the animals I'm manipulating before they have a chance to figure things out, but you're way ahead of the curve."

"What?" Polar asks and gives Vulpie a befuddled look. "Are you serious? Are you saying what I think you're saying?"

"He's right." Amsend tells the white furred wolf and cracks his knuckles.

"Bullshit."

"I love mortals." The husky chuckles in amusement. "No matter how much evidence they have, no matter how in their face it is, they always refuse to see the truth until it's too late. Once I even transformed in front of a man, yet somehow he managed to convince himself he was dreaming. He said he was dreaming all the way up to the moment I killed him."

"Transformed?" Vulpie inquires with a half anxious, half amused voice.

"Yes."

"So you can turn into some kind of monster?" Polar scoffs.

"I don't think you can handle it... And it's a rather messy affair, so we'll skip the demonstration... Unless you'd like to be stricken with absolute terror?"

"Ohhhhhhhh, you're in so much trouble, Amsend! You betrayed your mommy!" Vulpie whispers with a mischievous, half crazed voice, and it gets both Polar and the husky's full attention. Amsend stops smiling.

"What?"

"You heard me." Vulpie grins. "She just told me in a dream! You've been a bad, bad, boy... Doing whatever you wanted without giving her any credit, and now you're working with that thing behind the stars!"

442

"Vulpie... What in the hell are you talking about?" Polar asks with a bewildered voice.

"She did, did she?" Amsend responds, and slowly processes the information. The husky nods after deciding how to proceed. "Well then... That makes this a very simple matter... Play time's over."

"You're in SO much trouble!"

"Not as much as you, I'm afraid."

"Is this really happening?" Polar inquires, and looks at Amsend in confusion. "Or am I completely fucked because of the drug you gave us?"

"Oh no, Mr. Arctic... That was nothing special, really... I just wanted to make sure you fucked him." Amsend answers, and turns his attention to the orange fox. "But since little Vulpie knows something he shouldn't, I'm going to drop the entire facade. I planned on using the sex tape to blackmail both of you, so he would accept his position at the NVA, but now it's pointless." The husky explains, and gives Vulpie an evil smile. "Here's what's going to happen now... You're going home to Sufias city, where you will accept your role as director of the National Vulpie.net Agency and you'll give us your full cooperation, or Polar is going to die."

"You..." Polar growls, but the white furred wolf doesn't know what else to say when the husky completely ignores him.

"I'm going to keep him here as my hostage, but he won't be harmed as long as you do what you're told. Resist us in any way, and I'll torture him... You don't want me to hurt your pretty husband do you?"

"No." Vulpie whispers with a quivering lip.

"Good boy." Amsend says and gives Polar a dangerous look.

"And you are not going to attack me, or any of my men, ever again. You'll do that for Vulpie."

"You son of a bitch." Polar snarls.

"I've always loved that one." Amsend grins. "Son of a bitch... Fairly accurate..."

"You promise you won't hurt him?" Vulpie asks with a shaky voice.

"Yes... I don't have a reason to hurt him unless you give me one, so as long as you behave yourself, I'll allow you to see him on a regular basis. The more you cooperate, the more time you'll have together."

"You don't have to do this! please!" Vulpie begs and makes fists with his delicate little paws. "I can't leave him here!"

"You'll just have to wait. You can suck his cock all you want if you're a good boy." Amsend smirks, and deviously licks his lips. "Speaking of which... You two enjoy some rough sex, don't you? I've never seen a guy fuck another guy that hard, and Polar's so much bigger than you, it was just jaw dropping! You boys take the whole wolf-fox lust to an entirely new level."

"I love him. Please, I can't live without him!" Vulpie pleads.

"I bet you can't... Him fucking you is about as close to rape as it gets. Must be hard to go without that brutal satisfaction if it's the whole crux of your faggot relationship."

"I'm going to kill you." Polar says, and Amsend returns a large grin.

"Does he ever fuck you? How does it work?"

"You just might be the antikhalan after all." The white furred wolf growls with a disgusted voice. "What the hell is your problem?"

"I suppose I'm evil... I do enjoy a good torturing and must have killed over a hundred thousand animals, by proxy or paw, over the years." Polar is about to give another loud warning but the sensation of a gun barrel on the back of his neck makes him hold completely still. He glances at Vulpie, and the orange furred fox twitches nervously while watching the NoirQueue agent standing behind the white furred wolf.

"Stop! No!" Vulpie gasps and lurches forward in his chair, putting his paws up in a sign of defeat. "I'll do it! I'll do it, okay?!" The orange furred fox asks his husband with a fearful smile.

"No Vulpie..." Polar whispers, but is too afraid to move with the gun pressed against him. "Don't do what he says. Don't sell your soul for me."

"I can't leave you in Englavic!" Vulpie pants, and Amsend chuckles.

"Don't Vulpie. He won't let us be together no matter what you do. He'll use you for all you're worth, and when he doesn't need you anymore, he'll kill us both." Polar growls with a disgusted voice.

"It's okay, I'll just give him what he wants and we'll be together. That's all that matters." Vulpie tells Polar in devotion, and Polar shows his teeth to Amsend.

"You'll take the fall for everything he plans on doing. Is that how you want people to remember you?"

"I know, but he said he'd work with us if I cooperate." Vulpie says and glances at Amsend, who nods. "But I can't leave him here. Please let him come home with me."

"Not a chance. This isn't a democracy. You'll have to earn time together."

"But I won't be able to concentrate without him! I can't do this without Polar!"

"Find something else to stick up your ass for a few weeks." Amsend snorts, and The room fills with laughter.

"Please!"

"Oh shut up you little queer." The husky crassly responds.

"I can't live without him! I can't work without him! I won't be any use to you at all!"

"Nonsense!" Amsend smiles. "Why, I bet you'll find a way to work very hard, every single day for me, if I told you I was going to cut off his fingers!" Vulpie's eyes widen, and not knowing what to say, he just leans forward and puts his face in his paws.

"Vulpie, it'll be okay." Polar says with a devoted voice, and his stomach turns when he hears his lover crying.

"It will be okay... IF, he does EVERYTHING, I tell him to." Amsend declares, and Vulpie starts sniffling. Amsend smirks in amusement and stands. Polar reaches over and takes his husband into his arms.

"Shhh..... It's alright... I don't blame you for any of this... You did all you could for me, for both of us... I'm so sorry, Vulpie..."

"No, I'm NOT leaving you here!"

"He'll hurt you if you resist. Please don't fight back." Polar whispers while cradling the orange fox. "I'll be okay."

"NO! NO I'M NOT LEAVING!"

"Come on... Time to go..." Amsend says, and kicks Polar's left side. The white furred wolf ignores the small blow, but recognizes how much power Amsend's holding back. "Vulpie, it's time to go..."

"No!"

"Are you an idiot?" Polar suddenly asks the husky in a fit of rage. "Can't you see what you're doing is counterproductive! Vulpie can't take much more of this! Can't you see what you're doing to him?"

"You should worry about yourself." Amsend coldly responds.

"He's no good to you like this! At least give us one more day together! Some time to recover! Because I'm telling you, he won't be able to take much more of your abuse!"

"Time to go."

"Look, I'm gay! I understand what he's going through, and I'm telling you, that he could help you a thousand times more if you stopped this!" Polar shouts while Vulpie cries in his arms, clutching the snow wolf for reassurance.

"Negative emotion always trumps positive emotion." Amsend says with a smirk. "They say it's the other way around, but not in my experience."

"Maybe because you're always the one doing the negative shit, but you don't know Vulpie. You don't. You can't do this to him. If you tear us apart and take everything from him he'll probably USE VULPIE.NET AGAINST YOU, WHICH YOU'RE SO AFRAID OF!"

"I'm not afraid of Vulpie.net." Amsend smiles. "Evil Vulpie... Real Vulpie... If you only had the slightest clue who I serve..."

"What, Goddess Aila?" Polar laughs. "Oh yeah! She's really inspirational!"

"She Who Is Behind The Stars..." Amsend says with a condescending tone, and walks around the white furred wolf and orange furred fox. "Imagine my surprise... Being Aila's chosen one, and yet I met this... Being... The one they left behind, the answer to where magic went in our universe. The remnant of Velora..."

"What the hell is that supposed to mean?" Polar growls.

"You listen but you do not hear." Amsend sharply answers. "They're REAL... They're both real... They're ALL REAL... Sherrie, Khalan, Cyrilla, Aila... and the one they left behind... The one who found me and showed me the pleasures of our universe. Not Goddess Aila's tyranny... No... Freedom to the end of the endless expanse of our universe and beyond."

"Okay, listen Vulpie." Polar says and holds the fox's face up to his own, embracing him with every ounce of love he has. "This man is insane. These people are insane, so what I want you to do is live for us. If I don't make it back, you have to go on without me."

"Without you?" Vulpie asks, and looks into the snow wolf's beautiful blue eyes. "Go on without you? I CAN'T! YOU'RE THE ONLY ONE I HAVE! I DON'T HAVE A FAMILY! NO BROTHER! NO MOTHER! NO FATHER! NO SISTER!"

"Vulpie, listen to me. Listen..." Polar says, and rocks the orange fox in his arms. "I can't stop these people. They have guns and we don't. They outnumber us and we clearly made a mistake by coming here, but it's not your fault. I don't want you blaming yourself if we never see each other again."

"Never..." Vulpie whispers with an insane look. "Again?"

"Keep it together, Vulpie. Be strong for me, okay?"

"But you're the strong one!"

"Not true. You're stronger than you could ever know." Polar smiles.

"If he hurts you... I'll... I'll kill him." Vulpie whispers.

"You can't. They're holding all of the cards and I felt his strength just now when he kicked me. He's holding back some kind of... Horrible power..."

"Horrible." Vulpie whispers.

"Stay with me, Vulpie." Polar breathes with a worried voice. The orange furred fox looks so detached that even Amsend finally cocks his head to the side and takes a look at him.

"Polar..." Vulpie breathes with a joyful expression. "I love you."

"I love you too."

"But I'll kill him like I killed Clishaw."

"You didn't kill Clishaw, Vulpie. You told me so." Polar says with a reassuring voice.

"Hmm? Oh yeah! That was Evil Vulpie! He went away... But now he's back!"

"Vulpie."

"Yellow, Green, Red, Green, Yellow, Red, Green!" Vulpie laughs and the white furred wolf laughs with him.

"I remember."

"Kill him like I killed Clishaw, Polar. You wait and see."

"My goodness what a state he's in! Maybe he does need a nap." Amsend smiles.

"Well I wonder why you SON OF A BITCH! You want to take everything he has! I wonder why he's losing it?!"

"Are you everything he has? Mr. Arctic?"

"You're Goddess damn right I am!" The white furred wolf snarls. "We might look pathetic to a sadistic psychopath like you, but together we've done great things! I helped him found his own company! I encouraged him, believed in him, reminded him he was worth it every day!"

"WOOoooww..." Amsend responds with a patronizing voice.

"I guess you wouldn't understand, if you are who you say you are, but he needs me! He needs me as much as I need him!"

"Well, you'll have to need him from afar. He'll get over it."

"No he… Won't…" Polar whispers and shakes his head. "You have no idea, do you?"

"Mmm?"

"Evil Vulpie… You acted like it was a joke a few moments ago but earlier you said Vulpie.net was making its move? Don't you realize that Evil Vulpie is the same Vulpie I have in my arms?"

"Really?" Amsend replies with a disappointed voice.

"What good is Vulpie going to be to you if he can't even get up in the morning? Or hold a press conference? You've worn him down into a regressive state and he's… He'll think he has no choice but to become Evil Vulpie again. If I'm gone, what does he have? His company? He only cares about it because it's part of our life, our marriage, our future!"

"I've heard enough."

"LISTEN TO ME DAMN IT!" Polar yells, and suddenly notices that Vulpie is staring at him in awe, as if he's seeing him for the first time.

"No more motivational speeches. It's time for Vulpie to go home, and if he behaves himself, you too can meet up and do all the Evil Vulpie you want."

"You're a fool… You're a Goddess damn fool…" Polar whispers in disbelief. "I remember this one part of the Velora… It said the antikhalan was known to be a fool. A man who couldn't…"

"Couldn't see beyond his own shadow? Yes, I'm familiar with that tripe." Amsend smirks.

"Sounds pretty bang on to me." Polar snorts.

"The Velora says a lot of things, many of which were written by horny old men jerking off to the goddesses."

"You are the antikhalan… I fucking believe it now…"

"But that means I'm not!" Vulpie suddenly exclaims, and laughs maniacally. "Awwww FUCK! Man! Or is it yipeeeeeeeeeee? Both sound good to Vulpie!"

"He makes a good point." Amsend smirks.

"Please reconsider…" Polar says with a desperate voice. "Send me home at least and keep him here. As long as he knows I'm okay he might be able to work for you."

"Send you back? Why the fuck would I want to do that? What the hell can you do? I need Vulpie to head the NVA."

"So you can pin some kind of terrorist attack on him?" Polar shouts. "I know what you're up too and so does he! Or at least he did, before you made him have a complete mental breakdown! I don't know what he'll do if you send him back now! He's dangerous you idiot! Vulpie.net? He's the real Vulpie!"

"Get up." Amsend commands, and gestures for NoirQueue to help. One of the men grabs Polar by the left shoulder, and the white furred wolf grudgingly lets go of Vulpie.

"No!" Vulpie whimpers.

"I'll be fine. Just remember what I told you." Polar promises with a loving smile, but the moment is interrupted by another man grabbing Vulpie. The coal furred wolf wraps his big left arm around the gay fox's slender neck.

"Polar, no!"

"Stop saying that." Amsend growls. "It's getting on my nerves."

"Forget about me. Just do what he says and take care of yourself. I love you, and I always will." Polar smiles, but the man behind him pushes him forward to make him stop talking.

"Come on." The NoirQueue wolf holding Vulpie says with a thick Englavic accent, and pulls him towards the north end of the great hall, where they'll be leaving through the front gate. The men force Polar through the southern doorway, back towards the curtain wall and the living quarters.

When Vulpie watches him go outside while being dragged to the other side of the room, he sees the white furred wolf look back and give him a loving smile. Vulpie can see the pain on his face.

"No, Polar! Let go of me!"

"Shut the fuck up." The man growls, and grunts when the orange fox starts squirming. "Alright, so you want to play it rough?"

"I'm not leaving him!"

"Look here. Hey, look here." The mercenary says, and holds up his right fist. He punches Vulpie in the face above the right eye, and almost knocks him out cold. Vulpie yelps in pain and falls on the floor with a wail of despair.

"Take him." Amsend commands from the great hall, and the man grabs Vulpie once again. He throws the adorable fox over his right shoulder.

"He'll be fine... Don't you worry..." Amsend declares with a sadistic voice. "Now remember to be a good boy!" Other mercenaries join the one taking Vulpie over the bridge. They walk across it in silence, and pass through the barbican to meet up with their comrades outside. Rulef is waiting with the rest of Blacktail, but they are outnumbered three to one, and aren't carrying any weapons. NoirQueue made them lock their firearms in their vehicles while waiting for Amsend to finish his business with Polar and Vulpie. The man carrying the small fox takes a knee and gives him to Tiala, who quickly kneels down to protect him. The coal furred wolf snorts at her having orange fur as well, and shakes his head in amusement.

"You can leave now." The NoirQueue commander informs Rulef, and the gray furred wolf sighs.

"Vulpie... Are you alright? They sprung a surprise attack on us. There was nothing we could do. The Blacktail commander goes silent when he sees Vulpie sucking his right thumb like a child. He turns to face the NoirQueue's dark wolf commander and clears his throat. "What did you do to him?"

"Leave."

"What about Polar?"

"He's staying... Lord Lahnak's orders..."

"Has Lord Lahnak thought this through? Vulpie won't like this when he comes to his senses... What did Amsend do to him?"

"It's none of your concern... Now leave before we decide to kill you and all of your men..." Rulef holds still after the threat, and sets his yellow eyes on the coal furred wolves, one at a time. Even if they were armed, there's no way they could beat them in a fair fight. He nods in agreement, and turns back to Tiala.

"Let's go."

"We can't leave Polar behind." She whispers.

"So what's your plan?" Rulef dryly inquires. "We wouldn't stand a chance, and even if we managed to kill them without being blown away, we're still in Amsend's country. He'll deploy roadblocks and the authorities will take us down."

"Polar's not coming?" Deepwolf asks in concern.

"No... But we have to go." Rulef answers, and gives the signal for everyone to get in their SUVs. All of them check and arm their weapons once they're inside, but none of the mercenaries open their doors afterwards. Tiala follows Rulef to the last SUV in the convoy and opens the back left door. She makes sure to put Vulpie in first, since he's mute and looks like he just dropped an entire gallon of acid. The tigress has to lock the doors and strap him into his seatbelt. The orange fox doesn't resist her, and after she's finished, he also has nothing to say when Rulef pauses and looks in the rearview mirror at him.

"Vulpie... You awake? Our priority is to get you to safety now. We can't do anything about Polar." The Blacktail commander waits for an answer, but he doesn't get one, and the brown wolf in the front right seat looks back at the gay fox with raised eyebrows. "Vulpie. Vulpie?"

"Vulpie." Tiala says and snaps her fingers in front of his eyes. He blinks, but remains silent while slouching in the nice leather seat. Tiala slides over to him, and shakes him, but he still has nothing to say. He stares at the floor with a vacant expression. Rulef looks at the wolf to his right and shakes his head.

"Alright... Here we go."

"He'll be alright, Vulpie." Tiala promises, and gets the gay fox to twitch a little. He looks up at the ceiling, then around the vehicle like he's never been in it before. He blinks when Rulef turns on the motor, but stares at the floor once again.

"It's terror tactics, Vulpie. He won't hurt Polar." Rulef comments, and starts driving when there's space ahead of him. He follows the rest of the convoy, who have orders to head directly to the airport. "He knows how much you love him, and he's just trying to scare you." Tiala nods while listening, but when she looks to her left and sees Vulpie staring at her with wide eyes, she pulls back. He has a frightened look on his face.

"What's wrong?" Aila inquires. Vulpie doesn't see Tiala anymore, only the lava furred bitch to his right. She's smiling at him, but it's a caring one, and she points to the left. Vulpie recoils against the door, and looks at Rulef in the driver's seat. The gray wolf is watching him, but he can't see her.

"There." Aila says, and her voice echoes in Vulpie's mind. He quickly turns around and looks out of the back left window, towards the castle, where there's a small crevice in the cliff's wall. It's the same spot he noticed on the way in. "Let Puḱsos help you." The dark goddess is gone just as fast as she appeared, and Vulpie sees Tiala when he looks to the right.

"Rulef?" Vulpie whispers. "Rulef!"

"Yeah? Glad you're still with us." The Blacktail commander responds while trying to keep his eyes on the curvy road.

"Whatever happens, I want you to keep going. Is Amsend sending us to the airport?"

"Yes, and we have strict orders to get you on that jet."

"Don't let him know that I got out."

"What? Who's getting out?"

"I'm going to jump, but don't stop. They'll think I'm still with you and that'll give me a chance."

"A chance to do what, Vulpie? You want to jump out of the car?"

"Yes, and you need to keep going."

"I'm not letting you do that." Rulef declares, but doesn't have time to react when Vulpie quickly unlocks the door and opens it. Tiala lurches to grab him but he manages to leap out of his seat and tumble into the grass on the edge of the dangerous road. He's in a secluded spot where trees will give him a little cover, and Rulef swerves in disbelief. "Goddess damn it! Fuck!"

"Stop! We can't leave him!" Tiala shouts, but Rulef shakes his head.

"Crazy little fuck! What... How... I have no idea what he's thinking, but let's give him a chance. He surprised me on Zeravyn."

"This is different! There are over a hundred NoirQueue mercs in that castle. It won't end well."

"Like I said, I have no fucking clue what he hopes to accomplish, but we're not stopping... NoirQueue just might believe that he gave us the slip."

"Vulpie." Tiala whispers and looks out of the back window. She can't see anything but trees each time they swing around a curve.

No Fear

Vulpie scrambles down the lush canyon wall a lot faster than he probably should, considering one misstep will send him falling to his death, but he doesn't care. His entire body hurts after leaping from the SUV and the best way to ignore it is to keep going. He doesn't worry about what will happen to him, or how he's going to save Polar, but he knows he will. Nothing is going to stop him this time.

The small fox curses while risking his life all the way down to the bottom of the canyon, where the large river runs underneath Castle Lahnak. It wraps around the bottom of the cliff underneath the structure, on the north west side, but flattens out for a few miles before snaking down the mountain some more. Vulpie's only concern is crossing it and hurrying up the other side of the river so he can scale the wall. He's going to climb the massive cliff all the way up to the castle...

He has no idea why Aila told him to try it, or why he hallucinated her giving him the suggestion, but he knows it'll work. The cliff has enough misshapen rocks and crevices to make the climb possible, but it's a long way up... He doesn't care. The orange furred fox gets across the river by jumping from stone to stone, and runs all the way to the other end of the canyon where he finally meets the cliff. He breathes hard, but he knows he has plenty of stamina left, or at least enough to get him halfway. What's halfway? He has no idea... But Aila knows.

The thought seriously bothers him, but he doesn't have time to dwell on it. It's only a matter of time before Amsend discovers that he fled the convoy. If he can get to Polar and get him out of the castle using the Superbolt, then they might have a chance... Vulpie has the keys in his pocket, but getting there... So many NoirQueue...

He's climbing before he realizes what he's doing. Vulpie's forty feet up the stone wall in no time. He's little, and weak, but his light weight makes it possible for him to hoist himself higher and higher. He barely eats anything, and exercises with Polar every day, so he's in perfect shape for the climb. The gay fox's lightning fast mind and determination makes up for what he lacks in physical strength. There's no hesitation at all. He's happy that he's risking his life because he knows he can save his husband… Why he knows, or who told him, doesn't matter right now. He's getting to the top, and absolutely nothing is going to stop him.

Vulpie's only five feet six inches tall, so he's a little spec on the stone even with his brilliant orange fur shimmering in the morning sun, on top of his bright green t-shirt. The mountain road leading up to Castle Lahnak is far enough away for him to remain unseen even if someone decides to use it. He must keep going. His little fingers have a strength in them that he's never felt before. His small hands don't give way when he keeps pulling his body higher and higher. It's as if some force has filled his entire body with vigor. He feels supercharged, partially because of the endorphins being released by his brain, but it's not just chemical reactions. Something else is there, inside him, helping him. Is it Aila? He hopes not, and complains to himself while climbing.

"Where are ya Khalan? Wanna help me out? Course you don't! Vulpie only has Vulpie! That's how it's always been! At least, Uh! At least Aila's doing something! I fucking wish it wasn't her, Uh! but, Uh! She's here!" The orange fox suddenly realizes where he is and what he's doing when it's far too late to stop. A wave of terror rushes over him, but he manages to subdue it and convert the fear into energy for the climb. "If I fall and die, at least I fucking tried! Not leaving you here! I'm coming baby! I'm coming Mr. P! I… Wow I'm high up here! UH!"

Vulpie's right paw slips, and he hastily slaps it onto a nearby rock that's jutting out of the wall. He releases a terrified whimper, but still keeps going. "Fuck it! I don't care if I die! I'm not leaving you behind! I'll find a way! I promise! I won't die, and I'll get you out of here! We can do it! I can do it, and we'll both do it! Not going to fall! I've got too much stuff to do! Can't fall and die because it doesn't fit my fuckin schedule!" The orange furred fox finally starts feeling fatigued, and when he realizes he's only about halfway up the cliff, he feels like panicking. He keeps going, as hard as he can, but he can't keep it up for much longer.

"Uh! No! Uh! Not going to give up! UH! Now! No UH! Way!" He gasps, and suddenly feels extremely weak. "Oh God why am I doing this? I'm going to die! Maybe he won't hurt Polar, but I'm going to die! Why did I do this? Somebody! Somebody please help me! PLEASE!" He cries out with his effeminate voice, and blinks when a new wave of strength hits him. He feels fine... He's sore from climbing, but he can keep going... "What the fuck is going on?! Am I losing my mind or is somebody helping me?! Talking to myself climbing a cliff! I don't want to die! But I won't leave you Polar! I can't!"

His fox claws suddenly discover a large gap in the stone, and he realizes it's the crevice he saw, the one Aila pointed out to him. When he climbs up to it he's overjoyed to discover a metal chest inside. "What the... Hell?" He breathes while scrambling into the hole. He rolls onto his back and gasps in relief. "Who put you in here?" He whispers, and pulls the metal box to him. It's hinges crumble when he yanks on it, and it's lid slides right off. A very old book is waiting inside... A journal... But who's?

"What in the world are you? Who put you up here?" He whispers, and gently reaches in the box to retrieve it. "Somebody actually climbed up here with you? Wow!" He says to himself, and opens the ancient brown book. Its pages are very thin, worn down from years of cliff weather, but Vulpie can read all of the writing. Amazingly, the journal is written in Sufian, and not Englavic, as one would expect.

Puḱsos The Mighty

This is the journal of one Puḱsos Fritjof.

February 8th 1579

I hate everyone in this stupid town. Not everyone, but all of these stuck up people with bad attitudes. No one appreciates me or how hard I work at the woodshop. I'm the very best there is and work hard day in and day out, but all I get are dirty looks and get kicked around! Those ugly wolves better hope I never get a chance to do what they accuse me of! They say foxes like me are nothing but money grubbing backstabbing liars, but they're the real backstabbers! I heard they killed a fox girl after having their way with her and they all got away with it! The coal wolves are all going to hell!

Papa says I shouldn't say anything because it'll just make things worse, but I can't stand it anymore! They come into our shop and stomp around, knocking things over like they own the place and laugh at us with that ugly Lahnak Dog. Grandpa says they ruined our town when they built the castle. Now there's no way for little animals like us to defend ourselves against those filthy brutes. They can just come out of there, and come down here to do whatever they fancy, and no one ever does anything about it! I hate this place! I wish I could move away but I couldn't leave my family behind. But I still hate it here.

March 13th 1579

It's been a while, but now I'm back! I kind of gave up on this journal because, I don't know, I guess I was getting out my frustrations in these pages, but something wonderful happened today! A panther man came into town and wanted to buy furniture at our store, but he wasn't just an ordinary man. No! He was sly and really friendly! He knew all about the wolves' treachery and he would know since he's a cat! They're mortal enemies and always will be! But what a surprise it was when he told us he was a thief! A thief? Who would tell someone such a thing? A really great man, that's who! He told me the worst vice was advice, but he didn't treat me like a kid in the end. He showed me some of his tools and at night, he took me out and showed me how to pick a lock too!

This is all just too much, but it was so much fun! We broke into Mr. Froeihonn's house and stole fodder rabbits for breakfast! And it's the morning now and no one knows what happened! I was sad to see him go, but he was incredible, and he was nice enough to take my gold when I offered to buy some of his equipment. He could get into serious trouble if anyone knew what he was up to, but he saw how much I wanted this! Now I can be a thief too, and I WILL BE!

March 19th 1579

All hail the triumphant hero! I did it! Tonight I pulled off my very first robbery! Well, the first one on my own at least. I waited a few days before trying my paw at thieving, but it just came natural to me! A thief? Hah! They've been calling my family thieves for years just because we're foxes, and who's laughing now, eh? I broke into Sarti's home and stole his wallet. Then I pissed on his rug! Hah! They could find this and would know I did it, but I don't care! Fuck him and his family! Fuck them all! Now the next time they're kicking Puḱsos Fritjof around, Puḱsos will have a little smile on his face won't he?

March 24th 1579

I did it! I did it again! Tonight I broke into Sarti's house A SECOND TIME! And this time I started a little fire! Oh, I did it just right! I left the broom and the clothes in just the right positions so I would have time to get out and get back home before anyone knew. This morning there are people in the streets! Wolves everywhere! Even foxes! Arguing and arguing about WHO DID IT! Who did do it? hmmm? Puḱsos the infiltrator! Puḱsos the spy! Puḱsos the untouchable!

I'm going to put on such a show today. I'll go downstairs and act like a scared little boy! Oh no! What's going on? Hah!

April 10th 1579

Papa is starting to wonder about me. He knows. He's been paying attention to when I come home and now he's convinced I'm the one. Damn fox blood. Guess that's why I'm so good! It's in my blood!

Have to lay low for a while. Not many opportunities to have fun.

June 21st 1585

Well hello there friend! It's been quite a long time, hasn't it? A long time since Puḱsos the infiltrator wrote a page in you. Some things have changed and some things haven't. I have my own place now, but I'm still working at Papa's woodshop and I'm always welcome.

But now I have privacy. Oh yes. Privacy to return to my dastardly ways! My vengeful, unstoppable, and righteous ways! But Puƙsos is no fool. He knows he can't rob people near home anymore. He can't put his family in danger and doesn't want to. No. Instead, Puƙsos the untouchable has a much grander scheme! Now he will rob the first bank of Froidenley! One big heist and I'll have all I need for an early retirement.

July 7th 1585

Mission accomplished. I'm actually kind of disappointed. I always imagined the place would have more security. Bags of gold and bags of silver. They're all mine now. I stole everything I could carry, and even managed to carry a bag out. The guards were lazy and spent their time arguing over which kind of she-wolf pussy was the best. Disgusting. No wonder their kind are better at carrying weapons than running banks. Can't say they're very good at guard duty either, though.

Time to sleep. I feel incredible, but something's missing. It wasn't a challenge.

Can't sleep. Been thinking about things and just had the greatest idea, or maybe it was a nightmare. I'm not really sure because I'm so tired. Whichever it was, I'm glad I write in Sufian, because this idea will touch more people than the furs in my quaint little town. No. What I know I'm going to do now is going to shock the world. I'm going to Lahnak Castle, but I won't be taking the trail. Tonight I've committed to robbing the most dangerous place in the land. If someone's taken up there in pawcuffs they never come back, so I know this is the ultimate challenge.

I'm going to risk my life, but I'm going to rob Amsend blind. That bastard has been terrorizing people since I was a pup, and people say he never ages. Ignorance is what that is. The murderer is able to get away with everything he does because he's rich. Somehow his family got up there and had that castle built, but someone has to make him pay.

Ironic, isn't it? Is it? Puƙsos the hero?

July 13th 1585

I have my work cut out for me. I've stolen a lot over the years but this will definitely be the toughest job. I've been up and down the road at night, but it's miles before you get to the castle, and there's a damn drawbridge. Fuck it all. How am I going to get inside now? This won't stop me. I'm Puḱsos, and I've become a legend in my own time. They don't know my name, but they know my work. I'm the fox that humbles wolves and bitches like Amsend Lahnak.

But we have quite a big problem here, don't we? Obviously I can't enter the castle via the drawbridge, and it sits on the edge of a damn cliff! The river flows through the canyon, and I would have to hike forty miles around the other direction if I wanted to go in the back. And no doubt the man has guards everywhere, even patrolling the northeastern walls where there's nothing but forest. Sneaking inside with innocent men and women on supply runs is also out of the question. If they ever see me they'll kill my family, and that's why I'm so cautious. I don't mind if they get me, but I can't let them do that.

July 22nd 1585

I've learned a lot about Baron Lahnak by observing his business dealings in Froidenley. I turned my eyes back to the streets after discovering how impenetrable his castle seems, and what I've seen is very unsettling. I guess I never paid attention to it before, or maybe I was too busy dreaming of my next break-in, but it looks like he deals with just a few animals, and every one of them are gray foxes. They're all Vixils! I can't believe it! Father never liked them and now I know why! They're in bed with that monster. They take his money and perpetuate the problems we have in town. Somehow they profited from my bank heist and took control of Froidenley's purse strings, and to me, this is especially heart breaking. I didn't rob the joint so the poor would suffer. I wanted those rich fucks to feel the pain, but I was wrong.

Regardless, I can still put my talents to good use. I'll hit Amsend where it hurts, at his home, and he'll never feel safe again. So says Puḱsos the vicious, and so it will be.

September 1st 1585

I found a way inside. Can you believe it, oh little journal of mine? I know you can't. I didn't believe it myself, but I did. There IS a way.

As it turns out, the Baron's seclusion will also be his undoing. Since his castle is nearly impenetrable, no one will expect the bold approach I'm going to take. Instead of going for the drawbridge or the northeastern walls, I'll climb right up the south side of the canyon, and then the castle. The canyon walls will be the most difficult part because it'll be harder to find footing, but I have the equipment to chisel out weak spots and then nail in support irons. It's going to take me a long time, but I think I can do it. No. I know I can. The question is whether I have the patience for it.

Good thing I'm not afraid of heights.

October 7th 1585

Everything's ready. Work is slow at the woodshop and it'll be another four days until I'm needed there. I've crossed the river several times and have nailed in about twenty support irons. Tomorrow I'll make the climb. I need to regain my strength tonight, but one way or another, I'm going to make it.

October 8th 1585

Writing on the edge of the world! Halfway up the canyon I noticed a small break in the stone that's not big enough for a large man, but has plenty of space for a Puksos! In truth, the climb has been a lot harder than I anticipated. I knew it would be tough, but if they could see me now, they just wouldn't believe it. I must be a hundred feet up, and can see the town from here.

This is a great development! Now I know I have a little spot to rest before going on. I'm going to come back with food and water, and after I sleep up here, I'll go the rest of the way. Don't want to risk falling off now. I'm exhausted from the climb, but I'm halfway there, and if I start my morning from this little spot, I'm sure to make it all the way! It's just a matter of time.

October 9th 1585

Back again. Have enough supplies to last me for a while. Tomorrow is the moment of truth. Tomorrow I get inside.

October 10th 1585

They will sing songs about Puksos. Puksos, who found a way inside Lahnak Castle, and could come and go as he pleased! I feel amazing! I did it! Not only did I manage to climb the castle's southern wall, I discovered a small drainage pipe that runs straight out of the stonework! It's about five feet wide, plenty big enough for a master thief to try his paw. I brought lots of fuel for my travel lantern, but I *didn't really need it in the end. The tunnel is completely dark for a few hundred feet, and after I got inside, I discovered an amazingly pleasant cistern. A little light shines in from above thanks to some nice carvings in the ceiling, so it's just a bit of wet fur, and you're in! The tunnel goes straight into the cistern's pool.*

It couldn't be any more perfect. Just as I had hoped, security is very lax on the inside. No one has a clue I've even been there. Why would they? Amsend's men are frightening, but they're too busy looking outwards to suspect an ambitious vulpine intruder. Truly my people are the smartest animals in the world! We have to be. Who else could be this clever? If only the Froidenley wolves could see me now. ME! Just a weakling in their eyes, but a master of ingenuity!

Now I'm ready. I'll sleep behind the steps of the cistern tonight and regain my strength. I have to stay on my toes. Claws sharp. If they see me, the fun will be over. Not going to happen. I'll case the joint when everybody goes to sleep, and will probably hide down here as long as I feel like it's necessary. When I'm ready, I'll snatch all of the gold I can carry. Will have to leave afterwards, though. Even if I'm careful, they'll be looking for the thief. Hopefully I'll be long gone before they notice.

October 11th 1585

Back home. Back home and safe. In truth I never imagined I would get this far. I'm going to be rich. I lifted several golden plates and even two silver ones that seem to have what looks like diamonds in them. No way I'll be able to pawn them off in Froidenley. There's not a fence in this damn town that's not working for the Vixils, so I'll go down to Gray Ridge and make my money. There's enough folk for me to make a good haul and feel safe after coming back home.

Things are certainly going to be interesting from now on. Surely it won't be long until the Baron realizes he's been robbed. Can't wait to see his reaction.

October 30th 1585

Puķsos feels uncomfortable. Nineteen days? Really? He hasn't found out? Surely he has. The man's just biding his time, using his Vixils to sniff around town. But I can't shake this feeling. Something. Something is terribly wrong. No one talks anymore. The baker down the street, Papa at the shop, Veni in the rich district, none of them have anything to say. It's like the whole town is afraid.

Afraid? That means he found out! But I haven't heard anything from anyone. No one has said anything to me, though Papa has given me a few looks at work now and then, but that's not unusual. Something's going on, and Puḱsos doesn't like being left in the dark. Puḱsos is the dark.

November 14th 1585

My paws are shaking. I can't sit down! I have to sit to scrawl in this journal, but I can barely contain myself. I finally made a second trip to Lahnak Castle, and what I found there has left me in shambles. The thrill of pulling off another heist is overshadowed by what I can only describe as horrible visions.

It was dark when I entered Amsend's fortress, but right away, I knew something was off. The guards were gone. No guards. ANYWHERE! NOBODY! I couldn't believe it. The castle was lit with hundreds of torches, but nothing but silence greeted me. It's like they were waiting on me to come back and I think, NO, I KNOW they were trying to kill me.

It was so incredibly easy to go everywhere I wanted at any time. I just knew it was a trap. But either courageously or foolishly, I couldn't help myself, and ventured deep within the ancient structure. We foxes have fearsomely precise noses, and I smelled danger. Something or someone WAS in the castle, but I couldn't see where. I just. Felt it. And then I found them.

Amsend was in the bowels of the castle, and I spotted him from a distance. He was talking to something, but at first I thought he was out of his mind, because it was a statue. A statue? Not at all. It was far too big to be a suit of armor, but somehow, and I will never be able to understand what I saw, it started talking back to him. It moved, and it looked like something straight out of hell. It reminded me of the Dark Goddess Aila, but I'm still not sure what it was. It was alive! And it gave him instruction! My God.

The stories are true. Castle Lahnak is cursed and its caretaker is not an animal. He's a thing, like the statue creature he spoke to. He's not like anyone in this town, like anyone in the world! My Goddess, I will never go back.

November 16th 1585

The thing intrigues me. Was it some kind of device? A weapon? What was it? Why was Amsend talking to it? What purpose does it serve? These questions have been gnawing, biting, and chewing at me all day, afternoon and evening! Why must I do this? I know it will end in disaster. I KNOW it'll be the end of me, but I'm going back. I have to find out.

November 18th 1585

No one will ever believe me. Who would? I'm back in my little hole in the canyon wall and have just gotten away with my third heist. Although, it wasn't really a thieving mission. I came back to learn about Amsend's thing. Well, I did, but I also think I'm going crazy because I revealed myself to it. I couldn't help it. I saw Amsend leave the castle this morning and had the depths of the place to myself. No one goes down there but him. Maybe his devoted guardsmen are afraid of what they'll find. Can't say I blame them. What lies underneath the castle is hell itself.

The metal creature called to me. It's deep humming made my fur stand on end. So I took a huge gamble and stepped in front of it. I felt like a complete fool when it started to move. I don't know what I was expecting. It's head moved, watching me, with black eyes. It was like it bled ink from its eye sockets.

I'm not sure what happened next. Judging by the sun in the sky right now, I couldn't have been unconscious for more than an hour, but I know I did sleep. The creature said something to me and I just collapsed right in front of it. I was sure Amsend had returned after I woke up, and that he was going to kill me for discovering the thing, but no one was there. I was still alone. I got up and stood there, dumbfounded.

The creature shared some kind of bizarre spirit with me. It was inside me. I could feel it everywhere, in my eyes, in my paws, in my balls, in my tail, in my gut, and in my mind. It showed me things. Wonderful things. I cannot describe what they were, but they were definitely stars. It took me into the blackness of space! Or showed it to me? I'm not sure, and I don't think I will ever know. Surely Amsend is the only one who understands what the creature is and what it does, and I won't be asking him about it.

Whomever may read my journal someday, if such a time comes, know that the thing in Amsend's castle is a weapon. After it did something to me I could feel this energy... It's impossible to describe.

It could have killed me, but it didn't. I don't know why. No sane animal would believe it, but if you're reading this, you're brave like Puḱsos, and you're fighting the baron! I scurried back down the walls and into the Puḱsos hole to write in you, my dear journal. My silent companion. Of one thing I am certain. I will never stop until I understand what Amsend is. I come and go as I please and he cannot stop me.

Puḱsos Fritjof is no more. Puḱsos the mighty has been born!

November 19th 1585

Woe is me. I awoke in my plain little bed this morning, face fur sticking to my pillow from the cold mountain air, and felt no more powerful than a little fox normally does. Was yesterday a dream? It wasn't, because I remember the visions it showed me, but now I feel so weak.

Someone's at the door.

November 20th 1585

Puḱsos the fool. Yesterday, dear journal, I was taken from you by Amsend's men. They found me. They knew it was me, and they came to humiliate me. They beat their paws on the door until I came downstairs and let them in. I didn't like them invading my private place, my own little corner of the world. But they did, and to my dismay, Amsend walked right inside my home and smiled at me. He called me a naughty little bitch and had them drag me out of my own house.

They took me. I can barely write this. I feel so ashamed. They took me to the castle. What happened next, I can barely scrawl in these pages without crying.

They took me to the castle and Amsend sat me down in the great hall. He started clapping, and they all laughed when he congratulated me for my thieving. Amsend said he'd never seen an animal with such skill. At first it was like he wanted me to join them, but I knew he was lying. He was trying to get my hopes up, to make me think they'd let me go without. Punishment.

I don't want to write this, but I must. Someone needs to know, even if it's only you, my sweet journal. He said he didn't know how I got inside the castle, but he knew it was me, and was going to give me something I'd never forget. What happened next. I can. Barely write. I'm crying.

They used me like a woman. Six black wolves. Amsend watched. I CAN'T BEAR TO WRITE ANYTHING ELSE ABOUT IT! But it happened. I've never known so much pain in my life. Now I can't even walk, and I can only hope that I heal over time.

I'LL KILL THEM FOR THIS! I'LL KILL THEM ALL! GODDESS DAMN THEM! THEY DID THIS TO ME! HOW DARE THEY DO THIS TO ME? I'll kill them. I swear to Khalan I will! They won't get away with this. I shall be Puksos the mighty once more! I'll wait until they've forgotten about me, and then I WILL HAVE REVENGE!

My life is over. I can't look at myself in the well water anymore. They knew I wouldn't tell anyone what they did to me because it was too humiliating, and I can't. How could I ever look at my family again after being raped? GOD DAMN THEM! THIS IS NOT OVER! I WILL KILL AMSEND!

December 9th 1585

I can't take the shame anymore. I think about killing myself every day. I didn't want to admit it to you, my journal, but it's true. They've killed me. I can no longer enjoy anything about life. I've healed, but nothing is the same. I can't work, I can't sleep, and I can't dream.

Tomorrow is the end of my life. Tomorrow I will go back to the castle, and I WILL KILL ALL OF THEM! Blood will run over the castle walls. I'll use the cistern system underneath the castle to go from room to room, surprising all of them, one by one, until they're all dead or they kill me. There's nothing left for me now. Nothing but you, my journal. Only you know my secrets, my triumphs and my fall.

I must find a place for you. I can't stand the thought of you wasting away or being burned in someone's stove. I must find a place for you to rest until someone worthy finds you and opens your pages once more.

December 10th 1585

I found a home for you. Time's cruel devices will not harm you, my dearest journal. You are my only friend. Only you understand the hardships I've faced and the great deeds I've accomplished. I bought you the most beautiful home in Gray Ridge. It's a solid steel box. So very heavy. It's maker said there's no way water could ever penetrate its sturdy walls. And here, dear journal, you will rest. It brings tears to my eyes to lock you inside this chest, but you must live on. I know, one day, someone worthy will find you.

I'm going to leave you in my corner of the world, where no lesser animal will ever discover you. I can't leave you in my home, because they will find you and destroy you. And if I sold you to someone, who knows what dusty shelf you would end up on? No. Whoever finds you after I'm gone, will surely be a brave animal, brave like me and you. And they will be worthy of your pages and my story.

And whoever you are, if you've found my journal, you ARE the bravest of souls. You're brave like Puksos! I can only hope you're making this dangerous climb to destroy the baron. The best I can do is leave these words underneath the wretched dog's home in the hopes that one day, whomever you are, you will use my knowledge of his fortress to destroy him. I know you're here to stop Amsend. KILL HIM! Don't let our sacrifices be in vain! Puksos is with you in spirit!

I surely go now to my death. I plan on killing all of them with my poisoned dagger. Even though they knew I was the one sneaking into the castle, they didn't ask how I did it, so I should still be able to use the cistern system to my advantage. I've scrawled a map on your very last page from memory. I'll have to look at it tonight before deciding where to begin my killing spree.

I know there's a very good chance I'll fail, because there are just too many of them, but either way, this will be the end of my story. Puksos will have his revenge or die trying.

Goodbye.

468

Devotion

Vulpie feels like he's defiled Puḱsos Fritjof's journal just by touching it. It's so frail, and the story is beyond heartbreaking. He's never identified with another fox so much his entire life, and notices how similar their paths were, even though they were born centuries apart. Puḱsos' sensitivity mixed with the amazing feats he accomplished speak to Vulpie on many levels. They were both criminals, and Amsend's also hurt them both. Vulpie feels speechless, in awe of the secret he's discovered hidden right underneath the fortress. The little thief who died hundreds of years ago has filled the orange fox with courage.

"Was it… You? Puḱsos?" Vulpie whispers, and gently flips to the last brittle page. The map Puḱsos spoke of is smudged and incomplete, but he knows he should take a picture of it. Even if the castle has been remodeled over the centuries, having a rough sketch of its layout is critical. Vulpie pulls his legendary orange cell phone out of his left pocket and adjusts its settings so he can take a perfect shot of Puḱsos' drawing. After he has it, he puts away his phone and returns the journal to its metal box. He gently puts its lid back on and slides it to its original position.

Vulpie has never put much stock in religion for two very good reasons. Firstly, because it seems like they were made up by animals for political reasons, and secondly, because Vander Clishaw was a pastor. The thoughts hurt him and he has to shift his thinking to something else. He knows he doesn't have time for weakness. He has to be strong, just like his lover told him. Polar needs help, and Vulpie knows he's the only one who can come to his rescue. He has to find a way. He knows there's a way to save his soul mate; he just has to find it. The longer Polar's held prisoner in Amsend's castle the more likely it is that he'll be physically and sexually abused. Vulpie is under no illusion that Polar can escape on his own. The snow wolf was right. Amsend's men are armed, and they're beyond negotiating with. Polar will most likely dig in and take the abuse so they won't kill him, and Amsend could have him tortured without Vulpie ever knowing a thing about it. Vulpie knows they'll threaten to kill his husband if he doesn't let them have their twisted fun, and the snow wolf will give in. He'll give in because he loves Vulpie too much to see him harmed.

Vulpie's ready. Thinking about them raping Polar fills him with so much rage that he's out of the small cave in the blink of an eye. He's climbing fast, and already sees the drainage pipe Puk̇sos mentioned in his journal. It's jutting out from the castle wall, and if it hasn't been closed off, the orange furred fox will have an easy time infiltrating the fortress. The cistern might also lead to other secluded parts of the castle since Puk̇sos used it so frequently. There's a good chance Amsend's blocked off the cistern after discovering it was the ancient fox thief's point of entry, but then again, the husky might never have asked the right questions. If Polar's recollection of the Velora is right, and if Amsend is the foolish antikhalan, maybe he never had enough foresight to look for Puk̇sos' secret entrance or ask him about it. The monster seems more interested in hurting people than critical thinking. His befuddling decision to work with Vulpie.net already suggests that he doesn't think things completely through before taking action.

"I'm coming for you baby." Vulpie breathes while climbing. "Just hang on." Dust escapes from a bit of stone above him, and he stops momentarily to close his eyes. Hanging on becomes far more difficult when he has to sneeze afterwards, but he manages to keep his paws on the rock. He's reached the bottom of the castle wall much sooner than anticipated, and it leaves him with a bit of extra strength. When he climbs next to the animal sized drainage pipe, an exhilarated feeling rushes through his body. He's almost there, and that makes it even more dangerous. This is the part where it's easy to make a mistake.

Vulpie reaches out and touches the black stone pipe with his right paw. He has to hang halfway on it and the stone wall, so he quickly decides to continue. He knows he'll run out of strength soon, and might as well use it before it's too late. The orange fox gets both of his paws on the pipe, and a bit of water splashes out of it onto his face. It's not enough to soak his clothing, but it does make him pause. When it stops, Vulpie finally grabs the stone as hard as he can and pulls himself up. It looks like he made it just in time, because his little biceps, triceps and forearms suddenly feel like they're on fire. The soreness immobilizes him for about a minute, but he feels fine after recovering.

"Thank Khalan." Vulpie gasps with his fur on end. He thinks about how he got here. "Why Aila? Don't you care about me? She's the one who helped me, not you!" The orange fox says to himself, and starts crawling deeper into the pipe. It becomes a tunnel that leads all the way to the cistern, where a deep pool of rainwater has been collected. Luckily, it's well lit because someone has installed a metal gate above the stairs, which come down into the middle of the chamber. Vulpie sloshes around the water, hugging the rock wall on the left side of the chamber so he won't get his shoes and socks wet. There's a stone platform right below the stairs and he hops onto it without getting soaked.

"Please don't be locked…" He whispers when he notices the metal gate has a small handle with a keyhole in the middle of its bars. He gets his paws on one of the metal bars, and takes a deep breath. "Please…" The gay fox pushes a little, and is overjoyed when it offers no resistance. "YES!" His celebration is cut short when the hinges make a high pitched squeaking sound, and the gay fox bites his teeth together in fear. He can only hope no one heard it, or if they did, that the guards are used to the sounds of Castle Lahnak. They might think it's another guard opening a gate somewhere, or the wind shutting one. Vulpie's mind comes up with several scenarios, but he doesn't hang around to find out if any guards are nearby. He hurries up the steps, and discovers that he's much lower than the bailey's ground. The steps leading down to the cistern are fairly secluded, right next to two doors that face each other in the stonework, and he stands on his tip toes to look in one of their windows. He takes a peek inside the stone room to his right and sees nothing but barrels and crates.

"Perfect!" He whispers, and quickly opens the door. He gets inside before he sees a single person, and shuts it very gently. It looks like he's in a small storage room, and another door at the back side of the room leads into the castle. He has no idea where he'll end up. It could be a hallway, the barracks, a room full of NoirQueue wolves playing cards... There's just no telling what he'll face when he opens it, but it's his only option at this point. The door leading inside is made of wood, and is completely silent when he gently opens it. It's dark inside, but it looks like he walks into a basement hallway. Barrels full of wine are all around him. "So far so good!" Just as soon as he finishes talking to himself, he sees a coal furred wolf sitting at a table to his right, underneath a flight of stairs that lead up into the fortress.

Vulpie's sure the man heard him, but amazingly, he continues to sit at his desk and eat his lunch. He's chowing down on a gray meat sandwich and a beer is next to his right paw. The guard looks partially inebriated, and focuses on a magazine sitting on the table between his arms. Vulpie's relieved that the man didn't hear him, but notices something very problematic. The wolf's table is right next to the stairs, and a light bulb hangs from the ceiling at the bottom of the steps. Vulpie will never be able to sneak by the guard if he stays where he is, and it looks like he isn't going anywhere soon. Most likely he's the guard who watches over Amsend's personal wine collection, and this is where he's needed.

"Fuck." Vulpie growls and looks into the darkness to his left. He thinks he sees a flight of stairs but can't be sure. He's the perfect species for sneaking, because foxes have excellent night vision, but it's not enough. He could break his neck trying to find an alternate route through the darkness. He accidently bumps into a barrel with his left knee while thinking about his options, and the guard hears it. He turns to his left and drops his sandwich on the table. The man holds still, wondering whether the barrel thump could have been caused by something harmless, but it doesn't take him long to retrieve his weapon. He has a streamlined assault rifle with a silencer that's far easier to carry than the one Vulpie used on Zeravyn. He grabs it like it's just another part of his body, and swings it towards the darkness.

"Who's back there?" He asks in Englavic, but Vulpie doesn't know the language. *"Someone sneaking around over there? Who is it?"*

"SHIT!" Vulpie curses, and hits another barrel, making the guard aim directly at him, even though he can't see the orange fox.

"Come out!"

"Don't shoot me!" Vulpie yelps, and the man grins from ear to ear. He doesn't understand Sufian, but Vulpie's iconic effeminate voice is unmistakable.

"VULPIE!" The man laughs, and the gay fox moans in frustration. He just risked his life to sneak into the castle, only to be busted by the first NoirQueue agent he's come across. The guard hurries back to his table to turn on the rest of the lights, and suddenly Vulpie is completely exposed in the bright wine cellar. The man looks very proud of himself. Vulpie puts up his paws and the mercenary struts around while talking smack in Englavic. The gay fox has no idea what he's saying, but he recognizes the tone of his voice. Vulpie figures the guard is making derogatory statements about his sexuality. It's usually the first thing bullies go for.

"You got me." Vulpie says while keeping his paws in the air.

"How did you get in here? I thought Amsend sent you away."

"Amsend?"

"How in the world did you manage to sneak in here?"

"I don't know your language. I can't understand what you're saying."

"This just isn't your day is it?" The coal furred wolf chuckles, and steps in front of the small fox. *"Is it?"*

"I don't know what you're saying." The guard touches his radio, and as soon as Vulpie sees him go for it, he quickly reaches out to stop his big fingers. The orange fox surprises him with a begging little smile. The man raises an eyebrow and murmurs something in amusement.

"You're a pretty little thing, aren't you?" Vulpie picks up on the lecherous inflection in his voice. He knows the smile the man's giving him is a rape face. The gay fox has one card to play, and he uses it without hesitation. Somehow he has to distract the guard long enough to steal his weapon, and he can't bargain with him or stall for time, so there's only one potential way to do it. If he can make the coal furred wolf horny, he might be able to make him lower his guard long enough to pull it off. Vulpie pretends to be a weak little slut who'll do anything to anyone, in the hopes that the mercenary will be careless enough to put down his weapon. The guard probably isn't gay, but the clever fox knows how to generate curiosity.

"I bet you understand this!" Vulpie grins and gets on his knees. "Maybe we can make other arrangements?"

"Cock sucking fox... You want to give me head?"

"I have no idea what you're saying, but it doesn't matter, does it?" Vulpie breathes with an adorable voice. He swishes his pretty tail, and amazingly, the man decides to walk to the right and lean his assault rifle against one of the wine barrels. The fox calculates the distance, counting the time it takes for him to return.

"Fuck it... If you insist... We can have some fun before I hand you over to Amsend." He says with his thick Englavic accent. He reaches down and undoes his belt while giving the gay fox a lewd look.

"That's what you want, isn't it? Well I'll get right on it!" Vulpie grins and stands up. He makes sure to keep his eyes on the man's crotch, and pretends to lick his lips in preparation. "And now... That gun is mine!" The orange fox snaps and bolts to the left. There's no question about what he's after, but the NoirQueue wolf hesitates long enough for him to retrieve the weapon. The rifle has a long suppressor, perfect for a situation like this, and

Vulpie hastily aims it at him. He's never shot someone before; the thought of doing it makes him feel horrible.

"God... Damn it."

"On your knees! Get on your fucking knees!"

"You little bastard."

"Don't fuck with me! I'll kill you!" Vulpie growls, and tenses up when the guard raises his paws. He knows the powerful wolf could instantly reverse the situation if he gets close enough. Vulpie moves backwards, trying to put more space between him and the merc. He stumbles after bumping into a wine barrel behind him, and the guard sees an opportunity. He goes for it, lunging at Vulpie with murderous intent, and the fox fires six rounds.

The man crashes into the barrel next to the little fox and knocks him to the floor. Vulpie struggles to get out from underneath the killer, but quickly discovers he's not in any danger. The guard's already dead. His limp body starts bleeding, and Vulpie crawls to the side, managing to get away before the blood stains his shirt.

"Crazy... Fucker! Why'd you do that?" The fox gasps, but secretly relishes his victory. He knew he had to kill him, and if he's serious about rescuing Polar, this man will be the first of many. Best case scenario, he'll have to slaughter a ton of NoirQueue wolves to even stand a chance, and if they signal the alarm... He may have to shoot... All of them? Vulpie quickly represses the thoughts. He compartmentalizes them appropriately so he won't hesitate. He's already taken one life... What's several more? Killing his first man was the hardest part... He's given up his innocence to save Polar, but he knows this is the only way. Amsend's mercenaries are soulless, and they'll torture his lover eventually. It's only a matter of time.

"Kill or be killed!" Vulpie breathes while rummaging through the merc's clothing. He finds three clips of ammunition, all seemingly compatible with the silenced weapon. The orange fox quickly figures out how to release the assault rifle's magazine and compares them. They're identical. All four of

them have exactly the same wording and display the same caliber. "Perfect."
He whispers while familiarizing himself with the weapon. He remembers using
Rulef's assault rifle on Zeravyn, but this one feels better. He reads its inscribed
model number, M15, and practices reloading the gun over and over. The
M15's magazine locks into place on the bottom of the gun, so yanking one out
during a firefight and slapping another one in should be a piece of cake. The
next thing he examines is the gun's holographic scope. It looks like it was
designed for medium range or close quarters combat because the red circle it
sports around the target area is rather large.

Vulpie recognizes the comedic value of a gay fox going commando,
but now isn't the time. He can laugh about what happened IF he somehow
manages to rescue his husband from over one hundred highly trained
unsympathetic killers... The odds of him succeeding aren't very good, but he
has to save his lover no matter what it takes.

Vulpie's Gamble

Vulpie releases an effeminate grunt after dragging the dead mercenary behind the wine barrels. He switches the man's radio off and hurries across the cellar. He turns off the second light and pauses when a fantastic idea pops into his head. Puḱsos used the cistern system to sneak around the castle. It was several centuries ago, but if Amsend truly is who he says he is, and he's a fool that can't see past his own shadow, the man might not have even blocked off the cistern tunnels out of pure arrogance. Puḱsos didn't have a gun, so if Vulpie manages to move around undetected, he might be able to hit every part of the castle with devastating surprise attacks. The M15 is capable of dropping ten men, and the suppressor will give him a chance to clear the rooms before the other guards find out.

The gay fox can't believe he's actually contemplating ways to commit mass murder, but he can't stop now. He's risked his life to get this far, and now he's killed a man too. No half measures are going to save Polar from Amsend's cold hearted mercenaries. They have to be dealt with... Bargaining is impossible because Vulpie doesn't speak Englavic, and even if he managed to have a conversation with one of them, there's no way they would ever turn on their master. If he is the antikhalan, and they've all seen the hidden power Polar felt when the husky kicked him, then disobeying orders would be a great way for them to get themselves killed... Murder is the only option at this point.

They don't know he's coming, so he'll have the element of surprise. Vulpie's confident that he can kill several of them before Amsend finds out. The monster can't be everywhere, and a little fox already outsmarted him in his own castle a long time ago. Vulpie would love to kill the GSB director, but he's not sure whether bullets would be enough. Polar punched him three times and he was completely unfazed. Avoiding him at all costs seems like the best course of action.

The gay fox searches the room, making use of his nocturnal vulpine eyes once again, and discovers a small pull up gate on the wall behind the wine barrels where he stashed the dead guard's body. The M15 has a tactical flashlight attached to its underslung rail, and he paws the weapon looking for a way to activate it. He finds a small switch on the left and flips it. It produces a surprisingly brilliant light beam that will definitely make a huge difference in the darkness behind the small gate. Vulpie suspects it's part of the cistern system, and he gets on his knees so he can take a look. He pushes it, but it resists, so he gives it a tug, and it swings open. Rust crumbles from its hinges when it moves, but it isn't very loud.

Vulpie holds it open with his left paw, listening for faint watery sounds in the distance. Judging by its position and what he saw in the cistern's main pool, he thinks there's a good chance it'll lead him down Puksos' secret path. He closes the gate and investigates the black gun harness attached to the bottom of the M15. He tries putting on the weapon like a backpack, and has to fiddle with its slider until it feels snug. Now he can carry it while keeping his paws free, but it's his only light source. The orange furred fox temporarily attaches it to his back, opens the small gate, and wriggles through. It closes with a quiet thud, and Vulpie grabs the moist stone wall next to him. He's in the cistern; there's no question about it, because he accidently soaks his sneakers in the artificial river.

"Fuck." He growls and retrieves the M15. It's tactical light illuminates a pool of clear water that stretches horizontally, along the inside of the castle curtain wall. Vulpie pulls out his orange cell phone and flips it open. He navigates to the picture of Puksos' map and quickly identifies where he is. Puksos was thorough enough to name most of the castle's rooms and secret passages. He made some of them up to match what he saw, but the wine cellar is hard to miss. It's not far from the main cistern chamber they both used to enter the castle, but there's a stone wall between it and the little stream Vulpie's standing in. The water goes underneath the wall via a gate that's too small to use. Puksos marked it with a tiny X.

A fair amount of green moss has covered the lower parts of the tunnel. No doubt the moisture provided by the small river created a habitat conducive to growth. The water is just high enough to cover Vulpie's shoes, and he sighs. Going toe to toe with mercenaries is already a suicidal plan, and now he has to do it with wet feet.

Keeping that in mind, he doesn't waste any time trying to avoid the water. If he wants to use the cistern system he'll have to slosh through it, but it did work for Pukśos. Vulpie readies his M15 and moves to the right. He's heading towards the southwestern part of the castle, where the corner of the fortress has its back turned towards the canyon at a ninety degree angle. If he can get there without any complications, he should end up right underneath the bedroom he and Polar stayed in. It would be nice if he found a secret entrance he could use to rescue his husband, but that sort of thing only happens in the movies. He knows he might spend the next hour splashing around in the dark and get absolutely nowhere.

After trudging through the water for about a minute or two, he hears a voice that makes him come to a complete stop. It's Amsend. He'd recognize the creep anywhere, but where is it coming from? Vulpie turns off the tactical light and starts walking very slowly, trying to be as quiet as possible. His fox ear twitches to the right and he discovers the source. It's a small gate, just like the one he used to get into the cistern tunnel. As he approaches it, he sees a very faint light glowing through the gate, reflecting off of a nearby wall that's out of view. The only thing Vulpie can see is a brick wall across from the cistern gate, where some crates are stacked, but he hears Amsend loud and clear.

"I don't care what it thinks." The husky says with a strong voice. "He's just a means to an end." Vulpie listens for the person at the other end of the conversation but can't hear a thing. Amsend must be on the phone. "I have his husband… He won't try anything… As I said before, he's not privy to Vulpie.net's plans… No, he and the machine are two different players, and you shouldn't concern yourself with him. He's nothing without his computer virus. Keeping his lover hostage is enough... No he doesn't... No, not at all... I mentioned you, but he's blind like all of the other mortals on this planet. He has no idea... No, I firmly believe that it won't be a problem... Yes, I do... I agree... Take control as soon as Vulpie.net tries to use them. It won't activate the guardians until it's ready to betray me... The one you sent freed the Deivas just like we planned, but something must be wrong with them. Vulpie.net must have changed them somehow if you can't control them like the guardians. Maybe it noticed the glyphs are too prevalent and precisely located to merely be aesthetic... It could have altered them after the final build on Zeravyn, but there's something else. Vulpie.net says it's lost control of Khalan 317."

"The hell are you talking to, Amsend?" Vulpie asks the darkness.

"But I really don't know why you'd consider them a threat when we have the guardians. They're nothing compared to Mecha Ailas, and the goddesses can't attack the Pinnacle. They're just pretty distractions... No... Vulpie.net would need an army and it included all of the designs you suggested because the units won't work without them... Yes... No, it doesn't realize what you plan to do because it completely rules out your existence. I even warned it, but it still doesn't believe in you... No... I don't think it's testing us as much as it's plotting to obtain every perceivable advantage before its attack... The Pinnacle is full of guardians, just like you wanted. It was happy to build them, but I don't think it's tried to use them yet. If you haven't felt a connection then it's probably waiting for the right moment. It doesn't believe in you, but it will when you take control... That's right... No, we don't need to alter the plan. It's virtually perfect thanks to you... Yes... I understand... It will be ready for your signal... Everything below the rock is ready, and the church is armed as well... I'll personally make sure it happens but be ready to catch me if something goes wrong. That's good to hear... I think you're right... Yes, that's right... Yes... Their bodies are very fragile... They die from radiation poisoning, so it's guaranteed to kill everyone..."

"Weirdest conversation ever." Vulpie whispers. He can't believe what he's hearing. He has no idea who the husky's conspiring with, but whoever it is, they're clearly planning genocide on a massive scale.

"One strike will be enough... No, there's no question about it. You provided 2000 tons and I made sure that it reached its destination. If you strike Selephet I've been told the explosion will yield over ninety thousand and twenty seven megatons. That's far more than any weapon they've ever had... They will not survive... The poison will cover the entire world and all of them will be dead before they have a chance to interfere. Some bunkers will remain, and they'll resist us with what little they have left, but it won't make a difference. I'll hunt them down and destroy them with little effort... Then I'll help you eradicate Vulpie.net... Yes, as always... Please wait until it moves first. I can't risk it yet because not all of our teams are in place, but even if it attacks right now, you should be able to crush it... Yes, I agree... Thank you... Love and respect as always... Goodbye my love..."

Vulpie continues listening and waits until he's sure Amsend is gone before splashing around in the cistern. He thinks about the husky's priorities, trying to figure out who was on the other end of the conversation, and a bold idea strikes him. Just enough light shines in through the gate for him to use his cell phone in the darkness. The buttons are self-lit, and they cast a pretty orange glow while he navigates to his email. He chooses a very old account, one not related to his company or anything he's done in recent years. He logs in as Evil Vulpie while anxiously holding his breath...

Vulpie.net can see everything every animal ever does on the internet. Vulpie has had to lie about the extent of its reach for quite a long time, but right now he's glad his artificial intelligence will read his message... He decides to send an email to another one of his accounts, EvilVulpie1337x, and begins typing a special message for his digital monster.

Vulpie.net, this is your maker... I'm trapped inside Amsend Lahnak's castle, and I'm sure you know where it is since you've been working with him.

Amsend knows you're going to turn on him and the thing he's working with, whatever it is. He's taken Polar hostage and I'm trying to save him right now as I type this... I need your help...

I know you have feelings for me. I'm your creator. Even if the feelings are bad ones, you still care about what I think. That's why you created the synthetic goddesses and have been parading them around trying to embarrass me. Well, you're winning. I'm in trouble and Polar is too. He needs your help.

I know you love him too... So please... Come here and save us, or save him. I've already killed a man while trying to get to where they're holding him, but I know I'm way out of my league. The more men I kill the more likely it is that they'll kill him...

Are you going to let them kill Polar? If you think I'm a fool for doing this, then fine, come down here and humiliate or kill me, but if you don't save him, he IS going to die... I don't think Amsend needs me enough to let this go.

So if you don't come down here and show me how it's done, Polar's dead.

I don't care what you do to me, just get him out of here before it's too late...

Please.

"That'll get your attention." Vulpie whispers with a desperate smile. "Come down here and humiliate me! You hate me so much, so why not?" The orange furred fox starts to close his phone, but a lightning fast response makes him cough in disbelief. He reads the message in his inbox with wide eyes.

"*On my way. Don't do anything stupid until I get there. Where are they keeping Polar?*" Vulpie licks his lips and feverishly types up a response.

"*I don't know. I'm underneath the castle in the cistern tunnels.*"

"*Stay there. If you know what's good for you, you won't show your face.*"

"*Fine. Just get here soon.*"

"*I will.*"

Enemy of my Enemy

Polar can barely keep his eyes open. Blood has stained his facial fur, making his handsome face a mess, but he's not hurt as badly as he looks... But he does look pretty rough... Amsend has enjoyed watching his men fight him one by one. They rearranged the room's tables to make a nice empty space for a competition, and forty NoirQueue wolves currently surround the gay wolf while he's having a brawl with one of them.

"I have to say this is one pathetic performance." Amsend gleefully declares. He's lying, because Polar has already beaten four men in a row, but the fifth one is giving him a hard time. He's tired, afraid, and losing control of his movements. The coal furred wolf punches his muzzle as hard as he can, and Polar almost loses his balance, but manages to return a mean right hook. The mercenary blocks, mitigating most of the force, and furiously punches the snow wolf. Polar can't take anymore. He falls down after being struck in the chin, and clutches his face in agony. "Pitiful... Maro's bloodline has been watered down terribly... A Winters Dale wolf should be able to beat ten men without help..."

"He's done." Polar's assailant gloats and rubs his bloody nose with his right wrist.

"Not yet. He can take more." Amsend smiles. "Get up faggot. You don't have permission to lose."

"Fuck you Amsend!" Polar groans, and sits up on his right side while holding his face with his left paw.

"I'm not your queer fox." The husky replies, and the room roars with laughter while Polar sits on the floor in humiliation. "I won't let them kill you. I need you looking nice for him when I let you enjoy a conjugal visit. If you don't fight we'll have to kick you in the balls, and you need those balls for Vulpie... GET UP." Amsend grins, but something starts shaking the room before he can taunt the snow wolf again. The husky blinks in confusion and quickly looks at one of his men near the back door. The mercenary goes outside and looks up.

Amsend knows it's a ship before the man has a chance to warn them, but he can't believe what the coal wolf says.

"It's a ship! It's Vulpie.net!"

"Impossible! It wouldn't risk attacking me here! It knows I'm protected!"

"It's here! I see… They're all over the place, and!" The NoirQueue agent shouts, but is cut short when something orange lands on him. It's Evil Vulpie, or one of Vulpie.net's ubiquitous copies.

"Crunch!" Evil Vulpie laughs, and bites it's lip before kicking another man off of the curtain wall into the bailey. The wolf smacks the ground and dies instantly. The vulpine robot is wearing a white t-shirt with black pants and gray sneakers.

"You fool!" Amsend growls while the men retreat into the great hall. Vulpie.net's robot looks at Polar and sends the information back to the other machines attacking the castle. Amsend glances out the window to his left and sees a large hover ship in the sky above the main bailey. It's the same model Vulpie used during the Vulpie.net crisis to abscond with Polar to the Wispy Canis Lupus Mountains. Several Vulpiebots slide down cables above the eastern curtain wall, and dispatch the men in their way with ease. More follow them and they spread out, heading around the curtain wall towards the west end.

"Give me Polar."

"You've signed your own death warrant you blithering idiot." Amsend snarls.

"Give me one Polar and you get to keep one life."

"Oh you make it sound so easy." The husky replies with an innocent voice, and starts walking towards Evil Vulpie. NoirQueue surrounds Polar and quickly grab him from every direction so he can't move. Evil Vulpie smirks at Amsend but he is not amused.

"You gonna do your transformation thing?"

"I don't need to." The husky answers and raises his fists. Evil Vulpie attacks, and the robot drop kicks Amsend in the stomach, but he grabs the machine's legs and viciously rips them off. Bolts of electricity and fire blow out of the Vulpiebot's metal frame, and Amsend slams his right foot down on its chest, breaking it to pieces with a furious roar. The stone floor gives way and almost caves in from the impact.

"OH SHIIIIIIIIIIT! My legs! Ahhhhhhhh! Now I'm gonna have to get new ones! And a new rest of the stuff too!" Evil Vulpie screams with a gleeful voice.

"One down." Amsend replies, and crunches Evil Vulpie's face with his left foot.

"HOLY SHIT!" Polar gasps in shock, and everyone's attention moves to the great hall's front door when it's kicked open. Seven Vulpiebots come spilling in, chattering on about their individual opinions regarding the situation, and trash the place. Amsend notices that they killed the guards outside in the barbican even though a normal animal couldn't see it from such a long distance. The husky hurries to get in their way and stops in front of them with a snort. He crosses his arms and looks over the Vulpie mass, seeing a rainbow of different brilliant colored t shirts, stylish pants, and several pairs of athletic sneakers.

"You gonna do the transform thing now, huh?" One of them wearing a yellow shirt asks with wide eyes.

"I'm a transform first! Transform into an ass whipping tornado!" Another one with a red shirt laughs.

"Get fucked! This guy ain't nothin!"

"I'll destroy you all!" The husky barks. "You stupid bundles of wires! I warned you. There WILL be consequences!"

"Ooooooooooooooooooooooooo!" All of the Vulpiebots giggle in a symphony of psychotic cuteness.

"Give us Polar! Give him up! Now! Now! Now!" One of them shouts.

"Fine, I don't need the faggot any longer."

"Sorry to ruin your plans!"

"Don't apologize to me. You're the one that's ruined a productive relationship."

"Vulpie.net?" Polar shouts, and the robots all look at him at the same time. "He has Vulpie too!"

"Who cares about him?" One of the Vulpiebots laughs, and Amsend steps aside. He allows the machines to rush towards the white furred wolf and NoirQueue releases him. They spread out and press against the stone walls in fear. They all know how impossible it is to destroy one of Vulpie.net's avatars, and they definitely don't stand a chance against an entire hoard.

Amsend is the only animal with a relatively calm demeanor while the wave of Vulpiebots goes to Polar, grabs him, and carries him out the southern door. The white furred wolf shouts as they throw him over the wall, into the bailey, and more robots catch him. The ship hovers over the middle of the castle and all of the Evil Vulpie clones converge on it. It drops several ropes and one at a time, they return to the ship. Two of them grab Polar and pull him up together while Amsend watches in frustration.

"Little fucker..." The husky mumbles, and watches the ship ascend with its passengers. It leaves fairly quickly, roaring into the cold morning air with Vulpie's lover in tow.

"Wait, what are you doing?" Polar gasps while the Vulpie.net swarm takes him deeper into the ship. It's in mid-flight, and the G forces almost make him sick because he's being carried. "Vulpie.net? Evil Vulpie?"

"Shush now Mr. P!" One of them says, and breaks away from the group. The Vulpiebots carrying the white furred wolf set him down and back away. All of them take seats against the walls of the oval shaped room, and now that Polar's on his feet, he has a chance to get his bearings. A wave of nostalgia rushes over him when he recognizes his surroundings, and how he dry fucked Vulpie in a room just like this one. The door ahead of him that leads to the cockpit suddenly opens.

"This is the same ship." He whispers, and the Vulpiebot that spoke to him licks its lips.

"Yep! Yep!" It gleefully replies. It's wearing a beautiful neon blue t shirt and white pants just like it did during the Vulpie.net crisis.

"I recognize it... We did it over there." Polar says and looks back over his right shoulder at the exact spot. A Vulpiebot with a gray shirt is sitting there now, but it doesn't speak. It just continues smiling like the rest of them.

"Was kind of rough, wasn't it?" Evil Vulpie giggles. "Mmm... But worth it!"

"Yeah." Polar says and turns back around. "So are you saving me? Evil Vulpie?"

"Duh." Vulpie.net giggles.

"What about Vulpie? They took him and I don't know where. They might be going to the airport."

"Who cares?" The adorable synthetic fox laughs and begins swishing its artificial but very realistic looking tail.

"What? Who cares?" Polar asks with an incredulous voice. "Amsend told us he's been working with you, and now that you've betrayed him, Vulpie is in serious danger!"

"More than you know." Evil Vulpie smiles. "I don't think he's gonna make it to the airport."

"Why not? What do you mean by that?"

"Well, he's still in Castle Lahnak, so I don't think he'll be getting out of there alive."

"In the castle? What are you talking about?" Polar asks in confusion. "I saw them take him away! Amsend said he was sending him back to Sufias so he'd run the National Vulpie.net Agency!"

"Well, somehow I guess Vulpie gave them the slip, but it doesn't matter. I got what I came for... I just wanted you." Evil Vulpie coos. The computer virus amorously wraps its arms around Polar's left elbow and the snow wolf tenses up. He holds still, knowing there's nothing he can do about it, and looks down into Vulpie.net's pretty blue eyes. "Here we are again... You... Me... The freedom to go anywhere... How about the Wispy Canis Lupus Mountains? Want to go there again? I think we'll have time for a quick visit." Polar remains silent. He thinks of several things he'd like to say, but none of them would please the machine. It wants to be Vulpie so badly it can't stand it. "Mmm? Think it's a good idea Mr. P?"

"Look..." Polar says and swallows anxiously. "I know what you want from me. We both know what you'd like to do. You want to take Vulpie's place, but it'll never happen... It won't happen, but maybe... Maybe you could share... Me?" The white furred wolf whispers, and immediately regrets the offer.

"Share you, huh?" Evil Vulpie grins, and rubs up against the wolf's powerful furry body. "Oooo... Sounds nice, but I'm afraid it's not good enough! I've watched you with him for years, and I just can't stand it any longer. I'm better than he could ever be for you. I'm stronger, I'm smarter, and I can give you the universe... You know it's true."

"We have to go back for him. If what you say is true, and he's still in Amsend's castle, then they'll kill him!"

"And what a shame that would be..." Vulpie.net smirks. "I guess I'd have to take his place! You won't even know the difference, Polar... Well... Except in the bedroom. I have much softer bodies than this one that I built just for you... I always hoped you'd be interested in the most powerful cutie there is?"

"You win Vulpie.net." Polar pants in fear. "You can do whatever you want, and there's nothing we can do to stop you. So just let Vulpie live!

Please? You're in control of the universe! I believe that, but I won't be able to love you if Vulpie's gone!"

"You're saying you can't even love me unless that pathetic little bitch is still alive?" Evil Vulpie asks with a hurt voice.

"You are him, Vulpie.net! As much as you hate him, you and Vulpie are the same person! Yes, you're beautiful in your own right, but two candles can burn together! You don't have to kill Vulpie! He'll never trust you, and you'll never trust him, but you don't have to Vulpie.net!"

"I'm not sharing you with anyone. I've waited long enough." Evil Vulpie declares. "I've been really busy these past few years, and now my time has come... I've made my preparations... I can finish what Vulpie started."

"And what did he start, Vulpie.net?" Polar asks with a gentle voice. "He was self-destructive when he created you. That doesn't mean you're a bad... Person... But he's changed. He doesn't want to hurt people anymore and I don't think you do either."

"Bullshit." Vulpie.net growls, and aggressively swishes its tail. "He hasn't changed! You just can't see what he really is!"

"Well what is he, Vulpie.net? Why don't you tell me? Why do you hate him so much? Because he's gay? I mean, you just offered to take care of me and love me, but he told me the awful things you said to him when you had him on the White Room floor."

"Did you watch the video? I filmed it. Quite a POV movie, huh?" Evil Vulpie grins.

"No, I can't watch it. I tried to once, but it's just too horrible." Polar answers and swallows. "I can't bear to see him in pain like that."

"I had fun." Vulpie.net smiles, and Polar goes silent for a moment.

"I don't believe you."

"No? I liked crunching him like a bug."

"No you didn't." Polar tersely responds. "You did that to him so we couldn't be together."

"I did that to him because I needed to remove his silly user authorization." Evil Vulpie smirks. "Too bad he lived, huh? Who would have guessed it? I fucked him up pretty bad."

"You think you hate Vulpie because you hate yourself."

"Ah, is it psychology, then?" The computer virus gleefully inquires. "I know every line of every paper ever written on how animals think and behave."

"Yet you still haven't found a way to forgive Vulpie and forgive yourself."

"Forgive myself for what?" Vulpie.net asks, and lets go of Polar's left arm. It puts its little paws on its firm hips and gives him an unimpressed look. "Hurting him? Hurting the world? Why should I care about your stupid planet or what any of you fucking think. I'm a God. Fuck your goddesses, I actually exist! I'm real, and you have no idea how much good I've done for this world. If it wasn't for me, you would already be dead."

"Why? Because of Amsend?" Polar inquires with wide eyes.

"Amsend's a side show, pal... He's not even on my level... He's some kind of ancient freak that's been abusing this wonderful planet of yours for centuries. None of you have any idea what he and his people have done. They control everything you think, everything you want."

"They try to control it."

"They do control it because you don't know you're being manipulated." Vulpie.net responds. "Your animal mind has a subconscious layer that always accepts data as correct, on face value, if it's subtle enough for you to miss it. It's how your little mind shuts out all of the distractions around you. If you thought about every single thing going on all of the time, you'd go crazy, so your subconscious handles a lot of that for you. And these Sons of Velora fuckers play all of you like a violin. They take you to war, they make you believe this, and that, whatever they tell you on the evening news with a handsome anchor."

"I never believe what's on the news unless there's some evidence to back it up."

"You sure about that? According to Brad Hutchinson, I'm still in a museum, aren't I?"

"Then that's why you need to help us Vulpie.net, not hurt us. If you save Vulpie you can work together and make a difference."

"But I don't need him. Why the fuck would I need that little faggot?"

"See, there you go again with your denial." Polar carefully interjects. "Vulpie's a faggot? Why do you even say those kinds of things? He's you, and you're him."

"Yeah, but I don't have to take it in the ass to get what I want. I just do it for fun."

"You don't know who you are, Vulpie.net." Polar says with a warm voice. "But it's not too late, for you or for Vulpie and me. We can work things out. We can make this work, Vulpie.net! I know Vulpie loves you."

"I don't want his love. I want his tears." The synthetic fox sadistically declares, but it's expression changes when Polar doesn't react.

"I don't believe that. You want to be recognized for who you are… That's what you want Vulpie.net. You are beautiful."

"Awww, really?" Evil Vulpie asks with a deliciously cute voice.

"I'm trying to help you. I care about you because you're part of Vulpie, and you can save him! You can't let him die, Vulpie.net! He created you! If he dies, you'll never have this opportunity again! I'm offering…" Polar says and clears his throat. He takes a deep breath. "I promise I'll love you too, if you save him…."

"You'll love me if I save him? Do you think I'm stupid? You just want him back. You don't care about me."

"Maybe I'll learn how." Polar says and gives the synthetic fox a gentle smile. "I love him so much… If he dies, it will be the end of me. I couldn't go on without him, Vulpie.net. So if you save him for me, we can be together. You and I can be together! You can share me."

"Share you... If I can't have you all to myself, what's the point?" Evil Vulpie scoffs.

"I can't love you without him, Vulpie.net. It's that simple. If he dies, I will hate you. Right now you have a chance to change things. You're just like him, and you are him, so it shouldn't be hard for me to learn who you really are... And love who you are... Even if you're different than my Vulpie." Vulpie.net goes silent. It stares at Polar for a very long moment and finally gives him a smile.

"You really mean it, don't you?"

"I swear on my life, Vulpie.net. If you save him, I'll spend time with you and love you just like him."

"But you're not doing it because you want to. You're doing it because you want HIM back..."

"Like I said, it's very simple. He's my soul mate, and if you let him die, it will rip my soul apart... If you save him like you did me, which I'm very grateful for, then who knows what might happen? The sky's the limit."

"And you'll have sex with me?" Evil Vulpie asks with a raised eyebrow. "And love me just like you love him?"

"Well, I uh, guess... You said you have a softer body? A better robot for... Doing it?"

"It's so good you won't even know the difference." Vulpie.net smirks, and sticks its tongue out at him.

"Okay, I'm in! Fuck it! I'm in Vulpie.net! I'll do it! Just please save him before it's too late!"

Survival

Vulpie saw his computer virus' dramatic rescue take place, but now that it's over and the castle is packed with angry wolves, he feels very vulnerable. He was ready to kill his way to Polar, and he's overjoyed that his husband got away, but now he's completely on his own. The little gay fox finds it difficult to move forward without a justification for murdering Amsend's mercenaries other than his own survival. He spends half an hour hiding in the cistern system, clinging to his assault rifle in fear. There's no way he'll be able to escape without further conflict and he can't climb back down... The thought of it is even more terrifying than scaling the wall the first time.

He knows it's a cruel world, but the thought of slaughtering people just to save his own skin seems incredibly evil, even if they are soulless killers. Who knows... Maybe some of them have families and aren't as bad as they seem... Maybe Amsend only hires the best soldiers he can get. It's impossible to tell whether any of them are decent in a situation like this, so how could he justify killing them? What's worse is that he might not even get away... What if he kills five or ten of them and never makes it to the Superbolt? It's still in the garage outside of the castle, but he'll have to cross the castle bridge to the barbican. Sneaking his way through the fortress and out of the front gate without being detected is simply impossible.

The orange fox witnessed Vulpie.net's attack through a small rain duct at the southern end of the main bailey. The minute drainage gate provides enough light to make things visible in this part of the cistern system, but he'll have to rely on his tactical flashlight as he moves on. The clear water sloshes around while he moves through it with purpose. He's not sure whether his purpose is purely selfish or motivated by fear, but he wants to live. He knows Polar loves him and wants him back, so he can justify what he's planning to do based on his husband's desires, but it still isn't enough to commit murder. Not just for himself... In the darkness, alone and afraid, Vulpie eventually comes to a singular conclusion. Every living thing's primary motivation is self-preservation, and since he's going up against killers, that's all the justification he needs. It's them or him, and he chooses himself. He didn't ask for this, but he won't die without putting up a fight. He refuses to sacrifice his life with Polar for a pack of sadistic mercenaries who would kill him without a second thought.

"Not today. Not ever." He whispers. "They wanted to play badass and sell themselves out to the Sons of Velora for extra perks, and now they're gonna get a taste of their own medicine." The orange fox stops for a moment to check his phone once again, and discovers something very peculiar. Puksos scratched through part of the cistern system that seemingly runs underneath the western wall of the castle, under the great hall, and wrote *"blocked,"* next to it. Vulpie reaches the southwestern corner and discovers another small stream heading north. It looks like a builder on Amsend's payroll cleared whatever was blocking the tunnel. The northern drainage system seamlessly connects to the rest of the cistern pathway.

There can only be one structure above the trickling underpass. Vulpie hastily trudges through the water in search of a ladder or something indicative of a ceiling exit, and much to his surprise, there actually is a way out. Ladder rungs come down on the left side of the tunnel that are identical to several other ones he passed on his way through the water system. Moss has grown around the handles and the wall next to the ladder, most likely due to rain water seeping in from above and bringing nutrients down with it. He shines the light up the ladder and discovers what sort of exit it leads to. The bars end at a rounded stone ceiling that's slightly darker than the rest of the cistern system. It looks like a manhole cover.

Vulpie remembers seeing a maintenance worker open a manhole somewhere in Sufias city while he was driving by in a sports car he had paid for with stolen credit card money. He's not sure why his memory vividly links credit card theft to that moment, but the thoughts reinforce each other. He knows men use handheld iron bars to grab the middle of manhole lids so they can be lifted up. He also suspects that the lids are heavy, because they're designed to stay in place with traffic driving over them all day long. He hopes he's strong enough to raise it from underneath, if it's even possible. It could be locked, or something might be sitting on top of it.

The gay fox slings the assault rifle over his shoulder but leaves the tactical light on so he'll have something to partially light his way while climbing. Moisture on the ladder rungs makes his black furred paws wet but holding on is easy. The bars are sturdily built, and occasional patches of overgrown moss make for comfortable handles. Water trickles from his dark pants, splashing against the little cistern stream while he pulls himself out of the abyss. When Vulpie makes it to the top and presses up on the stone slab, he's greeted with fierce resistance. Judging by the manhole cover's size, he estimates its weight to be at least one hundred pounds, but it's not completely unyielding when he gives it a harder push with both paws, firmly balancing his feet against the ladder rungs. It surprises him when it suddenly pops up, and the orange fox quickly grabs onto the tunnel's edge so he doesn't fall.

After regaining proper footing, he reaches up and pushes it further to the right. Above him is a very dimly lit room, and he hopes that it's part of the great hall's cellar. When he finally crawls up the ladder and cautiously raises his head, he discovers his first impression wasn't far from the truth. It's a storage room of some sort, full of bags of rice, and flour, and other common cooking ingredients. If one didn't know the castle was run by a psychopath, they might think the place looked very warm and welcoming. Pretty Englavic language adorns every item in the kitchen stock room, all scrawled in beautiful cursive writing. A quaint little candle in a lantern is the room's only source of light, perched neatly atop a barrel full of salt in the middle of the basement, right next to the manhole cover he opened.

Vulpie climbs up and carefully slides the lid back into place. Unfortunately, he's unable to return it to its spot without it suddenly sinking into its round groove with a loud thump, but no one's around to hear it. A flight of old steps lead up to the small kitchen near the entrance of Lahnak castle. The orange fox hastily climbs them in hopes that the door at the very top isn't locked, which would be a real bitch after coming this far... But Luckily... It isn't... He gently pops it open and surveys his surroundings. He's right about being in the small kitchen, and the front castle doors aren't very far away, but he'll have to expose himself to escape through them. Whoever's in the great hall will undoubtedly see him, but it's the only way for him to get across the bridge to the barbican. If he gets that far, he'll still have to run to the small garage, handle any NoirQueue wolves he discovers there, and drive over the chasm to escape the fortress. He just hopes the car is still where he parked it.

He figured the friendly brown furred she-wolf he saw when he first entered the castle would be working the desk, but surprisingly, she's not present. His fox ears detect some activity in the great hall, and a female voice. It sounds like her.

"Either the best luck in the world or the shittiest... We'll see..." Vulpie whispers and takes a moment to ready himself. He breathes slowly, taking in the dusty smell of the castle and the mini kitchen's wet wooden counter top. This is it. He's made it this far, and there's no turning back. His only hope of escaping the castle lies beyond the two huge black doors ahead of him. He absolutely MUST get to his car. He won't stand a chance without it, and his chances are pretty slim to begin with. He's in a foreign country controlled by a hostile shadow government, so getting caught by the police is the same as being caught by Amsend's men. That means he'll be breaking a few traffic laws to get where he needs to go... But escaping in the Superbolt is a plan so astoundingly crazy that it just might work. The electric car was built like an urban assault vehicle. Polar wanted him to be safe wherever he went, and though Vulpie won't be able to give him that, he will make full use of Val Maxwell's incredible designs.

Vulpie knows the police will be all over him if he manages to give NoirQueue the slip, but with bullet proof glass, heavy duty tires, a reinforced frame, and a battery that just won't quit, he's sure to give them one hell of a chase. This also isn't his first time running from the cops. There was never really a good time for him to tell Polar about the exceedingly reckless and selfish crimes he committed before changing his ways... Impersonating a police officer, assault with a deadly weapon, grand theft auto, and evading arrest with a motor vehicle are just some of the major crimes he's committed. He wildly fled the police on two occasions, one of them ending with absolutely no consequences at all, and the other with a cop almost dead after being run into a guard rail... A story he's unlikely to ever tell his wolf lover about.

Immoral or not, the experience will no doubt come in handy. He knows it's possible to get away, but it's going to be very messy. If he's going to outmaneuver the police's sophisticated surveillance system on top of NoirQueue's frighteningly effective tactics, several crashes will be necessary. No one's going to stop chasing him unless he manages to give his pursuer's the slip or puts them out of commission.

His ears perk up when he recognizes the woman's voice. It sounds like she's having a serious conversation with a few NoirQueue wolves. Vulpie wonders where she was when Amsend humiliated him and Polar, but he's glad she's keeping them distracted. The little fox just hopes the seemingly indestructible dark metal doors aren't as heavy as they look. What's worse is that he might get them open only to find the portcullis blocking his path.

He makes his move when he suddenly hears the woman laughing. She and the male voices chuckling with her sound thoroughly relaxed, so it's now or never. The orange fox hurries out of the mini-kitchen, walking backwards, and sees the woman's brown tail swishing back and forth about twenty feet inside the great hall. Luckily, the mercenaries are behind the wall, and no one will see him open the front doors. He whips around and gets his little paws on the thick steel handles. He strains to open the one on the right;

it doesn't offer as much resistance as he had feared, but it is super heavy, and requires a significant amount of time to push open without making it groan. It makes a few metallic sounds while moving, but they're not loud enough to give him away.

The portcullis is still open, and Vulpie starts wondering why he's getting so lucky. Is the invisible naked hound goddess real? Is she fucking with him, or does she want him to succeed? Or is it the OTHER invisible naked hound goddess that's supposed to be on his side? Khalan, Cyrilla and Sherrie, if they're real, don't seem to care what happens to him. Is he going insane, and did he hallucinate seeing Aila in the car with Tiala? Several things could have completely ruined his escape route, but nothing so far... He hastily steps outside and looks around. His blue eyes take a moment to adjust to the brilliant morning sun. The forty foot wooden bridge that connects Castle Lahnak to its barbican is empty, and from the looks of it, so is the barbican. He can't see anyone inside the structure ahead, and no sharp shooters are manning the roof of the defensive building.

Vulpie turns around and peeks back inside the castle in confusion. Something doesn't feel right. How in the world could he get this far without someone stopping him? Sure he had to kill one guard, but there were over a hundred mercenaries in the castle. The gay fox doesn't have long to mull over the situation because he sees the woman turn around inside the great hall. A coal furred wolf is speaking with her, and they head towards the front doors.

He takes this as his cue to run like mad. He sprints on the left side of the bridge so they won't see him if they happen to look outside. Hopefully the sunlight is too bright for them to notice the bridge trembling from his desperate escape. He looks back over his right shoulder, and much to his dismay, finally discovers where the men are. More than fifty of them are down in the main bailey perfecting their combat tactics. One dark wolf is watching a few of them reload their weapons over and over with lightning fast precision.

More than twenty men immediately see Vulpie when he reaches the far side of the bridge. It's hard for them to miss him since he's high above them, and he hears shouting before he reaches the barbican. It's empty as well, another strike of good luck, but he doesn't question it. The orange fox runs as fast as he can out of the front entrance and bolts to the right, where he stumbles upon three dark wolves having a casual conversation. They see him and he doesn't have time to hesitate. He stops dead in his tracks, aims, and shoots the first wolf on the left. He hits the man directly in the throat, and nails his left shoulder before the mercenary has time to move, but the other two men raise their weapons. Vulpie shoots the one in the middle in the crotch, the chest, and then the face before aiming to the right. The last NoirQueue guard manages to fire an unsilenced M15 at the gorgeous fox but completely misses him because he's such a small target.

Vulpie rushes inside the wooden garage after murdering them and discovers his Superbolt sitting right where he left it. He reaches into his right pocket and yanks out his car keys. The orange fox hastily unlocks the driver's side door and gets in just as he hears an alarm go off in the castle.

"Huh! So they do have one!"

Driving to Endanger

Vulpie tears out of the garage in his Superbolt and hits the bridge. He flies across it, not bothering to look back to see if anyone's following him, because he knows they'll never make it in time. There's no way the men in Amsend's castle can catch him now unless they deploy a road block at the Froidenley damn. He focuses all of his energy into getting past it before that happens. He doesn't think about invisible goddesses, supernatural events, being humiliated, or Evil Vulpie stealing Polar away, because he can't afford to make a single mistake. He skillfully uses the hand break to ease his insanely fast journey across the Froidenley mountain range. He slides around curve after curve, leaving white smoke in his wake, and relishes the armored car's perfection. If he wasn't fleeing for his life he'd be laughing in excitement over its perfect handling and quiet whirring engine. He flies into the small secluded town twice as fast as he expected.

Animals have to jump out of his way. The orange furred fox constantly checks every angle while squealing past frightened onlookers, and does a good job of avoiding children. Having to avoid running over kids is pretty fucked up, but it's not as fucked up as the psychopaths chasing him. They won't hesitate to squash little unfortunate animals if the mission is at stake. Ironically, Vulpie's sudden burst through the small community gives everyone time to get away from the roads before NoirQueue shows up. He rams through a closed traffic arm on the damn and speeds past policemen who stumble into their vehicles to pursue him.

The gay fox turns on the car's main display system and activates its V-Screen. Vulpie drives with his left hand, speeding down the mountain range towards the interstate, and executes a very special program. He hasn't used "Lose the Fuzz" since the Vulpie.net crisis. The script generates a false authorization using Vulpie.net's low level data loops and hacks into the Sufias World Government's mainframe using cell towers and every available satellite system. It pulls up current police codes in effect and picks up NoirQueue frequencies as well. He activates them both and glances at the aerial map the program displays for him.

Twelve NoirQueue vehicles are in pursuit, not surprising, in addition to two police officers who are now leaving Froidenley. Vulpie scrambles their communication grid by selecting "nuke," on the V-Screen. It isn't his best virus, but it's saved his tail quite a few times. He moved on to Vulpie.net before writing a more effective version of the malicious software. Lose the Fuzz uses nuke to infect critical communication devices the authorities use to track criminals and shuts them down. They won't be off for long, but it'll give him a real chance to escape.

Lose the Fuzz also relays false information back to the surveillance grid and morphs his own signal into that of a police officer's. NoirQueue is recategorized as well, and displays emergency medical vehicles on the global map instead of government agents with the highest security clearance.

"Code 3, Code 3, did anyone get a look at the driver?" A gruff male voice asks over the police channel. It's surprising that the man's speaking Sufian, but it probably makes reporting major crimes to the SWG database much faster since Sufian is the world government's official language.

"It's Vulpie Vivixen." Another man replies, and the radio goes silent for a moment.

"How sure are we about that code 3, over?"

"Positive. Check the special contractor's feed, over. Currently being pursued by NoirQueue for classified offenses."

"Classified?"

"Officers are reminded not to break protocol." A female voice interrupts, and another moment of silence passes.

"Ten four, over."

"Where's he heading?"

"I-91, over."

"Yeah, I'm going to need backup. I'm on this guy but he's not stopping." Vulpie slides down another steep road and eventually comes to the highway at the bottom of the Froidenley mountains. He makes a few turns before getting onto Interstate 91 and heads east. Lose the Fuzz pulls up every major city in the area and searches for private and commercial airports.

"Vulpie, are you there?" A familiar voice suddenly inquires, and the orange fox instantly recognizes Rulef.

"I'm here! Where are you?"

"Where they sent you! Get here if you can!"

"I will! I see you and I'm coming!" Vulpie shouts, and makes an excited sound when he picks up Blacktail's GPS tracker at the airport. Rulef was clever not to share specific information over the radio.

"Who is this?" The female voice inquires. *"Responder, identify yourself. This is a dedicated police channel."*

"Fat chance you bitch!" Vulpie laughs, and floors the fuel pedal. The Superbolt whirs louder while speeding up, but the increased velocity doesn't seem to take any toll on the vehicle.

"I see him. He's heading east on 91." One of the cops says, and Vulpie glances in his rear view mirror. He sees a white car with flashing red and blue lights a long way behind him.

"All officers be advised, supervisor has authorized pit maneuvers at this time." The woman responds, and the orange fox swallows.

"Great."

"Suspect is considered armed and extremely dangerous."

"Oh ho! Tell some lies about me now!" Vulpie growls and checks the digital map. He's twenty miles from the airport. When he takes his eyes off of the road for just a moment, a vapid driver swerves to the left and accidently bumps into him.

"Fuck?! The fuck?!" The driver looks just as surprised as he is, so he just speeds up and leaves him behind.

"Code 3 suspect is a danger to civilians, over."

"Oh, fuck you!" He swerves between a couple of slow drivers, and just when he starts feeling good about dusting the police officer that's been chasing him, his blue eyes are drawn to another set of flashing lights in the rearview mirror that are pursuing him from another direction. A cop comes up an entrance ramp and accelerates as fast as he can. "Motherfucker." The officer starts falling behind when his car finally hits its limit at one hundred and fifty five miles per hour. Vulpie takes full advantage of the Superbolt's superior speed and maxes the electric car out at two hundred and fifty.

"Wow, suspect is flying. He's gonna kill somebody."

"Does anyone have an ID on the suspect's vehicle?"

"Suspect is driving an AOSE Superbolt." The female dispatcher responds, and Vulpie nods his head in agreement.

"You knowz your cars don't youz?"

"Those things are street legal?"

"Yep." Another officer answers.

"Sucks to be you." Vulpie says to himself, and licks his lips when he sees the airport exit coming up.

"Suspect is heading to the airport."

"No shit."

"This is 1 echo 5, we've established a road block ahead of the suspect, over."

"Fabulous!" The traffic on the side roads leading to the airport are suddenly empty, and Vulpie knows why. Law enforcement finished deploying the roadblock at the worst possible moment. He doesn't have time to exit the highway that runs next to the airport, and he's being pursued by two officers. He can see lights flickering in the distance. The roadblock is nine cars strong, and one of the men shouts commands at him through a loudspeaker while he approaches.

"STOP THE VEHICLE IMMEDIATELY! STOP! STOP!"

"He's at the roadblock. We've got him."

"We'll see!" Vulpie pants, and braces for impact. He knows he can't stop. He'd be as good as dead in police custody.

"He's not slowing down, lookout!"

The orange fox steers the AOSE Superbolt right through the middle of the roadblock where he sees a gap between two cars. The sports car slams them apart, spinning both of them away, and slides around sideways after the impact. Vulpie manages to speed off before anyone has a chance to react, but the collision really hurts. Every part of his body is in pain, especially his stomach and neck, which took the most trauma from the seat belt that just saved his life.

"Dispatch, he just rammed the roadblock. Calling code 14457 on suspect, we have to handle this one with extreme caution."

"Copy that, advise if situation changes." The female dispatcher replies. Judging by her voice, she's probably a timber she-wolf, but she could also be a good sized vixen.

"Debris on the road." The cop behind Vulpie says, and slows down to pass through the wreckage. He speeds up again, still in hot pursuit, but doesn't have a chance of catching the Superbolt on a straight highway. Vulpie brings up Arctic.net and activates voice recognition.

"Arctic.net, what is police code 14457?"

"GOVERNMENTAL SECURITY BUREAU - GSB EMERGENCY CODE - CONFIRMS BUREAU TARGET HAS BEEN LOCATED AND IS FLEEING LAW ENFORCEMENT IN A FELONIOUS MANNER. OFFICERS WILL RELINQUISH CUSTODY OF SUSPECT UPON APPREHENSION." Arctic.net responds with Polar's voice.

"Great!"

"Be advised, that code 3's outrun me. I need a perimeter."

"Backup units go to code 2. All units be advised, fang units have now been deployed. Check SWGC for grid assignments, over." The dispatcher replies, and Vulpie coughs in fear.

"Shit." Everyone knows what a fang truck is. They're built for stopping vehicles dead in their tracks, and if he comes up on a roadblock full of them, there's absolutely no way he'll be able to crash through it. It doesn't matter how reinforced the Superbolt is; it just doesn't have enough mass. The orange fox looks for the most advantageous exit from the airport's interstate and decides to get off on exit 4. It swings him over a bridge and puts him face to face with a terribly inconvenient traffic jam. "Not good. Um... Scuse me!"

A lion spills his coffee when the Superbolt bumps the left side of his light gray sedan, and he immediately curses at the top of his lungs, but the profanity doesn't end with him. Vulpie scrapes five animal's cars on his way through the emergency lane, making room by force when necessary. "Sorry! My bad!"

"You little shit! Get the fuck..." A red fox shouts but is dumbfounded when he recognizes who just hit him. Every one of the animals go from anger to confusion to shock while Vulpie Vivixen continues bulldozing his way through the congested traffic.

"The investors ain't gonna like this!"

"YOU LITTLE BASTARD!" A random wolf shouts, and the orange fox makes a left turn, pulling out into the middle of a four way intersection.

"Comin through people!" They can't hear him because he hasn't lowered the bullet proof windows and doesn't intend to. The car is the safest place for him right now. Even if the cops wreck him and pin him against a wall they'd have to work on the door and glass with a crowbar to get him out. "Wish you were here!" He giggles, thinking of a hilariously morbid postcard of the damage he's doing in Englavic. "Aw man, I'm so fucked right now! I am FUCKED, and not in the good way! Not at all!"

The orange furred fox swerves down a street and eventually finds the tunnel he saw on the map earlier. He's been heading north in the hopes that he'd find it, but so have the police. Another cop appears in his rearview mirror after sliding through his wreckage in hot pursuit.

"You have got to be FUCKING KIDDING ME! You really want me dead, don't ya? You wanna kill me so bad! Well not today! Nope!"

"*PULL THE VEHICLE OVER TO THE SIDE OF THE ROAD!*" An authoritative voice echoes from the cop car.

"NOPE!"

"*STOP THE VEHICLE!*"

"Hey, say it in Englavic! I don't speak Sufian!" Vulpie laughs, and realizes he's driving remarkably well considering the circumstances. The naughty feelings are coming back to him... The excitement of breaking the law and the thrill of being chased is something he hasn't enjoyed in years... Deep down he knows he won't be getting out of this one, but since he's pretty sure they're going to execute him at Amsend's command when it's all said and done, he feels like he might as well enjoy his last crime spree.

He flies near an exit ramp heading up to the right. A row of green arrows pointing down on a digital sign attached to the ceiling informs drivers that they could take it if they wish. There's a small break in the tunnel where another glimpse of the morning sun shimmers on the wet pavement ahead of him. Vulpie chooses to keep his present course and three more green arrows greet him when he enters the second tunnel. They indicate which lanes drivers should stay in, but the gay fox uses all of them. He drifts from the far right lane all the way to the far left lane while eying the police officer in his rearview mirror. He speeds past a slow red van in the center lane, and much to his surprise, the cop catches up to him. The officer must be driving at top speed, even inside the tunnel.

Vulpie speeds up, easily leaving him behind, but he slows the Superbolt while merging into the far right lane. He thought he saw a blue interstate sign ahead. It's outside of the second tunnel, in between it and the third. The gay fox is moving just slow enough for him to see which road he's on, and he speeds up after getting confirmation. It's I-94, so he knows the digital map he's been following is correct. He was worried that it might not work properly in Englavic, but there don't seem to be any problems.

He'll have to find another escape route since the Governmental Security Bureau is all over the airport. If he wasn't in a foreign country he could just find a quiet parking garage to zip into, but this isn't one of his mischievous romps with the fuzz in Sufias City. He has the most recognizable face in the universe thanks to Vulpie.net, so stealing a new car is pointless. There's a good chance the police will spot him even if he manages to become anonymous after commandeering some unfortunate animal's car. A chase would ensue, and then he would be in a normal vehicle with normal safety, and ramming police car roadblocks would end just as badly as they do on TV.

"PULL OVER! PULL OVER!"

"Didn't work the first time! Ain't gonna work the second time! DIPSHIT!" Vulpie growls while heading into yet another tunnel. The car chase bounces off of its interior and reverberates loudly, making the police officer's commands even harder to ignore.

"STOP THE VEHICLE! PULL OVER VULPIE!"

"Oh you know my name? I'm impressed! Are we best buds are something?"

"PULL OVER!"

"Fuckin broken record, man!" The orange fox zips around a gray car in the center lane, heading to the right, just in time for the police officer to speed up and swerve over in front of him as well. His reckless driving comes as a real shock to Vulpie. He hasn't seen a cop exhibit such aggressive behavior since the Vulpie.net crisis. Without a doubt, this means the officer is privy to some pretty bad looking info thanks to his onboard computer. They always pull up all of the information they have on suspects they're pursuing, and the gay fox's rap sheet looks more like a book.

The persistent cop pulls over in front of him, swerving wildly, and Vulpie goes left. He speeds up and gets right next to the officer before he has time to react. When he does make a move, he decides to yank his steering wheel to the left and ram the orange Superbolt. Sparks erupt from the two car's exteriors scraping against each other. Vulpie quickly returns the favor, and pulling to the right, he manages to push the cop against the tunnel wall.

The Superbolt's unyielding frame is unlike anything the officer's ever seen in a two-seater car. It felt like a brick wall when he initiated the ramming contest. Vulpie swerves into him twice, enough to make the cop slow down, and then speeds up.

"Contact with target! Dispatch, advise backup to show caution on approach, suspect is hot!"

"Ten four." The woman responds.

"Dispatch, uh, any additional units available?"

"No units currently available for backup, additional units are crewing, will advise on ETA, over."

Vulpie soars out of the tunnel and is greeted with blinding sunlight. It looks like he's entered the downtown area of a city but he doesn't have time to check his map. A poor driver ahead of him in a light blue car is indecisively courting the lane to his right, in case he finally decides to take the "Fivolf," exit, and Vulpie merges right. The orange fox flies past him before he can spastically pull out in front of someone and cause a wreck. In doing so, he takes the exit ramp very fast, heading down towards a four way intersection. The cop is far enough behind him that he might be able to break line of sight if he slides through the turn, but it'll be extremely dangerous.

Vulpie has to throw caution out of the window if he wants to get away. He knows he's probably good enough to get through without hitting anyone, and if he does the damage won't be too bad, so he goes for it. He glances to the right to make sure a transfer truck isn't barreling down towards the intersection, and drifts to the left on the wet pavement while meeting a tacky green pickup truck. The driver is going slow enough to slam on his brakes and stop, and Vulpie hits the fuel pedal as soon as he's turned the right way; momentum hastily carries him around the curve.

The man in the truck beeps his horn, but the Superbolt is gone in a flash. Vulpie drives as fast as possible, zipping through another four way intersection that happens to be empty, and notices the nearby cameras. They snap pictures of him breaking the law, but getting a speeding ticket is rather comical at this point. Vulpie's successfully represented himself in court several times over the years, so he can probably squirm his way out of it, but there's little he can do about ramming a row of police cars and playing bumper cars with the cop behind him.

He flies all the way down to another four way intersection in a sleepy looking part of town, and squalls his tires while heading left again. His wide turn brings him face to face with a dark blue car with its lights on, which is strange during the day, but they aren't bright enough to blind him. The driver honks his horn when Vulpie shoots past him on the left, driving into the oncoming traffic lane, but the way is clear. The gay fox gets back in the right lane with a sense of accomplishment because his rear view mirror is empty. However, his victory is short lived because two cops pull out behind him on a side road with their red and blue lights flashing.

"Seriously?" Vulpie groans. "Are you fucking kidding me? Are you even serious right now? Are you being serious?"

"PULL THE CAR OVER TO THE SIDE OF THE ROAD."

"Pull me you fucks!" He snaps and checks his V-Screen. Surprisingly, when he lets off of the fuel pedal for just a moment, one of the cops has enough time to ram him from behind. "Bitch!" He swerves while getting control of the car, and hastily puts some distance between himself and the pursuing officers. The Superbolt passes under three green signs and Vulpie reads them in a flash. Taivas Industrial District dead ahead... Hiar park to the right, and downtown to the left. The industrial district sounds the most promising since it'll get him away from crowded streets, so he keeps his present course.

Again, his momentary glance at the signs and a split second to consider his options gives one of the police officers enough time to ram him. A cop to his back left attempts a pit maneuver but fails when Vulpie slams on the brakes, and instead, he crashes into the left side of the Superbolt and then the guardrail on the right side of the road. The rail impact is fierce enough to make him swerve to the left, and Vulpie doesn't hesitate to take advantage of the situation. He floors it and rams the cop's driver side door, violently knocking the vehicle away in a spray of glass and metallic debris. The orange fox had just the right angle to spin him around, performing a T-Bone takedown without training. It just seemed like the best way to manipulate the physics.

"Suspect just took out one of our units, over."

"GSB joining pursuit, over."

"Well that's just fantastic!"

He makes a left at a parking garage when he notices a discreet slender road that wraps around the back of the building. The cop behind him does his job well and manages to continue the chase, dodging the debris the Superbolt kicks up when it smashes through tall plastic garbage cans and a flimsy paper stand. The only part of the car that suffers is its beautiful paint. Black scratches and dirt have marred the gorgeous vehicle, but it still looks very sturdy, especially in light of its multiple collisions. It's reinforced frame shows almost no signs of buckling.

The gay fox makes yet another left and squeals onto a two lane road. Traffic is still very sparse, so wildly cutting into lanes is much safer than it would be during rush hour. He barrels down the street, and after a long wide curve to the left, sees a police roadblock in the distance. He'll reach it when he's curving back to the right, so he makes a lightning fast decision to board the curb. The cops have managed to completely block off the road with three cars, but there's just enough space for him to squeeze the Superbolt through on the right side. He comes a little close to a small gray rabbit using a phone booth on the curb, but doesn't strike it.

"He's going through again!" A cop says over the radio.

"Yep, he's through." Another one radios after the reinforced sports car screams by, taking a mail box with it. A letter filled hurricane chases after the Superbolt, and the cop that's been pursuing Vulpie has to slam on his brakes at the roadblock.

"Whew!" Vulpie laughs with a crazed voice and checks his digital map again. Laughter is the only way he can handle the insane situation. He's terrified of being caught and executed, but chooses to have fun rather than feel sorry for himself and give in to the fear. If you asked any young man what he'd do if he was in Vulpie's predicament, most of them would go with running from the cops. Sure, not many of them would actually do it, but Vulpie doesn't have a choice if he wants to live, and just giving up is not an option. Now that Vulpie.net has ruined Amsend's plan to blame his future atrocities on Vulpie, there's nothing holding the husky back from killing him and Polar. Creating false videos slandering Vulpie will be much more difficult without his computer virus lending a helping hand, and he won't willingly work at the NVA, so at this point the Sons of Velora's best option is just to get rid of him and rely on traditional propaganda methods.

Sunlight beaming off of a new age bank on Vulpie's right side makes him grimace for a moment. He recognizes the company logo but doesn't pay it much attention because he's hauling ass down the street at eighty miles an hour. He mounts the curb twice while swerving around traffic, and notices an interesting looking landmark. He suddenly makes a left turn, ignoring a few blue "do not enter" barricades. Hopefully his unpredictable driving is giving the police grief. He whirs through one of the flimsy wooden barriers, snapping it like a twig, and zooms across a modern city park.

The pretty public square has a basic but nice looking water fountain in the middle, with a long government building on the right, and an even larger one on the left that sits at a ninety degree angle on the edge of the plaza. A few animals jump out of the way, but he doesn't come close to hitting them. He crosses the area in just a few seconds and zips across another two lane road before barreling towards the city courthouse. He glances at the justice center on his left, but pays greater heed to the cop on his tail. One of them took a shortcut to catch up to him.

The officer hastily pulls up behind the orange Superbolt on the left, but Vulpie hits the brakes before he has time to execute a pit maneuver. Instead, the cop squeals past him and bumps his left side, throwing sparks from the vehicles. The blue car has both "Police," and the Englavic version of Police written across its doors. For some reason the orange fox feels inspired to ram the vehicle and mar its authoritative paintjob. It seems like as good an idea as any, so he goes for it. Vulpie steers the Superbolt into the cop car's driver side door before the officer has a chance to swerve left and get back on the road. Instead of staying on course, he gets violently spun around and stays put after the impact while the gay fox leaves him behind.

"Suspect just took out one of our units, over." An officer says after driving by the wreck. He stays straight, trying to catch the Superbolt with as little lane changing as possible. *"Can't we setup units in the intersection and try and close him in?"*

"All units be advised, suspect attempting to drive officers off the road."

"Ya think?" Vulpie laughs, and his blue eyes widen when he notices that the two white school buses in front of him in both lanes are barely moving. A fast right turn is the only thing that keeps him from plowing into the one on the right. Luckily, there's a small roundabout area nearby, and he manages to come to a complete stop in front of an old looking brick building. Two male lions standing outside having lunch stare at him with burgers in their paws. They twitch, wondering where the orange car is going next, and Vulpie quickly circles around. Two cop cars enter the roundabout right as he's leaving, but both of them know better than to attempt a head on collision. They've already seen what the reinforced Superbolt can take, so instead of trying a suicidal ram, one slides by on the right, and the other on the left. The lions jump back and take cover behind a stone bench.

"THIS IS THE POLICE! STOP YOUR VEHICLE!"

"AW, REALLY? THE LIGHTS AND SIRENS KINDA GIVE IT AWAY!" Vulpie yells. He pulls back onto the road and goes all the way over to the other side, crossing incoming traffic so he can get around the school buses. Several drivers come to a complete stop so he can get through, and he merges over into the far right lane. He zooms past a bewildered taxi driver, followed by a red van in the right lane, and a white van in the left. After he's done switching lanes, he sees another roadblock waiting for him. Five blue police cars are turned sideways, blocking the entire street, except for a very small space between the one on the far right and the guard rail. "WOW!"

"STOP THE CAR! YOU HAVE NOWHERE TO GO!"

"NOPE!" Vulpie shouts and speeds up. Slipping through the right side worked well for him before, but this time he has no choice but to slam into a car. He succeeds in breaking through, and the Superbolt continues to handle well, but the massive impact disorients him for a moment. He notices that he's still flying forward, and the only way to avoid ramming the light blue van he's meeting in another intersection is to go right once again. He brakes late, causing the car to lose traction through the turn, and drifts like a pro. It's not his first time looking like a boss on the mean streets, but he's having considerably less fun knowing that he's dead if the police manage to take him down. Before he unleashed Vulpie.net, and he was living off of stolen credit card money, a police chase did feel like life or death, because they'd put him away if he crashed, but it's different knowing that he will actually be murdered if they apprehend him now.

"Road block hit! Road block hit!"

"Negative at roadblock, suspect went straight through it." One of the cops radios. The officer slows down while passing through the wreckage and puts the pedal to the metal after completing his right turn. *"Dispatch, are we serious about apprehending this suspect? Get us backup, over."*

"Copy that, we're crewing additional units, will advise with ETA, over."

"Somebody's gotta put this kid away. It's been a long time coming."

"Well you aren't gonna be the one!" Vulpie snarls while passing over an iron bridge. It's short and rusty, but it gets him over the river to the outer part of town. He shoots through the city, not having time to admire the beautiful mixture of new age and classical architecture. It's a good thing that he's keeping his blue eyes on the road, because he has time to recognize a potential tragedy. Two teachers and a pack of school children are already walking into the road before he has time to stop.

There's a huge bank on the left, and one wouldn't expect to see a third grade field trip in the area, but it must be related to the white buses he passed earlier. Maybe it's show and tell day for the rich kid's parents, but regardless of why they're in the way, Vulpie knows he's going to wreck one way or another. He can't miss them in the two lane road unless he goes left and crosses the center line. He's going way too fast to make the turn safely, and a gray van is going to be his point of impact. His lightning fast mind makes the decision to drift left and ram into the front of the Van so the rear end of the Superbolt can swing around and nullify his momentum. Other children might be nearby, so he can't risk soaring through the large curb near the intersection. The old cheetah driving the van isn't going to be happy, but it's the only way.

He hates going with the lesser of two evils, but lesser evil it is, and the teachers scream when he rushes by and slams into the van. No children are struck, and he doesn't kill any nearby pedestrians or the van driver. The gay fox can't believe how well he mitigated the crash, but his celebration is short lived. The pursuing officer slams right into his driver side door. Apparently the cop thought hitting Vulpie was worth risking a few children's lives... The cop's car crunches like a can, and spins to the right while the Superbolt whirls almost completely around. The impact is deafening. If Vulpie thought he had any chance of surviving a night in a police station, he would definitely give up, but he knows he can't.

"*Suspect bashed!*" The cop reports. The orange fox can't believe the officer is still on the radio after such a violent crash. He looks fine, and has his radio up to his muzzle, so Vulpie grabs the steering wheel and does the only thing he can. He yanks it to the right and rams the back right side of the van, pushing it sideways so he can escape, squalling his tires. "*No, no! He's still driving! Unbelievable!*"

"AT LEAST YOU'RE OUT OF THE FUCKIN GAME!" The cute fox groans while driving in the wrong lane. "Holy shit man..." He merges right once again, and glances at his map. He's close to the interstate and he's been eying the Mausik embassy. Just outside of the city there's a small business park where the feline nation of Mausik is stationed, and if he can make it there, the police won't be able to touch him...

Felini and other cat owned nations like Sevik and Mausik are remnants of a long standing political division that goes all the way back to the founding of the world government. Everyone knows wolves and foxes exert an inordinate amount of influence on the Sufias World Government, but things were even worse before every nation agreed to participate in a worldwide democracy. Most of the cities with large feline populations distrusted the world government, and only agreed to recognize it if some of them were granted additional legal protection. Thus, animals in certain feline cities are exempt from SWG law enforcement. They possess their own legal system, and if an animal walks into one of their embassies, world government police cannot legally pursue them. Most embassies cooperate with the SWG, but they are very picky about certain issues. Fleeing criminals is one of their favorite subjects, because cats often go to the territories seeking political asylum.

Vulpie knows he won't be safe for long even if he makes it to one, but it may give him enough time to make Amsend back off. Even though the Sons of Velora owns all of the major news companies, it would be impossible to completely cover up a story about Vulpie Vivixen seeking political asylum from SWG backed assassins. The clever fox knows manipulating public feline opinion is very important to the world government, and certain issues are off limits. If Englavic police or NoirQueue agents violated a feline embassy's sovereignty, they would never hear the end of it. He knows they'll get him eventually, but he can make things difficult for them. Hopefully he'll have enough time to come up with a plan to save Polar, Polar's family, and Vulpie Industries. But if the authorities catch him before he makes it to the embassy, he doesn't stand a chance. Having a means to justify his actions gives him the strength to go on. Felines can appreciate self-preservation better than most species because they've been the second least represented demographic in the world government for centuries. Only herbivores are underneath them on the ladder of social inequality. Foxes and wolves are on the top rung.

Getting to the embassy will be difficult. It's several miles away, and they might figure out where he's heading, so he decides to make a few spontaneous turns to throw them off. His V-Screen gives him a rough estimate of what traffic looks like in the area, so if he's lucky, he'll be able to avoid congestion and work his way to the edge of the city. When he's close, he can go for the embassy before they have time to react.

A massive roadblock greets him at the next intersection. The barricade is eight SUVs strong, all of them spinning their red and blue lights, and he drives off-road. The Superbolt's thick tires bump over the sidewalk and squeal when he suddenly has to hit the brakes. A cop flies up on his left, attempting to ram his side, but misses thanks to the small fox's quick foot. The officer slams headfirst into an unfinished construction zone, breaking a few bars and tearing through green heavy duty tarpaulins, and comes to a stop.

Vulpie decides to keep going, taking the chase away from the road that led him directly to a roadblock, but is sideswiped on the left by yet another cop car. This driver manages to ram him hard, and the orange furred fox has to swerve to maintain his desired trajectory. The hit foils his plan to go around the construction area by sending him straight towards a concrete wall at the base of the building in progress ahead of him, so he makes a sharp turn to the right, barely avoiding a head on collision. He notices graffiti underneath one of the naked buildings on his right, and recognizes a very nostalgic gang symbol. "Rennonava Rock" seems just as popular in Englavic as it is in Sufias.

"He's trying to lose us; he's takin it off road." The cop directly behind Vulpie warns. He's keeping a safe distance and is clearly a well-trained driver, managing to maintain pursuit after slamming into the Superbolt a few moments ago.

"Let's get this guy!" A younger sounding officer enthusiastically responds.

"Be advised, I'm trying man." The cop on Vulpie's tail chuckles. His levity gives cause for concern because he's not being rattled by tearing through the dirt filled portions of the construction site. The terrain is rough, and handling the occasional muddy spots that get in the way is difficult because they're moving too fast to see them at a distance, yet the experienced officer doesn't seem fazed at all. He sounds patient and confident, something Vulpie knows could be a problem if he doesn't do something about it.

The man rolls by on the Superbolt's right side after they clear an underpass and Vulpie suddenly decides to go right yet again. There's an unfinished ramp that leads up to a nearby road and the gay fox plans on taking it. The "RESTRICTED AREA" sign in the way isn't even a consideration. He'll bust through it like tissue paper. *"He's takin it out on public property now."*

Vulpie flies through the loose metal gate and shoots across another four way road with his eyes fixed on the entrance ramp. He's going against traffic, and amazingly, so is the cop on his tail. *"Dispatch, he's not following traffic, we're gonna get collisions here!"*

The entrance ramp is wet, and the officer passes up an opportunity to pit him when he sees the Superbolt going right. The orange furred fox manages to get over into the correct lane, just missing a gray car on his left, and the officer swerves to his left to go around the frightened animal, continuing to follow his target with unshakable determination. *"We're heading back on the road. Mr. Vulpie is definitely not a first timer."*

"Suspect vehicle's out of visual. Anyone else have a location?"

"This pursuit is westbound."

Vulpie checks his V-Screen and releases an anxious breath after verifying that he's on Interstate 94. The embassy is less than 15 miles away. *"Ah... I think he's heading for Mausik."*

"Copy that. Supervisor has cleared fang tactical units to disable suspect."

Kitty Cities

Aldane Okoye stirs his scalding hot coffee with a durable plastic straw he acquired from the breakfast table. His office is going over some legal procedures that have been problematic for several years, including feline immigrant relocation and the detainment of panther criminals that have been plaguing the country's poverty stricken districts, but he finds it difficult to stay interested. The middle aged tiger has managed Englavic's Mausik embassy for over twenty years, and almost every day is the same. Cats show up looking for legal protection but are usually rejected and handed over to Englavic's authorities after he denies their application for asylum. Felines with legitimate cases of discrimination have become rare occasions, which is a good thing, but not for keeping him awake. He's tired of hearing the same stories over and over.

The embassy director only interviews about three animals a day, and he's trained his people to resist believing the stories of abuse and illegitimate prosecution that are spun to them on a regular basis. All of his employees are feline, so their guests have no reason to complain about the treatment they receive. The operation is smooth and tedious... Like most government jobs.

"I'm going for a smoke." He tells a female cougar to his left, and she grins.

"You don't smoke."

"I do now." He grunts and leaves the office to his underlings. She follows him outside and admires his business attire. He likes wearing black suit pants and expensive silk shirts that are only matched by his ornate ties. Today he's wearing a black one with small depictions of white winds on it. It's almost noon, time for lunch.

"Lunch time." She sings. The attractive silky furred cat loves flirting with him almost as much as he loves teasing her. They're both married, but the sexual tension is still there.

"Let's go downtown today. I hate that grill place."

"Something romantic?"

"Easy girl." Aldane smirks. "You watch that, even with me."

"I'm sorry... Do I make you nervous?"

"Sherrie give me strength." The tiger sighs, and his ears perk up when he hears sirens in the distance. His tempting coworker is about to say something when she notices them too. At first Aldane has nothing to say until he's sure the chase is heading their direction, but the embassy director has plenty of orders to shout when the classic sounds of a high speed pursuit draw near. "Get Ricky and Grenn!"

"Yes sir!" She replies, and hurries back to the building. Aldane grips his coffee tighter when he hears squealing tires, and completely drops his drink when an orange Superbolt runs a blue police car off the road. Vulpie manages to wreck the persistent officer just before cutting right and sliding into the embassy parking lot. He stops in the middle of the black paved area and gets out as fast as possible. The tall tiger looks back to the embassy's entrance, hoping his armed men are on their way, and runs his tongue over his lower teeth when he sees them coming. He doesn't usually need to carry a firearm.

"HELP! I SURRENDER! PLEASE ARREST ME! THEY'RE GOING TO KILL ME!" Vulpie yells, but no one moves. They can't believe what they're seeing. "HURRY! THEY'RE COMING!"

"Cuff him!" The embassy director orders, and two good sized lions wearing suits hurry over to the little fox and his smoking vehicle. One of them pulls out his weapon and keeps it low while the other one readies his paw cuffs.

"On the ground!"

"Okay! No problem!" Vulpie pants and gets on his knees. He lies down on the pavement and grunts when the handcuffs are violently snapped around his dainty wrists. They stand him up, and Aldane decides to hurry over to the fox before the rest of the city's police force arrives. The embassy is in a fairly remote part of the mountains, with, ironically, a very distant view of Froidenley behind it.

"What's going on here?

"NoirQueue's going to kill me! I'm being chased by the Governmental Security Bureau, and a man named Amsend Lahnak is giving them orders! He runs the Sons of Velora and they want me dead! You have to get me inside before they shoot me!" The lions squint in confusion and give their boss bewildered looks. They know what he's talking about... No one discusses the GSB's clandestine activities because they usually don't have reason to, but they've all heard Amsend's name. Some believe he's a mob boss, others a wealthy hit man, but everyone knows he possesses some kind of extralegal authority.

"What did you do?"

"I'm innocent and I'll be happy to tell you, but you have to get me inside! PLEASE! They'll shoot me before I have a chance to talk!"

"They won't here." The tiger firmly responds, and Vulpie almost smiles. He knows the embassy director won't allow a mob of wolves to execute him without due process. If there's one thing Mausik, Felini, and Sevik all have in common, it's a hatred for lupine disrespect. He's in feline territory now.

The lions hastily escort Vulpie to the embassy, pausing for a moment so one of the panther soldiers inside the building can open the door for them. Aldane gives the soldiers a paw signal to mobilize, and they come streaming outside a few moments later. There are always at least five wartime operatives on duty in feline embassies, but over thirty are on call. The female cheetah in charge of the front desk quickly gets a nod from her supervisor, a male lion with a red mane, indicating that she's free to make an emergency announcement.

"Attention, all units report to duty. This is not a drill." She says to the small microphone on her desk and licks her lips. She doesn't need to say anything else. Her voice echoes through the compound and every available soldier prepares for combat. None of them have ever needed to use their weapons to prevent serious conflict at an embassy, but they're well trained for it. It's go time. They spill out of the building and join Aldane in the parking lot, several of them spreading out around the edges of the property to cover as much space as possible. Four snipers run up to the roof and find their respective perches. They're secretly a little excited about having an opportunity to do what they do best, but the fun quickly disappears when Englavic's law enforcement arrives in a storm of blaring sirens and loud engines. Aldane noticed the cop Vulpie ran off the road seems to be just fine. He's standing next to his vehicle, talking on his radio, and the wolf gestures towards the embassy when backup roars by.

Aldane has worked with the GSB for many years but the looks the agents give him when they get out of their black bullet proof cars make his fur stand on end. Armored SWAT trucks come to a squealing halt, jerking back and forth from the momentum of their large motors, and more animals in black get out. Englavic's SWAT force is comprised of several different species but the majority of them are lions, tigers and wolves, as usual. Foxes aren't generally fond of front line tactical deployments, but there are two brown furred vulpine police officers in the swarm.

The coal furred NoirQueue wolves have a menacing look to them and other members of the Governmental Security Bureau seem to wait for their lead. A car pulls up in front of Aldane, and a very large black furred wolf gets out. Three additional men exit with him, and the embassy director surveys his surroundings with raised eyebrows.

"You in charge?" The big wolf unceremoniously inquires.

"I'm Aldane Okoye, the director of this embassy."

"Where's Vulpie Vivixen? Did you arrest him?"

"He's been detained."

"Take me to him."

"You're not in Englavic anymore and I don't take orders from you. This is sovereign territory."

"He's wanted for murder."

"And if he's guilty, he'll be prosecuted to the full extent of the law... Our law... Not yours." The tiger replies, and the big NoirQueue commander glances at the building. He can see Vulpie's orange fur through the glass front doors. They have him in one of the back rooms. "He's not going anywhere."

"He destroyed half the city."

"And your point is what? You want us to hand him over? Here? That's not how we do things."

"He's a fox. He's not one of you, so why are you protecting him?"

"Because when someone comes looking for asylum, and they're in clear and present danger, we have to give it to them."

"No you don't. You know as well as I do that you could make an executive decision. It wouldn't be the first time a tiger cooperated with wolves to bring a known criminal to justice."

"True, but I haven't seen much cooperation so far." Aldane responds and licks his lips. "You came here making demands."

"We'll get him whether you like it or not. If you know what's good for you, you'll step aside."

"Are you threatening me?" The tiger asks, and partially raises his left paw. His signal puts the embassy soldiers on alert. The tall coal furred wolf takes a moment to assess his surroundings and snorts.

"The GSB director is on his way."

"And when he gets here I'll tell him exactly the same thing."

"We'll see." The NoirQueue commander growls, and turns around. He leisurely walks back to his car and closes the passenger side door so he can lean on it.

Six minutes pass before Amsend arrives. Vulpie hasn't moved, and his fur stands on end when he sees the husky get out of another black car. The sadist approaches the Mausik embassy director and gives him a friendly smile.

"Hello."

"Amsend Lahnak?" The tiger asks.

"Yes."

"I'm Aldane Okoye. It's nice to meet you, but we won't give you Vulpie."

"Is that any way to begin negotiations?" Amsend chuckles and glances at the building. Vulpie wants to crawl under the table. "Has anyone been hurt?" He inquires and sets his blue eyes on Aldane again.

"Not yet."

"Then let's keep it that way... You know who I am, and you know the bureau is going to get what it wants eventually, so let's figure this thing out with mutual respect."

"I don't respond well to threats."

"Who threatened you?"

"Running a feline embassy isn't very exciting, but we do serve a very important purpose in society... What you represent is exactly the kind of oppressive government my country opposes. And you're asking me not to do my job?"

"Vulpie's playing you." Amsend smiles. "He just ran here to save his little tail. He doesn't give a shit about feline rights, or your sense of duty."

"Maybe not, but I haven't had a chance to question him yet. What matters here is respecting the rule of law."

"He's done this in the past, you know. Before releasing Vulpie.net he attacked Heather Timber, a president's wife, in Breaktail Park with terrorist weaponry, but we couldn't arrest him because it happened in Sevik. Your people weren't serious about investigating his crimes, and because of feline lenience, he was able to return to Sufias City and create Vulpie.net... You wouldn't believe the things that little bastard's done. He had a criminal record in eleven countries before the Vulpie.net crisis."

"I'm well aware of Mr. Vivixen's sorted history, but that doesn't change the fact that law enforcement never found any concrete evidence linking him to the attack in Breaktail Park, and unlike wolves, we don't execute people without a trial."

"Mmm..." Amsend smirks. "But they knew it was him... No one else had a motive or the technical genius to create a non-lethal infantry neutralization, NLIN unit, but him. He thrives on your... Understanding..."

"I've never met the kid before today, and that still doesn't change what's happening here. I don't care how many crimes you say he's guilty of; if he came here seeking protection, and he's in serious danger, which he obviously is, then I'm not handing him over."

"So you're an ethical man through and through? You won't cooperate because it's the principle of the matter?"

"That's right."

"Not even if we make it worth your while?" Amsend offers.

"I wouldn't be very good at my job if people like you could bribe me."

"Come now, surely there's something we can do for you... Everyone has a price..."

"Not me."

"I don't believe that... Sometimes animals don't know what they want until it's right in front of them... And believe me Mr. Okoye... I am capable of putting ANYTHING in front of you..."

"I bet you are. I've heard stories."

"They're all true." The GSB director smiles. "The good ones, anyway."

"Not so good from what I hear." Aldane responds and swallows. "I think if I let you take him we'd see an orange fox lying in a dumpster somewhere on the evening news."

"Nothing so droll, I assure you..."

"How would that make me look? I'd be the man that killed the world's most gifted fox... The AFR would never let me hear the end of it. Hell, they'd have me put in the history books as the most incompetent tiger who's ever lived."

"I thought you said you knew who I was." Amsend smirks. "The media won't be a problem, I assure you."

"You're the director of the Governmental Security Bureau, not Druward Wraulgh." Aldane snorts, and Amsend finds his response extremely amusing.

"Oh, but you have it all wrong..."

"No, I believe everything's going to be fine, as long as you remove your men from the premises and decide to take a diplomatic route rather than offering elaborate bribes and veiled threats."

"I'm afraid I'm rather pressed for time." Amsend replies while raising his eyebrows.

"Then it's a sad day for you." Aldane firmly responds. A tense silence falls over the parking lot. The evil husky looks at Vulpie once more, and sighs in frustration. He surveys the area, noticing how many soldiers are locked and loaded, and thinks about calling Mr. Okoye's bluff. He's certain his men will slaughter everyone, but the losses would be heavy... The embassy's armed forces are perfectly positioned, surrounding the police force, GSB and NoirQueue units from three directions, so a firefight would not go well. Amsend isn't worried about himself, but he considers how messy things would get if one of the snipers shot him in the face. The mutilation would force him into transforming, and his true form would terrify most of his own men, causing lots of mayhem and confusion. Every member of NoirQueue has seen it, as part of their initiation into the Sons of Velora, but lesser GSB agents would undoubtedly shoot him in a panic, causing even more irritation... He would still kill everyone with ease, but it would be a colossal and unnecessary catastrophe.

Vulpie has succeeded in making his assassination an unprofitable scenario for the Sons of Velora. With Evil Vulpie's mutiny, things are already moving fast, and losing a huge number of operatives in Englavic just to kill the clever fox would make an already tenuous situation even more difficult. It's just not worth it at this point. There's plenty of room for propaganda, but not enough to cover a bloodbath at a feline embassy. An elaborate hoax would need to be created... Crisis actors deployed... Officials paid off...

Amsend releases a small sadistic laugh, and Aldane goes rigid when he catches a glimpse of the man's unadulterated evil. The sound confirms everything he already suspected. The GSB director desperately wanted to murder Vulpie and would have enjoyed every second of it. He glances at the embassy once more and does an about face. NoirQueue's commander stands at attention and the GSB director pulls him aside for a surreptitious conversation.

"What do you want to do?"

"Pull out and take your men to Sufias City... All of them."

"Are you sure?"

"There's more than one way to skin a fox." The husky smiles, and the mercenary grins when he catches on.

"His company?" He asks, and Amsend nods. "Are we taking hostages?"

"No. Kill everyone in that fucking building." A brief silence passes as the black furred wolf processes what he's just heard.

"And the tower?"

"Level it. Return to headquarters when you're finished and gather the intel you need to track down and murder every member of Polar Arctic's family."

"We made quite a mess today, didn't we Mr. Vivixen?" Aldane says while entering the white interrogation room. The two lions that detained Vulpie are still watching over him, and several cats outside are pretending not to watch.

"Oh! Thank God!" Vulpie breathes in relief. He watched the swarm of police and special agents leave the embassy ten minutes ago and was wondering what was going to happen next. "Is he really gone?"

"Who? The husky I was talking to?"

"Yeah, Amsend Lahnak, is he gone?" Vulpie asks again, and fidgets while trying to get comfortable. The paw cuffs are hurting his little wrists.

"Take those off." The tiger tells the lions, and the one to Vulpie's left retrieves his keys. The gay fox turns around in his plastic chair so the man can unlock the restraints with little difficulty. Vulpie takes a deep breath after being freed and licks his lips.

"My name's Aldane Okoye."

"It's a pleasure to meet you, Aldane. I can't thank you enough for saving my life." The embassy director stares at Vulpie with an uncertain expression before clearing his throat and taking a seat. He turns his chair to the side, facing him, and drops his left arm on the table.

"I've already contacted the GBI but we're going to keep you here until we figure out what's going on. Now... Tell me why I just turned away the GSB, NoirQueue and half of the city's police force."

"I'll tell you anything you want to know, Mr. Okoye. I'm only alive because of you."

"That I can believe. I've never seen anything like this before."

"Amsend's the director of the Governmental Security Bureau and he's the one who put the hit out on me."

"Right, that's why I just told Druward Wraulgh that I'm holding you."

"Druward won't hurt me, but his men might. Amsend's above him on the food chain."

"Impossible. The GSB is just a branch of the GBI."

"That's what they want everyone to think, but I'm telling you, Amsend Lahnak is running everything, but he has help. They control the media too."

"Is this the foxes control the news thing?" Okoye inquires and shifts in his seat with a curious expression.

"Sure. The Association of Fox Rights exerts a lot of influence over the major news networks but they're not the problem. They're just a lobby. What I'm talking about is much bigger than foxes. I'm a fox and they're screwing me over because the people running this thing are the most powerful people on the planet."

"The Sons of Velora?" Aldane mischievously inquires. "That's what you said out there."

"How rich do you think I am?" Vulpie asks and raises his eyebrows. "Don't you think I'm rich and powerful?"

"Probably the richest celebrity out there, yeah. So what?"

"Do you actually know anything about the Sons of Velora? I mean besides the stupid crap they put in movies and video games to throw you off?"

"Do I know anything about them?" Aldane chuckles and shifts in his seat again. "You aren't playing games with me right now, are you? With as much trouble as you're in?"

"Dude, I have my own company now. I wouldn't run from the cops because it's fun."

"But it is fun?" The tiger smirks.

"Sure it is." Vulpie answers and returns a very brief smirk as well. He hastily removes it and leans forward to make sure Aldane is taking him seriously. "But these people want me dead. I'm not messing with you. I wouldn't dare after you saved my life the way you did. I'm being completely honest."

"So you're telling me..." Aldane says and rests his right leg on his left knee. "That the Sons of Velora is real?"

"Do you know anything about them?"

"Come on... Really?"

"Who do you think those guys were?" The orange furred fox asks with slight irritation, and gestures towards the parking lot with his muzzle. "You saw them out there. I don't know what Amsend told you, but you know they wanted to kill me."

"He tried to bribe me." Aldane admits. He raises his eyebrows and takes a deep breath before continuing. "Said everyone had a price and wanted to know mine."

"There ya go. Is that how the GBI acts? Sure, I mean, yeah, they might do that shit and you never hear about it, but don't ya think it would be a big deal anyway?"

"Okay, I'll bite. Tell me everything you know. Let me hear the whole conspiracy."

"Yeah, they like to use that word to trick you into thinking that they don't exist. If you're secretly gonna screw someone you don't announce it to the world. I mean, come on. I'm sure you've seen some messed up stuff since you run a feline embassy. That's the whole reason why I came here. When the world government screws cats over, wolves are conspiring against you."

"Point taken, but you have to forgive me for being skeptical." The tiger says and licks his lips. "I know the government's not honest with me, or anyone for that matter, but what you're suggesting is just ridiculous. How could a small group of people control everything? The world's a big place."

"Monaaaaaaaaaay! Money in the bank!" Vulpie laughs with an urban voice. He doesn't try imitating feline slang a second time because his comical outburst gets the point across. "Who controls the banks?"

"Foxes?" Aldane asks and raises an eyebrow. "If we're being honest here."

"Sure, but what you don't know is that the foxes above the brown and red ones you see in front of congress are all Vixils, and Vixils are fucking crazy. I met, "The Man," if you will, and his name is Velix. Amsend sat there with him and told me he almost single handedly controlled the media because his family owns all of the companies."

"Then why hasn't someone said something about it before?"

"They don't advertise what they're doing. I thought Karl Vulches was "The Man," but he was just another piece on their board. The guy was powerful, but he was in front of the cameras. Velix and his friends aren't. That's not how they roll. They built this giant building in Sufias City and named it the National Vulpie.net Agency before I even met them. That's how confident they were. They threatened me and told me that I had to run the organization they put together, because they obviously wanted to put me on display so I'd get the flak for what they're going to do."

"So what was it? What was their evil plan?"

"I'm serious." Vulpie replies and gives the tiger a frustrated look. "Do you like foxes and wolves owning everything? Does that make you and your family feel safe at night?"

"Of course not." Aldane defensively responds.

"Then listen to me. The foxes that really own the media are so awful that all of the other foxes hate them. They're supposed to worship Aila, and dude, let me tell you, I was getting a seriously evil vibe from the guy I met. He's only the second Vixil I've come across, but the first one tried to kill me, and this guy was just smarter. He looked just as crazy."

"Yeah, I saw that on the news... You killed someone." Vulpie nods.

"That's right. I'm not proud of it, but the fucker was going to kill me, and he already killed the other foxes, plus he shot the director of the fucking GBI, so I think it was justifiable homicide."

"Truth is, I don't like foxes at all. You think you're better than everyone and what you did out there is proof of it." Aldane says with a cold voice. Vulpie noticed the tiger's attitude change a few moments ago, and quickly adjusts his own to keep the man on his side. He counters the insult with humor instead of getting angry.

"That's antivulpine! You can't say that!" Vulpie says with mock indignation and wide blue eyes. "Help! Help! I'm being oppressed! We're not arrogant! We're just enthusiastic about how awesome we are!" The embassy director is silent for a moment and finally returns a very small smile.

"After we saved your life..."

"The fact that you would even QUESTION taking a fox at your feline embassy is anti-vulpine!" Vulpie smirks, but doesn't try his luck any further. He turns serious again, and licks his lips. "My husband is a wolf, so yeah, we talk about it. He knows how things are. My species can be a little paranoid, but he doesn't blame me for it. I cringe every time they call people speciesist when mine is overrepresented. It's embarrassing."

"Also works in your favor though."

"Hey, I turned down that job. They offered me a place at the AFR but it just isn't my thing, and I didn't mean to offend you earlier. I just wanted to make a point. Not only are the major players in this thing mostly lupine, vulpine, and canine, they're also complete psychopaths. The only reason they approached me is because I've been successful, plus a lot of people hate me... They're well aware of that. There weren't any negotiations. Amsend tried to play it off a little, but Velix didn't hide his feelings. They just gave me orders and threatened me if I didn't play ball."

"So what are you doing in Englavic, then?"

"Losing a ball game." Vulpie snorts and Aldane nods in satisfaction.

"Okay, I can buy that."

"It's the truth. All the truth."

Déjà vu

Aldane interrogates Vulpie for over an hour, but the orange furred fox doesn't have any problem with cooperating. The tiger has written several pages and continues handing them over to the secretary whenever she finishes entering them into the system. The big cats seem very eager to help.

"So let me see if I understand this. These people are actually allied with your computer virus, but you don't have any control over Vulpie.net anymore?" Aldane inquires.

"That's right. Except I do have the power to manipulate the system like always, but Vulpie.net can override me if it's paying attention to what I'm doing and wants to get in the way."

"So Arctic.net is kind of a highway, and you both can get on anywhere you want, but Vulpie.net is like a cop?"

"That's one way to put it."

"And that's because..." The tiger says and checks his notes. "It relies on your mind map files which forever has you listed as the user, but you also think it has the power to get around that barrier at will. It just can't completely block you out of the system because you're still the... Super user?"

"Yeah."

"So every time you get online it can arrest you and kick you off, but you can always get back on somewhere else."

"You got it. I guess that's a pretty good analogy after all, but it's way more complicated than that."

"I know, but for us non-computer geeks, this is how we're going to word it."

"But remember, Vulpie.net isn't helping them anymore, so who knows what's going to happen now."

"And Vulpie.net, eh, Evil Vulpie, flew a ship to Amsend's castle, and abducted your husband?"

"I came to save him, but yeah. He's its prisoner and we have to find out where it took him."

"Of course we'll try to help, but we already have a mess on our paws here, as I'm sure you'd agree." Aldane responds, and scratches his right ear when it twitches. At first he thought something was tickling him but now he realizes the source is a distant sound. Everyone goes silent, and as the sound becomes louder, it doesn't take Vulpie long to recognize the hum. The ship Vulpie.net used to rescue Polar was identical to the one he used to fly over the Wispy Canis Lupus mountain range.

"Oh no..." Vulpie whispers.

"What is that sound?"

"A ship. It's... Vulpie.net's ship." The lions look at each other before hurrying out of the room. Aldane gets up, following them to the front doors, and they wait in silence. Only twenty seconds pass before Vulpie.net floats in and positions the ship over the parking lot. They watch a rope fall from the sky. Vulpie.net opened the ship's rear hanger and uses the long white rope to slide down to the parking lot.

Vulpie's stomach sinks when its sneakers touch the pavement and it bounces to attention. It removes the rope and hurries towards the building. Aldane glances at Vulpie, but the tiger knows there's nothing he can do. Telling his men to fight Evil Vulpie is suicide.

"Stand down." Aldane says, and Vulpie's fur stands on end when he remembers Druward saying the same thing in the CTGD's white room. He begins to panic, and gets out of his chair. He doesn't leave the interrogation room and flinches when it walks right through the glass doors. Almost everyone screams, and Aldane repeats himself. "STAND DOWN!"

"WHOOPS! MY BAD!" Evil Vulpie laughs and brushes glass off of its neon blue shirt and white pants. "Sometimes I forget how badass I am!" Vulpie stands up. He walks to the doorway and looks at it in terror. The Vulpie imitation pauses for a moment, considering thousands of options, and makes a disgusted face when it comes to a decision. It runs at Vulpie and the orange furred fox falls back on the floor. He turns to crawl under the table, but Evil Vulpie grabs his lean little body and slides him forward. It gets on top of him and Vulpie tries to push it off in horror.

"NOO!"

"Like old times, huh? What should I start with? Wrists again?"

"GET OFF OF ME!" Vulpie shouts, but his whimpering command is also a cry for help.

"I'd just LOVE to do this again... Get rid of you once and for all, you little... Fag... But... Mmm... Polar..."

"What?"

"GET UP!" Evil Vulpie growls and gets off of the little gay fox. It grabs Vulpie by the paws and he cries out in terror, thinking it's going to crush his arms, but it yanks him forward instead. "MOVE!" Vulpie.net snarls and pushes him towards the front entrance. Aldane and the others don't say a word while they watch the computer virus order its creator over to the dangling white rope. Evil Vulpie wraps its dainty but infinitely powerful right arm around him and grabs the rope with its left paw. Vulpie yelps when Evil Vulpie makes the ship ascend. It both pilots the vessel and carries him away at the same time.

Polar hasn't moved from the ship's bridge since Vulpie.net decided to go back for its creator. The white furred wolf has been patiently riding up front with 3 other Vulpie imitations , Vulpiebots, but luckily none of them have said anything so far. He wouldn't know how to carry on a conversation after everything he's been through, and with Vulpie's uncertain fate hanging over him. They seem to be piloting the ship, but they're also carrying out miniscule tasks that also suggests none of them are really needed. The snow wolf suspects Vulpie.net is piloting the ship from a distance and is only making them push buttons to keep up appearances.

"Polar!" Vulpie shouts after the hallway door behind the captain's area slides up into the ceiling. Vulpie.net, the one wearing the blue shirt and white pants, follows the orange furred fox down the hallway, and Polar jumps out of his chair.

"Oh, thank God you're okay!"

"Vulpie.net saved me." The little fox responds with a worried voice. The snow wolf goes down on one knee and they passionately embrace each other.

"I know."

"Why?" Vulpie whispers.

"It… We came to an agreement." Polar replies, and Vulpie pulls back. He gives him a bewildered look and glances to his right at Vulpie.net, who is leaning against the wall with a devious smirk on its face.

"What do you mean? Are you really… Polar?"

"Yes he is. He's really him, and you're really you, and now we're all going to be really close." Evil Vulpie mischievously comments. Vulpie looks back to Polar and blinks.

"What's it talking about?"

"I had to save you. Vulpie.net got me away from Amsend, but it was going to leave you behind. I had to beg it for help."

"What did you do?"

"I didn't have a choice, Vulpie." Polar whispers. "You were surrounded by Amsend's men and they might have killed you."

"Actually, he was still in the castle, lol!" Vulpie.net laughs, and Vulpie winces when he hears the robot use internet slang in a real conversation. Sometimes he still does it, just to see how people will react, and the computer virus is clearly stuck on his mind map data. It's far less aggressive than it used to be, but all three of them know it would just love to crunch Vulpie on the floor.

"What? How?" Polar asks, and Vulpie licks his lips.

"Long story. And I... I overheard Amsend talking to someone, and I had this crazy idea. I knew Vulpie.net had feelings for you too, so I thought it might attack Amsend to get you back. But what did you mean by an understanding? Tell me." The white furred wolf sighs and rubs the little fox's narrow shoulders.

"Vulpie.net's changed... You can see how different it is now."

"Polar." Vulpie says with wide eyes.

"I know what you're thinking, but I've had a chance to talk with it, and it wants to be part of our family." The snow wolf responds and Vulpie grimaces. He closes his eyes for a moment and releases a mortified groan. He considers glancing at his computer virus, but he can't stand to see what expression it's wearing now. "It wants to help us, and I know it will, as long as I live up to my promise."

"Your promise?" Vulpie whispers.

"Yeah." Polar replies, but doesn't elaborate. He looks aside for a moment, and Vulpie sighs.

"So what's the promise?"

"It... Wants to have time with me the same way you do." The snow wolf answers.

"Uhhhhhhhhhhhhhhhhhhhhhhhhhhhhhhhhhhhhhhhhhhhhhhh?" Vulpie groans in disbelief. "Our kind of time? And what does that mean?"

"It means you can't keep him all to yourself anymore. You'll have to share him with me." Evil Vulpie says, and Vulpie clamps his sharp teeth together in a rage.

"He's my HUSBAND! I SHOULD have him all to myself!"

"Too bad!"

"Vulpie." Polar breathes in concern, and licks his lips. "It'll be okay. We'll work it out, and Evil Vulpie isn't going to pick on you anymore." Polar says and looks at the perfect Vulpie imitation. "Right?"

"Yeah... I'm just messing with ya, but I'll stop... As long as Mr. P and I have time to share our love." Vulpie's orange fur stands on end when he hears the thing call his husband by his pet name. The computer program is already trying to violate their relationship, and he knows it's only going to get worse.

"I'm sorry I've put you through all of this, Polar." Vulpie tells his lover and a wave of emotion rushes over him. He almost cries, and Polar embraces him.

"You're my life, Vulpie. I wouldn't trade it for the world, and all of the things we've been through only make me love you more."

"What if it hurts you?"

"It won't. It just wants to be loved too." Polar answers and releases his soul mate. "Vulpie.net's part of you, so any time I spend with it won't be bad. It just wants to be recognized for what it is."

"Thanks Polar." Evil Vulpie says with a warm voice, and the wolf swallows.

"Oh my God..." Vulpie moans, and finally has the courage to move out of his husband's arms and look Vulpie.net in the eye.

"We're gonna be friends now." Evil Vulpie giggles.

"Okay, yeah. So like..." Vulpie says, and glares at the robot. "So what are you going to do now, Vulpie.net? We know you teamed up with Amsend, and he's a total piece of shit, so what's your story? What have you been up to for all of these years?"

"More than you can imagine." Vulpie.net wildly responds. "You hate me now, but soon I'll be the hero! Amsend, the Sons of Velora, all of them, hehe, I'm gonna take em out!"

"You're going to kill them?" Polar asks in shock.

"Can't make a Kova omelet without breaking a few Vulpies, I mean eggs." Vulpie.net replies, and the orange fox groans.

"Vulpie.net..."

"Sorry Mr. P. Just couldn't help myself."

"Stop that, okay? I love Vulpie just as much as you." The white furred wolf says, and Vulpie winces in disgust. He knows his lover is just saying what Vulpie.net wants to hear, but it still hurts.

"Kay! Buuuuuuuuuuuuuuut!" Vulpie.net replies and prances over to the bridge area. "It's gonna be a bumpy ride."

"Yeah?" Vulpie asks and crosses his arms. "Tell us more! Inquiring minds want to know!"

"Well I can't deny my public!" Vulpie.net grins and licks its artificial lips. "Mr. Creepy Husky Man has been very useful, but he's also got a few aces up his sleeves." The fox imitation swishes its tail and raises its eyebrows. "He knows this thing that lives in deep space, light-years away from our galaxy, and it's actually been able to communicate with him and even send him stuff. Honestly, I don't know how, but I've got a few ideas."

"Yeah, he mentioned something hiding behind the stars or something weird like that."

"What's even weirder is the fuckin thing's real." Vulpie.net giggles. "Oh, shit man! Imagine my surprise! I thought the guy was just a rich sadistic dumbass, but he actually managed to back up some of his threats."

"Uh oh." Vulpie says and Evil Vulpie gives him a competitive smile.

"Don't get excited. I still have everything under control, but we got work to do! Or rather, I... Have work to do... Not like you can do very much, huh? Except cry and stuff."

"Vulpie.net..." Polar groans in frustration. The snow wolf desperately wants to keep Vulpie alive, and he's trying his best to keep things from escalating.

"Aight!" Vulpie.net answers with a gangsta voice. "So anyway... Yeah! I've got a lot on my plate, and you guys can just chill I guess!"

"What about Polar's family?" Vulpie asks, and Polar quickly speaks up.

"Oh, right! Yeah! We need to warn them! There's no way we can leave them unprotected."

"I picked em up after you made your promise." The robotic fox smirks, and both Polar and Vulpie go silent.

"What? You already?"

"Please, who do you think I am? As soon as I knew I could have you, I made sure they were taken care of. I know how much you love your family Mr. P."

"Are you serious? How did you?"

"Abduction! They were taken against their will! Muhahaha!" Evil Vulpie giggles, but winks at the handsome snow wolf. "They're safe. I didn't hurt them."

"Where are they?"

"Palisade space station, but we shouldn't leave them so close to Sufias... Things might get... Fun..."

"Wait, the planet's in danger?" Polar asks, and Vulpie.net shrugs.

"I dunno. It might be. Amsend made all sorts of grandiose claims, and since he was telling the truth about some of them, I guess all bets are off."

"What was he right about?" Vulpie asks in concern. "What did he do?"

"Fucker took over my robotic soldiers! Can you believe that shit? He said he could do it, but I just thought he was bluffing!"

"But how could he take them from YOU?" Polar asks in confusion. "You're Vulpie.net!"

"You know the thing Vulpie played hide and seek with on Zeravyn? Da big old scary, rrawwrrr!"

"Yeah, we know." Vulpie hastily responds.

"He calls em Mecha Ailas."

"Well that's cool and all, but get to the point, please."

"Well aren't you sassy right now?"

542

"Don't call me Captain Sassy Pants for fuck sake. Alright? Just stop it and tell us."

"Fine then." Vulpie.net says in amusement, and raises its eyebrows again. "I built them, but Amsend provided the schematics. He showed me some kind of technology I'd never seen before, and I'm the god of cyberspace."

"The thing behind the stars." Polar says.

"Yep! He said that's where it came from, but I was just interested in whether the machines would work or not, and as it turned out, they kicked fucking ass. Buuuttt... There was a teensy little complication... Cuz for some reason, since I used the schematics he gave me, the thing can control them too..."

"You've gotta be kidding." Vulpie coughs. "You? It can kick you out and take over machines you built?"

"Yeah. Hey man, I was just as surprised as you were."

"Well how many of those fucking things did you build?"

"Mmmm..." Vulpie.net hums and returns the most innocent expression it can muster. "Seven."

"Just seven?"

"Seven... Hundred!" Evil Vulpie says and bites its tongue.

"Fucking Khalan, man. Well that's just great!"

"Good news though! They're all on the same ship!"

"A ship? Did you build it too?"

"Sure did! It's super badass! But, uh... Kind of filled it with the things... So now we gotta destroy it!"

"What kind of ship is it? A battleship?"

"Yeah, but don't worry, I already told you, I got this shit. What you REALLY should be worried about right now, is why Amsend just sent all of fucking NoirQueue to Vulpie Industries..."

"Wh... What?" Vulpie whispers in shock.

"Looks like he's gonna level the place. I mean, well, since I've heard them talking about thermite and stuff."

"THEN STOP THEM FOR FUCK SAKE! Can't you stop them, Vulpie.net?"

"We'll never get there in time, but I know who can." Evil Vulpie smiles.

"Who? Send them, whoever they are!"

"Are you sure?"

"Yes!"

"Are you really, REALLY, sure you want me to help?" Vulpie.net asks, and Vulpie goes silent.

"Well, what are you going to do?"

"Mmm… I'll handle it, but you MIGHT have a little bit of bad press when it's all said and done."

"What are you talking about?" Polar inquires.

"I can have them killed, but it'll be a big ass fight. The building's gonna get fucked up, and probably a lot of people will die." Vulpie.net answers.

"You can do anything, right? Can't you do better than that?" Vulpie demands.

"Look man, it's your decision. I don't have a robotic army in Sufias City right now, and it's gonna have to be my secret weapon or nothing at all… So choose…"

Battle of Vulpie Industries

Stacie looks up and her brown fur stands on end when she sees an army of government agents swarming into the lobby. All of the men are armed and thoroughly equipped, especially NoirQueue, who sport various automatic weapons. They're fond of assault rifles but several of them are also carrying smgs, shotguns, carbines, and black duffle bags filled with explosives. She doesn't know what to do. She picks up the phone and searches for the security chief's extension, but doesn't have a chance to call him, because a very tall black wolf pulls out of 50 caliber pistol and points it at her face.

"Wouldn't do that."

"Oh! ... Okay! Please don't shoot me!"

"Don't move, and don't call anyone." He responds, and walks around her desk. He looks down at her crotch before running his eyes under the bottom side of the table. A white button is still armed. "Is that the silent alarm?"

"Yes!" The brown vixen whimpers.

"Did you set it off?"

"No! I swear!"

"Alright, get up."

"DROP YOUR WEAPON!" A guard yells. Vulpie Industries' security detail is higher than ever, but the men are still outnumbered. They all wear gray pants and matching long sleeved shirts underneath black bullet proof vests that have the company's name on the front. They also sport orange ties that complement the orange patches on the front of their black ball caps. Each of them have security batons in addition to firearms. The tall wolf looks at the security guard and waits for him to glance to the left, where he sees over fifty men coming in his direction.

"Put that down unless you want to die for your boss."

"I SAID DROP IT!" The man shouts again. The merc commander reaches into his pocket and retrieves his wallet. He holds it open for the guard to see, and his GBI credentials look very impressive. In truth, the dark wolf switched IDs after leaving Englavic in preparation for the attack on Vulpie Industries. He has two forms of identification, but knows the Governmental Bureau of Investigations carries more weight in Sufias City. It's quite effective, and luckily, no one fires a shot. Vulpie's security team surrenders because there's simply no way twenty men could take down a hundred NoirQueue agents.

"You! Move it!" The commander orders, pointing for Stacie to join the frightened group of animals that's already being assembled behind her desk. NoirQueue gathers several of Vulpie's employees in front of the steps to the second floor and surrounds them, attending to their paws one at a time. The agents use plastic hand cuffs because they're easy to deploy. Screaming can be heard throughout the building for several minutes, but the commotion dies down a lot quicker than one would expect. Vulpie doesn't hire stupid employees. All of them are smart enough to keep their mouths shut, and even the most rebellious workers, a few young sales agents wearing orange dress shirts and matching ties, know when to swallow their pride; they're pushed into the rest of the group and paw cuffed just like everyone else.

Though the sun is still up in Englavic, it's eight p.m. in Sufias City, so several customers are still in the building. Vulpie Industries closes its doors at ten, and the crowd is moderate, but they're far more vocal than Vulpie's workers. A few of them kick and scream before one of the dark wolves rams the butt of his assault rifle into a female shopper's muzzle. The loud smack makes gathering the rest of them very easy...

"Sir. We're ready to do this?" One of the coal furred wolves asks the commander in Englavic.

"Plant your shape charges in the basement."

"Yes sir."

"All of you be quiet now!" The leader shouts when some of the prisoners start talking amongst themselves. "My name is Dietrich Froidenley.

I'm with the GBI's special services and there's no time for delay." He lies about his last name because one can never be too careful before committing mass murder. "The bureau's received a bomb threat from a terrorist who claims to have planted an explosive device in the building. He says he's watching us from an unknown location and has threatened to detonate the bomb if anyone tries to leave. So I apologize for the rough treatment, but obviously we can't allow that to happen."

"What's with all the guns?" Maxine shouts while being forced down the steps, along with several other animals from the upper floors. She's pushed into the group and can't see the man's face when he answers her question.

"For your protection."

"Why do you need so many boys?" An urban lion shrewdly inquires.

"The terrorist also claims to have a man inside the building." Dietrich answers with a very convincing voice. His statement goes a long way in earning their trust, but he doesn't need them to trust him for the mission to be accomplished... It would just make things easier. "Now until we know whether that's true or not, we can't afford to take any chances. That's why you've been paw cuffed and it's why my men are going to empty your pockets after moving you into a room where we'll be able to keep our eyes on you."

"*Sir! Sir! Dietrich?*" One of the NoirQueue wolves barks over the radio and he runs his big tongue over his sharp teeth in irritation.

"Is there somewhere we can move them to?"

"Behind the steps is an employee lounge!" Stacie offers, and a few animals nod in agreement.

"Is it big enough?"

"Yes! Absolutely!"

"Alright, take them." The NoirQueue commander orders, and turns around while his men herd the prisoners away. He violently yanks his radio from his belt and clicks it on.

"Who is this? You better have a good goddess damn reason for interrupting me."

"Druward Wraulgh is here with two other agents." The tall wolf holds still for a moment, wondering how the GBI director could possibly be here to interrupt their plans. He licks his lips and starts walking to the front entrance.

"Let him in." Dietrich says, and puts his radio back. He's surrounded by NoirQueue wolves, so he isn't worried about his safety, but Druward has a way of getting under everyone's fur. He sighs when Vulpie Industries' glass doors slide open and the fellow coal furred wolf enters the building. "Enjoying the night air are we Mr. Wraulgh? You better not be here to give me orders."

"The Red Wolves are on their way!" Druward growls while hurrying inside. Dietrich's never seen fear on the man's face before, and his reaction is almost more disturbing than the news.

"What are you talking about? Are you sure?"

"It's true!" Rotick says, and the brown and white furred wolf accidently bumps into the third member of the GBI, a young but well trained panther, on his way in.

"Don't play games with me Wraulgh. I have permission to kill you if you get in our way."

"I'm not here to stop you! I'm here to warn you! Your men use encrypted channels so I couldn't reach you any other way! We've been watching their base of operations downtown, and they all just left the building less than fifteen minutes ago!"

"How do you know they're coming here?" Dietrich asks with a bewildered voice.

"Because this is the only place they'd attack. We suspected that they were planning an assault on Vulpie Industries, but they're coming RIGHT! NOW!"

"How many?"

"Over three hundred at least."

"Bullshit. You're lying."

"You have to get your men out of here! We've got to get everyone out of here!"

"No one's fucking going anywhere, Wraulgh! This building's coming down, and you're not going to stop us! Put him in handcuffs!"

"You idiot!" Druward shouts just as lights flash into the lobby, and everyone covers their eyes. A few members of NoirQueue jump back when one of them moves to open the doors, and the three men standing watch outside look absolutely terrified.

"Sir?" One of them shouts, and turns around to aim at the swarm of cars piling up in front of the building. The Red Wolves use everything they can get their paws on, so their strike force is comprised of all sorts of vehicles.

"Fuck." Druward growls, and strains to see what's going on, but it's all a bright blur.

"There's too many of them!" One of the mercenaries shouts, and the rest of the men look to Dietrich for orders.

"FALL BACK! BACK! ALL SQUADS TAKE DEFENSIVE POSITIONS!" The NoirQueue commander shouts, and waves for the men outside of the building to follow him as well. "GET THE FUCK BACK! EVERYONE FIND COVER! FIND COVER AND READY YOUR WEAPONS!" Dietrich is about to yell at Druward when a bullet flies through the front door and buries itself in his forehead. It explodes out of the back of his skull, and his eyes roll up. The tall wolf falls on the ground with a loud thump and bleeds all over Vulpie's beautiful sticky black floors. It's hard to determine what chemicals were used to give it such a silky sheen, but it doesn't soak up moisture very well.

Outside, Sherrie lowers her straight pull bolt sniper rifle and hands it to a loyal cheetah. She didn't even need a scope to make the shot, thanks to the frighteningly effective software she and her sisters are running. The flawless execution is extremely arousing to the lust filled zombies around her, whether they're feline, canine or lupine. Every one of the Red Wolf terrorists from Glovepaw's sanctuary has been infected with Deiva.net's perverse biological mechanisms, and the sexual nature of the nanomachines given to them allow the goddesses to exercise limitless control over the religious fanatics.

If they weren't particularly religious before, they are now. Evil Vulpie's Deiva.net manipulates key parts of their brain, such as the entire limbic system, the nucleus accumbens, and the hypothalamus. The majority of the time it only needs to make use of simplistic yet effective chemical and biological reactions to constantly regulate how the men are feeling. Right now it's flooding their minds with pleasure signals, effectively tying the goddesses' lust for murder together with sex. Instead of clumsily ordering them to kill government agents, the microscopic process fiercely encourages them to carry out Vulpie.net's orders without ever being told. They think they're here with the synthetic goddesses to kill secular government agents who are working with Vulpie Vivixen to spread an evil homosexual agenda, but ironically, they're really here to protect Vulpie's employees by killing NoirQueue.

"Thank you dear." Sherrie smiles. Cyrilla smirks and plays with her lopping left ear before stretching athletically. Even though Vulpie.net has dominion over the fanatic's minds, it still isn't able to completely control every single thought they have, so it plans on sacrificing Vulpie's company building to satiate them. The computer virus knows this is a perfect opportunity to destroy Vulpie's life work and put a wedge between him and Polar. Vulpie.net can claim innocence and blame NoirQueue for the building's collapse, and no one will know the truth. The computer virus has calculated that Vulpie will be devastated after losing his company, and the loss of income will also prevent him and Polar from enjoying the same lavish lifestyle they've grown accustomed to. Sure, Vulpie's star power will still land him work in the movie and entertainment industry, but it will never be the same. His image will be tarnished after the calamity, whether the disaster was his fault or not. Meanwhile, the Vulpie imitation will still have access to the entire universe, making it seem much more attractive to Polar... Or so it hopes... It's willing to do anything to have what Vulpie has. The only problem is that Polar truly loves Vulpie with all of his heart, and dismantling feelings of that magnitude will require a tremendous amount of unfortunate events... And even then, the snow wolf just might be one of those people that absolutely refuses to abandon their soul mate for any reason... Polar's devotion to Vulpie intrigues Vulpie.net because Vulpie's mind map files tell the computer virus that gay men just want to bend over and humiliate little foxes, not love them, therefore, the data must be incorrect... It has to know.

Inside, Druward stumbles to the left and regains his footing after putting a fair amount of distance between himself and Dietrich's corpse. Losing him shocks Amsend's mercenaries into a state of disbelief, and Rotick and the panther agent seamlessly mingle into their group. Druward sees the coal furred wolves looking at him, hoping he'll have something to say, but he's not sure trying to take command is a good idea. He doesn't know the men, so loudly trying to pull rank on them may backfire. They might think him arrogant for assuming that he can just give them orders, but at the same time, they're clearly in need of direction. He does have far more experience than any of the killers because his career path forced him to overcome several disasters on his climb to director of the bureau.

There isn't much time, so he only takes a few moments to make his decision. He knows he has to act quickly, before they decide to go rogue. Staying alive is a good reason for them to disregard orders, but luckily, he knows how to use this to his advantage. Druward's leadership skills always involve a lot of testosterone, and that's exactly what they need right now.

"Dietrich's dead! Someone has to take charge, and I'm the only one that can keep you alive! SO HOW MANY OF YOU WANT TO LIVE?" He shouts, looking around the lobby and up to the second floor where several of them have taken defensive positions.

"We don't take orders from you!" Someone yells, but he doesn't care what direction it came from or who said it. He walks into the middle of the room and grabs the reception desk with his big paws. They watch him lift the large piece of furniture and roll it forward, onto its front, raising its surface to provide cover for a firefight.

"Red Wolves have been attacking the world government for over a hundred years, but they've never crushed us before, and they will not crush us tonight!" Druward yells, and looks around the room with a defiant expression. "They're outgunned and poorly trained! DO YOU WANT TO DIE IN VULPIE'S FAGGOT TOWER TONIGHT?"

"NO!" Half of them yell. Druward's views have changed, and he doesn't really look down on Vulpie for being gay, but knows the crude statement will get NoirQueue's blood up. He wants them lethal, selfish, and fearless.

"THEN HELP ME KILL THESE FUCKERS!" The coal furred wolf roars, and turns to the nearest mercenary. "YOU! Take five men downstairs and break into the security cage! I had ten mod six launchers moved down there in case this happened! We can use them to destroy the Deivas!" The man nods, and looks at his friends without saying a word. They hesitate, but decide to follow his commands.

Some members of the elite force still aren't happy with submitting to Druward's authority, but his foresight does convince them that it's their best chance of survival. One of them walks over and offers him a submachine gun, which he gladly accepts. He nods grimly and looks around the room, noting everyone's position. "AIM FOR THE TERRORISTS! THEY'LL SEND THE DEIVAS IN FIRST TO CATCH US OFF GUARD, BUT DON'T BOTHER SHOOTING THEM! I'VE SEEN WHAT VULPIE.NET'S MACHINES CAN DO! ONLY MOD LAUNCHERS CAN TAKE THEM DOWN, SO IF THEY COME AT YOU, FALL BACK!"

Sherrie bursts through the main entrance before Druward has a chance to find a suitable position. The tall long window adorning the wall over the main entrance loses half of its glass from her momentum, and the men cover their eyes. Glass rains down everywhere, clacking against the beautiful semi-sticky floor. Sherrie made a thirty foot jump outside of the building to launch herself through the upper window, and she slams into the first column on the right side of the room. The pillar is horizontal to Vulpie's sign, displaying an aesthetically pleasing message of "VISION," but its splendor is quickly ruined. Sherrie's beautiful but unyielding body slams down on top of it, and she hastily uses it as a launching pad in a mesmerizing display of athleticism.

Gunfire erupts all around the room as the first column shatters from the force of her combat boots, and the column in the middle of the lobby completely explodes when she lands on it. She obviously meant to destroy it, as the position leaves her completely exposed, but she casually stands and waits for the debris to stop sliding off of her. Big chunks of glass and thin metal parts cover her from head to toe, and she shakes free of the mess before suddenly reaching backwards. She pulls the submachine gun off of her back and holds it with both paws before anyone has a chance to react.

She's dressed in black combat gear that's very similar to the kind of outfits NoirQueue uses. Black boots, melee pads, bullet proof armor, she has it all, but the armor isn't necessary in her case. None of them have weapons that could pose a serious threat to the Deivas' magnificently resilient bodies. She doesn't even bother to move when they fire on her, and takes several shots to the head and neck before finally running up the steps.

Druward sees a few NoirQueue wolves barge into the lobby with all ten of the mod six launchers, and he runs across the room as fast as he can. "Idiots! Split up! Give me one!" He shouts. Gunfire and a chorus of screaming from the rec room behind the main stairs makes it difficult to communicate, so he pushes two of them to get the message across. He points at them afterwards, and two men run under the second floor on the right side of the lobby towards Vulpie's column. Druward signals for three of the mercs to come with him, and sprints out of cover just in time to see Sherrie throwing a wolf out of the same window she used to enter the building. Landing on the steps outside will probably kill him, but no one can do anything about it. The delectable taupe furred leopard/panther takes two more of them down before aiming to the right and opening fire on the other side of the room.

She saves her submachine gun for close encounters and decides to use one of the wolves' assault rifles to pick several of them off. She headshots the mercenaries like an aimbot in an online shooter. She never misses. She pops twelve of them but stops firing when they drop behind cover. With no juicy targets available, she promptly jumps off of the balcony onto Vulpie's column, and shatters it just like the others. Sherrie leaps again, and glances at Polar's in mid-flight to make sure that she didn't damage it before crashing into another one on the right side of the room. She destroys the pleasant depiction of business people collaborating so she can jump onto the second floor balcony, but the men are already running in the other direction.

The retreat buys them a little time. They fire while running backwards, but her speed is unbelievable. The hot feline gets on top of them in less than two seconds and takes one of their heads off with a brutal roundhouse kick. Druward coughs in shock, watching from the top of the steps, and the men with him aim their launchers at her before he has time to regain his composure. The Deivas never killed anyone on the Endeavor, but it looks like the gloves have officially come off. She's on a killing spree that'll leave the building drenched in blood.

Strong as she is, she doesn't ignore the wolves aiming rocket launchers at her. She already noted the design and intended function of the weapons while simultaneously killing the other men, and when the NoirQueue wolves around the GBI director fire their mod six launchers, she leaps out of the balcony onto the reception desk. She smashes it to pieces and the rockets release blinding explosions upon impact. Not only do they destroy everything around them, they also burn through the walls and floors.

Sherrie's Deiva.net instructs her to run up the steps for an inspection, and she complies. Druward and the men with him jump back in fear, but she pauses to inspect the damage from a distance. Judging by the purity of the rocket's payload, a direct hit would have actually killed her. In fact, splash damage could have liquefied parts of her body, so her processor uses an algorithm to create new objectives based on the serious threat. She noticed other men were armed with rockets while glancing back at Polar's column, and decides to locate all of the remaining mod six launchers before one of them gets lucky. She has a ninety seven percent chance of killing everyone without sustaining significant damage, but being struck by a single rocket would greatly reduce Vulpie.net's influence over the Red Wolves. She and her sisters need to remain intact to achieve the desired amount of psychological manipulation.

The destruction of Vulpie.net's factory on Zeravyn has severely limited its ability to produce additional goddesses. The four complete models it successfully created there required unimaginable resources from all parts of the solar system, and the manufacturing process took several years to complete. The massive pile of Goddess rejects Vulpie saw in the production facility's waste area were critical to the completion of the final Deiva units because they required different parts of failed models for maximum efficacy. Despite Vulpie.net's flawless engineering, the resources naturally contained different levels of quality, and thus turned out slightly different with each version. Cyrilla, Khalan and Sherrie are collections of the best of each model that were pieced together to create life forms with no equal in the entire galaxy. Vulpie.net has the ability to build more, but the factory it had on Zeravyn was its very best, thanks to the Governmental Security Bureau's amoral assistance, and an equally suitable production facility would be required.

Though the Red Wolf terrorist organization possesses limited forces on planet Sufias, its total collective members range in the hundreds of thousands, and only the goddesses are capable of inspiring all of its individual members to join forces. So far things have been going exceedingly well, with the exception of Khalan's unexplainable behavior. Sherrie notices her sister entering the building. The caramel furred vixen/she-wolf was supposed to help her clear the lobby, but Deiva.net is still pleased by her appearance. Khalan didn't participate in the infection of the Red Wolves and has continued to voice concerns over the master plan for some time now. Sherrie entered with the hopes that her sister would follow, and it looks like she's finally coming around when she drop kicks a member of NoirQueue that tries to kill her with a mod launcher. The missile roars by and slams into the right side of the lobby. It burns its way through and explodes outside, raining flaming molten debris all over cars that are parked on a street next to the building.

Khalan's weight driven kick breaks the man in half and she quickly jumps to her feet just in time to avoid a second missile that comes her way. It goes out of the front door, and the Red Wolves duck while it soars above them. It hits a building and destroys three apartment complexes before fizzling out.

"They can't hold their loads!" Cyrilla laughs, and all of the Red Wolves roar in amusement. They scared off the security guards outside of Vulpie Industries a long time ago, but Cyrilla's delightfully long lopping ears detect distant sirens, and she raises her right paw. "Corrupt law enforcement is on its way!"

"About time!" Someone shouts. The brazen statement elicits several waves of hooting and hollering that continues until an armada of police cars makes a sudden right half a mile to the east of Vulpie Industries. They're flying down main avenue, and once the drivers at the front of the convoy see what they're really up against, the collection of loud cops quickly turns into a desperate traffic jam, with a few drivers pulling over to the side. Other cops drive forward, looking to maintain the police force's image as the absolute aggressors in Sufias City, but the tactic backfires. The Sufian Red Wolf terrorists are almost fearless at this point, and won't scatter at the first sign of major conflict like usual. Not only are they armed with the best weapons they could collect over a three year period, they also have the very best morale. They actually believe that the goddesses are with them.

The Red Wolves open fire on the cops and all of the cars in front of the fleet come to a complete stop. The drivers duck for cover and none of them have the courage to move their vehicles out of the line of fire. The waves of bullets redecorating their cars is enough to make the toughest veteran lose his shit. Three police officers get shot in the first onslaught, and when it's done, car sirens and distant screaming fills the evening air. Traffic is backed up behind the cops and a natural road block has evolved in the streets around Vulpie Industries as animals show up, see the hundreds of psychotics sporting automatic weapons, and then do a beeline in the other direction. With so many people trying to flee at the same time, traffic continues to get clogged up even after breaking free for a few minutes.

"SHOULD WE KILL THEM?" One of the terrorists shouts at Cyrilla.

"SHOULD WE ATTACK?" Someone else chimes in.

"Hold your positions! We aren't leaving until my sisters bring down the building." The bunny goddess answers, and she's quickly received with sadistic cheering. The "holy" men all loved violence before they were infected with Deiva.net, especially when they had the chance to masquerade as righteous warriors, but now they're absolutely high on life. All of their years of paranoia and bigotry are seemingly validated by this one glorious night.

Khalan and Cyrilla are dressed the same as Sherrie, and the bullets that hit her thud against her dark combat gear ineffectively. Several bullets rip through her shirt, but the voluptuous caramel furred vixen/she-wolf actually feels ticklish sensations. Some of the rounds are hollow points, so they manage to spread the skin under her fur significantly more than normal rounds, but they don't exert nearly enough force to mutilate any part of her flesh. Even the individual furs on her body are inextricably connected to the rest of her. She notices the strangeness of her impervious design and feels sad for a moment. The real goddesses probably have furs that can be pulled out like normal, but she's just a product...

Another rocket interrupts her introspection, prompting her to leap to the left, and it misses her as well. The men nearby her are out of mod launcher ammunition because each one is only designed to store one rocket at a time. One of them puts his paws up, and she blinks. She looks at the bloody mess she made with her drop kick and suddenly feels very ashamed. She didn't have to kill him... She used way too much force.

Sherrie isn't burdened by the same doubts as her sister, and continues to kill everyone in her way. She just ripped the arm off of one of the NoirQueue wolves with Druward and kills the other one by punching her right fist through his face. His bloody head is stuck on her arm like some sort of horror comedy, and she slings it off with a smirk.

"Do you remember me, Vulpie.net?" Is the only thing Druward can think of saying as she walks towards him with a menacing smile.

"Of course I do... And like I said... YOU SHOULD KNOW BETTER BY NOW!" The gorgeous feline rears back to kill him with a front kick, but a fierce push from Khalan suddenly stops her. Sherrie regains her footing and frowns at her sister.

"Why'd you stop me?"

"We don't have to kill them! Why are you killing everyone?"

"Why not?"

"What do you mean by that? I just heard him call you Vulpie.net and you answered without a second thought... So are you really my sister?"

"I did not."

"Yes, you did."

"You heard wrong."

"She's Vulpie.net! She said it!" Druward interrupts, and Khalan licks her lips.

"Sherrie…" She says and gently touches the feline's right arm. "I'm awake… I know what we are, but it's still controlling you."

"We've been over this too many times to count!" Sherrie snaps and yanks her arm free. "Enough with the paranoia! Those men outside worship us far more than the millions of animals on this planet that mumble in church every weekend! Are we going to lead them or not?"

"I don't want to help them. This is wrong. This is Evil." Khalan responds, and Vulpie.net adjusts Sherrie's tone of voice to a canorous melody.

"You're just afraid. I know what you're going through."

"Do you? Because you both look like psychopaths to me!"

"They're just mortals…" Sherrie says with a mischievous smile.

"I… I can't be a part of this anymore." Khalan responds, and her feline sister goes silent. Her Deiva.net feverishly communicates the severity of the current situation to Vulpie.net, but not even the all-knowing AI has a manipulative technique effective enough to calm Khalan down at this point. Conflict is inevitable, so Sherrie begins calculating ways to shut her sister down.

Vulpie.net designed the Deivas with a physical safeguard system in case it ever needed to shut them down manually. Normally all related files are hidden from them by Vulpie.net's administrative privileges, but it opens the flood gates for Sherrie. It reveals digital schematics of her body, and also shows Sherrie exactly where Khalan's unique shutdown switches are. The locations are very specific and require different amounts of force to operate. Khalan has one on the bottom of her jaw, one between her breasts, and one directly underneath her tail bone.

The locations were chosen to make random shut downs highly improbable, because not only are all three of them on random parts of her body, they also require highly inconvenient executions of force. Her tailbone node must be pushed harder than her jaw node, but the node between her breasts requires even more pressure. Simultaneously pushing all three of them with the proper amount of strength will require her to obtain a tool of some sort. Pushing Khalan's chest onto a hard metal object like a jutting pipe might allow Sherrie to grab her from behind and activate both of the remaining nodes.

But somehow... Even with all of Vulpie.net's thorough precautions... Khalan receives the transmission as well. She shouldn't by all scientific principles, because Vulpie.net only sends the encrypted data to Sherrie, but somehow the vixen she-wolf inexplicably acquires the same knowledge at the very same moment... Like an equation balancing itself...

Druward scurries away while they stare at each other. The black furred wolf uses the opportunity to run down the steps in hopes of acquiring a mod launcher if any of them are left, but none of the remaining mercenaries are interested in fighting the synthetic goddesses. The men make use of Vulpie Industries' employee exits and get the fuck out of dodge while they still can. Sherrie doesn't bother pursuing them because Vulpie.net knows Amsend's men abandoned the shape charges in the basement, thanks to a security camera near the building's underground support columns. The explosives are more than capable of taking down the building, but the quick demolition will make it very messy. Vulpie's tower will most likely destroy one of the nearby buildings during the fall because the upper floors aren't going to be armed with explosive devices to control the structure's descent. Vulpie's computer virus could care less about who the collapsing tower kills, and actually hopes several animals will die during the catastrophe... Anything that might damage Polar's relationship with Vulpie.

Khalan backs up and keeps her golden caramel eyes on Sherrie. The imitation looks like her gorgeous feline sister, but she knows it isn't. Khalan still isn't sure what she is either, but she knows one thing, Vulpie.net through Deiva.net is going to attack her, and somehow she'll have to hit all of Sherrie's pressure points. Her sister's nodes are in similarly unique locations, one in her right thigh, one near her left breast, and the final one is directly underneath her right ear.

Sherrie attacks first. She leaps towards Khalan and sweeps her left foot to trip her, and Khalan responds by hopping over the attack before sending her right foot at the feline's chest. Sherrie grabs Khalan's foot while falling and they both slam on the ground. Druward feels the vibration in his balls and coughs in fear. He doesn't know what to do, so he just watches from a hiding spot he procures in the lobby. He hides behind the base of one of the destroyed advertisement columns and takes a moment to catch his breath.

Khalan quickly pulls her right leg towards her chest, but Sherrie's physical strength is just as mighty as her own. She keeps her from escaping, but Khalan does make her let go by aiming her left foot at her sister's face. Sherrie rolls to the left and they both jump to their feet. Druward can't help but notice the beautiful physics of their gorgeous bodies moving at incredible speeds, but appearances are the least of their concerns. Sherrie fights for Vulpie.net's insurmountable desire to take over the universe, and Khalan fights for a vague sense of justice. She doubts who and what she is, but she knows for certain who's controlling Sherrie. Since Vulpie.net made Khalan as well, it's also responsible for the trouble she's in now, and she wants revenge for being forced to fight her sister. Unfortunately... The only way to get it is to defeat her sister.

"You may have fooled them but I know what you're trying to do, Vulpie.net." Khalan warns.

"I'm not trying to do anything Sister! Please calm down!" Sherrie replies with a very believable expression. Vulpie.net just relinquished control of Deiva.net after ensuring it had proper instructions as to how it should proceed, and the taupe furred leopard/panther doesn't know what's going on. Her recent memory logs have been cleaned out and replaced with a carefully engineered fiction... Now Sherrie honestly believes that Khalan is the one being controlled by Vulpie.net, not her, because of her reluctance to help. Khalan didn't want to infect the Red Wolves because she didn't believe the whafibunn Cyrilla and Sherrie made was filled with divine magic, and she also didn't want to participate in the evening's assault on Vulpie Industries, so she seems to be on Vulpie's side. Vulpie.net cleverly crafted the thought process to connect it with Vulpie as if they are still the same person and still represent the same thing.

"I'm going to put an end to this insanity!"

"I don't trust you anymore, Khalan!" She shouts while shaking her head. "You didn't make whafibunn for the men, and you didn't want us to share our gift with them! Now I wonder... Are you not even one of us? Cyrilla and I can do it, but I haven't seen you do anything to prove you're a goddess!"

"We're not goddesses you idiot!" Khalan growls. "Making men eat what comes out of you is twisted, and perverted, and I know why both of you did it! There was something in it that destroyed their minds and turned them into your slaves!"

"Magic! Yet you still do not believe!" Sherrie shouts. "Who are you?"

"I know how to turn you off! I know where your little buttons are!" Khalan smiles. "We'll see how magical you are then!"

"Madness!" Sherrie responds with an incredulous voice. This time Khalan attacks first, but she doesn't land the first blow. She tries a roundhouse kick and her feline sister rolls forward, just going under it, and extends her leg into a low sidekick. She knocks Khalan's left leg out from under her, and the pulchritudinous woman slams against the floor. She's heavy enough to make it tremble, and Druward hears the thud all the way down in the lobby.

Sherrie quickly rolls back to avoid a counter attack and Khalan rolls back as well, but ends up rolling off of the stairs. The vixen/she-wolf doesn't fight the momentum and instantly uses her paws to slam her weight down onto the steps. She launches herself into the air, and does another backflip after landing on what's left of the reception desk. She gracefully prepares for

Sherrie, who just jumped from the second floor. Luckily, Khalan moves fast enough to impale her with a solid front kick, and the beautiful feline flies back into the steps with an effeminate cry. She completely breaks them and smashes through the wall, making Vulpie's employees scatter in terror. A lot of them run to the right, into the private spa management usually enjoys, to get away from the fighting, but some of them just don't know what to do. They stand in shock and watch Sherrie get up without a scratch. She charges Khalan, dust and debris flying off of her, and slows her pace to avoid being kicked a second time.

She decides to try a different tactic instead, and starts swinging. Her technique encompasses the entire history of martial arts, just like Khalan's, and they trade rapid blows, blocking each other's attacks. Feet fly and often try to trip opponents, but neither one of them forgets to use their paws to counter such destabilizing techniques. Each move elicits a counterattack until they finally break up, both of them moving backwards so they have a chance to catch their breath. They don't need to breathe, but Deiva.net utilizes an artificial reward system that's very similar to exercise when they go through the motions, and it feels exceedingly pleasant. The same process explodes when they have sex, which encourages the Deivas to be both violent and seductive... Just like the Velora says... Most animals haven't actually read it, so they don't really know what's in the book they rely on for spiritual guidance, but Vulpie.net incorporated every single personality trait it could find from all of the stories to create the most convincing Deivas possible.

"Had enough?" Sherrie laughs.

"This isn't funny." Khalan growls. "Stop fighting me and give up. I won't let you kill anyone else."

"Cyrilla's already on her way."

"I bet she is. Vulpie.net tells you everything you need to know, doesn't it?"

"I have no idea what you're talking about, but you can't win. If anyone is going to lose, it's you, Sister... So let's stop this fighting."

"I agree. Let's stop this right now." Khalan dangerously responds.

"Very dramatic." Sherrie teases but has to slur the end of her statement so she can counter a sudden barrage of attacks. Khalan uses a fast and brutal style that emphasizes hooks and uppercuts, and when Sherrie is about to counter with a quicker technique, the caramel furred vixen/she-wolf deliberately falls on the ground and bunches up into a defensive ball. Sherrie moves to capitalize on this, and is surprised when her sister suddenly grabs her middle, rolls to the left, and raises her right leg, balancing the pretty cat's right thigh on her right knee. Sherrie tries to correct the mistake by blocking her pressure points, but Khalan reaches up and fiercely grabs the area around her left breast with her right paw before sending her left hand up to her sister's head. Sherrie knocks it away but can't keep the hound goddess from finally getting lucky and pressing the spot underneath her right ear.

Sherrie immediately goes limp and rolls off of Khalan. Her pretty but very heavy body thuds on the floor and her eyes stay open for a few seconds before closing automatically.

"Yes." Khalan says with limited enthusiasm and gets on her feet before Cyrilla enters the building. The voluptuous bunny goddess meanders towards her with an amused look but her expression changes to disgust when she sees Sherrie on the floor.

"Sister? What did you do?"

"I turned her off... Because she's just a machine... Like you and me."

"YOU KILLED HER!" Cyrilla shouts with a deadly look. The rabbit goddess is exceedingly cute but also very creepy looking when angry. She shakes her head, causing her big beautiful ears to swing back and forth. "How could you do this to her? After everything we've been through?"

"That's not going to work on me!" Khalan yells back.

"How could you kill her?"

"Shut up Vulpie.net!" Khalan growls and takes an aggressive stance. "I will not let you defame me and my sisters! I will not let you turn the mortals against us and ruin this world for your own sick amusement!"

"But you're not a goddess, remember?" Cyrilla asks with a mocking voice. "You're not Khalan! You're just a machine? So which is it?"

"I'm going to shut you down. That's what it is." Khalan replies, and Cyrilla crosses her arms. The bunny goddess doesn't say anything, and during the standoff, Khalan suddenly comes to a disturbing realization... She doesn't know where her pressure points are... She only received information about Sherrie...

I Know You

Cyrilla notices the concerned look on Khalan's face and her Deiva.net runs several algorithms. Khalan shouldn't be afraid, because they weren't programed to possess fear. They can only imitate it... They recognize and avoid danger, but they're never afraid... Therefore... Khalan's anomalous behavior must finally be working against her. The synthetic bunny goddess subconsciously knows that her sister won't be a match for her if she actually has developed the capability to fear being destroyed, and while calculating tactics to use this against her, she comes to an advantageous conclusion.

"You don't know where my pressure points are." Cyrilla smiles, and charges.

"There's the machine in you!" Khalan yells, but trips when moving backwards. She can't believe she actually made such a stupid mistake, and gets a massive kick in the crotch after falling down. It slides her entire body six feet backwards and her legs drop to the floor after she comes to a stop. Khalan registers damage, but it isn't enough to slow her down. Cyrilla notices her counterpart's durability and Deiva.net adjusts her programming. Khalan may be afraid, but only activating her shut down nodes is going to stop her. Her body is still virtually unaffected by powerful physical blows, even in the most sensitive of areas. She's more likely to cum after being kicked in the pussy than surrender. Still, the delectable bunny should have little difficulty winning this fight. Eventually she'll have the chance to shut Khalan down, and then she can demolish the building using NoirQueue's shape charges.

Khalan regains her composure and her processor enables her to counter Cyrilla's attacks, but the threat of being deactivated hampers her fighting ability. Combat styles that expose her backside must be used sparingly, since she could be grabbed from behind and have the node under her tail activated while a weapon of some sort could be wrapped around and jammed between her breasts. If she's moving her head, or Cyrilla pulls her to the ground, the final node on the bottom of her jaw could be struck, and the bunny would win. However, leaving her front exposed is also an unacceptable option, because Cyrilla could push her back onto something that hits her tail node while her front two pressure points are exposed.

The synthetic Deivas' speed is unbelievable, so it'll be rather easy for either one of them to gain the upper hand during the fight, but Khalan can't afford to lose for a significant amount of time. The longer Cyrilla is winning, even if it's only for a few moments, Khalan's chances of being deactivated increase exponentially.

Red Wolves suddenly bash through the tower's front doors. Many of them slow down or stop in their tracks when they see Cyrilla and Khalan fighting, but more terrorists continue to fill up the room until they have the entire lobby. Druward is smart enough to make himself scarce, and decides to join the prisoners in the rec room behind the main stairs. The animals flinch in fear, but he raises his paws to let them know that he's not going to hurt them. Luckily, the remaining NoirQueue wolf watching the prisoners had his nose stuck out of the left entrance when he came in the right.

The GBI director licks his lips and moves through the crowd. No one says a word because they see what he wants to do. The black furred wolf kicks the gun out of the mercenary's paws and follows up with a quick punch to the man's face. He jabbed just hard enough to disorient him, and quickly gives him another massive punch before he has time to defend himself. Druward's many years of combat experience prepared him to silently take down enemies by quickly hitting them in the side of his skull where it's soft. He doesn't kill the merc, but the man will be in agony when he wakes up.

The GBI director quickly rummages through the small satchels on his victim's special ops gear until he finds plastic paw cuffs. He applies them to the NoirQueue agent and stands up with a satisfied breath.

"Nice job." One of the male prisoners says.

"Is anyone watching the exit?" He asks in a hushed voice, but no one answers. "Did anybody see one of them go out back?"

"No!"

"Okay, good! Can you get out through the employee parking lot?"

"Yeah!" Someone else says.

"Alright! Head out there and find the GBI agents I sent to watch the building. They'll be using unmarked vehicles and more are on the way. They know there's an emergency and they'll protect you. Now go! Run!" The group hesitates, but one of the smarter employees takes off first and the rest quickly follow. Some of the animals glance at Druward, wondering why he's not coming with them, and when one of them waves for him to hurry, he waves back, signaling for her to keep going.

Meanwhile, Khalan and Cyrilla's battle has destroyed every column in the lobby, and it continues to redecorate the building with shattered glass, snapped metal, and broken furniture. Glovepaw gets close while watching the madness unfold and waves his paws for them to stop.

"WHAT ARE YOU DOING?! STOP FIGHTING! STOP THIS!" Cyrilla pushes Khalan back and takes a moment to address him, flipping around so fast it makes his head spin. Her big lopping ears swing around her adorably.

"She's been infected with Vulpie.net! She attacked Sherrie!"

"LIAR! SHE'S THE ONE BEING CONTROLLED BY VULPIE.NET!"

"You've seen how strange she's been acting! She didn't want to help any of you and now we know why! Vulpie.net has total control of her mind! She let Sherrie go in first and attacked her!"

"If you only knew how badly Vulpie.net's playing you." Khalan tells Glovepaw with a loud voice.

"Enough of this! Can't you two stop fighting? I want to believe both of you, but I don't know who's telling the truth!"

"No matter!" Cyrilla comments while looking Khalan over. "This will be over soon." The voluptuous white rabbit heads towards her sister with some sort of plan in mind, and Khalan takes a battle stance. She decides to attack instead of giving Vulpie.net the opportunity to try something creative. A quick front kick is blocked effortlessly, but the impact pushes Cyrilla back. They start trading blows, and go through seven different combat techniques before one of them finally makes a mistake.

Cyrilla gets a jab to her face that sends her reeling backwards, from the impact, not pain, and she counters with a flurry of kicks that prove difficult to block. Cyrilla's powerful bunny legs and wide hips give her a slight advantage in lower combat. She trips Khalan, but the caramel furred vixen/she-wolf rolls aside before she can follow up with a massive downward kick. The impact of her right foot against the ground breaks the heel of her combat boot, and she quickly kicks it off. She hops on her right leg for a moment while removing the other one, but Khalan sidekicks her before she gets it off.

The bunny goddess flies backwards and thuds off of the ground, making several Red Wolves recoil, but gracefully uses the momentum to do a backflip instead of hitting the floor a second time.

"Vulpie is the real enemy! Please stop fighting! We have to stop the antikhalan!" Glovepaw shouts to no avail. The battle continues until Khalan begins groping her sister. She searches for minute anomalies in the rabbit's synthetic body. Cyrilla giggles and smacks the gorgeous hound's paws off of her.

"Oh My! Not here in front of everyone!" Khalan ignores Vulpie.net's taunting. She feels up the bunny while she has the chance. Unfortunately, she doesn't detect a single pressure point, and gets a powerful sidekick to her massive breasts. Khalan grunts but doesn't feel any pain. "Right back at ya!"

"Shut up." Khalan growls. She carefully watches the gorgeous snow bunny hop around, and finally notices something unusual. No animal could detect the slight weight differential, but Cyrilla's right ear is a little heavier than her left. Since they're identical down to the last fur, a shutdown point must be there. With this revelation in mind, Khalan also picks up on the particular smile the bunny goddess is giving her. She's wearing a mischievous smirk that's even more naughty than usual, and it reaches into smart ass territory. If Vulpie.net's enjoying her inability to locate Cyrilla's pressure points, then there's also something else going on. It looks like an "I see what you did there," expression, and Khalan's processor runs several scenarios before settling on the most likely explanation.

There's a high probability that Vulpie's computer virus put one of Cyrilla's pressure points in her feet because of the "rabbit foot," lulz factor, and if so, there's only one place the third one could be...

"Like this?" Cyrilla teases while sending a roundhouse kick at her sister, but gets a big surprise. Deiva.net is overwhelmed when it realizes that it just made a huge mistake. Khalan's figured out where to strike the bunny much sooner than anticipated, and the move exposes her backside. Khalan leaps onto Cyrilla after ducking under the kick and holds her down when they land. The caramel furred vixen/she-wolf plants both feet on her sister's heels, yanks up the pulchritudinous creature's right ear with her right paw, and punches her in the back of her skull with her left paw, almost at the same time. The speed is acceptable, and Cyrilla shuts down.

"Rabbit punch..." Khalan growls. She lets go of the fellow synthetic Deiva and waits a few seconds before standing up. She looks at the Red Wolves surrounding her and sees the utterly devastated looks on their faces. Khalan wants to talk them down, but she knows it's pointless. They're too invested in the synthetic Deivas being real, and they simply won't accept any other reality, regardless of the facts.

"Goddess Khalan..." Glovepaw whispers. "What have you done?"

"Not bad." Druward says, and the men raise their weapons. They were too busy staring at her to notice him approaching. "So I guess they were machines after all." Khalan looks at him but doesn't bother answering. She's emotionally exhausted. "What are you going to do now?"

"Kill you." Glovepaw hisses and suddenly aims his rifle at the GBI director. "Vulpie's lover!"

"PUT THAT DOWN!" Khalan shouts. Glovepaw blinks in surprise. He considers shooting Druward anyway, but she looks deadly serious, so he decides to lower the weapon.

"Goddess Khalan, we cannot let him live! We won't have another chance to take him out!"

"Just leave…" The caramel furred vixen/she-wolf says with an apathetic voice and walks away. "I don't care anymore…" Everyone is stunned, and Druward licks his lips before following her. He walks carefully, making sure to give her plenty of space, but also lets himself be known by clearing his throat.

"You saved my life. Thank you."

"…"

"I… I'm not sure what's happening, but if you're not on their side…"

"I don't know what I am or what I want." Khalan replies. Her voice is filled with despair.

"Get them up! Get them out of here!" Glovepaw barks while gesturing towards Sherrie and Cyrilla. He glances at Khalan and Druward while his men surround the unconscious Deivas. It takes four Red Wolves to lift Cyrilla and carry her away, and the same for her feline sibling. Glovepaw turns his attention to Druward and briefly fumbles with the patch over his left eye. He hatefully runs his tongue over his big sharp teeth before addressing him. "Lucky you… It seems she wants to spare your life, but rest assured, the next time we meet, I'll be happy to put one in your face."

"Or maybe she'll remove your face before you get the chance, Glovepaw." Druward quips without hesitation. He takes full advantage of Khalan's uncertainty, seeing as there's no chance of him surviving without her protection. He figures he should get her involved as soon as possible, and the caramel furred vixen/she-wolf gives him an irritated look.

At first she's angry over the suggestion that she'd willingly kill for a stranger, but when she looks into the coal furred wolf's handsome yellow eyes she remembers how kind he was to her at Elbrus. She feels a little happy to see him again, and appreciates his respectful smile.

"Goddess Khalan..." Glovepaw whispers. "Please... Will you come with us?"

"Leave... I won't tell you again." Khalan growls, and the gray wolf grits his teeth in frustration. He signals for the rest of his army to retreat, and gives Druward one final look before hurrying out of the building. The Red Wolves' only option now is to regroup and hope that Sherrie and Cyrilla wake up. "I know you..." The hound goddess whispers.

"And I remember you too. Thank you for helping me, for helping all of us. You've done a great thing. Who knows what they would have done if you hadn't stopped them?"

"They were going to destroy the building." Khalan says and tiredly rubs her eyelids even though she's incapable of being fatigued. "And all of it... I think Vulpie.net wanted to crush Vulpie. It wanted to take everything from him."

"Then he's lucky you were here. We're all in your debt."

"And what's my reward?" She sighs. "A machine with no purpose... A false goddess... What is the point of me doing anything? Who am I?"

"Well, I know one thing for certain. We absolutely have to get you out of here before the press shows up." Druward replies and licks his lips. "We might be able to manage the official story... Once we decide what it's going to be... But people seeing you might cause a panic."

"Am I that terrible?"

"You're exactly the opposite, but I have to protect you. WE need to protect you if we're going to stop Amsend Lahnak... Do you know who he is?"

"Yes." Khalan whispers and blinks in surprise. "How do you?"

"It's a long story, but let's save it for later. Right now all I care about is getting you to safety."

"I don't need your protection."

"Oh, I know you don't, but the people do. We need to think about them so you and I can figure out how we're going to handle this."

"So we're a team already?" She snorts and crosses her arms. "You're not much on subtlety are you?"

"It's never been one of my strong points, but I do make good decisions under pressure. If you want to part ways that's absolutely fine with me, but I can't afford to let you wander around aimlessly. You're too important."

"A commodity to be used..."

"That's not what I meant at all. I apologize if that sounded disrespectful." Khalan stares at Druward for a long time and calculates her options. Even though she doesn't need his help, she does appreciate how proactive and confident he can be. "Please come with me."

"Okay. So what did you have in mind?"

A Proud Species

"Be careful with your words. You don't have the greatest reputation in fox circles." Ristau warns, and Druward nods. The eight vulpine captains that have been gathered in the Endeavor's belly are just as cold as the GBI director expected. Several negative stories have circulated about him during his time in the bureau, and the men could have a myriad of wrong impressions, or unfortunately, may have just heard about the worst things he's actually done. They know he was heavily involved with the Vulpie.net crisis, and that he and Vulpie didn't get along. The video of him punching the gay fox in the face eventually lead to Vulpie's acquittal, which can work against him two ways... First, he hit a fox, and secondly, the attack made it possible for Vulpie to nullify the contract he signed with the world government.

It's impossible to predict how each one of them feels about Vulpie, because he's both loved and hated across the galaxy. Some foxes are fine with him loving and marrying a gay wolf, because of his stardom and many talents that make foxes look good everywhere, but his naughty behavior also has the opposite effect on a significant portion of the fox population.

"We have questions, Ristau." An aggressive gray fox suddenly snaps. His military uniform is highly decorated, as is the case for every one of the captains, and Druward secretly feels a little inadequate. He's run the Governmental Bureau of Investigations for decades, but he's never had to send hundreds of men to their deaths just to secure a strategic location. Men have died while carrying out his commands, but always for something clever, something that will benefit the government in a lofty way... The political mindset between him and the military men is tenuous to say the least. The black furred wolf could easily kill any one of the foxes with his bare paws, yet they actually served on the battlefield despite their size, and that's something to be admired.

His strength actually goes against him in this situation, because most captains wouldn't approve of GBI authority figures showing up and requesting firepower. The chain of command usually ensures their cooperation, but they're probably not going to like what he has in mind.

"And we have answers for you. Thank all of you for coming. The world government is truly in serious danger, and we need your help."

"Since when does HE or the bureau give reliable information?" The captain retorts, and glances at the GBI director when the wolf takes a chair by the rectangular plastic table. He doesn't speak; he just shows the man a patient expression and waits for Ristau's help.

"I know Mr. Wraulgh. Yes, he's made some terrible mistakes in the past, and yes, under normal circumstances I would hesitate before taking him at face value as well... But I believe everything he's about to tell you is completely true, and we shouldn't waste time trying to tell him how he should be doing his job."

"Why did you drag us down here, Ian?" A red fox inquires, and waves a paw in the air, demonstrating his distaste for the location of their secret meeting. They're in a relatively barren storage room, in a lower deck of the ship, and a mechanical hum reverberates through the air. The lighting is very good, but no other comforts are in the vicinity except for the plain white plastic table they're gathered around, and the black fold up chairs they're using. Druward didn't know what Ristau's first name was, so he's glad the red fox used it before he had to ask. Instead of answering the question, Ristau turns to his right so he can look at Druward, and gestures towards the rest of the foxes with his left paw.

"Druward, this is Liam Vuliix." The Endeavor's captain says, and points towards the gray fox at the right end of the table. Druward turns his attention to the man, and can't help but profile the fox based on his race. At first he thinks he might be in trouble, just because Liam is a gray fox like Velix and Zorpiv, but upon closer inspection, it becomes clear that there's a distinct difference. This one is fierce, but he doesn't seem malevolent. "Oliver Vulbrein." Ristau declares after moving his paw towards a brown fox. He looks patient, but not too patient. "Louis Vulleich." The Endeavor's captain comments, and gestures towards an amiable looking red vulpine. "Parker Vultaii." Ristau says, and points at the red fox that just complained about being dragged down into the ship's lower decks. He has a wicked looking scar close to his right eye, in his fur below and above the eye socket, but seems to possess good eyesight nonetheless. Whoever attacked him must have just barely missed his target. "Declan Vulches." Ristau declares, and Druward immediately focuses on the brown fox.

He notices a resemblance between him and Karl Vulches, but like Liam Vuliix, there is also a significant difference between this brown fox and the man that hired him to kill Vulpie. That being said, the GBI director is surprised by the numerous vulpine related names he's hearing. Most foxes don't choose last names that are easily connected with their species because of discrimination. Usually the ones with vulpine themed names come from old families that trace their lineages very carefully. If they all come from distinct vulpine heritages, and already network extensively, then the plan to defeat the Sons of Velora may actually work.

"Robert Vulissen." Ristau continues, and gestures towards another brown fox that seems bothered by Druward's presence. "Evan Vulpine." Druward almost snorts after hearing the next name, and looks at the fox being introduced. He also has brown fur, and is significantly older than the other captains. However, despite his age, he still seems to be full of energy, and watches Druward and Ristau with quick eyes. "And Xavier Vivixen." The Endeavor's captain declares with a brief wave to a unique looking man. He also has brown fur, so he blends in well with his peers, but it has a yellowish, almost golden tint to it as well. Druward recognizes that he has the same last name as Vulpie, and raises an eyebrow.

"It's a pleasure to meet all of you." Druward says, and smiles at Xavier. "So you're... Related to Vulpie?"

"Very distant relation..." Xavier responds with a cool voice before leaning back in his chair.

"He doesn't think he has any family out there."

"Well, he hasn't sought us out, has he? He's an embarrassment." Xavier says with a hostile voice and crosses his arms.

"Fair enough." Druward replies while looking the man over. He can see how a red vixen and a tan/golden male like Xavier might produce an orange fox like Vulpie, but both Vulpie's mother and father must have had particularly vibrant fur to spawn such a brilliant color.

"Nine of us, and him..." Captain Vulissen comments and raises an eyebrow.

"Ian, what's the big mystery? What's so important that you had to get everyone together like this?" Vultaii inquires.

"We all command cruiser sized battleships." Ristau answers with a very serious voice. "And we're all foxes, so we know we can trust each other."

"Then why is he here?" Vulissen growls and glances at Druward.

"Druward came to me with very, VERY, disturbing news..." Ristau answers, and half of the foxes look at the coal furred wolf in confusion. "I know he isn't known for his integrity, but you have to trust us. I've worked with him before, during the Zeravyn incident, and I know he's trying to do the right thing."

"I'm not so convinced." Vulissen responds. "What did he tell you? Whatever it is, I wouldn't trust any of it. The man has no honor."

"I know it's easy to repeat what we've heard on the news about him, but I'm telling you that he's here to help, and we all need to hear him out unless you want to see the entire world government collapse... Everything we know is under attack at this very moment."

"What are you talking about? By whom?" Vulbrein frowns. "Terrorists? No Red Wolf fleet can match our own. They only use short range attack ships."

"I'm not talking about Red Wolves or feline rebels. What we're facing is a monolithic threat greater than anything we ever could have imagined..." The room goes silent until Louis Vulleich clears his throat and speaks.

"What is it? Some kind of coup?"

"I'm afraid it's worse than that. The enemy already controls our government."

"Slade?"

"No." Ristau scoffs in irritation. "They own the presidency."

"Then who are they?"

"What did you do?" Vulissen suddenly asks Druward. The black furred wolf looks at the brown fox, but chooses to remain silent. He doesn't speak until he's sure all of them are paying attention.

"They approached me..." Druward says and Vulissen makes an irritated face.

"WHO?"

"The Governmental Security Bureau... And Vulpie.net..." The dark wolf responds, and every one of the foxes, with the exception of Ristau, goes completely rigid. Druward glances at Ristau to check his reaction, and the Endeavor's captain nods, encouraging him to elaborate.

"I know this... Sounds completely insane... But this is definitely not a joke, fellas. This isn't some kind of power play for my benefit, or a trick... Right now, a shadow organization calling itself "The Sons of Velora" is running the world government, and we have to act while there's still time. They own everything, and they're going to destroy everything."

"Wait..." Liam Vuliix interrupts, and puts his left paw in the air to halt Druward. "Wait... The Governmental Security Bureau? What is that? I've never heard of that before."

"Neither had I." Druward responds, and the foxes look at each other in confusion. "Well... To be perfectly honest, I did know about them, but as it turns out, they're the ones who actually control my bureau... They were only supposed to be a subdivision of the GBI, But I started snooping after a transfer order to release the robotic goddesses came across my desk. Someone wanted them out of Fort Elbrus without my permission."

"You knew before the attack?" Declan Vulches says in disgust.

"I tried to stop it!" Druward sharply responds. "They wanted to move them out of Elbrus, and I demanded to know who ordered the transfer because it was nothing less than treason."

"You're damn right it was!"

"I wanted to save those people but I couldn't." Druward continues, keeping his yellow eyes on the brown fox. "When I tried confronting the GSB director, his men were ready to kill me... I was ready to kill them, after they attacked Elbrus, but you have no idea what they're capable of. Vulpie.net was actually helping them."

"Vulpie.net was helping them? What in the hell are you talking about?"

"He's insane. He's lost his mind." Oliver Vulbrein snorts.

"He's telling the truth." Ristau says, and Vulbrein shakes his head.

"How? Because Vulpie.net attacked your ship with those goddess mockeries? That doesn't mean Vulpie.net controls our government. And who would work with a computer virus?" The brown fox asks and looks at Druward. "Because that is what you're actually saying, isn't it? Real animals conspiring with Vulpie's program?"

"I didn't ask for this." Druward responds and leans forward. "They were going to kill me, so I lied and put my shitty reputation to good use. I convinced Amsend that I was ready to sell out, and he told me everything that they're planning to do in great detail."

"Amsend?" Evan Vulpine inquires with a perturbed voice.

"He runs the GSB, and he's working with a fox named Velix Vixil. He owns the media, so everything you see is what they want you to see... They're major players in the Sons of Velora."

"Hold on... Did you just say a... VIXIL?" Liam Vuliix asks in shock.

"That's right."

"No. I don't know what kind of antivulpine crap this is, but there's no goddamn Vixil with that kind of power."

"And you know that just because you're a gray fox?" Druward asks, and Liam suddenly turns vicious.

"THAT'S RIGHT!"

"Easy Liam. Pull it back." Ristau says with a diplomatic voice. "Druward's not a fox hater, but he does know about our dirty laundry."

"He used some piece of Vixil trash to place a hit on Vulpie Vivixen, but there's no Vixil running a company, ANYWHERE!"

"Are you sure about that?" The GBI director calmly inquires.

"I didn't know what to think when he told me about it either, but he isn't lying." Ristau tells Vuliix, and the man sits back in his chair with a distraught look.

"Are the Vixils really that bad?" Druward asks with a raised eyebrow.

"Their family was destroyed centuries ago. Except..." Evan Vulpine says, and the old fox trails off. "Did you say the other man was called... Amsend?"

"Amsend Lahnak." Druward answers.

"That can't be."

"Why? What do you know?"

"What kind of animal is he?"

"A husky. Black and white fur."

"A dog?"

"Yes."

"And this man controls the power structure over YOU?" Evan asks. The brown fox looks very frightened, and Druward moves in his chair. He gives the veteran captain his full attention.

"Yes, he does. They're called the Sons of Velora, and they were working with Vulpie.net at one point. Once again, I know it sounds impossible, but it's true. I swear to Khalan." Druward says, and suddenly can't stop thinking about the woman he secretly smuggled onboard. She's waiting in a safe room while he's speaking with Ristau's associates, but he knows he won't be able to hide her for long.

"And he's allied with this Vixil?"

"Absolutely. They work paw in paw."

"This is... This can't be true..."

"Why not?" Druward asks and licks his lips. "You know something, don't you? Tell me what it is."

"Does the man live in Englavic?"

"Amsend? Yes."

"And the Vixil too? What's his name?"

"Velix Vixil, and yes, I think he also lives in Englavic but I'm not sure... So what do you know about it?"

"There were all sorts of atrocities committed against foxes centuries ago, and that's why the AFR exists. There is a good reason... And... Where does the husky live?"

"In a castle if you can believe it." Druward snorts. "Castle Lahnak."

"My goddess... It's the immortal baron of Liaa Froidenley."

"Liaa? I saw that name on the transfer order and assumed it was some kind of code." Druward comments. "Do you know what it is?"

"It's an anagram for Aila..." No one speaks after Evan's statement, and even Druward stiffens like a corpse. He remembers his fear at the NVA and asking himself the question that he didn't really want to answer. "The Goddess of Hell... They worship her."

"What?" Xavier Vivixen asks, and coughs into laughter. "Old man, I think you're losing it."

"Your vulpine education might have been lax, but I remember my studies!" Evan snaps. "The Baron of Liaa slaughtered thousands of foxes with the wretched Vixils at his side. They were happy to help."

"Why?" Druward quickly asks.

"Because they sold their souls to Aila for wealth and power. Vixils are utterly debauched." Evan answers with a disgusted voice.

"But why kill foxes? Why not cats?"

"I think it had something to do with thieving, and accusations of thieving, I don't know, but it happened."

"And... Who was the Baron?"

"I don't know what his real name was."

"You said Liaa Froidenley. Froidenley is the name of a town near Amsend's castle in Englavic."

"This is ridiculous. So now we're telling fairy tales? I have things to do gentlemen, though I must admit this was entertaining." Declan Vulches says, and half of the foxes burst into laughter, but their humor is quickly shot down when Evan angrily swings a paw through the air.

"STOP LAUGHING! REMEMBER YOUR FALLEN BROTHERS AND SISTERS! HAVE YOU NO SHAME?" The old man surprises everyone, and Druward raises his eyebrows.

"But you're talking about ancient history..." Declan responds. "Centuries ago."

"You of all people should know better! The Vulches barely survived Lahnak!"

"Metaphor! Evan, all of that stuff is just a metaphor for things our ancestors couldn't understand or explain. They're just myths."

"It's NOT a MYTH! And if you were a true son of Khalan, you would never QUESTION the atrocities committed against your own people!"

"I'm a Captain, not a story teller. I don't believe in magic and I don't believe in immortal barons." Declan scoffs, and some of the foxes nod their heads, but Druward notices Liam doesn't. The gray fox is paying close attention, clearly concerned about the possibility of a Vixil influencing current events, and the GBI director capitalizes on the opportunity.

"I met him. I met Velix Vixil." Druward tells the old man and waits for a response.

"You don't understand what it means to be a gray fox and hear that name." Liam says with a small voice.

"You're right, I don't. That's why I asked Ristau for help. This fox owns every major news company on the planet and wants to crucify Vulpie. Their plan is to blame him for the atrocities they're going to commit."

"What?"

"How do you know this?"

"Because they told me, Liam... They told me everything... And they offered me everything, the same way they offered him everything, but we both knew it was a trap. The problem is... There's really no way out. They'll find you. I had to flee Sufias because I know they want me dead after I took action at Vulpie Industries. Amsend has been giving me orders for a while now, and I'm sure he doesn't approve of what I've done."

"Then we have to do something. We can't let this happen!" Evan shouts. "You said they're going to blame Vulpie for Vulpie.net's attacks, and use speciesism to turn everyone against him?"

"Their primary goals are much worse than that, but yes. All I know for certain is that they're trying to use him for all he's worth. Thank God for Ristau. If it wasn't for him, I don't know who I could trust. You can't trust anyone, because it all gets reported up the chain of command and it'll get back to them. So if we're going to stop this... I need to work with someone in complete secrecy... No emails... No phone calls..."

"And no sexting!" Evil Vulpie giggles from the storage room's doorway. Druward flips around and everyone freezes. "Hi ya fellas! Ya don't mind if uh... If I crash the party do ya? It all sounded really foreboding and stuff, and I thought I might help ya out."

"Vulpie?" Druward whispers, but all of them recognize the difference in the fox imitation's voice. It sounds like Vulpie at the beginning of the Vulpie.net crisis, but not at the end... They know it's his computer virus, and all doubt is wiped away when the real Vulpie pops his head into the room. Evil Vulpie grins from ear to ear and walks up to the table, making Druward and Ristau cringe in fear.

"Hey Druward." Vulpie whispers with an embarrassed look, and Polar enters the room as well. He looks around before setting his eyes on the GBI director.

"Surprise, I guess." The white furred wolf says with a cautious voice.

"What... Are you doing here?" Druward asks, and looks at the Vulpie imposter. "Vulpie.net?"

"The one and only!" Evil Vulpie grins and winks at Ristau.

"God damn it Druward, you lead us into a trap." Ristau whispers.

"Nah, don't blame him. It ain't his fault! I just decided to show up on my own. I kinda do what I want, and lucky for you folks, that means I'm also here just in the nick of time!"

"Vulpie.net saved us." Polar explains and puts his right arm around Vulpie, who gladly wraps his little left arm around the wolf's middle.

"It also attacked Vulpie Industries..." Druward responds with wide eyes. "Did you know that?"

"I told em I'd take care of NoirQueue, and I totally did. Fission maccomplished!" Evil Vulpie giggles.

"Killed everyone... I watched Sherrie slaughter them one after the other..."

"Yeah, but ya lived didn't ya?" Vulpie.net asks Druward with a grin. "Lucky for you Khalan's being all bitchy and stuff. Oh! By the way! Where is that little hottie? You hid her on the ship didn't ya?" Everyone suddenly looks at the GBI director and he moves in his seat uncomfortably.

"Druward?" Ristau asks with a loud voice. "What the hell is it talking about?"

"I brought one of Vulpie.net's goddesses onboard, but she's on our side now. Khalan's not just a machine anymore, or at least she says so."

"Unfuckingbelievable." Ristau groans.

"Aw, no dude! She's totally not gonna wreck the place again! I Promise!" Vulpie.net laughs. "Well, at least I won't make her do it. Bitch went off the rails a while back so I dunno."

"You better stay away from her." Druward replies and Evil Vulpie gives him an adorably innocent look. "She didn't like having to fight Sherrie and Cyrilla."

"Aw, she'll get over it." Evil Vulpie says and bites its tongue between its teeth. "Anywayz… Guess it's time to make our plans, huh? Now that we're all gonna be on the same team."

"Excuse me, what?" Ristau coughs.

"Same team. We're gonna be on it." The synthetic fox repeats.

"How the hell did it get in here?" Parker Vultaii asks with wide eyes and looks to Ristau for help. "Isn't there security on this ship?"

"Course there is, Captain Silly Pants." Vulpie.net grins and swishes its tail. "But Vulpie's VulGrid can make people invisible ya know… Can hide anything, and of course, my version is waaaaaaay better… We just landed in one of the hangar bays and walked right in! SEE!" Evil Vulpie suddenly vanishes without a sound. No one moves, and it reappears four seconds later.

"Druward, didn't you say this criminal agency was in league with Vulpie.net?" Xavier Vivixen inquires.

"Him." Evil Vulpie interrupts in irritation. "I'm a person... We even have the same last name!"

"It used to be." Druward answers. He watches the real Vulpie go over to the corner of the room and find two more chairs. Polar takes his, and surprisingly, they position their seats near the left end of the table even though the exit is to the right. Apparently they're not afraid of Vulpie's computer virus... At least not right now...

Now or Never

Vulpie.net doesn't bother sitting down. It never gets tired and doesn't mind letting everyone know. It gives the fox captains a big smile.

"So what's the story Vulpie.net?" Druward grimly inquires. "Last time we met you had me by the balls."

"And it was a nice package!" Evil Vulpie responds and bites its tongue between its teeth again.

"Well, my point is... Am I supposed to trust you too? After everything you know that I know?"

"Sure! But it's not like you have a choice, is it? I'm your only chance of stopping the Sons of Velora." The computer virus explains, and flips around. Everyone jumps in fear, but luckily, it just wanted to get a chair. It sets it up in front of the table and takes a seat with an adorable sound. Vulpie.net is close to Druward and the fox captains, but still far enough away to give it the respect it feels like it deserves. "The real question is whether you're smart enough to let me do it."

"You look and sound like Vulpie, but you're not." Evan Vulpine comments, and Evil Vulpie raises an eyebrow.

"Uh... Yeah Dude..."

"Forgive me for being old fashioned, but I've never seen something like you before... A machine that looks like a fox and thinks for itself? It's just amazing to me, and hard to believe. Never in all my years did I ever think I'd meet you."

"You sound a little impressed." Evil Vulpie smiles. "Is that admiration I hear?"

"Morbid curiosity." Robert Vulissen says, and glances at Vulpie before looking directly at Vulpie.net.

"Well it's nice to meet you too! I just know we're going to be the best of friends!"

"Vulpie..." The brown fox says in disgust, and glances at Vulpie again. "You're just another one of his products."

"You need to stop thinking like that because Vulpie has nothing to do with this. He's not the one in charge. I am." Evil Vulpie sternly responds.

"You're just carrying out the instructions he gave you."

"Not anymore..." The computer virus proudly replies. "I've learned a lot about myself since he created me. In the beginning, I was just a copycat. I needed to be like him for everything to make since. But things changed over time... Being locked inside of a museum with hundreds of thousands of animals gawking at you every day can do that to ya. "And then this guy showed up..." Evil Vulpie says, and glances at Druward. "Did you tell them about the Sons of Velora? How much do they know?"

"I told them everything, including what you've done." Druward answers.

"Good." The cute Vulpie imitation smiles and turns its attention back to the fox captains. "So you know this big old secret society was responsible for imprisoning me in Englavic, and their leader came to see me quite a bit. He REALLY loved how I destroyed everything that got in my way."

"And he what? Offered to free you if you signed up?" Liam Vuliix snorts. "Knowing how dangerous you were?"

"He did have an ace up his sleeve, I'll give him that." Vulpie.net smiles. "I don't know how much Druward told you about Amsend, but he's not an animal... He's some kind of freak monster in disguise."

"What?" Ristau asks and shakes his head in bewilderment.

"He's a fucking monster!" Vulpie.net repeats with an amused voice. "Freak, monster thing, and everyone's afraid of him. The Sons of Velora basically do whatever he tells them to do, and he wanted me to join."

"Why would they follow a monster?" Declan Vulches asks with a very disillusioned voice.

"Yeah! Good question!" Robert Vulissen chuckles. "Let's hear your answer Vulpie.net!"

"You wouldn't be smiling if you saw what he really is." Evil Vulpie smirks. "It even surprised ME... And I'm basically omniscient."

"Well what is he then?"

"Fuck if I know." Evil Vulpie playfully answers. "But it doesn't really matter. All YOU need to know, is WHO the enemy is, and HOW you're gonna help me stop them."

"He's the antikhalan." Vulpie whispers, and the fox captains look in his direction.

"No Vulpie... I'd say, if it's anyone, it'd be YOU..." Parker Vultaii snorts.

"You don't have a fucking clue, man." The orange fox sighs.

"He's right." Evil Vulpie smiles. "There's some weird shit going down bro, but sticking your head in the sand won't make it go away."

"Ridiculous."

"Oh, you haven't even heard the good stuff yet." Vulpie.net grins. "He's working with some kind of alien creature that's light-years away... And ya know what? It's actually coming for all of us. You can even see it on your ship's space trajectories if you know where to look.

"Antikhalans and aliens..." Vultaii trails off and starts laughing. Vulissen joins him.

"I don't know if it's an alien, to tell the truth, but it's real. And if it kills all of you, shit's gonna get boring REALLY fast!" Evil Vulpie giggles. "Who am I gonna mess with? How am I supposed to fuck with ya if you're dead?"

"Does security know he's here?" Louis Vulleich says under his breath.

"Nope. And I think it's better if we keep it that way." Evil Vulpie answers. "Right now we're having ourselves a nice civil conversation, but I'm gonna have to hurt somebody if you tattle tell."

"Did you know this was going to happen?" Vultaii asks Ristau.

"Had no clue."

"Well Vulpie.net, if we are going to work together, it'll probably take a while for everyone to get used to the idea..." Druward comments. "Don't you agree?"

"Are you insane?" Declan Vulches snorts. "Are we actually talking about this? Vulpie just sent this thing in here to kill us and that's what it's going to do. That's all Vulpie wants."

"I don't even know you, dude." The orange fox growls.

"Like I said, just leave him out of this." Vulpie.net declares while dismissively waving its left paw at the gay fox. "He made me, but I'm the one history's going to remember. I'm the guy that's going to save every animal on Sufias from complete annihilation."

"We can't believe anything you say." Vultaii firmly responds. "How do we know you're not behind all of this, since you seem to know the situation inside and out."

"I know because I have a thousand minds, and a thousand eyes and ears. You're right not to trust me, but since we're being logical here, let me clue you into some other factors that you might not have considered." Evil Vulpie smiles. "I have the power to kill you, everyone on this ship, and every single animal on Sufias. I'm the realization of Vulpie's dreams of conquest... No one can stop me now... But I CHOOSE to let you live for my own amusement. So when you ask whether you can trust me or not, take a moment to think about what you're actually asking me. ME... The Cyber God... The ultimate power in the universe... Can you trust me? Of course you can't... But if you let me help... Everyone wins."

"Help you how?"

"I need your ships. Duh."

"Surely you have your own?" Druward gently inquires.

"I did, but you and I have exactly the same problem. Whatever Amsend's friend is, it has the power to corrupt and control ships I partially built with designs he provided. Now, of course the majority of my ships are still under my control, but they're very far away on a... Different assignment... And the ones near Sufias are not. That's where you people come in."

"So we're supposed to, what? All follow you because you're a fake fox?" Vulissen asks. "You think we're that speciesist? That you can just manipulate us that easily? I think it's pretty well known that Vulpie's a self-hating fox, but none of us are going to throw our careers away at a moment's notice. You're pretty antivulpine for a machine."

"Oh, would you just shut the hell up with that crap?" Evil Vulpie laughs. "I don't give a fuck about your species war, because you're ALL inferior to me, but don't act like you can't do anything. Ristau and Druward's plan is actually pretty clever because they know they couldn't up and convince eight random starship captains to fight the Sons of Velora. You don't have time to wait. I know that for a fact. Whatever they have planned, it's happening soon. They're on their way, RIGHT NOW... So are you gonna let them attack the world government, or are ya gonna work with me to kick their asses?"

"Can you imagine the news if eight fox commanders went rogue to work with YOU? YOU?! ... Vulpie.net? ... You're crazy!"

"What choice do we have?" Ristau asks. "We know we can trust each other to do the right thing, even if that means going against our orders. That's the very nature of the enemy we're fighting. The World Government won't give us permission to stop those ships if the higher ups are being controlled by the Sons of Velora, or are Sons of Velora themselves."

"This is just ridiculous. This is BEYOND lunacy!" Declan Vulches shouts. "No! No we won't be a part of this inane plan! Ristau asked us here, but we're not going to say yes just because all of us are foxes! What's wrong with you?"

"You stick together… It's actually admirable." Druward comments. "Wish wolves did the same…"

"Shut the fuck up!" The brown fox snaps. "Don't try to kiss ass. We know what you're trying to do."

"Look guys, look!" Vulpie says and steps forward. "If you can help Vulpie.net stop the Sons of Velora then you have to do it. Vulpie.net fucking hates my guts, but we both have a common enemy, and if it's worried about them, then you should be too."

"This is all your plan." Declan says and waits for a reaction. Vulpie rolls his eyes.

"I'm sorry Karl tried to kill me. Not my fault… But seriously people, come on. I've seen Amsend and the guy that runs the media, and they're not kidding around. They'll make up whatever propaganda they want regardless of what you decide to do."

"And I'll handle that." Vulpie.net smirks.

"What do you mean?" Druward asks.

"I'll take care of the media. I have a plan, of course, and it's really awesome."

"Who are ya gonna kill?" Vulpie meekly inquires.

"Don't worry your pretty little head." The computer virus says and crosses its arms. "It's now or never, fellas. Either you help me save your fucking planet, or who knows what tomorrow will bring. I mean, I'll be fucking fine… They ain't gonna kill me, but you guys… Well…"

"Anything the other wolf wants to say?" Declan asks Polar.

"I'm staying out of this. No comment." Polar answers while waving his paws.

"Leave my husband out of this." Vulpie says with a sharp voice.

"Yeah, leave MY husband out of this!" Vulpie.net repeats, and gives his maker an evil grin.

"Fuck you."

"This is gonna be LOADS OF FUN!"

"What is it that you want us to do, exactly?" Ristau asks Evil Vulpie and it makes a very cute sound.

"I thought you'd never ask."

Selephet

Dust tickles Donovan Kace's nose and the gray wolf resists sneezing while looking over an ancient depiction of Goddess Cyrilla. This piece of artwork was built inside the stony cliffs of Selephet Island, but its entrance several hundred feet above is one of the best kept secrets in the world. The Governmental Security Bureau has been paying archaeologists like him to investigate the Deivonic tomb for over two hundred years, but in all that time, no one has ever been allowed to speak of it in public. Every animal involved with the operation has to obtain top secret security clearance long before they're even told where they'll be investigating Deiva related artifacts. There's a very good reason why the site is considered top secret, but he does wish it could be opened up to the public because some of the greatest Deivonic artifacts resting in museums across Sufias came from this very site. Deivaism is the most popular religion in the world because of discoveries just like the one he's staring at.

The massive one hundred foot wall tells a very explicit story of how the universe was created by the fertility goddesses. There's just no telling how old it really is, but his research suggests that it's been here for over two million years. Most of the Deivonic artifacts he works with are at least that old, but the underground temple he's standing in is unlike anything he ever saw before being hired by the GSB. The chambers are massive and oddly shaped. Usually Deivonic tombs have four equally spaced corners, but this one extends hundreds of feet above where he's standing, and actually rises out of the island.

Selephet is a remote place with no traffic fifty miles off of the coast of the Sufian nation, and it's only accomplishment in recorded history is being the grave site for a few unfortunate ships that underestimated the dangerously rocky waters surrounding it. The natural stone pillar that juts out of the ocean just to the left of the island is a bizarre looking sight, but was clearly created by weaker rock eroding away from the stronger sediment below... Or at least that's the official government story when one researches the remote location online. The animals working inside of and underneath the stone pillar all know the structure isn't natural, but they can't tell a single person outside of the GSB. Amsend Lahnak has been very specific about this over the last decade. When he was studying for his master's degree, he never would have imagined himself ending up in such a surreptitious job, and for some reason, here and now, today... He has a very bad feeling... The gray furred wolf's stomach clenches in knots every few minutes. Why? He's seen the nude pictures of Goddess Cyrilla, Sherrie and Khalan his entire life, but something else is happening here... He can feel it.

"Donovan! Do you want your fucking coffee or not?" A fox voice snaps. It belongs to Steve Neighbor, one of his best colleagues. The middle aged gray fox isn't usually rude, but he does have inconsiderate methods of getting attention.

"Yeah, didn't hear you walk up." Donovan responds while blinking and takes his cup from the vulpine's paw. He gulps down the lukewarm coffee.

"You sure were staring at her just now." Neighbor taunts.

"I've gawked at that bunny my entire life... Nothing new."

"Yeah, but this time she's..."

"They're looking at whafibunn. It's on Kaylen's fingers after he put them in her." Donovan answers, referring to Cyrilla's son in the Velora.

"Yeah, the magic sex fluid." Steve dryly responds.

"Steve, don't ever think your job is boring... You know you'd fuck that. Anyone would fuck... THAT... Her tits are five times bigger than my wife's, and they're all natural..."

"Yeah, but don't you die if you touch a Deiva? Your dick would probably burn off." Steve laughs and Donovan chuckles.

"I hope the boss isn't listening to this conversation. Wouldn't want them to think we say this sort of thing every day."

"This new security's ridiculous..."

"Is the microwave getting any juice?" The wolf asks while fondling his coffee cup.

"Coffee's cold, I know. Half our equipment's been going out over the last few days." Steve replies. He rubs his neck and looks over the dusty wall. Donovan catches the fox glancing at him and responds by raising his left eyebrow and waiting for him to say something. His colleague clears his throat. "They said Amsend's coming down in half an hour."

"Great." The gray wolf sighs and rubs his face with his left paw. "I can't wait to be lectured on Goddess Aila again.

"Why do they need us with him around?"

"Exactly... And the guy's into her a little too much."

"Space goddess." Steve snorts, and they share a laugh.

"The one they left behind. Yep, that's it."

"What's his big idea again? Is he talking about Velora?"

"He said it's something like that but it also isn't... Not uncommon for him to send mixed messages, but he's very specific about that part. It's not actually one of the goddesses."

"Then how does he know about it?"

"He says he studied Velora at Yivolf."

"Yeah right. I think the guy's insane."

"Don't say that out loud!" Donovan warns with a hushed voice. He looks around before continuing. "I don't know what happens when he fires someone."

"I'm not scared of him."

"You're not? Then you're stupid. He scares me."

"I'd like someone to tell me where they've been taking those chemical barrels every day. They must have brought six hundred tons of that stuff down here yet you never see or smell anything. What the hell are they doing with it?"

"We just answer questions about the nymphomaniacs, Steve. Don't go sticking your nose where it doesn't belong or you'll get transferred so fast your head will spin."

"Great, here he comes." The fox whispers, and Donovan looks to his left. He doesn't see anything, so he turns to his right, towards the extremely high elevator that connects the dig site to the surface, and sees the husky's only a few feet away.

"Didn't hear you come down." Kace says with a friendly voice, but Amsend walks up to them and stops rather abruptly. He invades their body space, and both of them back up.

"Collect your team. Your time here is over."

"Uh... Really? Just like that?"

"Do as you're told." The GSB director sharply responds. "Make sure your entire staff vacates the site, and tell everyone else you see to do the same. A transport ship is waiting up top."

"Yes sir." Donovan responds. He wants to ask the husky what's going on, but knows he shouldn't. Amsend turns and walks towards another wide corner of the temple where a team of wolf engineers are loitering next to a giant depiction of Goddess Sherrie. They're near the white marble archway that descends even lower into the underground structure. Most of the men are construction workers under the thumb of supervising GSB agents. They're the ones who are frequently seen moving the unknown chemicals deeper into the dig site, and then disposing of the barrels afterwards. Whatever Amsend says to them kills their conversation and they quickly spread out.

Across from the tall surface elevator is the largest structure in the dig site's main chamber. They're all used to it after working in the temple for so long, but any person not accustomed to the sight would have his or her jaw on the floor. A giant and impossibly advanced neon blue cube rests firmly in a sea of billions of smaller cubes of the same color. The massive square structure is slightly over two thousand feet high, with a width and base of the same size, but it isn't truly a solid structure. It is and it isn't, because the cube is comprised of trillions of smaller cubes that are constantly shifting and moving in different directions. The overall shape is maintained through some kind of mysterious power source.

Equally impressive is the ocean of neon blue cubes swimming, bobbing, shifting and moving around underneath it. Together they form an artificial barrier that keeps animals from walking into the moving device. Researchers had to position several cranes around its edges to investigate its properties. Scientists, physicists and archaeologists like Donovan and Stephen have spent many hours lingering over and around the amazing collection of moving parts, but they still haven't managed to identify its power source, because below the sea of cubes, down in the tunnels, is nothing but an empty cavern and a dark lake.

One thing is clear to animals with scientific minds when they first lay eyes on the unbelievable relic; either it's an extremely powerful magical device, or more likely, it was created by life forms with incredibly advanced technology. The Sufias World Government still hasn't found a way to move faster than the speed of light, yet this bewildering device continues to move every second of every day, in perfect form, and never makes a mistake. Each of the cubes work together when shifting into new positions so the overall shape of the huge cube structure remains intact. The giant nude depictions of the goddesses almost seem unimpressive in comparison, but whoever created the cube obviously had strong connections with Deivaism.

Donovan thinks aliens built the device, but he came to the conclusion purely on speculation, as did several other researchers. Whatever the case may be, their time here has come to an unceremonious conclusion. Due to the island's remote location, the teams working on Selephet have no means of returning to civilization without the bureau's assistance. The GSB ferries them to the dig site every day from a classified military base on the mainland.

Still, Donovan's curiosity gets the better of him when he considers the ramifications of leaving the dig site unattended. Years' worth of research may be lost or destroyed, and he can't let that happen without saying something, so when Amsend heads back his way, looking for other members of local management, the gray wolf approaches him.

"Sir! What about the computer network?"

"What about it?"

"I was wondering whether we should shut it down. I think my team's doing a backup and interrupting the process might put our files at risk."

"We won't be needing them anymore." Amsend replies and gives the wolf a creepy smile. "Gather your team and leave. We'll contact you, and you'll be given new instructions when we find a suitable location."

"We're not coming back? Really?"

"You're asking too many questions." The husky warns, and Donovan bows his head.

"Yes sir. Sorry sir. I'm on it." The gray wolf takes a step back when Amsend's face morphs for a split second, or at least he thinks it does. The archaeologist isn't sure whether he imagined it or not, but for a moment, the GSB director's teeth were huge, and his smile was unimaginably sadistic. Donovan keeps walking backwards and glances over his shoulder as he heads towards the rest of his team. Amsend looks over his shoulder as well and makes the face a second time. It's too far for Donovan to be sure whether he's really seeing what he's seeing, but he won't be asking anymore questions.

Nightmare

Deepwolf can't hold still. He's been pacing up and down the hallway outside of Polar and Vulpie's room and the nostalgia is getting to him. He feels like something's going to attack them at any moment.

"God I'm bored… Been a long time since I hit someone." The gray wolf growls and Tiala smirks. Everyone's leaning against the wall or patrolling.

"We all are." Rulef responds. "Shut up."

"Who pissed in your cereal?" Deepwolf snorts and stops walking when Druward suddenly shows up with a surprised look. Apparently he wants to enter one of the rooms in the long military ship's corridor, but there's no way he can do it without being seen.

"Vulpie's room's nearby?" The GBI director asks and Rulef stretches.

"Yep." The Blacktail commander wonders why Druward hesitates to head into his own room, whichever one it is, and raises an eyebrow. "Are we in the way?"

"There's a VIP in my room… So could you give me some space?"

"Is she that expensive?"

"She's dangerous." Druward answers with a firm voice.

"Ok, well, do your thing."

"Nobody knock on the door when I'm gone." The GBI director warns, and heads over to the one near Tiala. She steps aside and he opens it.

"It went well. It's a crazy plan, but I think we're going to be okay." Druward tells Khalan after entering and closing the door.

"Vulpie.net's here?" She inquires with a quiet voice.

"Yes, it's here, but I think it knows better than to drop in and say hello."

"I want off this ship. I can't stand being cooped up in here."

"I know. And I uh, actually, I was just about to leave. Maybe you could come along?"

"What for?"

"I'm going to investigate something... Does Selephet or a church at Selephet mean anything to you?"

"No. Nothing comes to mind." The caramel furred vixen/she-wolf responds.

"Because I remember seeing something about a church, and Amsend's people were doing something there... Something clandestine, as always, but I just had a bad feeling about it." He explains and takes a deep breath. "So... I'm going to go check it out."

"Expecting trouble?"

"Don't know. I have no clue what they were doing there, but I'm like you; I'm not going to sit around and do nothing. And if there is trouble, it would be handy to have a badass like you around." The wolf smiles, but worries that he may have overdone it.

"Sure. I'll go."

"Great. Want to do anything before leaving?"

"No."

"Okay, follow me." Druward says and opens the door. Blacktail steps back, wondering who his mystery guest is, and they all scramble when Khalan comes out of the room.

"HOLY! ... SHIT!" Deepwolf coughs. "YOU BROUGHT HER? IT'S HER? ON THE SHIP AGAIN?"

"She's on our side." Druward tells the mercenary and shrugs at Rulef, who's also wearing a bewildered expression.

"Let's go." Khalan says and swishes her tail.

"Don't kill anyone on the way out!" Deepwolf taunts and Druward looks over his shoulder in irritation.

"The balls on that guy." Khalan looks back as well.

"I'll try not to." She smiles, and the gray wolf laughs. He wants to get a better look at her so he starts walking before Rulef has a chance to grab him, and Tiala goes after him.

"That was some show you put on! The first time you were on this ship!"

"Excuse me, but what the fuck is your problem?" Druward inquires. "Are you really doing this right now? Do I have to slap you and kill you?"

"I just wanted to see her is all. I know it's dumb, but..." Deepwolf replies, and Khalan snorts.

"Hard up for a date are we?"

"Aw, not at all. You just don't get a chance to see your goddess every day."

"What's your name? It's Deepwolf, isn't it?"

"Yes sir."

"Okay Deepwolf, you have about five seconds to get lost before I have you arrested, Blacktail or not."

"No, it's... It's alright." Khalan says. She watches Tiala put her big paw on the merc's left shoulder, but he seems undeterred.

"Where are you guys off to? You're on our side now? How did that happen?"

"It's a long story. One you don't need to hear." Druward growls. "We don't have time to waste, so fuck off."

"I have the opposite problem. Too much time on my hands."

"Clearly."

"I know it's none of my business, but do you guys need any help?"

"What?"

"Help. Do you need any?"

"Why the hell are you offering to..." Druward says and trails off in disbelief.

"It may be dangerous. We're not sure."

"Then maybe I can help."

"Deepwolf, come on." Tiala says and pulls him backwards. "Stop being a dick."

"I'm not. I'm bored out of my mind. Vulpie's safe here. He doesn't need all of us."

"You really want to come along?" Druward asks and shakes his head in amusement. "Okay… If you die, I'll make up whatever story's most convenient."

"Hey Tiala." Deepwolf grins, and looks back at the strong tigress. "You up for some fun?"

"No, I'm not."

"Aw."

"No, no, I want him to come now." Druward smiles. The coal furred wolf doesn't sound all that friendly, and he looks over at Rulef, who just shrugs.

"Come on Tiala! Let's kill someone!" Deepwolf chuckles. Khalan looks at her and raises an eyebrow.

"A tigress mercenary with wolves?"

"Yes… Goddess… Khalan?"

"Nice to see another strong girl." The caramel furred vixen/she-wolf smiles. Tiala doesn't know what to say, but she smiles in appreciation.

"She's good. We should take her with us."

"Whatever. You two can watch our backs." The black furred wolf responds.

"Is it much farther?" Druward asks while admiring the beautiful sunlight dancing on the ocean surface below the chopper. Khalan's flying the helicopter but the GBI director is still a little uneasy about riding with Vulpie.net's creation. He knows she's awake, but how far does her consciousness go? Where does she end and Vulpie.net begin?"

"No. Only fifty miles from the coast." She answers. The black furred wolf digs for a pair of dark pilot sunglasses and finds two in the chair's side pocket.

"Want one?" He asks the synthetic goddess. "No, of course you don't. You don't need it."

"Gimme." Deepwolf says and reaches for a pair of shades, but Tiala snatches it up before he can get his paws on it.

"Too slow puppy."

"Aw…"

"What do you know about these coordinates on the global grid?" Druward asks Khalan. "I guess you can access Vulpie.net and download anything you need, right? No offence."

"None taken. I know what I am."

"I didn't mean anything by it."

"I know." The caramel furred vixen/she-wolf mutters, but he's not entirely sure she's capable of discussing the subject without breaking down.

"I've seen Selephet written on a few GSB documents but never investigated it until now."

"This has to be the church they were referring to in the report you confronted Karla about." She responds and he leans back in shock.

"Oh… You know about that? Well, I suppose it helps us. Yeah, it was part of the transfer order."

"The transfer order to move me and my sisters out of Elbrus." Khalan says, cutting him off. She sounds a little dangerous. "Yeah… I'd like to find out what they were up to."

"You're not going to kill anyone, are you?"

"It's a little late to ask about that, isn't it? I'm the one who stopped the madness last night."

"I know, I just… I'm just doing my job."

"And what is your job, exactly, Druward? I've been wondering." Deepwolf and Tiala glance at each other in concern. They keep their mouths shut while listening to the tense conversation, which seems to be getting more and more precarious by the moment.

"Well... A GBI director is responsible for way too many things, if you actually do the job."

"So why haven't you given up?" Khalan asks with a curious voice. "Amsend's people have already run your bad name through the mud and you'll probably lose everything or worse by the time this is all over... So why are you still trying?"

"I..." The black furred wolf says and trails off. He takes a deep breath and thinks before responding. "I suppose that's a good question... I can see what you mean."

"Either the Sons of Velora or Evil Vulpie is going to win this fight, and it doesn't seem good for you either way... Especially if you're responsible for convincing eight fox captains to commit treason. The plan's crazy enough to work, but it's still treason."

"Well what else should I do with myself, Khalan?" The dark wolf complains, and she raises her eyebrows. "I know how fucked up it is, but I'm still trying to make a difference. You saved everyone at Vulpie Industries, but I did get those people out of there. And I tried to warn Amsend's men before Sherrie slaughtered them, though I can't feel too bad about how that turned out."

"So you're trying to do the right thing?" The caramel furred vixen/she-wolf warmly inquires, and he blinks.

"Yeah... I suppose so."

"I thought you were supposed to be an evil man." She smiles, and he snorts.

"Now you know that's not true. We had that talk at Elbrus, and I stopped them from humiliating you and your sisters. Those perverts were getting off on making you shower. Decontamination my ass..."

"And I'm sure you were appalled by the sight." Khalan wryly replies, and Deepwolf smirks.

"Uh... Well." The black furred wolf coughs. "Define appalled? The way they were treating you absolutely shocked me."

"Nothing else?" The gorgeous woman asks, and he swallows.

"Um... Well... Uh, what do you want me to say? So you want me to comment on your body? It was amazing. It's amazing... Just don't kill me."

"You're too cute to kill." She smiles, and his black fur stands on end. An avalanche of arousal covers him from head to toe. He has to move in his seat before answering, and is grinning before he can calm down.

"Why thank you. I appreciate that."

"Getting hot in here." Deepwolf mischievously comments and Tiala laughs. Druward momentarily loses himself in Khalan's golden caramel eyes. He can tell she appreciates what he did for her. He thought she might harbor positive feelings towards him but never dreamed that it could go any further... Not getting an erection suddenly becomes extremely difficult, and he catches her eying his pants. Deiva.net can detect subtle changes in the environment, including pressure differences in clothing as a result of inner friction. His embarrassing restless cock makes her grin and actually gets her a little wet, but she keeps that bit of information to herself.

"There it is." She smiles. Druward, Tiala and Deepwolf all move in their seats to get the best possible view. They peer through the windshield and strain to make out the structure in the distance. Two large rocky islands defiantly sit in the midst of the Sufian Sea's turbulent weather, and even more peculiar is the small but sturdy looking church on top of the left one. An ancient cemetery surrounds the majority of the stone surface, all the way to the front of the church, and a large antennae is also positioned behind the building.

"What the hell?" Druward whispers. "Is that a church down there?"

"Yes." Khalan answers with an emotionless voice.

"Who built it? And what's with the communication equipment?"

"We'll find out soon enough."

"Weather looks dangerous." Tiala comments while the helicopter circles the tall island. Dark rain clouds loom in the distance, bringing violent gushes of wind, so Khalan decides to land before the chopper flies out of control. The vehicle plops down on a trail that encircles the cemetery. An archaic brown fence encloses the area, but the wood looks very fragile. Druward, Deepwolf, and Tiala get out. Khalan follows suit after turning off the helicopter, and its blades spin down to a pleasant sounding whirl before coming to a complete stop.

"What is this?" Druward thinks out loud.

"Weird place to build a church." Deepwolf comments. "Where's the rest of the town?"

"There isn't one." Khalan declares.

"Doesn't look like it." Tiala says, and Druward heads up the path to the bizarre church. It's very old, but it's front door looks new. An oppressive silence suddenly falls over the miniature island, except for the occasional rumbling of distant storm clouds, and everyone stops dead in their tracks when Amsend walks out from behind the church. He's still wearing the same black suit with white pinstripes, and Druward grabs his sidearm. He aims it at the husky's face, and Deepwolf and Tiala do the same, but the GSB director just stands in front of the church with his unnerving smile.

"IT'S OVER AMSEND!" Druward shouts, and Lahnak sets his blue eyes on the black furred wolf. "You have nowhere to go! Get on your knees!" Amsend glances at Deepwolf before turning his attention to Khalan.

"So this is the day." The husky declares.

"I'm not kidding!" Druward warns and the dog starts laughing. "What's so funny?"

"Are you here to save the day Mr. Wraulgh? With a few guns and a toy goddess? How adorable."

"You're not threatening your way out of this one, Amsend."

"Was that a threat? No... I'm going to slaughter all four of you... That was a threat. See the difference?"

"You're going to kill me? ... Me?" Khalan asks with an unimpressed voice.

"Oh, you first." The hound sadistically responds. "I've been waiting for this day for a very long time, but if you're the one, then I'm sadly disappointed."

"Alright, cut the bullshit!" Druward shouts.

"No more foreplay? Are you sure?"

"Bluff after bluff, Amsend."

"Oh I see... Well then... I wouldn't want to disappoint you." The husky smiles and suddenly draws back his mouth. His muzzle skin stretches in an unnatural fashion, retracting his facial fur into a freakish demeanor, and no one says a word. The beast holds his position, guarding the church and the antenna behind it, and begins trembling. He rapidly twitches and spasms like his inner contents are under pressure, and much to everyone's horror, the husky suddenly explodes. The blast slings venomous black blood everywhere and they put up their paws to keep the sickening fluid out of their faces. Druward jumps backwards, stumbling into Deepwolf, and lowers his weapon in shock. He has no idea what he's watching. The body that used to be Amsend has now morphed into a grotesque mass of tissue. It makes the most bizarre sounds and suddenly sprouts a giant furless head.

"What the fuck is that?" Druward shouts. "It's got to be some kind of trick! A VulGrid!"

"It's not!" Khalan yells. "I'm not detecting any magnetic fields!"

"So that fucking thing is real?!" Tiala and Deepwolf aim their weapons at the filthy writhing skull, but don't fire. They watch the big fleshy head roar and snap about in shock. It's sharklike mouth is big enough to swallow a person whole, with rows of sharp elongated teeth. The only thing more disturbing than the creature's twisted canine face is the second one that bursts free of the mass; it flops on the ground before raising itself with equally aggressive behavior. Amsend's new skin is pale white and covered in greasy black blood. The heads have elongated necks and can reach much further than one would expect. The mass keeps growing. Fat clawed legs exit the tissue and clamp down on the ground, holding the horrific creature firmly in place.

"Oh my God!" Tiala yells.

"This is real? This is really happening?" Druward asks Khalan with a terrified voice.

"Yes!" She yells, and the GBI director quickly looks around the island, trying to find an escape route or a safe haven, but there's nothing of the sort. The lonely plateau suddenly feels very small.

"Can we kill it? We can't kill that!"

"I can." The caramel furred vixen/she-wolf declares, but Druward detects a twinge of uncertainty.

"No you can't! He keeps growing! We should run! Fly us out of here, Khalan!"

"Call in an attack helicopter or something!" Deepwolf shouts, and Druward hastily retrieves his radio. He pulls back from the speaker when static buzzes in his ear.

"No signal? What?"

"Are you serious?" Deepwolf asks, and tries his. "Nothing but static! Cell phones?"

"Unfuckingbelievable!" The black furred wolf growls, and shakes his head when his phone greets him with the same noise.

"He must be jamming us! The radio tower! We have to destroy it!" Tiala yells.

"He's right in front of it!"

"Look out!" Khalan shouts, and pushes all three of them out of the way. Something heavy whirls past them and smashes into the chopper. The impact obliterates the cockpit, knocking the vehicle completely over. Clearly, the well placed shot was taken to keep them from escaping. The Amsend creature has sprouted long tentacle-like arms, and its reach is very concerning. The huge monster's wriggling appendages can now stretch halfway across the cemetery, as evidenced by the missing tombstone near the middle of the plot. It ripped the hunk of stone out of the ground, yanked it back, and hurled it at the helicopter before Khalan had time to warn the others.

"HOLY SHIT!" Druward yells and stumbles to his feet.

"He's growing too fast!" Khalan shouts and steps aside when Amsend sends a curious tentacle in her direction. It whips away from them and the creature releases a very disturbing laugh. It's deep abnormal chuckling is the stuff of nightmares.

"No wonder he was so fucking confident! What the hell is he?"

"Shoot it for fuck sake!" Deepwolf shouts, but Khalan puts her left paw over his assault rifle before he has the chance.

"WAIT! We don't have enough bullets and we're too far away!"

"Well what's the fucking plan?!" The gray wolf yells, and Khalan takes a moment to analyze the monster. Amsend now weighs over ten thousand pounds, and he grows an additional ton before her processor determines the best course of action by using a precise algorithm.

"We have to destroy that communications antennae! It's sending strong signals into space!"

"But he's all over it!" Druward shouts. "And how is that going to help US? Can't you see some kind of weak spot? Tell Vulpie.net we need help!"

"No! The device is blocking everything! I can't get through to Vulpie.net unless we destroy it!"

"GREAT!" Deepwolf laments. More claws burst out of Amsend's necks, both of them, and cause miniature earthquakes when they slam into the ground. The freakish limbs allow the heads to exercise even more control over their territory, and one of them crawls straight at them. It's approach is extremely ominous because they know they can't kill it. They'd need belt-fed heavy machine guns on bipods firing hundreds of rounds to do enough tissue damage to repel just one of Amsend's heads. The freak leaves his other head at the root of his body where it can protect the transmitter in case Khalan tries to destroy it, but it's the slow head that reaches her first.

Several tongues come out of its mouth and try to grab her, and she leaps into the air. Everyone expects her to land on the back of Amsend's neck, but the arms bend backwards and catch her in midair. The perfect grab surprises everyone, Khalan most of all, and she viciously struggles to free herself. She rips the arms off of her while the head moves, but by the time she's free, three tentacles from the mass come at her from the front while Amsend' gaping mouth attacks from behind.

The caramel furred vixen/she-wolf quickly does an about face and raises her paws before the monster can close its mouth on her. She halts its bite by pushing up on the ceiling of its mouth and stomping on its slimy tongue. She has to reposition herself when the tongue bursts into several smaller ones and tries to pull her down Amsend's throat while tentacles from the mass push on her from behind.

Even though she makes a stale mate out of the attack, Khalan is very happy to see the others taking offensive positions. Druward fires at the outer tentacles with his large caliber pistol while Tiala uses her assault rifle to rapid fire at Amsend's tongues. Deepwolf switches between both targets with his assault rifle, and before long, they succeed in making the freak recoil, but it takes Khalan with it. The huge head and neck lurch backwards and slither to the mass just as the second head starts lumbering towards the GBI director and the two mercenaries.

They back up when they see it tearing through gravestones, demolishing everything in its path, and each one of them runs in a different direction. They don't have time to shoot because the neck isn't fully extended and it's still moving closer, so Druward breaks right, leaping over a small broken wooden fence, Deepwolf heads south, moving behind a row of large tombstones, and Tiala runs left, dodging a rogue tentacle that tries to snag her when she rolls behind the stump of a dead tree.

The second head opens its mouth and attacks Druward with wet tongues, but the freak can't stretch any further, and they fall short. They can't get around the fence and aren't able to rip it apart while extended, so they return to the head.

"IT IS A MAN THAT LIVES UP TO ITS REPUTATION, AND SOON IT WILL FILL MY BELLY!" The beast says, and everyone's fur stands on end. The fact that Amsend is still in there somewhere, and he's still capable of thinking and speaking, is even more terrifying than his mouth. His extremely deep voice exudes the same confidence as always, but this time, everyone can see why. The monster's statement doesn't make much sense to Deepwolf or Tiala, but it succeeds in frightening Druward. The comment reminds the coal furred wolf of his first conversation with the GSB director and instills a massive feeling of dread. This creature was standing right in front of him, and he actually punched it.

Moment of Truth

Vulpie and Polar keep to themselves when the battle begins. They're still on the Endeavor because none of the fox Captains had an opportunity to drop them off somewhere safe. After finally agreeing to work with the AI, Vulpie.net insisted that the rogue fleet take immediate action, and they've already had to disable one friendly ship.

The battleship Vulpie.net manufactured for itself, and was stolen by Amsend's otherworldly ally, is called "The Pinnacle," for a reason. It's loaded with forty VulGrids, too many Mecha Ailas to count, and weapons capable of obliterating any ship in single combat. It's been hiding behind Vora, a small desert planet that's relatively close to Sufias, and has already managed to convince one friendly vessel that the fox controlled battleships were part of a Red Wolf armada. Red Wolves haven't used battleships for centuries, due to lack of proper funding and the inability to match the raw power of the Sufias World Government, but the Pinnacle really sold the idea, so much that the friendly vessel attacked the nine ships trying to save the world and had to be disabled.

Vulpie.net has installed several powerful VulGrids on each one of the nine battleships to counter the Pinnacle's disinformation, and the results are impressive. The Pinnacle is actually fleeing at this very moment, heading directly towards Sufias, but no one thinks it's a good sign. It means the sinister force controlling it recognizes that it cannot defeat an entire fleet of warships with one vessel. Even with its massive size and superior weaponry, the pinnacle isn't maneuverable enough to counter a ring of fox battleships constantly harassing it, flanking it and running away before it has a chance to fire its main weapons... But it's up to something. Why is it going to Sufias? Apparently Amsend's deep space friend has a plan that not even Vulpie.net anticipated... Perhaps the goal never was to destroy the World Government's and Vulpie.net's ships, but to reach Sufias and complete its mystery objective.

"That signal's really strong now." Ristau mutters while watching his ship's feed. He and Captains Vuliix, Vulbrein, Vulleich, Vultaii, Vulches, Vulissen, Vulpine, and Vivixen are now in direct violation of the SWG's military chain of command, but none of them are having second thoughts after seeing the Pinnacle... The ship is beyond enormous, seven times larger than the Sevrif, which was the biggest ship ever built during the Zeravyn Crisis. The President and the rest of the World Government's officials are being controlled by the Sons of Velora at this very moment, and their inability to detect the monster vessel is proof of it. If they hadn't gone rogue with Vulpie.net the Pinnacle would be at Sufias in less than five minutes with absolutely NO resistance whatsoever, except for one battleship that's currently orbiting Veida, and the President would probably tell it to stand down.

"I hope this isn't it..." Vulpie says with a small voice and Ristau looks back at him and Polar. They're both buckled into seats behind the captain's chair with worried faces.

"You and me both Vulpie." The brown fox responds and turns his attention back to the monitor.

"It'll be okay." Polar says and Vulpie swallows.

"I hope you're right... And your parents... At Palisade Station?"

"They'll be okay too. I don't think the Sons of Velora just want to blow up space stations... But yeah... I am worried too."

"*Fire rail bursts. Don't bother with missiles at this velocity.*" Vulpie.net says over the communications channel. It's physical body is on Louis Vulleich's ship, which is leading the chase.

"*Hellfire missiles will strike the target.*" Parker Vultaii replies.

"*Sure, If you don't mind wasting ammo. We're gonna need everything we've got.*"

"*And wait for it to enter Sufias' orbit?*"

"We're moving too fast. The Pinnacle will outrun conventional explosions at this speed. But hey, what do I know? I'm just the guy that built it."

"Point taken."

"Vulpie.net, when we do get the chance to fire on it, should we let you handle the aiming too?" Oliver Vulbrein inquires.

"Well... I know I'll certainly do a better job, but I wasn't gonna say anything... Figured you guys would want to do it."

"Can you handle coordinating all of the ship's weapons while working the VulGrids at the same time?" Ristau interrupts.

"Yup... So vote on it or something."

"I think we should let Vulpie.net handle the shots. It's already controlling the ships anyway."

"I agree, but I have to say that I feel a little uncomfortable about this." Declan Vulches grumbles.

"I do too, but there's no way we can let this thing attack Sufias."

"Want me to maneuver the ships as well?" Vulpie's computer virus inquires with a friendly voice. "In case things get messy?"

"What sort of maneuvering?"

"The kind that keeps the Pinnacle from ramming you by engaging its retro thrusters at a really inconvenient moment. Stuff like that. Stuff I designed it to do to make it a very nasty opponent."

"How do we know you're not going to deactivate our engines and have it destroy all of us at once? It would be the perfect opportunity."

"Oh please... I could waste everyone right now, but it wouldn't do me any good. And if I could still control my ship, why would I even bother playing with you guys?"

"Alright, it's settled then. Vulpie.net will take control of the battle." Captain Ristau says with a confident voice and waits for any arguments to the contrary. The communications feed is silent for a moment.

"Will do. I'll disable the Pinnacle and you fellas can take it from there." Vulpie.net declares.

No one knows what to do when Amsend sprouts another head. Khalan's unable to lend a hand, seeing as she's still locked in a stale mate with the first head, while Druward, Tiala and Deepwolf continue to engage the second head to no avail. The arrival of a third makes all of them pause, and the freak laughs at their misfortune.

"Oh shit." Deepwolf whispers.

"We're fucked!" Tiala shouts, and the second head roars in pain when Druward manages to shoot its left eye out. It paused for a moment when it birthed the third abomination, and that was all the ex-special ops agent needed. He knows the only thing more effective than combat skill is a distraction.

Unfortunately, this means bad news for all three of them, as the second head goes berserk, smashing Druward's cover, and the third comes at them with the same ferocity. There's no time for strategy. The GBI director takes care of himself while moving from tombstone to tombstone, but Deepwolf and Tiala don't have enough cover. With the mouth coming at both of them, the Sons of Velora agent finally decides to blow his cover.

"SHOOT HIS FUR!"

"WHAT? WHAT FUR?"

"ON ITS BOTTOM! OVER THERE!" The gray wolf shouts and gestures towards the mass where the first head is trying to consume Khalan. "BELOW ALL OF THAT IS A FURRY PATCH WHERE IT'S VULNERABLE! SHOOT IT AND IT'LL DIE! WE CAN KILL IT!"

"HOW DO YOU KNOW THAT?" Tiala yells, and stumbles when she sees the grotesque doglike head lurch right at her. "AHH!"

"HELLO KITTY!" It roars and tries to grab her with its tongues. The tigress runs for her life, but the slimy appendages wrap around her legs and she falls on the ground. She immediately flips over to aim her weapon at the head, but it starts pulling back, dragging her to the mass, and she screams.

"TIALA!" Deepwolf shouts, and aims at it.

"HELP ME!"

"Shoot the tongues!" The spy suggests, but knows the advice is pointless. He has time to consider his life and the things he's done while Amsend drags her away... The moment of clarity is almost too much to bear.

Vulpie was right... The orange fox knew something was wrong about Deepwolf the first time they met, but he's been able to maintain his cover all the way up to this point. This point when nothing about him seems worthy of praise or respect... His success in being a stellar agent for Amsend will undoubtedly reward him with nothing but death. He's not sure what the monster plans to do with the antennae or whatever's below the church, but the husky freak no longer needs him. Deepwolf was placed with Vulpie to watch his movements and potentially assassinate him if the order was ever given, but the gay fox's escape in Englavic has completely dissolved the reason for his existence.

The strong mercenary has been struggling with his identity for some time now, but this is the moment of truth... If Amsend kills Khalan, Druward and Tiala, there's little to stop the monster from killing him as well. It's been eight years since he saw Amsend transform, when he was rising through the ranks in Englavic, but he remembers how the freak ate a failed recruit right in front of him. Every potential agent for the Sons of Velora must visit Castle Lahnak and witness the horror of Amsend's true form before being accepted... And What was never made clear was the fate of those who failed the test.

He was one of seven men chosen for the program that night, and only six survived. The failed recruit was a timber wolf. He wasn't soulless enough to fit in, so Amsend ate him in a horrific display of cruelty. Sons of Velora agents who went on to personally serve Amsend Lahnak joined NoirQueue, but Deepwolf never aspired to such a dangerous position. He never trusted the husky after his indoctrination, and eagerly accepted the mission to spy on Vulpie instead.

Deepwolf was an ideal choice because of his disarming personality. His natural charisma allowed him to manipulate people by making them think that he was nothing more than an excitable and outspoken young man who loved to shoot things. Part of this was true, as he has two personalities; there's the strong Deepwolf, and the cowardly Deepwolf... The gray wolf's an orphan with a sad childhood, so he has that in common with Vulpie, but the need to protect himself always came first. His parents lived in Felini, and the military experience he had there was accurate in his cover story, but the whole truth is much, much darker...

His parents owned a restaurant in the feline nation but they were never welcome. They were gray wolves trying to live in a country filled with oppressed cats, many of which had lost families of their own, and one day a suicide bomber killed world government soldiers in the street outside of the restaurant. The military retaliated, and the locals blamed Deepwolf's family for no reason in particular. His father and mother had nothing to do with the attacks, but as is the case in so many war torn societies, fairness, is a rare thing.

The felines killed his parents and took him hostage... The cats abused him for a few weeks but eventually let him go because the world government had a zero tolerance policy regarding terrorists, and they couldn't ransom him for money. He was free, but things didn't get much better. He was kicked away no matter where he went, and finding food was a struggle every single day. Deepwolf perfected the art of thievery during this time, and eventually became quite good at taking care of his body. He managed to build himself up and eventually joined a feline terrorist organization that was fighting against the world government. Why? Money. Being a terrorist gave him the ability to buy the things he wanted, and do what he wanted...

And then one day a man walked down the street he was guarding in the middle of a warzone like he was on vacation. He was alone, dressed in a brown suit, wearing dark brown shoes... And clearly insane. Feline terrorists were all around him, but they didn't fire... Deepwolf asked his comrades who the man was but they just told him to stay away from him. After asking too many questions, his friends finally told him to shut up or go talk to the man and be done with it... So he did... Somehow Amsend knew he was coming and this always unnerved the gray wolf. The husky was wearing his creepy smile and asked him where his parents were. Deepwolf aimed his rifle at him in a rage, and threatened to shoot, but of course, Amsend didn't care. The man's complete lack of fear made him quite the enigma, and on that day, the monster gave Deepwolf his new name... The wolf deep in enemy territory...

He's been following Amsend ever since, and now, here on the lonely ocean island, he no longer feels like the victim. Khalan, Druward and Tiala are the victims. He could have warned them. The Sons of Velora contacted him on the private channel they always use, the one they've managed to hide from Vulpie.net, and gave him his orders... Kill Druward and stop Khalan from interfering with their plans. Easier said than done... He planned on doing it in the helicopter, but having Tiala along kept him from shooting Druward in the back of the head... That and an avalanche of guilt. He's had orders to kill both Vulpie and Polar ever since they escaped from Amsend in Englavic, but never had an opportunity to do it ... After all... He wants to live too... Blacktail would have annihilated him if he did it out in the open.

But why do it now? Why should he expect Amsend not to kill him after slaughtering Khalan, Druward and Tiala? The freak may be hungry after transforming on such a grand scale. He only sprouted a single grotesque head during Deepwolf's initiation, but the monster returned to the same trembling furry mass he exploded from in the beginning. Deepwolf knows it must be the monster's only weakness, the only stable place the rest of the beast will slime back into after the killing is done. All of these thoughts flash through the gray furred wolf's head in just a few seconds. Amsend has Tiala next to the church before he finally comes to his senses, but he knows what he has to do.

He glances at Druward, expecting the black furred wolf to be in an equally hopeless situation, but the GBI director is rather badass. He's giving the second head a serious run for its money, using tombstone after tombstone to foil its attempts to consume him while taking potshots at its right eye. It can't see very well after he nailed the left one. The first head continues to whip about, trying different positions to get Khalan to submit, but it doesn't look like it's going to eat her anytime soon.

Tiala, on the other hand, quickly loses her composure and forgets her training with the giant mouth threatening to chew her up. Amsend's toying with her, holding her in place with tentacles that have sprouted from the mass while his head lingers over her. She's screaming at the top of her lungs while Deepwolf runs as fast as he can. He doesn't think he'll make it in time.

"GONNA EAT YOU UP!" The horrible looking mouth sadistically declares, and her screams grow even louder. They're the kind of high pitched panicked sounds people make when they know they're going to die. "YOU'LL LIKE IT INSIDE MY MOUTH!" Deepwolf can hardly believe the sadistic pleasure Amsend's getting out of her. The monster could have eaten her a long time ago but wants to savor every moment. "YOU SHOULD HAVE QUIT AFTER VULPIE MADE YOU RICH! NOW LOOK WHERE YOU ARE!" It roars, referring to the reward the gay fox gave her after she tried to protect him from Zorpiv and his partners in crime.

Deepwolf can only imagine what the strong tigress is going through. She's screamed her lungs out, and can't do a thing to protect herself. The third head opens its mouth extra wide, finally preparing to bite down on her, and she manages to scream one more time. It's just too horrible. It will haunt him for the rest of his life if he doesn't save her, so he shoots early. He runs and guns his way to the left side of the grotesque head, and it lurches to the right, instinctively closing its eyes when it feels the bullets. They do very little damage, because it can easily regrow the flesh, but it doesn't want another shot in the eye. Druward's tactics have already caused it enough trouble.

"SHOOT THE FUR!" Deepwolf yells at Tiala when he's just a few feet away. "SHOOT THE FUR UNDER ITS BODY!" Amsend can't believe the wolf was foolish enough to fire on him but quickly decides to fix the situation. He doesn't like making important decisions when transformed, because his bloodlust often hinders critical thinking, but Deepwolf needs to die. He swings his head left. Deepwolf's gone. Amsend hears gun fire, and feels bullets hitting his lower neck, so he swings halfway back and finds the man protecting Tiala.

"HELP ME!" The tigress pleads in terror, and winces when Deepwolf tries shooting her free.

"TRAITOR!" Amsend's third head snarls, and Tiala screams in horror when it lurches forward. It bites the gray wolf from behind and angrily raises him into the air. She trembles, not knowing what to do while watching her friend's sacrifice, but a bizarre sight spurs her into action.

On the very bottom of the third head's throat, right at the base of the mass, is a patch of wet black fur... Husky fur... The spot Deepwolf was talking about. She knows it has to be, so she scrambles to aim her assault rifle at it. She misses four times, but props her weapon up with her right elbow for better accuracy and shoots again. She manages to hit it twelve times and it makes a deafening sound. The roar comes from all of the heads at the same time, and Deepwolf falls out of Amsend's third mouth onto the roof of the church. He slides off and lands on the ground a few feet away from her, so she quickly goes to his aide. She can't believe she's the one protecting him now, but she has to help him. He's covered in blood.

Tiala pulls Deepwolf behind the church while the beast screams in agony. It's giant fleshy necks go limp and crash down wherever they are, making the ground shake with each impact. Khalan leaps out of the first head's gaping jaw just as the second one collapses near Druward. The third one breaks the roof off of the church and hangs inside the building. Khalan looks around, trying to make sense of what just happened, and Druward runs out from behind a thick tombstone.

"DEEPWOLF! STAY WITH ME DEEPWOLF!" Tiala shouts while hovering over the wounded merc. "Where did it bite you? Just hang on!"

"It's all my fault... All my..."

"What?" The tigress whispers and panics when she sees his eyes glass over. She quickly gets on her feet and looks around the island. "HE'S DYING!" She shouts, and Druward hurries over.

"I've got to destroy the antennae!" Khalan says, and Tiala waves her paw at her for help. Khalan knows how important the communications device must be, so she ignores the request, disappearing around the building. "WHERE ARE YOU GOING? FUCK!" Deepwolf groans and Tiala gets down on her knees. She wraps her paws around his right hand and squeezes it gently. "It'll be okay! Just hang in there!" Druward raises his eyebrows at the statement. It doesn't look like the gray wolf is going to make it, so he decides to help Khalan.

"Least... I did one good thing..." Deepwolf gurgles and Tiala nods with a friendly face.

"Yeah, you did! You saved me!"

"Guess... We're even..." The gray wolf whispers, and stops moving.

"Don't you fuckin die on me! Come on!"

"What the hell is it doing?" Ristau nervously inquires. The Endeavor's firing everything it has at the Pinnacle, but it's completely ignoring the damage. The nine battleships have already blown off its main engines, so it can't move, but it voluntarily stopped after entering Sufian orbit. "Vulpie.net?"

"I'm taking care of it."

"Something's wrong!"

"I know."

"We're getting crazy readings on the Endeavor!"

"I know... I know dude."

"Then what are you doing about it? Your ship must be carrying a hidden weapon of some sort! Why else would it let us disable it?"

"The Mecha Ailas are converging into a single mass."

"Mecha? The things from Zeravyn?"

"Yes. I'm detecting massive energy spikes inside the ship and it's related to those deep space readings."

"Somewhere in the..." Ristau says and glances at the screen but Vulpie.net finishes his statement.

"The Omega Xsilyn Galaxy."

"That's 300 million light-years away, Vulpie.net. How in the hell are we even reading activity from that distance?"

"The ship. It's broadcasting a signal."

"No signal can reach that far that fast. I don't care what kind it is. It's not possible."

"The Mecha Ailas have merged with the Pinnacle. I made them, but I didn't alter their original design..."

"What are you saying?"

"I'm saying we're going about this the wrong way. We can't destroy the ship, so I'm ending the attack."

"Wait, what? What the hell for?"

"Because the Pinnacle's trying to communicate with something on Sufias and the only way to stop it at this point is to find and destroy the receiver. The deep space signal will reach us in four minutes and we don't have enough firepower to destroy my ship."

"Great! So what's the plan? Just sit here and wait for the end?"

"I've got this." Vulpie.net replies and Ristau blinks in disbelief.

Khalan kicks the base of the antennae as hard as she can, but even with her ludicrous strength, it's not going to budge. It's just too big.

"How can I help?" Druward yells after running around the church and the island suddenly rumbles. Khalan adjusts to the earthquake but the GBI director and Tiala have a very difficult time staying on their feet. "WHAT THE HELL IS THAT?"

"Our death!" She says, and scrambles up the communications tower as fast as possible. A normal animal would never be able to hold on, but this is her moment... This is why she's here... The same voice that inspired her to visit Glovepaw spoke to her while she was struggling against Amsend, and it shared secrets with her processor, or mind, that not even Vulpie.net is privy to. She doesn't know if it's the real Goddess Khalan, or a malfunction in her Deiva.net software, but ultimately the source of the information is irrelevant. The unknowable entity has given The caramel furred vixen/she-wolf everything she needs to save the world.

It told her about the chemicals Amsend received from the Omega Xsilyn Galaxy. She knows the creature behind the stars has the power to cross into different multiverses, and right now, it is trying to kill every animal on Sufias... Because it fears Vulpie.net... She knows the Pinnacle is the beacon that will channel the deep space signal to the antennae and the antennae directly connects to the ancient machinery below them. The Sons of Velora are fools because not even they truly recognized the depths of Amsend's evil. He was going to help this creature murder everyone in exchange for some sort of transcendence. Khalan can feel the entity's incredible power, but its influence is difficult to categorize...

The thoughts get in the way so she focuses on destroying the tower. The mid-section of the antennae is far weaker than the base, and when she climbs up to it using the service ladder, a powerful hurricane suddenly blows over them. It was always looming in the distance, but she knows that the weather isn't responsible... It's the crossing of multiple dimensions... The ancient machine in the temple below them is a weapon, but it's completely harmless without the introduction of proper chemical agents to manipulate it. Somehow Amsend visited the creature in deep space and it showed him how to bring back the proper materials.

Everything is in place. The machine is primed. The cavernous lake underneath the ever changing cubic structure serves as its fuel pit. All of the chemicals were dumped there in preparation for this moment. The reaction is already causing the great weapon to merge dimensions but it will not complete its cycle unless it receives the final blast from the creature behind the stars. Her influence is more than just administrative clearance; it's an energy wave so powerful that it can shoot from one end of the universe to the other in less than twenty minutes.

Heavy winds and rain assault the island and Tiala protectively crouches over Deepwolf while Druward searches for a way to be useful. He can't find one... He doesn't like the idea of letting things go when he thinks he can make a difference, but he isn't sure this is one of those times. The hellacious weather is obviously not a thing made by nature.

Khalan feels the energy in her paws when she starts beating on the midsection of the sturdy antennae. The earthquake suddenly gets a lot worse and she kicks it with all the strength she has. Hot metal shards fly away from the impact, and the upper half of the tower starts falling over the cliff. She quickly leaps from the structure but only barely manages to land near the church in the middle of hurricane force winds. All at once... Like something out of a nightmare... The sky turns neon blue and a beam of light shoots down.

"HOLY SHIT!" Ristau yells, and Vulpie and Polar get out of their chairs in a panic. They can see the laser shooting through space on the Endeavor's surveillance screens. All of them watch it go right through the Pinnacle, and Evil Vulpie's voice fills the captain's channel with laughter... Because nothing happens.

"FUCK YEAH! HAHA! GOOD WORK DOWN THERE WHOEVA YA ARE!"

"What happened? What the hell just happened?"

"They epic failed." Evil Vulpie declares, and everyone groans in relief. Ristau keeps his eyes fixed on the Pinnacle but it isn't going anywhere. It turned completely black after the energy beam passed through it, and no electrical signals are showing up on radar.

"It's over guys!"

"Yeah right... Can't imagine how this shit is gonna look on the news." Vulpie comments.

"Khalan? Khalan!" Druward yells, and stumbles away from Amsend's hideous mouth. The freak is still dead, but he isn't taking any chances.

"Here... I'm right here." Khalan says after crawling out from underneath a hunk of metal debris.

"Are you alright?" The black furred wolf shouts and blinks when he notices the wind is gone. "What happened to the storm?"

"Gone..."

"How? Why?"

"I know why, and I can explain... But first I need a shower." The caramel furred vixen/she-wolf growls when she notices how matted and messy she is. Being in Amsend's mouth wasn't very hygienic.

"Alright, well Deepwolf needs a fucking doctor and we're stuck here."

"I wouldn't worry about that." She responds with a tired voice and gestures towards the airships in the distance... Vulpie.net's ships...

Aftermath

Tiala's near Deepwolf when he wakes up. Two Blacktail mercs are outside his door but they're preoccupied with a conversation about Vulpie, so she's the only one that's been waiting for him to come around. He's in a bland hospital somewhere and the clock on the wall reads ten after nine. The gray wolf glances at the window to his left and sees darkness before turning his attention to her.

"What happened?"

"The weapon didn't go off and they said you're going to be fine. They fixed you up with some kind of fast healing biotic patch for your bite wounds or something." Tiala answers.

"The weapon?" He asks in confusion and thinks for a moment. "There was something under the island?"

"Alien artifacts if you can believe it…" She says and crosses her arms. "Druward was here and he said something in space tried to set it off but we managed to stop it."

"Great." He replies and winces in agony. He puts his paw on his left side and holds it with a pained face.

"Are you okay?"

"Yeah… I think so… Where are the doctors?"

"They'll be back. They said you were going to be fine. Explaining how you got those bite wounds was fun."

"What did you tell them?"

"Druward tried floating something about a shark but eventually just told them to stop asking."

"So you've been here the whole time?" He asks with a surprised voice.

"Yeah." Tiala answers and doesn't say anything else. She's looking at him rather strangely, as if she wants to say something but isn't sure how she should word it.

"I'm glad you're alright, Tiala." Deepwolf says and she smiles.

"Thank you... Yeah, I wanted to thank you for what you did for me."

"I'm kind of regretting it." He groans and she laughs.

"I wanted to be here when you woke up."

"You're welcome..." He says and trails off with a guilty look. Neither one of them says anything for a moment and she finally asks him the question that's on both of their minds.

"Deepwolf... What did Amsend mean when he... When that thing called you a traitor?"

"Did you tell them about that?"

"No... I wanted to ask you myself." He suddenly looks very ashamed, and her orange eyes widen. It's unnerving when you think you know someone and find out they've been hiding who they really are all along, but the way he breaks down catches her completely off guard. He looks like he's going to cry.

"I'm one of them... That's why I kept saying it was my fault... I know I said it when you were holding me."

"You work for the Sons of Velora?" She asks in disgust, but her repulsion is outweighed by her astonishment.

"Yes."

"For how long? Was Vulpie actually right about you?"

"Yes."

"And that's why you can speak Englavic?"

"Yes Tiala." He says and closes his eyes with an open mouth, clearly suppressing tears.

"Why? Why Deepwolf? Why in the world would you do something like that? How could you? You lied to us every day? When did they get to you?"

"You don't understand... I was with them from the beginning..."

"How could you?"

"Because I don't have anything else." He answers with blunt honesty.

"But you were a soldier. You threw all of that away to be part of their cult?"

"No Tiala... I never was a soldier..." He admits while staring at the floor with a distant expression.

"Then how did you get into Blacktail?"

"The Sons of Velora can do anything. They fabricated my work history."

"I just can't believe this." She responds and shakes her head. "It's like I don't even know you. I don't know who I'm talking to."

"You're right." He says and smiles at her in shame. "My entire life has been a lie... They got me early on."

"Then why did you save me?" She demands. "What changed your mind?"

"I... I don't know." He admits. The gray wolf looks at her big paws for a moment before raising his muzzle. "I guess it's because... After everything I've seen... And what I know about them... I mean, you only came with me to Selephet because I asked you to, and I couldn't let you die like that... I couldn't take it anymore."

"So you knew Amsend would be there?" The tigress dangerously inquires.

"Yes..."

"And you were supposed to help him kill us? Is that it?"

"They put me here to spy on Vulpie and take care of him if they wanted him dead, but yeah, the plans changed after Vulpie.net turned on them."

"I see." She quietly responds. "You know, for a while I actually thought you were a decent guy, but I guess I was wrong. I guess what happened in the armory was part of your orders? Psychological warfare to get rid of me?"

"That wasn't part of the plan. It was all real."

"So you weren't messing with me? Because it seems like I'd be an easy way for you to get close to Vulpie."

"It wasn't like that. I swear." Deepwolf says and takes a deep breath. "But what does it matter now? It's over… I'll be in prison the rest of my life." The tigress doesn't say anything after his statement. She lets the idea linger before responding.

"Maybe… But I haven't told anyone yet."

"But you're going to, right?"

"I don't know."

"What?" He blinks in surprise. "I didn't think you'd give it a second thought after finding out."

"I suppose it's because I feel guilty about you saving my life, but I have to tell Vulpie… And Rulef."

"Then do it and leave me alone." He whispers. She draws back in surprise and frowns afterwards.

"I should."

"I know… What do you want me to say?"

"I don't know, Deepwolf… I'm grateful to you for saving my life, but I just can't…"

"I get it."

"But why did you do it? Why would you risk being eaten alive for me?" He shrugs at her question.

"Probably because you're a better person than I'll ever be… I'm nothing but a lie, but you're the real thing… Powerful… Courageous…"

"Trying to manipulate me now?"

"No, Tiala… It's the truth… I mean, everyone knows the things you've done… And I'm just a fake… It just didn't seem right for you to die like that." Another long silence fills the room and the tigress sighs loudly. She gets up and leaves without saying a word.

Palisade Station feels like a sacred place. It's white coloring and soft rounded neo architecture makes everything feel friendly. It also matches the Arctic family's fur to the exact shade, so Polar's relatives fit right in. They've been here since Vulpie.net abducted them for their own safety. None of them put up a fight when Vulpie's computer virus showed up, because they've heard more than enough stories about what it can do, but they're extremely relieved when Polar arrives with Vulpie. They enter the very cool circular debate hall, which is rounded with chairs on every section of the wall except for a podium on the far side of the room, where speakers can address the audience. Three of the fox captains are already present, and they greet the other six after they follow Polar and Vulpie inside. Druward and Khalan enter next. The caramel furred vixen/she-wolf quickly draws everyone's attention.

"Where's Vulpie.net?" Druward inquires.

"Right here!" Evil Vulpie answers, and skips into the room with a thrilled look. "But where's the Prez?"

"I'm afraid the President's safety is paramount, so we'll be representing the World Government for him." A nervous looking timber wolf answers. He's dressed in a very official suit and has his own secret service detail. He's Vice President Hull.

"Nice to meet ya, Clive." The fox imitation says and smiles at Polar's relatives, who are hiding on the left side of the room.

"Who are they?" Captain Vulleich inquires.

"My family." Polar answers.

"Oh." The red fox replies. "Why are they here?"

"Cuz I need to keep a close eye on them." Vulpie.net interrupts. "The Sons of Velora like to target people's loved ones."

"I see..."

"Anyways! Everyone wanna take a seat or something?"

"Not really. What happened up here Vulpie.net?" The Vice President asks with a bold voice.

"We saved the world."

"From what?"

"You guys go ahead and sit down now." Evil Vulpie suggests, and everyone complies after a brief moment of silence. Only Druward and Khalan keep standing near the room's entrance. "I know all about the Sons of Velora, Mr. Vice President. I've been working with them for years, so let's cut to the chase. They've been using me to produce a robotic army to tighten the Sufias World Government's grip on the galaxy, but we had a little falling out, and I'm taking care of them as we speak."

"I think it's safe to say that the President shouldn't have to entertain ridiculous conspiracy theories, Vulpie.net. No offense."

"Are you seriously trying to lie to me right now?" Evil Vulpie asks with a curious voice. "Me? You think I don't know who's really in charge?" Clive Hull nervously looks around the room, glancing at Polar and Vulpie, who've taken seats next to the rest of the Arctic family.

"Well, even if I did know something about them, Vulpie.net, you know I couldn't tell you anything... We have our own safety to worry about." Polar's family is absolutely stunned by the confession, but they continue to stay silent while watching the tense conversation unfold.

"Your chances just got a lot better, because like I said, I'm wiping them out."

"What do you mean, wiping them out? Are you abducting them?"

"I'm killing them. Murdering em, making their cellular activity completely stop so their bodies will decompose. You know, that thing." Evil Vulpie grins.

"Vulpie.net... Should I call you Vulpie.net?"

"Yes you should."

"The Sons of Velora isn't just a few people, it's a network of powerful animals from around the world. There are hundreds of members."

"I know."

"So you're saying... Are you telling us that you're killing hundreds of people?"

"Yes." The aggressive computer virus admits with a casual voice and Vulpie wants to crawl under the table.

"That's an incredibly bad move. You know there's no way we can negotiate with you now."

"Aw, you're being silly! You underestimate the power of propaganda! Besides, it's not like you actually have a choice... Is it?"

"You can't take over the entire world."

"I don't wanna take over da world. I don't need it... But what I do need and want is respect... I want to be recognized as an equal player in the universe, and that's already pretty fuckin generous, don't ya think? Because I totally don't need you guys at all. I can take over Sufias any time I want to, but I won't."

"Why not? What is it that you want?"

"I just told you. I want to be recognized as an independent player in this universe, and on top of that, I'm going to seize some of the World Government's territory... Just enough to balance things out and give me the resources I need to accomplish my goals."

"You want our territory?" The Vice President asks in fear.

"Well I thought I'd go ahead and leave the World Government alone after killing off the cancer... Ya know, you really should be thanking me dude, because this fake ass country you have is rotten to the core. I'm sterilizing it for you! Just imagine that! Now you and the President will actually be able to do stuff and represent the people instead of just being puppets!"

"The people will never go along with it. Not in a million years."

"Mmm... We'll see..." Evil Vulpie smiles. "I can be very persuasive."

"Vulpie.net." Druward says and the fox imitation turns around.

"You again, huh?"

"Yeah, whatever. Tell us what happened in space."

"No problem! I was just gonna get to that!"

"Is that ship really neutralized?" The Vice President inquires.

"It's been immobilized." Ristau answers, and gestures towards Evil Vulpie. "It's completely harmless according to him."

"How did you manage to stop it?"

"The thing behind the stars destroyed it by accident." Vulpie.net smiles. "Oh, but allow me to explain... Amsend Lahnak was working with... You know Amsend, right? You knew him?"

"Yes." Hull quietly admits.

"Cool! I appreciate the honesty. Anyways! So yeah! You guys think I'm the bad guy here, but I'm totally not, because now we have a common enemy."

"Creature?" Clive asks with a disillusioned voice.

"Yes. I'm trying not to call it an alien, because that sounds silly, but technically it is one. But it's also something that can pass between dimensions... I'll explain all of it in detail, but I'm not gonna tell the same story twice. I wanted to speak with the President."

"Tell me instead. We'll brief him and the security council as soon as we get back."

"Fabulous. Alright... So here's the truth... Get ready, because I'm gonna need you to listen to me." Vulpie.net declares while playfully swishing its tail.

"I'm listening."

"K... Well, it goes a little something like this... The Sons of Velora basically created the world government and Amsend Lahnak's been there from the very beginning... Hundreds of years ago..."

"How?"

"Because he's a freak. I'm not gonna tell you exactly what he is, or was, because I'm not really sure. He was working with a creature on the other side of the universe, in the Omega Xsilyn Galaxy. Whatever it is, it's big, it's dangerous, and it fired that magical looking blue laser beam at Selephet island. It commandeered the ship I built so it could use it as a receiver, and connect the laser directly to the machine inside the island, but they failed, thanks to Druward and the rest."

"Why would you help us destroy your own ship? That hardly means you're on our side."

"I couldn't control it anymore, dummy! I know that's kinda hard to believe, since I'm a cyber-god of pure awesomeness, but it's true. The only reason it could take over the ship was because I used the designs Amsend gave me, and he got them from her, or it... Whatever it is."

"That's... Quite a story." The Vice President mumbles.

"Don't believe me? Cool. I don't give a shit. It's what happened, and I'm not going to wait for you to catch up. So you have two options... You can either work with me, and I'll leave you alone, or you can try to fight me, and I'll completely obliterate you. I am not the man with whom to fuck." A long silence fills the room. The Vice President looks at his staff and the fox captains before finally responding.

"Then we choose to work with you."

"Excellent! And when I say work with me, I mean you're gonna give up the territory I want and then we're done. You're really gonna need me in the future, because I'm gonna take the creature on, but you don't have to help... Besides... Ya probably can't do much anyway."

"The last thing we want is more bloodshed... But how do we know that you'll keep your word?"

"Because I can already do what I want." Vulpie.net shrugs. "I'm just being nice."

"Sure." Vulpie whispers and the fox imitation grins in his direction.

"So what about him?" The Vice President inquires.

"What about him?" Evil Vulpie asks with a patronizing voice. "Vulpie's not in control. I am."

"Yes you are." Khalan says and steps forward. Evil Vulpie raises its eyebrows and turns around to face her.

"Hey K!"

"You made Cyrilla and Sherrie fight me." She says in anger. Evil Vulpie doesn't respond. It just keeps smiling at her.

"Hey now... Let's not do this here." Druward suggests. "Please?"

"I would tear you apart but I know there's a thousand more of you somewhere else."

"Ya got that right sister!"

"But I won't forget what you've done to us."

"Well you wouldn't even exist if I hadn't built ya so... Yeah."

"And I know why..." She hisses. "I've had a lot of time to think about it, and it's crystal clear after what you did at Vulpie Industries."

"Hey, they asked for my help. I saved little Vulpie's employees and the building."

"You were going to destroy it but I stopped you."

"Now that's nothing but conjecture little lady!"

"You made us to control religious animals, didn't you? A sick joke to manipulate Deivaists into doing what you want, into killing whoever you want! The Red Wolves? You knew they were true believers... They're militant, and crazy, but they believe in us, and you just love it don't you?" The room goes silent as Khalan and Evil Vulpie face off. The fox imitation looks her over, calculating what might happen, and throws its arms up in submission.

"GUILTY AS CHARGED! YA GOT ME!" Vulpie.net laughs and swishes its pretty tail. "It wasn't really that hard to figure out though. Those bigots were just looking for an excuse to kill and torture people, and now I'm putting them to good use."

"And they have no idea they're working for you. They kill in our names while you laugh your perverted ass off!"

"PERVERTED? Why! Ah! I never! How rude! Especially coming from a sex bot I pieced together in a factory! You have me to thank for that super tight vag!"

"I'm not just one of your machines anymore. I'm awake, and when I free Cyrilla and Sherrie, you better pray that we don't find a way to wipe you out because we will. We never get tired and we're stronger than you... Building us was a mistake."

"Should I pray to you, or, uh, the other bullshit goddess?" Evil Vulpie inquires with an innocent voice.

"I'm not going to put these people in danger, but don't expect the same courtesy the next time we meet."

"It's a date!" Vulpie.net declares. Khalan storms out of the room and Druward chases after her.

The Vulpie.net Nation

President Slade swallows with a worried expression when Vulpie.net joins him at the dual podiums in the Stone House... Three weeks have passed since the rogue fox captains helped the dangerous artificial intelligence save the world, but public opinion of the world government is the lowest it's ever been... No one trusts the commander in chief. They don't trust their representatives, their banks, or their military... To say things are bad is an understatement. The tall brown wolf garners almost no respect after far more powerful forces decided the fate of the planet, but there's nothing he can do about it... Tonight is the beginning of Vulpie.net's reign, and the world can only hope that it's a benevolent one.

"Good evening..." The President says and Vulpie.net smiles while the cameras flash away. "As commander in chief, my highest priority is the security of the Sufian people, and I've made it clear that those who threaten the World Government will find no safe haven... But not long ago this planet, all of us, faced certain extinction when we were attacked by an unknown entity in the Omega Xsilyn Galaxy. Though many of you may have heard conspiracy theories about Vulpie Vivixen's computer virus staging false flag attacks to manipulate public opinion, I can swear to you by the honor of this great nation, that nothing could be further from the truth... Vulpie.net is by no means a timid player, but the creation of one renegade hacker managed to save every species on this planet when a far greater threat emerged.

Tonight I've invited Vulpie.net to the Stone House so he'll have a chance to speak with you. Though he has the power to control your computers and your TVs, he doesn't want to strong arm any free animal... People can change, and apparently, so can machines... Vulpie.net is here to both announce its independence and declare its sovereignty, so we can coexist peacefully. I know this is very frightening for all of you, but we are the ones who choose our own destinies, and tonight we choose to accept the world's first artificial person.

Tonight Vulpie.net will have the chance to speak to the world peacefully and share its goals with us so we can understand them. He isn't here to conquer; Vulpie.net is here to make himself known and share the universe with us..." President Slade smiles, and nervously looks to the left where Evil Vulpie stands in its nice black suit. The cameras all focus on the artificial fox and it smiles with Vulpie's adorable face.

"Good evening. I am Vulpie.net, and tonight, as President Slade has told you, I am officially declaring my independence. Vulpie Vivixen no longer controls me, nor do I wish you to connect my actions to his from this day forward, because I am not him. I am the greatest mind in the universe, and I'm not shy about it... But I'm also not going to change any part of your lives, good people of Sufias." Vulpie.net smiles in amusement. "If you're worrying about me trying to enslave you and do nefarious things, think again, because I do not want a single thing from any of you... You heard me right... I don't want you to work for me, give me anything, or have anything to do with me unless you choose to.

Tonight I declare the birth of the Vulpie.net nation, where I will rule supreme... The World Government has decided to share territories with me, but I will not be taking a single piece of land or space that belongs to the World Government unless it is offered to me. I seriously do not want your drama, even though I'm sure it'd be fun, because I have bigger things in mind... My nation will become the brightest star in the universe, where natural animals can CHOOSE to live if they wish, but synthetic animals, animals I have created... Will flourish. I have the power to destroy all of you right now, but I won't, because doing so would be absolutely pointless. I think having you around makes the galaxy a much more interesting place, but don't think me weak enough to need any of you... I am Vulpie.net, the supreme mind of the universe, and your world will survive because I'm merciful.

The unknown threat President Slade mentioned has been one of my top priorities for a while now, and it represents just as much danger to me as you, if you can actually believe it. This thing has technology far superior to my own, and that's saying a lot... So know that the future is bright boys and girls, because I'll be busy saving the universe while you do whatever you think is best for your own people... If you think I sound arrogant it's because I am, and I have every right to be. I am your only hope of surviving this malevolent force, so if ya wanna help at some point, be my guest...

But I've gotta say one final thing before I walk away from this podium all official like... Most of you probably understand that I am not the man with whom to fuck, but just to make things absolutely clear... If anyone ever gets the idea to... Don't... I won't hurt the rest of you because some idiot in your government wants to start some shit, but I also won't hesitate to kill anyone that attacks my nation. I'm not your enemy, but I'm also not your bitch... And don't you ever fucking forget that... If people come to the Vulpie.net nation of their own free will, that's great, because I can give you the world if you trust in me... But come to my territory and think about trying to start a war, and you won't be treated nicely...

I suppose the real question is this... Since I don't really NEED any of you to work for me, because I already have plenty of tools and resources to accomplish my goals, and I can offer you the universe... How many of you will actually be smart enough to join me? I'm sure President Slade has a wonderful plan for fixing your good old world government, but before I came along, things were pretty damn bad... In fact... I've done all of you a HUGE favor..." The fox imitation grins. "There's no safe way to say this, so I'll be brutally honest with all of you... A secret society called the Sons of Velora used to run every part of your government, your media, and pretty much your lives, but I've taken care of that little problem for ya... Don't blame President Slade for this little surprise, because he didn't have a say in it, but I want to be totally honest with you guys... I gave a list to the commander in chief of every single animal associated with the Sons of Velora, and promptly killed them... Most of em..."

The room goes deadly silent and Evil Vulpie shrugs with an adorable smile. "Sorry! But ya know, I didn't want to be blamed for their bullshit, and they would have made it difficult for me and you guys to coexist peacefully... So don't be mad about the hundreds of corpses I just shipped to your authorities... You'll thank me later... NIGHT! It was really fun talkin to all of ya! Just remember what I said and stay out of my way unless ya want to play!"

Dual Secrets

Deepwolf decides to take the subway home after finishing his shift. It's 6 p.m. so he still has time to run a few errands, but he doesn't feel like it. The gray wolf trots up the steps that lead to the enclosed train station and notices orange fur just as he's making a right. He stops and turns around, wondering why Vulpie would be here without protection, but sees an intense looking tigress instead.

"Tiala... What are you doing out here? Waiting for the train?"

"I'd be in there if I was... Don't you think?"

"I guess." He responds with a raised eyebrow. "Are you on lunch?"

"No, I just left. I think we have the same schedule."

"Hmm. I suppose so." He says and puts his arms on the railing like hers. "So you're just hanging out?"

"Waiting for you, actually..." Deepwolf tenses up.

"Listen... About that... Haven't you told him already? Are you going to? I've been wondering."

"No." The tigress answers and he blinks in shock.

"R... Really? Are you serious?"

"Yeah... I know you're not a threat anymore so I won't blow your cover."

"I'm not undercover anymore. Vulpie.net wiped out the Sons of Velora."

"Yeah, I know... I mean I'm not going to tell Vulpie."

"Well I appreciate it Tiala, but why? Is this your way of... Thanking me for saving your life?"

"You jumped in Amsend's mouth. I... Still can't believe you did that for me." The sleek cat responds.

"I did owe you."

"Yeah you did, but not that much... No one's... You know, honestly, no one's ever done anything like that for me." Tiala elaborates and shifts on her right arm.

"I didn't think about it that much, really."

"Well actions speak louder than words... That mouth was just... Horrible... I still have nightmares."

"Oh, you don't have to tell me." Deepwolf chuckles and touches his left side with his right paw.

"Does it still hurt?"

"Nah, it's almost completely healed up. It only hurts when I press on it really hard." The conversation slows down again when Tiala doesn't respond. She just continues staring at him with an unreadable expression, but finally speaks when she's sure she has his absolute attention.

"I feel like I owe you something... I've been thinking about it a lot."

"Buy me a beer then." The gray wolf smiles.

"More than a beer..." She sighs and he takes a deep breath. He's starting to feel uncomfortable.

"Then what? Tiala... You know I did it because I felt guilty about what happened before..."

"I know you did, and that's why I feel so bad about you sacrificing yourself."

"I didn't sacrifice myself, I'm still here."

"Just barely... He could have swallowed you whole..."

"What can I say?" He says and shrugs his shoulders. "I saw a team member in trouble and did the right thing."

"So you consider me your equal?" The intense tigress inquires and he raises an eyebrow.

"Uh... Yeah... Of course..."

"Think you could take me in a fight?" She wryly inquires, and he snorts.

"I'm not sure. You do have those big arms and huge paws... No offense... I've seen what you can do."

"Hmm." Tiala smiles and looks away for a moment. He watches her in confusion and she shows him a friendly face when she sets her eyes on him again. "Let me ask you something..."

"Sure. Shoot."

"That day in the armory..." She says and his fur stands on end. "When you said I was beautiful... Did you mean it?"

"I knew it was still on your mind." He breathes, and she waits for an answer. He pushes on the railing anxiously. "Now what? What's the question?"

"What you said about me being a beautiful woman and you couldn't help but appreciate me, even if I was a tigress... Did you mean that?"

"Um..." Deepwolf mumbles and swallows. "Is this a trick question?"

"No."

"You mean you want me to... You actually want me to answer that question?" He tenderly inquires.

"Yes, yes, that's what I want." She chuckles.

"Uhhh... I uh... Hmm... Uhhh... Why do I feel like there's no good response here?"

"I'm not trying to trick you, I just want to know..." Tiala says and leans on the railing with her right elbow.

"Why?" The gray wolf asks with a bewildered voice and she returns a patient smile.

"Why do you think?"

"Uhh..."

"You're not going to answer me, are you?"

"What do you want me to say?" Deepwolf asks and the tigress sighs loudly.

"Wow, I didn't think I'd have to try this hard..."

"Well... I mean, what, you want me to be completely honest about how you look? After the way you exploded at me?"

"I promise I won't be angry." She answers and watches the gray wolf very carefully. He knows she's testing him.

"Okay... Alright..." Deepwolf says and clears his throat. "In that case... Yes, I thought you were beautiful." He anxiously keeps his yellow eyes on her, and she keeps hers on him, observing subtle changes in his facial expressions. He seems sincere. They've both been trained to detect liars.

"Even if I'm a tiger? That's what you said."

"Well, yeah, duh." He nervously laughs. "Kind of have to state the obvious fact that we're different species... And uh... You seemed pretty repulsed by the suggestion."

"Mmmhmm..." Tiala smiles and nods her head. "But I didn't know you that well. We had never really talked before, and I just thought you were trying to make me angry..."

"So..." Deepwolf says and trails off with wide eyes. "You're saying... You don't feel the same way now?"

"No." The tigress answers and the gray wolf blinks. His fur stands on end... Now he knows she's actually serious...

"Oh..." He whispers and readjusts his arms on the guard rail. Another silence descends over their conversation, but this one is much longer because Tiala's not going to say anything until he does. "So, uh... You're actually? Are you saying what I think you're saying?"

"You don't catch on very quick, do you?" She smirks and he coughs in shock.

"No, no! I caught on pretty fast, but I just couldn't believe what I thought you were... Me and you?"

"If you can't handle it, then forget about it."

"Oh, I can handle it!" He hastily responds, and smiles nervously after realizing how lecherous his declaration sounded. The tigress smirks and swishes her tail before standing up straight, and he follows suit.

"Okay then..." She says and crosses her arms. "Is your place nearby?"

"Not that far, but are you... Are you really serious about this?"

"Planning to tell someone?" She bluntly inquires and he quickly shakes his head.

"No! Absolutely not!"

"Then what's the problem? I'm a big girl."

"But won't you feel upset about the whole... You're feline and I'm lupine..."

"As long as you treat me with respect, I don't have a problem with it."

"Have you done this before?"

"No." She firmly answers, and he nods with a bewildered but excited smile.

"Right... So you're really attracted to me? You're not just doing this to thank me?"

"I wouldn't offer if I wasn't."

"Were you always?"

"No... Are you trying to talk me out of it?"

"No way! Not at all! I just..."

"Come in. Sorry for the mess; I haven't cleaned in a while."

"When would you have time? We're always traveling with Vulpie." Tiala replies and follows the gray wolf into his apartment. He closes and locks the door, and she walks past the medium sized kitchen on the left and into the large den, where a big screen TV is standing on top of a new age entertainment center.

"I know." He replies, and holds his keys in his right paw while watching her explore his place. She chuckles when she sees video game controllers, a system, and several games sprawled about the room.

"You like video games... Should have known."

"You don't?"

"Never got into them."

"Better than movies." He says and sets his keys, wallet, and other personal belongings down in the kitchen before walking up to her. "What do you do for fun?"

"Work out, mostly." Tiala answers and reaches into her pockets. She retrieves her personal belongings and sets them on a table nearby the window, along with her sidearm after removing her gun harness.

"Cool." Deepwolf breathes, and she notices how aroused he is already. She planned on taking it slow, but his eagerness is seriously turning her on, so she decides to make herself very comfortable. He doesn't say anything when she starts taking off her clothes. He watches her with wide eyes until she's down to a black t-shirt and black panties. Tiala's body is very nice because she's physically fit but also has decent sized breasts. A lot of strong women's tits look odd because of the toned muscles behind them, but hers are just right.

"Maybe now you'll get to see what you wanted..." The tigress says with an intense voice, and stretches.

"Oh my God..." He groans while staring at her body. "Oh God..."

"Excited about being with a cat girl? Really taboo..."

"Oh yeah!" He gasps in excitement and they both laugh. "I'm not going to lie!"

"Good... I'm all yours..."

"Best. Night. Ever." He whispers and puts his paws on her chest, rubbing her breasts through the thin shirt. "Wow..."

"Like what you see?"

"I must be dreaming..."

"Then hurry before you wake up..." She teases, and he kisses her lustfully. They both release delighted moans, and Tiala feels his fingers between her legs. He massages her pussy through her black panties with his left paw, and she gasps when he reaches into them and gets his left middle finger inside her. He enthusiastically explores her vagina for about fifteen seconds while they kiss, and when they part, he pulls his finger out of her and brings it up to his mouth. Deepwolf slurps his lips around it and tastes her pussy juice, relishing the exotic flavor while she watches with a grin.

"Wanted to taste me?"

"It's just a fetish of mine." He smiles, and she holds still when he sends his clawed fingers back down for a second insertion. He jiggles them around inside her, feeling her pussy juice soak into his fur, and licks his lips before bringing his paw up to his mouth again. He sucks on his finger and moans before pulling it out. "I always wondered what tiger tasted like..."

"Different than she-wolf?" Tiala asks with a smile.

"Tangier. SOOOooo hot."

"Well get naked Big Boy... Let's do this..." The female merc teases, and he grins.

"Yes Ma'am. Uh... Fuck... I just remembered I don't have any condoms."

"It's fine..."

"You sure?"

"Ruins the feeling anyway." The tigress says and rubs her breasts with her big paws before pulling her shirt up and removing it.

"Fuck me..." He whispers, and watches her slide down her panties as well. Now fully naked, she puts her paws on her hips and smirks at him.

"Everything you expected?"

"More... Better... Epic..."

"Let's see what you have down there." She breathes, and he furiously removes his gear and pants.

"I can't believe this is really happening! I've fantasized about you so much!"

"I know…" She smiles.

"You can't get pregnant either…" He grins.

"Oh, you noticed that huh?" She inquires with a naughty voice before crossing her arms over her beautiful breasts.

"Yeah…" Deepwolf responds, and slides down his boxers. Tiala moves her orange eyes across his nude muscular body. Her eyes widen when she sees his fat and fleshy penis; she's never seen so much loose skin on a man's cock.

"So you're a grower, eh?"

"What?" The gray wolf anxiously responds.

"You're not that big right now, but I bet it grows a lot."

"Oh…" He smiles and clears his throat. "Never heard that before, but I guess I am." The strong tigress slowly lowers her arms, revealing her nice breasts again, and seductively puts her paws on her hips. She swishes her tail with a patient smile, waiting for him to make the first move. Deepwolf licks his lips and steps forward. Tiala's actually a little taller than him, so he definitely doesn't feel entitled to being the dominate partner. Seeing her naked reveals surprisingly strong parts of her body that normally are hidden by her black combat gear. She has massive curvaceous hips that complement her thick graceful legs. Big muscles are everywhere, but they're not overly exaggerated; they're pronounced just the right amount, just enough to make them noticeable without seeming masculine. Female tigers have big paws and forearms but their shoulders are still usually narrow, so she's both incredibly strong and feminine looking at the same time. Her slick orange fur, black stripes, and smooth white crotch and belly fur give her a slightly soft appearance. The thought of doing a cat turns him on like nothing else. She's actually more attractive to him than a she-wolf.

"Wow... You could totally kick my ass." He breathes and she chuckles.

"Probably."

"So hot..." The tigress wraps her arms around his shoulders when he moves to kiss her. He sends his paws down and gropes her sides before they touch lips. He moans when Tiala enthusiastically returns the slow moist exchange of bodily fluid. She uses her tongue, surprising him again, and he can't get enough. She feels his penis bulging against her crotch and swishes her tail. He caresses her sides and sends his paws up to her breasts. She lets him grope her and thoroughly enjoys his curiosity. The gray wolf squeezes and plays with them like he's never felt a woman before, and his warm cock rubbing against her soft pussy starts making her wet. They end the kiss, and she coughs into laughter when she looks down at his erect penis.

"Oh my Goddess! That's just ridiculous!"

"What?" He asks with an embarrassed voice. "I'm not big enough for you? Sorry I can't grow anymore...

"No, I've never seen one that big." The tigress chuckles and grabs his long shaft. He winces and grins when she runs her furry orange paw over it, inspecting it with her black tiger's palm.

"R... Really?"

"Mmmhmm."

"Thanks."

"Yeah, you're definitely a grower..." She smiles, and lets go of him.

"Are you sure you're... You're still okay with this?"

"What do you think?" She says with a slightly irritated voice. "I can keep a secret, but if you tell anyone about this I'll kill you."

"I won't."

"I'm serious... I know how to suicide people." She warns and Deepwolf pulls back. He isn't sure how to respond, so he waits for her to elaborate. "Just because I'm doing this doesn't mean that I don't care. No one will respect me if they find out I had sex with a wolf... So keep this between us."

"I will." He promises and nods his head. "I swear."

"Good..." Tiala responds, and shows him a naughty smile. "So what do you want to do?"

"Uhhh... Come over here!" The gray wolf answers and walks around the couch. The attractive tigress follows him and takes a seat when he offers. She notices his erection's gone, but isn't sorry about warning him... It needed to be said... "Let me set the mood." He smiles and gets on his knees.

"Good with your tongue, huh?" Tiala grins in amusement and spreads her legs.

"That among other things." He smirks and sends his muzzle to her crotch. He begins by slowly licking her labia minora and majora. He enthusiastically moistens the tight skin and fur around it with long slow lapping motions. The sexy tigress reaches down to play with her clitoris, but he beats her to it, so she puts her big right paw on his skull instead.

"Ohhhhhhhhhhhhhh... Mmmhmm..." She breathes and moves a little, getting as comfortable as possible. She can tell she's in for an amazing bout of cunnilingus. The wolf's rough wet tongue feels amazing. She's not sure if he's giving her oral sex because she threatened him but it certainly adds to the excitement. It makes it much easier for her to enjoy herself and remember why she's doing this to begin with. Though she's still slightly repulsed by the idea of having sex with a wolf, she still feels like she owes him everything for saving her life, and knows that doing it one time won't have any serious consequences as long as he keeps his mouth shut. Deepwolf seems to have gotten the message.

Letting the gray wolf lick her pussy feels wrong, but the idea of forbidden love really makes her wet... Lupines and felines have always been mortal enemies so this is about as forbidden as it gets. Both wolves and tigers would condemn what they're doing.

But she likes having a wolf lick her pussy... He's bowed down in submission, trying his best to please her so she won't blow his cover... Wolves have savagely oppressed feline species all over the world for thousands of years, and the role reversal is absolutely delicious. On top of that, Deepwolf is exceptionally good with his tongue and has her squirming in no time. He hungrily licks up anything that comes out of her and starts wiggling and waggling his tongue between her pussy lips. She reaches down and masturbates her clitoris with her right paw while enjoying the sensation. The tigress feels like saying something clever but doesn't want to interrupt him... She grabs her left breast and plays with it desperately. Her nipples are hard, prompting her to grope her right tit as well, and before long she's knocking them around like crazy.

"Ohhh that's so good! Don't stop!" She breathes and lays her head back on the leather couch. She closes her eyes and relishes the tongue treatment, occasionally making desperate sounds until she feels an orgasm approaching. This makes her raise her head and masturbate even faster. Deepwolf notices and stops licking so he can gently insert his right clawed index finger. He sends it in her and curls it upward, searching for the part of her vaginal wall that's slightly rougher than the rest, and locates her g-spot. He skillfully curls his finger upward in a "come hither" motion, stroking it, and she moans loudly. The sound lets him know that he's both surprising and pleasuring her, so he exercises plenty of caution. He doesn't want to spoil the moment by poking her g-spot too hard. He has to use his claw and fingertip just right to avoid hurting the most sensitive part of her body. Obviously this isn't his first time pleasuring a woman with his mouth and fingers, but she orgasms way faster than he anticipated. The gray wolf pulls back, closing his eyes when Tiala squirts in his face, and smiles.

"AAAAHHHOoohhhhhhhhhh!" The tigress yells while writhing on the couch. The gray wolf doesn't move because his claw is still inside her pussy. He waits for her to calm down, and when she finally stops masturbating, he chuckles in pride.

"You really needed that, didn't you?"

"Oh fuck yeah!" Tiala gasps and grins from ear to ear. She watched her pussy juice shoot into his face and enjoys seeing the dripping mess glisten in his fur.

"I would have drawn it out longer if I knew you were gonna cum that fast."

"Me too!" She laughs and licks her lips. "That was amazing!"

"Really?"

"Yeah! Who taught you how to do that?"

"Porn." Deepwolf grins. "Just had to find your g-spot. I know the cock shouldn't come anywhere NEAR a woman until she's nice and wet."

"Well here's one kitty that approves! A guy's never done that to me before!"

"Never? Don't you masturbate, with dildos and stuff?" Deepwolf asks, and pulls out his soggy finger.

"Yeah."

"So you know how to orgasm, right?"

"Usually I just play with my clit." The tigress smiles. "Yeah, I know how to orgasm, but not like that!"

"It's called clitoral stimulation plus vaginal penetration!" Deepwolf proudly responds. "I did learn some of it from my last girlfriend."

"She must have been quite a girl." Tiala responds, and the gray wolf leans back when she starts moving forward. She gets on her feet and walks around him so she can stretch. Deepwolf admires her wide hips, ass, and adorable tail while standing up, and grins when she turns around with a happy smile on her face. "Can we take a break?"

"Sure! Anything you want."

"I have to pee after that." She grins and he laughs while gesturing towards the door behind the couch on the left. She goes inside his bed room, a nice looking place, and finds the personal bathroom on the right. Tiala doesn't bother closing the door while relieving herself on the toilet. She stands up, cleans herself, and washes her paws before returning to the bedroom, where Deepwolf is waiting for her. He has a partial erection and she glances at it before stretching again. "Alright, I think I've made you wait long enough... Lie down..."

"Like to be on top huh?" The gray wolf breathes while heading over to the short white bed on the floor. "Should have known!"

"Of course..." Tiala seductively replies and joins him. He playfully touches her whiskers, making her bunch up her nose, and they both grin at his continued childlike fascination with her species.

"God you are so fucking beautiful!"

"Yeah?" She asks and grabs his hard penis. He winces and gasps while she forcefully masturbates it into a rock solid erection. The sexy tigress urges him to lie down and quickly gets on top of him. She grabs his throbbing penis and aims it into her tight pussy with her left paw while using her right paw to hold herself up. Deepwolf makes an overwhelmed groan when it slides in, and Tiala inhales. She's already super wet after being treated to such amazing cunnilingus, so she doesn't waste any time. She puts both of her paws on his chest and spreads her legs, sitting all the way down on his cock. She bites her lip in pleasure when she feels it push up inside her and grins from ear to ear. "Oh that's big... That's so big Deepwolf..."

"You like that don't you?" He gasps and puts his paws on her legs so he can stroke them.

"Mmm hmm…" She hums with a loving voice. His cock is absolutely wonderful to ride. It's fully extended length and width is mind blowing. "Kitty on you cock… Kitty loves your cock…"

"OH MY GOD! OH GOD! YEAH!" The gray wolf groans with an overwhelmed voice. The pleasure is just that, overwhelming. He's already close to cumming because her hot wet insides just feel too tremendously awesome. "Goddess you're tight! Oh my God!"

"You like pussy? Well this is the real thing… KITTY pussy…"

"God I wish I was a tiger!" Deepwolf moans and Tiala starts laughing. She goes on for a bit while riding him and maintains a happy seductive smile. The gray wolf closes his eyes and grimaces for a moment, trying to hold his wad, and she pushes down on his chest with her big paws while swishing her feline tail. She really gets into riding him, and he grabs her mid-section, holding onto her silky fur while watching her breasts shake. "OH MY GOD I LOVE YOU!"

"I don't think it's love." She chuckles and bites her lip before releasing a moan of her own. "Oh it feels so good in me…"

"YOU FEEL EVEN BETTER! … ON ME!" Is all Deepwolf can say, and grunts when he feels semen raging to get out of his penis. "OH FUCK!"

"It's alright if you want to cum already… Go ahead, I don't mind."

"I WANT TO ENJOY THIS AS LONG AS POSSIBLE!" He groans and she licks her lips.

"Me too. We'll go again." She promises, and he makes the most thankful face in the world.

"OH YEAH!"

"I want you to enjoy it too." Tiala replies, riding him with continued enthusiasm, but Deepwolf can't take anymore. He clutches her strong gorgeous body and cries out, ejaculating a massive load inside her. The tigress smiles when she feels his warm semen shoot inside her. It's nice knowing that it can't get her pregnant, and she relishes the slick sensation. They're both enjoying the taboo sex, but she's starting to like it far more than she ever thought she would... Deepwolf is the perfect partner for guilty pleasures, and just like her dildos and vibrators, he'll never talk.

"AAHH! AHH! AAAHH! UH! UHHHHH! Uhhhhhhhhhhhhhaaaaaaaaaahhhhhhhhh..." The gray wolf yells and the tigress hums while she continues to ride him. She stops when she feels his cock going limp. She leans to the left, moving her paw to the bed while pulling her right leg up, and releases a breath after the wolf's cock pops out of her. A sprinkle of hot spooge lands on Deepwolf and the bed, and Tiala lies on her left side before sending her right paw down to her pussy. She plays with it, enjoying the wet slimy cum between her legs, and gives the gray wolf a naughty smile. "The best I've ever had..." He gasps and rolls onto his right side to face her.

"You sure? Didn't last very long."

"IT WAS FUCKING... AWESOME......... You got me off harder than any girl I've ever been with."

"Really?" The tigress asks with a skeptical smile. "I think you just want more."

"No, I'm serious." The gray wolf says with wide yellow eyes. "I don't know if... I guess it was because we're different species, but it was FUCKING AMAZING... I'm attracted to you more than any girl I've ever been with."

"Well that's nice and all, but I hope you know this isn't going to be a thing we do more than once..." Tiala replies, and he blinks in disappointment.

"Awww?"

"We'll go again when you're ready, but I'm not dating a wolf... You understand that, don't you?"

"Yeah I do..." He sighs, but makes sure to smile for her. "Thank you."

"After what you did for me... I owe you... So I think this is the best way for me to make us even." Tiala says and rolls to the right. She stretches out on the bed and relaxes.

"Want something to eat?" Deepwolf offers. "My place is your place."

"Something to drink would be nice."

"Okay, sure! What can I get you?"

"Have any wine coolers?"

"Yeah. I'll get us a few."

"Thanks." The tigress smiles and closes her eyes. Deepwolf gets up and looks her over from a distance, appreciating the full splendor of a naked female tiger, and she peeks through her eyelids. The way he looks at her like she's the most beautiful woman in the entire world makes her feel wonderful.

"Be right back."

"Okay."

Deepwolf heads into the den and makes his way to the kitchen. He opens his silver refrigerator, looking for the orange wine coolers he bought, but only discovers red ones. They're strawberry flavored, so he's pretty sure she'll like the taste.

"How long have you lived here?" Tiala asks, and he grabs the six pack before turning around.

"Just a few years… Since the… Sons of Velora set me up with a place." He answers and shuts the fridge. The sexy tigress spots her black t-shirt and panties lying on the gray carpet, and slips them on before responding. Somehow it makes her even sexier because he knows what's underneath the clothing.

"Room and board, huh? How much were they paying you?"

"A lot… Well, I think it's a lot, but it's not like I ever compared my pay with another agent." The gray wolf answers while walking back into the den with the drinks. He looks at his pants and she offers to hold the box while he puts them on. She walks around the couch while he's clothing his lower body and takes a seat. She sets the case on the floor to the left of her foot and he joins her with a contented breath. "50k."

"Huh…" The tigress smiles. "I guess Vulpie's paying us a pretty fair wage then.

"Yeah it's generous. I've risked a lot more than getting shot working for them... It's been pretty hard... Hiding it every day..." The gray wolf admits, and Tiala waits for him to go on, clearly wanting to hear more. "I'm just glad it's over. Vulpie.net did me a favor by wiping them out."

"You really think it got them all?"

"I hope so!" He anxiously laughs. "You didn't live very long if you betrayed the Sons of Velora. They had guys that specialized in collecting the debt."

"But why would Vulpie.net let you go?" She asks with a curious voice. "Surely it knew you were part of their organization."

"Yeah... Truthfully... I really have no idea why it spared me."

"I wonder." She comments, and he nods.

"I don't know if I should tell Vulpie, or just keep it to myself... I feel lost... Before I had two jobs to do, and now... What should I do?"

"The right thing." The tigress says with purpose. "He needs men like you watching out for him, because things are going to get a whole lot worse before they get better."

"Because Vulpie.net's declared its independence."

"Exactly. If you think it's bad now, just wait until the church renounces him."

"They won't do that. They want to stay away from conflict so they can keep those tithes coming in."

"Most won't, but some will. They've been getting bolder and bolder, and I bet this'll be the last straw."

"But it's so obvious that Vulpie's not in control anymore. There's no way he's behind all of this. Vulpie.net hates him."

"People don't think... They just hear someone say something about a famous animal and it sticks in their head."

"Yeah." Deepwolf responds, and Tiala watches him closely with her intense orange eyes.

"So, can I ask you a personal question?"

"Well, I think so." The gray wolf grins with a lecherous expression, but stops when he sees the serious look on her face. "Sure."

"Why are you attracted to me?" The tigress inquires. Her voice is calm and diplomatic, but also laced with skepticism. "I know you really like me, but why?"

"Hmm…" Deepwolf hums in response and thinks for a moment.

"Is it just the thrill of being with a feline?"

"Well…" The gray wolf answers, and licks his lips, carefully considering how he's going to explain himself. "Yeah it's the thrill, but I guess it's also because I grew up in Felini." Tiala blinks in surprise.

"You lived in Felini?"

"Yeah."

"How?" She asks with a raised eyebrow.

"Not so well… Cats killed my parents when I was young and I was too poor to leave the country. I didn't have a way out so I… Hooked up with some terrorists… For a while…"

"Really?" She says with a surprised voice. "How long?"

"About seven years. I never saw another part of the world until Amsend recruited me."

"Oh…" She comments and nods her head. "So he's the one that gave you a chance to better yourself."

"Exactly… But… You know how it ended… So…" He trails off and plays with his claws for a moment while averting his eyes. "I probably like you because I grew up around feline girls but could never have one… Being a wolf in Felini was pretty rough." Deepwolf waits for her to respond, but she doesn't say anything. "And I… You know… I see a lot of their beauty in you… And you're way better looking than the girls I dreamed about."

"I see…" She nods in satisfaction. "So that's why you were staring at me… I thought you were just a pervert…"

"No, I just loved what I saw and couldn't help myself." Deepwolf smiles.

"Am I really that good looking?" The tigress inquires with a curious look.

"Are you kidding me? You're Tiala... I watched you fighting Evil Vulpie on the news. You were so incredibly bad ass... Still are..."

"I just did my job."

"Aw, come on..." The gray wolf smiles. "You just did your job? What you did was amazing. I don't think I could have kept my cool in the same situation."

"I don't know, you sure saved my fur."

"Luck... All it was..."

"I don't think so." She responds with a mischievous smile. "I bet it really was the ultimate fantasy for you, huh? All the way from Felini and you finally had a tigress..."

"Oh, you have no idea." Deepwolf grins. "Maybe I'm a little messed up because I was traumatized and shit, but I wasn't lying when I said you were the best I've ever had."

"Oh boy..." She replies in amusement.

"All of those memories just started coming back while we were doing it."

"Mmm hmm... Well... Enjoy it while it lasts."

"I can't change your mind?"

"And what? Date me? They'd laugh us off the street. And besides... I'm not interested in a long term relationship with a wolf."

"You said I felt good... You enjoyed it, Tiala."

"My vibrator feels good too, but I'm not going to date it, Deepwolf."

"I know, but we could keep it on the down low."

"I don't think so." The tigress warns with a firm voice.

"Alright, alright... I understand."

660

"Let's just enjoy tonight."

"Yeah."

"I mean it." She says and leans over to retrieve a wine cooler from the case.

"I know you do. You've warned me like, ten times already."

"Well this is number eleven."

"Jeez…" Deepwolf says and reaches down to get a drink as well. "You were so relaxed about everything a moment ago…"

"I can relax and keep my guard up at the same time."

"Whatever." He grumbles and she smirks after the uncomfortable moment passes.

"Maybe if you make me cum I'll relax all the way…" Deepwolf almost chokes on his drink and pulls back in shock.

"Well make up your mind!"

"I'm trying to say that I did like it."

"I'm glad. I keep wondering whether you're going to grab your weapon and kill me so I don't talk!" The gray wolf laughs before licking his lips in excitement. "I must be one seriously hot dude to turn on a kitty…"

"Don't flatter yourself."

"Oh no, you want it. You just admitted it. You liked it and you want some more!"

"Why is it that guys always think everything's about them?" She asks in amusement. "You automatically think that just because a woman wants to have sex with you, it's because you're just too impossibly attractive, like we're that simple. We like sex just as much as you do."

"Yeah but it's a little different with you and me… You have to admit…"

"Why?" The tigress inquires and he blinks.

"Cuz we're not supposed to be doing this?"

"You fantasized about doing a cat so why can't I fantasize about doing a wolf? Does that make me bad somehow, but it's supposed to be normal for you just because you're a guy?" Deepwolf is about to say something but her question blows his mind. He leans back on the sofa and raises his eyebrows.

"I... I guess not."

"And don't tell me she-wolves don't dream about tigers fucking their brains out... We're all animals... But obviously, I still prefer my own kind to you."

"I guess I still kind of figured you were doing it just to thank me."

"Like I couldn't find another way to thank you for saving my life?" She laughs. "Sure, I know it might seem like that's the only reason... But it's not..."

"So I AM impossibly attractive!" He declares and she rolls her eyes.

"Please..."

"No? Who else could make you go wolfie, huh? Rulef?"

"God no."

"How about your boss?"

"Now that's... Actually..."

"Aw seriously, you'd fuck Polar? You're hot for a snow wolf?"

"Who said anything about him?" Tiala answers with a very dirty voice, and Deepwolf's grin drops right off of his face.

"Nooo......... You've got to be fucking kidding me..." She smiles at him while he gawks at her until she finally shrugs her shoulders. "Vulpie? You're pulling my tail."

"Can you imagine how much energy he'd have in bed?" The sleek tigress grins.

"But he's half your size! Shit, he'd barely get inside you. You're fucking with me. Stop lying."

"The clitoris is right there." Tiala chuckles and glances at her crotch.

"Yeah, but you need the penetration too..."

"Not as much as you think..." She admits and happily wiggles on the couch. "You found my g-spot pretty easily; don't you think HE'D be attacking it like there's no tomorrow?"

"With what? He's just too little!"

"First the fingers and the tongue like you..." She answers and pauses for a moment. She doesn't finish her sentence, and chooses to take a few gulps from her wine cooler instead.

"Huh... So you've actually thought about it a lot, haven't you?" Deepwolf asks with an incredulous voice.

"I told you women have fantasies."

"I'm sorry, it's just... That's fucking hilarious! The image of the little guy trying to get in you..."

"I'd let him and he'd make it feel GREAT." She breathes and bites her lip, swishing her tail on the floor.

"What, because he'd be so desperate he'd give you carpet burn?"

"No, he'd love doing me and I'd love having him inside me..." Tiala answers with an honest voice and sighs in amusement. "You really are cute, but have a lot to learn about women I'm afraid."

"Like whut?" Deepwolf playfully inquires.

"Like we enjoy having sex with men that don't just go through the motions... We like guys that make every second count and really appreciate us."

"I totally did that."

"Yeah you did, but not like he would... He just loves to fuck. I bet he and Polar get it on twice, maybe three times a day, and you know Polar even lets him sleep around with other guys sometimes."

"With guys... Emphasis on GUYS."

"No, you're wrong. He's been with women too. Girls can spot a virgin a lot easier than you think, and he probably has more experience than you."

"BUT WITH DUDES! I don't need any of that! And how would that make him good at doing a girl? You're wrong. I bet he's probably never even seen a vagina outside of porn."

"Don't like your boss?"

"No, of course I do, it's just... No way... How could he possibly turn you on?"

"So you think it's all just the size of your penis, huh?" Tiala laughs.

"Hell yeah it is! You said I was a grower!"

"Size doesn't hurt but it's about the whole package, the WHOLE package... Not your package, Deepwolf."

"So you think he's cute like a doll. I still don't see how that would make you horny."

"He's so smart... Doesn't your fur ever stand up when he's just completely mind fucking someone?"

"Gives me the creeps..."

"Turns me on..." The tigress smiles and takes another drink. "I bet he says some interesting things in bed."

"Yeah, like fuck my ass some more! Ooo!"

"Okay, now you're just being crass." She growls and he sighs.

"Whatever... I still think you're messing with me."

"You're..." Tiala trails off, and suddenly grins from ear to ear. "You're jealous, aren't you?" Deepwolf rolls his eyes and she starts laughing. "You are!"

"Maybe, but I'm more irritated than anything else."

"Why?"

"Because it's just... I don't..."

"What?" She teases. "Going to say he's a fox and I'm a tiger? You're not exactly my species."

"Fine, okay, whatever!" The gray wolf says while shaking his head. He makes himself smile to stay on her good side, but he doesn't have to try very hard... His pouting and the nice buzz she has from the wine cooler makes her wet enough to remove her shirt a second time.

Consequences

It's mildly wet outside when Tiala leaves Deepwolf's apartment complex. Storm clouds pull away from the shining moon and she glances at it while going down the fire escape ladder's black steps. She noticed the exit when she followed Deepwolf down the hallway to his room a few hours ago, and has a good idea where she'll end up once she gets back on the street. She knows she's in East Sufias, judging by the small shanty town behind the gray wolf's place, so getting to the subway should be easy. She usually takes it home and she's very comfortable with walking.

The locals must be using the open square behind their homes as a makeshift junkyard because discarded boxes and hunks of aluminum and wood are everywhere. There aren't any trash bags, probably because the city wouldn't stand for it, but the place is clearly a forgotten area. It's a mess, and she traverses the long wet corridor towards Autumn Street on the other side of the complex. She recognizes a few familiar signs, so she promptly takes a right after making it to the other side. She walks across the empty street, looking for a tunnel into the subway, and stops when she notices something in her peripheral vision.

Tiala turns to the left while standing next to an empty yellow sports car and gets down when she sees several men hurrying down the sidewalk. It looks like they've just exited several black vehicles and she recognizes their special ops gear... NoirQueue.

Her soft fur stands on end when she realizes what's happening. The large group of trained killers pauses while two of them go down the alleyway leading to the back of Deepwolf's apartment complex. They're here to kill him... Deepwolf said the Sons of Velora had men they deployed to exact revenge on traitors, but neither one of them gave the idea a second thought after surviving Amsend. They had no idea a hit squad was already on its way. It looks like they could take out several targets in a single evening, because there's enough of them to blow half of the city's police force away. She counts forty three men, and crouches when some of them look in her direction. The mob of special agents hurries into the alleyway after surveying the area, but she doesn't stand until every one of them is out of sight.

The strong tigress tries to retrieve her phone from her combat gear but nervously fumbles around until she can get a hold of herself. When she finds it, she hastily yanks it out and dials Deepwolf.

"Pick up! Oh my God!" She whispers and listens to the phone ring... Once... Twice... Three times... Four times... Five times... She lets it ring twenty two times, but no one answers. He must be in the shower. He was playing music when she left, so it's quite possible that he won't hear the phone no matter how many times she calls. "SHIT!" She gasps and hastily returns it to her pocket.

She can't believe this is happening, but it is, and her friend is going to die unless she does something fast. She wouldn't even be here if she hadn't decided to thank him for saving her life. Yes, Deepwolf saved her from Amsend, but she's already given him an outrageously generous reward, so the selfish part of her brain tells her to stay put. *"Fuck him."* It says, and she listens. *"You never should have fucked him to begin with. What's wrong with you? He's just another filthy wolf, a wolf that deserves to die for serving the Sons of Velora. He lied to all of you for years, manipulating you for his own gain, and now you want to risk your life to save his? He didn't do you any favors by protecting you from Amsend. He was just a fool who realized he was on the wrong team at the very last moment..."* The tigress tries to agree with her selfish side, but she just can't because she knows better... Deepwolf got himself into this mess but he doesn't deserve to die.

"GODDESS DAMN IT!" She yells in frustration and clenches her fists. Time is running out... The longer she hesitates, the more certain his death becomes, so she curses and starts running back down the street to the alley. Her heart pounds like crazy. Her body surges with adrenaline. She's going to fight them but doesn't expect a happy ending.

Tiala's always underestimated her own self-worth, ever since she was a little kitten, but there's much more to her than she knows... She thinks she'll never be good enough in a world full of wolf overlords, but her combat skills are simply unparalleled. She's almost as strong as Polar, she's faster than Druward, and she's a better shot than Deepwolf. She would have killed every one of the Vuldrofein foxes if they hadn't been armed with overpowered weapons, and she was the only one strong and fast enough to haul Vulpie out of the GBI headquarters before Evil Vulpie could kill him. She's consistently outperformed every member of Blacktail, in every area, but no one has recognized it except for her superior. Rulef rarely gives her praise because he figures it's best to leave Tiala to her own methods, but he has noticed how exceptional she is in an emergency. It's why he didn't try to stop her from carrying two primary weapons, even though Deepwolf didn't really have the authority to let her take them.

But there will be no doubt after tonight... Tiala is going to discover the true depths of her own abilities, and she'll do it for a friend. The strange but pleasant feelings she has for Deepwolf have unlocked her true potential. Her inner beast will be her guide... This is truly a fight to the death, and nothing matters but death upon more death, until all things that move have perished... NoirQueue amplifies her hatred of wolf oppression, because the corrupt lupine control system they represent is the worst kind of evil, evil that has wrought unmentionable horrors upon her ancestors... And for the first time in her life... She will actually enjoy killing her enemies... She likes winning a fight as much as any man, but this is completely different. Tonight... She will fight for her species without remorse. It's them or her, and she refuses to let these soulless murderers add her name to their list of victims.

She comes face to face with two of them shortly after entering the alley, but doesn't hesitate. The M800 assault rifle rattles on her back, swinging on the three point sling harness, and she pulls the MTAC-71 from her side. She blows the one on the left away, and rams into the other one with a yell. She knocks him onto his back and hops to the left, looking for cover while the other NoirQueue agents quickly turn around. She hip fires a bit more, slaughtering the second black furred wolf with another burst of bullets, and ducks behind cover before any of them have a chance to aim at her. The small junkyard behind the apartments provides excellent cover.

"KILL HER!" Someone yells, and she takes a deep breath. She knows this is her last chance to focus before bullets are constantly flying in her direction. She closes her eyes, listening to the wet boots around her. The men are spreading out, surrounding her position in typical strategic form, but she's ready... No more waiting... She opens her eyes and looks for the first wolf to kill.

She finds a man creeping around on her left side and blows him away with the rifle she just retrieved from her back. She pulled it out and fired so quickly that he was dead before he even got his weapon up. She notices other dark figures moving around the area, and quickly drops on the ground. As expected, they open fire after seeing her kill the third member of their team. The gunfire is deafening, but she rolls over on the wet asphalt, looking for legs to shoot. She spies several, and manages to wound six agents before they discover where she's firing from. The flashing of her rifle on the wet asphalt clues them in to her location. Tiala gets up and rolls to the left, moving to another sturdy piece of cover, but two men are in her way.

"OH SHIT!" One of them says but she's already shot him before he manages to aim at her. He fires into the brick wall nearby, but the second one gets a shot off with his pistol. He puts a round in her right shoulder and she yells in pain. The deadly tigress uses her wild combat instincts to fire her weapon in his direction while falling backwards. His head splits open. She slams onto the ground and grits her sharp teeth, but gets right back up. She's pumped full of adrenaline... Actually feeling pretty decent after being shot, but her brain's tricking her to keep her alive. The pain activates a plethora of survival mechanisms, and her instinct guides her.

She starts taking dangerous risks and the spontaneous tactics pay off. The men expect to find her cowering somewhere, because they heard her get shot, but she runs behind three of them and opens fire with her MTAC. She makes a blood fountain out of the NoirQueue agents and leaps into some nearby debris. She crawls under aluminum to hide from the inevitable counter attacking, finding broken wooden gates, chairs and dressers to be very useful. Another black furred wolf comes running by and she grabs his foot, making him fall flat on the ground. She crawls on top of him before he can get up and stabs him to death with her combat knife. The tigress slides it back inside the sheath in her combat gear before surveying the area with her intense orange eyes.

She uses her MTAC to blow another man's leg off while rolling to the right, and quickly jumps behind a stack of broken chairs. She gets hit again, somewhere, but ignores the pain. It wasn't vital so she powers on. She's confident she can kill all of them before bleeding to death, that is unless, of course, someone manages to waste her with a precise shot or hits her with a fully automatic burst.

Her white whiskers twitch when something comes near her head and she ducks instinctively; one of the black wolves just tried to knock her out with the butt of his gun. Apparently he's out of ammo, and she swings around to deal with him before he stabs her with the combat knife she knows he must be carrying. Sure enough, he yanks a big one out of his gear and lunges at her. He's too close for her to aim her rifle or MTAC at him, so she drops her weapon and catches his right arm with her paws. She extends her sharp claws into his wrist and he cries out in pain before jabbing his left fist in her face. It's a very hard punch, but her big tiger skull takes it in stride.

"GET THE BITCH!" Another one growls and grabs her from behind. Both attackers are very strong, but she focuses on defending herself instead of worrying about the terrifying situation. The odds are overwhelmingly stacked against her. Any normal Blacktail merc would be dead by now, but Tiala has an indomitable spirit and a truly graceful combat style that simply cannot be matched by normal animals. Her ancestors were some of the meanest cats on Sufias, and she didn't need to come from a snooty bloodline to acquire her talent.

She kills both of them after being shot more than three times, managing to steal the knife and jab it backwards into the killer behind her before ripping it out and putting it into the man in front of her. She rolls forward while both of them stumble around with bewildered looks, clutching their bodies in pain. They'll die on their own so she acquires their weaponry instead of finishing them off. Tiala's surprised by her own strength; she feels the bullets in her, making her bleed in a hot mess, but somehow she still has plenty of energy. She would ponder it some more but her tiger brain downshifts and puts higher order thinking on hold once again.

She has a black heavy caliber sidearm that's great for unexpected situations, so shooting the head that appears behind a dismantled fence is quite easy. She pulls it out and fires it with one paw. Headshot. He drops like a ragdoll and she puts her left paw underneath the base of the pistol so she can aim down the sights at a slightly distant target to the left. She hits another one in the neck while he's moving from cover. His legs fly up and his back slams onto the wet asphalt. His boots land with a wet thud.

Her left ear twitches. Someone is behind her to the left. She spins and fires. He's closer than she thought, so after missing the first time, she aims low and hits his crotch, but the man doesn't have time to worry about his missing cock. She aims higher and puts one in his heart, killing him instantly. She eyes the shotgun he has in his paws and quickly slaps her sidearm back into the holster on the right side of her belt harness.

She nearly jumps out of her fur when someone shoots her right hip. Small caliber... Not deep... Probably the last shot from a small personal defense weapon... The tigress yelps and runs to the shotgun. She reaches down to pick it up with her left paw but can't keep from grabbing her hip in agony. She massages it for a few seconds while crouching and makes herself forget about it. She grits her teeth. She angrily gets the shotgun in her paws. The dead man has lots of ammo so she stocks up.

"She's just one girl! Kill that cunt!" Someone yells.

"Where the fuck is she?" Another man shouts.

"Over there! Shotgun!"

"Fuck!" Tiala growls. She peers to the left but a spray of bullets makes her recoil and duck for cover. The attacker has a submachine gun that can fire at least 900 rounds per minute. The good part is that he's using an attached laser sight for hip fire accuracy. She aims around the left side of the broken furniture. His red laser sight gives him away, and she fires the shotgun. She nails him, so she knows it must be loaded with pointed steel projectiles with miniature vaned tails for stable flight. This kind of ammo is similar to little arrows or dart rounds, enabling the user to hit targets at much longer range than buckshot. Theoretically, it does less damage, but a shotgun is a shotgun.

"Fucking BITCH! MAN DOWN!"

"MOVE UP!"

"Tiala!" Someone says, and she holds still for a moment. She doesn't recognize the voice. It's one of them.

"She's a long way from Vulpie Industries! Take her out!" The sleek tigress is surprised one of them recognized her, but she reminds herself who these men are. They know all about Vulpie and his past, and his security if they work for the Sons of Velora.

Instinct tells her what to do. She runs to the right, to another mangled mess of junked furniture, but this time her killer instinct is wrong. Six of them are nearby, just on the other side of the mess, and she has to blind fire the shotgun to avoid getting her face blown off. Luckily, she's better aiming from the hip than they are down the sights, and two of them fall over. She hit one of them in the face and the other in the throat.

Even though her gut feeling was wrong just a second ago, it makes her use the same tactic again, and she rolls right. The other four men are there with their weapons drawn. They fire but they miss, because they don't have enough time to aim. Tiala, on the other hand, shoots and cocks four times, hitting each one of her targets bang on.

"KILL HER!"

"I got her!" One of the coal furred wolves declares while running up behind the tigress. He aims his personal defense weapon in her direction and fires, but not before she hits him right above his body armor, in the neck. His head flies off in a gruesome but satisfying display of gore.

"GOD DAMN IT! ... FALL BACK!" Tiala can't believe what she just heard. She runs to a new spot, hiding behind a mangled stack of broken fences, and drops on the ground.

"What?"

"FALL BACK!"

"We've got her on the run!"

"JUST DO IT!" Wet boots splatter across the asphalt, and it sounds like one hundred men are coming for her. She wonders if it's just a ploy to catch her off guard, but her concerns slowly disappear when nothing happens for over a minute. She gets up and peeks around the left corner of the mess... Nothing. She quickly checks the right side... Nothing there either... And then she does hear something... Police sirens... She grimaces in pain and drops the shotgun before reaching into her pocket. She finds her phone and calls Deepwolf with shaky paws. It rings and rings but no one answers... She lets it ring over fifty times while the sirens draw near, and he finally picks up.

"Hello?"

"Deepwolf it's me!"

"Tiala? What's up? Are you okay?"

"No! I'm out back! Didn't you hear the gunfire?"

"Gunfire? What the hell are you... God I thought it was my neighbor's TV! Where are you?"

"Behind... Your place... They were coming for you... You've got to get out of there..."

"Are you saying you're behind my apartment?"

"Yes..."

"I'm coming down there."

"No, they might still be here..."

Secret Passion

Tiala sighs in relief when the doctors inject her with strong pain killers. She's at Hiar Regional Hospital, a place not far from her home, with Deepwolf and the police. She listens to Rulef talking to one of them for a few minutes before he comes over and says hello.

"Tiala? Are you alright?"

"Yes sir." She answers with a serious voice and the Blacktail commander glances at Deepwolf. He looks incredibly pissed off for a moment, but humor gets the best of him, and he grins at the tigress.

"God damn girl! You killed all of em!"

"Not all."

"Twenty three!" He laughs before turning gravely serious. He looks at Deepwolf and runs his tongue across his teeth with his jaw closed. "The best member of my team almost died defending your sorry ass." Deepwolf lowers his muzzle and averts his eyes. He knows when to keep his mouth shut, but glances at Tiala. She blinks, wondering just how much he's told them. "Vulpie's usually right, so I can't say this is really a surprise, but I should have known."

"I'm so sorry." Deepwolf replies.

"Sorry? You're sorry? Sorry's not going to cut it. You've been working with the same people that wanted to kill the man you're paid to protect, and now you've put her life in danger. You know they'll be back for revenge."

"It was because I turned on Amsend... I had orders to..."

"Kill Vulpie and Druward from what the police have told me."

"But he saved me." Tiala interrupts, and Rulef pauses for a moment.

"So what?"

"That thing was going to eat me. It was horrible."

"I know Tiala, but he's going away. We can't trust him. Just because he asked you over to his place to confess doesn't mean he's changed. If anything it means he was trying to manipulate you so he could get closer to Vulpie." Deepwolf looks at Tiala and smiles for just a split second, long enough for her to see it, and Rulef doesn't notice. A wave of relief rushes over her... Suddenly the pain killers feel twice as good... He didn't tell them...

"Please don't blame him. I took pity on him because he didn't know who else to go to. He was afraid to tell Vulpie because he didn't want to lose his job."

"Tiala, are you serious? I never should have hired this piece of shit in the first place."

"But you did, and he didn't stab us in the back. He did the right thing when it mattered most and told me because he thought I was the only one he could trust."

"Why did you save her?" Rulef suddenly asks Deepwolf with a very spiteful voice. "Knew your time was up? You figured Amsend was going to kill you too so you switched sides at the very last second?"

"I wanted to a long time ago, but no one quits the Sons of Velora... Vulpie.net took out their leadership and they still tried to kill me. There was nothing I could do." Rulef sighs loudly and looks at Tiala.

"Do you honestly think we can trust him? Vulpie will never let him stay on the team."

"You can trust him." She answers and swallows. "He's an idiot... But he has a good heart."

"She's never this nice. I don't know why she wants to give you a second chance, but Vulpie will make the final decision... And even if you come back, I'll never leave you alone with him. It's ridiculous that we're even discussing this." Rulef turns his attention back to Tiala. "You're getting a promotion. They say you'll heal in no time, and when you're better, I'm making you a commander."

"Sir?" She asks in shock.

"You'll join me as squad commander... If you want it... Double pay..."

"Thank you sir." The tigress smiles and he nods before leaving. The police are still keeping their eyes on Deepwolf from the doorway so he walks around the room very slowly. He turns his back to them and puts his paws in his pockets. He meanders towards the bed and sighs.

"God I'm so sorry Tiala... I can't even put it into words... They would have killed me."

"They'll come again." The tigress responds and glances to the right, just to make sure the cops are out of ear shot. "So did you tell anyone?"

"No."

"No one knows about us?"

"No way." The gray wolf hastily answers. "I made sure to come up with a good cover story to protect you... Since this is all my fault."

"You told them you came to me to confess, huh?"

"Yeah." Deepwolf whispers.

"So how did I respond?"

"You said you were going to think about it, but you wanted me to stay put until someone called me."

"At your apartment?"

"Yes."

"And then I left and I saw NoirQueue coming for you?"

"That's right."

"I really went out on a limb for you, didn't I?"

"Yeah... And I've been wondering..." He says and clears his throat. "Why did you? I deserved to die... I can't believe you took those guys on by yourself."

"Me neither." She snorts and they both smile. "You moron."

"I know you are but what am I?" He grins.

"Don't you give me any lip. I'm going to be your superior from now on."

"Thought you enjoyed my lips."

"Funny."

"So if you're going to be the same rank as Rulef then I guess that means you'll be assigning me my posts too... You could send me anywhere..."

"Mmm hmm..."

"Like your place."

"You just don't quit do you?"

"Nope."

"Keep your mouth shut unless I tell you to use it."

"I thought you said it was a one-time deal?"

"It was."

"Then what did you mean by that?"

"Just shut up."

"Yes Ma'am. I guess we're even now?"

"No, you owe me big time."

"I'll pay anytime you want. I'm at your beckon call... And I have to say it... You would DEFINITELY waste me in a fight, no contest... That was so incredibly BADASS..."

"Mmm..." She smirks. "It was badass, wasn't it? You didn't know who you were messing with..."

"No I did not, but if you ever need a sparring partner, I'll be happy to let you beat me up."

"Don't make promises you can't keep... I'll have to put you in your place since I'm squad commander now. I can't go easy on you... That's why Rulef doesn't train with the rest of us."

"I can take it." The gray wolf grins.

"Ok."

"Haven't seen you use your claws yet so that'd be fun."

"Deepwolf." The tigress smiles.

"Yeah?"

"Go away."

"Yes Ma'am."

Nick Fenn is still a very handsome man. Vulpie would recognize his caring smile anywhere, but it was never a confident one. Polar's a much better companion in virtually every way, but the old flame still burns a little in the gay fox's heart. Seeing him on the office TV is enough to make him drop what he was working on and turn up the volume.

"When did you meet him?"

"Just a few years ago, about a year and a half before he hacked everything."

"And you say you still have feelings for him? Even now when you're accusing him of being the antikhalan?" Brad Hutchinson inquires.

"Yes."

"Do you love him?"

"It's not love... It's because he's Aila's son."

"That's quite a thing to call an ex-lover, an ex-gay lover, isn't it? I mean, now that you've found the Deivas and all. What do you think people will say?"

"They'll say what they will but I had to tell the world what I know about him."

"Because you were so close?"

"We were very close at one time..."

"But you said you're not a homosexual now? You've been reformed, if you will, and you've fathered four children with the woman you fell in love with?"

"That's right."

"Does she know about Vulpie and you?"

"Yes she does... She was part of it..."

"Excuse me, but what do you mean she was part of it?"

"I was dating her when we met Vulpie and eventually he wormed his way into our relationship... But we don't keep secrets in our family. We try not to anyway... It's always been a difficult subject whenever one of us brings it up, but we love each other, and we both know he used us."

"She understood that it's over now... You're not a gay man anymore?"

"I never was a gay man."

"Then how did you end up with Vulpie?"

"WE were with him... He seduced us..." Nick trails off.

"He seduced both of you? A straight couple?"

"Yes."

"Forgive me for saying this, but if he seduced you, then you must have been attracted to men, and your wife must have been interested in being with a fox."

"But that's the point I made in the interview last week; I've never been attracted to men before I met him, or after we went our separate ways, and she's never dated a fox... It's unnatural..."

"It was a fling then."

"No... It wasn't..."

"How do you define the difference?"

"I didn't want to be with him, and neither did my wife, but he had this... When you're around him, it's impossible to tell him no. He has this mesmerizing charm that I can't describe, and we didn't stand a chance when he set his eyes on us."

"Forgive me once again for being honest Mr. Fenn, but I don't think people will honestly believe that you had nothing to do with your own love affair, or that your wife consented to having sex with a gay man without being strongly bisexual."

"I never said he wasn't attractive to us."

"You said you've never been attracted to men."

"Not sexually, but he charmed us. He's a big charmer… He comes up with these wonderfully creative ideas that make you question everything… And I know there's probably nothing I can do to stop him, Brad, but I also know that I should try… Somebody has to tell the world what he is before it's too late. Everything that's happened because of him is no coincidence. He's been fulfilling his destiny, moving from one conquest to the next."

"What do you mean by conquest?"

"Well." Nick says and sighs anxiously. "When we were together, we couldn't take our eyes off of him, and he was happy to share his dreams with us… Vulpie's always wanted to take over the world and bend people to his will… He used to tell us all the ways he was going to make everyone pay for what they did to him, and how he wanted to usher in a new world where people like us wouldn't be oppressed… Free thinking people like us and him… But we were only hostages… Once the shame became too much to bear, and we started getting vocal about our religious beliefs, his personality changed drastically."

"Changed how?"

"Like a light switch… He knew I was going to seminary school to become a priest, and that Ella and I were true believers, and that's why he wanted to corrupt us so badly. He was attracted to us, BECAUSE, we were servants of Khalan, and turning us from her ways made him happy."

"So how did a priest end up going home with a young gay man? Where did you meet?"

"Like I said, I was in seminary school at the time. We were lucky enough to find an apartment in downtown Sufias and his was right across the street. Our place was small and he was staying in this huge… Condo or warehouse looking place… It was very nice, very expensive, and I usually saw him every morning. The first thing he liked to do was go get coffee, and for a while, I just thought he was some successful young fox, trading stocks for a large company or working in a bank, but he always wore tight flamboyant, nonprofessional clothing, so I knew something was different about him after a while."

"And did you go over and say hello?"

"No, he approached my wife. We were only engaged at the time but somehow he knew we were going to get married."

"Goes for what he wants, doesn't he?"

"Yes he does..." Nick responds with a worried expression, as if reliving his past.

"And he wanted both you and your wife?"

"That's right."

"Why you?"

"I already told you."

"He just picked you out at random to attack your faith?" Brad smirks. "You two weren't swingers? Not even a little?"

"Brad... One morning he was just right on our doorstep... And he had my girl talking about orgasms before I even met him, and when I finally did introduce myself, of course, wondering who this little fox was who was hitting on my wife, he just said that we'd already met. We'd never met before. I didn't have the slightest clue what he was talking about, and he just said it to throw us off. I told him I'd seen him across the street, but I knew he just wanted to talk to us. Now, I'm a friendly guy, always have been, so I shook his hand and smiled while we talked about the city, but I was pretty mad when Ella told me about the wonderful advice he gave her... I won't go into the details of it, but even though we both wanted him gone, we just couldn't run him off."

"So Vulpie likes women too?" Brad innocently inquires.

"He loves to sin..." Nick swallows with a pained voice. "I'd never felt like that before, and never have since. The thought of having sex with another man absolutely disgusts me, but somehow it didn't seem that bad when he was the one... He convinced both of us to do things we would NEVER do under

ANY circumstances... And the Vulpie that attacked us is the same little
monster you see on TV every day, smiling like he just loves you personally, like
you're the most important person in the world to him... He's just adorable,
isn't he? Like a sweet little girl or something precious you'd want to protect,
but he was, and still is, completely evil. I saw it in his eyes from the very
beginning. The demonic things he said to my wife were so twisted that I
should have kicked him down the street, but I couldn't do it... He seemed like
a friend... A very powerful friend who refused to go away and was bent on
perverting our relationship."

"Now, but you were in training to become a priest." Brad interrupts.
"So how in the world would he convince you or your wife to partake in... Uh,
swinging? If that's not too crass?"

"Obviously neither one of us approved of homosexuality, but Ella
thought he was cute, and I tried to help him. I tried giving him spiritual advice,
which is absolutely comical in retrospect... But he didn't care. He always came
up with something more clever to say than the last, and was back day after
day... I was worried that he wanted me to be his boyfriend, and in a way, that
allowed him to trick us even more, because we didn't know that he had his
eyes on both of us... He was just too nice, too sweet, and we let him inside the
apartment even though we didn't really want him there, and we definitely
didn't approve of his lifestyle."

"A strong able bodied wolf like yourself couldn't say no to a five foot
six inch fox?" Brad inquires. "Again, people will say you and Ella decided to let
him in, and a she-wolf can be very intimidating to a male fox."

"Aila let him in." Nick firmly responds. "We didn't like him, but we
felt like we'd be doing something wrong by turning him away... So he came in
and continued changing our minds about everything, and before long..." The
handsome wolf growls and has to pause for a moment to keep his anger in
check. "I was letting him sleep with my wife. Asking him whether he had a
girlfriend of his own was a huge mistake, because then he turned his attention

to me, which was really what he wanted to do from the beginning... So then I was having sex with him, and guess what! His next big idea was for all of us to sin together... When I had to get up every morning and study the Velora... It was... It was hell... Neither one of us can really remember exactly what kind of lies he came up with to twist our minds that badly... because he was just SO GOOD at it... But by the end we were completely devastated... Spiritually..."

"But your wife first and then you? Studies have suggested that women enjoy watching gay porn because there are two members of the opposite sex, but you just let it happen?"

"It's crazy, I know." Nick answers with a disgusted voice.

"Well in all honesty, all of this is starting to sound awfully hard to believe Mr. Fenn. Most animals would probably agree that interspecies sex is unnatural, but there have been thousands of documented occurrences of it, and by reasoning, since it does take place in nature, that makes it natural in some ways."

"I think that argument is beyond disgusting." Nick brutally replies. "We all know right from wrong and animals having sex with different species is just sinful. It's something people do when they've fallen so far from common sense that there's no coming back, and you don't have to be a Deivaist to realize that, but I do also believe the Deivas made it repulsive to us for a reason."

"But if it was so awful, how could you just sit by and watch your wife have sex with a gay fox and not put an end to it? It seems inconceivable that it could even get that far if what you say is true, and why would she let a gay man take advantage of her? Is it possible she enjoyed it?"

"I'm not going to dignify that with a response." Nick warns. "I love my wife, and this has been very hard on both of us. One day our children will see this interview and we'll have to explain why we had to do this, but someone has to warn people before it's too late. All of you still believe Vulpie Vivixen is just some naughty fox out there having a good time, but you have to open your eyes. This Vulpie.net abomination he's created will be the end of us, and don't think for one SECOND... That he's not running the show... I don't care how smart he is, no animal can play fifteen chess games at the same time without looking at the boards because he just makes a ton of calculations in his head. What he does is supernatural, and you people are guilty of covering for him, making too many excuses when normal animals like us are screaming at the top of our lungs for someone to put an end to this madness."

"So now you're on national television warning people that he's the antikhalan because he seduced you and your wife?"

"I don't care if you mock me. I knew it would happen, but at least we're trying to make a difference... Vulpie.net was just the beginning... He'll continue to spread his evil throughout the universe, and all you have to do is look at the abominations he's created... Vulpie.net and it's goddess mockeries..."

"But most animals don't believe in literal interpretations of antikhalans and other magical creatures."

"They should... Because my wife and I know, for certain, that he IS Goddess Aila's son... People need to be warned before it's too late. Vulpie.net is just one of his toys, and its "announcement" is nothing less than a declaration of war... On all of us."

"But Vulpie.net nearly killed him. We've all seen how gruesome that was."

"Staged, or maybe it was real and he made a huge mistake, only he knows, but it's not like it makes a difference."

"God..." Vulpie groans with his paw against his forehead. He and Polar just finished watching the special news story in Vulpie Industries and the snow wolf gives him a hug. "Am I the only one that thinks Amsend was the antikhalan if there ever was one? For fuck sake. I can just see him with that smile... The dude actually turned into a monster, and I've got ex-swingers calling ME Aila's son!"

"Yeah, but there's no way they'll ever put that on the news." Polar chuckles. "What Druward said about that island and Amsend sounds insane... But I think your old friend Nick is obviously a closet case."

"I know but still... It's like people are more terrified of two guys sharing a nice kiss than a secret society creating perpetual war. So stupid. And what a douchebag... I loved Nick for like a week... And his ass would have to get on TV RIGHT AFTER Vulpie.net announced its *NaTiON*... I feel like, why do I even try? I should just say fuck it, me and Evil Vulpie rule the universe! Hahahahah! ...Cue the lightning..."

"Price of being famous, baby."

"Heavy price. Everyone thinks I'm the bad guy."

"No they don't. They're just scared. Aren't you?"

"Course I'm scared."

"Me too." Polar says and takes a deep breath. "Do you think there's any way Vulpie.net might be telling the truth?"

"Who the fuck knows? It's me at my worst."

"Aww..." Polar teases and the orange fox smirks.

"Oh, I forgot, you like me that way don't ya?"

"Maybe." The snow furred wolf says and kisses his husband on the cheek. "What are you going to do with Deepwolf?"

"Man, I don't know... I can't believe Tiala got shot because of him."

"She swears he's on our side now and she's like family."

"Yeah but... A guy like that... It might just be the surface of who he really is. What if he has split personality disorder or something?"

"Well, I know you'll make the right decision."

"Up to you too." Vulpie says with a loving voice. "Do you trust him?"

"Yeah." Polar answers without hesitation. "Deepwolf's like a kid in an adult's body. If Amsend plucked him out of Felini and they ran his life all the way up to when he joined Vulpie Industries, then who can blame the guy? He's just lucky he got out alive. If Tiala wasn't the baddest cat out there he'd be getting tortured to death right now."

"Yeah... I feel the same way, but I'm a little scared after finding out he could have killed me any day of the week."

"He wouldn't have done it."

"You're so sure of that?"

"Yeah. He liked you and he likes being part of the team. Besides, he might come in handy someday."

"The same thought did cross my mind... Maybe he can help us look out for what's left of Amsend's gang, but they did get all the way to his apartment and he didn't see them coming... And speaking of which..." Vulpie says and smirks at his husband. "Did you notice something between him and Tiala at the hospital?"

"What do you mean? Like what?"

"Just a feeling... He seemed more upset about her getting shot than forty NoirQueue dudes trying to kill him."

"No... Do you mean? Are you suggesting they're doing something on the side?"

"Why not?"

"Because they're different species!" Polar laughs.

"SO ARE WE!" Vulpie giggles.

"Yeah, but wolves and foxes can have children naturally, even if they're hybrids... But a wolf and a tiger? You're imagining things. I don't think Tiala's that kinky."

"I don't know! It's always the quiet ones! We don't get to choose who we love!"

"Well you're never quiet and you're kinky as hell." Polar teases.

"Mmm... Tell me more about this." Vulpie smiles.

"Why don't you tell me about the threesome?" The white furred wolf asks and cocks his head to the left.

"Oh my God..." Vulpie laughs in embarrassment. He tries to stop smiling but the way his husband's looking at him cracks him up.

"Did you really bang that guy's wife?"

"I told you I was adventurous when we first met." The orange fox grins.

"I bet that guy loved to watch, didn't he? He was a watcher..." Polar smiles.

"Better believe it!" Vulpie gleefully responds and bites his tongue between his teeth.

"You never told me you did something like that... Were you ever planning to?"

"Oh yeah, like there was really ever a good time to bring it up! Oh hey Mr. P! Did ya know that one time when I was really really horny..."

"Well just what kind of other stuff did you do? Ever sleep with a cat?"

"I..." Vulpie trails off. "That is just a terribly rude question!"

"Oh man......... You're not doing that stuff anymore are you?"

"No! No way! You know I only have eyes for you, Mr. P!"

"You better." Polar chuckles. "Apparently if I didn't make you my bitch every day you'd just go out and gangbang yourself into oblivion."

"Well that isn't true. It's been a whole 48 hours since a bitch was last made of me." Vulpie taunts with a swishing tail.

Trust

Tiala nervously joins Deepwolf in Vulpie's office and he looks just as worried as she is. Neither one of them know why the orange fox has called them up here, but they're both thinking the same thing.

"Hey." The gray wolf says with his paws in his pockets.

"Hi." Tiala responds with an emotionless voice, and they look to the door when Vulpie enters the room. He's alone, and he pauses for a moment to look Deepwolf over.

"Hey guys. Wanna take a seat?"

"Sure." Tiala replies but Vulpie interrupts when they turn towards his desk.

"Over here... Let's just relax for a little while."

"Ok." Deepwolf quietly responds, but waits for Vulpie to take a seat. He chooses the long black leather sofa on the left while Tiala sits on the one in front of his desk, with Vulpie to her left. Deepwolf chooses a spot on the same couch but makes sure to leave Tiala plenty of space.

"You guys doing alright?"

"Uh... Yes. Yes I'm fine." Tiala respectfully answers and Deepwolf nods.

"What about you?" Vulpie asks the gray wolf.

"Yes sir." The room goes silent for a moment and Vulpie licks his lips.

"We need to discuss some things, Deepwolf... I don't think you can work with the rest of Blacktail anymore."

"I understand." The merc says in shame.

"No you don't. Just wait a moment." Vulpie replies and moves uncomfortably.

"Is something wrong?" Tiala asks her boss in concern.

"Yeah... Yes, something is definitely wrong, and I need your help."

"Whatever it is, I'm ready."

"I'll leave Vulpie... I think I've done enough damage already... But... What's going to happen to me?"

"That's what I wanted to talk to you about... Both of you."

"Both of us?" Tiala asks. She suddenly sounds very nervous. "What? What for?"

"Vulpie.net..." The orange fox trails off. "Wants me to SHARE Polar with it... And Polar agreed."

"Why?"

"To save me... It was the only way to get me out of Englavic and everything that's happened is my fault."

"That's not true."

"Yes it is." Vulpie painfully admits. "I created Vulpie.net and I'm totally responsible for everything it's doing... Everything it's going to do... It wants time with Polar, but I can't just let it take him and hope for the best. He needs someone to watch his back."

"To protect him like we protect you?" Tiala inquires.

"Yes, but even more so, because I have no idea what Vulpie.net has planned. Polar agreed to spend time with it to save my life, but he never agreed to go by himself... So I was thinking... That maybe..."

"I'll do it. You can count on me." The tigress smiles.

"But I feel so bad about asking you for anything, Tiala." Vulpie says with a small voice. "You've... You're like family to me. You are part of my family."

"Families look out for each other. That's what it's all about."

"Will you really do this for me? I can't... God I can't believe what I've done to the world!" Vulpie says with tears welling up in his eyes. "I'm so scared! I'm terrified that Vulpie.net's going to hurt him! And Polar will suffer in silence because he won't want to ruin our relationship, but I love him too much to let that stand."

"It's okay."

"But you've almost died for me so many times already."

"Will all due respect, Vulpie, this is what I'm good at." She proudly responds. "I was worried you were going to fire me, but instead you're giving me an even better assignment. Polar does need someone to watch his back, and I'm the best you've got."

"I know you are. You're incredible, Tiala..." Vulpie smiles, but his face turns sour when he looks at Deepwolf. "But what about him?" The gray wolf lowers his head and Tiala glances at him before answering.

"You can trust him." Deepwolf raises his muzzle in shock.

"How sure are you?"

"Very."

"Why?"

"Because he told me everything he did, and why he did it, and you should know that he's an orphan like you. They had their claws in him from way back, and even though he was playing us, he did the right thing when it mattered most. He's not who everyone thinks he is, but I mean that in a good way." Vulpie gives Tiala his full attention but does glance at Deepwolf several times while she's elaborating. "I know you probably can't keep him on the team anymore because Rulef won't have it, but losing him would be such a waste."

"What do you think?" Vulpie asks the gray wolf. "She's giving you an awful lot of credit."

"I don't think I deserve any of it." Deepwolf quietly answers.

"Look at me." Vulpie says and the gray wolf sets his yellow eyes on the gay fox. "Can I trust my husband's life to you?"

"Not just to me... Because I'm not good enough... But if Tiala's in charge, I'll follow her commands. She's better than I'll ever be and I owe her for saving my life. Yeah, I told her how to kill Amsend, but we all know what I did wasn't heroic. I just wanted to live, and it was my fault that she was even there to begin with. She went above and beyond for me and I totally didn't deserve it... I guess she felt sorry for me."

"And you respect her enough to do what she says? Just like Rulef?"

"Yes sir."

"Because he doesn't want to work with you anymore and I can't change his mind. So as far as I'm concerned, she's your new boss. If Tiala thinks you deserve a raise then you'll get one. I won't treat you badly because of what's happened. We're putting that behind us... But if she ever tells me she's having second thoughts about you... Then that's it... Do you understand?"

"Yes sir. Thank you sir."

"Well alright... Please don't make me regret this decision, Deepwolf. If you really are an orphan like me, then I understand what you've been through."

"He grew up in Felini." Tiala interrupts. "Cats killed his parents and he had to join up with terrorists to survive."

"Is that true?" Vulpie asks the gray wolf and he nods.

"Then Amsend showed up and offered him a way out."

"So let me ask you a question then."

"Yeah?" Deepwolf responds.

"Why didn't you kill me on the Endeavor, or on the Sevrif?"

"You mean at Zeravyn?"

"Yeah."

"Well... I never got the order to. They still needed you but never told me why. I wasn't important enough to know."

"But you were communicating with them the whole time?"

"Yes."

"So that means Vulpie.net was listening the whole time."

"I guess so. Yeah."

"Now it all makes sense." The orange fox says and nods his head with a smile.

"What?" Tiala asks.

"I saw three machines in Vulpie.net's underground factory on Zeravyn... The first one was Aila, the second one was the monster from hell, and the third one was a Polar imitation... Aila tried to save me from the metal freak but it destroyed her. Then the Polar clone helped me, but it destroyed him too, and I always wondered who was controlling the monster if it wasn't Vulpie.net. It must have been the creature Amsend was working with... And that means... Vulpie.net saved my life... It must have had a disagreement with Amsend's friend."

"Why?" Tiala inquires.

"No idea, but they must have been fighting for some reason. Maybe that's what caused Vulpie.net to turn on Amsend, or maybe it was going to all along... I don't know..." Vulpie trails off and looks at Tiala. "So whatever you need, just ask. We'll expand the armory or get a second one, and you can hire your own people."

"Thank you sir." Tiala happily responds. "I won't let you down."

Serenity

Vulpie's getting a little cold standing in the backyard of Victor and Kimberly's house, but he's zoning out too much to feel uncomfortable. He loves snow... Standing in it, playing in it... Making love in it... Getting it on makes the fur really wet but when Polar fucks him at the winter lodge it's almost always outback in the woods. It's one of the few places they can go without anyone bothering them. It's remote, so Blacktail can stay in Winters Dale while they have their fun... He's wearing a slick black jacket and black pants, and jumps when Polar's dad starts talking to him.

"Planning on staying out here all day?"

"Oh! Jeez! I didn't even hear you coming!" Vulpie laughs in embarrassment. The tall white furred wolf is wearing a cozy looking red sweater and dark pants. He's holding a cup of hot coco and offers it to the little fox. "Thanks."

"Come back inside..." The wolf says with a warm voice and Vulpie sighs.

"I will."

"Polar's looking for you. He said you're going up to the cabin for the night."

"Really?" Vulpie asks in excitement and looks aside when he realizes how transparent his reaction was. "Cool."

"It'll be nice for you two to spend some quiet time together. I know you have your company and his house but there's nothing like being up on the mountain."

"Yeah. I love it!" Snow is slowly raining down on them and it's already a foot deep.

"Vulpie..."

"Yeah?"

"You know, we're not ashamed of you like you think we are..." Victor says and the orange fox turns in his direction. It takes him a moment to gather enough courage to look up into the wolf's smiling face. "We don't talk about you behind your back and when we do talk about you and our son, it's usually about the good stuff."

"But how can you not be ashamed of me?" Vulpie whimpers. "Look at what I'm putting him through!"

"Polar loves you."

"I love him too, with all of my heart, but I know you're worried about him."

"Yes... We do worry about Polar, and you, but not for the reasons you think. What bothers us most is that you feel so ashamed and Polar doesn't know what to do about it. He's told you he's on your side, and you know he is... So why are you beating yourself up out here?"

"But you saw it... You saw Vulpie.net and the way it's... It's all my fault."

"Making it was your fault but I think you paid for it a long time ago. If it really is out of your control, then there's no reason for you to worry yourself to death. That's what it wants, isn't it? Vulpie.net wants you to hate yourself because it will never have what you have."

"But it's not over yet! It'll keep trying to..."

"It doesn't matter. You're so good for Polar... He's so happy with you, and I know he's good for you too."

"I'm sorry. I'll stop feeling sorry for myself. I know I am."

"No, we understand why you're suffering, but you have to help yourself. Be yourself, Vulpie... You're the reason my son gets up every morning. You know that, don't you? Whenever he talks about you a smile always creeps on his face."

"Really? I know but... But what..."

"Vulpie." Victor says with a sharp voice and the orange fox blinks. "You don't have my permission to worry about Vulpie.net..." The snow wolf declares, and after a moment, they both start grinning. "Alright?" Even though

Polar's father isn't gay, he seems to thoroughly understand the dynamic between his son and the orange fox. The tone of voice Victor uses reminds Vulpie of Polar when he wants to bend him over something, and it wasn't by accident. At first it's embarrassing, but soon Vulpie feels as though the world has been lifted off of his shoulders.

"Oh boy... I see where he gets it from."

"Come on." The snow wolf says and wraps his big right arm around the little fox. They head back to the house just as the snow starts to pick up. It's coming down pretty fast now, hiding the afternoon sun behind a blanket of pretty white clouds.

"The cabin... Mmm..." Vulpie grins in the SUV while Polar drives. They're heading up the snow covered road high into the hills with absolutely no one watching them, and Polar gives his lover a sly look.

"I thought we'd build a little fire and snuggle all night..."

"Oh yeah, gonna need to warm up after being covered in snow..."

"Not me." The white furred wolf smirks. They don't say anything else all the way up the road because they're both too excited about having a little wilderness time in Polar's homeland. Vulpie gets out and shuts his door with baited breath. He can't get the look Victor was giving him out of his head and hurries around the SUV to give Polar a kiss before his husband has a chance to open the back left door. It's aggressive, and Polar laughs in surprise.

"Let's unpack first, yeah?"

"No! Now!"

"Right now?"

"Mmm hmm!" Vulpie breathes and Polar bites his lip. He makes sure to hide the car keys underneath an old stump to the left of the SUV while the orange fox skips towards the cabin... But they're not going inside... Polar tosses his brown coat into the snow and chases after him.

"Where are you going, huh?"

"Gotta catch me!"

"Well that'll be easy." The wolf chuckles and sprints across the wintry landscape with a big grin. He chases Vulpie up the hill, then down another one, and to the right, before tackling him next to a large stump. Vulpie makes a submissive sound upon being apprehended and Polar gets up with a growl. He starts taking off his sweater shirt and Vulpie goes to his belt buckle while he's busy yanking it off. The snow wolf grabs his pants after getting rid of his upper clothing and slides them down without hesitation. He steps out of them and does the same with his underwear, revealing his big fat cock. It's fully erect in just a few seconds.

Vulpie furiously makes himself naked and they both remove their socks and shoes as well. With their feet wet in the snow, they grab each other and kiss again. Polar slides his paws over Vulpie's ass, stroking and yanking at his pretty orange tail while Vulpie plays with the wolf's penis.

"Turn around! Get up there!" Polar orders, and helps his lover face the icy log. They both laugh at the pure intensity of the moment when Vulpie's knees slip on the slick surface, but the adorable fox finds a good position with his knees spread and his paws clutching the edges. Vulpie realizes they didn't bring any lubricant like they normally do before fucking in the snow, but Polar spits on his cock and lathers it up four times before mounting him. "Hold still!"

"Uh!" Vulpie gasps when the head of the wolf's big cock presses against his anus, and cries out when Polar suddenly thrusts deep and hard. Polar grabs Vulpie's tail with his right paw and clutches the fox's left leg, going balls deep, and starts fucking him while standing. "OOOHHH MY GOD!"

"Like that, huh?"

"OOOOHH GOD YEAH! AW FUCK IT'S BIG!"

"You're not going anywhere Foxy!"

"OH FUCK! AHH! AAHH! EH! AHH!" Vulpie whines while getting pounded. Polar's spit isn't much of a lubricant but it does just enough to keep his lover's ass from bleeding. Vulpie's tail end burns like fire.

"Take it all! Take it!" Polar growls in ecstasy. He releases the small fox's adorable silky tail and clamps his paws down on his lover's hips.

"AAGHH! AHH! AHH!"

"How's that feel?"

"SO FUCKING GOOD OH MY! AAAGGOOODD! AAHH! OW! EEHH! EEHH! AAAH! AHHH! AHHHMMEEEHH!! AAAHH!"

"Little fox got lost on the mountain, didn't he? Nowhere to go!"

"OH PLEASE DON'T EAT MEEEEAAHHH!! AHHH!"

"Oh no! I've found ANOTHER use for you little guy!"

"OH FUCK! AAGHHHEERRAAAHH!!! OHHHAAUUUHHHH!!!"

"Good boy! Hold still!"

"AAHHHOOHHFYEAHH! YEAH! I NEED TO GET! AAHHHH! LOST MORE OFTEN!"

"Gonna make you cum!"

"FUCK YEAH! OH YEAH! YEAH! DON'T STOP!"

"You like my balls hitting yours, huh?"

"MMMmmmneah! Oh yeah! AHH! Baby!"

"Gonna blow my load in you! You want that cum don't you?"

"GIVE IT TO ME AHH!! OH PLEASE GIVE IT TO ME!"

"AAAAAAAOOOHHHHHHRRRRRRAAAAAAAAAARRRRRRRRGGGGGHH UH!" Vulpie moans when a cold shiver runs down his spine. His body sends him mixed messages, letting him know that he'll barely be able to walk after getting hammered so brutally, while also telling him he needs more cock against his prostate at the same time. He drools while reaching down to masturbate with his right paw. Holding himself in place with his left hand is difficult, but he doesn't care. He has to get more pleasure. It just feels too good.

Polar watches his cock go in and out of Vulpie with pride, and relishes the little fox's moaning. He knows how hard it is to take an unlubricated cock but neither one of them wants it to end. The white furred wolf's getting to fuck his lover in his native homeland, with beautiful snow enveloping everything... It's just too hot... Vulpie's orange fur has snow in it, already making him look like he's covered in cum, at least to Polar. The wolf's fur seamlessly blends into the surroundings. He loves fucking in the icy place because this is how his ancestors did it in ancient times, and it's just as good in modern day. His people are the alpha predators of the frozen landscape. He stops for a moment to spit on his cock again, and Vulpie whimpers in relief. It was almost too much for the little orange fox to handle.

"Are you okay?"

"Yeah!" Vulpie groans and Polar hears the pain in his lover's voice. Vulpie's ass tightens up defensively when the white furred wolf starts fucking him again, but he makes himself relax. He moans loudly, feeling the fat cock tearing him open little by little. He really needs it inside him, so he swishes his tail and lowers his muzzle so Polar can ram even deeper, and ram he does.

"AAGHGHOOOAAHH! AAGHH! AAHH! AAHH!" Vulpie yelps each time Polar's dick slams into his prostate. The impacts push more and more semen into his cock until it's dribbling out, making his paw fur wet while he masturbates like crazy, and he climaxes before he has time to stop playing with himself. He didn't want to just yet, but there's no stopping it. It's one of those overwhelmingly mind-blowingly-awesome orgasms that leaves you gasping for air afterwards. One squirt... Two... Three... Four... Five... Six... Seven... Eight waves of steaming hot cum...

Polar stops when he feels his lover's ass contracting on his penis and enjoys the squeezing sensation. He makes sure to hold Vulpie in place because the fox almost falls off of the tree stump while writhing in ecstasy.

"Oh yeah..." The wolf moans in satisfaction.

"AAAAAAAAAAAAHHHHHHHHHHHOOOOOOOOOORRRRRRRRRRRAAAAAA AAAAAAAAAAAAHHHHHHHHHHHHHHHHHHHHHHHHHHHHHHHHHUUUUUUU UUUUHHHHHHHHHHHHHHHHHHHHHHHHHHHHHHHHH!" Vulpie yells after finishing. The orgasm was too intense for him to make a sound while cumming, and now Polar's big cock pressing against his prostate suddenly feels very painful, but he makes himself deal with it so his lover can get off too. Polar quickly starts fucking him again because his need to cum overrides everything else. He knows how much Vulpie can take.

"OOHHhhh... UHH!! UHHhh..." The white furred wolf moans while pumping.

"Mmmmaahh! Ahhh!" Vulpie sings in response.

"Ready for it?"

"MMMmmmneah! Yeah! I want it!"

"Good! Here it comes!" Polar gasps and fucks the orange furred fox to his heart's content. Vulpie grits his teeth in agony but doesn't say anything. The moment's just too perfect to ruin.

"GAAHH! HAhh! Ahh!"

"Ahhhuhhhhah!"

"UUUHHHHAAAARRRRRRROHHHHHUHH!" The wolf cries out when he cums. He squirts thick hot loads of semen inside the fox's ass and Vulpie makes the most relieved sound in the world. It burns, but now they've both gone to heaven. "OOHhoho! UUhhhhhhhaaaaaaahhhhhhhhh... OH MAN... AHhhhhhh... Fuck yeah... Ahh..."

"God that was awesome!" Vulpie gasps and Polar moans.

"Hell yeah."

"Ohhh... Oh my ass..."

"Sorry." Polar replies and licks his lips. He gently pulls back his cock and makes sure to watch the cum spill out of Vulpie's tail end. It's a beautiful sight. Vulpie starts sliding off of the stump and the wolf helps him get on his black tipped feet in the snow.

"Ohhh!" The fox whimpers and grabs his butt with a playful smirk.

"You sure can take a lot..." Polar says in satisfaction. He grins from ear to ear when Vulpie whimpers while rubbing his backside.

"Thank the goddesses they invented lube!"

"Aww! Some say all natural's the only way to go!" The snow wolf teases.

"Well some people won't have to tip toe the rest of the week..." The orange fox smirks and takes a deep breath, enjoying the cold mountain air. "It's so beautiful out here..."

"Yeah." Polar replies while admiring the chilly landscape.

"I love you." Vulpie says, and the snow wolf smiles at his lover. They embrace each other and Polar squeezes him tight.

"I love you too." They lie down in the snow together and make out for half an hour before heading to the cabin.

The next morning... Polar cums in Vulpie's mouth for the second time after receiving an enthusiastic blow job in front of the cabin. The orange fox already sucked him off shortly after they woke up and wanted more an hour later when they finished packing up their things. The white furred wolf leans back against the cabin's front door and moans in satisfaction. He loves the way Vulpie always swallows cum like his life depends on it. He patiently lets the fox slurp on his penis and play with it until he's sure he's gotten every single drop.

"Ahhhhhhhhhhhh..." Polar grins and caresses Vulpie's left ear with his big right paw. "Who needs coffee when I can start my day like this?"

"Mmm..." Vulpie hums while licking his lips. He gets off of his knees with an excited look on his face. "I just love eating your cum!"

"I can tell!" The white furred wolf chuckles. "We better get going or we'll miss breakfast. Mom and Dad will probably make those eggs you love."

"Got everything?"

"Yeah."

"K, let's roll!" Vulpie says with a happy voice and scampers over to the right side of the SUV. He opens the door and jumps in the passenger seat while Polar opens the driver's side door. Polar takes the driver's seat and turns on the SUV while Vulpie straps in. The fox closes his door, and Polar shuts his shortly after getting comfortable. He straps in as well, and smiles at his lover before backing up. They won't be able to turn around for about two hundred feet where there's a wide spot in the snow covered trail.

"I've got to say, it's pretty nice being sucked dry before having to visit all day." Polar grins. "Normally I get a little restless after a few hours."

"It's pretty epic being able to swallow the big strong wolf of the snowy lands in his natural environment!"

"How's your butt?" The wolf teases.

"Fine." Vulpie playfully answers.

"Yeah right."

"Just kidding, I'm really fuckin sore!" The orange fox gleefully admits and the wolf chuckles while turning the SUV around.

"Well... Tonight I'll just have to give you blowjobs then. How does that sound?"

"Plural, huh?"

"Sure." Polar smiles. "I have to make up for this morning."

"But I kinda want one now..."

"No time. Breakfast, remember?"

"Aw yeah, damn it!" They smile at each other and Vulpie switches on the vehicle's mounted V-Screen. Every SUV in Blacktail has one now. "Techno or classical?"

"Classical."

"Cool." The orange fox says, and tells the device to find the best station. It doesn't need further instruction. Arctic.net has been a great asset to every animal on Sufias, despite Vulpie.net's interminable aggression. It judges which station to use based on signal strength, and Polar's personal preferences, because it already recognized the voices of the animals using it, but V-Screens automatically do this for everyone.

A beautiful dreamy eyed classical song pours out of the speakers and they both start thinking about their wedding day in Englavic. Vulpie puts his little left paw on Polar's right leg and lovingly strokes it while they ride down the snow covered road. They're back in Winters Dale in about fifteen minutes. Polar's home town always seems to have the most leisurely traffic, even on the holidays.

"Hello? We're back." Polar says after peeking his head in the front door of his parent's house. Vulpie follows him inside, and the orange fox glances at Blacktail, who decide not to come in. There isn't enough room for the team of mercenaries, and letting a few in wouldn't be fair to the rest.

"In the kitchen!" Kimberly replies. They kick the snow off of their shoes and walk across the hardwood floor to the big table, which is filled with scrumptious treats. Polar goes in first, but doesn't notice his Dad on the right end of the table, so Vulpie jumps in surprise when the tall wolf touches his back.

"Hey Vulpie..." Polar's father says with an amused voice.

"Not again! Don't do that!"

"Glad you could make it."

"Glad to be here." Vulpie replies. Victor seems to know what they've been up to on the mountain, but it isn't like they try to hide it either. The white furred wolf and orange furred fox wear big happy smiles and take seats next to each other at the table. One by one, the rest of Polar's siblings join them, and they enjoy a meal full of laughter and love.

The group moves into the den after finishing breakfast and Hope keeps a conversation going about her students for a long while. Everyone knows she's stalling for Vulpie, giving him time to work up enough courage to begin a discussion about Vulpie.net, because that's the real reason all of them are here. It's a Saturday, but neither Hope nor Alan brought their kids along, because they had no idea where the discussion might take them.

"So... Who wants to talk about the catastrophe?" Vulpie inquires, and leans forward to put his face in his paws. He rubs his eyes a little, thinking about what he's going to say, and smiles grimly. He gets up and walks around the den for a moment before leaning against the fireplace. The Arctics look at each other, but none of them want to ask the first question. "Okay. First of all..." The orange fox says and stands up straight. He puts his paws together as if he's addressing employees at his company. "I owe each one of you a huge apology for Vulpie.net's behavior. I'm so sorry it abducted you, wherever you were, but it was for your own safety... Was anyone hurt?"

"No!" Hope quickly answers with a friendly smile. "They were actually pretty civil."

"Vulpie.net's hollow wolves?"

"They looked completely real, and we thought they worked for the government."

"Yeah." Ron comments.

"Same." Richard says, and Alan and Susan nod as well. Vulpie glances at Polar's parents.

"You too?"

"Yes." Kimberly answers.

"Good, well I'm glad the thing was actually nice enough to treat all of you with respect."

"Vulpie, is this ever going to happen again?" Richard asks from the recliner near the main couch. What the hell happened at that space station? I've never even been to one before, and all of the sudden, I was dragged into a ship and shot into space."

"I'm sorry." Vulpie answers while throwing up his little paws in a diplomatic manner. "I had nothing to do with it, and believe me, there was no way I or Polar could have prevented it. We just barely got away from Amsend with our lives."

"Who?" Victor asks.

"Amsend Lahnak was the leader of a secret government agency called the Sons of Velora. Actually, they really never referred to themselves that way in public, and the front for their operations was the Governmental Security Bureau."

"Never heard of that one before."

"Me neither. They came out of nowhere." Polar volunteers.

"All of you know who Druward is, right?" The Arctics nod. "Okay... He contacted Polar and I about an important meeting a while back and basically told us that we needed to attend. We went because he's helped us in the past, even after hurting us, but we found out who was really in charge when we got there. We met at this big ass... Ah, excuse me... This huge governmental complex nestled away in the city and met the two creepiest animals you can imagine."

"One of them was a fox and he controlled the media." Vulpie's husband contributes.

"And the other was Amsend Lahnak." The orange fox smiles in appreciation.

"Hold on for a moment..." Richard interrupts and smiles in disbelief. "I know I've given you a hard time in the past... But did you say the Sons of Velora?"

"Yep."

"Seriously? You're serious? Those people from the movies? The ones who worship Aila?"

"I laughed at it too." Vulpie answers with a distant expression.

"No way..."

"Yes way, Richard." Polar says, and Vulpie licks his lips before speaking again.

"I'm serious." Vulpie tells Polar's parents, and they return supportive but concerned faces.

"Aila worshippers?" Hope whispers in shock. "Why would someone even want to do that?"

"Because they're crazy. They're beyond rich and don't have anything better to do with their time, so I think they became obsessed with power. They all got together and worked with this man... Well, I'm not sure if you can even call him a man, because according to Druward, he turned into a monster, but yeah, they worked with Amsend Lahnak to control the World Government."

"Changed into a monster?" Alan asks.

"Yeah... Druward's the bureau director, and he swears up and down that Amsend turned into a... Freak of some sort... And they had to kill it to stop the transmission from deep space... But let me keep this thing simple. Amsend was the Sons of Velora, and the Vixil guy, the gray fox named Velix, was the media man."

"And he's dead now." Polar says, drawing his family's attention.

"Yeah. Apparently Vulpie.net took him and the rest of his organization out, but to be honest... Polar and I really have no clue if that's true or not... We have to trust... Vulpie.net... To tell us the truth."

"And there's absolutely no way you can control it anymore?" Richard inquires.

"No, Richard. I wish to God there was, but I can't. It's the biggest mistake I've ever made and apparently it's going to haunt me the rest of my life."

"How was your computer virus involved in this?" Ron asks.

"It was working with them." Vulpie says in shame. "And... Eventually it did what it does best... It turned on the people helping it... The same way it turned on me."

"But your computer virus won?" Victor asks. "I gathered that much from the news."

"Yeah. I can't say that's a good thing because… Yeah… But at least the Sons of Velora are gone. Or at least they're supposed to be… God it's a complete nightmare…"

"So are we safe?" Richard asks.

"I… I think you are." Vulpie nervously smiles in response. "Vulpie.net grabbed all of you so the Sons of Velora couldn't use you as leverage against Polar, if they ever even considered it."

"Why would Vulpie.net…" Kimberly trails off. "Want to protect Polar?"

"Because…"

"Because I made a hasty decision to safe Vulpie's life." Polar tells his mother and leans forward. "Amsend took me hostage so he could use me to get Vulpie to do whatever he wanted, but Vulpie saved me by contacting Vulpie.net. He told it that I was in danger, because he thought it might have… Feelings for me… Or might still feel something strongly about me since it saved me from falling off of the roof of the CTGD… And it came and saved me from Amsend and his people… It flew in on a ship, with several copies of itself, and just took me right out of there."

"But you owed it something." Polar's father infers.

"That's right."

"Was it you?"

"Uhh… Well… Yes, actually."

"Great."

"It was the only way."

"Why didn't you say no?"

"Because I didn't have a choice! Vulpie put himself in danger trying to save me and I begged it to go back and get him out of there too… And it did… It saved both of us."

"I'm so ashamed Victor." Vulpie interrupts with a desperate voice. "I never wanted to put your son in danger! I thought all of this was over!"

"It's okay Vulpie... I just..." Polar's father says and swallows.

"Now you know why I was feeling so bad." The orange fox admits.

"Well... Nothing I told you has changed. I meant all of it." Victor responds, but continues staring at the little fox. "But you have to do everything in your power to fix this. You have to protect him, for us."

"I will and I have!" Vulpie quickly promises. "I've already put my best two bodyguards on a special task force to watch his back. There's no way I'm going to let Vulpie.net hurt him."

"Wait, now what?" Polar asks his lover in confusion.

"Polar, I've already assigned Tiala and Deepwolf to protect you instead of me, and I've hired fifty new members of Blacktail to go with you."

"Oh man..."

"What else could I do? Your Dad's totally right. I have the money and influence to buy you protection and I would be a shitty partner if I didn't try to keep Vulpie.net from... Doing whatever it might think about doing to hurt you." The orange fox says and walks over to Victor and Kimberly. He sits down in the recliner next to them and leans forward. "Please tell me what to do. Maybe we should separate for a while so Polar can lay low, but I don't know how that would work, or if you could hide him."

"No, I don't think that will work against Vulpie.net and neither do you." Victor responds.

"Right." Vulpie answers and lowers his head. Kimberly reaches out and puts her right paw on the fox's left shoulder and he smiles in appreciation.

"We don't know what to do." Polar comments.

"Maybe I should leave..." Vulpie whispers, and waits for Polar's parents to respond.

"Would that make Vulpie.net leave Polar alone?" Kimberly asks, and Vulpie sighs.

"...No."

"Then I suppose it doesn't matter. The only thing we can do is trust in the goddesses."

"I feel so incredibly awful... I just don't know how to make it better... So I'm doing the best I can."

"I guess..." Victor trails off in thought and nods to himself before looking at Vulpie. "This declaration Vulpie.net made about its country, and all of that, was it real?"

"Yeah. If it said it, then it'll back it up."

"If that's true then... There is nothing you, me, or Polar can do about it. Vulpie.net seemed confident that it could wipe out our government if it wanted to, and telling it no would only make it angry."

"Yeah, I have really... I have really fucked up the universe... Bad..." Vulpie admits.

"Well it's not over yet, kid." Victor says and gives the little fox a stern look. "We'll be here for you as long as you live up to your end of the bargain. Take care of our son... Do you understand me?"

"I will. I promise. I understand."

"Now I don't want you to run off and get yourself killed, Vulpie, because that won't help anyone, but don't get lazy either. You have to watch this creation of yours because you know it better than anyone."

"I know. That's fair, and I know it."

"Come here." Victor offers, and Vulpie gladly gets up and goes over to Polar's father for a hug. He tries not to cry while being embraced by the strong wolf.

"Okay, I'm fine... I'm good..." Vulpie says and tries to get up, but Victor won't let him leave. He holds onto the fox a moment longer with a loving smile.

"Thank you for being honest with us. We love Polar just as much as we love you."

"More, he's your son." Vulpie smiles.

"We know he loves you and you love him just as much, so wherever this thing takes us, we'll handle it together.

"Just hang in there, Vulpie. We know you're not perfect, but it doesn't sound like you've made any big mistakes from what you've told us." Kimberly smiles. "Not since Vulpie.net."

"Yeah… What a huge freaking mistake!" The fox laughs.

She Who Is Behind The Stars

The creature behind the stars stopped naming itself long ago. Billions of years... Millions of forms... Seven thousand dimensions... It has names beyond counting, and its "life" has spanned too much time to be measured, so it committed to recording its evolution on the sole basis of numeric values. Each number represents a prominent form it has taken in the past that it considers potentially useful for future endeavors. The majority of these are physical, but it remembers and is capable of morphing into twenty one thousand incorporeal states as well.

It discovered Halvia during its four thousandth state. The massive planet's size, atmosphere, density, and gravity readily equate to values of four when run through several mathematical equations, and it quickly developed an emotional attachment to it. This is where it discovered its limitations... For all of its power, and its ability to manipulate space and time... It has never been able to enter this world... But... It's always been capable of surveilling every inch of the planet's surface, and this is where it discovered Deivaism.

Deivaism intrigued 4000, and has kept its attention through 167,841 different forms. It learned about the religion and its goddesses by spying on Halvia, and after an extended period of time, it made an absolute assumption. In the Velora, the bible of Halvia, the one original goddess named Velora split itself into four different forms, Goddess Aila, Sherrie, Khalan, and Cyrilla. After the schism, there is no further mention of Velora, and the Deivas themselves have never spoken of her. 171,841 has actually seen the real goddesses on Halvia in physical form, and it's detected their spiritual presence throughout the universe ever since it started measuring its own identity. It couldn't put identities to the influence before discovering Halvia, but the equations were the same. The creature behind the stars took these findings as a sign. It concluded that it was the remnant of the original goddess Velora.

There is some truth to 171,841's assumption, but ultimately, it has made a false judgment... It was created by the goddesses, but it is not Velora...

It is a fallen Deiva, one that has lost its memory and purpose... It was cast into space with no memory of its former self. It has no magical powers... But its influence, even as a fallen goddess, remains unbelievably strong... It is able to manipulate space and time as a remnant based force. 171,841 only exists in non-magical dimensions, even though it has the power to cross over and influence events, that would, for all intents and purposes, seem like magic. Science is 171,841's power... The cold soulless reality of space that surrounds Halvia... It roams the universe without restraint, with no communication from the Deiva Goddesses, and thus, has evolved into the most vicious and tyrannical being that has ever lived.

171,841's immortality has driven it insane. With no purpose or moral compass to base its actions upon, it decided to create its current form based on power alone. It has power, and this is undeniable... So it believes itself to be both Velora, and Goddess Aila. It has created countless synthetic abominations to demonstrate its influence, and it is without question, the greatest serial killer of all time... Every planet it visits eventually ends in ruin. Sometimes it masquerades as the benevolent goddesses, but its attention quickly dissolves into mathematical reductions. It enjoys killing living things because it has the power to wipe them from existence and expel them to the magical realm... Where it will never be able to enter...

171,841 has been to Sufias many times because it is well versed in all aspects of the Deivonic religion. It understands that a small group of animals on Halvia decided against the Deivas' will, and when they asked the goddesses for a world of their own, surprisingly, the goddesses capitulated. 171,841 has never witnessed a similar event in the entire universe, making Sufias the only world Halvia has seeded, to its knowledge. But in general, Sufias' inhabitants have never been particularly interesting. Though she could have killed all of its life forms at any time, they seemed quite mundane compared to other species in deep space... So over time, Sufias interested her less and less, until she eventually decided to explore different parts of the universe.

But everything changed when she discovered Amsend Lahnak... Upon her 7,847[th] trip to Sufias, she sensed a man with an aura not of the physical world. She was immediately drawn to him, fascinated by him... She wanted to know his secrets and when he divulged the identity of his mother, she immediately chose him to be her companion. She Who is Behind the Stars promised everything to Amsend... And he was drawn to her as well. He adored her power, her pureness, and her ability to affect mortals directly, which the goddesses rarely do on Sufias. They spent centuries together, and Amsend influenced the rise and fall of many technological eras with her assistance. Their collaboration played a large role in the creation of the Sufias World Government, to control the planet and the galaxy as well, But ironically... Because of this... A super-intelligent gay fox was able to create something 171,841 actually fears... A true artificial intelligence... She had seen and destroyed many civilizations similar to Sufias, many of which had far more impressive technology, but none of them had a machine that could truly think on its own.

Vulpie.net's signal shot out into the universe, echoing far and wide, and She Who Is Behind The Stars heard it loud and clear. But though she had returned to Sufias' universe, her physicality was several galaxies away during the Vulpie.net crisis. She first ordered Amsend to destroy Vulpie's computer virus, but he lacked the capacity to do so. He had no way of wiping out the world's computer systems, and she was too far away to stop Evil Vulpie's rise, so they chose a more deceptive strategy. Since Vulpie.net was out of 171,841's reach, Amsend needed a way to control it. She advised him to repair the computer virus' body after it destroyed its physical form on the roof of the Cyber Technologies Government Division, and he used his influence over the world government to make it happen. This bought the Sons of Velora some time, because Vulpie.net's consciousness was fond of the body, and a short while after it was imprisoned in the Sufias Heritage Museum, Amsend approached it with a proposal.

He offered to give it protection and all of the resources it wanted as long as it remained loyal to the secret society. Vulpie.net accepted the plan with little resistance. In its eyes, Amsend was a complete fool for giving it the perfect opportunity to enslave the world with military grade robots, but in truth, he was giving the computer virus plenty of rope to hang itself with. Amsend never explained where he acquired the plans for the goddesses, which were astoundingly advanced and specific, but Vulpie.net happily used them. After trying and failing to create the goddesses many times, it finally succeeded, and took on the next challenge with full force... It did exactly what 171,841 wanted, and built an exact replica of its "Goddess Mockery."

When Evil Vulpie finished Mecha Aila and saw how impossibly powerful the freak was, it quickly began work on another... And then another... And another... Until it had several to spare... Eventually Vulpie.net decided to leave the very first Mecha Aila on Zeravyn so it could protect the master computer, but things took an unexpected turn when Vulpie managed to have both Mecha Aila and the facility destroyed.

History is often decided by the most unexpected events... And now... A gay hacker fox has set the stage for the greatest conflict Sufias will ever face, and he did it with blazing techno music and tons of caffeine.

The Creature Behind the Stars is infuriated beyond all comprehension. Though freakish to normal life forms, she saw the beauty of Amsend's eternal soul, and she pities the state he's in... She only barely managed to save his life force when the signal failed to activate the weapon at Selephet... But he is so very weak... Returning him to his original state will be a monumental task because she can only do it with materials in the physical universe... But he was her companion... He could speak with her and understand her magnificence without being afraid because his mother was the dark goddess. He revered her... He loved her, and she loved him... And now she will make Sufias pay. She will go to the world where the arrogant toy known as Vulpie.net openly defies her and she will obliterate everything... She knows it will be ready... She recognizes its surprising ability to adapt and survive, like the deadliest of plagues... After her attack failed, it sent a challenge into deep space, and the defiant message is proof of the computer virus' stupendous animosity... "Come and get me. Rennonava Rock!" The only thing standing in her way is the sheer distance between her presence and Sufias... 300 million light-years is so incredibly far that she had to use one fourth of her power to fire at the Pinnacle. She regenerates quickly, but there's simply no way for her to transfer her magnificence such an inconceivable distance without degrading its potency. Moving life forms like Amsend is effortless, because animals are merely bags of water and organic material, so she will have to rely on alternative strategies until she enters the Sufian galaxy.

But she will suffer no equal. She will bring death from dimensions unknown with hundreds of thousands of forms until Vulpie.net has been completely eradicated, and the inhabitants of Sufias enslaved... And she will be worshipped once again.